THE MALACCA CANE

⚜⚜⚜

THE MALACCA CANE is a story of Italian upper and middle class life in which the scene moves between Turin and Rome. It starts before the First World War, when Emilio Viotti is a little boy both cosseted and smothered among the fading elegancies and the snobberies of provincial life, and ends in the hectic atmosphere of Rome's modern film industry, in which he has become an important figure. It is at one and the same time a portrait of a man, his loves and his moral dilemmas; a panorama of half a century of Italian history taking in two wars and the rise and fall of Fascism; and a protest against the values prevailing in the society it describes. It is conceived on a far larger scale than any of Mario Soldati's previous novels, and is as enjoyable as it is impressive.

MARIO SOLDATI

The Malacca Cane

Translated by Gwyn Morris

ANDRE DEUTSCH

First published 1973 by
André Deutsch Limited
105 Great Russell Street London WC1

Copyright © 1973 by Mario Soldati

Printed in Great Britain by
Ebenezer Baylis and Son Ltd
The Trinity Press, Worcester, and London

ISBN 0 233 96115 1

TO CARLO PONTI
in memory of a mutual friend

AUTHOR'S NOTE

I thank my friends Giorgio Bassani, Mario Bonfantini, Aldo Buzzi and Giorgio De Blasi whose advice helped me write and revise this novel.

Apart from historic personages and events, which I have always tried to describe accurately, all the action and all the characters represented here are imaginary.

PART ONE

�֎✖✖

With her gloved right hand his mother brusquely grasped the greasy leather border and lifted the heavy curtain, letting through in turn the enormous bodies of the two great-aunts, rustling with black crepe and shrouded in mourning veils. At the same time, with her left hand, she held him firmly by the shoulder; then pushed him forward.

The little country church was still empty, dark and cold. No sooner were they inside than the usual silent tussle began between him and his mother. He always tried to be last in order to sit next to her at the end of the pew, but she wanted him to kneel between his two great-aunts. His great-aunts stank of urine. Emilio detested them. Next to them he could never daydream; he had to pretend to be praying all the time. But his mother always insisted on it. And the reason for her insistence Emilio had discovered two months before. A colonel in the artillery, accompanied by Prince, the old gardener, had appeared mysteriously at the french windows of the dining-room. It was early one afternoon in July. In the heat after lunch everyone in the villa was asleep – his two little cousins because they were small, the others because they were grown-up – everyone except him and the servants. The cook was washing up. The maid was finishing clearing away. Emilio himself was waiting for Pierino, the gardener's nephew three years his senior, to come and show him his bicycle, and was taking advantage of the lack of supervision and everybody's absence to play a forbidden game: war with his lead soldiers on the old red-tiled floor, banned because his legs and knickers always got covered with red dust. Absorbed in the game, he had not heard the crunch of riding-boots on gravel until the last minute, when the colonel had appeared, a blaze of black and orange against the green background of the sunlit garden.

Tall, haughty and bewhiskered, he stopped, looked down at Emilio and his soldiers, then turned to Prince with a slight movement of the head and a tilting of the chin that signified a question.

Prince, an old grenadier and veteran of the war of '48, replied impassively: 'It's the niece's little boy.' So Emilio had realized that the colonel was looking for one of his great-aunts; it was almost certainly not Aunt Vittoria but Aunt Elisa, because her only son was a cavalry captain and was away at the war in Libya.

There was something solemn and out of the ordinary about the colonel's unexpected arrival and his bearing – Emilio had realized this at once, if only because it frightened him and stopped him from turning to Prince, as he had intended, to complain about Pierino not appearing.

His mother had been wakened. The colonel had gone with her into the great drawing-room which was always kept closed and dark even during the day. It was his heavy duty to inform the family of the death of Captain Sanfront.

An only son. And a bachelor. And Aunt Elisa was rich; so also was her husband, old Count Sanfront. And now, the heirs . . .

That evening Emilio's father had not returned home as usual on the seven o'clock train. He had stayed in Turin, so his mother had said, to be with Uncle Sanfront when they told him the news.

From Aunt Elisa, who was there with them in the country at their old villa at Rivoli, the colonel's visit had been kept a secret; they had told her to start with that her son had been wounded, and that the news had been brought from Turin not by a colonel but a subaltern. Aunt Vittoria had undertaken to reveal the truth to her gradually: she had shut herself in with her sister in her bedroom, allowed no other member of the family near her, intended to spend the night with her either sitting at her side or sleeping in her bed.

There was an atmosphere which Emilio had never experienced until then – until, that is to say, he was ten years of age. Everyone, including the servants, was silent or spoke in whispers; they walked about on tip-toe; they were continually wiping away tears, whether real or false. His two little cousins' evening meal was brought forward a good half-hour, and they were put to bed immediately after. He himself had not felt particularly sorry. Certainly he had liked cousin Amedeo – a tall, ruddy fair-haired fellow, with a big blue cloak. But he so rarely saw him. When he came visiting, he was always in a hurry to leave. He would kiss Papa and Mama on both cheeks, take tea or a vermouth; four more kisses and away he would go. In those few minutes Emilio, who was fascinated by his uniform, never failed to come to his side. He would have liked to touch his big cousin. He used at least to stroke the tassels hanging from his long sabre. And his cousin never failed to push his hand away gently, doing it as if the tassels had caught in a chair. He never looked at the boy, not even then, but continued to talk to Papa and Mama. He had never played with him. He had never given him a present.

So, why should he feel sorry? Indeed, with the sudden change in everybody's mood and the upsetting of the evening routine, the news was rather exciting: even, to be honest, pleasing. He calculated and hoped that the next day the grown-ups would be too distracted by the unusual turn of events and too busy fussing around Aunt Elisa and the old Count, who would doubtlessly leave Turin and come and join his wife at Rivoli, to pay much attention to him. And he, at last, would be free to spend a little more time with Pierino, who that day had shown him his marvellous red bicycle and had promised in great secrecy to teach him to ride it.

Dreaming of this, he raised not one word of protest when his mother told him that he could not wait up for Papa, and that he too would have to go to bed straight after supper.

But because it was earlier than usual, or perhaps as a result of natural reaction to the strange talk and tears and silences he had witnessed, he woke up after a while. He did not dare call out. He lay on his back in bed, motionless, staring wide-eyed at the rectangle of the window high above striped by the shutters – scarcely visible and yet so reassuring.

He listened hard. Raising his head from the pillow, he heard in the distance an incessant crying – almost a wail – coming from great-aunt Elisa's room. Then at last: rapid footsteps on the gravel path in the garden, the rattling of the glass door, the familiar hoarse voice. Papa had arrived. What time could it be? Perhaps midnight, perhaps later. How had he got back? In Uncle Sanfront's Isotta-Fraschini? He hadn't heard the car. Still, perhaps it hadn't come into the garden but had stopped outside.

The sound of feet on the stairs. The voices of Papa and Mama whispering together excitedly. Now they were coming along the corridor. Now they were going into their room, the one next to his. The door, as usual, was ajar: he could see the cleft of light.

Papa and Mama continued talking in an excited undertone.

13

Then came the familiar noise of Papa taking off his boots –
thump, and after a long pause, again – *thump.*

His mother was saying: 'Sssh! I'll see if he's asleep.'

In the sudden silence which followed he heard the old door creak
on its hinges. His mother entered. As always she was coming to see
if he had been properly tucked in.

He closed his eyes, held his breath. She came to the bedside and
leant over him but less tenderly than usual and a little more
hurriedly. She brushed his forehead with a kiss, and for a moment
Emilio smelt her perfume enveloping him, a perfume so sweet, so
soft, a perfume which he would have liked always to be near,
especially in church.

Now his mother was drawing aside, going from the room – still,
however, leaving the door ajar. He heard her saying to Papa: 'He's
fast asleep.'

He opened his eyes and lay perfectly still, staring at the crack of
light. And then, very softly, Papa and Mama began talking again.

The heirs, now . . . Now that cousin Amedeo was dead the heirs
to the Sanfronts could be Papa and Mama and then one day,
Emilio himself. Or else Alberto, Aunt Vittoria's son, a cousin of
Amedeo's like Papa, and his wife Marie Rose and then one day,
instead of Emilio, his cousins, the two little girls, and the little boy
Vittorio, who was the same age as him and who always spent his
holidays in France with his mother's parents.

It was also possible that the inheritance, as would be right and
proper – 'right and proper – very fair, very fair!' he heard his father
say again and again, his deep hoarse voice at one point becoming
shrill with excitement and his mother hissing 'Sssh, Luigi, you'll
wake the boy' . . . it was also possible that the inheritance would be
divided in equal parts between Alberto's family and Papa's, as they
were both related to the Sanfronts in the same degree. And if
Emilio's grandmother Cristina had still been alive this without
doubt would have been Aunt Elisa's final decision.

The three Racagni sisters, Vittoria, Elisa and Cristina, daughters
of General Racagni, had once been very close. But unfortunately
Cristina, his father's mother, had been dead for some time; Emilio
could scarcely remember her. And gradually, over the years, the
two surviving sisters, instead of showing their dead sister's husband
or his son at least a part of the affection that they had for her,

lavished it all upon each other. As they grew older they became inseparable, living together in the Palazzo Sanfront in Turin. When Commendatore Ceroni, Alberto's father and Aunt Vittoria's husband, had retired as head of a department at the Ministry of Public Works and returned from Rome for good, Uncle Sanfront, with his wife's encouragement, had promptly given up to the Ceronis the entire second floor. Now, with the death of her only son, what remained to Aunt Elisa but the Faith and a morbid attachment to her sister?

'It's up to you!' Papa was saying, his voice growing clearer in the night-time silence of the villa. But Emilio was now having to struggle to keep awake in order to listen to the end. 'It's up to you. You're the one to get in with her!'

'Me?' replied his mother with a bitter little laugh. 'Aunt Elisa has never been able to stand me. She was jealous of me. She used to say that Amedeo liked me too much, that I flirted with him. No, no, she hates me. It had better be you – you're her sister's son just as much as Alberto. He's only another sister's son.'

'Even when my poor mother was alive,' murmured Papa, 'even then Aunt Elisa preferred darling Vittoria to her, poor thing. Afterwards, well, you can imagine . . . No, I can't do it. Anyway, this is the sort of thing that women do better. It's up to you now to make yourself useful, make yourself indispensable, make her fond of you . . . I don't mean straight away. First of all, she must get over the shock. But then, little by little, make her fond of you. In the meantime, you must stay beside her. Even if Aunt Vittoria is there, it doesn't matter. You'll simply both be there. Aunt Vittoria is old. There are a great many things that can only be done by a young woman in her prime like you. In other words, you'll have to make sacrifices and fight all the way. No hesitation, just fight and fight. Not for us, but for Emilio, for the sake of his future. He mustn't be robbed of what is due to him. It wouldn't be fair . . .'

And that is why that summer, after the news of Amedeo's death, Emilio's mother had joined silent and strenuous battle with Aunt Vittoria and the Ceronis.

She supervised the cooking so that no dishes which Aunt Elisa did not like were ever served at table, even if intended for the other people present. For the same reason she had decided to give up serving wine as long as they stayed in the country – or rather, kept house with Aunt Elisa who had always detested it and could seldom bear to see it being drunk without manifesting her own distaste. Emilio's Papa, reluctantly to be sure, had approved of the decision; he managed instead by taking refuge in the kitchen after a meal, unseen by the two aunts, and throwing back a couple of glasses there.

Then would come the time for Aunt Elisa to go to bed. Every evening her two nieces – that is to say, Emilio's mother and Marie Rose, the little girls' mama – would engage in a secret, violent battle for possession of their aunt's hot water bottle. Emilio's mother almost invariably won because at the critical moment Marie Rose would be busy with the children.

Mama would rush out of the kitchen clutching the bottle in its woollen cover like a trophy. She would go to Aunt Elisa, help her to her feet, and holding her under her right arm while Aunt Vittoria made a show of holding her under the left, assist her step by step up the stone stairs as far as her bedroom door. And here, shortly afterwards, Marie Rose would regularly have her revenge. She was admitted into the room with Aunt Elisa where only Aunt Vittoria had been before; she was admitted, indeed summoned, to help undress the old woman and say the evening prayers, while Emilio's mother was not allowed to set foot across the threshold. Worried and humiliated, she would have to go downstairs, sometimes passing her blonde rival on the stairs and having to meet her veiled look, her subtle, confident smile.

And to this she could not resign herself. At the last moment, still supporting her aunt under her right arm, she would try to slip into the bedroom. But without more ado Aunt Vittoria would push her away from her sister, and glaring at her from under her thick, black eyebrows, her lips protruding in an habitual sneer, she would dismiss her with a curt, sarcastic goodnight which clearly meant 'Come along, be off with you, you don't fool me.'

Emilio's mother was lucky if she managed to give Aunt Elisa a peck on her cadaverous cheek and the old woman's only response was a sigh slightly deeper than all her other endless sighs.

Emilio saw everything, and understood everything. He agreed with his father and mother, of course. Agreed in principle: at least a half of the legacy should be theirs, the Viottis'. But he did not agree with all this wheedling which, according to Papa and Mama, was necessary to get into Aunt Elisa's good books. With the infallible instinct that children have for things which do not directly concern them, he knew that it was all a waste of time. But then he had always hated his old great-aunts – especially Aunt Vittoria who was invariably callous, bad-tempered and unpleasant to him and to everyone else unless they happened to be a Ceroni or a Sanfront – almost as if people had always given her cause to take offence.

Aunt Elisa seemed a little kinder. Perhaps she was. But she showed it – with a little kiss, a *marron glacè*, a silver crown – only when her sister was not present, which happened very rarely and after her son's death, never. Vittoria dominated her. In her presence Aunt Elisa never dared to smile, even before her son's death when she would have been able to do so. She never said anything. She just looked about her sadly, with her large blue eyes in her pale, sagging face that must once have been very beautiful, and seemed to be imploring: 'Forgive me. I can't tell you anything. I can't give you anything. I would like to but I can't. I'm completely helpless.'

And now the bitterness of grief for the loss of her only son had destroyed even this hint of sweetness in her. She had become like her sister, gloomy and sour. All that emerged now was resentment against all those living in this world when her son was dead – resentment directed especially against the nephews of the same generation as her son: Alberto Ceroni and Emilio's father. Aunt Vittoria must have divined this particular feeling of her sister's and naturally, after Amedeo's death, must have seen to it that her own son Alberto, the civil engineer, did not come to Rivoli even on Sundays.

This might seem strange, considering that his wife and daughters were there on holiday, only a short distance from Turin. But there was in fact an explanation. Alberto had important work to do concerning a dam in Veneto province. Everyone took the explanation for granted, including Emilio's papa and mama. Only Emilio, though he did not say so to anyone, secretly thought it an excuse: and perhaps once again he was right.

About a month after her son's death, Aunt Elisa appeared again about the villa, shuffling along, leaning on, almost clinging to Aunt Vittoria who seemed no less exhausted than her sister. She took to coming downstairs for her meals again, and Emilio did not miss the look of hate she gave Papa every evening when, having come home from Turin on the seven o'clock train, he took his place at table, unfortunately opposite her, and came suddenly forward into its revealing cone of light.

What depressing dinners they were that dreadful autumn – with not a word spoken. They were not depressing to Emilio, though. He was young – not so young that he could not appreciate the importance of money and the inheritance but still young enough not to worry about it. Life (the life in which, as Papa kept on saying, 'he would have to make a career') was a huge, far-off adventure that, inheritance or not, would surely turn out marvellously, and be endless good fun.

What would he be? A lawyer? A doctor? An engineer like his uncle? He wasn't worried. But one thing was certain; he wouldn't be a government lawyer like Papa, nor a magistrate. He had been into court once, and there he had suddenly seemed to notice how hoarse his father's voice was and thought this must be due to the great strain of being a lawyer and talking so long about all those boring things.

No, there were a great many other careers in life. He wasn't worried. Meanwhile, his secret calculations had proved correct. The day after the news of Amedeo's death he had had his first bicycle lesson from Pierino. A fortnight later he was an expert. But for the time being he was only allowed to ride round the garden or in the wooded enclosure behind the villa.

His mother propelled him into the pew and made him kneel between his two great-aunts.

There was always, in every moment of his life as a child, one thing which he wanted more than anything else. At that particular moment, the one thing he wanted most was to go on a real bicycle ride with Pierino – a ride from Rivoli to Villarbasse, then on to Trana and Avigliana. Tomorrow was Pierino's last day there – then he was going back to Turin. He had found himself a post – assistant in a photographer's studio. It was his first job. And tomorrow being Pierino's last day Emilio's mother had finally given him the permission that he had longed for.

Feeling the bench hard under his knees he thought with glee of the following day and how he would pedal for hours and hours, free and happy, with Pierino. He gazed contentedly at the candles which the nun was lighting one after the other on the altar. One after the other. Each candle lit was a moment of time passing, advancing with marvellous inevitability towards tomorrow. Time never turned back, it had just begun to move and it all lay ahead.

The warm flickering glow grew steadily stronger, glinting on the gold of the shrine and the candelabra. Gradually, with a soft shuffling of feet, the little church filled with peasant women and with ladies who were holidaying in the vicinity. The rosary began. Emilio recited it loudly, putting into this, too, all the enthusiasm, impatience and assurance of his hopes.

His heavy, evil-smelling old aunts – symbols of death and power – between whom he was clamped, no longer existed; he had forgotten them, thinking of Pierino and the bicycle, wallowing in the sonorous *cantilena* of the Ave Maria and staring at the flames on the altar. And there, much sooner than he had dared hope, appeared the priest clad in his golden mantle – a sign that the service was now drawing to a close.

The incense began to smoke and spread its mysterious antique perfume.

Swelling and resounding in the baroque vaults of the little church, the deep voice of the priest intoned: *Tantum ergo Sacramentum.*

❀❀❀

About 1912 the vogue for long summer holidays in the mountains
or at the seaside had just begun. Many Turin families, though
well-off, were quite content to spend the summer in the Canavese
alpine foothills, or better still, as it was nearer the city, on the
ridge between the Avigliana lakes and Rivoli castle, between the
valleys of the rivers Dora and Sangone: on those majestic rolling
heights, still covered to this day with age-old woods, which seem to
block the mouth of the Susa Valley with their huge amphitheatre
and which, the air being clear of the dank mists which breathe from
the lower reaches of the Po and also (in those days) free from the
smoke of the industries along the Riparia, offered from the top of
even the most modest hill-crests or through the windows of the
sparse dwellings an extraordinary close-up of the alpine arc.

The houses were almost exclusively picturesque old villas, built
in the seventeenth and eighteenth centuries, and farmhouses
belonging to them: low buildings whose reddish roofs were hidden
in the tall, leafy trees of the great parks and woods and merged in
other seasons with the lichen and tangle of the naked boughs.

Every summer and autumn the city nobility, following an ancient
custom, moved into the villas. And those belonging to im-
poverished families or families in decline were usually rented to the
wealthier and more ambitious *bourgeoisie – parvenus* from the
professions, business or budding industries who wanted to acquire
immediately the habits of nobility. Emilio Viotti's family was in the
middle of the social ladder. Related to the Sanfronts, it descended
through Emilio's paternal grandmother from General Racagni – a
nobleman himself even though his name did not rank as nobility.
General Racagni, not a particularly affluent man, had left the villa
at Rivoli as an undivided legacy to his three daughters.

The Sanfronts possessed (besides a villa in the hills just outside
Turin on the road to Santa Margherita), a castle at Sanfront in the
Cuneese district – too far in those times and anyway too incon-

venient for holidays. They, too, while Amedeo was in school at Moncalieri and had his summers free, came for holidays to Rivoli from La Consolata dei Santi and shared the villa with the Ceronis and the Viottis. But once Amedeo had taken his diploma and entered Modena Academy, Count Sanfront – who had made the annual sacrifice of leaving Turin and his club and spending the vacation with his brothers and sisters-in-law purely for the boy's sake – resigned himself very willingly to the other sacrifice of being parted from his wife. She, indeed, would never have foregone spending at least those months with her adored sister Vittoria who lived for the rest of the year in Rome: they had known the villa as children. Emilio's grandmother had died early on. The Rivoli holiday ménage was dominated by the imperious, sinister couple of old great-aunts whom the Viotti and Ceroni nieces coddled with every conceivable attention because of the inheritance, whom Emilio hated and the two little cousins regarded with religious awe. Count Sanfront, however, whom the whole family loved to call 'Uncle Sanfront', 'my uncle Sanfront', was only rarely to be seen: and when he did appear, though old and ill, he inspired in all, but especially in the children, a kind of fascinated respect. He was a typical eighteenth-century aristocrat, formally deferential to institutions but deep down a libertine, full of vitality, capricious – sometimes warmly human, sometimes despotic, always charming. Tall, well-built, ruddy-complexioned, he had a thick, bristling moustache which like his hair had once been fair to ginger and was now snow-white. In bowler hat and dark blue fitted overcoat, he walked briskly, strutting like a military man, with a malacca cane which stabbed the ground and swung to the horizontal on alternate steps, and which, when he came to the villa on a short visit, he relinquished only at the last moment before passing from the hall to the drawing-room. The sight of it laid across a chair or erect in the bamboo umbrella stand was the unmistakable sign of his presence.

The villa dated from the first half of the eighteenth century and was in a rather bad state. Built on low ground among fields and woods, between the road to Villarbasse and a swift mill-race, it was quite far from the old centre of Rivoli – that medieval cluster of houses and churches, alleys and walls which huddle together and clamber up the eastern slope of the hill towards the ridge dominated by the Savoy castle. But in the second half of the nineteenth century Rivoli, which today is a town of more than ten thousand inhabitants, had already become a large village; it had extended gradually wherever the land was flat – towards Rivalta, Villarbasse, Turin, Alpignano – in every direction except towards the castle. Officials, middle-class townspeople, artisans, even *nouveau-riche* farmers had begun to nibble at the parklands and estates of the nobles, to build their little villas and cottages, felling the trees in age-old parks, to convert the proud remains of these into charmingly attractive gardens.

With the exception of Villa Rignon, Villa Cavalli and Villa Nuvoli, the pedigree families no longer shielded the aristocratic serenity of their ancient pale-yellow façades from the inquisitive gaze of early Sunday trippers. Now, through the railings, you could see everything – the slender, elegant french windows, the oval parterres, the fuchsia beds, the glorious display of hydrangeas and peonies, the tall magnolias, the cedars of Lebanon. But some of the squires, although forced by financial necessity to sell piece by piece all their grounds save the garden immediately around the villa, had maintained privacy by enclosing what was left with a sufficiently high wall bristling with broken glass. No longer, then, the impressive wrought-iron gate but a stout, rustic wooden front-door painted green. No longer the lodge-keeper and his family but just a gardener who also acted as caretaker.

This was the situation at Villa Racagni at the time of the Libyan campaign. And the cluster of four families who spent their vacations there was curiously typical of Turin society in the last few years before the Great War and the big growth in industry. The old villa itself and the two aunts summed up the Racagni family – petty nobility without large estates or capital, entirely committed to the military prowess of its menfolk who, moreover, despised any other career: result, a fatal, inevitable decline unless those generals and colonels were dishonest.

The Viottis and the Ceronis were civil servants, magistrates, professional men: they represented the class which was rapidly becoming rich and rising in the social scale. Emilio's paternal grandfather was from the countryside near Vercelli. For many years registrar in his native Trino where he still lived on a pension, he had married a Racagni, or as people said *bien au-dessus de lui*, and had therefore set his two sons to study for the Bench. Only one was successful, the elder, from 1907 Public Prosecutor at the Court of Appeal in Genoa. The other son, Emilio's papa, possibly encountering difficulties in his studies, had lowered his sights: yet even so he had done extremely well. While still a young man he became a government lawyer, a Treasury Counsel.

Uncle Ceroni, Aunt Vittoria's husband, had achieved a triumphant bureaucratic career. In 1865, when he was little more than twenty and already a civil servant, he had followed the transference of the capital to Florence and immediately after 1870 to Rome. There, at the Ministry of Public Works, he had become a departmental head. Whenever they spoke of him, his wife and sister-in-law, Aunt Vittoria and Aunt Elisa, raised their voices until they reached a strange double violence: admiration for the honest, incorruptible bureaucrat and contempt for anyone who accused and suspected him of being otherwise. 'Anyone' was always a vague, indefinite being, formless and nameless. Emilio finished his first year at grammar school without meeting the proverb *excusatio non petita*: and in any case he would never have been malicious enough to apply it spontaneously. Yet even he, a mere child, was struck by that vehement, furious attitude of theirs. Struck but not convinced. Uncle Ceroni's bald, spherical head, his round face and his round gold spectacles, his bulbous, protruding green eyes, his sarcastic snigger, his stiff, taciturn manner – there was something unpleasant about them, especially to a child. If Uncle Sanfront was the generous, amusing, impulsive aristocrat, Uncle Ceroni was the mean, tedious, calculating civil servant. Emilio instinctively compared the two and it goes without saying that he was all for Uncle Sanfront.

Uncle Ceroni, though he had lived in Rome for more than thirty years in an apartment in Via Cavour, returned to Turin on reaching retirement and sent his son Alberto to study at the Polytechnic there. No doubt at all. The authority of the old Ministry of Public Works official, his very name, helped the budding engineer to pass his first examinations, to snap up a share of the contracts. What then? Simply one more proof that the Ceronis were not more ambitious, but tougher, more obstinate, more fortunate than the Viottis. A comparison between Alberto's marriage and that of Emilio's father led to the same conclusion. Marie Rose, Alberto's wife, was on her father's side a Piatti of Piea and Moransengo –

23

important names, quality, a dowry: on her mother's side, a du Buisson de Courson-Cristot, an old Norman family belonging to the Papal nobility. Whereas Emilio's mother was the daughter of a lawyer from Bagnone, and so half Ligurian, half Tuscan – a likeable but muddle-headed man and, as is often the case with ambitious and not particularly intelligent provincials, very presumptuous: Emilio's father had met her at La Spezia, his first post.

There remained the Sanfronts. Here was the ark of security which the Viottis and the Ceronis had always dreamt of entering – realizing, though, that it could only be a dream. Now, since the death of Count Sanfront's only heir, the dream had suddenly become reality. It was the gold-dust that rubbed off on anybody who lived near the central hoard. It was the rare (and for them the only) chance of reaching the banks of the new world by crossing one of the few bridges linking the wealth of the agricultural feudalism dependent on the House of Savoy with the modern wealth stemming from big industry. The difference between being a Sanfront and being a Viotti or a Ceroni had been measured once and for all by Luigi Viotti, Emilio's papa and Alberto Ceroni when they were children of about the same age as Emilio was now, and had watched a carriage and groom coming to the green front door of the old villa punctually at nine o'clock every Monday, Wednesday and Friday morning: it was there to take their little cousin Amedeo to the Gerbido, near Turin, where the Sanfronts had stables and the little boy was given riding lessons.

Well before the end of the century, new houses for the farm-workers and even cow-sheds had been built adjoining the wall round what was left of the park – the few flower-beds, the shrubberies, the last avenues, the last clumps of woodland. The crowing of the cocks and the tiresome gobbling of the turkeys, the swarms of flies and from time to time the stench of dung were considered humiliating to the Racagni name and estate by the old aunts, while for the ambitious second generation they reduced the symbolic and social value of the family property. But to the third generation, little Emilio's, it was the very decadence, the slow degradation and decay, the agreeable absence of neatly trimmed hedges and closely clipped lawns, of flower-beds and pergolas in full bloom, of valuable carpets, waxed floors, polished furniture, brasses like mirrors, all necessitating a tedious respect, which invested the old villa with a special beauty and enchantment.

Sometimes in July and August, during the early hours of the afternoon, when neither the shrubs in the garden, nor the tall trees in the wood behind the villa offered enough shade from the glare and heat, Emilio was allowed to venture into the enormous rooms on the ground floor: three or four in a row – dark, cool, ideal for games and fancies, with vast semi-desert red-tiled floors, furniture, pictures and strange old tapestries.

In all that gloom which became half-light only after a few minutes, the sun sliced high, narrow strips of golden dust, dancing, gently whirling, and illuminated the opposite wall in patches of wide, alternately coloured stripes: bottle green and ruby, orange and crimson, Prussian blue and wine red.

On the marble mantelshelves of each chimney-piece, so high that Emilio could hardly reach them, stood two great bronze candelabra and in the middle of a group of mythological figures around the clock, or under a glass bell, a bunch of artificial flowers, delicately pink, lilac, yellow and green. The mirrors were silver-black, speckled, mysterious. The firescreens embroidered with designs of flowers and fruit: subtle shades of a single colour – for instance, cream to light brown and light brown to coffee. And portraits of the family ancestors. Some dating back to the eighteenth century – the men in powdered wigs with dirks at their side, the women with small oval faces, vermilion cheeks, eyes bright and piercing. But the majority belonged to the Napoleonic or early Restoration periods: soldiers, diplomats as was clear from their sashes and decorations.

Emilio had learnt to recognize each one. And although, the previous summer, in a rare – no, unique – moment of familiarity, Aunt Elisa had told him their names, he had forgotten them all and rechristened them in his own way: the Admiral, the Bad Man, the Good Man, the Silly Fool, the One with the Red Hair, the Old Man, the Wizard, the Second-Lieutenant ...

He had his favourites, or rather, his favourite. Except that he would never have thought of him as a favourite. He believed he hated him. It was, of course, the Bad Man: of all the characters, he was the one who interested him by far the most.

He was a man of authority, no doubt. A minister or a general in mufti. The Bad Man. But when Emilio stopped to look at him, why did the Bad Man seem to look back at him, a mere child, with his

25

large, black, severe eyes? Why did the pale-faced man purse his thin lips so tightly as if he were going to spit at him? From infancy, perhaps from the age of four or five, Emilio when alone in the second room, used to talk to the Bad Man.

'What do you want now? D'you want to be alone? Do you want to order *me* about, too? I'm ready to obey you.'

Then there was the great stairway of rough stone. And on the floor above, the bedrooms, all with bold floral designs in pink and pea-green, or yellow and dark blue. The beds with their canopies and curtains of threadbare damask. Marble fireplaces here too, one to every room, but slightly lower and smaller than those on the ground floor. And the deep sleep which overcame him every night in bed. His mother would tuck him in, kiss him on the forehead, put out the light and leave the room. He would listen to her footsteps receding down the stone staircase and fading rapidly into the distance. But he was already past hearing. Before he had time to be scared of the dark and the dead silence, he was asleep.

If the Bad Man, that magical character in whom Emilio pretended to believe for fun, had the leading part indoors, the same role, in the avenues and by the flower-beds, in the orchards and the wood in the park at the back of the house, was taken by a real, live man, but one even more fantastic and fascinating in his way – Prince, the gardener. He was an old man of more than ninety. Though his back might be a little bent with age and his legs slightly bowed, he was still very tall – taller than Uncle Sanfront, almost as tall as Cousin Amedeo when he was wearing his helmet.

Bony, tough, vigorous, stone-deaf, he walked slowly, swaying from side to side, but with even, rhythmical steps – he marched, in other words, even though they were only very short marches. He marched and the shears beat against his buttocks like a bayonet, even if he had only to go and open the door when finally he heard the bell and he had merely to cross the few yards of entrance-hall.

Next to the hall, against the external wall of the villa, was a hut, a sort of shed but brick-built. Originally a greenhouse, it had been converted into a potting shed, a rough kind of workshop where Prince kept his tools and spent most of the day. In the far corner a wooden ladder, worm-eaten and falling to pieces, led up to a loft. Emilio had climbed up there once and been left breathless by what he saw. In the rays of the sun, yellow, warm but masked by the dust-caked window-panes, stuffed with old newspapers where they were broken, Prince's room appeared before his eyes – the bed with a mattress of maize leaves and a few filthy blankets; a chest of drawers, a rusty iron wash-stand, a metal-studded trunk. On everything dust and more dust. A smell of tobacco and sweat. A piece of paper glued to the window had come unstuck and buzzed as a trapped bluebottle tried to fly free.

The room inspired the same sense of wonder that the child felt every time he went up to the old gardener and stood quietly watching him at his work: while he weeded in the orchard or pruned the rose-bushes of their dead stems and rotting leaves, or when he sprayed the espaliered Victoria plum with sulphur.

Prince's neck was a maze of black wrinkles – a skin that seemed thick and strong like leather, but not in the least repulsive or beastly. You thought of his long life, first as a soldier and then as a farm labourer, always in the open air, always in the sun.

His face, too, was very wrinkled – but it was copper-coloured. And the pure whiteness of his drooping moustache and little goatee beard, his thick quizzical eyebrows, the wisps of hair which strayed from under his hat, accentuated that ruddy complexion, creating an effect of extraordinary energy and youthfulness.

Not even he was sure of the year he was born. Sometimes he would say 1816, other times, 1818. He had served in the '48 war with the 1st Regiment, Sardinian Grenadiers; then in the Crimea where he was promoted to corporal; finally in the '59 campaign. After which he had been discharged with the rank of sergeant. He had acquired the nickname Prince perhaps because of his military and majestic gait, or maybe his character had something to do with it.

Sometimes Emilio's papa would question him. The idea was obvious – to give the boy an opportunity to commit to memory that living historical, patriotic monument. But it was very difficult to get the old man to reply except by a slight shake of the head and the shadow of a fixed smile barely distinguishable between moustache and beard.

'What d'you say, Prince, is it true that you were at the battle of Pastrengo?' the lawyer would bawl in his ear, hoarsely and with the geniality of a man who has fully earned his holidays. Prince would nod. All he would say was: 'Was I there? By Christ, I should say I was.' And he would laugh with his crafty eyes. Then suddenly he would spit out his quid of tobacco – thick, liquefied, brown – which he had kept till then under his lower lip. You could see then that his artful, ironical expression was not only due to the old-fashioned Grenadier sergeant's beard but also to the plug of tobacco against his gum in direct line with it.

He had hardly spat when with thumb and forefinger he was ferreting in his waistcoat pocket; he would fish out another little heap of tobacco, roll it into a ball and pop it into his mouth.

The lawyer deplored the old man's violent and outrageously blasphemous exclamations in archaic dialect even more than his Zouave habits; he was afraid that as little Emilio was present he would have to call a halt. He would break off his imprudent interrogation, take his son by the hand and start to move off. 'Good day to you, Prince.'

But Prince noticed nothing and remained unmoved: he went on chewing 'baccy, weeding and cursing as he had always done – and also getting drunk, according to the aunts, but Emilio did not believe it.

When, the year before – at the end of September 1911 – war was declared on Turkey, Emilio who lived in the family atmosphere, all military ardour and conformity to the government, could not understand why no one had thought of letting old Prince join in the general enthusiasm for this new war being fought for the glory of Italy against the wicked Turks, in exactly the same way that the previous ones had been waged against the wicked Austrians. Amedeo, now a lieutenant – instructor at the Pinerolo School – had applied to be sent to the front. One afternoon in October, he and a group of his young brother officers who were leaving with him for Libya had come to a party in their honour.

The cream of Rivoli society and the holidaymakers of rank had been invited: the Cavalli of Olivola, the Rignons, the Nuvoli, General Zunino, lawyer Piolti, Signora Midana, all of them.

The cook had made a vanilla ice taller and thicker than a *panettone*: and a sweet of *savoiardi* sponge fingers covered with cream and chocolate so big that to serve it the huge Savona on the dining-room sideboard had to be pressed into service, the one that Emilio thought would never be used. And it was only just large enough.

There was tea with *bignole*[1] *di Stratta* and the first *marrons glacés* of the season. There was French champagne, *passito* wine from Caluso, and a drink whose name Emilio's mother repeated very often with mingled pride and complacency – *marquise*, or muscatel from Asti containing diced apples and pears and a few grapes.

The ice-cream was served in large shells, real sea-shells, and the champagne in tall, slender Bohemian goblets, all from the Sanfront ménage, which Aunt Elisa had sent for expressly from Turin, together with a quantity of lace table-cloths and napkins.

Everywhere for three days there had been an extraordinary cleaning-drive and the floors of the big rooms had been waxed. The french windows were thrown wide on to the garden. For the first time in Emilio's recollection the drawing-rooms were flooded with light. Marie Rose played patriotic songs at the piano. The young officers sang in chorus. His mother sang, too. But Papa was less daring: leaning on the upright piano, a long-stemmed glass in his left hand, he beat time with his right and when the piece finished merely shouted with the rest: 'Long live Italy, long live Italian Tobruk.'

Emilio ate *bignole* apart from the others, almost hidden in a corner behind the big green sofa. He was quite happy in the general confusion to be forgotten by all, even by his mama. Aunt Elisa was the nearest, sitting on the sofa with her back to him. Because of her age and her naturally majestic mien, because she was the mother of Amedeo, for whom the party was being given, and because she was the Countess Sanfront, guests as they arrived paid their respects to her first.

Round Aunt Elisa sat a group of ladies of her age in conversation. But next to her there was an empty armchair, her sister's place. Aunt Vittoria, as usual at parties, was even grumpier than usual. It was as if, for some mysterious reason, she considered the general gaiety unseemly and shameful. She wandered about among the armchairs and the sofas, the buffet tables, the bustle of waiters and guests, throwing baleful glances of contempt at this person or that, especially the younger and noisier elements, not speaking to anyone except Aunt Elisa to whom she returned every now and then, but very briefly, to reoccupy her seat. Then she sat on the edge of the chair; rudely indifferent to the feelings of the ladies in the group,

[1] *Bignole* – cream pastries, a type of éclair.

she interrupted their conversation and, bending over to whisper in her sister's ear, told her of some trivial, unpleasant incident. Emilio, unseen, was so near that he could hear everything.

'The Nuvolis' dog has done its business right in front of the entrance. People shouldn't bring animals to parties.' Or: 'The housekeeper has broken two glasses.' Or again, in an anxious tone: 'Elisa, it's already five o'clock' – words that Emilio promptly translated as 'Elisa, surely we're not going to miss Benediction, are we?'

Each time, Aunt Elisa sighed as she agreed; but not (this, too, was perfectly clear to Emilio) because she was annoyed at her sister's intervention – on the contrary, she sighed to show that she always left everything to her but did not shrink from what aroused indignation or anxiety in her; no, she shared her ideas, conformed to her wishes, followed her example. Emilio, from a little boy, knew very well, because his parents were always saying so, that Aunt Elisa was beautiful and good, but Vittoria was ugly and bad.

Suddenly Emilio noticed a disturbance among the guests. Some were moving back, some settling down again, some getting up. The officers, still singing, had turned towards the hall door through which an instant before Uncle Sanfront had entered. Now he was advancing towards the centre of the room. Three gentlemen of his age followed him. Emilio knew two of them because they were on holiday in Rivoli: Count Cavalli d'Olivola and General Zunino. The third was the big engineer, Badia, with his enormous side-whiskers, Uncle Sanfront's bailiff and his inseparable friend.

Emilio noticed for the first time that Uncle Sanfront's snow-white hair was distinctly yellow at the temples. Uncle Sanfront took a glass of champagne, raised it, looked around, smiling, arrogant, dignified, and seemed to be waiting for something.

He waited for the beginning of a verse and struck up at the right moment in a stentorian voice:

Naviga, o corazzata:
benigno il vento e dolce e' la stagion . . .

'Sail on, o warship:
Favourable is the wind and fair the weather'

Even Papa, then, hesitated no longer. Emilio wondered if he too could or should join in the chorus. He hastily finished the *bignola* he had in his hand and was about to open his mouth to sing. But just then Aunt Vittoria spied him.

'What are you doing here? Hiding to eat *bignole*, eh? Then tomorrow you'll have to take castor oil. Leave the room, go and play. This is no place for children. Be off with you!'

Emilio, crushed, a lump in his throat, looked desperately through the crowd of guests for his mother.

Mama, in a new white silk gown with an enormous artificial rose on her shoulder, was busy serving the officers, talking and joking with them. Emilio saw that there was nothing for it and beat a retreat. He circled the room, slipping behind the groups of officers with their black backs, silver buttons, pomaded necks, and the bitter-sweet scent of violet and lilac lotions.

He went out into the hall. The box of lead soldiers was in the drawer of one of the two corner-cupboards. But half-way there he was drawn, as had happened on other occasions, by Uncle Sanfront's malacca cane which was standing, a little askew, in the centre compartment of the umbrella-stand. It was light-coloured, almost luminous: and the gold ring under the handle glittered. There was no one in the hall. He felt an instinctive desire to touch the cane. He went up to it, stroked it. How smooth it was! It gave him pleasure to fondle it. He took it gently by the handle. He drew it from the stand, slowly, carefully. In the middle of the ring a crest was engraved: a helmet and below, six small balls and three towers – the Sanfront crest, as he knew from their writing paper, from the doors of the carriage and the Isotta Fraschini. But, more than the ring and the crest, he liked the wood, so light, polished and smooth, dotted irregularly with little reddish specks which suddenly reminded him of similar spots on the back of Uncle Sanfront's large, plump, pink hand. He had noticed them a moment before, when Uncle Sanfront, standing in the centre of the room, the object of the company's attention, had raised his slender glass before joining in the chorus. He pressed the cane to his cheek, the better to feel its smoothness. And, after pleasurably rubbing it two or three times against each cheek, he felt an inexplicable urge to sniff it. But the cane had no odour. So he tried sniffing the handle. Surely Uncle Sanfront's hand must have left a smell? Yes, he thought he could detect some sort of perfume – perhaps from toilet soap and not so different from that given off by the bodies of the officers when he had passed behind them shortly before.

Meanwhile, he kept his eyes fixed on the entrance in case someone caught him. Inside they were singing a martial tune from Bellini's *Puritani*:

> '*Suoni la tromba, intrepido* . . .
> *io pugnerò-o-o da forte* . . .'

He put his lips to the handle of the cane and slowly began to lick it. But he stopped abruptly. Not merely because he derived little pleasure from it, but because down in the sunlit garden, he had seen Prince passing with his customary rhythmical step.

He replaced the malacca cane. He thought of Prince – it was very strange that nobody had remembered him. All right, he was deaf. But he had certainly seen the carriages, the cars and all the guests arriving. And by now, a little of the noise they were making must have got through to him.

He went back boldly into the drawing-room, found his mother and took her by the elbow. Her arm was completely bare to the shoulder. It was plump, soft, warm. And the skin was much smoother than the malacca cane. It was like silk.

But Mama was laughing and chatting to two officers, one from the cavalry, the other an artillery man, and she did not seem to grasp what the boy was saying to her. Yet it was so simple – he wanted permission to take Prince a glass of *spumante*.

'Yes, dear . . . yes, tell me . . .' his mother kept on replying, but she neither looked at him nor understood what he wanted. She was too busy listening to the two officers. Finally, she said yes. But then she stopped him as he was running to the buffet and told a footman (the footmen, too, belonged to the Sanfront ménage and had come expressly from Turin) to get a glass of ordinary red wine from the kitchen and take it to the gardener.

The footman made a face, he had enough to do serving the guests. Mama did not notice, she was already back with the officers. But Emilio gave the man no peace until he went to the kitchen, filled a glass with wine from the demi-john, then, with the glass on a plate, left the kitchen and passed through the deserted dining-room to the french window, grumbling aloud as if he were talking to himself: 'Now then, where the devil's this gardener?'

32

'I know,' said Emilio, and taking the plate and glass which the footman was only too glad to hand over, he hurried out into the garden as quickly as he could, careful not to spill a drop.

Prince drained the wine in one long gulp, but so slowly that it seemed as if he would never finish. Then he returned the glass to Emilio, thanked him and wiped his mouth with the back of his hand. All extremely slowly.

'Tripoli,
bel suol d'amore . . .'

In the villa, the gay, high-spirited singing had begun again. The sun had just set, leaving the arbours and flower-beds in clear, transparent shadow, and for a few minutes continuing to kindle with a steady glow the great red espalier, the virginia creeper which covered the high wall dividing the villa from the adjoining farm.

Emilio gazed at Prince. He wanted at all costs to hear some word of enthusiasm from him.

'Hey, Prince, aren't you glad they've taken Tobruk?'

Prince was quick to reply, laughing aloud. He had probably been drinking before, and that last glass had been enough to make him merry. The old man replied in words that Emilio was at a complete loss to understand, nor could he even guess their meaning. But he caught his mood clearly enough – something between indignation and sarcasm. Years after when he thought of the gardener's reply he enjoyed trying to recall it. 'Me? Me, I'd be glad if they all stuck it up their arses!'

Perhaps, relying on a memory coloured with imagination, Emilio tended to exaggerate. At any rate, he had understood one thing very well at the time – the war in Libya left Prince completely indifferent.

It had been a tremendous surprise. With the plate in one hand and the empty glass in the other, he turned his back on the old man and made his way disconsolately back to the villa. He had hardly taken two steps when he heard someone calling him.

It was lawyer Cavalli, not Cavalli d'Olivola, another Cavalli – no relation: a little old man who lived in a villa near San Rocco and, so they said, was a great friend of the grandfather from Trino. He was emerging slowly from behind the bamboo grove, kicking out with his right leg and buttoning up his trousers. As usual he had a

Virginia cigar in his mouth – but it had gone out. His narrow imperial beard, pointed moustache and upward-slanting eyebrows gave him a Mephisthophelean air. But he was a very kind man and always cheerful. He liked playing with children, told them fairy tales, made marvellous smoke rings with his cigar.

Emilio showed him the plate and the empty glass, explaining the reason. Then with the smugness of a young master of the house he repeated what he had heard his papa say so often.

'Did you know that Prince was in the Risorgimento Wars?'

Lawyer Cavalli had turned to look at the tall figure of Prince slowly and majestically crossing the orchard in the direction of his cottage.

He relit his cigar and said: 'That fellow was never in the Risorgimento. Vittorio Amedeo, that's it – he was one of Vittorio Amedeo's grenadiers!'

Emilio said nothing, ashamed of not quite knowing who Vittorio Amedeo was and how he came to be involved. Then he associated these words – half-mysterious to him – with those used by Prince which were utterly mysterious. Perhaps therein lay the explanation, he thought. Lawyer Cavalli, from the nearby bamboo grove, had heard and understood. All that autumn, he dared not confide in Prince: he had to wait for the following summer and the extra-ordinary arrival of his thirteen-year-old great-great-nephew.

Ah, yes, with Pierino there, everything would change!

III

Yes, the memory of the sun in those far-off summers and that golden air; that immense peace which seemed as if it would last all Emilio's life; it sheltered, almost jealously hid, another memory. It was not a fact, not even an image. It was a daytime, joyous, vibrant sound, which rose into the sky and seemed to fill it, mingled with the memory of the sun, the heat and the calm and perhaps alone expressed its mysterious, deepest meaning.

Yet whenever he recalled the villa at Rivoli, his childhood and adolescence that ringing, vibrant note would be muffled almost to silence in the mute, golden décor of his happiness.

Only when he thought of his dear friend Pietro Giraudo and their first meetings; only when his memory reached back beyond the villa at Rivoli to Pierino as a boy, lean, skinny, bony, curly, with his bare arms already hairy, scorched red by the fire, Pierino blowing the bellows for his uncle at the old blacksmith's shop in Via Larga, just fifty metres to the right of the green front door of villa Racagni: only then would he suddenly hear the sharp ring of the hammer on the anvil. That sound which despite its proximity and violence annoyed no one, not even the aunts who were so quick to take offence; that sound which harmonized so well with all the rustic noises of the neighbourhood, the hens clucking, the cocks crowing or the staccato lowing of the oxen when in the heat of the day they were brought back from the fields and driven into the sheds; a sound so much gayer and livelier than that of the bells even on feast days; active and in a major key, a sound you immediately associated with the idea of profitable toil and the creation of something useful: a sound which seemed a song, rhythmic yet irregular, monotonous but free, a single note ringing out with constantly varying intensity and repeated at unexpected intervals and in unusual combinations.

Emilio, like all the residents of Via Larga, had become accustomed to the sound of the anvil. And now he no longer noticed it except

35

during the first two or three days whenever he came on holiday with the family; or later if some incident distracted him from his games, breaking their inexhaustible sequence; Boby, the dog hiding in a hedge or a bush and refusing to come out or his ball pitching over the farmhouse wall . . .

He gazed at that wall: the stretch of virginia creeper, a thick mat of red leaves, the grape-vine, greeny-blue with sulphate, yellow leaves thinning, here and there the bunches, each in a strange gauze bag (to protect them against the wasps, Prince had explained): that wall bristling along the top with pieces of multi-coloured glass, the pomegranate roof of the farmhouse protruding on the other side, the tall, leafy branches of a tree, an elm which, while walking past the farm-gate in Via Larga, he had seen and learnt to recognize in one corner of the threshing-floor; and overhead the vast blue sky. He looked – sky, tree, roof, wall, seemed to ring out in unison with the clang of the anvil, still and joyful in the pure, clear light.

The blacksmith was Pierino's uncle. But Emilio did not know this at first. He only knew that a sister of Prince's, now dead, was the smith's grandmother, and therefore Prince was the smith's great-uncle.

So whenever he passed the smithy (he often did but always with the grown-ups), he instinctively sought a resemblance to the old gardener in the smith's black, chubby, whiskered face, in his shiny, round forehead. But try as he might, he could not see one.

It was the smithy itself that interested and excited him with its mysterious fairy-tale atmosphere, its complicated equipment, the smoke, the flames, the glint of metal in the gloom and the marvel of red-hot iron gripped in the tongs and soft under the hammer, soft and spouting showers of sparks. Perhaps there was another reason why all these things seemed mysterious to him. He never went out alone but always with Mama or the aunts or holding Papa's hand; and he could not stop where and when he wanted to. And so he had only caught glimpses of the forge, a little at a time, until he built up a complete picture in his mind which retained the vague charm of an almost imaginary vision.

When Emilio passed by, the smith, serious and stern, with his sweaty brow and thick black moustache, never looked up from his work. Emilio, while still at some distance, noticed the quick, surly way the man glanced from beneath his bushy eyebrows and thought he understood. It was neither coincidence nor shyness that made the smith look down. He did it deliberately. Indeed on the rare occasions when he was seen moving from the anvil to the forge or vice-versa, which meant that he had to look out into the street and greet Papa, Mama or the aunts, he seemed to do it reluctantly with a nod and a flat 'Evenin''.

Was the smith a bad man? wondered Emilio. He had even asked his father. And Papa, pouting with disgust, had replied: 'Of course he is. He's a socialist.'

Emilio was not quite sure what *socialist* meant. But he did know that it was something that infuriated Papa so he dared not ask for an explanation. He rightly sensed that Papa would be loth to give him one, anyway. In the depths of every hate there exists the firm intention and the specific pleasure of hating, and there also exists the conviction that hating is all the easier when you do not know the person, when ignorance allows you to imagine just how hateful that person is. So you avoid speaking about him; you even avoid getting to know him too well, almost as if you were afraid of understanding or forgiving him, if not actually of endorsing his point of view.

'He's a socialist,' said lawyer Viotti, and the tone in which he said the word was enough to warn Emilio against certain individuals and to discourage him once and for all not only from having anything to do with such people but also from finding out about them and the meaning of the terrible word. Just as if he had said: 'He's not been found, he's still free – but he's a criminal, a murderer, a parricide. That's all. Don't ask any more.'

Gradually Emilio came to understand that *socialist* meant *enemy*, an enemy of Papa, of Mama, of himself. An enemy of gentlemen, and therefore of his family, old Uncle Sanfront, cousin Amedeo who was a cavalry officer fighting in Libya. Much more than that – an enemy of the officers and men who were then fighting against the cursed Turks. In a word, an enemy of the whole of Italy.

In the smith's glance and greeting, he thought he saw only hate. That scared him and attracted him at one and the same time, rather like the forge. They had told him that the blacksmith's grandmother was Prince's sister. As he had a grandmother then he must have a father and a mother, too. Perhaps he also had a wife and children . . . On reflection, it all seemed more and more strange to Emilio.

The word *socialist* was uttered by the Viotti, Ceroni and Sanfront families with such horror that quite involuntarily Emilio came to detect in it a savage resonance, a fearful significance – it was worse than *gipsy*. Socialists, he apprehended, were people who knew nothing of family and affection; were rebels, greedy for money, who only wanted one thing – the destruction of all that was good in the world. Now as he watched the moustachioed smith at work, Emilio, though unable to overcome this prejudice or suppress a feeling of horror, began to have doubts and to feel attracted as if by an out-of-bounds precipice.

One day it happened that, intent on unwrapping a sweet, he had fallen a few steps behind the slow trio of his mother and aunts. The smith in his leather apron was there striking the anvil. The blows rang out loud and clear. Emilio would have liked to stop and look. With the excuse of the sweet, he lingered for a moment. Then the smith looked at him; a different, new sort of look that Emilio had never seen before. Behind his drooping black moustache he was smiling: and suddenly he winked. He winked, and nodded his great, bald, sweating head at the trio slowly receding along the cobbled path – at the obvious tiresomeness and absurdity of those two huge aunts.

Emilio was unable to resist returning his smile. But he immediately felt guilty and ran to join his mother and aunts. His heart thumped partly because his conscience told him that he had betrayed his own family with that smile, partly because of a mysterious fear that a *socialist's* wink might not stop there but might have all kinds of consequences and implications.

The next day he saw the skinny little curly-haired boy blowing the bellows in the smithy. This was something else new. Up to then he had seen an old, lame man doing the job, Giacu was his name, he sometimes came to the villa for the heavy work such as washing the floors or cleaning the windows, sweeping away the cobwebs or bottling wine.

It was while he was walking to the Castle with his father that Emilio saw – or rather, glimpsed – the boy working the bellows in the shadows around the forge: a bony back clad in a light-brown woollen vest, a red, scrawny neck and a head of chestnut curls. But on the way back he saw the boy clearly. He was standing at the anvil near the door, gripping with long tongs a piece of red-hot iron which showered sparks as the smith hammered it.

The little apprentice had an intelligent, merry face, a long pointed nose, hollow cheeks, and – his most striking feature – big brown, rather melancholy eyes which as they momentarily met Emilio's gaze danced with laughter and irresistible charm.

He must be a little older than Emilio, but not much. Who was he?

A few days later he had a huge surprise. It was one evening at the beginning of July. They had finished dinner but were all still sitting around the table which had not been cleared. The aunts were certainly not in a gay mood but neither were they gloomy. This was before Amedeo's death, so a little conversation was still permitted. Papa asked if, exceptionally, he might light a cigarette before leaving table. Aunt Vittoria grudgingly said yes, turning slightly to see that the smoke would disperse immediately. It was hot and the french windows leading to the garden were wide open.

The restful white glow of the paraffin lamp illuminated a small rectangle of gravel outside the dining-room. The flowerbeds and hedges were plunged in darkness. But above, the tree-tops stood out against a clear sky – pale green in the far distance beyond the Alps where the sun had gone down.

Crickets chirped and frogs croaked in the ditch behind the villa and every now and then, as if to emphasize that profound peace, the horned owl hooted its single note.

A moth wheeled around the light, striking the shade with little thumps that set it vibrating.

Uncle Ceroni, who was very stingy and hardly ever smoked, took advantage of the special concession granted by his wife to cadge a cigarette from Emilio's father.

Mama rose. She took the pan and the curved brush and began to go round the table carefully sweeping the crumbs up from the cloth. As though at a given sign, Aunt Marie Rose also got up. She said that she was going upstairs to see that the children were not too hot in bed. She went out into the hall. Then a voice was heard greeting her.

'Good evening, Signora.'

'Good evening, Pierino,' replied Marie Rose.

Emilio was sitting with his back to the hall-door. He was just in time to turn and, with a start, catch a glimpse of the little boy he had seen at the smithy standing cap-in-hand as Marie Rose passed.

Although he had immediately recognized the lad, he concealed his feelings (which he could not explain even to himself) and pretended to take no notice. Later, he was about to ask with studied calm who the caller was when his mother, who had sensed something, told him.

He was the smith's nephew, son of his sister and so the old gardener's grand-nephew. He seemed a bright little boy. Fourteen years of age, son of a workman employed in a printing or typographic establishment in Turin, a few days before he had taken his technical school diploma, passing all his examinations with flying colours. But as his health was not too good, his parents before putting him to work thought it would be wiser to send him to his uncle in the country. His uncle fed him and gave him a job in the smithy but only for a few hours a day so as not to overtire him. The smith's wife had come to ask the aunts if the boy might sleep at the villa, up in the attic in one of the servants' rooms which surely were not all occupied. The smith had three children, two of them very small, so there was really no room for the boy which made it extremely inconvenient – 'You know what it's like when you've got little ones.'

Without consulting either Marie Rose or Mama the aunts had consented. 'But on one condition,' Aunt Vittoria growled, before Emilio's mother could say anything, 'and it's just as well that this fine fellow knows it too' (and the aunt's thick lips pouted sarcastically as if to spit). 'Fine fellow' referred to Emilio, for Aunt Vittoria, seizing upon his innocent little shortcomings, never missed an opportunity to label him as rebellious and dangerous – a 'fine' fellow.

'The condition is that every morning the smith's boy must get up at six o'clock precisely, the same time as Teresa and Maria' – (the housemaid and the cook) – 'and go back home to his uncle, and he must not show his face again here until bedtime.'

'It is an act of charity,' added Aunt Elisa, slowly raising her lovely blue eyes and gazing sternly at Emilio. 'An act of charity and we have done it gladly. But a word to the wise . . .'

Still eyeing Emilio severely, Aunt Elisa left her remark unfinished. But what her harsh, fixed, almost terrified stare meant was clear: 'You must have nothing to do, no contact, with the smith's nephew.'

Uncle Ceroni concluded in a loud voice: 'That's all we need! A socialist's nephew! Why, his father may be a socialist, too!'

'What has socialism to do with it?' with another growl Aunt Vittoria turned to her husband. 'Children aren't interested in politics. It's because of his education that he mustn't play with the urchin.' And as she said 'his education', she indicated Emilio with a contemptuous tilt of the chin.

'Tell me the company you keep and I'll tell you who you are. This would only be a school of sordidness and vulgarity. Because, listen, these people are the lowest of the low, the son of a labourer, nephew of a blacksmith, grand-nephew of a gardener . . . a peasant, after all. What can we expect? Let us have no illusions. They're the dregs!'

It seemed to Emilio that despite the extreme violence with which Aunt Vittoria had expressed herself, Papa had an objection to make. Indeed, he coughed as if to pluck up courage and timidly raised his hand to attract her attention. But Mama stopped him with a whispered '*Après*'.

In the family French was used whenever there was any risk of the servants or children understanding something they were not meant to.

Of course, Papa's opinions were certainly not very different from those held by Aunt Vittoria. Emilio guessed that his father, with the apologetic cough and the timid hand held up in the bright, white circle of light, had no intention of defending the people, but might possibly wish to point out the desirability of his son's having a playmate.

Shortly afterwards, when asked by his mother to perform the regular evening rite (going around saying goodnight to everyone, then up to his room and into bed), Emilio obeyed. But once outside the door, he stopped. He sat on the bottom step of the great stair-case and very slowly began to unbutton his boots – a plausible enough excuse if anyone found him and accused him of eavesdropping.

They had immediately resumed their discussion of the smith's nephew. Papa must have said something quietly along the lines that Emilio had imagined, for there was another growl as Aunt Vittoria responded with one of her usual proverbs: 'Better alone than in bad company.'

Then Mama joined in the fray: 'At least he could go to the Lanzas!'

'Who? The Lanzas? The tallow candle people?'

'They've got a little boy of about the same age. The child looks nicely brought up . . .'

'But do you mean the candle people?'

'Yes. The mother sent me a formal invitation. I met her at the station the other evening. She said "Send your little boy along to play with mine".'

'Are you talking about the candle and toilet soap people?'

'They've got a magnificent villa and a park that must be four times the size of ours.'

'They're still tradespeople.' Few words in Aunt Vittoria's vocabulary were uttered with such a definite, immutable tone of contempt.

'Tradespeople?' Papa ventured timidly; 'I should call them industrialists.'

'Industrialists, tradespeople, it's all the same' – Aunt Vittoria dismissed the argument. 'They're only shopkeepers. Riff-raff. Dregs, dregs. Just like the other lot. The only difference is in the banknotes. What vulgarity!'

Papa responded with a mournful grunt. And even Emilio could not help smiling as he thought of Uncle Ceroni's and Aunt Vittoria's greed for money.

Just a few days later when the news of Amedeo's death in battle arrived, the 'vulgarity' of masses of banknotes in the form of a legacy from sister Sanfront suddenly became quite attractive. But it is true that Aunt Vittoria even in this case could have claimed to be consistent with her theories and rejected all criticism: these banknotes were different from the others, sacred banknotes, hallowed by the crest of nobility. In any case, as can well be imagined, Signora Lanza's invitation did not suffer the affront of a rebuff.

Emilio was taken to play in the great park. But the little Lanza boy was, if possible, even shyer, more 'the young gentleman' than Emilio. He had no bicycle and did not climb trees though he was turned out like a real sportsman; bottle-green tweed jacket, knicker-bockers and woollen stockings to match, despite the heat. The jacket had a lot of bellow pockets, big and small, and was garnished with both vertical and horizontal martingales – and buttons all over it.

The only real attraction of Villa Lanza was a marvellous croquet lawn. But Ernestino behaved oddly when he played, getting excited when he was winning, and bored as soon as he began losing. In addition, he was taciturn, hesitant, melancholy and uncommunica-tive. He looked cold and reserved with his hair neatly trimmed *à la Umberto* and his sad, scared eyes. He ran stiffly and with no spring in his step as if he were practising a gymnastic exercise. He always walked on tip-toe even along the street or in the garden, as if afraid of waking someone in the next room. Perhaps that was the explanation, and his ridiculous, timorous gait owed its origin to a tyrannical family rule.

No, Ernestino was not much fun. On this point, though for different reasons, Emilio agreed with Aunt Vittoria – 'Better on one's own'. And every night, before going to sleep, he was plagued by the thought that the thin, curly-haired fourteen-year-old boy he had seen in the smithy was sleeping under the same roof in a little room on the second floor that might well be above his own.

This boy was not very strong, according to his mother, but Emilio had quite a different impression. And when one day he happened to see him come out of the smithy, pushing a splendid red bicycle, spring lightly into the saddle and zigzag off along Via Larga, then cross the great square and finally disappear as if by magic up the narrow street leading to the castle, his admiration knew no bounds. He began to long to make friends with the boy even though he was older and undeniably 'working-class'.

One Sunday morning after Mass he slipped into the kitchen – he was thirsty. The cook was busy making *sfoglia* pasta on the centre table. Emilio dipped the ladle in the pail and drank. Then, as there was some water left, he went to pour it away outside the door which stood wide open on to the wood behind the house. And there on a chair in the shade of the great trees sat the blacksmith's nephew, a huge book open on his knees.

Emilio took courage and went up to him.

The boy looked up from his book but did not get to his feet. Emilio was glad – he would have felt terribly embarrassed.

'I know you,' he said. 'You are Prince's nephew.'

'I know you too,' replied the boy.

'What's your name?' asked Emilio.

'Giraudo Pietro,' said the boy. 'But they all call me Pierino.'

Emilio suddenly felt a lump in his throat. He wanted to talk to him straightaway about the bicycle, to make friends. But the aunts had forbidden it. What could he say? And what would happen?

He turned round, hesitating. The back of the villa, which the late morning sunshine was beginning to desert, loomed high, sombre,

43

bluish, streaked with mould and damp-stains. Many of the windows were false, simple ornamental rectangles etched in the plaster. The real windows were few, here and there, corresponding to the corridors or the toilets, and the blinds were always drawn. So there was no risk that the aunts or his mother might be looking down.

As for Maria, the cook, she was still busy rolling out the paste for the *sfoglia*. Once she eyed the two boys but Emilio could detect no disapproval or malice in her glance. He was almost sure that she would not carry tales.

And so, feeling awkward there with Pierino who also had no idea what to say and did not dare return to his reading, Emilio looked at the book. It was massive, larger than an album and very thick. The pages with their two columns of print were illustrated.

'*The Common People* by Vittorio Bersezio,' said Pierino proudly. 'It's very fine. When I finish it, I'll lend it to you. So you can read it, too. What class are you in?'

'I'm just going up into the fifth.'

'So you'll be able to read it all right.'

But Emilio was thinking of something else. He flushed with embarrassment at what he had to say and found it easier to slip into dialect.

'I saw you on the bike yesterday. Is it yours?'

'Yes,' Pierino replied firmly. 'Papa bought it for me to go to work.' He added what Emilio knew already, that he had taken his technical school diploma and he meant to settle down to a serious job at the end of October. He worked his uncle's bellows just for sport. And the boy said it, smiling and blushing, half shyly, half with the pride of using the fashionable new word: 'Just for "sport".' Though, he hastened to point out, rising to his feet with a kind of quaint solemnity, the sport that interested him was quite different – real amateur cycle racing. And it was not unlikely that one day he might make a success of it.

Then Emilio asked the boy if he would teach him to ride a bicycle.

'Why, can't you? Of course I will. Have you got a bike?'

'Not yet. But if I show them I can ride they'll buy me one straightaway.'

Emilio stared at him. Pierino was such a nice boy – so tall standing there between the sun and the shade of the wood, with his chestnut curls, pointed nose and big laughing eyes.

Pierino said: 'I'll soon teach you to ride. But not on my bike. It's too high for you. You must hire one from the cycle-shop. Ask your mother.' Emilio looked at him questioningly for a last confirmation of the promise he had made. But, meeting his laughing eyes again, felt like weeping for joy. How stupid! Yet he could not help it. He averted his gaze and merely said 'Ciao, then.' And fled into the villa.

This is what happened. The news of Amedeo's death in Libya had upset the daily routine at Villa Racagni and the grown-ups no longer paid much attention to what Emilio was doing. To start with, the two aunts shut themselves in their room for more than a month with the blinds and shutters always closed, Aunt Elisa only concerned with her grief as a mother and Aunt Vittoria with Aunt Elisa's sorrow.

His father and mother had forbidden him to play with Pierino less from their own conviction than from fear of contradicting Aunt Vittoria. They were thus open to argument, as they would not otherwise have been. And each time they finally gave in, convinced that the aunts, cloistered on the floor above, would notice nothing.

So Emilio had to fight every time to obtain 'permission to play with Pierino'. And in these discussions with his parents he detected another attitude of confused embarrassment – reticences and hesitations which only ceased to be mysterious when they eventually vanished.

For some time a celebrated surgeon, Professor Fornaca, had been coming every afternoon from Turin 'for Aunt Elisa's heart'. During one of these visits, Emilio who was gloomily pushing his little cousins on the swing in the arbour, noticed some strange goings-on. The housemaid ran out of the house, shouting to Maria that she had to go to the smithy. Then the smith's wife, whom Emilio only knew by sight, came hurrying back with her and they both went into the villa. Almost at once she came out again, alone, and rushed off across the garden. Finally and incredibly Pierino raced in on his bike with a loud grating of tyres on gravel. He passed Emilio without seeing him, braked, jumped off, leant the bike calmly and neatly against the wall, took off his cap, tidied his curly hair and disappeared through the main door.

It was not difficult for Emilio to solve the little mystery. Papa and Mama had been led to have doubts about Pierino's state of health and they feared that he might be suffering from 'weakness of the lungs' – such was the term used in those days. Perhaps it was not wise to leave Emilio too long in his company? Fortunately Professor Fornaca's reply had allayed all their fears, and the next day Pierino received official sanction to teach Emilio to ride a bicycle as well as a deposit for the hire of a suitable model.

The avenues and paths in the garden at the front of the villa were gravelled and so hardly indicated for the operation. But the paths in the wood at the back were of beaten earth; there was, in particular, a large, rectangular, shady clearing, a hundred metres long, also of beaten earth, which seemed made to order. The only difficulty was overcoming the initial moment of fear.

'Even if you fall, you won't hurt yourself,' Pierino kept on saying to him. 'It's only earth and grass. You can't hurt yourself. Off you go, pedal away.'

And he would hold him by the saddle and run alongside. He would push him, let go, catch him again, support him when he faltered and looked like falling, keep him straight. Emilio felt that arm so different from his mother's against his side, that bony arm as hard as iron.

Pierino's body, so close to him during the whole lesson, gave off a stale smell of sweat which was not exactly pleasant. Perhaps Pierino doesn't take a bath very often, thought Emilio. Gentlemen in those times took it for granted that the common people never washed, a habit which became a problem or a cause for anxiety only in the case of servants. (And therefore 'the quality' found, or pretended to find, a solution: they firmly believed in the existence of certain individuals who, even without washing, did not smell offensively and they tried to recruit their domestic help exclusively from these.)

This unsavoury physical fact never affected for one moment the tremendous liking that Emilio had for his first friend. Emilio did not think of it as an 'affinity'. This was an idea that had not yet entered his head. He was only aware of an affection for Pierino, realizing at the same time that it was quite a different kind of affection from the one he felt for his mother, whom he always wanted to hug and kiss. It was a new affection rather like what he felt for his father, but stronger. An affection of glances, words, doing something specific and real together – repairing a cycle tyre, oiling the chain, sweeping the dead leaves from the paths in the wood to prevent them from fouling up the spokes and the gears. Yes, this was the supreme good. It was also the greatest happiness that Emilio had ever experienced.

46

A happiness obviously and entirely linked to the bicycle. But a happiness which certainly depended on Pierino and not on his bicycle.

One day Pierino told him that in October he was starting work as an apprentice in the Musso and Filippa photographic studio, 11 Via Cavour, Turin. The printing establishment where Pierino's father worked was a regular customer of Musso and Filippa. His father had known M. Filippa for years. As Pierino had always said that he wanted to become a photographer . . .

Emilio did not let him finish. He ran up to get his Brownie camera and a box containing all the materials for developing and printing, dishes, bottles of acid, fixatives, frames, paper and so on which he had never had the patience to learn to use. The Brownie was a present from Uncle Sanfront for his last birthday. All the rest a present from his father who always tried, without much success, to keep him occupied at some quiet pastime in a corner of the room.

At once Pierino seemed most interested. He examined everything seriously and carefully. He was quite an expert. He showed more than a hint of contempt for the Brownie which, he said, was too much of a 'baby's toy'. He advised Emilio to get someone to give him for his next birthday a Vest Pocket which had adjustable diaphragm and focus.

The enjoyment, the delight of those long afternoons in the dark room which Pierino, with his enthusiastic aid, had artfully rigged up in a cubby-hole under the stairs. The pleasure of the red transparent paper and the opaque black paper which Pierino had bought when he made a special journey to Turin! and when for the first time in the almost pitch darkness as he looked on patiently (for now ensconced in the dark room with Pierino, he had the patience of Job) he slowly made out the faint outline, a black smudge on a white ground, of Boby crouching down by the box hedge. His eyes fixed on the lens, set in a delicate white mask that was really black, the little fox-terrier showed up in negative with his head keenly and quizzically on one side.

47

IV

❧❧❧

The memory of that first bike-ride, October 1912, was almost obliterated by another trip with Pierino, a few years later, in June 1915. Both times they had started and finished at the villa. Pierino was now seventeen, Emilio fourteen and a half, almost fifteen. From Rivoli they had reached Pinerolo, and from Pinerolo on to Sestrières, toiling up the steep Chisone valley road. Then from Sestrières down to Cesana and Oulx, and finally to Bussoleno, where, too exhausted to pedal any further, they had caught the train, putting their bikes in the luggage van.

More than a hundred kilometres, certainly. And while Pierino's bike was a racing model, Emilio's was an ordinary tourist type. The roads were what you would expect at the time – from Fenestrelle up to the top of the hill, and from there as far as Susa, all earth and gravel. On the harder slopes Emilio had to get off and push. Pierino who was tougher, fitter and more experienced managed to keep going a little longer, then he would get off and wait for his friend.

Despite the difference in way of life and background, and the few opportunities they had of seeing each other, they had remained friends. Pierino was still with Musso and Filippa. Working as he did not only in the laboratory, developing and printing, but also in the studio and outside, he was well on the way to becoming a fully fledged photographer. Once, M. Filippa had lent him for a fortnight as second assistant to a cameraman at Fert. So, at the studios in Via Luisa del Carretto, near the Casale gate, he began to learn how a film is shot.

Emilio had completed his primary studies and was due to go to grammar school the following October. He was studious and reserved, partly because his father's caution and his mother's conceit combined to prevent him from striking up intimate friendships with other boys *when you never knew who they were*. As for those who belonged to aristocratic or good middle-class families, Emilio did not care much for them. Perhaps it was something to do with the spirit of contradiction in many boys of his age – their mania for independence and the way they find every possible excuse to oppose the wishes or even the mere opinions of their parents. Emilio's father and mother did not approve of Pierino but they had not dared to break a habit which seemed long-standing, or to revoke the permission which they had solemnly given. Perhaps snobbery had something to do with it, too, because Pierino was not just any working–class boy – he was 'our gardener's nephew'. This, at least, is what Emilio's mama would have said to any lady visitor who happened to enquire where the boy was. 'He's gone for a ride with our gardener's nephew,' even though ownership of the garden, with the villa, depended on a fondly optimistic hope of eventually inheriting the property.

Hostility on the part of his parents, therefore, but not an absolute ban – ideal conditions for Emilio to seek Pierino's company and experience a growing affection for him.

Compared to Pierino, even his closest school-friends like Tarchetti and Bertolé paled into insignificance. All right! Bertolé and Tarchetti already talked about women. But what were those yarns, confidences, descriptions, usually whispered in the stench of a latrine, or in the classroom during a break before the next lesson? What were they in comparison with a bike-ride up the alpine slopes, through flowering meadows, in the bracing, intoxicating, perfumed air of springtime with Pierino at his side, laughing as he pushed him along by the saddle?

The tyres on Pierino's Stucchi crunched on the gravelly surface. Emilio stood up on the pedals and pushed with all his might until he got to the top.

Oh, the joy in the sheer effort, the joy even in his aching muscles alternately stretching and contracting, in his fight for breath as his heart pounded faster, so it seemed, way up in his throat, in the sweat streaming down his cheeks until he could taste it bitter-sweet on his lips, in his eyes burning from the dust and the glare of the sun.

Now Pierino was silent. He was pulling Emilio from the front. Emilio could see his scrawny, red neck, a young peasant's neck, and the white cloth cap bobbing gently against the background of blue sky and black, rocky mountain. But soon, with the strain of pedalling, Emilio had to look down. All he could see was his own front wheel, the rear wheel of the Stucchi and the ground crunching as he passed over it. The ascent became slower and more difficult. Gradually but inexorably the back wheel of the Stucchi began to pull away, gaining ground at every turn of the pedals. Or was he, Emilio, falling back? He looked up. Pierino was well ahead, up there at the bend. He seemed to be able to tackle the hill without a trace of effort. His spare figure clad in brown vest and black shorts swayed rhythmically while his hands rested lightly on the handlebars.

Before disappearing round the rocky bend Pierino shouted to him in his powerful, man's voice, a real workman's or farm labourer's voice – so it seemed to Emilio: 'Come on, Emilio! Go it, boy!'

The guttural cry, echoing down the valley, reached Emilio with a strange, savage violence bordering on cruelty. What was meant to be a spur of encouragement struck him more as a wounding stab of humiliation. He began to suspect that Pierino was really a nasty type: for a moment he attributed this nastiness to the sportsman's thrill at winning, just as he attributed his own resentment to the smart of defeat. Then he thought it over. His own suffering went beyond his failure on the bike and the realization of his inferiority as a cyclist: suddenly he saw that there was something fatally, irremediably alien about his friend, the friend he liked so much. In other words, Pierino was not nasty. He was simply different. It was as if, once he had shot away up the steep slope leaving 'the young master' well behind, in his enthusiasm and strenuous effort he had involuntarily betrayed with that sarcastic shout his true nature – the age-old plebeian strength in his blood, the rigour of his childhood and upbringing.

Of course, the irony was unconscious and symbolic. Emilio could push and 'go it' until he burst but he would never catch his friend up. Pierino's world was one which Emilio sadly felt he could never share. On the other hand, Emilio's admiration for Pierino grew from this constitutional diversity. What would he not have given to be like Pierino – speak in dialect, work, earn his living and pedal like him!

When they got to the pass at Sestrières, they stopped for a few minutes at the rustic stone fountain to quench their thirst. Pierino, mouth wide open, gulped water easily and expertly from the icy jet. Emilio tried desperately to imitate him but merely got soaked to the skin. Pierino burst out laughing.

He laughed heartily, uninhibitedly, showing a gap where a tooth was missing, and his lean face with its irregular features was clearly likeable, handsome in a sort of way. Hearing that frank laughter Emilio immediately felt relieved of the suspicion that had flashed across his mind. Pierino a nasty type? Of course not! No, Pierino was a good scout, Pierino loved him like a brother, like a true friend.

The strong, bracing wind was like cool, intoxicating refreshment to their weary, sweating limbs. But the experienced Pierino made Emilio change into the reserve vest he had strapped to his carrier and slip a newspaper folded into four between vest and shirt as protection during the descent: 'Or else you'll catch cold. Your mother will say it's my fault, and she won't let you come again.'

There was in these words and the smile that accompanied them not only a sense of protection for the younger boy but also a sly dig at the lad's delicate upbringing – an only son coddled by his doting, over-anxious parents. In addition there was the assurance that it would do Emilio a lot of good to 'come out of his shell'.

The spectacle of the Alps, as Emilio Viotti saw it first for a few minutes from the Colle del Sestrières, in the limpid splendour of a June morning, was unforgettable. Opposite, beyond the green wooded valleys with their blue shadows which beckoned the way down, was a circle, horizon-wide, of lofty mountains, some of them rocky, others mantled in sparkling snow. Pierino, who had been to Sestrières before, pointed out a great, sheer towering peak straight ahead – a grey pyramid of rock and stone dominating the valley. 'That's the Forte of Chaberton. It's the last Italian Forte. All the other peaks you see are in France. And that' – he pointed to the central mountain, higher and further away, gently rising from a base of snowfields and glaciers and crowned with a huge dome, white against the sky – 'that's the Pelvoux group. Have you ever been on a glacier?' Emilio confessed sadly that despite their nearness to Turin, he had never been to the mountains. Since he was a baby he had always spent his holidays at Rivoli. The last two years, before going to Rivoli his parents had taken him to the seaside, to Alassio for a couple of months. He had learnt to swim. But he had never been in the mountains.

Pierino explained that he had taken up a new sport, though cycling would always remain his favourite. He had entered a few amateur races and the previous year had even won the *Giro delle Langhe*, arriving at Alba well ahead of the rest which had earned him the Federation Gold Medal. Then he had begun to go mountaineering with his boss who was a member of the Alpine Club. For example, he had been one of a rope on the Gran Paradiso glacier. As slowly and calmly as ever, he took from the back pocket of his knickerbockers a brown leather wallet. Emilio looked at it hungrily, full of admiration and envy. He too had a wallet. But not so fat or so worn, not so *real* as that one. And the slow, solemn way in which Pierino handled it seemed to endow it with extraordinary and mysterious properties.

The wallet contained some snapshots of a party of mountaineers on a glacier.

'That's Monsieur Filippa. That's a guide. And that's me.' Then he briefly described the burning sun, the rarified air, the crevasses, the rope and how to cross a glacier.

Emilio, after studying the photos, turned instinctively to look at the Pelvoux. There in the distance – high, incredibly white, expanses. The more he gazed at them, the stronger grew a sense of wonder that he had never experienced before. He tried to imagine what they were like close to or when one was actually on them – it must be terrifying and marvellous. He stared at them for a time in silence, dreaming. Up there, too – he thought – there was life. Perhaps the finest life of all – the freest, the most complete. With the sun, the sky, the ice and nothing else.

He started at the sudden sound of a cow-bell, mellowly diffused in the air. Following the sound he looked round the meadows – immense, green slopes in blossom down to the ridge, with cows grazing – almost motionless splashes of black and white and black and brown – not far away but as unreal as a mirage.

'How peaceful,' said Pierino with a sigh, carefully buttoning the trouser-pocket where he kept his wallet. 'It doesn't seem possible that we're at war.'

Emilio immediately forgot the view, forgot all the emotions and dreams which had absorbed him just before.

'Why do you sigh? Aren't you glad we're at war?'

'Not a bit,' murmured Pierino, standing stock-still.

'War is a fine thing!' Emilio repeated automatically what he had been hearing in the family and at school for months and months. 'Italy will win and we'll take Trento and Trieste.'

'No, my papa says that war is bad. Bad and unfair. Men have died and many more will. We shouldn't make war. The rich wanted it but the ones who suffer most are the peasants and the workers.'

'After all, the officers die too.'

'Yes, but more soldiers do. You don't understand these things.' Pierino's face had become serious. With his thin lips pursed like a grown-up's, he looked straight ahead at the distant peaks. Emilio felt more sharply, more painfully than before all that separated him from his friend. In fact, how could Pierino be his friend if he hated the rich?

'Let's go! We've still got a long way. Jump on!'

Emilio looked up and saw the best answer to his anguished, unspoken question – Pierino once again smiling at him, calmly and affectionately. Then he jumped on his bike, turned round for a moment expecting Emilio to do the same, and shot off down the slope, high on the pedals.

Cold, blue air, speed banishing thought, a supreme illusion of lightness as if the body were weightless, a delicious prolonging of the imaginary moment before take-off in a flying machine . . . Emilio felt himself floating in a cocoon of speed. And bent low over the handlebars he felt his head and chest cleave the air like the figurehead and prow of a ship. The only effort required was in his hands which, on approaching the bends, had gradually to grip the brakes and apply them each time with tenacious violence. Pierino, who was more expert, rode like the racing cyclists – he neither slowed down nor braked, he took the bends at full speed; then slammed the brakes on, skidded round on his back wheel and was off again like a flash. It was a trick that Emilio would never have attempted. And it was another reason to admire Pierino in and out of sight two, three, four curves further down on the way to Cesana – a tiny black silhouette on the zigzag pink road flitting between the clumps of pines.

Suddenly he disappeared from view. Emilio caught up with him in a village at the Monginevro fork. He was waiting, astride the bike and with one foot resting on the parapet of the bridge. The poplars on the old square rustled gaily in the sun and wind blending with the roar of the torrent. They set off again at more than thirty kilometres an hour. The joy of riding in unison, taking it in turns to lead down the gentle slope! The two boys, busy pedalling with all their might, paid no attention to the view and perhaps because of this it remained

53

all the more vividly imprinted on their memories. On the right, a fir-wood – kilometres of cool shade. On the left, the steep, winding cut of the river Dora, and on the opposite bank in the glare of the sun, precipitous slopes, wooded or craggy. High above, beyond the peaks, there appeared for a few moments a small point half silvery in the sun's rays, half in light blue shadow.

'The great Hoche' – said Pierino without slowing down – 'it's not a high mountain, but a very difficult one. A third-class climb.' They saw it again a little later from the meadow by the Bardonnèche where Pierino had chosen to picnic.

From there, the great Hoche, etched against the golden sky of early afternoon, was merely a black triangle. And Emilio wondered – would he ever experience the dangers and joys of a real climb? He reminded himself that he was fifteen with his whole life before him. In the endless future there seemed to be room for everything. It looked as if no adventure, no experience would be excluded.

Meanwhile Pierino in his slow, deliberate way had spread a newspaper on the grass and neatly laid out the food that he had brought in a special case.

It was a brown fibre lunch-box, strong and deep, one of those cases by which Emilio had learnt to recognize workmen when he saw them coming home every evening in a tram or on a bike. That same morning at half-past five, while cutting through Via Lagrange on the way to his rendezvous with Pierino at Porta Nuova, he had met long streams of them, all on bikes, wearing blue linen suits and peaked caps, all with their lunch-boxes tied to the handle-bars or the carrier. Past the old grey houses and along the street beyond Corso Vittorio which, under a new name, led straight to the Nice Barrier and the Lingotto factories, the bread-winners of Turin were seriously and silently going to work. The sun lit up only the roofs and the squares. The city was still immersed in the cool shade of a summer morning. The trams clattered by, packed with workmen, skirted, then overtook the unbroken line of cycles and with a vigorous clanging of bells forged ahead also in the direction of the Nice Barrier. And peace returned to the sleeping middle-class dwellings, a silence punctuated by the gentle clicking of a thousand free wheels.

The Musso and Filippa studios were in the centre of the city, in Via Cavour. Pierino lived with his family at La Madonna di

Campagna. He went to work by bike and did not come home at midday. And so, like the workmen, he took a lunch-box which his mother prepared for him.

For this trip, he had personally chosen the menu. Besides an onion omelette and other family specialities, he had brought mortadella, cheese, sardines and a large round loaf of bread.

The cook had given Emilio four white rolls, ham and butter and four brioches with butter and jam. Pierino laughed.

'Poor chap! Look – this is what we'll do. You keep it for a snack.' And he fished out of his pocket, even more solemnly than he had fished the wallet, a large, thick, nickel-plated knife with a lot of complicated gadgets. He opened the biggest blade and began to divide his lunch into two portions.

The penknife was certainly a wonderful thing. Any penknife is, for all boys and for many grown men, too. But what fascinated Emilio most was Pierino's calm manner, his skill and confidence, the almost religious rationality of every movement, even in ordinary matters like this.

He cut the loaf methodically into equal slices holding it against his chest, country style. The he made sandwiches of omelette, mortadella, sardines. A round blue enamelled tin contained aubergines prepared by his mother. He screwed off the lid and used it as a plate. In a tiny waxed-paper packet there was some salt. He opened it and put it in the middle.

Why was everything so lovely? And why was the food not only so good, but also so different in taste, mysterious and somehow richer, a taste of rightness?

Pierino seemed to value everything – to consider that every moment and detail of life was important. You could be quite sure that he would always live it to the best of his ability without a trace of discouragement. And the result was that Pierino transformed every action into something beautiful, as if without knowing it he possessed a magic touch.

Passing through Oulx they had bought two bottles of beer at the Golden Lion. It was not far – after lunch they would take the empties back.

'I bet you don't remember,' said Pierino, going to fetch one of the bottles which he had put in the stream up against a little dam of stones to keep cool.

'What don't I remember?' asked Emilio, puzzled. In reply, Pierino held up to the sunlight the sparkling, golden bottle, dripping with water, and laughed in his affectionate, teasing way.

Then Emilio remembered. That other outing with Pierino, years before. Round the lakes of Avigliana. Emilio was still a child, or almost. He had just learnt to ride a bike. When he got back he was sweating, thirsty, worn out. His legs were aching. It was the first real trip.

Finally, he again saw the red roofs climbing the hill up to the towering mass of the Savoy castle – Rivoli! And the station square where the steam-tram came in from Turin. And there were the dusty horse-chestnut trees, the Three Kings Hotel, the little garden among the plants in tubs, the coloured tin advertisement with a bearded, bald old chap drinking a glass of Bosio and Caratsch beer, a look of supreme contentment on his face.

A beer? Emilio hesitated. He had never drunk beer. As a general rule, at the Viottis' the only beverage was water. Papa was allowed a small quarter-bottle of wine at meals – from two demijohns which Uncle Sanfront always sent just before Christmas. And once when Emilio unwisely expressed his curiosity about beer, the unknown drink, Aunt Vittoria leapt into the breach. Pouting her thick lips in utter disgust, she seemed as usual to spit her words. 'Beer! That filthy stuff! The very idea!' And turning to Emilio's father and mother, she accused them indirectly of bringing the child up badly so as to humiliate them deliberately in front of Aunt Elisa and show that they were unfit to inherit. 'For a child of his age he certainly has very refined tastes. Beer, indeed! A waggoners' drink!'

Emilio's curiosity had remained, but mingled with suspicion and a kind of fear. Waggoners' drink? A drink for strong, energetic people, even if they were 'vulgar'. By offering him a beer, Pierino clinched the fact that he too was one of those people with whom, according to Aunt Vittoria, Emilio should have nothing to do, but who, the boy felt, were as good as his own family, if not actually better – more alive, more positive, nicer people.

Now, three years later, it was Pierino who first reminded him of the occasion. And Emilio, as usual when someone revives memories of something that we have not thought about for a long time, recalled the exact moment: an October afternoon and the hot sun on the pale yellow front of the Three Kings, the little garden among

56

the plants in tubs, the Bosio and Caratsch advertisement, Pierino's bony forehead fringed with unruly, sweaty curls and his teasing, inviting smile: 'Come on! Have a go!'

They had sat in the garden. Pierino had ordered with his usual assurance. The deep clink of the brimming mug. The pleasantly bitter taste of the beer, scented with barley.

He looked at his friend. Pierino had put his mug on the table. Now he was mopping the sweat from his forehead with a carefully folded handkerchief. He gazed at Emilio, laughing: 'Well, d'you like it?'

And it was the first time that Emilio felt a strong liking for the boy. He simply felt it without telling himself so. Between friends, it is not the thing to make or even think declarations of loyalty. But they happen without the two friends knowing, expressed in an unconscious rite, an involuntary symbol, sometimes of the most ordinary kind such as a glass of beer. It is noticeable that when put to the test these pacts – perhaps because of their implicit nature – are almost invariably stronger than those between couples of different sexes.

And so, three years later, the symbol reappeared. The rite was repeated. Emilio and Pierino sat drinking beer together again, looking into each other's eyes without thinking of anything in particular, just happy to be together.

PART TWO

I

In the distance, a girl dressed in yellow came into view on the pavement of Corso Casale.

She approached rapidly, walking in the shade of the brown or green awnings in front of the little shops, crossing every now and then the short patches of sunlight between them – then for an instant the yellow shone brightly. Was it Vévé?

Her size. Her springy step. Blonde. And she was coming at the right time to the right place.

With his heart thumping in the blissful torture of hope, Emilio gazed at the girl dressed in yellow coming towards him. And could not believe it was true. Should he go to meet her and so shorten the waiting and uncertainty. No, of course not. Though that was mere superstition. An absurdly retrospective superstition. As if a few steps towards the girl – supposing it were Vévé – could suddenly change her into someone else. Or, more subtly, as if they could have been foreseen by some obscure god who, as a punishment for his impatience, had kept Vévé from her appointment and sent in her place another girl resembling her from a distance to walk along the pavement of Corso Casale at that particular time. And now it looked in any case as if the god were in a teasing mood and enjoyed keeping him on tenterhooks. For the girl dressed in yellow, Vévé or not, stopped abruptly to look in a shopwindow. Was it natural for Vévé to stop and look in a shopwindow just a few yards from their rendezvous? Quite natural. Emilio took from his waistcoat pocket the Vacheron and Constantin watch which had been presented to him after he had passed out of grammar school. Barely five minutes late. Perfectly natural. Vévé had admitted to him how she loathed waiting because it hurt her pride. Perhaps she was afraid that *he* would be late, like all the other times. Or it was just coquetry. The shopwindow was a milliner's – some pretty little hat must have caught her eye, but even more attractive than the hat, was – possibly – the calculated ploy of being seen by Emilio dawdling, and not appearing too eager, or at least a little more self-possessed than she really was. At last she seemed to make up her mind, and left the window. A second later, she hesitated. She turned back a half pace to take another look. And at that moment of dancing poise, one leg slightly bent, one arm slightly at an angle, her white-gloved hand half-raised, she stuck out her high, round bottom so that Emilio would have recognized her even from much further away.

He ran happily towards her.

He had met Vévé a few weeks before; on his way to the insurance firm to see a university friend, who was older than himself and had taken his degree, he had noticed her at the typewriter in the next office. Vévé was blonde, pale, but strong – blue eyes, sparkling white teeth, a frank and generous smile. His friend introduced him. It was nearly midday. Emilio chanced waiting outside the employees' entrance and offered to see her home.

'Thanks, but just for a little way,' said Vévé, laughing. He accompanied her as far as the end of Via Po – a vermouth, two *bignole*.

After that they met almost every day. Emilio went to fetch her from the office, but not at midday: he went at seven o'clock in the evening so that they had a little longer to stroll under the arcades. It happened several times that Emilio was delayed by a university lecture and had to run all the way – not far, fortunately – to the insurance office. Once, Vévé had got annoyed and had not waited for him.

Their courtship, despite Emilio's persistent attentions, was confined to innocent walks in the arcades between seven and eight – the time for the evening glass of vermouth. At eight, no later, Vévé caught the tram to go home. She came from a humble family and lived at Barriera di Casale. Emilio, on the other hand, lived on the second floor of an old mansion in Piazza Maria Teresa, Borgo Nuovo.

As Vévé had to be home by a quarter past eight there was no question of going to the cinema. One evening she agreed to go to the Valentino Park. But it was in May and light until late. Emilio had only been able to steal a brief kiss on their way back, as they sat on a bench at the top of the mound in the Cavour Gardens. On Sundays, Vévé had to spend the day with her family. At least so she said, smiling artfully as if to hint at something quite different. In fact it was unlikely for a girl of such beauty and charm not to have any suitors. It was even improbable that Vévé did not have a lover or an unofficial fiancé. This was what Emilio thought, stifling almost immediately foolish presumption. And he had not been discreet enough to hide his incredulity. But Vévé had told him laughingly, with a shake of her blonde curls: 'No, there's nobody. You're in luck. You've happened along between one and the other.'

'How, between one and the other?'

'Well, until a few days ago, before you turned up, there was an engineer who courted me, and how he courted me! But he was one of those chaps who at first seem charming and intelligent and then are quite the opposite, and as false as Judas. And so I sent him packing the night before you came to the office. You're as false as Judas, too, but you're nicer than usual. More intelligent, too. Your stocks are rising.'

'And the other one?'

'What other one?'

'You know, the one after me. You say I'm lucky and I've happened along between one and the other. You've told me about the one. What about the other?'

'The other? Oh, he doesn't exist yet. But he'll come, of course.' And their glances, like duellists' blades crossing for the first time in the instantaneous immobility of a lightning flash, met in a mutual exchange of desire and suspicion, love and fear.

You're on the defensive, said Emilio's eyes – you talk of my successor because you're afraid, not of failing to find him, but of not wanting this successor; you think that perhaps you'll love me and I'll love you; but you're scared that I'll get tired of you first, you're afraid that one day, maybe in the distant future, you'll be thinking of marriage and I won't.

Vévé's eyes said: you're afraid that even if I love you, I'll be thinking one day in the distant future of marriage; this fear is natural because you belong to a higher social class than mine.

It's possible – replied Emilio's eyes – that in a few years I may marry you: but at the moment it's a ridiculous idea. I'm still a long way from getting a position and earning my own living. I could only think of marrying you if one day my family became rich with the Sanfront legacy. For now, I like you more than any other girl I've met, I want you and perhaps I'll love you.

Vévé's eyes concluded: you're not capable of real love. I'm awfully

63

scared of suffering, maybe in a few years. But I like you more than any other boy I've met, I want you and I'll certainly love you.

An embarrassing silence followed that moment of truth, as soon as they lowered their eyes. Emilio instinctively felt for her hip – the high waist, the solid, plump flesh through the chiffon blouse. And all his thoughts and doubts vanished in a trice. The future was immense, free, indistinct, like a clear sky, like the sky on that day in May. You did not need to look at it, but it entered your soul with the air and the sun. The future lay in the long hours before them till evening in the meadows and woods of La Collina.

It was the afternoon of Ascension Day – not a Sunday! This was how Vévé, laughing mischievously as usual, had explained why she was free. It was the first time that she could stay so long with Emilio, and – more important still – not just in the city streets.

Vévé suggested their route – Santa Margherita, L'Eremo,[1] La Fontana dei Francesi.[2] There, at the Beccaccia Inn they would have tea and biscuits. Emilio agreed unreservedly – it was obvious that Vévé knew La Collina better than he did.

'A fine Torinese you are, I must say!'

'We always go to Rivoli in the country,' murmured Emilio, and he felt himself blushing. It had happened before – Vévé would break into dialect and, knowing that he could not speak it very well, he would reply in Italian. But this time he found it perfectly natural to overcome his little inferiority complex – to overcome it by talking frankly about it.

They strolled slowly up the avenue towards Villa della Regina. He kept his arm round her waist. The strange ease with which she let him hold her tight and the way her ripe body seemed to press questingly against his, one breast in close contact with his side, led him to hope that she had adopted a new attitude towards him, perhaps consciously, and he was eager to recognize the signs of imminent surrender.

'I was born in Turin,' explained Emilio, 'but my mother's family come from La Spezia – and we always speak Italian at home.'

'You're a gentleman, we know. You're a young gentleman,' said Vévé, laughing confidently and hugging him round the waist. She was twenty, like him. But just then Emilio realized that she was much

[1] The Hermitage.
[2] The Fountain of the French.

more experienced than him and not only in the roads and paths of the Turin Collina.

Emilio at twenty was in his second year at the university, but his experience of women, both physical and sentimental was still meagre.

His father's ambition for him was exclusively and fanatically set on a career. He had always wanted Emilio to become a great lawyer. His mother's ambition, on the other hand, was fired by the cherished hope that he would bring off a sensational marriage to some incredibly rich girl of aristocratic family. The Sanfront legacy, for which both parents never ceased to hope, would one day facilitate both career and marriage. Meantime, it was essential to feed this illusion at all costs. As far as their standard of living was concerned the Viottis had to appear to belong to the cream of the upper middle class in Turin. A box at the Regio (shared with the Ceroni cousins); reception day once a week; the hiring of a private carriage to go to Mirafiori a couple of times during the racing season: a cook and a parlourmaid; suits for Papa, but not often, from Prandoni; Mama's dresses, hardly more frequently, from Bellom; shoes from Cappa . . . The family budget provoked a silent struggle and was kept a close secret from Emilio who had only recently become aware of it. Besides the lawyer's salary there was the income from his rice-fields at Trino Vercellese – a slender one because it had to be shared with a brother and a sister – and there was the revenue from Mama's dowry which Grandfather sent every two months from La Spezia. But altogether was it enough?

Papa and Mama, realizing that substance was important as well as appearances, and that their extravagant (though calculatedly so) way of life would not in itself guarantee the brilliant future they visualized for their son, had always put the greatest emphasis on his studies and education. From the beginning they had lavished all their attentions upon him, strictly, obstinately, implacably. English and French courses, piano and fencing lessons. Then, while he was at the university, they bought his books, kept in constant touch with his professors. Continual attention, care and supervision.

Emilio, for his part, had responded as well as his parents could have possibly expected. Up to and including grammar school, he was always top of the class. At the university, nothing but praise. His distractions and diversions were few and he never sought them with much enthusiasm. That is why he had gained little experience of love. His studies seemed to rob him of both the time and the urge. Just a few innocent flirtations with girls of good family during the summer holidays or in the winter evenings at the *carré*,[1] given by La Radicati di Primeglio; at La D'Agliano's *carré*, a kiss and a peck from some little seamstress in the dimly-lighted passages adjoining the ballroom; one or two inevitable, hasty attempts, generally incomplete, at the Massena, the Raffaello or in one of the two houses in Via Principe Amedeo where parties of students usually met.

It was like the old times again, especially in Turin, the days of the Medieval students celebrated in song by Oxilia and Camasio: the last rocket (relit after the forced interruption of the war and finally extinguished by the grey uniformity of Fascism) in the long firework display of the *belle époque*. Though the grim, tragic period did not begin with the March on Rome, but later in June, 1924, with the assassination of Matteotti. So the Turin students' last carnivals were in '23 and '24 – a blissful interval for the bourgeoisie between the Bolshevist peril and the actual onset of dictatorship, when the régime had already – as people said – saved the fatherland but not yet invented the doleful, grotesque, hypocritical ritual known as the Fascist style. The carnivals from 1919 to 1922 should have been a little less giddy; these were the years when the workers' organizations in Turin were facing their first great trials culminating in the autumn of 1920 with the desperate attempt to occupy the Fiat workshops. But how many of the students at that time gave a thought to the workers? Their mothers and aunts offered *novenas* at the Consolata church so that the National Bloc would win the elections. Their fathers, professional men or employees, even though they believed in Agnelli and Giolitti and for the moment did not go so far as to approve of the Fascist squads' early expeditions, yet they feared that the government was not strong enough; they made a face and shook their heads; they gritted their teeth more than they dared admit. Not to mention the terror of those, like the Treasury Counsellor, who had always considered Giolitti 'a sort of socialist'.

But what about their sons? Apart from the more intelligent ones, or the sons of the more intelligent and enlightened fathers, apart from an élite surrounding Gobetti, Gramsci, Ruffini and a group of

---

[1] A series of exclusive parties organized during Carnival by Turin aristocratic families in order to find eligible husbands for 'débutante' daughters.

writers, painters, musicians, most of the university students took no interest in politics. As if assured by an infallible instinct that in the end nothing of what their parents feared would come to pass, they thought only of their own affairs, studies and enjoyment – especially enjoyment – and never bothered their heads with the workers' demonstrations of unrest. The topography of Turin favoured a certain ignorance of this subject. There were two residential districts, adjacent, concentric yet strictly separated by a long perimeter of arcades and avenues that might as well have been a barrier of invisible, unscalable walls. On one side, the middle-class area, on the other, the working-class outskirts of the city. The latter encroached on the former at a number of points but the only important one was the Labour Exchange in Corso Siccardi.

Sometimes the students heard the crackle of machine-gun fire, far away in the direction of Barriera San Paolo. Half an hour later, if they happened to be near Corso Re Umberto, Piazza Solferino, Via Alfieri, they could distinguish in the subdued murmur of the city traffic the familiar, insistent and poignant note of the Green Cross bell. The bell came nearer. And then hospital orderlies wearing armbands raced up, silently pushing ambulance stretchers high on their rubber wheels. They crossed Piazza San Carlo, turned into Via Ospedale. There was something tragic about the ringing of the bell, the scuffle of their feet, their panting faces. Suddenly quiet, the crowd made way for the stretchers, looked at them, counted them – six, seven, eight, another and yet another . . . and sometimes the fog, as it enshrouded them, seemed to increase their speed in that final leg of the journey; to reach the hospital a minute earlier might mean a life saved.

But what did most of the students of those days care about the workers and their struggles? It was the last happy season of a class that had held sway for a century. For the Turin students it meant the little milliners and dressmakers, the Collina and the afternoon strolls along the deserted old streets that threaded tortuously between the walls; it meant the kisses, promises, declarations of love, the farewells; it meant the carnival nights beneath the arcades in Via Po, and the triumphant revel in Piazza Vittorio. It meant masquerades, choruses, tangos, one-steps; on the pavements, carpets of confetti, in the sky, pergolas of coloured streamers; on the white haunches of the Peter roundabout horses, the bottoms of the prettiest girls in town. Interminable, crowded, intoxicating nights – riotous nights of joy. And the aim, the climax of it all, the brothel.

On the rare evenings when he went out with his friends Emilio did not opt out of the final stage. Brought up as a rooted conformist, he simply said to himself – 'They're all going so I will, too.' The first time, he was clever enough to give the impression that it was *not* the first time. And as for the pleasure he experienced, keen and genuine though it was, it always paled in comparison with the promise of imagination and desire. He therefore did not find it difficult to show an indifference that he considered chic on these occasions.

But his pals considered him more of a swot than a snob. Emilio applied himself to his studies with a coldness matched by diligence. Methodically, never passionately. As if his parents had only been able to instil in him the ambition to succeed. Discipline, icy strictness – comprehensible and even partly excusable attitudes up until leaving school, but while preparing for a freely chosen profession, unpleasant and almost odd. In fact, Emilio did not admit the truth even to himself.

He had taken law apparently to satisfy his father's constant wishes but really because he knew that he had no leanings towards one particular profession more than another. Four years of law would open up many avenues and provide the quickest and most practical solution. The Bench, the Bar, administration, university teaching, diplomacy, business? In his heart of hearts, he knew full well, even though he dared not admit it honestly to himself, that once he had taken his degree, he would have only one object in mind – to make money as rapidly as possible in order to enjoy life. On the other hand, if he had wanted to, had been able to reflect upon this problem even more coldly than he thought he usually did when examining every fact, plan, invitation of life, he would have realized that the only happy days of his adolescence (which was already drawing to a close) had been spent with Pierino. And in no way had they been conditioned by money, nor were they concerned with what can give money or what money can give. He would have realized that to be happy with Pierino or like Pierino there was no need to belong to the upper middle class, go to the races and the Regio Opera House, keep servants in striped jackets, dress at

Prandoni's and be shod by Cappa, own a carriage and an automobile, travel abroad, know Paris, London, New York, speak English and French with a good accent, be invited to the richest mansions in Turin and to receptions at the Royal Palace or to the Radicati and D'Agliano *carré*; no need to inherit the Sanfront legacy, marry a girl of noble family one day, go hunting, play golf, bathe at the seaside, indulge with a guarantee of perfect secrecy in adventures, escapades, mistresses. No. No need for all this to be happy like Pierino or with Pierino. But perhaps, because they had really been together very infrequently, Pierino had remained during Emilio's adolescence a wonderful, enchanted island, but almost divorced from reality and therefore unimportant.

Six years had passed since the ride to Sestrières. Though feeling the same bond of friendship for each other, they had seldom met. Of course, Pierino had been called up for military service. At first, due to the after-effects of pleurisy, he was declared fit only for sedentary duties and sent to a photography unit in the Engineers; then almost immediately he was posted to the front as a cameraman.

Two years at the front, two years of war from 1916 to 1918. Shortly after Caporetto, Pierino came on Christmas leave to Turin. He stopped by to see his friend.

Emilio was studying in his room. On hearing his father's joyful exclamation in the hall, that long hoarse 'oh', muffled through the walls of the huge apartment, he jumped to the conclusion that it must be an unexpected visitor – some old friend, a colleague, a magistrate, maybe his brother who was Public Prosecutor in Savona. What a surprise for Emilio to be called out by his father and an even greater one to find Piero – or rather Sapper Corporal Piero Giraudo – there! Papa, so genial, so cordial to Pierino? To a working-class boy? This was something completely new. The explanation lay in the uniform, the rank and the fact that he was back from the front. An embrace and Emilio felt his friend's beard pricking and the cloth of his cape, rough and virile, which produced almost the same effect. Suddenly Piero was no longer a boy, he was a man. As thin as a rake. His cheeks and temples sunken; his hair closely cropped; his chestnut curls gone. His broad forehead seemed even bonier and more stubborn, a real peasant's forehead. But in his eyes was the same irresistible twinkle of friendliness and kindness, the same old smile; and his unexpected presence there, amid the massive, sombre, polished Umberto-period furniture, in the immutable order of the old, middle-class apartment against the familiar suffocating background of the tall bookshelves stuffed with notebooks and countless copies of *La Giurisprudenza*, was like a breath of life and liberty. Oh, but Pierino did not talk about cycling or sport this time. He smiled continually but certainly did not suggest that war was lovely. Modestly, he said he had seen little of it and then only by chance. The real war was being fought by the soldiers in the trenches – weeks and weeks in mud and snow. And when they had to attack, then they all had to be brave, even those who were shitting themselves with fear, because behind were the *carabinieri* ready to fire upon them He was lucky to be a cameraman. And in the heat of shooting a scene, if there was any danger, he never even noticed it – he was there to do his job, not make war.

These sincere words did not suit the barrister and his patriotic zeal. His face soon darkened with disapproval and finally, mumbling an excuse, he went out of the room, leaving the two friends alone together.

Then Pierino told Emilio about a girl he had known in Preganziol, just outside Treviso where his unit was stationed – a girl called Lucia whom, for the first time in his life, he thought he loved and who had made him happy. He explained how it happened. Between duties he had leave to sleep wherever he wanted. Lucia was the daughter of the landlady who had rented him a room. The father was away. He had been taken prisoner on the Carso. Lucia was beautiful, very young, shapely, a brunette with lovely blue eyes. Piero fished out her photograph.

Every morning she brought him coffee in bed. And so it began with one little kiss, then another and another. One evening, instead of going out, he stayed in with the excuse of keeping her mother company. All night he heard the thunder of cannon close by and the constant rumble of trucks passing in the street. There was also the danger of air-raids which had already claimed a number of victims in the city. To pass the time they played cards. But eventually the mother began to yawn. She did her best to keep awake. At ten o'clock she retired to her room and soon after they heard her snoring.

'You can imagine how we felt. At first we both went on playing.

But instead of looking at the cards, we looked into each other's eyes. Until . . . but she wouldn't even kiss me again like in the morning – or at least so it seemed. She refused and got up from the table. The chair fell over. "Stay where you are and let's play cards, or else I'm going to bed, too," she said. I couldn't insist because I was afraid of waking her mother. I wanted to have her, see, but I thought – fine! Suppose she's a virgin, though. And it seemed just like heaven to be alone with her and look into her eyes and not say a word. Just like that she was a thousand times better than all the other girls – tarts or not – I had been with.'

'What happened then?'

'Well, the time came when we both felt sleepy and we said good-night. She gave me a kiss, just a peck, nothing like the ones I had in the morning. And so we went to our own rooms. As soon as I was in bed, of course, I didn't feel sleepy any more. And as it turned out, neither did she. Because hardly a quarter of an hour later, I heard a noise, a tiny noise like a cat would make. I turned in bed and thought I was dreaming. In the almost pitch-dark I seemed to see the door opening ever so gently. I saw a light form slipping into the room. From the breathing and a hint of scent I guessed it was her. It *was* her, because she locked the door. Well, Emilio, my boy, I still thank my lucky stars, for there's nothing in the world more marvellous!'

'And . . . was she a virgin?'

'No, fortunately.'

'If you love her, you shouldn't say "fortunately".'

'As a matter of fact I'm sorry about it. But the responsibility . . .' said Pierino, still smiling, and his instinctively wise face looked for a moment like an old man's. 'It's the responsibility, see. Anyway, I can't marry her. When I go back it's almost certain that they'll transfer me to Venice. And that means – so long, Lucia. A pity, but it's better that way.'

The war over, the Fert, Ambrosio, and Pasquali film studios, which had worked very little during all those years but never closed, began to operate at full pressure, turning out one film after another, some of them big, important productions. Piero Giraudo, in spite of his youth, rapidly became one of the ace cameramen. Thoughtful, methodical, controlled, he did not lose his head like many of the others. He realized that the boom could not last, could not withstand the growing influx of American films. So he immediately started to save; by the end of 1921 he had put away enough to set up house and was already engaged to a baker's daughter in Via Santa Giulia in the Vanchiglia district. Piero lived with his mother two blocks away in a small mezzanine flat. His father, a printer to the last, had died of Spanish 'flu in the January of 1918.

Piero had noticed Nuccia in the shop every morning when he called on his way to work to buy fresh rolls. Whatever the weather he cycled to the studios. He had his usual lunch-box on the carrier just like the workmen, the same as when he was an apprentice at Musso and Filippa. His colleagues went by tram, a few by car with the director and producer and they lunched at the studio restaurant with the actors and actresses. He never did, to economize and – so he said – for health reasons.

Nuccia had light chestnut hair, rounded limbs and a plump face, very pretty with an unusual expression – charming and roguish, almost provocative but at the same time rather fixed, doll-like. When a young man spoke to her she gave the impression of being hard of hearing; she looked at him straight in the eye and laughed, as if he had mentioned something indelicate. She was a nice girl, of course, but a little odd, not quite all there.

Perhaps this strangeness was the very reason why Piero Giraudo, so logical and sensible in everything he did, had fallen in love with her. In the most honest and generous hearts love is very often born like that, by a law of radical compensation and the instinctive need to contradict one's own nature and get to know in some way, even at the price of bitter grief, quite a different part of reality which that nature would otherwise never learn.

The few times that Emilio had seen his friend since, there was, alas, no chance of a bicycle-ride. Piero was working hard and found it difficult to take a day off. They had met on a Saturday or Sunday in the late afternoon for a game of bowls, a drink, a snack at an inn in the suburbs. Recently Emilio had come across him by pure chance. He was at work shooting a scene on the Santa Margherita road, just above Villa della Regina, with a panoramic view of the city – exactly at the point where Emilio was strolling up the hill now, his arm tight around Vévé's firm waist.

It was fresh in his memory – one afternoon last November. A big, mustard-coloured sports Ansaldo with red morocco seats, engine

72

roaring, climbed slowly up from Villa della Regina. Reaching the square it turned and stopped. Beyond the stone parapet, through the thin veil of golden haze (it was Indian summer) you could see the regimented brown-red roofs of the town, the straight, deep furrows of the streets and the equally straight but broader and longer yellow-splashed avenues, and the church cupolas and the steeples and over all the silhouette of the Mole Antonelliana, so black and strange but so familiar and dear to anyone who was born and lived in the city.

From the Ansaldo stepped a lean, smooth-faced young man wearing a check cap and a light grey Norfolk jacket, knickerbockers and woollen stockings. He ran round the car, opened the door and helped the lady who had been sitting next to him to alight – a tall, most elegant woman in a blue costume, a cloche hat and long veils floating to the ground.

She took the young man's arm and slowly walked over with him to the parapet – but . . . surprise! From a clump of robinias which fringed the square like the wings of a stage and where something white had been flitting between the trees for a few moments, out came a gentleman in a straw hat and white flannel suit with a moustache, yellow gloves and a malacca cane. The couple stopped dead as if struck by lightning and the gentleman advanced towards them, one step, then another, and another, jerkily like a robot. Until he stopped, too, removed his straw hat with a flamboyant sweep and with an evil smile – called out, stressing each syllable: 'Na-tur-al-ly.'

Emilio had taken the tram to the terminus and was continuing on foot to the Sanfront Villa along the Santa Margherita road. A duty visit – the following day was Aunt Elisa's birthday.

Piero Giraudo was there among the technicians of the little unit. Emilio recognized his voice, even before seeing him. Perched on a high platform behind the camera, two electricians were trying to focus a large reflector lined with tin-foil on the robinia grove.

'Up with it! Up again! Not enough! Up!' shouted Piero in that throaty, common voice, a peasant, old-world, authoritarian voice which he had only when he shouted.

'Ah, there you are! Good for you! Stay and watch us shooting this scene!'

Emilio had stopped, fascinated, forgetting all about Aunt Elisa and the inheritance, and he stayed with Piero until the end when the sun went down and work was abandoned for the day.

The director, a dark, thickset, vulgar character in a fawn overcoat, leather gloves with raised seams, broad-brimmed hat, monocle, poured a continuous stream of instructions to the actors in precise Italian through a red megaphone.

'Get out, Gustavo, now run round, quicker!... a bigger smile, Maria, a bigger smile... More sensual, more passionate. Look at him, look at him as you get out! That's it. Lean on his arm immediately... Lean heavily on him...'

'Ready,' came a voice from the clump of trees.

'Action!... You two, smile, look at each other! *Cavaliere,*[1] come out! Slowly. Slowly. You two, stop, don't move. Forward, *cavaliere*. Slowly. One. Two. Three. Slowly, slowly, damn it! Five. Smile. Six. More evil, more evil, really savage. Seven. Straw hat off! Evil, now – dialogue!'

'Na-tur-al-ly.'

Emilio was concentrating on the actress who was a famous star. For a moment, he toyed with the idea of getting an introduction to her. I'm a student but I'm a gentleman, too, he thought. I could easily be introduced and have a chat with her. But he was too proud – or rather, too greedy for life and too sure of success – not to despise such childishness. He did not want to know actresses until he had the money to invite them to dinner and all the rest of it. And then, in spite of all his affection for Giraudo, Emilio would have been ashamed to be introduced by him. Giraudo was a fine cameraman – this was clear, too, from the way they all jumped to obey him as chief unit technician. But he was still working class, a man of the people. This is what Emilio thought, or rather felt, without even noticing that the sight of a famous actress was enough to bring back the prejudices he associated with his mother and father and the old aunts.

In fact, shortly after, while his assistants were changing the film, Giraudo came up to him and whispered in his ear: 'Come on, I'll introduce you...' and he smiled as he looked over towards the star. Emilio blushed.

He flushed with rage! But he knew that Piero was naïve enough to think that shyness might be the reason for his colouring up.

[1] 'Cavalier of the Crown of Italy' – a civil honour.

It seemed impossible that Piero had lived so long in the film world!

The sun, violet through a veil of mist, was sinking behind the ashen mountain-peaks. In the distance, the triangular Monviso, the highest of all, as familiar and dear to the people of Turin as the Mole, was streaked with orange, crimson, purple.

Piero, viewing the shooting scene through a dark glass, called out in his voice for great occasions: 'The light is no longer actinic.'

This was the signal for the director to declare – 'That's it. We stop shooting. Thank you, darling. Good night and thanks, gentlemen. Back tomorrow morning.'

He slipped an enormous gold cigarette case from his hip-pocket, selected an oval gold-tipped Laurens, put it between his lips, offered them around and lit up. Then he waved everyone goodnight with a circular motion of his gloved hand. He kissed the star on both cheeks. Followed by some of his assistants he walked springily over to a big 510 which was hidden beyond the bend in the road, behind the trees. The unit dispersed in a few minutes. The actors drove off in the Ansaldo that was used in the film scene. The technicians dismantled the platforms and loaded everything on to a truck which had also been parked under the trees.

Giraudo came up. He jumped on to the truck and gingerly handed down his racing model 'Legnano' to Emilio.

'Let's go down together. I'll come with you as far as Via Po. I bet you've never tasted Barolo *chinato* [Barolo wine with quinine]! Then I must pop in at the studio to see the rushes.' Emilio looked at the time. It was too late to go to Aunt Elisa's. She would be in the drawing-room for the rosary, surrounded by the servants. The rosary was recited every afternoon at the same time in its entirety, that is to say, all fifteen decades which took more than an hour. Aunt Vittoria, who was living with her sister and her expectations of the inheritance, fussing around her, watching and watching over her, would never let him in – or, worse still, would spitefully make him stay, kneel and recite the rosary with the others. But at home when they knew that he had not been to see Aunt Elisa! He could just hear the usual exasperated duet, the same old monotonous theme, the frenzied invocation to the money and security which the Sanfront inheritance would bring. Papa, hoarse and dejected, Mama, shrill and tearful.

75

'But you promised . . .'

'Is this the way you show your gratitude? After all we've done for you.'

'And then we complain if Aunt Elisa doesn't invite us more often!'

'We're not asking much of you, surely! But it seems that you won't even do a little thing like that!'

'You ungrateful boy!'

'Can't keep his word!'

'Stupid, that's what he is, stupid!'

He would explain that his practicals in forensic medicine had kept him late at the hospital. He would promise faithfully to visit Aunt Elisa the following morning, yes, and take her some flowers . . . No, no flowers. After Amedeo's death in Libya, flowers were taboo at the Sanfront house. They were considered a sinister symbol of death. If a friend of the family ever committed the indiscretion of sending them, they were immediately despatched to the cemetery or to La Consolata. Emilio could not ignore the rule. If he arrived at the front door carrying flowers he would be turned away by the butler. He laughed as he explained it all to Piero while they walked down to Villa della Regina. Piero held the bicycle in his right hand. On the left was the parapet, and beyond, a panorama of the city, an immense grey-blue monochrome print dotted with yellow lights from the windows, and chequered geometrically by straight rows of street lights.

Piero listened, then talked about his work and himself. All at once he mentioned Nuccia but without describing her. After a brief hesitation, he hastily and dispassionately admitted that he wanted to marry her, that he was already engaged.

Emilio felt a deep dislike for Nuccia. But why? He had not experienced anything like that in the case of Lucia, the girl at Treviso. And Piero had told him every detail about Lucia, while he dismissed Nuccia in a few words. Between the two confidences, their friendship had not strengthened, if anything it had degenerated. So there was no question of jealousy. It was the instinctive aversion sometimes akin to hate that every real friend feels for the woman who is destined to become the wife of *his* best friend.

Hurt by the news, unable to criticize or cast doubts upon Nuccia whom he did not know, Emilio retaliated with a prejudicial

remark. Why did Piero want to get married? . . . and so soon . . .?
What need was there? Surely not the need for a woman – in his
job there must be plenty of opportunities! Fun and games, love
affairs - he could certainly find all he wanted in films and without
too many sentimental or financial risks, at least at first. If only he,
Emilio, could live in that world! Piero listened, laughing, and shook
his head.

'What a kid you are! All right, fun and games . . . but once you've
sampled them . . . either you become immoral and then nothing
satisfies, neither money nor anything else, or you begin to cool off
and then like everybody else you want a home, a family, yes, and
little ones running around and you want to sleep every blessed night
with your wife and no worries, no nonsense. And after all, if you
want to be unfaithful, you always can. No harm in that. Well . . .
let's say, nothing tragic. Understand? You're still only a kid. But
you'll soon get the idea. Otherwise, why should everybody get
married?'

'But not at twenty-three, Piero.'

'I'm twenty-five. And I've been through the war. Anyway,
believe me, there's no fixed age. If it has to happen, you just feel it,
and it happens.' He paused a moment then concluded with a laugh:
'I suppose it's the same when you die.'

'Well, you said it – I didn't,' replied Emilio.

At the time he believed with a certainty that seemed prophetic
that he would never follow his friend's example. Neither at his age
nor later. He would never marry. Never? Not unless . . . Emilio
always made this proviso, although he avoided formulating it
clearly . . . unless he could pull off a big deal – a bride with a dowry
of millions, just like his mother wanted for him! Then marriage
would offer freedom – the freedom of wealth – not its suppression
and limitation. A wife and children who represent only a small
proportion of one's budget cannot possibly be an embarrassment.

But he could not tell Piero this conclusion. Firstly, because it
was not clear-cut, only a vague aspiration; secondly, because he did
not think that Piero would understand and approve of a marriage
of convenience, coldly planned and engineered. But here Emilio was
wrong. Conscious and fearful of his own cynicism, but at the same
time instinctively determined not to fight it, he found it comforting
to picture Piero Giraudo as his exact opposite, a kind of saint with

77

whom at bottom he had nothing in common, and who could not, therefore, exert any appreciable influence over him. Emilio wanted to preserve this first image of his perfect friend. He wanted to ignore the true facts about him, his real difficulties, everything which, he felt, would bring him dangerously close. Otherwise, he would have discovered that Piero was perfectly capable of understanding a marriage of convenience. He knew, for instance, that his future father-in-law's business was doing well and this certainly had a bearing upon his decision to marry Nuccia. She had only one brother, and her father would make her a substantial monthly allowance. Piero was a sensitive man, perhaps even an artist, but he was no saint. Above all he was not a dummy but a human being and he made mistakes like everybody else. Which he proved ten minutes later, when they reached Piazza Gran Madre.

Two truckloads of Royal Guards drove into the square. One truck stopped and an armed patrol jumped out. The other shot off down Corso Moncalieri. These were days of strikes and riots at the Lingotto, at Barriera San Paolo, Barriera di Francia and Barriera di Milano, along the northern outskirts of the city, but the central districts and especially the zone beyond the Po and near La Collina where Emilio and Giraudo had stopped were, on the other hand, as quiet as could be. Two trucks full of Royal Guards might well mean that – surprisingly – a meeting or procession was feared in that part of the town. Piero cursed impatiently. Emilio thought it natural for a Socialist, an idealist like Piero, to be angry but, to be honest, he told him that he could not agree. Not that he liked the Royal Guards, either. There was something dismal and stupid about them. Yet, when all was said and done, they did give him a sense of security.

'What do you want them to do? Let the others start a revolution? It won't be long before we have total Bolshevism!' These were the usual clichés which appeared in *La Stampa* and *La Gazzetta del Popolo* and which Emilio heard at home and at the university from the majority of his fellow-students and professors; but not from the painters, writers and musicians whose company he had begun to keep out of snobbery, in the hope of being invited one day to the house of the powerful industrialist Golzio, and also because he was sincerely fond of one of them, Gino Serra. He knew their political ideas – definitely anti-fascist though not in any way Socialist.

He expected a rather similar attitude from Piero. But to his great surprise Piero explained his irritation quite differently.

'That's what I say, too. It's time that they stopped these strikes. One of these days, there's going to be real trouble. Meanwhile the Stock Market's tumbling. Not that their claims are anything but justified. But both sides should get together and agree to give and take a little. And let those who want and need to work, do so . . .'

This would probably have infuriated Piero's father if he had been alive. After earning and saving his first wages, Piero had evidently abandoned his former political ideas. His father had been a printer, but his grandfather, from Baldichieri near Asti, had been a peasant and the conservative streak in his inheritance was surfacing. And Emilio should have felt pleased to learn that his friend now tended to share his own ideas. Emilio was not politically-minded, but he considered himself a Reformer. Bissolati and Bonomi, they were his ideal. They could reconcile patriotism, humanity, justice, liberty, peace and all the rest. But Piero's unexpected pronouncement stirred a vague sadness within him – almost disappointment. It did not last long. He did not pause to reflect. He took no notice of it. How could he? Piero Giraudo was a friend, of course. But he was also a strange family idol, the object of sincere yet abstract veneration, a secret alibi for his own conscience.

They crossed Piazza Vittorio, boundless in the first shadows of evening. They had started to talk about football. Emilio was, naturally, a supporter of Juventus, the team for the gentlemen, the pioneers of industry, the Jesuits, the moderates, the grammar-school set – in other words, the rich middle class. Piero, just as naturally, was a fan of the Toro,[1] the team supported by workers, shop keepers, immigrants from the neighbouring countryside or from the provinces of Cuneo and Alessandria, the technical-school set – the petit-bourgeoisie and the poor. Piero was passionately partisan. Without risk he could sublimate all his mortified socialism in hatred for Juventus and love for the dark-red shirts of the Torino team. While Emilio, like his schoolmates, his family's friends and his relations including Alberto Ceroni and his son Vittorio, who was Emilio's age, thrilled to the 'snob' black-and-white of his club's shirts.

[1] Toro = the Bull, the symbol of Turin.

79

It created no serious conflict between them. On the contrary, it strengthened the relationship, providing a safety-valve for their differences of opinion, taste, and origin. Just as they had done on two or three occasions previously, this time too they quarrelled good-naturedly about football. They felt that they were disagreeing frankly, as true friends ought to do.

They came to an old, smoky, cosy wine-shop under the arcades in Via Po where *barolo chinato* was a speciality of the house. The wine was new to Emilio.

'This is "the father" of vermouth,' said Piero, carefully extracting a one-lira note from his wallet. It was his turn to pay and he was a stickler for protocol. And in the end the *barolo chinato*, with its bitterish aftertaste and its rich colour ('garnet' exclaimed Piero, chaffingly raising his glass and studying it against the luminous gas-mantle; 'Garnet! Up with the Bull!') restored his idol intact to worshipping Emilio.

Outside the church of Santa Margherita, as you come from Turin, the road forks: on the right it goes down to Valsalice, on the left it continues to climb gently up to the Hermitage, but no longer clamped between the interminable boundary walls of the old villas. It runs freely among trees and meadows with a view of the steep, grassy slopes of Val San Martino and Mongreno, and of unkempt woods stretching up the opposite side of the majestic bowl to the summit of the Superga.

Because of the heat Vévé had taken off her jacket. Through her transparent white blouse more white showed up against the rosy skin – the swelling cups of her brassière. Emilio tried not to look. To gain assurance, he spoke of a possible trip to England (though he knew full well that lack of funds would prevent him from going), and he tried to keep his eyes on the road in front, the Collina and the pale greens of spring, the flowers in the meadows, the blossom on the trees, and to listen to the gay, riotous song of the birds. If his glance should fall on Vévé's breasts, he knew that he would become speechless and breathless.

It was like walking beside something terribly precious, even being responsible for its safety, with the possibility of losing it at any moment by no more than an ill-considered movement or word. A difficult responsibility! For an instant he felt a mad urge to run away, leave Vévé there and never see her again. Not that he did not want her – quite the contrary, for her beauty and sweetness, by their very existence, were sufficient reasons for life, joy and trust. He had never experienced anything like it before.

He suddenly felt his eyes prickling with tears. He asked himself – 'Is this love I feel? Is it really love?' They were tears of confusion, humiliation, a kind of langorous desperation. He wondered – 'What have I done to deserve her walking at my side and listening to me talking?' And in his heart came the secret, ineffable, intoxicating reply – nothing. Nothing more than he had done to create spring-time.

The purpose of the walk – tea and biscuits – was to be satisfied at the Hermitage Col. But about half-way there, Vévé, with a high-spirited laugh in her charming, open Turin accent, suddenly said: 'Listen, dear, you can say what you like – but I'm starving! Come on!' She left the road, leapt over the ditch, raced up the grassy bank and led the way along a footpath which seemed to vanish into the meadows.

Tall and sturdy, Vévé was also agile and lithe. Emilio ran after her but not so fast that he was prevented from admiring her figure yet again: the firmness of her breasts, shoulders and bottom, the extraordinary modelling of her legs and calves, strong and rounded, yet tapering gradually and harmoniously down to a pair of slim ankles.

Sun-drenched, a vineyard seemed to slope down from the sky. The neat rows of poles. Branches bare save for the first leaves of palest green. The vines stopped short at a long, low, yellow house. To the right of the door, along the trunk and branches of a thick vine, traces of copper sulphate. Faded green shutters. Dark red roofs. And in a corner, against the wall, a stone basin, running water.

'The Fountain of the French,' said Vévé. 'Believe it or not, this is an inn.' She called out: 'Madamìn, Madamìn!' Then, 'Perhaps you don't know why it's called that? You're blushing? Bravo. You're not a real Torinese, but you're so sweet when you blush . . . Well, they call it Fountain of the French, because when Turin was once besieged by the French . . . the Piedmontese soldiers were defending it, of course, and the front line was just here. Above were the French. Below, our lads. But, you see, there's no water on the ridge. So the French had to come down here for a drink. They came at night. Our troops waited and fired on them. That's the story, at any rate. My father told me when I was small. We always used to come here on Easter Monday.'

On the crest of a surge of affection, Emilio let his curiosity get the better of him. In the past he had preferred not to know, and had sheltered behind discretion, but now he asked: 'What does your father do?'

'He's a tram-driver,' Vévé replied unhesitatingly.

The *madamìn* rushed up with a basket of cherries. She was gathering them from the tree behind the house. That was why she had kept them waiting. She apologized. Vévé ordered two bottles of beer and mortadella and asked if they could buy some cherries.

They had a large paper bag full for a few pence. Emilio thought they would be eating their snack there at the Fountain, but Vévé said to the *madamìn*: 'I'll bring the empties back later, if that's all right.'

And, almost running back to the road: 'Come on. Let's find a field with a bit of shade.' And she was off again briskly up the path to the Hermitage.

'At the Fountain of the French,' thought Emilio, 'there's certainly not a scrap of shade.'

They entered a wood on the right, following a rough path. Beyond the wood was a small bowl-shaped meadow. The grass was tall and full of flowers. They sat in the grass at the edge of the wood which protected them from the heat of the sun and the prying gaze of any passers-by or farm labourers. But there was nobody about. Nobody. Blackbirds were whistling loudly. Two cuckoos exchanged calls, monotonous notes, yet gay and free. Somewhere in the distance, a barking dog seemed to join in the merriment.

The idea was to begin with bread and mortadella and finish with the cherries. But the fruit, smooth, red and white, ripe and firm, was too tempting not to be relished immediately and between Vévé's rosy lips was too inviting for Emilio not to try immediately for a delicious kiss. The ploy was as old as the hills, but Vévé and Emilio fancied that they had just invented it. One kiss? So many kisses. So many and such lingering ones, such strong, intense kisses. And above all, such *new* kisses. With those kisses the two lovers believed that they were telling each other (and perhaps they were) all that they had been unable to express in words, or even in their thoughts. Lying closely embraced in the grass, their lips pressed together, they experienced a revelation not only of each other, but also of themselves. It was like a great discovery – the discovery of the world, of life.

'I've wanted you so much!' murmured Vévé in a moment of pause, looking into his eyes and stroking his hair with a white hand that was both strong and delicate. 'Did you feel the same way too?'

But her words, or her caress, or perhaps the pause, seemed to disturb him. He gazed into her eyes and at her mouth differently from before, even when he was kissing her. Vévé's eyes seemed suddenly to have changed colour – their twinkling blue had deepened, and the expression on her face, from happy and laughing had become sad, yet in some strange way, happier still.

'Yes,' whispered Vévé, without turning her eyes from his. 'Yes, darling, yes.'

He penetrated her very gently and slowly for a long, long time, as he had never been able to do with other women.

They rose from the meadow as if the cool, the silence and the shadows of evening had suddenly awakened them from a dream. It was late for both of them. They had to get back. The bread and the mortadella and the bottles of beer were still there. They ate and drank as they walked back. They left the empties with *madamìn*. Emilio told himself that he was happy. Then he thought that Vévé must be happy, too – but in a very different way.

He felt light-hearted and confident. He no longer experienced that humility, that gratitude, that conviction of being a chance and undeserving beneficiary of a miracle. So something extraordinary and miraculous had happened to him? Well, the future would be full of similar miracles. Among the girls of the Turin upper middle class, among those whom his mother intended for him, he would easily find one as nice as Vévé, if not better. Why not combine business with pleasure?

And what about her? She must be thinking that she would never be so happy again. That, at least, is what Emilio imagined. But she was silent and pensive, and as they strolled back down the hill he tried to make her tell him what was wrong. Finally, when they reached Santa Margherita, Vévé muttered: 'Nothing, I would just like to die.'

83

II

Old Uncle Sanfront was off to Rome. He held the office of Privy Chamberlain of Cloak and Sword and once a year he had to serve in the Vatican. He was accompanied as usual by Badia, the engineer, his friend and bailiff, a handsome, thick-set man of medium height with a big, strong, humorous face and a marvellous halo of white hair with enormous matching side-whiskers. People said that he was younger than Uncle Sanfront, but to Emilio he had been exactly the same for more than fifteen years – a fairy-tale character in the garden of the villa at Rivoli, and now an anachronistic and almost ridiculous figure. Badia had a mania for telling jokes and no longer thought it necessary to restock his repertoire. In his dry, eighteenth-century way, Uncle Sanfront, although older, was infinitely more alive and modern. Badia had a grandson, about Emilio's age. Giorgio Badia had been at grammar school with Vittorio Ceroni, Emilio's cousin – they were friends and both in their fourth year of engineering.

Aunt Vittoria, who was Vittorio's grandmother and godmother, had managed with Aunt Elisa's help and Badia's consent to persuade Uncle Sanfront to take the two boys with him. A trip to Rome! A chance not to be missed! But Aunt Vittoria was interested not so much in her grandson's cultural development as in the opportunity, from the point of view of the inheritance, that he might have of becoming better known to Uncle Sanfront, and better liked. It was this chance – not Rome – which must not be missed.

Uncle Sanfront agreed on one condition. Emilio should come, too, because he was as much a grand-nephew as the Ceroni boy. Aunt Vittoria did not like this but she dared not object. In any case, the old lady had cunningly foreseen the danger when she broached the idea. According to her, there was all the difference in the world between Vittorio and Emilio. Uncle Sanfront would make a direct comparison to the former's advantage.

The grandmother's affection, or rather, the great-aunt's hate, was almost blind. Vittorio was less serious-minded, less studious and less intelligent than Emilio. All you could say was that he was more likeable. At that age, Emilio, perhaps because of his parents' ambitious upbringing, seemed unsociable, tensely eager as he was to make a successful career.

His cousin Vittorio, on the other hand, though essentially a moderate conformist, conservative and religious, seemed gay and carefree. He attended the Politecnico as often as was absolutely necessary and no more. He was behind with several examinations. As though he knew that one day his father, mother and grandmother would shove him through his degree, and expecting as he did to be settled in a splendid job thanks to his family's important business connections, he thought at present only of having a good time.

As far as pleasure was concerned, Giorgio Badia was his mentor and inseparable companion. The only son of an only son, while he was an adolescent his parents and grandparents foolishly vied with each other as to who could spoil him the most and eventually he became completely dissipated. He spent his nights at the Maffei or the Alfieri, in brothels or at the poker-table; he alternately took cocaine or caught gonorrhoea, and periodically disappeared for a week under the pretext of retiring to the family villa in Alassio to study – but instead he was in Montecarlo with some cocotte or other. The gentleness and imperturbable serenity of his manner, the true and sincere affection that he showed his parents and grandparents were matched only by their credulity. For they refused to believe reports of his debaucheries and, slaves of a habit that went back to his childhood, continued to lavish more and more money upon him. It was surprising to find this weakness in the old engineer, a tough businessman and a harsh administrator. But Giorgio Badia was what is termed 'a daddy's boy' – one of the last, a final spark from the Bengal lights, a late blossom of the bourgeoisie and the *belle époque*.

The plan was to travel by day. Departure from Turin five o'clock in the morning, arrival in Rome in the late afternoon. The two old men and the three young ones took their seats in a reserved compartment.

Giorgio and Vittorio did not normally share confidences with Emilio. This time, however, they explained their intentions to him because they could not carry them out without his help. Vittorio and Emilio had never been to Rome, unlike Giorgio who knew where and how they could have a good time. The idea that both Badia and Aunt Vittoria had in mind (Uncle Sanfront did not care a rap) was that the three boys should devote their entire stay in Rome to visiting museums and ancient monuments – and of course there was the audience with the Pope which had been arranged a long time before. It was not a question of deceiving anyone, but simply of not offending the engineer, keeping up the pretence of being what he thought they were – nice boys ignorant of the facts of life. They had to make him think that they were going to the museums while instead they were having a good time from morning to night, or rather from night to morning – except for the audience which they could not avoid because they had to go with the two old men.

The farce began in the restaurant-car. In a notebook which contained names and addresses of quite a different kind, Giorgio made a show of meticulously entering a detailed itinerary of things to see in Rome. He kept consulting Uncle Sanfront, who was the only one who knew Rome at all well, having lived there for a few months in his youth. But Uncle Sanfront did not or would not remember. And the engineer's persistent efforts to seek enlightenment were really comic.

'Excuse me, Signor Conte, but what about the Medici Tombs?'

'What a bore you are! I cannot remember exactly now. Leo X, he was a Medici. That's positive. But the Tombs . . . I don't think they're in Rome . . .'

'Anyway, I'll write it down – Medici Tombs. We'll find out . . .' concluded Giorgio. And he scribbled an obscenity in his note-book. Meantime they were passing through the deserted expanse of the Maremma, a cold, metallic green beneath the sky high above, grey with the winter sirocco. The five passengers all had the same sensation of depression and gloom – the impression of crossing a land 'at the ends of the earth', so different was the landscape from the one they knew.

As the hours passed so did this sensation grow. Until even the green vanished, to give way in the shadows of early twilight to an infinity of formless, colourless undulations unrelieved by tree or brook as far as the questing eye could reach. At times they would see a tumble-down hovel surrounded by a fence, dung and mud and

86

catch a glimpse of grey sheep lying in the open. A tiny, red light glowing from a dark doorway, the figure of a shepherd or a farm-labourer, motionless and ragged, only stressed the air of desolation. Even the sea, when the railway skirted it – even the sea was miserable and stripped of its majesty. The breakers beat feebly on an iron-hued shore, narrow and hollow beneath banks of brush and poor tufts of grass.

Emilio who, in any case, was a little sceptical and not too enamoured of the amusements promised by his cousin and George, felt his heart miss a beat. Was it possible, he thought, looking out of the window, was it really possible that Rome would appear at the end of all this?

Rome appeared. Unheralded. With no introduction apart from a succession of orchards, shrubberies, huts; dirty, squat houses, all with terraced roofs; more houses gradually becoming denser and higher but also without conventional roofs; lighted windows, washing hanging out to dry, dark clumps of trees, silhouettes of umbrella pines, cypresses, ruins of ancient walls. The rails became progressively more numerous, there was a stationary, crowded tram, another and another, a row of stationary trams, a great, ancient Roman gateway, and a monument with round holes which he remembered seeing in a photograph, and now the train was slowing down and here was Rome.

The air was mild, relaxing, enervating. An excited commotion in the crowd of passengers, in the gait, the coats, the faces of the porters seemed superficial and of no real importance. A clumsy confusion, good-natured and yet somehow aggressive. An atmosphere of general lassitude and discouragement as if life were no longer worth living except for the moment while it lasted.

'Watch your bags' was the engineer's solemn warning in a whisper while the porters were taking them – a warning that he had repeated *ad nauseam* on the journey. Rome isn't Naples but you never know!

Their hotel was the Continentale, at the side of the Termini station. In those times the Piedmontese, when they came to Rome, tried not to leave the vicinity of the station – an enclave that had been built by their forefathers. Uncle Sanfront, because of tradition and instinct, followed this rule and broke it only when it was unavoidable, when he had to go to the Vatican, the Lateran or San

Paolo. The Quirinal, if he happened to be invited to a Court reception there, presented no problem since it bordered on the enclave and could be reached by way of Via Nazionale or Via XX Settembre without crossing other districts. The same applied to the British Embassy and the basilica of Santa Maria Maggiore.

Something happened to Emilio that he could not possibly have foreseen. The days in Rome passed slowly and monotonously – he felt in a strange state between sleeping and waking. There were naturally good reasons for that and Emilio had no need to think of others. On the very first evening he made an essential discovery: while Giorgio and Vittorio were well provided with money, he had almost none.

Uncle Sanfront and the engineer were on the first floor, the three young men on the third, Giorgio and Vittorio in a double room, Emilio in one with a communicating door. After dinner they all said goodnight and there was a tacit understanding that the boys, too, would go straight to bed. Instead, they washed, changed and left the hotel.

At the Sala Umberto they ordered champagne and invited three dancers to their table. Then, supper at the Gallinaccio. Finally, to bed in a *pensione* in Via Due Macelli. Everything was squalid, sordid, spectral. Emilio's meagre experience of similar places and escapades in Turin made him look upon his home town as a second Paris and Rome, in comparison, as the most miserable, forsaken and provincial of Balkan capitals.

Largo Tritone by night, in the rain: the crooked, haphazard intersections of streets, wide and narrow; the dismal entrance to the tunnel, up above the dark mass of the Quirinal gardens; the Messaggero building with its massive, cement ornamentation, small, squat and ridiculously pompous; the wet, deserted asphalt – and down there in the corner, the sole, warm touch of humanity, the faint lights of the Gallinaccio with its display of fennel and fettuccine in the window. It would have been difficult to imagine anything more desolate.

The dancers were two Marseilles women and one from Hungary, middle-aged, skinny, bored and grasping; a good opportunity for Vittorio to show off his French, but it did nothing to inspire either the toasts or the supper.

Emilio paid his share and the money his father had given him for the entire trip barely covered it. If he continued to spend like this for the rest of the time he would have to rely on his cousin and Giorgio. And he hated the idea of that. Worse still, he found their company tedious, always the same jokes, the same suggestive remarks, the endless naïve and vulgar talk.

Emilio was surprised without quite understanding why – was he better or worse than the other two? Was it only a question of Giorgio's golden vice; honestly, there seemed to be cause for hoping the contrary. At least, he thought, one had to take into account the difference between the Maffei and the Alfieri in Turin and the Sala Umberto in Rome.

They got back to the hotel shortly before seven o'clock in the morning. They had just turned in when there was a violent knock on the door: Engineer Badia, dressed in his best – overcoat, bowler hat, umbrella. Against all that black, his white whiskers and pink face looked somehow unreal. He began to clap his hands loudly and pace up and down the room.

'Come on, get up! Time to be out seeing Rome! What are you doing idling in bed?'

Dead tired and still half asleep they had to get up. That morning they were supposed to take in the Forum, the Palatine and the Colosseum! They piled into a taxi, determined to catch up on their sleep at the *pensione* in Via Due Macelli.

Emilio accompanied them as far as the front door of the *pensione* and then went off on his own. At midday when they met for lunch, he said that he would not come with them again. Giorgio and Vittorio understood. All right, they would pay for him and he need not feel obliged to return the money. Emilio refused. They were not to worry, he would manage and so as not to ruin things for them he promised to stay away from the hotel for the same length of time as they did. Giorgio and Vittorio did not insist. It was clear that this solution suited them admirably. And by the way, did Emilio have any objection to going alone to *The Valkyrie* on Saturday evening? Then he could tell them all about it. The engineer who was on the board of the Regio Theatre in Turin had accepted the ritual gift of a box at the Costanzi, thinking to offer the boys free, instructive entertainment. But wild horses could not have dragged Vittorio and Giorgio there.

So Emilio spent those solitary days visiting basilicas, catacombs,

ancient monuments and museums. He kept a promise that he had
made to his parents and went to see in turn all his relations in the
capital, especially the Sassarini family, the one they called Uncle
Pippo, from La Spezia, a second cousin on his mother's side, who
was a departmental head at the Ministry of Finance.

One day, feeling unable to take any more pictures, monuments
or relations, he happened to be strolling aimlessly along streets
which he had expressly chosen as a possible escape from picturesque
surroundings and antiquities. He had taken a tram and alighted at
the terminus. Now he was walking in a trance past dusty gardens of
oleanders, mean little villas the colour of rotten apricots, shabby and
dilapidated even though they had been built only a few years
before, knolls covered with yellowish undergrowth, landslips, tufa
quarries, and here and there the sepulchral solemnity of a tall
pine-tree. As he walked he seemed to see everything through a dull,
grey screen. Was this the Roman sirocco? Although he did not miss
their company for a moment, was it the financial humiliation that
his cousin and Giorgio had inflicted on him?

A despondency, a depression that he had never experienced
before . . . It called in question everything about him, his sensibility,
his intelligence, his ability to secure a position and a family, even to
earn a living. He could find consolation in only one thought –
Vévé's unwavering affection and the joy that she would continue to
give him. But he rejected the thought. He had been glad to come to
Rome if only to have an excuse to get away from her for a few
days . . .

In the first months he had hoped that it was only a passing fancy.
And this hope had been fostered almost immediately by the holiday
recess, no longer at Rivoli but in Alassio for the whole of August
alone with his parents, then at Saint-Vincent with his aunts and
cousins. But back in town, the October mildness blanching the
avenues of lime trees and the woods on the Collina seemed to recall
fleeting time and irresistibly urged him not to waste it. He began to
see Vévé again with increasing pleasure, even when the weather
prevented them from going for walks on the Collina.

On the Collina, it is true, or in the streets or avenues at the foot
of the hill, there were plenty of little restaurants with rooms on the
first floor. Formalities were reduced to a minimum. Here you

found a friendly welcome, clean and cheerful surroundings, curtains and covers of flowered cretonne, majolica stoves, big brass beds, carpets, sofas. Altogether a most civilized amenity, almost worthy of Nice or Aix-les-Bains. But for this reason the places were very crowded, and Emilio and Vévé (of the two he was the more cautious) avoided going to them too often in case they were seen. So their meetings were mostly confined to long conversations and long silences as they sat holding hands at the back of some stuffy, dark café and at night to lingering kisses in a corner or against the railings of some palatial villa, in the deserted streets above the Casale gate, the district where Vévé lived.

When they left the café, they would take a number 3. She always got off at the stop before last, while he went on to the terminus. There was the danger that the driver might be, if not Vévé's father, perhaps one of his mates. Then they would meet a hundred metres further on in a secluded street and enjoy what is perhaps for two young people the most delightful and beguiling game of all, which can reach to infinity and give free rein to the imagination. But at that time the centre of Turin was little more than a provincial town. What with the cafés, the trams, the deserted streets, they were bound to be seen by somebody eventually. It had to happen and it did. The news soon began to circulate among the middle-class gossips and malicious trouble-makers in the town.

'Who? Viotti, the boy? The Treasury Counsel's son . . . impossible!'

'But it's true. He's been seen and he's quite shameless about it.'

'And who is she?'

'No class. A dressmaker or even worse.'

And Papa and Mama Viotti came to hear of these rumours. When they were all three at table they would drop hints tinged with a mixture of sarcasm, discretion and menace – nothing more for the moment, since they cherished the illusion that it was merely a fleeting attachment. But what would happen when they knew? And could Emilio really blame them?

He was afraid of 'attachment': at the same time, if he had been honest with himself, he would have understood that it was all he wanted. But he went on believing there was no question of marrying Vévé. He imagined leaving her, falling in love with another girl, or her falling in love with another boy. He failed to understand the difficulty, the unnaturalness, of stifling such a spontaneous feeling, so he went on trying to stifle it and actually thought that he had been successful. Meanwhile, he continued to think about her, about their regular meetings, so delicious even under those conditions, and about the exciting memory of the few occasions when they had really been together.

Over the door of one of the squalid little villas in the Roman suburbs was the tobacco monopoly sign. Up four steps, a cement ramp flanked by two sickly vegetable gardens with a few rows of tomato plants and a surrounding wall. Emilio went in to buy cigarettes. The shop was only a kind of landing, a narrow, foul, shabby passage. On the counter, two jars of pastilles – licorice and Valda. A revolving picture-postcard stand. Dust. Swarms of flies, despite the season. And a nauseating smell of fug and frying fat. A small glass window was open on to the adjoining kitchen. Two filthy little urchins with bare bottoms were playing on the brick floor.

He felt something yield within him. He took a postcard, wrote the address and an intimate, affectionate note. This was breaking a promise that he had made to himself. He dropped the idea of the cowardly, tacit warning that he had intended to give Vévé – once in Rome not to send her even a postcard, a kind of dress-rehearsal for a goodbye. He bought a stamp and went out. The red postbox bearing the royal crest was on a peeling wall at the far side of the earth and gravel square. With the card hovering at the edge of the slit while he was debating whether to post it – an action suggesting sensuality, tenderness, weakness – or whether to tear it up in deference to a sense of duty, what his eyes rested on became impressed upon his memory. It was a small downward-sloping depression, perhaps more accurately a very wide, irregular ditch about half a kilometre long. Its flanks were of a colour between yellow and red, the earth tufaceous, clayey. It seemed scooped out by human hand rather than the work of nature. And on both sides flat grass and scrub, like a plateau a few metres higher than the depression, stretching as far as the eye could see – all on the same level except for some darker strips winding here and there through the grass and shrubs, evidence of other invisible depressions. It had the same contours as the terrain on which Rome was built, offered almost the same view that could be enjoyed, masked by trees, monuments, houses from the Pincio and the Janiculum. Rome was not so much the city of the seven hills as the city of the seven hollows.

Emilio stood looking. For some mysterious reason this landscape deeply saddened and at the same time fascinated him. If someone had asked him why he had gone out there and not to some other place in Rome, just as sad perhaps, but not so ugly, he would have been unable to answer.

In the same mood, he found the audience with the Pope equally unreal and dream-like. Uncle Sanfront was in uniform. With him were a dozen relations and friends who had come especially from Turin. They had all been kneeling for some minutes when Benedict XV entered. Small, thin and brisk, he kept turning round to chat animatedly in French to a group of priests who were following him. He hurried past the kneeling visitors from Turin without pausing and as quickly as he could, blessing each one and stretching out his ringed hand to be kissed. When he came to Uncle Sanfront he stopped, and from the way he turned sharply towards them as they knelt a short distance away and his glance glinted like a diamond for an instant behind his thick-lensed spectacles, Emilio saw that the Pope, evidently previously informed, had asked Uncle Sanfront about his nephews. When he passed he blessed them and gave his hand to be kissed mechanically without looking at them. He had resumed talking to members of his suite. Emilio caught this remark: '*Oui, mais la petite vieille, qu'est-ce qu'on peut faire? Elle est malade, n'est-ce pas?*' The Pope's voice was nasal. His mouth had a sad and scornful expression. Who could the sick little old woman be? It might be a figure of speech – perhaps the Pope was alluding to an institution or a nation in decline.

Emilio had already heard *Das Rheingold* and *Tristan* at the Regio Theatre in Turin. Of all the arts, the one that he preferred was music. Oddly enough, he had inherited this passion from his father. Yes, the Treasury Counsel had an ear, and a love of music was perhaps the only likeable and spontaneous side of a character otherwise subservient to a strict conformity. In his youth, probably because of his family name and a cherished tradition in Trino, the birthplace of the famous violinist, he had studied the fiddle. He knew and sometimes, in spite of his chronic hoarseness, softly sang Piedmontese songs. Especially the one beginning '*All' umbreta dël*

93

büssun', an eighteenth-century melody of classical and sober character which seemed magically to evoke the lost perfection of the period in which it was composed. Magically? More subtly, at any rate, than the music of the great composers which with its complex construction always overlaps the time when it was written.

Up to a few years before, Emilio had studied the piano, practising from half-an-hour to an hour every day. When he went to university he gave it up. He considered that he knew enough about general culture and did not want to waste time precious for his studies.

At the Regio the opera was always something of a social occasion. Perhaps because he went with his parents, uncles and aunts. Here in Rome he was all alone in a box. For one reason or another, he was in ecstasy. From the overwhelming, breathless opening and the precipitate entrance of the wounded, fugitive hero who collapses exhausted in Hunding's sinister dwelling, Emilio seemed to be hearing music for the first time in his life. Of course, this was music with a literary and pictorial background – opera. But Emilio felt himself responding to something whose existence he had never suspected, in the same way that the door of Hunding's hut flew open as the warm, vital spring breeze invaded it. The music penetrated his innermost soul just as friendship and love had done on more than one occasion. It was a miracle this time, too. And at that moment, he did not believe that the future would deny it. While he listened, he let his fancy roam. He saw himself as Siegmund, and Vévé as Sieglinde. Suddenly he looked through his opera glasses; he saw the singer taking the part of Sieglinde, her avid, determined face, large dark eyes, sharp nose and pale cheeks wreathed in a halo of Titian-red tresses – a very different type of beauty, indeed the opposite to the frank expression and rounded contours of Vévé's face. A strange, striking beauty which in the mysterious illusion of the glasses, disturbed him. He had the absurd idea that the singer had noticed him and in some way, with a severe, disquieting flash of her great, dark eyes, she was responding to his desire.

On his last day, he accepted an invitation to lunch with his Uncle Pippo. The Sassarini family occupied a third-floor apartment in Via XX Settembre, opposite the Ministry of Finance. Lunch was at a quarter past two, as was usual in Rome. Uncle Pippo was a bachelor and lived with two sisters, the daughter of one of them and her husband, Franco Beltramo, also employed at the Ministry. They had two little girls, between five and ten years old. The Sassarinis were from La Spezia, the niece's husband from Alessandria, but they had lived in Rome since the beginning of the century and were now completely romanized even in the way they spoke – except for Uncle Pippo who was almost sixty.

The cries of joy which greeted him, the hugs, the eager kisses, the congratulations on his studies, the interminable meal, the mountain of *fettuccine*, the *abbacchio*,[1] the beetroot, the fennel, the Frascati wine; the noise, the chatter, the excitement, the slight touch of hysteria; the naughty, spoilt children; the questions, the good wishes to be taken to Mother in Turin; the continual complaints that she never came to Rome to see them – all this was to Emilio a depressing and irritating revelation of a decline in morals, a decadence which had sapped the family dignity with the languor of the climate and security of employment. Happy people, though. 'We're in Rome,' they seemed to say, and they seized every opportunity to say it over and over again: 'We're in Rome, we have the sun, there's no need of heating [but it was quite cold] the Ministry is opposite, the King within a stone's throw, the Pope a little further away. What more could we want of life?'

Emilio saw the Sassarinis again the following summer. They were on their way to spend a holiday as usual in Coazze and had stopped for a few hours in Turin. Uncle Pippo and Franco Beltramo seemed rather anxious: in the papers was the news that the Fascists had attacked the town-hall in Ferrara and occupied it without meeting resistance.

'Yes, of course, of course,' said Uncle Pippo stroking his pepper-and-salt imperial and moustache à la Cialdini. 'Law and order come first. But . . . what about the danger of Bolshevism? We can't go on putting up with these strikes. These people are riff-raff, rabble. You give them an inch and they'll take a yard. There should be no Fascist squads either, we're all agreed on that. But what I say is, as long as they have a go at the cooperatives and the *Avanti* offices, good luck to them. Let them burn the whole lot to the ground! But it's too bad when they start on town halls! Bah . . .' He stopped and heaved a deep sigh, conscious that his argument did not hold water, but unable to think of another one.

[1] Lamb.

Beltramo, a staunch supporter of Giolitti, a thin, pale man with gold spectacles and short-cropped hair said: 'The government should be firmer with everyone, that's the point. Fortunately Taddei's at the Home Office. And Taddei is a man of action. He'll do something. We must give him time. He'll put them all in their place. A man of action.'

But the emphatic way in which he said the word 'action' – pronouncing it 'ection' – betrayed a facile optimism and inner lack of confidence. Emilio was instinctively very perplexed. He too would have liked to believe in Taddei's energy.

Uncle Sanfront, engineer Badia, Giorgio and Vittorio, without being Fascists were decidedly favourable to Fascism. During the return journey, Uncle Sanfront said that Fascism was a painful necessity and it all depended on the King: in any case whatever the King did would be for the general good.

Emilio had no liking for the Fascists. Yet there was something in their violence that he did not find entirely unpleasant; and without admitting it, he felt in common with all young people of his age, an irrational, almost sensual longing for a change whatever it might be. On the other hand, his birth and education, rather than his thinking, had bred in him a holy terror of a socialist revolution. Taddei . . . ? The King . . . ? To be honest, he did not know what to think, nor what to hope for.

Taddei did not or could not do anything. True, that same year, one morning in late October, the newspapers announced that Taddei had declared a state of siege. But the King had not signed and the following day the news broke that Mussolini had been summoned to the Quirinal.

That evening Emilio was studying in his room. Papa burst in, shouting. There was a big demonstration, processions in the streets, we are saved! Mama appeared – she was happy. To Emilio's great surprise she cried to him: 'What are you doing here? Why don't you go out? There's no danger! Off you go!'

Emilio put on his raincoat and went out. The streets were wet; the trees in Piazza Maria Teresa were still dripping after a shower but it had stopped raining. He could hear shouting in the direction of Via Po. He met the procession in Corso Cairoli.

There were, or seemed to be, thousands of them. They were

carrying torches, banners, flags, They were advancing at a quick march singing *Giovinezza*, *Il Piave*, *All' armi siam fascisti*, the Hymn to Garibaldi. They were shouting 'Long Live Italy! Long live the King! *Eia Eia Eia alalà.*' A squad of blackshirts wearing the fez and carrying cudgels passed by. Their faces, especially those in the first two ranks, were typical – hard, vulgar, fanatical, unshaven or with long beards, hair brushed back. After the blackshirts came a disorderly group of young and not-so-young men, townspeople and students, singing, shouting in reply and trying to march in step. Then more detachments of blackshirts and civilians and so on. And then blueshirts, the 'Nationalists'. It may have been the attractive colour, or the fact that there were fewer of them, or because their faces seemed less criminal, but Emilio felt impelled to join them. He understood clearly that this instinctive action of his did not spring from any rooted conviction. He knew that Federzoni was the leader of the Nationalists and that he was patriotic and loyal to the King. But were those his own ideas? Emilio had no political views, he took no interest in politics – if he had been honest with himself he would have seen that to be the plain truth. He should have stopped and looked and then gone straight home, and he knew it. But something stronger than himself had urged him to join the march and was now urging him to sing. The tunes, the words that he hardly knew – he was straining to pick them up from the others and they were coming from his throat.

The column turned into Corso Vittorio. The trams had stopped. In the damp and festive night, the lights, the clamour, the singing, it seemed to Emilio that as far as the eye could reach, away over to Porta Nuova, the Corso was crammed with people. He did not think of all those who were not there. It was as if they had never existed. At the corner of Via Accademia he saw Piero standing with his bicycle outside the window of a cycle shop.

He left the procession and ran over to him. From the serious expression on his face, he could see to his surprise that Piero was annoyed.

'I thought you would be glad.'

'But don't you see that they've all been bought, that it's a farce? With the best intentions, I don't doubt. Moral: now we must wait and see what the other one can do down in Rome!'

'Who? . . . The King?'

'No, not the King. *Him*. We'll soon see what sort of man he is.'

He disapproved of the Fascists but wanted to have confidence in their leader.

III

Without taking his arm from Vévé's rosy, rounded shoulders, Emilio turned to look for the cigarettes on the table. He noticed that dusk had closed in. The studio was plunged in almost nocturnal gloom: on the easels or leaning against the walls, the paintings had lost their colours, and framed in the open windows was a landscape study in blue: high over the hill, a strip of dark blue sky with a sapphire star; violet woods studded with isolated, twinkling lights in the houses and villas; the slate-grey outline of Monte dei Cappuccini; the azure foam of the great rapids; and a light blue haze – river fog or smoke from chimneys – veiling the other bank below.

Mingled with the constant roar of the rapids, a scattered and subdued hum came from the city. From time to time he could hear quite distinctly the clatter of the tram at the corner of the bridge or the distant sound of bells. He seemed to be breathing as never before – deeply, calmly, in rhythm with Vévé's breathing as she lingered, clasped in his arms, and with the breath of the city, nature, the approaching evening, the living world.

His happiness was complete but it seemed to contain a share of pain. Emilio told himself that he wanted nothing more. Is this all? he wondered. He knew that in this question there was no suggestion of disappointment. He reassured himself – yes, this is all, you can be quite sure of that. You will never want, either now or in the future, anything more than this peace. Then what was the pain he was feeling? Oh, it was not really pain, but the sadness of finality, the certainty that he had drained the cup of happiness. Joy and sadness inextricably united, as perhaps some poet had imagined it of the gods, but which is not given to mortals.

A glance at her watch and Vévé started up in dismay – she had to dress and run, once again she would be late home. It was an agonizing awakening but one which also brought a kind of relief.

That winter and spring their love seemed new to them every day.

Gino Serra, Emilio's painter friend, had lent them his studio on the banks of the Po. They could use it whenever they wished. His health was poor and the doctor had advised him to work as much as possible in the open air, so weather permitting he would be off on his bicycle to paint on the Collina, in the country or down by the river. Emilio was introduced to the porteress (whether she believed it or not) as a painter sharing the studio with Serra, and Véve as one of the models who came during the day – nothing odd about that.

It happened once that the lift was out of order. Emilio told Véve with a smile that they would have to walk up seven floors. She seized his arm and murmured, 'I would do it on my knees.' The half-shadow on the first-floor landing, by the lift-cage with its iron floral design painted pink. The notice: maintenance repairs. On the right, the porter's lodge – cherry-wood cornices, ground-glass panes. The staircase rose in semi-oval flights, floor by floor around the lift, and the steps and the banister base were in Baveno granite. It was March. A Sunday morning. It was raining. The river was in spate and reached half-way up the wharf walls – there was no need to look, the mighty roar of the rapids was sufficient indication. When they had jumped off the tram they had seen along the Lungo Po a diffuse silvery light reflected from the rain, the river, the clouds, the spring air. But between the Lungo Po and the landing was a long, narrow entrance hall, a flight of seven steps, a door, a partition with its ornamental, translucent glass. So it was almost pitch dark. For fear of the porteress who kept an eye on them from her cubby-hole, they had stopped by the lift but at some distance from each other. He could not have seen Véve's face clearly. Surely in his memory of it imagination must have played a large part. In the shadows on the landing her sparkling blue eyes looking at him, her half-open, quivering lips. He had felt her seize his arm violently. 'I would do it on my knees.' As she spoke he could not help closing his eyes as though overcome by an attack of giddiness which seemed comic an instant later. Even her words seemed comic. It is the sign of real happiness when it finds us. We feel unworthy, ashamed, above all, ridiculous. We take it seriously when it is lost. They climbed the stairs together, arm-in-arm, passionately embracing as soon as they were sure that the porteress could no longer see them.

But soon, so as not to arouse suspicion, they had to avoid arriving at the studio together. Emilio got there first – two or three hours before, unless he had a lecture. He brought books and notes intending to swot for his examinations. What a hope!

On Fridays and Saturdays Vévé left the office sometimes at five, sometimes at six or seven or even later. She had moved to another department with more pay but there was this nuisance of overtime on Friday and Saturday, the erratic hours depending not so much on the work as on the whim of her boss. By tram it took her barely five minutes to get to the Lungo Po, but up to the last minute she was never sure of being able to come. If she left the office at seven, it was too late.

Serra's studio had no telephone. Emilio would wait, torn with suspense. He tried to study but was distracted by wanting Vévé, wondering if she would come or not. He kept on looking at his watch. The time crawled by. When at last the moment drew near, it seemed to Emilio that the page before his eyes no longer made sense and the Italian or Latin had been magically transformed into some obscure language. He had begun to listen for the distant clang of the lift gate and the hum of its ascent, heard through the walls in the silence of the house and the dead quiet of the city. It started as an almost imperceptible hiss, gradually approaching. Slowly it became a rustle. At the various floors, the ascending cage engaged the gate mechanism with two consecutive dull thumps. By these thumps Emilio counted the floors. Two, three, four . . . Now the rustle was changing to a sizzling, then a rasping noise. The double thump was louder. Emilio would rush to the door, open it the merest fraction and stand listening. Five, six, it was here! No, it had stopped at the floor below. The gate opened, closed. The lift was off down again. From the floor below he could hear the sound of a door-bell or the jingle of keys in the lock. Absurdly enough, he began to hate that faceless, nameless person who was not Vévé.

They had agreed that in any case Emilio was not to wait for her after a quarter past seven. Sometimes she arrived later, but he had not given up hope. He would embrace her at the door, hardly believing that it was true. And at whatever time she arrived, as soon as he saw her, held her close in his arms and kissed her generous lips, he experienced the same feeling of astonishment and wonder as the first time on the Collina. A year had passed and he was still not sure that he really knew her.

What, for instance, was that strange look, as sweet as honey yet malicious, almost devilish, which he noticed at times? Vévé, lying on her back, gazed at him with a glint in her eyes that was intense, searching, ironic and happy, completely different from the way in which she normally looked at him. Even her face seemed changed, as if swollen with pleasure. And her eyes appeared to be oblique and almond-shaped.

Still staring at him, she said: 'Isn't it true that I'm everything to you? Mother, daughter, sister, lover, everything? I'm the woman meant just for you. One day you'll get used to the idea – you won't be able to live without me. And I won't be able to live without you. What shall we do then? We don't want to get married.'

'We *can't*,' Emilio corrected her.

'No, that's not true. We don't want to. *I* don't want to. Because, look, we could say without any promises to each other that maybe we'll get married one day, when you're earning and have got a good job. But *I* don't want to, see?'

She raised herself on one elbow. And now she made *him* lie on his back. Now *she* looked down at him through the short, smooth blonde hair falling over her forehead – but with those eyes that were still so different from usual, which seemed to laugh with an inner malice while her lips bore no trace of laughter. She repeated slowly: 'I'm the one, *I* don't want to marry you – not tomorrow or ever. D'you understand or don't you?'

Emilio said nothing. He did not want to think. Whenever he thought about it, he told himself that he had fallen into the trap which, right from the beginning, he had hoped to avoid – an attachment, as his family put it. Or that Vévé was being dishonest when she said that she did not want to marry him.

Vévé had talked to him about her life and kept him informed of what went on every day at home – her sister's engagement, her mother's heart-attack, her father's boozing bout. She was the third of four children. The two boys, older than her, were workmen, one at Savigliano and the other at Fiat but fortunately they were both married with children and did not live at home. The sister, Egle, was younger and learning to be a dressmaker. She was not really cut out for study. Vévé, on the contrary, was. Just think, she had entered the insurance firm before finishing in training college and had taken her teaching diploma without leaving her job. She studied at home in the evenings. Now she would do better to stay on at the office – with her diploma she was not just a typist but a secretary. Practically speaking she was responsible for the entire department. And her wages were correspondingly higher.

Her father was no longer young. He was a Communist and had been in trouble because of his politics. The family had lived for years in Via Segurana off Corso Casale. Their flat was a modest one, overlooking a courtyard, but the district was quiet, near the Collina and the Val San Martino tram depot. So Papa did not need to get up very early on winter mornings, and at his age this had its importance . . .

Vévé did not want to marry him? Well . . . perhaps she was testing him to see if he would argue with her, protest, promise her something. But he would say nothing. He did not think of the future. After all he preferred to believe that Vévé was honest with him. He felt happier that way.

At the studio by the Po he was in the habit of spending evenings after dinner twice a week with Gino Serra and others of his group of anti-Fascist artists and intellectuals who were protected by their patron, Golzio – an industrialist who had become immensely rich and powerful during and after the war.

Emilio was Serra's friend and felt no need to become intimate with anyone else apart from Ferrau, a young musician already a university teacher, extraordinarily well informed and passionately fond of all the arts. Maestro Ferrau was small, pale, witty. His eyes were piercing, yet there was warm humanity in them, too. He looked at you and listened with the idea of getting to know you, or learning more about you. C. the famous painter was too 'grand', too elderly and probably too reserved and isolated in his art to be a real friend to anyone. The others were pleasant and amusing, altogether they represented for Emilio something new, fresh and open – a release from the petty aristocratic and bourgeois milieu in which he had been brought up. For instance, he had never expected to be able to talk about Wagner, Debussy and Ravel to someone who understood and shared his views. He had never foreseen that (with Ferrau's encouragement) he would put these views into writing and publish them under the title 'Musical Transparencies'.

Paolino Rousset was another painter, reputedly an intimate friend of the Golzio family. A regular guest at their town house in Corso Presidente Wilson and at the castle of Casalgrasso, he sold many of his paintings to Golzio. Although he had no particular liking for Rousset, Emilio sought his company and his confidence. He took to walking home with him when they left Serra's studio, then visiting him, commenting upon and praising his pictures even if he found nothing special in them. He thought that he was being sincere and perhaps gradually he became so, forgetting that his original motive in saying 'Shall I come along with you?' was the hope of being invited one day to Golzio's. His rapport with Serra had been similarly tainted, though Gino Serra's humanity and his radiant youth had finally subdued, even erased, the ulterior motives in Emilio's mind.

Gino was very delicate. He may have been suffering from an incurable disease but he never referred to it or complained. He was one of those charmers who seem to live in a state of grace. As if they know that they have no time to make mistakes, they seek and find Beauty and Justice where you would least expect it and unfailingly sense what is ugly and bad. Gino's artistic judgments were simple and direct – he could immediately detect an ambitious brush-stroke, a fraud, artiness or lack of inspiration, and he was equally clear-sighted about politics. The Fascist régime had taken over and almost all Italians, including many genuine old liberals, flattered themselves that the danger of Bolshevism had passed and tried to pretend that the danger of dictatorship would soon pass. But Gino Serra had already seen and foreseen everything – the absurdity of Mussolini and the weakness of his adversaries, whether or not they were temporary allies of the government. But he made no mystery or it, nor did he play the prophet. Indeed, his arguments were generally confined to spontaneous remarks. For instance he would say: 'I don't trust those spats. He wants to rule the roost, that's all.'[1]

He used to sing the old Piedmontese songs, which was how Emilio met him. One evening Emilio had gone to the Caffé Nazionale almost opposite the University in Via Po. He had an hour free between two lectures and there was no point in going home. He sat down with his notes at one of the small, marble tables. The café, neo-classical in style, was dark, smoky, fusty-smelling, great sombre canvases on the walls, indistinct landscapes and eighteenth-century mythological scenes alternating with oblong, age-blackened mirrors.

[1] Mussolini, as Prime Minister, habitually wore light-coloured spats.

At a nearby table, a painfully thin young man wearing light tortoiseshell spectacles, with a large yellow nose shining like alabaster, sparkling white teeth, a charming smile and flashing eyes was singing softly to two friends, accompanying himself on the guitar, the song of the shepherdess:

> *A l'umbreta dël büssun*
> *bela bergera a l'é 'ndurmia . . .*

> 'In the shade of the bush
> a beautiful shepherdess was asleep'

the Treasury Counsel's favourite! Gino Serra sang it better, especially from the second verse when the French soldiers came on the scene, *'tre zoli Fransé'*. Better because of the sly refinement of the allusions to love which he delicately traced in melodic arabesques which were completely absent in the version sung by Emilio's father.

> *J'àn bin die: – Bela bergera,*
> *vui j'avì la frev.*
> *Ma se vui j'avì la frev*
> *faruma fé 'na cuvertüra.*
> *Cun ël me mantel,*
> *ch'a l'é tantu bel,*
> *faruma fé 'na cuvertüra,*
> *passerà la frev.*

> 'I said: "Beautiful shepherdess,
> you have a fever.
> But if you have a fever
> I'll have a coverlet made.
> Out of my cloak
> which is so lovely,
> I'll have a coverlet made,
> and the fever will pass." '

There was a last verse which Emilio did not know. The lawyer never sang it because he thought it indecent. The young shepherd jumped out of the hut and started playing the viola. Then – extraordinary affair – he and the Frenchman each took her by the hand and they all three danced in the perfect harmony of love:

L'àn ciapà bela bergera,
l'àn fà-la dansé

'They caught hold of the beautiful shepherdess
and made her dance'

Emilio wanted to learn that verse, and that was how his friendship
with Serra began. The painter with his quick perceptions could not
doubt the sincerity of the enthusiasm showed by this middle-class,
well-educated student, sharp-featured and passionate of eye, in
seeking his company. Serra realized that good training helped to
repress or at any rate to conceal an extraordinary appetite for life.
And Emilio, happening to notice his own profile in the mirrors,
realized that Serra understood.

Serra saw only one fault in Emilio, just one flaw in his good
training. Emilio had introduced Vévé to him. He had not introduced
her to the others. Serra chided him.

'Why don't you bring her along to meet us this evening?'

Emilio flushed.

'Impossible. With all those people. Society women!'

'Why not? Are you afraid that she won't know how to behave?
She's a hundred times better than the others. More intelligent, no
doubt about it. More cultured, too, I think.'

'It's not that. Everybody would see her and talk would get around.'

'People know already, old chap!'

'Not officially. If I brought her here one evening, the whole thing
would take on a different complexion.'

'Who would have thought that you were so Torinese!'

Emilio blushed again. Had he been caught out in flagrant pro-
vincialism, he wondered?

Serra, who had been about to carry on his banter, stopped short.
He must have noticed that the boy's colouring up was accompanied
by a depth of sadness which indicated a reluctance to admit the
reason.

Emilio discovered only later that Serra and his friends belonged
to what everybody called 'the Golzio set'. That had strengthened
his liking for Serra and he spent more and more evenings with the
group. For some time he had been wondering whether he could
ever bear the long, patient work and pittance of a deputy and then

a procurator – a necessary apprenticeship if he decided on the career of barrister after taking his degree. His father, who still cherished illusions on the subject, had recently persuaded a jurist friend of his, the celebrated barrister Flores-Torèl, to accept him in chambers as an unpaid junior. But Emilio had left after a couple of months with the excuse that if he practised he would have no time for study. And he added that he felt 'the call' more to theory than to practice, to the study and history of jurisprudence, even to a career as university professor rather than to the bar. His father's view was that as long as the boy took his studies seriously, all well and good. No question of incompatibility – the profession did not exclude teaching; on the contrary, it was an integral part . . . and so on.

Emilio's real reason was different: Flores-Torèl was in the habit of working late every afternoon!

And there was yet another, deeper reason, also to do with Vévé. Without Emilio realizing it, his first great *amour* had changed his character in a few months, fired his ambition, spurred the need to make a lot of money as quickly as possible. He still did not know what he wanted to do in life; but he had taken a step forward. He knew what he did *not* want to be – for instance, a barrister, a magistrate or an office employee. Diplomacy might tempt him – foreign parts, travel, a new life. But the preparation for that was long, too – another year for a degree, then two at the Institute of Political Science in Florence – examinations and all the rest of it. Besides, unless you were exceptionally clever or lucky, the only way to make a rapid and brilliant career was to have money – almost all the ambassadors were rich aristocrats. With the Sanfront legacy – or even half of it – it would be easy. But meanwhile, cousin Alberto Ceroni had been made a count by the new Pope – perhaps he owed it to his wife, Marie Rose, the last descendant of the du Buisson de Courson-Cristot family. It was anyhow an honour and a guarantee which seemed to have brought him closer to Uncle Sanfront. And Aunt Vittoria now greeted Emilio's parents with a curt, mocking sneer. Sheer folly, then, to hope for more than half of the legacy. Still, that would be more than sufficient to enter the diplomatic service. But would the Viottis get it? And when? No, a diplomatic career would mean another two or three years' study and five or six more 'in the ranks' with the possibility of finishing up as Vice-Consul in Varna or Rosario.

His only hope, therefore, was to try to go into business. And since he had no flair for commerce or figures, he believed or rather felt, that the only kind of business where he could succeed would have to be concerned with art and artists. He thought vaguely of advertising, cultural relations, an organizational post. Until in the mist of these aspirations the name of Golzio gradually emerged and began to shine out like a summer sun. If only he could get an introduction, a recommendation!

He had never mentioned it to Serra. The painter went to see the great industrialist and patron of the arts from time to time, and Emilio knew it, but when he was alone with Serra he entered a special state of mind, disinterested, elated, vibrant – ready to hear a Mozart record or browse through a Cézanne album, and then he stopped thinking about his plans. Or if he did think of them – and eventually he did – he feared that by being the first to refer to them, he might spoil the opinion that Serra seemed to have of him. This opinion, thought Emilio, was still full of enthusiasm, full of confidence in his intelligence and his truly sincere love of art. Better that it should remain so. Later, Serra could mention him to Golzio in good faith. It was a subtle but accurate calculation imposed by Serra's finesse.

Paolino Rousset was a different type. He had a foxy face, ironic, intelligent, friendly, but one which an unkind assessment might interpret as crafty, foolish, egotistical. Sharp nose, curling lips, black toothbrush moustache, receding chin. He was tall and thin, with short arms. If the face was foxy, his general appearance was more reminiscent of a flamingo or a heron. Emilio saw at once that Rousset was not as human and intelligent as Serra. It showed in the pompous way in which the painter replied when he asked to visit his studio: 'But of course, my dear fellow, you're very welcome. Come tomorrow . . . no, I can't make it tomorrow. The day after tomorrow . . . wait a moment, that's no good either. Let's say Friday. Friday at three. The light is good in the early afternoon. You'll see! I expect you on Friday.'

Well, one can be a good painter and yet be guilty of vanity, and even, in a sense, be lacking in intelligence. At least, that was what Emilio wanted to think. But when he first saw Rousset's pictures, he was frankly puzzled, though he did not hesitate to praise them. Only conventional compliments, true, and after all what harm was there in that? He was merely obeying a rule of society, the code of good manners. Yet something within told him that he had overdone the praise, to say the least, and he regretted it not so much out of honesty as because of a vague, deep-rooted fear of strange, future consequences – one of which might well be remorse for his dishonesty, while the others were completely unpredictable for the present. He had overdone the praise.

With Gino Serra the idea would never have crossed his mind. He liked his pictures, and didn't much like Rousset's. He had a fleeting suspicion that Rousset's were a little cold, too polished and technically thought out – colours put together like a pattern book. Gino's pictures seemed painted in one natural flow – tree, sky, street, light – all that Gino had wanted to say was there, firm and clear. And Emilio had never dared to praise them to Gino. He would look at them for a long time in silence. At most he might murmur 'Beautiful!'

But he had gradually perfected the compliments he paid to Rousset. He had convinced himself, making excuses for what he considered three-quarters spontaneous, one quarter calculated. He did not see that flattering remarks are like lies and cherries – one leads to another. The tempting voice of a tiny devil whispered in his ear: 'Now it's done. A word more, a word less, what does it matter?' He gazed at Rousset's pictures until he believed that he believed in them, and the rest was easy. He only had to read a few books by Venturi or Berenson, or some of Zanzi's articles in *La Stampa*.

Although Rousset's paintings soon came to seem really beautiful, his company was less easy to appreciate. His conversation was so bankrupt of ideas. But here too Emilio decided to give him the benefit of the doubt. At first he had suspected Paolino of not being very intelligent. Now he was persuaded of the contrary. Paolino was by nature melancholy and taciturn – that was all. Indeed, on reflection, was not this melancholy the secret lode which inspired his painting, a vein so secret that until then Emilio had doubted its very existence?

To avoid silence, Emilio generally did most of the talking as they walked at night from the Lungo Po to Corso Vittorio. He talked about art, politics and sometimes about himself. He found himself revealing personal confidences that he had never told either Serra or Piero Giraudo. He spoke to Rousset of his fears for the future and of Vévé, who was increasingly occupying his thoughts and his time. Rousset said nothing, or responded with mysterious sighs and brief exclamations suitable for any topic or situation: 'Ah, yes . . . That's right! . . . Bravo! . . . Well! . . . That's life! . . . Of course, of course . . .'

Sometimes Emilio, too, fell silent. Then there were interminable, embarrassed, excruciating pauses. Rousset did not seem to mind, but Emilio was trying to convince himself that those silences had some significance. There was this painter walking by his side. He had his own problems and his affections. His art and a reputation to be won. A fiancée in Rome. Did he have nothing to say? Perhaps his silence meant just that – a failure to communicate even between friends.

Who then was this man – Emilio wondered – a little older than him, thin, tall, with a sharp nose and short arms who until a few months before had been a total stranger? He was certainly a human being. But as Emilio walked in silence with him, elbow to elbow or arm in arm, he felt at times as if he were giving off a negative electric charge, a repellent form of energy, a kind of vaguely metallic effluvium. It was not remotely a physical sensation but something more, something alarming if one thought about it. It seemed impossible for any man to be so irremediably independent and different from all others, and for there not to be some force, love or intelligence capable of capturing and uniting people.

Although Emilio kept them strictly to himself, these lofty and mystic considerations eventually helped him to continue with his less-than-sincere compliments.

And eventually Rousset, too vain to separate the true from the false in Emilio's praise, had an idea. 'Come here, Viotti,' he said, one day, and led the way to a writing-desk on the veranda at the back of the studio. The glass windows were framed by curtains of rough canvas. In the golden glow of the May morning they could see a uniform, vast expanse of red-brown roofs, dotted here and there with bell-towers, and the Tempio Valdese, and the domes of the synagogue, and the iron arch of Porta Nuova; the wide, deep, straight furrow of Corso Vittorio with the pale-green tips of the lime trees barely visible; and in the background, the huge circle of the Alps.

'Here you are,' said Rousset and showed Emilio a small, printed sheet folded in two, bearing his name in large type, a reproduction of one of his pictures and two pages of text. 'This is the leaflet for an exhibition that I gave last year at Piacenza. The presentation, as you see, is unsigned – I wrote it myself!' He raised his short little arm, made more grotesque by the sleeve of his artist's smock. He put his small hand on Emilio's shoulder and gazed earnestly at him, his eyes as bright and black as boot buttons. 'Why don't you try to jot down the nice things that you've said about my pictures? In a month's time I'm having another show at Alessandria – you ought to write the presentation for it. You'd be doing me a favour.'

Emilio was immediately on the defensive – he did not feel competent. Rousset insisted, saying that he had read his article 'Musical Transparencies' which was well written.

Finally he accepted. And a week after he had written and delivered the two pages, one night as they were leaving Serra's studio, Rousset suddenly put his hand on Emilio's shoulder again and said with a ring of solemnity in his voice: 'What are you doing on Monday? Come to Golzio's place after dinner. There'll be some music. You're invited.'

When he arrived with Paolino Rousset and walked up the shadowy marble staircase into the large room on the first floor (also marble and shadowy) he was surprised to see that most of the guests were the same friends who met at the Caffé Nazionale or in Serra's studio. They were all there. Only Ettore Cuomo was missing – but of course he was a Neapolitan! And he was not sufficiently well known for his writing and work to overcome that grave handicap. How extraordinary that none of them, a few evenings before, had mentioned the party and that nobody, not even Serra, had betrayed the secret! From their jealous caution, Emilio gauged the extreme importance that they attached to an invitation from Golzio.

They could not even conceal a certain disgruntlement at seeing him. 'Oh, you're here, too. How nice to see you. Bravo.' Two exceptions. Serra, who whispered with a smile: 'I knew about it. I'm glad.' And Ferrau who winked at him – that wink meant everything and was another proof of his generous nature. Two exceptions, not to the provincial narrow-mindedness of Golzio's protégés, merely to their spite.

Besides all these friends whom Emilio already knew and, of course, Golzio and his wife, there were only a few elegant women, a group of journalists and some university professors. Among these he saw Professor B who taught history of law and who happened to be responsible for setting the subject of his thesis.

The furnishings in the house were the work of C and of Rousset, who had collaborated with C. The style was ultramodern – or, as it was called at the time, 'twentieth-century'. Bare, light-coloured walls, the first room in marble, the others in fabrics. Huge curtains of rose or lilac silk sweeping down from ceiling to floor in voluminous folds. Indirect lighting. Massive antique tables, enormous chests; and above, *objets d'art* and precious exhibits standing isolated – Chinese vases, jade lions, Indian sculptures in reddish stone. On the walls – on a gold background – paintings by Matisse, Modigliani, Spadini – a Renoir, a Van Gogh.

Golzio's appearance seemed to blend perfectly with the décor. Medium height, thin, as pale as ivory, his white hair slicked down, cold eyes, thin lips fixed in a polite smile, he certainly looked older than he was. This was partly the result, perhaps, of a physical defect which had deformed his hands into hooked gnarled prongs with yellowish skin stretched over them, very much like claws. The only sign of his relative youth and his undeniable energy was the extreme mobility of his head which he kept on turning sharply to the right, to the left, behind, glancing at those around him regardless of the course of the conversation. He did not look at anyone for more than a few seconds.

'Pleased to meet you. I've heard about you. They told me. My congratulations,' he said. He squeezed Emilio's hand and the young man, taken by surprise after what he had been told and all he had seen since he had entered the room, by the strong Canavese accent – a waggoner's, a peasant's accent – promptly turned away in embarrassment and looked admiringly at three bronze cocks standing on a granite altar nearby.

Golzio, following Emilio's glance, exclaimed just as promptly: 'Those cocks, eh? Ceylon, sixth century.' He added, 'Don't you find that the old habit of arranging pieces almost at random, one here, another there, is an absurd idea? Don't you find it much more restful to lay them out like this at equal distances, symmetrically? Repose. To me, Art is above all synonymous with calm and repose.'

The surrounding chorus of intellectuals – including the decrepit senator Queirolo – mumbled their approval, to which Emilio endeavoured to contribute as clearly as he could, since Golzio seemed to be talking to him. Before the murmuring died away, Emilio felt that he must seize the opportunity to make an impression. With something of an effort he tried to make an opening. 'It would be interesting to discover the reason for this wide-spread prejudice ... the prejudice ... that asymmetry is the thing ...' But Golzio, as if he had not heard, went on to talk about the altar.

'It's Romanesque or pre-Romanesque, unearthed in the country – Carpugnino, province of Novara. A stroke of luck.' Emilio simply could not understand how an accent like that fitted in with the splendour and refinement of the house.

Later that evening, Ferrau ventured an explanation. The splendour and refinement were a direct consequence of his economic power, while his economic power was a direct consequence of his only real quality – age-old peasant shrewdness, which Golzio had inherited from his Canavese parents and forefathers and which for some mysterious reason (though there was surely a rational explanation) he had retained, primitive, genuine, earthy, throughout his upbringing and education. That was why – concluded Ferrau – his accent had not been influenced in the slightest by Torinese or city Piedmontese.

Golzio had explained 'the stroke of luck' which had brought him the altar of Carpugnino: 'I found it myself. I had been visiting the place to see if it was suitable for a new factory. As it turned out, it wasn't. But in an orchard behind a farm, half-buried in the ground, covered with weeds and filthy dirty was that thing there. I took it away without thinking any more about it. It looked like a basin, an upturned basin. My idea was to take it to Casalgrasso and put it in the garden. But as it turned out, it was valuable. Just look at the time and money you waste on antique-dealers sometimes, and end up with a fake. ...'

'Not always, Ingegnere, not always,' said a tall, massive man with a small round beard. His sensitive voice and smile were a peculiar contrast to his almost gigantic stature.

'Not always, I agree, professor,' Golzio retorted chaffingly but abruptly. 'Give me a little credit, too.'

Professor V was the famous historian, critic and expert who

advised Golzio what to buy and presided over this new and important collection of paintings, sculpture and *objets d'art*. Rousset introduced Emilio to him. And V, to Emilio's surprise, said that he had read and admired the two pages he had written for Rousset's exhibition at Alessandria, and even the article 'Musical Transparencies'.

The highlight of the evening was not a concert but a ballet performance by Clotilde and Alexander Sakharoff. The guests went down to a gallery on the floor below which had been converted into a soberly appointed little theatre. The walls and the armchairs were upholstered in pearl-grey velvet. The velvety carpet was a slightly darker grey. The low stage was sealed off by the white stucco cornice of a broad arch and a white tweed curtain.

Signora Golzio was waiting in the theatre and apologized for not appearing sooner. She had been busy looking after the Sakharoffs who had just arrived from London. And from her tone it was made clear that the Sakharoffs were not staying at a hotel but were house-guests.

Signora Golzio, too, was an ivory figure. Small, slender, straight, frail, perfectly in harmony with the neo-classical, twentieth-century style of all the rest. Her hair was raven-black, lustrous, slicked down with a white woollen bandeau and gathered at the nape of the neck in a shining, compact chignon. Her dress: a straight, glossy tunic of pearl-grey shantung, sleeveless and reaching to her feet. No jewellery – no bracelets, ear-rings, rings – absolutely nothing except a Rajah's solitaire diamond on the middle finger of her right hand. Her eyes could not be seen – two slits between lashes thick with mascara. Heelless sandals with rough leather straps like a monk's. The nails of her feet and hands were beautifully kept, but unvarnished. In Paris or London her style would have perhaps been judged a little odd and nothing more. In Turin, or rather in that group of ten or twelve wives of intellectuals, regular guests at the soirées in Corso Presidente Wilson, it had an upsetting and nerve-racking effect. Superficially, the other women surrendered unconditionally to the necessary enthusiasm; but each one secretly wondered how far Signora Golzio was following the latest Paris fashion and how far she was exercising her personal initiative and determination to shock them, the good lady intellectuals of Turin.

Rather similar was the reaction of that enlightened yet provincial audience to the Sakharoffs' dancing. Many were seeing them for the first time, and it was Emilio's very first experience of Russian ballet. Serra and Ferrau had told him a little about it. You could not judge or even enjoy the Sakharoffs without knowing the Russian ballet which Diaghilev had developed in Paris from 1909 on. The Sakharoffs were simply a fragment, a miniature sample, an already withering branch of that luxuriant growth. And, Emilio did indeed think he detected in those refined inventions, those erudite illustrations, something shrivelled and forced – a great deal of taste and culture but a great deal of conscious effort, too. It was true, as he whispered to Serra in an interval, that the artistes' age no longer favoured those leaps and bounds, that natural abandon to the surge of the music which is always the effect, however studied it may be, of great dancing.

'Me Lan Fan,' Professor V then murmured with a smile. 'Me Lan Fan at seventy dances like the most marvellous, supple girl.'

'Who is Me Lan Fan?' asked Ferrau who was not ashamed to admit his ignorance, presumably because it was very limited.

'The greatest mime, dancer and actor in the world.' The briefest pause and Professor V added almost breathlessly – 'and perhaps of all time.'

'You've seen him?'

Professor V's reply clinched the matter: 'In Pekin.'

This comparison with the obscure Chinese ballet genius was sufficient for Emilio provisionally to classify the Sakharoffs; yet, back home that night, he noticed that the final scene stuck in his memory with a precise clarity reserved only for perfect works and performances. To the magnificent, melting music of Lully's delicate minuet, Alessandro Sakharoff, dressed as *Le Roi Soleil*, made larger and taller by his enormous wig and costume of gold, yellow and coffee, advanced and strutted in slow, complicated, stately evolutions. Two huge beige silk bows adorned his slippers, quivering incessantly like two great butterflies. The scene was a bigger success than all the others and had been encored three times. After that the guests had been individually introduced to the famous ballet-dancers.

Lying in his gloomy bed of carved walnut, in his little old bourgeois room of the King Umberto period, Emilio had put out the light but was finding it difficult to get to sleep. His imagination, like an inadvertently shaken kaleidoscope, conjured up jumbled, composite images of the precious, living world where he had finally . . . gained a foothold? No, not yet, but he had at least taken a look at it – the gold panels, the jade lions, the silk curtains, *Le Roi Soleil*, Signora Golzio's solitaire diamond, Me Lan Fan, the Asiatic face of Professor V, all to the confused accompaniment of Lully's minuet and Golzio's country accent. A clearer, unimportant recollection suddenly broke in upon his reverie. On the landing of the marble staircase, while they were going down to the theatre, law-history Professor B, whom Emilio had asked a long time before to set him a subject for his thesis, approached him and said in a loud voice, a real professor's voice: 'Your name is . . . ?'

'Viotti, Professor.'

'Ah, yes, Viotti, good. You're still waiting for me to give you your thesis, aren't you?'

'Yes, Professor.'

'Don't suppose that I haven't been thinking about it, you know . . .'

It was perfectly obvious, however, that he had *not* thought about it. The Professor peered at Emilio for a moment through his pince-nez. He had white, close-cropped hair, a little grey moustache curled at the ends, a high, starched collar in which his scrawny neck was lost just as his delicate, almost feminine hands tended to disappear inside his round, stiff cuffs. He raised his right hand, fore-finger outstretched, as if he had suddenly remembered something. He was play-acting. In fact, as though changing his mind, he went on – 'No, no . . . better not now. We must meet and discuss it first. Come and see me whenever you wish. Better for you to come to my house. We can take our time there.' It was evident that B, surprised to find Emilio at Golzio's and not knowing why someone so young should be admitted, had thought it advisable to treat him with a certain respect. B was a coward. After the show, while waiting at the buffet for the Sakharoffs to change, Professor V, notoriously anti-Fascist, happened to mention the liberals and socialists who were supporting the government.

'It's very simple to me. They're all very naïve. They can't see that we're heading for ruin.'

B moved away instantly. But Golzio, turning to V with a jerk that was immediately contradicted by his extremely calm tone of voice, said, 'I wouldn't say that, Professor. Look, I'll be very frank with you. We must always keep an eye on the Stock Exchange. France and England don't think badly of us. Give it time, Professor, give it time. If I said to you – Professor, put the Hermitage up in three months, what would you say? That I'm mad. And you'd be right. By the way, I'm told that they've opened a fascinating exhibition of Impressionist pictures in Amsterdam . . .'

He was obviously anxious to change the subject.

'Too powerful to speak out against the government in public,' thought Emilio, drowsing off. 'But in private . . . I wonder . . .'

He had been invited to Golzio's. About the same time he had committed a *faux-pas* – a defeat, a small one, but the sort of thing that had never happened to him before during his three years at the university. He sat an examination in Science of Finance and Professor Einaudi had given him the choice of being satisfied with eighteen, the lowest qualifying mark, or retiring and taking the examination again in November so as not to spoil his average of thirty.

Emilio retired and breathed not a word to anyone. He knew perfectly well that the reason for his insufficient preparation was not the time he had devoted to Vévé instead of studying, but the recent change in his state of mind. Perhaps he was beginning to feel the indifference which inevitably steals into the happiest, most requited passion, when the desire is born to transform it into a complete, lasting bond, simultaneously with the opposite desire – to be rid of it, although the mere thought of such freedom seems absurd. In practice, he continued violently to reject the idea of marrying either at once or in the future. The future, when he could safely marry her, seemed too remote. On the other hand, he felt that he could not go on like this – neither for his own sake nor for hers.

She, true to type, never complained, never hinted at a change, much less at breaking it off. It was an attitude of exceptional sincerity and generosity for a girl of her age and class. Emilio did not appreciate it enough. When he confided in Serra, the artist was silent; then murmured: 'Why don't you marry her? You'll never find another girl like that.'

But Emilio remembered that he was twenty-two and this was enough to make him burst out laughing. Serra was intelligent – but he was a sentimental character *à la* Gozzano, that was what he was!

He went to Fert to see Piero and ask his advice. In a corner of the set, he waited for him to finish work: the scene was the interior of a luxurious apartment, vaguely Moorish in style – huge carpets, bear and tiger skins, period folding chairs inlaid with mother-of-pearl, velvet, palms, chenzias, bamboo canes with white plumes, panoplies, leather pouffes, *abat-jours*. Piero was busy arranging brocaded curtains mounted on runners under the glazed ceiling. He was pulling them backwards and forwards so as to diffuse or focus the sunlight. Enormous, humming arc-lamps were helping to disperse the darker shadows.

Work ceased when the sun went down. The studios emptied in a moment. The two friends walked up and down for a long time in the deserted courtyards which gave on to the hay-scented country-side.

Emilio had never talked to Piero about Vévé before, apart from some joking remark. And Piero surprised him once again by saying exactly what he would never have expected him to say: 'Don't get married, don't do anything silly. It's different for me. Me, I feel like being a father and so I'm doing the right thing to get married soon – perhaps this autumn. But not you, you're not the type! At least wait until you've got a job and start earning.'

Meanwhile, to make matters worse, Professor Bonadé, lecturer and barrister who was on the university committee, happened to meet his father while strolling in the arcade. Although they hardly knew each other, they talked about the examination. And so Papa had found out. The heavens opened – tears, threats, despair! In a stormy scene, Papa and Mama for the first time showed openly that they were in full possession of the facts; they even came out with Vévé's surname.

Emilio had not given way, he had not promised to leave her, he had not promised anything. But his mother's tears, his father's hoarse bawling (you'll not get a sou from me! Get on with it! Go to work! After all we've done for you!) formed a heavy accompaniment to his anguished doubts.

He said nothing to Vévé. He knew that she was too proud to tolerate a string of prejudices which were more social than moral. And then, the real trouble was not the scenes with his mother and father, nor his failure to take the examination. The real trouble was much more serious – it was the need that he felt to make a decision, to change. But change in what way? By marrying her? Or by leaving her? And if he lacked the courage to admit his uncertainty, what was the use of telling her all the rest? Proud and impetuous as she was, merely to mention the subject would be like saying goodbye to her and Emilio certainly did not have the courage to do that.

But Vévé had guessed without being told anything. From her first suspicion she reacted very simply by trying to ration her dates with him. And Emilio, out of love or pique or a mixture of both, tried on the other hand to see her more often than before. He rang her at the office, knowing all the time that she was not allowed to take telephone calls there. He went to wait for her outside the office, not so far from the main door as they had agreed and as he had always done, and not only in the evening but at midday too. Vévé scolded him, and became alarmed. They quarrelled for the first time. Emilio wondered – was this what he wanted to do, gradually create a situation of mutual intolerance which would naturally end in the break-up of their relationship?

For the moment their quarrels ended differently. And with kisses and caresses throughout the languid, voluptuous twilights of that week in June, how soon the light faded in the attic windows! How suddenly a violet hue tinged the high, steep Collina with its wooded hillocks and deep ravines! Even more quickly came the moment when bad thoughts and bitter words and the tears of a few minutes before seemed only a pretext to love in a new way and with greater abandon.

The feast of La Consolata was approaching. These were the loveliest evenings in the year. The scent of the lime trees, mysterious, intoxicating, rising from the avenues and the public gardens, pervaded the city. The song of the nightingales, barely audible across the Po from the first, gentle slopes of the Collina, the warm, quivering air – it all spoke of love. And Emilio and Vévé could not escape the spell, enclosed in their own feelings which, after a whole year of happiness, had not changed from that first day of cherries in the grove and their first real kisses. Since that day she had sensed how it would end and secretly resigned herself to it. And now, with plebeian and generous disregard for what had not yet happened, she tried as hard as she could not to reflect upon it. He too had stayed the same from that day. In a year, he had learnt nothing. Because of optimism, lust for life and money and a chance to see the world, he still attached no importance to his happiness.

And if a friend – Serra, for instance – had been wise enough to warn him that he was risking losing it, the warning and the wisdom would have been useless. Emilio would not have believed him. All that year he had been in a seventh heaven of happiness, and never more so than in the last few days. And during those days he had been making plans and schemes and unwittingly striving never to be so happy again.

He climbed the little oval, rococo staircase which led to Professor B's mezzanine flat in the courtyard of Palazzo D'Azeglio, thinking less of the thesis that the Professor was about to set him, than of the summer which had begun and the uncertainty it brought with it. Soon he would be off with his people to Alassio, but what after? Instead of going with them to Saint-Vincent as in previous years he would have liked to return to Turin alone and get down to some intensive study without delay – prepare Science of Finance and two more examinations, start work on his thesis in order to graduate at the first session the following year. But if he did that he would be alone in the house without his parents and more opportunities to see Vévé would create a serious obstacle to his studies. So much for leaving her!

The solution, unexpected as always in matters of doubt and love affairs, came from Professor B.

Professor B, a provincial who had recently scaled the heights to a university chair in a big city, a scholar as vain as he was erudite, had for many years submitted his vanity to the acquisition of learning. Now that he was in Turin, he was reversing the process, using his learning to satisfy his vanity; that is to say, striving ceaselessly for recognition and honour, giving lectures and society *conversazioni*, presiding over a women's cultural circle, chairing debates, attending concerts, receptions, exhibitions with the utmost regularity and ceremony.

The walls of the little mezzanine room were lined with crammed bookshelves. The windows, high and narrow, protected by baroque wrought-iron bars. They were open. Through the half-closed blinds, the blazing summer sun could be seen shining on the yellow-ochre walls of the courtyard. It was hot and dark in the room. The writing-desk was cluttered with huge piles of books, magazines, papers, bundles of proofs. And there behind it was the Professor, his face and the upper part of his body in the green half-light of an office lamp, his forearms in the yellowish glow, resting on a sheet of ruled foolscap paper, his right hand – or rather, just the fingers – protruding from a round cuff, clasping a penholder.

'I beg your pardon, I'll be with you in a moment,' he said in his piercing voice. Pointing to what he was writing, he went on: 'It's a lecture, in German, for the University of Heidelberg. I've reached the peroration. Sit down, please.'

Emilio sat on a small, upholstered sofa facing the desk and waited. He could see Professor B's bent head and white short-cropped hair between two stacks of books and pamphlets, and heard his pen scratching from time to time. He could see the yellow courtyard through the green shutters and hear the 21 tram rattling past in the street – the same one which took Vévé home. And then the silence and quiet hum of early afternoon in summer. The place, the moment, were particularly distressing. In the heavy, stifling air, with that musty smell of old papers, among all those books powerless to teach one about life, in that peace lasting a few minutes while the Professor finished writing his lecture, Emilio seemed to sense a mysterious vibration, a final cryptic warning, a last, almost ironical hint of the possibility of salvation. The 21 tram passing? Follow its clatter, let himself be carried away to the Casale gate, to lie there in her rosy arms and on her swelling breasts, there and no betrayal? Or was it a presentiment invented later, a mirage in reverse – the funeral knell of fate unconsciously applied to a memory, when that fate had already been decided?

How many times in his life he recalled that moment, those five minutes of waiting in the mezzanine flat at Palazzo D'Azeglio! As if it were possible, by dint of thinking about it, to make something that has happened, not happen. There is a doubt still sadder than the irrevocability of fate – the absence of a true faculty of choice, except in the romantic fantasies of the memory. Alas, what was could not be otherwise, and precisely because it should be so, we have never been warned of it.

'Viotti,' said Professor B, replacing the penholder and putting on his pince-nez, 'I've a great idea for you. But first I must know if you think it possible, that is to say, if your family situation, with which

I am not acquainted, would allow you to be away from Turin for some time.'

'How long?'

'That depends on you, on how quickly you carry out your research and how well you stand up to the work. In any case, I should say at least seven or eight months. Just enough time to present your thesis in a year.'

'And where should I have to go?'

'Oh, I'm glad to tell you that it's the most marvellous of all destinations: Rome.'

Emilio did not hear the knell of destiny. He thought – seven or eight months, that's not serious, it's just enough. Because, in a flash, he had seen the solution to all his problems. Eight months apart? Well, one of two things – either we'll see that our love has lasted and then, all right, we'll get married; or that it has faded and then – so long! True, it might fade for me but not for her, or vice versa, but either way it would only be a question of time, it would soon fade for the other, too ... An experiment: in other words, a way out.

He was so absorbed and excited by this idea that he did not even hear the subject of his thesis. He covered up by taking a notebook and pencil from his pocket and asking the Professor to repeat it.

'Survivals of Lombard law in the Communal Statutes of the territory of the Duchy of Spoleto' was the title of the thesis. The documents and texts, for the most part still unpublished, were in Rome in the Senate library. As for the examinations, there was no need to worry. He would be back in Turin some time in November, or he would sit them together with his degree examination in June or July of the following year. A couple of months' attendance, even less, between May and June would be sufficient. But the draft of his thesis would have to be completed before then. The work consisted more of research than of original study, more of analysis than of synthesis – the draft, therefore, could develop simultaneously with the research, apart from an introduction and a conclusion which he would write afterwards.

The important thing was for his parents to agree and give him an allowance to live in Rome. Emilio knew that they would and he knew why. So it was all settled then? Yes, but ... a brief hesitation, a sudden idea: would it not be possible for him to leave for Rome at once? Work all summer, return to Turin earlier, in the spring and so increase the number of attendances? But of course it was possible! The Professor approved of the idea and fixed another appointment for the following day. He would prepare a study programme and a short bibliography.

Leaving Palazzo D'Azeglio, Emilio went straight to see Serra, not at the studio but at home in Via Napione where he lived with his widowed mother and his sisters. The painter had been in bed for a few days, suffering from a crisis in his illness.

In spite of the heat, he was covered as far as the chest with a cashmere shawl and supported by an untidy pile of cushions amidst records, photographs of pictures, art books, a novel by Giraudoux, a volume of *A la recherche*, a Rimbaud, and an open album with a half-finished sketch. He showed it to Emilio with a sigh and an even wearier and gentler smile than usual on his damp, shiny, alabaster-yellow face. The sketch was yet another attempt to 'fix' the french window of his room, so different according to the time of day or the changing seasons.

Emilio looked at it. The french window opened on to a broad terrace. A cool green awning hung down to within about a metre and a half from the ground, a protection from the blinding white glare of the sky, a hint of which could be seen on the left through a narrow slit. At the far end of the terrace, arranged along the parapet against a white lattice, there were two rows of vases with leaves and flowers. But the dominant feature was the paving with its lozenge-design, alternately light and dark, which seemed to be clouded and covered with dust by the violence of the sun.

'The tone,' murmured Serra – 'if you can't see it with a stick of charcoal, it's no good using colour. Tell me, I can see from your face that something's happened. Have you left her? You're crazy!'

'Not yet. But we're not splitting up. Just for a few months.' Emilio smiled and explained in detail his idea of 'the experiment'.

Serra shook his head: 'I look at you and wonder how you can be such a child. Have you told her?'

'I'm going to, tonight. That's not what's worrying me. She's prepared for it. She knew. Look, she knew before me! Now you lived in Rome for a long time and must help me to find a place there. I don't want to end up in a students' *pension*. Something not too expensive, just a tiny flat . . .'

'A *pied-à-terre*? In Rome? If they're decent, they're dear. Then, you'll have to eat out. Wait a minute! Rousset's going at the end of the month. He could ask his girl-friend's mother, a wonderful old lady, to look for a room, something to suit you. She found him his studio. He says it's marvellous – near Villa Massimo. But he's got a job and is earning. What you need is a room and board with some nice family we know – not the usual *pension*.'

Emilio had said that he was not worried about Véve and this was the truth. When she undressed, he began hugging, kissing and caressing her. Suddenly he stopped, and it crossed his mind that it was dishonest or at least indelicate not to tell her at once.

Véve received the news about Rome and his idea of a trial separation without the least surprise. She remained motionless for an instant, staring into the void beyond the foot of the bed as if she had seen somebody enter the studio whom she was sure she knew but did not recognize. She did not smile. She said very quietly and almost immediately: 'When do you leave?'

'Monday,' replied Emilio.

Véve frowned. Was she counting the days? Emilio did the same – there were four to go. And since Véve said nothing and continued to avert her gaze, he began to fondle her again, cautiously, gently, as if afraid of a sudden violent reaction. He explained: 'Look, it's not goodbye, it's not a separation . . .'

'Of course it's not, Milio! Who says it is? Your parents, perhaps. I can only say that . . . that I don't like it, that's all. It means that I'll wait for you and you'll wait for me. We'll write. Then, when we meet again, if we still feel inclined . . .'

As if someone were listening, she went on, whispering in the conventional language, so secret and tender that all lovers gradually create for themselves. And as she whispered, Emilio smelt her fresh breath, the delicate perfume, the clean tang of her skin, and he began to make love with a kind of controlled frenzy that was sweetly gentle. They gazed into each other's eyes, tensed in the pleasure and mutual desire of possession and abandon.

Now Véve's blue eyes were sparkling with that happy smile which transformed them. Telling her of his decision to go to Rome was like telling her what he had always kept a secret, if only because he had never clearly told himself: that is to say his need to leave Turin for a time, to embark upon a glittering life (he no longer thought of a 'career', his father's term) and to earn a lot of money!

So Vévé looked at him with those eyes, that smile, even though, suddenly and finally, she knew all, yes all about him. Just as, Emilio imagined, he had known all about her. Her office boss? Yes, her boss, Bianchi-Mina had courted her, a bachelor of about forty, an elegant, interesting man. But this was all water under the bridge to Emilio. Vévé had told him everything and had even pointed out Bianchi-Mina in the arcade, through the windows of Baratti and Mulassano. Perhaps they had never gazed into each other's eyes as they did on that occasion. Perhaps it was the supreme joy that only the assurance of not deceiving and not being deceived in return can give.

Suddenly, while they were still blissfully engrossed in each other, Vévé said: 'I'm not afraid, you know. Love, you'll never forget me. Even if we were never to meet again as long as we live.'

IV

❧❧❧

In any case, there was no call to take things too seriously. He was going to Rome, at last he would be away from home for a few months on his own – that was all. He attached no importance to Rome. Now if it had been New York or Sydney...! He felt a burning impatience, a longing to get away at all costs and for no particular reason. Separation from Vévé? A seven or eight months' 'experiment'? Nonsense! The next morning, walking briskly up Corso Vittorio in the blazing June sun to Rousset's, he realized that it was simply not true and his calculations were illusory, he was not leaving in order to get away from Vévé; on the contrary, leaving Vévé was extremely painful. No, he was going away because he had to. Because the moment to go, no matter how or where, had arrived.

And was it not equally painful to leave Turin? Corso Vittorio, Corso Umberto, Corso Siccardi, Corso Vinzaglio, the great airy, sunny arcades, the splendid shops, the gilt signs, the sparkling windows, the fine, broad, straight avenues stretching away into infinity with their four parallel rows of tall trees, black, living columns, flowering, perfumed cupolas through which the bracing solstice wind, sweeping down from the neighbouring peaks and glaciers, rushed impetuously. What need was there of walls, arches, marble, real columns and real cupolas? Through the green foam of the trees and the dazzling sunlight he could see in the distance a red tram coming down the Corso. He was suddenly sure, as if a mysterious hand had pressed his heart in warning, that he would not find in Rome, Paris, Sydney or New York – if he ever went there – a city so beautiful, so bright, so logical, so close to the ideal: a city to be loved like Turin. The red tram passed gaily, clattering, swaying, gleaming in the sunshine with its windows, numbers, destination boards, its light-coloured woodwork. He did not need trains and trans-Atlantic liners. Why go away? Truth, beauty, youth were here.

Lean and swarthy, Rousset emerged almost furtively from behind a pillar in the arcade where he had come to meet him.

'So you're off to Rome, too! You've done the best thing. Serra told me that you're looking for board and lodging. Look, I've got an idea. But I won't tell you now because, first, I must write to my future mother-in-law. You'll see, it's a different life in Rome! The light! The air! And you breathe centuries of history there. It's still the capital of the world. What can compare with it here? It's delightful. But provincial. Provincial.'

Rousset had been looking about him. Emilio did the same thing. He could not think of an apter, more modern solution to the problem known as town-planning! Trees and trees. Nature canalized geometrically between buildings which did not stifle it. Nothing provincial about that. But Rousset went on praising Rome until Emilio stopped listening to him. He was distracted by a sudden, new idea. He was beginning to understand. To get away from Turin was inevitable, and yet useless and painful. Basically, life was absurd. What did Piero Giraudo think about it?

Emilio went back to Fert that afternoon. He had decided. He went to tell Piero and say goodbye to him. He met him coming out with his bicycle. It was Saturday. Work had finished and Piero was off to play bowls at the Martinetto.

'Come along and play a couple of games. When you've had a hard day at work it's the best sport of all.' He still pronounced 'sport' in the same way as when he was a boy, isolating it from the other words as if it were a religious expression.

The Martinetto bowling-alleys at the end of Via Cibrario were the best in Turin. Weather permitting, Piero went there regularly every Saturday. On Sundays, if he did not feel too tired, he did his hundred, hundred and fifty, even two hundred kilometres on the bike. Otherwise, bowls on Sunday, too.

Spacious, beautifully level, well-kept and always neat, the rinks (and there were quite a number of them) benefited from the shade of gigantic lime trees. Between the trees, wooden benches and tables – at the far end, a pergola and a booth where they sold drinks, and the canal nearby flowing clear and fast.

It was the first time that Emilio had come to play at the Martinetto, but soon he felt as if he had known them all for years. Professional men, artisans, clerks, workmen, retired senior officers, magistrates, even bricklayer's labourers met there to build and achieve on the rink, with woods in their hands, a temporary ideal society which strangers to Turin, at that time so riddled with prejudice and class distinction, would have thought inconceivable. But an ideal society none-the-less real where cordiality and good humour reigned supreme, where the only language was dialect, the only law that of the game, the only glory to aim and bowl well, the only animosity the one that divided adversaries during a match, the only claim, to be able to drink good wine.

Emilio lost himself in the game, and forgot facts and feelings recent and past, thoughts or *the* thought which harassed him most, the eager longing for life that consumed him, the desire and fear inspired by his imminent departure – in short, all self-knowledge.

Not that he had much of a flair for bowls. Poor aim, little skill and almost no practice. But for this very reason he started in with a kind of sensual, desperate determination. From the first bowl, he seemed to become another man. And with a modicum of luck and the help of expert partners like Piero and Bürin he managed to put on a decent show. People who did not know him well, for instance his opponents that day, might have taken him for an experienced player.

Bent in the delicate effort of gauging the force and speed that he had to transmit to the wood, his eye fixed on the distant 'jack', a yellow spot on the grey, deserted rink which just then seemed boundless, he felt his heart pounding with a deep, inarticulate, giddy joy, as if the whole of life and all its possible values were magically condensed and contained in the simple movement that he was about to make and which he could make by choosing from a vast range of similar gestures (but each different from another), according to the various combinations of force, trajectory, lift, turn, half-turn, straight delivery, the spot where the wood would strike the ground, the angle, the effect, the aim.

From the other end of the rink he heard Piero's voice, again that throaty, peasant's voice which Piero had when he shouted: 'Aim high, Emilio – high so that it drops straight down on to the jack.' He heard that voice which seemed to echo in his heart like the voice of youth and happiness.

They were playing three against three. He was partnered by Piero and Bürin, an electrician, thin, pale, smooth-faced, with a big nose and wearing a cyclist's cap. The other team consisted of a little old man with a white goatee beard whom everyone addressed as 'lawyer'; a middle-aged gentleman, heavily-built, rubicund, with ginger whiskers, a retired colonel of the Alpine Regiment; and a young bricklayer whose tall, massive physique and thick, black, American-style moustache made him look twice his age. Oh, how many times did he try, later, to remember exactly the events of that game! For some peculiar reason he kept telling himself that if he managed to remember the stratagems, openings, weaknesses, strokes of skill and luck which had helped his trio and their opponents to score points, and the number of points each time – if he had managed to remember all Piero's successful shots (and all Lawyer Peccoz's damnable ones, too) – well, he would have won the key to a mystery. It was a Saturday. The day after tomorrow, Monday night, he was leaving for Rome. Fate was changing horses. While he was playing, Emilio did not once give it a thought, not even for a moment. He was immersed in the game. It was only some time later that he began to think that the game might be mysteriously linked to his destiny. Actually, they played not one but three games. Emilio's team won the first and lost the second. The deciding match incorporated the features of the other two – at least so it seemed when he thought about it afterwards.

He aimed first, Bürin second and Piero was the one to knock away the opponent's wood. He seemed to remember that each time he bowled, the members of the other team looked bigger and taller. Perhaps it was an image that remained imprinted on his subconscious at the anguished and decisive moment when he was bending down to take aim and, looking up, had seen them as tall as giants against the soaring background of lindens in bloom and the sky above. The 'decider' was going badly, as badly as a cruel joke, as a painful and malicious hoax. At first, he, Piero and Bürin had scored six points and the others, none. They only had to make six more. Emilio's heart was in his mouth – the goal was in sight, they were certain to win.

To curb his enthusiasm, Piero motioned to him as if to say 'Don't get excited, we haven't won yet,' as he passed by and slowly crossed the rink to examine the ground around where the jack had stopped.

And Emilio, controlling his enthusiasm and impatience, got

ready to bowl. Fascinated, he looked at his opponents who were standing perfectly still looking at him. Oh, he was to remember them so well, those three faces quite different from each other. But all three were the eternal faces of executioners!

Lawyer Peccoz, the skip, was very much like Pirandello, but taller and thinner than Pirandello, even more acute and shrewd. His eyes were two ironical, diabolical slits, while Pirandello's were frank, melancholy and Mediterranean. In later years Emilio knew Pirandello personally. In fact, he had dealings with him. And it was quite possib'e that, again in his subconscious, the autocratic, albeit mournful likeness of the Sicilian writer became superimposed on the mischievous, though harmless, modest and provincial image of the Torinese lawyer and hence – especially after Pirandello was dead – the one had blurred the other, eventually endowing it with a sense of greatness and violence that it did not possess.

Lawyer Peccoz was the *bocciatore*[1] of the team, but he also had a marvellously high delivery. He took two steps and bent forward, using his whole body, first to the left, then to the right. Two steps, two rhythmic measures as if he were going to perform the 'splits' in a ballet. On the third 'beat', with his feet firmly planted on the ground, he thrust forward his right shoulder, raised his arm, released the wood underhand from his side, spinning it in the opposite direction to the throw, in a very high curve so that it grazed the leaves and flowers of the lime trees before plummeting down to within fifty centimetres of his opponent's wood which it knocked away and replaced. Looking up with his Mongolian-type slit-eyes, the lawyer followed the wood's flight and smiled. He went on smiling even when the shot did not succeed.

What was it, a rictus, a fixed, withdrawn Chinese smile? Or a subtle expedient to mask his disappointment and his failure – to hearten his team-mates and worry his opponents? Or yet again the genuine, instinctive sign of unshakeable confidence in himself and final victory?

Colonel Soria, a cigar clamped between red lips beneath his bristling, ginger moustache, a squat, plump man, was the first bowler or *puntatore*. He made hard going of his bowling. First he prodded the ground with his toe. Then, puffing and blowing, he would drop to one knee. In a kind of slow-motion lunge, he would

[1] A bowler whose function it is to knock away his opponent's wood.

flex his left knee, rest his forearm on it and let his plump, purplish left hand dangle. His blue trousers strained across his enormous backside, threatening to split at any moment. With his right hand, he balanced the weight of the wood to and fro, scarcely brushing the ground. The colonel swung it until he felt that he had gauged the distance and then released the wood. With an affected flourish, he turned his hand over and it remained motionless, the little finger with its white, sharp nail pointing upwards and two rubies sparkling on his ring finger. Emilio hated those rubies, that little finger, that purple hand, those ginger whiskers. And he both hated and feared the colonel's blue eyes. At the same time, they fascinated him. The colonel rose painfully to his feet, half-closed one eye to relight his cigar and with the other, though not moving his head, he momentarily stopped studying the end of his cigar to look at Emilio – an eye of lapis-lazuli blue, impassive and magnetic, a sudden, surprise glance which probably had a very definite aim. This aim, Emilio felt, was to unmask him, to reveal his inadequacy or nonentity as a player, to expose the freakish trick that a combination of luck, Bürin's skill and especially Piero's methodical conduct of the game had produced in bringing them up to that incredible score of six-nil.

'Signor Peccoz, Colonel, may I present my friend Viotti, law graduate, who won the Alessandria tournament last summer,' Piero had said when he challenged them to a match. Whatever the result of the game, he meant to tell them the truth afterwards. In his jokes, as in everything else, Piero was serious, logical, dependable.

But now, as he caught the colonel's eye, Emilio felt defenceless. Absurdly enough, it was almost as if he were being accused, not only of not winning the Alessandria or any other tournament, but of other indeterminate, deadly sins. Sins that he may have committed without knowing or that he was sure to commit in the future. Not really sins – faults, rather, or one single fault, but so grave, so deep, so congenital that Emilio feared that he would never understand its true nature and simply be left with a vague, nagging, forlorn doubt.

'You're a fake,' – the colonel's stare seemed to say. 'You're not a graduate and so you're not Dottor Viotti. You've never been to Alessandria. You're an incompetent, a weak character, a man without true feelings, desires or joy – and you're not likely to amount to anything in life.'

The third opponent, the bricklayer, inspired possibly greater respect than the lawyer and the colonel. He was equally proficient at all types of bowling. Tall, robust, young, he did not seem to deliver the wood so much as carry it and put it down exactly where and how he wished. When the other two failed, he always came to the rescue – and although unable to turn the tables in any particular 'end' he managed at least to shorten his opponents' lead. Against him, victory seemed impossible. Yet, victory was in sight – six-nil. Piero, Emilio and Bürin needed only six points to win, while the other team had to make twelve points or prevent them from scoring six more.

Emilio bowled the jack and muffed it . . . too short. Piero had whispered to him to throw it short – he was tired and beginning to miss on the long shots. So Emilio had to throw the jack a shade further than the regulation distance, just a shade further. He threw a second time but again the jack stopped short. He prepared to throw for the third time – his last chance. Then the jack would pass to his opponents.

With the clear and malicious intention of flustering him, Lawyer Peccoz made a point of reminding him of the rule. He twanged nasally: 'Take care, we've reached the Court of Cassation. You *have* graduated in law, haven't you?'

'I'm an undergraduate,' Emilio felt bound to confess.

'No talking on the rink,' warned Giraudo.

'We're not concerned with the rink, just the jack,' sniggered the colonel.

Indeed, there was nothing easier than throwing the jack. But Emilio could not calm his nerves. As if he had suddenly lost all sense of weight and distance, an explicable lapse made him throw the jack too hard. It rolled, struck the board at the end of the rink and the shot was disqualified. According to the rules, the colonel took it. He had a brief, whispered consultation with the lawyer. The sun had just set and the clarity of the June twilight lingered beneath the great shadows of the lime trees. The other rinks were deserted now. The colonel flung the jack high over two of them. Piero protested but had to accept it. The rules allowed these tactics. The jack had stopped in the centre of the third rink, the one nearest to the canal. No more bowling along the ground, every wood had to be thrown high, very high. This was the rule, the game and they had to abide by it.

It was Emilio's turn to bowl the first wood. He was not used to throwing high. He aimed straight but too short. The wood bounced off the second board and came back.

A glint of joy lit up the lapis-lazuli eyes. The whiskers seemed to quiver. The colonel had found his rivals' weak spot.

Piero and Bürin went on playing as before. Piero would take his three springy jumps, as rhythmic and graceful as ever, and rarely missed his target. But it was not enough.

In that first game, the other team scored four points. Then two, three and two again. The colonel had the jack and kept throwing it over the other rinks. His team had notched up eleven points when Emilio's were still only six.

The last time, the colonel threw normally, inside his own rink, out of courtesy, but also in sheer bravado as if to show that with partners like his, he felt sure of victory.

The bitterness of defeat was short-lived. It had already vanished in laughter and congratulations by the time they had drunk the ritual bottle of old Barbaresco at the end of the game. With the twilight, the scent of the lime trees had become stronger. In the semi-darkness of the pergola, the six players could not distinguish each other's faces. They could only make out the glint of their glasses.

Their remarks were lost in cheerful, confused shouting. Piero had explained the joke. They drank the health of the champion of Alessandria. 'Let me tell you, and I've played in more than one competition,' said the bricklayer pompously, clinking glasses with Emilio, 'you've got the makings of a bowler. And I'm not saying it to cheer you up. You need to play more often, that's all.'

The bitterness of defeat lay in his heart like the dregs at the bottom of the bottle of old Barbaresco. Oh, to be able to drink in the fortunes of life, stopping each time just before the end.

He said goodbye to Piero at the No. 4 terminus. When would he see him again? In a few months, at any rate less than a year. He would not be in Rome for longer than that. Yet at the last moment, when the tramdriver pressed the pedal and rang the bell, indulgently enough but with a note of impatience, to signal his departure,

Emilio suddenly felt that the separation might not be so short, so easy, so unimportant as he could reasonably suppose.

'Ciao. Look after yourself,' muttered Piero, motionless on his bike, one foot tensed against the pavement. In the light of the only street-lamp at the terminus, his eyes sparkled with their usual smiling affection tinged with a hint of sadness.

Emilio felt the need to embrace him. He hesitated for a moment. It would be the first time for six years, since Piero came home from the front in his grey-green uniform. And the bike was in the way. He kissed his friend on both cheeks. He sensed the stiff beard, a faint smell of garlic, the metal pedal against his shin. At the same time, he realized that he was very fond of Piero.

He jumped on to the tram which was already in motion. He looked back – Piero had slipped into his toe-clips, arched over the saddle, shot away in a curve, disappearing with a wave, swallowed up in the blue haze along the avenue. There in the distance he could still see the black alpine peaks against a strip of sky, yellow-green, light-green, penetrating, breathtaking. What does the human heart desire? Where does it hope to go, escape, lose itself? The love of a friend, the emerald sky over the Alps at eventide, it was like remembering a forgotten boon and finding new hope.

During the long tram journey to Piazza Vittorio, he kept on thinking of that last look in Piero's eyes. Surely they were not just tears of friendship. Piero must have been moved at the idea that on his return from Rome Emilio would probably find him already married: moved at the sudden thought of fleeting time that nobody can arrest.

Indeed, that was what it was. In the pale yellow light of the tramcar, empty but for the reassuring and affectionate shapes of a few townsfolk, with the tram jolting and swaying along the cool, dark avenues and the broad streets flanked by great, deserted arcades and an interminable line of shops, shuttered and bolted, the bowling-match, despite the sharp taste of the wine, as pleasant as it was persistent, seemed remote and irrevocable – as if all his youth were over.

The following evening, the Sunday before the feast of La Consolata, straight after dinner, he went to Vévé's. It was partly calculated, partly sincere. He had felt a genuine desire to meet her parents. At the same time, he was convinced that Vévé, even if she denied it, would grieve at the separation, so he thought to soften the blow by a visit and an introduction to her parents – in no way signifying a betrothal, of course, but simply the possibility of a future engagement.

It took him a long time to persuade Vévé to accept this ambiguous proposal, which smacked too much of a futile and offensive consolation prize. Finally she consented but on one condition – the condition was that Emilio should introduce her to *his* parents. Taken by surprise, Emilio hovered. He stammered: 'Y-y-yes, of course . . . but I'd have to prepare them . . . and there's no time . . . I'm leaving tomorrow.'

Vévé replied with a laugh: 'Look, I'm sorry for you,' then with sudden decision, shrugging, she concluded: 'All right, come. They met the others, they may as well meet you!'

'The others?'

'Yes, the engineer, I told you about him, remember? Then there was another one before him . . . If you really must, come along. But, mind, you mustn't say, or even think, that you're doing it for me. Understand? Look in my eyes, if you dare, and tell me you understand.'

He looked at her. Vévé's blue eyes were blazing. Pride? Love? It could almost have been hate. They were in a little café on the Lungo Po and it was Sunday morning. With the effort of controlling her voice, Vévé's full, rosy breasts were gently heaving beneath her snow-white blouse, and her generous mouth, still half-open, irresistibly suggested the sweetness of her kisses.

Emilio stretched out his hand and laid it on Vévé's which, white and strong, were holding her handbag on the table. She drew back and jumped up sharply.

'Tonight then. No later than nine o'clock, because Papa goes to bed early.'

Vévé's home was exactly as he had imagined it from her description. The main building faced on to Via Segurana. Above the ground-floor were two more modestly equipped ones. The same plan applied to the two wings which, at right angles to the back of the building, flanked the courtyard. Two small flights of stone steps with iron railings led up at both corners to the two upper floors. Two long open galleries, also with iron railings, ran the length of the building and at the ends were four wood and corrugated-iron lavatories – two for the tenants on the left-hand side and two for those on the right. The flats, three or four on each side, could only be entered from the galleries. On the ground floor there were stores and workshops, closed at that time in the evening.

Apart from the luxury dwellings, you could say that all the houses built in Turin after the transference of the capital and up to the First World War, more or less followed this pattern, sometimes with an even denser concentration of flats usually rising to five or six floors.

Five or six rows of horizontal galleries intersected vertically by plumbing and W.Cs: dismal tenements which, in any other city and inhabited by any other people in the world, would have given a much worse impression, one of squalor, filth and despair, like cages or prison cells. But not in Turin. For only rarely were the court-yards, rectangular or square, closed on more than three sides. The fourth almost invariably opened on to wide expanses of meadow-land or the huge backdrops of the Alps or the Collina. In any case, even when they were not so fortunately placed, thanks to a strict code of cleanliness and Turin's passion for order, geometry and symmetry, those courtyards became magically transformed. Finely executed ironwork in delicate traceries, decoration and perspectives harmoniously reflecting both the ideal and the rational, were gaily, colourfully, discreetly enhanced by potted geraniums and boxes of plants methodically lining the galleries.

Véve's courtyard, dimly lit at that hour, with grass sprouting between the cobbles, was narrow, long and closed at one end by low railings. Beyond in the gloom you could make out tall trees – pines and magnolias in the grounds of a villa. And high over the invisible tree-tops, the distant lights on La Collina, perhaps those of Mongreno. Still higher in the sky, a slim, crescent moon. No hint of prison, no squalor, no misery, therefore. Perhaps a kind of gentle melancholy and provincial ennui . . .

'Stairs on the right, fourth french window along the landing, there's a majolica door-bell with the name: 'Gariglio.' Véve, anxious that everything should go smoothly and to avoid the usual gossip between the porter and the other tenants, had given him detailed instructions.

But Emilio had stopped for a few minutes just inside the

entrance, looking and listening with bated breath. The courtyard was deserted and dark. He could see french windows here and there along the left and right hand landings, ablaze with light and wide-open. And he heard the light clatter from kitchen and table, voices of families lingering over supper, babies crying, laughter, someone singing quietly. It was Sunday evening, but also the eve of another feast-day.

Véve came home here every evening, here was her humble and secret life, her family, the scene of her affections and habits. It seemed impossible. What connection was there between the girl's freshness, gaiety, energy and the old courtyard? Between the snow-white, beautifully-ironed blouses taut across her swelling breasts, her young, frisky, soap-scented body and the squalor of a communal W.C.?

But a moment's reflection convinced Emilio that any house, even the most luxurious and modern, a flat in the new blocks in the exclusive quarter of La Crocetta, or a town house in Piazza d'Armi – marble staircase, felt runners, mahogany, mirrors, glass-ware – would be unable to match her vital, brilliant personality. The very instant that he mentally associated Véve with it, such a background in comparison would be bound to seem shabby and futile.

Emilio felt that this was not a private impression concerning himself and Véve alone, but the inevitable and almost tragic contrast between sublime love and the reality of life. Emilio had only seen Véve away from her background and home, had become used to her, fallen in love with her in the street, in cafés on the Collina, in Serra's studio. Véve, a free creature, almost a creature of fancy whose life was love. So that sense of defeat and constraint was natural on seeing her at home for the first time – a feeling, he kept on telling himself, that would have been no different and just as strong if her home had been more palatial, much more palatial! For the real Véve had neither home, family, nor parents.

He found them sitting around the marble table in the kitchen which was also the dining-room. No need to ring the bell because the french window was open and the kitchen gave directly on to the landing.

A small reddish carbon lamp hung with its enamel shade over the centre of the table which was clean and empty apart from a tray where, arranged on a lace napkin, were glasses, a bottle and a corkscrew. Vévé, her mother and her little sister jumped up when they saw him. Vévé ran out to meet him and took his panama. Her father, who was sitting at the far side of the rectangular table facing the french window, did not move at first.

He got up just in time to shake Emilio's hand. He was a man of about fifty, slightly over medium height, bald, clean-shaven with sparkling blue eyes like Vévé's, rosy cheeks and fleshy, regular features, delicate yet strong, a man who struck you at once as handsome despite his age and baldness, and aristocratic though he was poorly dressed and his big hands were calloused. While his frank gaze, intelligent smile and the calm way that he motioned Emilio to a seat, conveyed a natural, mysterious authority.

As often happens, and as Vévé had told Emilio, this air of authority was probably due to extreme shyness.

They sat in silence, looking and smiling at each other. Vévé who could have and should have said something, did not open her mouth – out of sheer devilment, of course. When he looked up, Emilio met her ironical glance. She was sitting away from the table, in the shadow, on the corner of a black iron divan bed whose mattress and cushions had covers with a red and brown flowered pattern. From the shadow her eyes seemed to say: 'You wanted to come. Well then, make the best of it!' Over the divan, in the centre of the dark wall were three large framed photographs: Marx, Lenin, Trotsky.

Her mother, a small, thin, grey woman who also had extraordinarily refined, regular features, was busy opening the bottle with a corkscrew. Her younger sister Egle, a pale, plump brunette, sat next to Emilio and kept staring at him with a look in her big, hazel eyes and a timid smile which could only mean sincere approval.

Meanwhile, their unbroken silence and frozen immobility created in the small kitchen an atmosphere of mingled embarrassment and solemnity exactly characteristic of the nineteenth century, provincial tradition of betrothal – the very atmosphere that Emilio had fondly hoped to avoid.

'It's a two-year-old wine. A two-year-old bottle,' driver Gariglio said at last, taking a glass from the tray which his wife passed to him and offering it to Emilio. Then he took another glass and gave it to Vévé.

'. . . and a twenty-year-old daughter. Actually she's twenty-one but it's the same thing. I don't know if Vévé has told you about me. But I'm not very keen on proverbs. They're called the knowledge of the people. All right. But mark you, the knowledge of people who in those days were not permitted the luxury of knowledge.' After a brief pause, he added: 'As if things were different today,' and burst out laughing. High spirits? No, there was a sarcastic ring in his youthful laugh which, just like Vévé's, revealed flashing white teeth. He raised his glass against the light, studied it closely with satisfaction. Next he put it to his lips, but before drinking he paused and looked at Emilio in silence. For an instant he seemed to scrutinize the boy, but then motioned his glass towards him and said with an easy laugh: 'Well, now . . . A penny for your thoughts!' Emilio smiled hastily. He must have unconsciously had a worried expression on his face!

Vévé immediately piled on the agony, laughing like a fool. 'Penny for his thoughts, Papa? What can Monsieur Viotti be thinking about?'

'Oh, well . . . that's his business. Who d'you take me for, Gabrielli?' Gabrielli was a famous illusionist who did a thought-reading act around the halls. Suddenly the driver changed his tone. He clinked glasses with Emilio and said seriously: 'My best wishes for your studies Signor Viotti. My daughter tells me that you're going to the capital for a time . . . Good luck! And don't pay any attention to that simpleton down there if you want to drink another bottle of wine in this house.'

'Ernesto!' said his wife warningly.

'My wife is always afraid that I'll talk too much. And I wonder if that's why we are where we are? Is it because all the wives and mothers from Piedmont to Sicily are afraid that their husbands and sons will talk too much?'

'Of course,' murmured Emilio.

But tramdriver Gariglio seemed to be listening to some inner objection and hastened to correct himself.

'Yes, it's talking just for the sake of it. Our wives' fear is not the cause of our cowardice, it's simply a consequence, like so many others, of our economic slavery.'

And so saying, he got up and went to a small bookcase near the divan, and in those few steps he seemed to stagger slightly. Emilio recalled that Vévé had told him that Papa sometimes came home drunk. Perhaps the tone if not the substance of his conversation, the intense sparkle in his eyes and even the high colour in his fleshy cheeks betrayed an addiction to alcohol. He came from the bookcase with two volumes, one thick, the other very slim and showed them to Emilio. But Emilio, before looking at the titles, saw that the tram-driver's big hands were trembling.

'I bet you haven't read them,' Gariglio said, laughing. And he put the two books on the table. They were *Das Kapital* and the *Communist Manifesto*.

'No,' admitted Emilio.

'A pity. A pity because, you see . . . well take *Das Kapital*, I read it, yes, I read it but I must confess that it's too difficult for me. You need an education. Now, Vévé, she's read the *Manifesto*. And I swear she understands it better than me.'

'Boring, but sound,' was Vévé's gay verdict. She jumped to her feet, glancing at her watch with its white leather strap round her pink, blue-veined wrist which, even after a whole year, Emilio could not see without feeling a wave of emotion. 'We'd better go if we want to catch some of the illuminations.' The tramdriver wagged his finger at his daughter reprovingly and with comic gravity.

'A woman *with modern ideas* like you shouldn't show so much interest in religious celebrations.'

'Fine thing!' her mother chaffed. 'Now we can't go to see the illuminations at La Consolata! Who said so? Marx, Marx again?'

The tramdriver, smiling at Emilio, replied: 'The day when women learn to talk sense, we'll all be really free. But I won't live to see it. And neither will you, Marietta, never fret. But you will, monsieur. At least I hope so.'

Throughout his childhood, on the eve of La Consolata, Emilio had gone to see the illuminations with the entire family – Papa, Mama, uncles, aunts and cousins. He would trot along holding the hand of one of the grown-ups. The whole way along Via Po the façades of the buildings, the cornices, the ledges, the tympana of the windows and mansard-roofs were picked out with innumerable dots, flickering green, blue, red, yellow lights. In Piazza Castello there were blue and yellow lights on the left, while on the right the Military Academy, the Teatro Regio, the Prefecture, the Arsenal, the Royal Palace, Palazza Chiablese were all in darkness as usual. The celebration was exclusively a religious one and the darkness had a polemical significance. The dispute between Church and State had lasted since 1870. The lights began again at the corner of Via Palazza di Città and blazed forth as far as the Santuario. That was old Turin – straight, narrow alleys between towering houses, usually as black as mountain ravines on moonless nights, but on that night lit up with arabesques, spots, haloes, stripes, monograms of the name of Mary. The peeling plaster, the broken stone, the patches of damp, the rusty railings of the little baroque balconies, all these blemishes were suddenly revealed by the unaccustomed reflected glare which pried everywhere, even beneath the dark, protruding cornices and up above the lichen-coated, cat-haunted tiles, around the high attic windows decked with geraniums and other signs of genteel poverty. Piazza Palazzo di Città, Via Milano, Via Corte d'Appello, piazza del Carmine – the liveliness of the crowd, the lights and the gay originality of the decorations intensified all the way to the Santuario. The whole scene throbbed in a fever of holy intoxication, of absurd rapture – as if, miraculously, joy and virtue were in complete accord, as if liberty, novelty and the bizarre had been consecrated, as if order had gone by the board. The child who every other night of the year had to be in bed asleep was not only allowed to be out and about, but was even invited to admire the lights, enjoy himself, have fun! The cupolas of La Consolata were a blaze of light – slightly frustrating, for the simple reason that they were the climax of the illuminations. After that you could not expect to see any other building more brilliantly lit up. La Consolata was the *non plus ultra*.

Inside the church, even devotion seemed to be celebrating, or at least there was no longer anything gloomy or boring about it. People talked loudly as they walked past the glittering walls lined with countless ex-voto tributes. Laughing groups stopped to examine some of them more closely. Their footsteps echoed on the marble floor. Nobody prayed – just a few hasty, perfunctory words of supplication, that was all. There was no space to kneel. You had to queue for the holy water, so many people abstained. But they could all walk about the church with a light heart and emerge into the open air free of any twinge of remorse. Perhaps they felt that they had peeped into Paradise; and naturally, once in Paradise, there was no more need for religious devotion.

Some traces of this happiness, so much a part of the feast of La Consolata, had lingered in Emilio's heart. But not in Véré's for, having received little or no religious education, she appreciated only the pomp and pageantry of the celebration.

They caught the tram and got off at Piazza Castello. They continued on foot along Via Palazzo di Città. Vévé had no inhibitions about leaning on his arm and when they had to push their way through the crowd she instinctively pressed close to him. Emilio felt a mingled sensation of pleasure and pain, of gratified vanity and fear.

At Vévé's side, he seemed to re-live the rapture of his childhood, unholy in a different way but no less intense – he was proud to be seen arm-in-arm with such a pretty girl. At the same time he feared the spiteful gossip of his relations and acquaintances who were bound to see him. And what if he were to marry her against his parents' wishes on his return from Rome? Wouldn't he be doing the right thing? Wasn't Serra right when he said that nowhere would Emilio find a girl so pretty and so much in love with him? And if Vévé were already his wife, would he be any the less happy?

But he was leaving for Rome in the morning. He had no idea what the future held. Perhaps his happiness that evening was due to the certainty of his imminent departure – the happiness of the wanderer or the traveller, supreme yet tinged with the regret that foreshadows its loss even when it is in his grasp; a happiness which does not involve the future or curb freedom.

For once Vévé had obtained permission to stay out after midnight. On entering the little square of La Consolata, like everyone else they were momentarily startled by the explosion of light as they paused to gaze at the cupolas and the façade. Emilio squeezed Vévé's firm waist and thought of the wild joy that shortly awaited him at Serra's studio. Lost in a sensual flight of fancy he forgot what he felt to be his duty not to deceive the girl, never to raise her hopes. They mounted the steps to the Santuario. Pressing her more tightly, he whispered in her ear: 'Shall we get married in church?'

Vévé wrenched herself free and replied coldly, seriously: 'You know very well that we'll never marry.' Then she had second thoughts, summoning up a laugh – 'At least not in church. Think of my father!'

'And you think of my parents.'

'I don't care a damn for your people,' continued Vévé, lowering her voice, and at that moment they entered the church.

A crowd packed the only space, large and oval in shape. The cupolas, the high altar, the apse were ablaze with lighted lamps, tapers and candles, the glitter of gold and the fresh colours of flowers.

In the centre, a small, dark rectangle – the venerated and miraculous image of the Vergine Consolata.

'You do believe . . . a little . . . don't you?' Emilio asked with a degree of concern.

'Me? *You*, perhaps. But not me, no, not a bit.'

'That's not true,' teased Emilio. He was almost certain that even if she did not go to Mass on Sundays, Vévé still believed in God.

'Do you want proof?' asked the girl, suddenly stopping in the middle of the central nave while the crowd drifted slowly by, and looking straight at Emilio with her sparkling, blue eyes which were just like her father's.

'There's no proof . . . Forget it,' murmured Emilio, a little alarmed.

'Of course there is. Look – the habit of blaspheming is itself a kind of faith. When things go badly people take it out on the Eternal Father, Jesus Christ, the Madonna and all the rest. Now swearing is a stupid habit and I don't like it. My father never swears. But to prove that I don't believe, well here goes . . .' She stopped when she saw that Emilio had gone pale.

'That worries you, eh? Anyway, it wouldn't be in very good taste to do it here.'

'Come on,' said Emilio, seizing her plump arm, 'let's go out and get a taxi.'

'No, darling, there's no point,' replied Vévé without budging an inch. Now her eyes were sparkling with malicious delight. 'Let's go to Pepino's and have an ice and leave it at that. No, it's useless making that face. What do you expect? It's fate. You're leaving and today I understand that I can't.'

She was there with him in her red cambric dress, a few inches away, and he had his arm around her. Yet she was suddenly far away, very far away, lost perhaps for ever in the months, in the years, in the rest of his life. Emilio had considered that evening as possibly their last opportunity to be happy together. Now he realized that the occasion was already in the past. And she was laughing – perhaps she was thinking the same thing – she was laughing as she said: 'It's a good joke, eh?'

Perhaps it was a joke – born of pride, revenge and a fear of suffering. More than likely. From the start Emilio had this doubt.

And the doubt remained. They did not take a taxi. They walked slowly as far as Piazza Solferino and sat down at Pepino's. It was the most melancholy ice-cream that they had had in their lives. Every now and then Vévé tried to make a joke but it was hopeless. Even the vaguest reference to the fun and enjoyment of the last year or so rang like a hollow knell and left them more silent and sad than before. They said goodbye in Via Segurana. Now that he had been up to see her people there was no reason why he should not take her to the door. They kissed for a long time but not in the way that Emilio thought they might. At least for him it was a completely different kiss from all their others. For the first time it was not a lovers' kiss but more like one between brother and sister, father and daughter or mother and daughter – a serious, chaste, melancholy kiss, a kiss between friends or a wedding couple.

He looked into Vévé's eyes, saw the usual merry sparkle and not too much emotion in them. It was he who felt tears in his eyes and a lump in his throat. He had to make a great effort not to break down.

Vévé noticed and said gently, but firmly and practically: 'It'll hurt a bit, but the pain'll soon pass, you'll see. Ciao, eh?' And she vanished inside.

Via Segurana, a cobbled street with stone pavements, wide, deserted, ill-lit by a few lamps, flanked by squat houses and garden walls, led down to Corso Casale. There, a red tram passed against the black backdrop of Michelotti Park. The noisy clatter rapidly faded into the distance, ceased at the first stop, started up again, then disappeared entirely. Emilio stood listening outside the front door. Silence now, and from the Collina behind him the ecstatic, desperate song of the nightingale. The night breeze bore the lingering, mysterious, voluptuous perfume of the limes.

He travelled in a sleeper. At Porta Nuova, Papa and Mama were there to say goodbye to him, full of emotion but delighted, too, and a group of friends and colleagues – Serra, Ferrau, Rousset, Ettore Cuomo who, as a kind of foretaste of the 'other Italy' kept shouting to him from the platform: 'Good luck, Don Emi! Good luck!' and the unusual accent was enough to gladden the entire company and cloud the faces beneath their shiny cap-peaks of the Turin porters who, in those days, considered every departure as definitely a serious matter.

Rousset had given him a note for Signora Calandra, his future mother-in-law. But he had already written to her about Emilio, and, in any case, he too would be leaving for Rome in a few days. After all, it was quite an ordinary departure. No, it was not an ordinary departure. This he realized at the last moment, when the train was starting to move and he could see his friends smiling at him – Serra tenderly, Ferrau understandingly, Rousset knowingly. Cuomo was still shouting, his mother was weeping and waving her lace handkerchief, Papa had taken off his straw hat and held it high in the air as a last warning. The little group rapidly began to get smaller and smaller and even before it vanished from sight he had forgotten about it and was beginning to think of the future with its confused, violent music that spoke of gold, the night and liberty.

V

❀❀❀

Signora Calandra was preparing to leave for the theatre – it was a spectacular and voluptuous ceremony. Emilio had caught a glimpse of it several times but continued to be fascinated by it.

He spent his days, in the morning from half-past nine to one o'clock, and from four to seven every afternoon, at the Senate library. Tedious hours poring over manuscripts, the hard slog of copying – a monotonous task broken only by moments of perplexity while deciphering difficult passages and, after he had done so, by a modest pride of achievement. The Lombard abbreviations posed many problems and in order to be able to cope he had to acquire a smattering (it only covered the Early Middle Ages) of palaeography.

And the long, slow tram rides – number 13 from the Pantheon to Porta Pia, number 9 from Porta Pia to Sant'Agnese; the misery of having to cross half Rome four times a day and get used to the winter there, universally considered to be a mild one but to him an unhealthy, exasperating alternation between sirocco and icy north wind – warmish, sticky rain or piercing, blinding cold. And the faces he saw about him, especially in the tram – the faces of clerks, servants, the lower middle class, with their gloomy expressions, their impenetrable resistance to any new or strange idea; the ignorant, complacent, presumptuous resignation of citizens or inhabitants of the Eternal City. And the sloppy, aggressive cadence of their speech, so expressive of that presumption . . . In fact, he would have felt sorry for the Romans if, unsure as he was of his own future and considering himself an exile, he had not been full of rancour and closed his mind to any other feeling.

He got off the tram at the stop before Sant'Agnese. A few steps along damp, deserted Via Nomentana, then up Via Guattani. It was the end of the day, half-past seven in the evening – the time when the cup of daily bitterness is brimming for so many people in cities all over the world, when the heart (and not only the exile's) aches at the sudden, painful, irrevocable realization of life's emptiness.

Childishly, Emilio felt a desperate nostalgia for Turin and the arcades of Piazza Castello. He longed to see the Baratti and Mulassano shop windows, the orderly, cordial crowds strolling up and down, and Vévé with her neat springy step hurrying to meet him in the rose-pink light of the Galleria Subalpina. But Rome was a city without arcades or rendezvous – a multitude of solitary, uncommunicative families retiring every evening to the uncertain lukewarmth of their lairs, satisfied with a half litre of wine and early to bed for a long, long sleep. Months of rain and wind, a winter free of fog and snow.

The black thuias in the cool, glistening gardens along Via Guattani dripped stickily on to the cement pavements. Emilio fished out his Yale key before he got to the gate, impatient to be safely home.

He had spent the summer at a *pensione* in Via Arenula whose sole advantage was its proximity to the Senate. Finally, in mid-September, he had been accepted by Signora Calandra, Rousset's future mother-in-law. It meant that he wasted about three hours a day to-ing and fro-ing by tram. But in return he was staying at a pretty little villa in its own garden and with those of the neighbouring villas all around. He was the only guest, treated like one of the family and paying not much more than he did for his fetid lodgings in Via Arenula. He had a large room, comfortable and elegant, at the back of the house but on the same floor as those occupied by Signora Calandra and her daughter Elena, Rousset's fiancée. Signora Calandra had taken him in not for the money but to do a favour to a friend of her future son-in-law and also because, being a talkative, gay, expansive woman, she dreaded loneliness and loved company, especially at table. For Elena was rarely there. She came to see her mother sometimes, but Emilio lived for months in Via Guattani without actually meeting her. The girl never appeared – she shut herself mysteriously in her room and did not come out even for meals. Emilio got to know from the maid that 'The Signorina had arrived'. He would hear footsteps or other slight sounds from the next room. A day or two later he would learn from the same source that 'the Signorina had left'. She had gone to Turin, it seemed, or to Capri, Aix or Santa Margherita – to stay with friends, or on a cruise, or perhaps to a nursing-home, because she suffered from nervous debility. Or so Emilio was given to understand by one of Rousset's fleeting, sybilline confidences and the rare hints that her mother dropped.

147

Emilio had his meals alone with the elderly Signora. The prospect of these têtes-à-têtes twice daily for months on end had made him doubtful of accepting Rousset's proposal, but to his delight and surprise he soon realized that his fears were groundless and that Signora Calandra's conversation and company, together with the brief intellectual joys he derived from reading the more abstruse passages of the Lombard manuscripts, were ample consolation for his Roman exile.

Signora Calandra was the widow of an admiral, a distant relative of the famous Davide and Edoardo Calandra, the sculptor and the author – bronze reproductions of the former's works and bound volumes of the latter's writings were scattered throughout the villa in Via Guattani. Signora Calandra came from Turin and although she had lived in Rome for more than twenty years, though she was passionately fond (or said she was) of Rome, its climate and society and hated (or said she did) Turin, *its* climate and society, though she claimed to have adopted even the Roman dialect and accent, she was still – probably unconsciously – a gay and glorious incarnation of Turin; the essence of the Turin that was aristocratic, bourgeois, nineteenth-century, artistic, gossipy, ironical – bottled Turin, which for Emilio had a delicious, fragrant *fin de siècle* bouquet. So the little villa in Via Guattani was a haven, a nostalgic, hospitable refuge from his gloomy days in Rome. This explains why he fingered his small Yale key with an almost sensual impatience. And when he arrived at the gate, saw all the windows in the basement, on the ground and first floors ablaze with light with shadows flitting behind the curtains, and heard the bell ringing inside and voices calling, then he knew that Signora Calandra was off to the theatre and savoured with the melancholy promise of a lonely dinner (Signora Calandra would be having supper out after the show), the joy and lascivious charm of some of Boucher's pictures.

Signora Calandra's elderly lover, Doctor Bonansea, was waiting in the drawing-room on the ground floor. To avoid creasing his tailcoat and his starched shirt he was pacing slowly up and down on the soft Bukhara carpets past the gilt furniture. He bent down to knock off the ash of his Minghetti cigar in the vase of a *chenzia*. He paused for a moment at each mirror, studying his big, pale, round face and his high forehead with its halo of thick white curls.

Gina, the maid from Veneto, a hip-swinging brunette in cap and Saint-Gall embroidered apron, rushed down the wooden stairs, snatched a mysterious-looking steaming jug from the service-lift, ran up again and into the bedroom, the Signora's inner sanctum. And Emilio, from the gloom of the landing, caught a vision of the elderly Signora (through two open doors and as if in a magnesium flash-light) half-naked, wrapped to the armpits in a spotless towel, her plump, milk-white shoulders contrasting with her raven, shingled hair.

The cook hurried up to the bedroom to lend a hand. Emilio, following from his room the sound of voices and scurrying footsteps, pictured the final preparations. Gina and the cook would be squeezing the flabby, powdered old flesh into the corset, fastening her silver sandals, gently helping her into her gown. Then the jewels, the perfume, the glossy kid gloves . . . It was dinner-time now. Emilio went downstairs and found the elderly admirer still waiting in the drawing-room. In a little while the Signora appeared, her generous figure swathed in sparkling blue paillettes, sapphires and diamonds half-hidden by thick black curls in the lobes of her ears, around her smooth unwrinkled neck a rivière of diamonds ending in a great cabochon sapphire upon her ample bosom.

Emilio gazed at her in admiration, strangely moved, without knowing the precise reason for his emotion and admiration. Signora Calandra was between fifty-five and sixty. Rather small and fat, slim ankles, shapely legs and hands, lovely shoulders and arms, dark, roguish eyes, dyed hair – quite apart from age, her beauty could not be compared to Vévé's. So why was he fascinated by her? She was a strange mixture, new to him, of conformity and broad-mindedness, of personality and calculation. Signora Calandra evidently preferred Rome to Turin because however careful she might be in Turin, she could not hope to enjoy the liberty and licence that she safely took in Rome – entertaining old doctor Bonansea and her other lovers far into the night at home, and even in her own room; going to the theatre with one or another of them and being seen with them in restaurants and *trattorie*. Moreover, the secret of the extraordinary pleasure that she found in this liberty and licence, and of the inexhaustible enthusiasm that she brought to her life in Rome, lay in the thought that it would all have been taboo in Turin and of how her friends back there must envy her because she was in Rome.

When, a widow at thirty-five, Signora Calandra had 'discovered' Rome, bought the little villa in Via Guattani and settled there for nine months of the year (she spent July at Viareggio, August and

September at her castle in Quara, Canavese) she had felt exactly as if she were starting a holiday – a long, long holiday lasting a lifetime. She credited Rome with this magic power of transforming life into an eternal holiday, not realizing that the responsibility was Turin's. Of course, she knew fewer people in Rome than in Turin. Rome was big, scattered, full of tourists, artists, foreigners, politicians, clerics. Rome was a city without regulation promenades or fixed rendezvous. Yet the licence in Rome was essentially a negation of the conformity to convention in Turin – freedom from the strict moral climate there. It was certainly a holiday, but mainly a holiday from Turin.

The few ladies of the Roman bourgeoisie whom Emilio had met, daughters of parents who had settled in Rome at the end of last century or even earlier, saw Rome quite differently and would never have dreamt of seeking amusement there as the Signora did.

Was it the holiday smile hovering round Signora Calandra's thin lips and sparkling beneath her heavy eyelids that fascinated Emilio? Or was it her wealth, the thing that made it possible for her to lead such a life? By upbringing or by intuition, Emilio was already convinced of the importance of money: his father and – even more – his mother had taught him little else. But, living under the same roof as that complacent old woman, as calm as she was passionate, who thanks to her money could so love and enjoy life; imagining her twice-weekly nocturnal escapades and her ritual occupations during the day – massage, beauty treatment, manicure, pedicure; witnessing her majestic departures for the theatre, seeing with his own eyes the jewellery which seemed to enhance and vitalize her flabby, tired flesh; what other aim in life – Emilio asked himself – could he possibly have, what other ambition could he reasonably be expected to cherish with ever-increasing passion, than the accumulation of wealth?

Gina appeared at the door. She held her mistress's ermine coat tightly against her chest. Doctor Bonansea had just uncorked a bottle of Moet et Chandon and was filling the glasses. He gave a toast.

Signora Calandra lifted the cover, studded with tiny diamonds and sapphires, of her wrist-watch: '*Mamma mia*, how late it is!' she exclaimed *alla romanesca* in her slightly husky voice which with its French R sound reminded him of a cracked fine glass. 'How late it is! I haven't even time to finish my champagne. And it's bad for you to drink quickly, isn't it, Doctor?'

The doctor nodded. 'Everything should be taken slowly. And you should always arrive late at the theatre – that way you'll get more admiring glances.'

'Absurd man,' laughed Signora Calandra. She took another sip, then turning to Emilio said: 'Listen, Viotti, let me be frank. I hate wasting real champagne when I think of what it costs. You finish it. You don't mind do you?' Giving him her glass, she looked at the young man from under her heavy eyelids, slyly, silently, enticingly. It was not the first time that Emilio had noticed the Signora looking at him in that way. It had happened when they got up from table and he was pulling out her chair for her; when they went into the drawing-room and he was arranging a cushion to support her; when from the shelves where the blue or claret gold-bordered H.M.V. albums were kept, he turned to ask her preference or suggest a record; when after the music and conversation he bade her goodnight on the landing and kissed her hand. Or for no particular reason and without any contact. And her dark, velvety glance, so sudden, profound and serious clashed so violently with the rest of the Signora's jovial, playful nature that it worried Emilio every time.

Signora Calandra noticed it. She thought that she had offended him. In her sensual glance there had also been a glint of economy. She tried to reassure him: 'Oh, Viotti what am I saying? Drink the whole bottle. Have it with your dinner, of course.' This was not generosity. Champagne had to be finished once it was uncorked. Emilio knew that, and he thanked the Signora with a forced smile that naturally did not escape her but just as naturally did not bother her in the slightest.

Gina accompanied her and the doctor to the car. Then she came back into the house. Emilio, who was already sitting at the table, pointed to the bottle of champagne: 'Finish it up with the cook.'

Gina blushed: 'Oh, no, no.'

'Why not? It's good French champagne, fifty lire a bottle. More than five lire a glass. Don't tell me that you don't like champagne.' And so saying, he smacked her bottom.

In return, Gina slapped his face. But it was only a game that they played whenever the Signora went out.

'But I don't. If you must know it makes me feel sick. I'll give it to the cook.'

151

She snatched the bottle and walked off, swinging her hips. Emilio sat watching her. He thought of Vévé and what would happen a little later. When the cook had finished washing up and was ready for bed, Gina would tell her that she was going out, that she had a date at the corner of Via Nomentana with a frontier guard from the nearby barracks. Instead, she would open the gate, slam it shut, take off her shoes, tip-toe back and up to his room. Then they would make love. This too, was a game they played every evening when the Signora went to the theatre.

February, March, the early Roman spring. Rousset put in a few appearances, one evening in three or four, duty visits to his future mother-in-law. Each time he found an opportunity to take her aside and whisper to her, so that Emilio, busy changing a record as quickly as he could 'to continue the piece', was unable to hear what they said. But he guessed that Rousset was asking about Elena's movements and her state of health.

They had been engaged for years. The marriage was supposed to take place the following summer. But perhaps there were some difficulties and from Elena's side. This, at least, was Emilio's impression, one he gained from Gina who always spoke highly of her Signorina's extraordinary beauty. 'She's a princess,' the girl would say. And he concluded from what she told him that the painter did not deserve such good luck. Emilio, his curiosity aroused, would then go and look at the big oval photograph signed Dall'Armi and framed in silver, which stood on the small grand piano in the drawing-room. A great mass of fair hair merged into the hazy background, crowning an exceptionally high, broad forehead. The eyes were sparkling and crystal-clear. The mouth, thin-lipped. With one hand she was clasping a light-coloured boa to her breast. Her tapering fingers were almost hidden in the feathers. And a large pearl adorned her ring finger. The artificial pose, the studied expression and the *flou* style of the famous Turin society photographer, made it difficult to pass any real judgment.

One of the reasons which had induced Rousset to settle in Rome was that his fiancée lived there, so it was odd that now of all times she should almost always be away. Every so often Rousset could hardly avoid giving Emilio some sort of explanation. After mentioning vaguely 'nervous trouble', he would close his eyes and sigh deeply: 'What can you expect, she's a very intelligent girl. Extremely intelligent as you'll see! Extremely intelligent and beautiful, but very obstinate and shy, too. In my opinion she's not ill, she just thinks she is. She's shy of life. It's obvious that to take a step like marriage requires a little courage. My view is that when we're married, she'll be all right. But she insists that she cannot marry until she's better. Well, there it is, my dear Emilio, it's a cross and I must bear it!'

Most evenings, apart from those when Signora Calandra went to the theatre or out to dinner with a friend, Emilio spent alone with her. Gradually, at table and later in the drawing-room, between one record and another, they began to exchange confidences. He told about Vévé and himself, his voluntary departure (almost flight) from Turin, the uncertainty about his future, his family's financial situation, their hopes of inheriting the Sanfront legacy, his reluctance to study law and his lack of interest in an academic career.

Signora Calandra, lying comfortably back on the cushions in a yellow velvet-upholstered armchair, her slender legs resting on a special cushion, listened with half-closed eyes, smiled and always had an encouraging word.

'Don't worry, Viotti. You're young and life is wonderful. You'll find a solution. I'm sure that you'll make a lot of money. Look, I shan't even wish you good luck. I'm sure you'll succeed. But now don't think any more about that girl. Love is the most beautiful thing in life. But in your situation you'd be foolish . . .' The cracked-glass voice hesitated for a moment. Motionless in the chair, her bare, jewel-laden forearms stretched out on its velvet rests, Signora Calandra slowly raised her heavy eyelids. Her dark eyes studied Emilio as if to judge him afresh – a strange boy, could she be frank with him or not . . . but of course she could, and laughing heartily and exaggerating the Roman accent in an unsuccessful imitation along with her aristocratic Rs, she went on 'in your situation you'd be foolish . . . forgive me if I use a vulgar expression . . . you'd be foolish to drop anchor at the first port of call!'

At these words Emilio's heart missed a beat. He thought of Vévé. For the first time her memory had been directly attacked, insulted. What should he do? How should he react? If he felt offended at Signora Calandra's words, why not show it? Why not get up and leave? Or at least why not say nothing? He smiled weakly as if he were ashamed to admit that he was still in love and murmured: 'I understand, I understand.' And he realized that he had been living in a long and comfortable state of illusion. From the moment he said goodbye to Vévé a little less than a year before, he had believed that his love would last, despite time and separation, keen, ardent, immutable, and that he could pick up the threads again when and how he wished. But, the real situation was different. Perhaps he had taken Signora Calandra into his confidence to fan the glowing embers of a dying fire but instead had only hastened its conversion to ashes. How would he have reacted a year ago if someone had referred to Vévé in such a vulgar way? But then no one would have talked like that about Vévé to his face so the matter would never have arisen.

He immediately contradicted himself. It was not that at all. The stab of pain caused by Signora Calandra's remark had been like that of a doctor's probe. He still loved and wanted Vévé more than any other woman. He had gone on writing to her – twice or three times a month, although he had kept it dark from Signora Calandra. And Vévé had always replied. A calm, regular, deeply tender correspondence in a time of waiting and trial.

That very night, in a few minutes, as soon as he was up in his room, he would write her a longer, more affectionate letter than usual. After all, their separation was nearly at an end. He would be back in Turin in May to take his finals and his degree. His love was as strong as it had been for the past year. Even stronger – he had passed the test. So the smile and the meek 'I understand, I understand' meant nothing at all, no need to fret, they were just a form of natural reserve, a shy mode of defence. Did he have to be honest with Signora Calandra? Wasn't it enough that he should be honest with himself? And he was honest with himself to a fault. No, he needn't worry about his feelings for Vévé. His work and career, yes, he should think seriously of those. And in fact Signora Calandra began to talk of nothing else: 'Now you must concentrate on getting a good degree, that's all. You'll see that once you've graduated everything will be easier. I believe you already know Golzio, don't you? Well, do you really think that he wouldn't give you a job? Go and see him personally without making an appointment through anybody, not even my future son-in-law. Take my advice, I've known Golzio well for years. And my daughter's a close friend of his wife. D'you see that postcard on the *étagère* . . . yes, that's the one. It's signed by Signora Golzio . . . Renée. Elena's staying with them now at their villa in Santa Margherita. When you get your law degree, ring Golzio, speak

to his secretary, ask her to fix an appointment and you'll see . . .'
Golzio, Golzio, Golzio, was there no hope of any other prospect?

The future was grey, amorphous, insipid like the sirocco-swept afternoons of those April Sundays. The library was closed. He had almost finished his thesis. He was tired of studying and reading. Even Signora Calandra's company was beginning to pall.

Lunch had been specially lavish – two courses followed by a sweet. In the dining-room, the conversation was flagging. A wan light filtered through damask-bordered Madras curtains. The gold and velvet of the furniture, the carpets, the records of symphonies and popular songs would have put anyone to sleep but a young man of twenty-three who in any case had slept until midday. Signora Calandra retired for her inevitable siesta. Emilio went out. And found outside the same drowsy atmosphere.

He walked to Villa Borghese and along the Pincio. The glare in the sky was so dazzling that he could not bear to look up. Impossible to distinguish in that grey-white haze even vague shapes or outlines, darker or lighter patches. The air was warm and sticky. The mere act of breathing seemed painfully difficult. The grey and yellow cupolas and terraced roofs (a uniformly sandy shade darkening here and there to apricot) stretched way out of sight but there was nothing vague about them, because the surrounding limits like the low rims of a huge basin full of fragments and debris were clearly visible – on the left, the modest ridges of the Janiculum and the Vatican, on the right the slightly higher Monte Mario. There was no suggestion of distance, no hint of a gateway to the infinite, no apparent hope of escape. The city was large. Beautiful too, perhaps. But it was all there in being as if the world outside did not exist.

Emilio, looking down from the Pincio terrace that Sunday afternoon, thought of Milan, Genoa, Venice and other cities he had seen. But he thought chiefly of Turin. And he realized that only Rome had that exclusive, immobile, unchangeable, centralized look, like a great penitentiary which the convicts had made their whole world for all time, or all that was worth knowing for all time, in the whole world. Down in the round pit of Piazza del Popolo weaved the traffic – horse-drawn cabs, pedestrians, trams, a few motor-cars; a slice of life girded by the double exhedra, the twin churches with their leaded tiles, the great gate, the flights of steps between statues, balustrades, immense shock-headed pines creating an overall effect of grace, harmony and exquisite beauty tempered with one no less pervasive but secret and mysterious of weariness, suffocation, anguish. Perhaps in the past, at the time of its creation, that spectacular view of stones and trees was livelier, gayer. Today, in its immobility and perfection, it seemed to have imprisoned time and did its part to make Rome like a prison. The bowl of Piazza del Popolo with human beings and vehicles circulating at the bottom of it was like a marvellous but quite obvious improvement on a convicts' exercise-yard.

To the north, in the shadows, the damp wall of the Pincio jutted out over the Muro Torto road. The wire fences fitted later were not in existence yet. The spot had a sinister reputation for suicides. 'Why don't you jump off the Muro Torto' was an elegant variation on the most famous Roman insult. Emilio looked down for a long time. Not that he felt seriously tempted to commit suicide, but these were the only occasions in his life when he even thought about it.

He had lost confidence in the future. He felt neither intelligent nor strong enough to reach what he considered the only desirable goal. But he was intelligent enough to realize it and suffer for his weakness. Never, no, never would he have the tenacity, the necessary energy to push ahead – the tenacity and energy of a Golzio, for instance! However things turned out, he could never hope for anything better than a modest post and a dull life as a clerk or a small-time lawyer. He loved Vévé, of course; when he made love to her he was happy and satisfied. But he was convinced that married life with her, unless he rapidly and quite improbably came into a fortune, would destroy all feeling and happiness. That was the way he had been brought up, that was the way he tended to look at life. He hated and despised the worthy bourgeois families, the working class, the soldiers, the servant-girls, apparently blissfully strolling in the Villa Borghese. He told himself that perhaps one day he would have to put up with being like them. Free of his lust for money, once he lost all his torturing hope of leisure and comfort, what point would there be in living? But he would very probably cease to be aware of his poverty; he would forget his former ambitions; he would no longer prefer death to failure. So wasn't it better to finish it all now? After all, it didn't take much. Life, in his heart and around him, was as insubstantial as a dream. Coloured silhouettes, the Sunday crowd: fatuous smiles and shouts. A dream which he could very well interrupt and by so doing solve all his problems. It would mean suffering atrociously for a moment, then never again. And with his chest pressed against the wall, he looked down again at the grey, hard, empty asphalt, so near and yet so far since it was sufficient for the longest of all journeys.

Then another thought struck him. If he should decide to commit suicide, why not seize the opportunity it offered to render his country a service? Why not die for an idea in which be believed? When he first came to Rome he had made the acquaintance of a young man of about his own age at the Senate library, Bernardi by name, from Brescia, who also specialized in the history of Law. He was a thin, slight, fair-haired boy in rather poor health. His face was as pale as ivory: two strange inflamed patches often appeared on his cheeks. His expression was frank and smiling and seemed both to seek and offer affection. On leaving the libraty, Emilio gradually took to walking part of the way with him, deep in conversation. At first they talked about their studies, then soon turned to politics after overcoming their natural caution and reserve in a place like Rome where there was a constant fear of spies and *agents provocateurs*. Bernardi was more anti-Fascist than Emilio. He could see no hope of salvation in Mussolini and even then had no illusions about the future of Italy, which in his opinion would be disastrous. He said it unhesitatingly, yet without losing for an instant his calm, his mildness, his affable smile.

Bernardi's ideas were based not only on reason, ideological concepts or philosophical and historic culture but also and more firmly on taste and instinct. He hated vulgarity and violence with all his being. One evening, a few months after they had started meeting regularly, he unexpectedly confided in Emilio. It was a mild twilight at the end of February. The day had been warm, sunny, spring-like as often happens in Rome during that month.

They had left the library together but instead of making for the tram-stop at the Pantheon where Bernardi usually took his friend, they crossed the narrow street and came out into nearby Piazza Navona. They began to stroll slowly up and down in the centre of the square, skirting the great fountain now on one side, now on the other. The strident cry of the swallows – early arrivals, too – mingled with the shouts of urchins playing in a corner of the vast open space and the splashing of the fountain. The clear, cloudless sky, locked in the oval rim of the houses, varied in hue from deep blue to something between pastel blue and pale green and against this light background, the two bell-towers, the cornices, the pediment, the statues stood out in dark relief, gigantic, sharp as an etching. It hung in the air like an inner, anguished peace. It was again the melancholy hour when life seems useless and at the same time charged with a mysterious threat of disaster.

'Oh, well,' sighed Emilio and turned to his friend as if expecting a similar sigh of comfort and approval from him.

Bernardi, who never sighed, went on smiling and staring in an amused way straight in front of him, though there was nothing to see but a wide empty space as far as the flattened curve of the old buildings.

Emilio suddenly asked him: 'How do you manage to be always happy and contented?'

The patches on Bernardi's cheeks seemed to flush even redder. His brown, almond-shaped, ever-smiling eyes half closed as if to hold back tears or look further into the distance. He did not answer at once. He hesitated and just smiled. Emilio did not dare to repeat the question. Suddenly Bernardi began to speak. His first words were halting and muffled, suggesting that they were particularly painful to utter.

'I'm happy because . . . well, think for a moment that recently I was on the point of dying – I saw and almost touched Death. Then someone told me: "No, not yet. You can get up and walk. The time will come. But for now you can live." From that instant, you see, every minute that passes is a wonderful boon to me. That's why I'm happy. Yes, I was in a sanatorium in Switzerland. Last year. They thought I would die.'

'But now you're better?'

'For the time being.'

'Isn't it bad for you to live in Rome? If you'd stayed up in the mountains perhaps you'd have recovered completely.'

'I know all about my illness,' Bernardi said with a smile, 'and I've done everything possible. Don't worry. I've no wish to die one minute before I have to. I'm only sorry that I don't know when it will happen.'

'Why?'

'Can't you guess? Because then I'd buy a revolver and practise target-shooting. Then I'd find a way of getting into the front row at some public ceremony . . .'

Emilio understood. Bernardi had stopped, looked around, then added quietly: 'Three bullets for him and the fourth for me. I've often wondered about doing it. I'm sure I'd save Italy and go down in history. The trouble is that I'm a coward.'

And now Emilio, looking down from the Muro Torto, asked himself, 'Why shouldn't I do it?' Mussolini's big, smooth face, his bulging eyes, the wide brow, the bony jaw, the top hat and spats made an ideal target. It would be a final, heroic escape from the bitterness, mistrust and hate that he felt for a future which seemed dominated by the power and violence of money. Oh, to hear the children shouting as they played on the lawns, the mournful bells in the distance, the motor-car horns, the trams clanging and clattering down Muro Torto . . . Death, death! And what lay beyond? Never before had he felt so sure that there was nothing after death, so he could forget the religious instruction of his childhood and Father Pesso's exhortations at the Immacolata Sunday school and Father Righini's sermons at the Spiritual Reunions at Villa Santa Croce. He was even surer of something else – that if he were to commit suicide he would not be punished in any case. Punished . . . why? He hadn't asked to be born, had he?

Rousset's fiancée, Signora Calandra's daughter, the mysterious Elena, suddenly returned about the middle of April. Several days passed. This time she showed no signs of wanting to leave again. In the little villa in Via Guattani, the rhythm of life had changed. The Signorina still did not come downstairs to meals. Emilio had not seen her yet. But Signora Calandra, the maid and Rousset himself all said that she was almost completely restored to health.

Rousset would hurry in, smiling, ask to be announced and wait in the drawing-room. He would be there for a half-an-hour, even longer. Eventually he would be summoned upstairs to her room but on each occasion he stayed for only a few minutes. True, he called twice or three times a day – never in the evening. They said that Elena was better but she suffered from insomnia, and had to take medicine so that she could sleep soundly from early evening. After dinner Signora Calandra, settling comfortably as usual in her yellow armchair would ask Emilio to choose the least noisy records. She would do so with a sigh – it was not clear whether this meant that she was still worried about her daughter's health or that she simply felt put out at not being able to hear her favourite *Rosenkavalier* waltz.

Rousset, too, had changed. He made no attempt to conceal his delight. One day, as he was coming out of his fiancée's room, he met Emilio on the landing. Full of importance and mystery, he drew him aside. His eyes glittered in his ferrety face, his nose seemed even sharper and shinier. Wonderful news! Elena had agreed to fix the date. 'The eighteenth of September in the Basilica of Sant'Agnese. The papers are all drawn up. Marvellous isn't it? Ever seen the inside of Sant'Agnese? It's the most impressive church in Rome! And guess who's promised to be a witness, go on, guess!'

Emilio was not interested enough to want to guess.

'Well, it's Golzio! Golzio in person!'

'Congratulations,' said Emilio. He instinctively disapproved of the mixture of aestheticism and sentimentality which Rousset, like so many other artists, considered the happiest of all combinations. Worse still, that emotionalism was inspired by Rome, which Emilio now rated as a sink of corruption and deceit.

The next day, Elena came down to lunch and Emilio finally made her acquaintance. Rousset had been invited, too, and was beaming with pride. Elena really was very beautiful. Yet her beauty and even her expression were or seemed to be identical to those in the silver-framed photograph – they were or seemed to be just as artificial.

Emilio was surprised and perplexed. Elena sat opposite him. What was the significance of the flashing smiles and the knowing glances that the lovely 'princess', as Gina called her, turned in his direction right from the beginning of the meal? Come on! They had never met before. The knowing air, the roguishness, the glances, the smiles had to be imaginary – unintentional flirtatiousness, a party ploy with no more meaning than miming before a mirror, the habitual game of a smart woman – or, indeed, a real princess – obliged to be condescending to her inferiors – which is to say everybody. Gina had not been far wrong. As a small boy, Emilio had once been taken to a charity reception, pushed vigorously along a red carpet by his mother and presented to Maria Laetitia Bonaparte, the old Duca d'Aosta's second wife and widow. In preparation for the occasion Mama had made him practise bowing and kissing the hand as required by etiquette. With her great aigrette-trimmed hat, Laetitia (as she was known in Turin), offering her hand to kiss, stooped over him and to his utter amazement smiled as if she were really interested in him. But his surprise soon became wonder when he saw that Laetitia had forgotten him in a flash and bestowed an identical smile on the next child. Still, it was absurd for Elena to behave like that at home, in front of her mother and fiancé and her fiancé's friend. Emilio was positive that he had done nothing to encourage her attentions. He had greeted her and was now looking at her and talking quite naturally. But she said: 'I expect you've been hearing about me for months, haven't you, Viotti? Well now you're lucky enough to see me here in the flesh. Ah, yes! Mother and Paolo begged me, so I gave in. I came down from the mountain. But I must confess that I would rather have stayed in hiding up on my Olympus. So much for the background in which I live!' And with these words she eyed her mother, her fiancé and the dining-room with an all-embracing air of feigned scorn, then gazed at Emilio and deliberately winked. It was just a way of telling him not to take her too seriously, of course. Signora Calandra had already contributed with one of her most high-pitched, extravagant, cracked-glass laughs. Yet Emilio felt that Elena's conceit was more than mere banter.

Suddenly he noticed that Elena was being served first. This, too, was absurd. But Signora Calandra, the maid and Rousset all seemed to think it perfectly normal. Was it perhaps because she had been ill and was now gracing the table for the first time after a long absence?

But no, that evening and the next day, Elena was regularly served before her mother. Absurd – and Emilio, recalling the respect, the caution, the gravity with which Signora Calandra, Rousset and even Gina had always spoken to him of Elena, realized that at home she was considered an exceptional, a superior being! Left fatherless from an early age, an only, spoilt child – that might have accounted for her strange manner if only Signora Calandra had been one of those mothers who adore their daughters to compensate for their own thwarted or lost love. But Signora Calandra lived her life to the full, determined to harbour no regrets. Clearly her affection for her daughter was not at all morbid. She never scolded her. She never insisted on her changing any of her opinions or decisions. She allowed her complete freedom of action. In fact, it was more an oddly mysterious form of respect than real affection. Just as if Elena were the secret daughter of some important personage. Or as if she were financially independent of her mother. Emilio began to wonder whether Admiral Calandra had left his estate to his daughter, appointing his wife as administratrix until Elena reached her majority. But Gina exploded that theory. Elena was twenty-three and her mother still had the money.

Several days had passed since Elena's appearance at table, since her descent among common mortals. Rousset was now a regular guest at lunch and dinner. The scene was always the same. Elena sitting opposite Emilio, smiling and talking in the same supercilious, artificial tone as before, throwing him sly glances. She only changed her *toilettes* – in all the latest fashion and in the evening, décolleté and jewels.

Emilio and Rousset, after Signora Calandra hinted that it would please Elena, also changed into dark suits every evening. Emilio noted Elena's beauty, elegance and wit. He admired her for them but she left him cold. And he did not care whether this coldness resulted from the fact that he disliked her, or the thought that she was his friend's fiancée. Any flush of passion or sneaking temptation was stifled by a fitful series of visions that continually flashed into his mind: Rousset clasping Elena in his skinny arms; Rousset kissing her with his tiny rodent's mouth; Rousset with his pointed nose nuzzling in the misty halo of her golden hair . . .

Soon the sight of the two at table began to get on Emilio's nerves. He was no longer curious about Elena's mysterious coquetries. He was even less amused by Rousset's air of stupid complacency. He would have found some excuse to leave Signora Calandra's for other lodgings (certainly a frying-pan-into-the-fire move) but for the fact that he was returning to Turin in a couple of weeks. And one evening when Elena and Rousset officially invited him to the wedding ceremony at Santa Agnese, it was with something like joy – though he pretended to be sorry – that he told them that he could not accept. In all probability he would be travelling abroad in September.

The next day, coming home as usual at about two o'clock in the afternoon and going up to his room before lunch, he was surprised to find a glorious scarlet rose in a large glass on his bedside table. In all the months that he had been there no one had ever decorated his room with flowers. The May sunshine filtered through the open window and the half-closed blinds: a warm reflection shone on the glass and in the grey shadow of the room suffused the rich hue of the rose, calm and still, with an unnatural light. It seemed a sign more than a kind thought, a warning: but with reference to what and from whom?

He immediately thought of Gina. He had occasionally given her little presents such as he could afford to show his gratitude. The girl had been very nice and very generous to him without asking for anything in return or referring at all during the day to their fleeting secret rendezvous every so often at night. She always addressed him formally when they were alone and even when they were in bed. Now that the day of farewell was approaching, perhaps Gina wanted to express a certain tenderness, a certain affection and at the same time gently remind him that she expected to be 'paid off' with a rather more substantial gift?

Only right, he thought. He would not disappoint her. He wanted to tell the girl immediately and thank her for the discreet, delicate way she had chosen to make her request. But since 'the Signorina' had returned Emilio had been unable to see the maid alone even for a moment. Elena's continual, capricious and finicky demands had doubled Gina's work. And as Elena's room was next to his, Gina could no longer come to him as she had done in the past. When he came down to lunch he had another surprise. Rousset was not there.

'I didn't feel very well,' explained Elena, 'so I phoned him not to come. I'm tired. I couldn't get to sleep last night . . .' She left the sentence hanging in mid-air and stared at Emilio with that superficial smile of hers. It was obvious that she expected Emilio to ask why she had come downstairs.

But Emilio said nothing. For some days all Elena's conversations had seemed lies to him. At first he would have liked to know what lay behind them and what she hoped to gain. Now they appeared to be just a game with no need of explanation.

Emilio's silence only made Elena more determined to justify her actions. Laughing and still gazing at Emilio across the table, she exclaimed: '. . . but barely ten minutes ago, I suddenly felt fine and so here I am. Are you glad?'

'Very glad, Signorina – very glad that you're better.'

'No, don't avoid my question. I'm asking you if you're glad of my company.'

'Doesn't your mother count?' Signora Calandra broke in, laughing as if someone was tickling her – an impression accentuated by the way she usually sat at table, with her napkin stretched over her ample bosom, tucked under her armpits, her elbows gripping it tightly against her plump thighs.

'Your mother has been an extraordinarily pleasant table-companion to me all these months. I shall never forget it.'

'Neither will I,' Signora Calandra giggled again, and this time she shot him a wicked glance. A glance which meant nothing of course, but one which Emilio noted with satisfaction as a blow to Elena's vanity, suggested all kinds of goings-on between him and the old lady.

'Thank you,' said Emilio.

'I must thank *you*,' replied Signora Calandra. She seemed to enjoy teasing her daughter for she added: 'You know, Elena, Viotti has always been a perfect cavalier.'

'Enthusiastic rather than perfect,' Viotti piled on the agony.

Signora Calandra rounded off the teasing: 'Well, let's say that we've been good company for each other.'

'And no need of me, I suppose?' snapped Elena.

'No need of you,' her mother laughed aloud, pretending not to notice the sudden serious tone in her daughter's voice. Elena leapt to her feet. For a second she fixed her lovely gold-flecked eyes on Emilio, not her mother. She threw her napkin on to the chair and rushed out of the room, slamming the door. Perhaps Elena was not so beautiful as everybody said and as she had seemed to be that first day. She was tall and thin. Narrow shoulders, slim waist, prominent hips, rather big-boned. Angular and nervy, refined, capricious, intellectual, snobbish, she was the exact opposite of Vévé, in other words the opposite of all the qualities that Emilio now appreciated in a girl: a round, full figure, a calm disposition, a manner that was not vulgar but free and easy, simplicity, frankness, natural sincerity.

'Is she offended?' asked Emilio more out of courtesy to Signora Calandra than because he felt any concern. For his thoughts had flown instinctively to Vévé as he made the comparison with Elena. Vévé had not replied to his latest letters and in fact had not written to him for more than a month. No, it was Vévé he felt concerned about.

'Offended?' sighed Signora Calandra. 'Take no notice. She's a strange girl. Anyway, it's all my fault. I know her and I shouldn't have teased her. But she'll get over it soon. She's always like that. She just needs to get married, that's all.'

'In that case,' murmured Emilio, 'you've no worries. It's only a question of a few months.'

'No, no worries. No worries at all. Still . . . poor Elena!' and she sighed again.

In the same way as when her daughter was not at home, Signora Calandra seemed to be hinting at some mystery – a nervous disorder, maybe, or perhaps something even worse.

Oh, Emilio refused to be taken in by it. There was something forced and insincere about Signora Calandra's sighing over Elena. A lovely girl, an only child, heiress to a tidy fortune, assured of her future, shortly to be the bride of a successful artist who was a nice young man and very much in love with her – what need was there to sigh over her? Just another habit, an urge to complain in the belief that her life was much more difficult and complicated than it really was. And all because a difficult and complicated life is chic while a simple one is not.

This was the true significance of Signora Calandra's sighs, according to Emilio. Whenever she could, she herself showed clearly that she did not take them seriously. A few hours later, about eight o'clock, Emilio found Rousset waiting for Elena and Doctor Bonansea for Signora Calandra in the drawing-room. The doctor had his dinner-jacket on – so it was the theatre and supper afterwards. And Signora Calandra came downstairs late as usual with the usual ceremonial fuss and gay prattle – even though Gina sadly, almost apologetically, informed Rousset that the Signorina still did not feel well (a bad migraine), that she would not be available for dinner nor could she receive him in her room. She thanked him for coming and wished him goodnight. Rousset, as black as thunder, probably forgetting that Emilio was present, rounded on his future mother-in-law with more than a hint of asperity.

'And what are you going to do about it, Signora Calandra? Not a word? You're off to the theatre and not a word . . .? This looks like a relapse to me.'

'The doctors have prescribed Elena complete rest. For several days now she's come down to dinner with us. She's overdone it and is suffering the consequences. As her mother I feel that she's very wise to stay in bed and see no one. Don't you agree, Doctor?'

Doctor Bonansea nodded his great curly white head in assent.

But Rousset persisted: 'Excellent, Signora! But you're going to the theatre all the same.'

'Oh, that's enough, Rousset. Don't be such a bore. There's nothing seriously wrong with Elena. And I don't have to account to anyone for my actions. My daughter is free and independent, too. At least until the day she becomes your wife.'

Then with a little laugh she tried to close the argument humorously: 'You see, Doctor, what these people from Turin are like? Rome for ever! And paddle your own canoe! Eh?'

Signora Calandra, the Doctor and Rousset left. Emilio sat down alone at the table. It was the first time that it had happened to him for quite a while. When Gina came in with the soup tureen, his immediate thought was to thank her for the rose. He smiled at her and was about to stretch out his arm to caress her when the door opened and Elena appeared. She was wearing a red chiffon dress which enveloped her like a vaporous flame and through a scarf of the same material and colour he caught a glimpse of her thin shoulders. She came slowly forward. 'My headache's gone. If you don't mind, Viotti, I'll join you for dinner. Gina, set a place please.'

Later, on reflection, Emilio could not remember exactly how that meal tête-à-tête with Elena had gone – what they had talked about, how she had begun to express her feelings for him, his reaction to her confidences. But were they really confidences? Perhaps they were only vague, hesitant advances. That was it! Advances. He would have been an idiot not to realize it. But he remembered that not once during dinner or immediately after had he considered them part of a deliberate plan. He had regarded them merely as another sudden, momentary, perverse caprice of a blasé girl with experience of life and doubts, or even second thoughts, about her imminent marriage. But he had readily discarded this supposition not so much out of a moral sense of loyalty to his friend as because he felt an instinctive, physical revulsion at the thought of any relationship with Rousset's fiancée. And this revulsion was so deep that it never crossed his mind that Elena's indisposition could be a pretence and her sudden decision to come down to dinner a planned manoeuvre.

There came a moment when, before the end of the meal, the conversation turned somehow to the subject of spiritualism. Emilio recalled how he would have welcomed any topic as a relief from sentimental or personal chatter and a way of bringing such a strange, embarrassing, altogether distasteful evening to a successful conclusion.

'Have you ever seen a ghost?' asked Elena after a pause, still gazing at him with her big, sparkling green eyes.

'No, have you?'

'No. But I believe in them.'

Emilio was not interested. He talked to keep the conversation from flagging.

'And why do you believe in them?'

'Because some English friends of mine have told me fantastic stories. And because I feel it's true. And beautiful, too. Have you ever been at a table-turning?'

'No, have you?' asked Emilio.

'No, I haven't. But I know how it's done. My English friends told me all about it. Why don't we try?'

'I'd love to.'

'Perhaps . . . you're afraid?' Elena said hesitantly, looking away to a dark corner of the lounge where an arch with slender gilt columns divided it from the dining-room.

'I. Afraid?' Emilio retorted, surprised. 'I've never tried it but I don't think I'd be afraid. Plenty of people there . . .'

'It'll work with a few, too. Just two around the little table.'

'Even so, you'd not be alone. I suppose I'd only be afraid if I were alone.'

'Why don't we try?' repeated Elena.

'All right, I've told you – I'd love to. Whenever you like. Let me know. I'll come.'

'Why don't we try tonight?'

'Tonight? Where?'

'Here, after dinner. Just we two. I think I know a little about being a medium.' Elena smiled as she turned to look at him again – even more intensely (if that were possible) than before.

Elena's eyes – no doubt about it – were glorious: green, flecked with gold and steel, and so sparkling that it seemed quite natural to suppose that they were powered with a magnetic charge. Her long lashes – natural or artificial? – cast a fleeting, mysterious shadow. And her pencilled, arched eyebrows rising almost to her temples gave her a touch of the devil.

Why then did Emilio not feel attracted? Perhaps because she seemed always to reflect Rousset's ferrety face.

Actually, for about a quarter of an hour, Emilio had begun to forget Rousset. The unpleasant visions of the couple locked in passionate embrace flashed less frequently across his mind. For a quarter of an hour Emilio had been admiring Elena to the exclusion of all else but without a trace of emotion – admiration, but no feeling of affection nor any desire for contact, a caress, a kiss, an embrace. Rather as if she were a cat. Many people do not hesitate to fondle cats like human beings. Emilio was not one of them. He admired Elena, and especially her green eyes, with a mixture of suspicion and disgust. And when finally he thought of Rousset again, he began to feel sorry for him. Elena was beautiful, intelligent, broad-minded, original, rich. She was what is called 'a superior type of woman'. In any case she was definitely superior to Rousset, sex for sex. On the other hand, to have to put up with all those 'bogus princess' airs and graces for the rest of his life! Emilio decided that he could not possibly do it. But he also decided that Rousset probably did not notice her affectation.

After dinner they went through to the drawing-room. Elena made herself comfortable in Mama's yellow velvet armchair. Emilio sat at her side. They waited for Gina to serve the coffee and clear the table. And they kept on talking about ghosts. Elena regaled Emilio with some of her English friends' weirder stories.

Gina, who seemed much slower than usual that evening, extinguished the chandelier in the dining-room. From the far corner behind the piano the red dome of the only skylight dimly lit the huge lounge. Gina asked the Signorina if she needed anything or whether she could go.

They were alone.

The three-legged table was old, light, inlaid and covered with a lace cloth. On it there were little Chinese ivory figures, an ash-tray, a glazed porcelain snuff-box. Elena cleared the table and brought it into the middle of the room. They sat opposite each other. Elena stretched her hands palm downwards across the table and rested them lightly on Emilio's extended palms.

Elena had thin, soft, ivory-coloured hands with long fingers, pointed nails, and wrists too slim in ratio to the length of the fingers – a child's wrists on a woman's hands.

Emilio thought again of Vévé – Vévé's hands, large, strong, pink and white, peasant's or washerwoman's hands of course, but so gently and tenderly caressing and so capable. A mother's hands, the loveliest hands in the world, Emilio suddenly realized as he compared them to Elena's strange ones. It occurred to him once more that Vévé had stopped writing to him. He shut his eyes and Elena and the darkened drawing-room with its gilt decorations, carpets, damasks and the ridiculous table-charade vanished for a moment. Why had Vévé stopped writing?

He felt Elena withdrawing her hands and opened his eyes. Elena was gazing at him and laughing soundlessly.

'No, we'll get nowhere this way,' she said. She rose slowly, crossed the room to the piano and turned off the light. An instant later, her tall, willowy figure was silhouetted against the glimmering glow from the street filtering through the closed blinds and the thick evergreens in the garden. Elena did not move.

'I can't see.'

'I can see you perfectly,' replied Emilio, just to say something.

'Then come and fetch me. I can't walk a step in the dark. I've always been the same, ever since I was a baby.' And when Emilio went to her: 'Take me back to my chair.'

Emilio obeyed. The skin under Elena's armpit was smoother than silk. Close to her in the dark, he was aware of the fresh, powerful, heady perfume from her body through her filmy gown.

They resumed the experiment. Once again they sat at the table, palm to palm.

'What do I have to do?' said Emilio after a while. He was beginning to get bored.

'Nothing. Just think. Think as hard as you can.'

'About what?'

'I'm the medium,' murmured Elena and Emilio seemed to detect an amused note in her voice, a stifled laugh that she could not wholly repress. 'You must think hard, wish hard with all your might that what I want will happen.'

'And what *do* you want?'

Elena hesitated a moment before replying: 'Well . . . the spirit to materialize of course, the one I call.'

'And pray who may that be?'

'Don't joke about it, Viotti,' retorted Elena, playfully slapping his palms as punishment. Then she dropped her voice – 'or it'll be useless. You've got to believe. Now be a good boy and concentrate. Think. Think as hard as you can.'

'Can you see me now?' Emilio asked.

'Yes, a little. But it's better to keep your eyes closed. Emilio closed his eyes and immediately reverted to thinking of Vévé. Over the deep silence, he could hear the trams in the distance passing along Via Nomentana and a nightingale trying its first notes in the garden. Through the open windows came the warmth of a May night. So there were nightingales in Rome too. Ah, the nightingales on the Collina in Turin! What was Vévé doing at that very moment? It was the middle of spring. Perhaps Vévé had found someone she liked (even if she did not love him) just as he . . . yes just as he had found Gina. Or she may have given in to one of her colleagues at the office or some exceptionally persistent boss – given in not for love or by a sudden impulse, but simply through weakness as she had done two years before with the engineer who wanted to marry her. He himself was submitting to this stupid game only because he did not have the strength to say 'No' and in spite of the fact that he cared nothing for Elena and even felt a sort of repulsion for her! It was quite possible that Vévé, though she might still love him, had been unfaithful. Highly probable when he came to think of it. Luckily there were only a few more days to go now . . .

Elena's palms trembled very slightly, almost imperceptibly – a continual, regular twitching rather like an involuntary nervous tic. And every now and then she gently stroked his as if seeking a more sensitive spot, caressing him or perhaps trying to say something. Was it deliberate coquetry? Or instinctive fondling? In either case the manoeuvre was useless and, despite the favouring darkness, the impressive silence and the effect of the perfume, it left Emilio completely indifferent.

This Elena, what was she? An episode that did not concern him. The minutes passed and in his imagination he kept on seeing more and more clearly Vévé's open, healthy, passionate face – her deep, blue eyes. And he felt certain that he loved her. An unhesitating certainty with no reservations. He would always love her.

'What are you thinking about?'

Elena's sibilant whisper broke into the silence, his emotions, his thoughts. Wish hard, with all his might for the spirit to materialize? What nonsense! If Elena was really a medium she must have sensed that he was thinking of something entirely different. Emilio lied.

'I'm afraid of what you told me to think.'

Silence and stillness fell once more. In the faint light filtering through the shutters, Emilio could see Elena's eyes glinting colourlessly. He seethed with impatience. Not that he was afraid of being hypnotized. The idea had occurred to him but he laughed it off. He was getting bored. Or was it uncomfortable? Both bored and uncomfortable, that was it. How long would he have to wait for Elena to tire of the experiment and admit failure? He yearned to get back to his room. He had to study for his examinations, not waste time with spiritualism, of all things! He waited a few minutes, then decided. He would tell the truth – it was late and he had work to do. He searched for the words and the right polite tone. He was about to speak when suddenly Elena seemed to be activated by a supernatural force, and grasped his hands. She gasped: 'There, did you hear?'

'No, I heard nothing.' Emilio was quite sure.

'What do you mean? Didn't you hear it?'

'What?'

'A knock, it was quite clear. The table moved. Let's keep quiet. Listen!'

Emilio was baffled. There had been no knock. Elena was either pretending or imagining. The longed-for end of the stupid experiment now seemed further off than ever! Yet Elena's hands had not resumed their ritual position; they still grasped and squeezed his own. Emilio felt her nails in his flesh. Only after a few minutes did her grip slowly relax. And Elena's hands instead of coming to rest palm to palm as before slowly glided forward – the slim tips of her fingers slipped into his shirt-cuffs and began to stroke his wrists so tenderly, so delicately that for the first time Emilio felt a wave of desire and for the first time he was left in no doubt as to what Elena wanted. He hesitated. He realized clearly what he could do and no heroics involved – what he *should* do, in fact. Calmly get up, apologize and politely ask if he might go to his room. *Should* do? But was it such a vital decision? To refuse an adventure that seemed neither crystal-clear nor natural nor even particularly exciting – wasn't he running the risk of giving it too much importance? Oh, it was easy either way – to say yes or no. Like turning a key to right or to left.

So he turned it and immediately forgot everything else. Involuntarily he began to stroke the hands that were stroking his. Elena leaned towards him in the dark: 'My love!'

Emilio saw her inviting mouth smiling at him. And the table fell noiselessly on to the soft, Bukhara carpet as, a few instants later, they both knelt and quietly sank upon the thick pile, locked in a tight embrace.

He had torn off her expensive dress, absolutely ruined it. He felt a violent but very short spasm of pleasure. When he got up he registered the impression (and it must have been so in reality) that he had enjoyed with his body but not with his soul – above all not with his mind, which had remained inert, detached, sad, as if from his small corner he had been able to witness everything that happened in a mirror. He had possessed Elena, yet she still seemed to mean nothing to him. Did Elena feel the same way about him? This was a question that Emilio should have asked himself, but it never occurred to him because he did not love Elena and cared nothing for her feelings.

They went up to her room, undressed, got into bed and spent the night making love continually in the same violent, rapid way, even after they had become tired.

Elena, perhaps in order to beguile the long pauses, abandoned herself completely to her new lover with lingering tenderness.

But each time Emilio felt that he had to overcome a slight but definite obstacle – a sort of frontier, a gully, a narrow, deep cleft. On one side natural instinct, on the other will-power. He had never deserted natural instinct with Vévé. Now, every time before taking Elena he had to exercise his will-power, divert from the mainstream of spontaneity – in other words, turn the key.

He discovered that this effort of will brought its own tang. It was a new tang that he had never experienced before – bitter and dry, the sad pride of being two people, of not giving himself to what he was doing and even condemning what he was doing.

As he entered Elena's room he thought of Rousset. And he began to realize that the new flavour included the pleasure of violating the idea of friendship, breaking this bond without remorse – or almost. After all, he wasn't a real friend, he was such a stupid, ridiculous man! Everything that he disliked about Elena before – her skinny shoulders, her slim wrists, her studied smile and affected, snobbish ways, he continued to dislike. But of course the new flavour also brought the sour delight of feigning affection and aping attentions for something that in his heart of hearts he despised.

They were amused when they heard Elena's mother coming home from the theatre and the voice of the doctor who took her to her room where he stayed for a while. Doctor Bonansea was obviously trying to talk quietly but his voice boomed comically through the wall like a *basso profondo's*.

'Love,' said Elena when they saw that it was daylight and the time had come for them to part. Emilio was sitting on the edge of the bed. She was lying back, naked. Her white shoulders buried in the salmon-pink pillows seemed almost pointed. Her gold and steel-flecked eyes gazed into his, laughing, blissfully happy.

'Love,' she repeated, voluptuously stroking his hair with her long, slender fingers. 'From the first moment that I saw you, I've wanted you night and day. I tried to tell you, to make you understand. But you didn't want to know, you couldn't see . . .' Emilio was about to protest but she stretched out her slim arm and closed his lips with her finger-tips.

'Yes, I know what you're going to say – it's because of Rousset. But Rousset means nothing to me! That's what you wouldn't accept! I've known him for years and he's always been crazy about me and says he'll wait for me. But, look, in all those years I've never done with him a fraction of what I've done with you tonight. I don't think I'll even marry him. He's nice and kind. But I don't love him. He's so stupid. And what do you care about Rousset? You're not such good friends. That's why I was so annoyed. I couldn't stand it. You never looked at me, you didn't listen to me, you didn't even notice me! The last few nights . . . I'm not making it up . . . I couldn't sleep. All because of you. And so yesterday morning I decided that I couldn't go on living without telling you. I went into your room and put a rose on your bedside table. I meant the rose to tell you what I was unable to myself. But still nothing from you – you were as cold as ever. You didn't even understand the rose, did you? You're so intelligent and so cold. Who could have put such a lovely rose on your table in that beautiful glass? Like a still life by Berthe Morisot. Who could have put it there? Mother? Gina? Oh, my poor Emilio. But I wanted you even before. Even before I knew you existed. Yes, because I've always wanted a man like you.'

'How, like me?' asked Emilio with a half-gratified, half-mocking smile. Whatever answer Elena gave, it was of no importance to him.

'How like you? Intelligent, intelligent and . . . intelligent,' and she looked at him admiringly and went on stroking his hair.

'Maybe,' Emilio remarked, still smiling incredulously. 'But I wish intelligence would be some use in life.'

Elena slipped her hand down to the nape of his neck and drew him towards her, mouth to mouth. She gave him a lingering kiss and then, detaching her lips from his, whispered: 'In the meantime it's helped you to take me. If you were not as intelligent as you are, do you think that I would have paid any attention to you?'

'It's not that,' said Emilio, struggling free. 'In two months I'll have my degree and what am I going to do with it? What am I going to do with a degree and all that intelligence you've been talking about? I have ten years of police court work before me. Your honour, your worship, I quote Article 438, Article 521, case remanded? Case remanded. What an end for an intelligent man!'

But Elena smiled: 'Not a man. A child. And it's time for children to go bye-byes. Ciao, sleep well, my love. Don't make a noise as you go out. Quietly.' From the bed, in the rosy light of the night-light on the sheets, she followed him with her eyes until the very last moment when Emilio softly closed the door behind him.

Two hours later Gina awakened him, bringing him on the breakfast tray an express letter that had just arrived.

It was from Vévé. He looked at it for a while without opening it. He had a premonition.

In her big rounded, upright writing, lucid like her, Vévé said: 'Dear Milio,

'I haven't written or even answered your letters because since you left Turin to go to Rome something new has happened in my life.

'I've been seeing and getting to understand a man whom anyway I knew before you and told you about. He was so gentle and affectionate that at first I felt quite bewildered. Then gradually I began to realize that I loved him – that maybe I was in love with him without knowing it even before I knew you.

'Not that I haven't been honest with you – that's not what I mean and I don't want you to get the wrong idea. I've loved you, Milio with all my heart. I think I showed you how much. I don't think you can deny that at least. I loved you. If only you had loved me as I loved you . . .

'Anyway, we were happy, so happy that, dear Milio, I have no regrets. I'll write it again in case you're not convinced that I'm sincere – I have no regrets. And I thank you, Milio, I thank you again and I'll always thank you for what you've given me. Perhaps you're the type who could never give more. That consoles me and I'm less jealous of the woman or women you've met in Rome all these months or, more important still, those you'll meet in the future. Because, you know, I believe that a woman who's loved a man is still a bit jealous of him even after she's stopped loving him. At any rate, you've given me something perhaps you knew nothing about and didn't even want to give me. Something you can't take the credit for but thanks all the same. For the first time in my life you've given me the great joy of loving with my whole physical and moral being, *en bloc*. That's amusing because it reminds me of 'monobloc'. My boy-friend knows a lot about machines and motors and is always using technical terms.

'Now, love . . . love is a monobloc – could be a song-title, couldn't it? I pity you, I'll always pity you because I don't think you'll ever experience this great joy. And so you'll always be a bit miserable.

'I know you won't like this letter. I know it'll hurt you. But don't blame me. If you want us to stay good friends and I hope we will, don't ever blame me.

'You went to Rome, disappeared. Left me. Your parents, your studies, your career, your inheritance, etcetera. I know it all. I've heard it hundreds of times. And if we meet again, I mean, if you want to see me again, I only beg you to spare me the usual rigmarole. So you went away. Let's have a trial separation, you said. And I said, all right, let's have a trial separation. You've written regularly, it's true. And I've answered just as regularly.

'But after all Rome isn't at the South Pole and Turin isn't at the North Pole. Just one night in a train. And you could have slipped away at least once during all these months and without your people knowing, surely?

'Or perhaps you think not?

175

'Fancy, I toyed with the idea a few times of paying you a surprise visit in Rome. At the office we had three and a half days off for Carnival – from Saturday to Wednesday morning. I very nearly came. Then I said to myself – the trial separation was his idea, he started it, not me. So it was up to you to finish it. Not me. And I was right. Because I suffered. I suffered loneliness and pain. But in this way I dug down inside and learnt to understand myself. I know who I am and what I want. But I've learnt to understand not only by reasoning. I've done it through sheer desperation.

'Now, everything is clear in my mind. It happened one April evening when . . . But why am I telling you all this? What does it matter to you?

'I can hear your protests, your cry of pain from here. But it is not a sincere cry. It's prompted by pride and wounded vanity that I couldn't wait for you, that I've found another man. In that cry of yours there's just a little love – or, rather, affection – but very little.

'Anyway, pride or affection, I'm sorry, dear Milio, I'm honestly sorry to hurt you. I almost wish that you didn't love me at all and then you wouldn't feel a thing. But somebody else I love like I loved you for two years, somebody I appreciate and respect more than you, would have no reason to live if I refused to marry him.

'I was so desperate last winter that I felt that I wanted children, I was made to have children and since in our backward society children born out of wedlock have a difficult time, I had to get married.

'You may say – why didn't you be honest with me at the time? Simply because, dear Milio, then I felt it in my heart. But only now, as I've told you, am I clear in my mind. Then what good would it have been my saying it, if you hadn't felt the same way first? Hand on heart, have you ever thought – not of marrying me (I know that you have), but seriously of the only thing that counts in marriage – having children by me?

'You should have understood, Milio and you didn't. If this is any consolation, remember that the fault or let's say the cause (because I'm sure you'll soon forget and everything will turn out all right for you again) the cause of what's happened lies in yourself. So you only have yourself to blame. Me, I don't blame you; on the contrary, I thank you because, by being far away and not making up your mind, you have opened my eyes and given me the opportunity to be happy with the man I love and who will shortly be my husband. He's Ingegnere Umberto Bianchi-Mina. Yes, my former boss. He's thirty-seven. I lied when I said he was older. I didn't want to make you suspicious.

'I love him and he loves me. I want to make him happy just as he wants to make me happy. We've discovered that we agree on so many things . . .

'Like you and I? Yes, like you and I but in a different way. With you everything seems a joke even when it's a serious matter. With him, everything seems serious even when it's all a joke. I want to have children and I'm obviously getting older.

'Again I beg you to forgive me.

'You know that in a way I'll always love you.

Your Vévé.'

How many times did he read that letter? He did nothing else the whole day. In the library he spread it out on the pages of his completed thesis (he only had to check a few quotations) and, instead of working, read and re-read what Vévé had written in a vain attempt to discern a ray of hope.

He did not feel up to lunch with Elena and Signora Calandra. He rang Gina to warn her and went to a restaurant in Sant' Eustachio. While he tried to eat he took the letter from his pocket to re-read a sentence, a word which he thought he had not taken in before. And each time he read the whole page and even the previous and the following ones.

The sunshine on the cobbled square, a carriage passing, a hawker at the end of his round crying his wares, a small, chubby, white-haired priest entering the restaurant and sitting opposite him, the waiter with his dirty, white jacket and unshaven chin, the yellow wine sparkling in the carafes, a cat rearing up on his hind legs to snatch the bacon fat that the priest was holding on his knife-blade - it all seemed unfriendly, senseless and sad, as if life, even in its humble details and most trivial circumstances, were only the mask over a secret horror.

All afternoon he walked the streets of Rome – ancient and modern Rome, on both banks of the Tiber – stopping at every corner to read or look at the letter, unconscious of where he was and without so much as a glance at the walls, the mansions, the streets, the sunshine, the river, the trams, the parks, the crowds, or the loneliness around.

Vévé's letter left no hope. And she was perfectly justified. Vévé was right in everything she had written. He and he only was the cause, he was to blame for this disaster which he would never have believed could be so serious. And yet he felt insulted, cheated. A stupid idea but none the less real. So he loved her – loved her *with all his heart* just as, alas, she said she had loved him. He had loved her like that without realizing it! What did it matter that Vévé could not be blamed? The affront, the deception, his ignorance of his own deep feelings; Emilio blamed it on everything and everybody – Turin, Rome, his relations, his parents, his studies, his friends, himself, Vévé and her circle, Ingegnere Bianchi-Mina, the office in Via Maria Vittoria, her tramdriver father . . .

As darkness fell he drifted back to San Silvestro. He went into the post-office. He filled in form after form and tore them all up in desperation. He was terrified of offending Vévé. The telegram would probably arrive while she was at the office and the family might be upset and start to worry.

In the end he realized that he was suffering *physically* from heart-ache and the telegram was for the moment the only possible medicine – a thread of hope to grasp.

He presented it at the counter. It read: 'Received your express letter Stop Returning permanently Turin weekend Stop please postpone decision until we meet Stop letter following Yours Emilio.' This was the final draft after many attempts. It contained no term of affection that might irritate her. Better keep it on the serious, almost business basis she very likely was used to with Ingegnere Bianchi-Mina. And since he wanted to see her, touch her, repossess her, marry her, save her and himself, he had to meet her as soon as he got back to Turin. Fortunately her letter did not seem to exclude that possibility. He simply had to talk to her. He would surprise her, bewilder her, overwhelm her, win her all over again. This was his thread of hope.

The post office clerk scribbled some figures on the grey form and the receipt. He stamped it, blotted it and tore it off with his metal rule. Reality continued to be hostile and senseless. But in the red glow of the electric light bulbs, in the stale ink-impregnated air of the old office, the clerk's weary, elderly face, his thin limbs swathed in a black sateen dust-coat, his measured, habitual movements which Emilio watched imploringly through the glass, seemed to form part of a ritual sacred perhaps to the inscrutable decrees of some divinity – the God who holds sway over the happiness and destinies of men.

❧❧❧

VI

At last the sky began to brighten. Framed by the windows and the blinds flapping to and fro with the speed of the train, gardens, vineyards, cottages, orchards rushed past in the pale light. In the distance, over towards the sea, a black streak, the pine forest, lined the horizon. Viareggio, already. Monday's dawn was breaking at last.

Before dusk he would be seeing Vévé again. Monday. Monday the twenty-first. As soon as he had fixed Sunday night for his departure from Rome, he had written arranging to meet her at a quarter-past-seven the following evening on the mound in the Cavour gardens, the old rendezvous where they had exchanged their first kiss. Whatever the outcome of their conversation he would see her again! At least he hoped so. He even thought he probably would. That was all. In any case, just to see her seemed an immense, inestimable boon. See her, talk to her, look into her blue eyes and at her generous mouth. In his wallet he had a small snapshot of her taken when they went to the festival of San Michele. Even now on the train that was speeding him to her, he kept looking at the little photo. And all the time he kept imagining cruelly how those eyes had rested lovingly on another man and smiled at him, and how he had kissed that mouth.

Ingegnere Bianchi-Mina with his slight, dandified figure obsessed Emilio. He could not remember his face. He had never seen him at close quarters. It must be smooth, sharp-featured and he seemed to recollect a moustache and a vague impression of greying, pomaded temples. But he recalled quite clearly the shaped, twill overcoat, the pigskin gloves, the malacca cane which he pictured as having a little gold ring under the handle just like Uncle Sanfront's. A British mannequin imported for the admiration of the Turin public, a model of the richest, most stupid and provincial bourgeoisie in the city. It was absurd that Vévé, a woman with natural impulses, a rebel, should love a man so alien to all her tastes, such a despicable creature.

Despicable? What evidence did Emilio have to call him despicable so categorically? Faults in his appearance might not be important, they might be outweighed by unsuspected qualities. The mere fact that he had fallen in love with Véve and that he was prepared to marry her, a working-class girl, daughter of a tramdriver, instead of some rich heiress, daughter of an aristocrat or an industrialist, in other words someone from Bianchi-Mina's own world, was a point in his favour. It was probably just a caprice like Elena's feeling for Emilio. But in good faith since he was ready to marry her. And only one thing mattered – Véve had taken the caprice for love and given love in return.

Or perhaps not. Perhaps Véve's was not true love. Some sentences – or rather some of the turns of phrase – in her letter seemed to suggest this possibility. For example, where she mentioned that with Bianchi-Mina everything became 'serious, even laughing matters'. Wasn't there just a hint of boredom, reading between the lines? Didn't this new affection of hers for Bianchi-Mina appear a little too ostentatious? And deep down were there not traces of her bitter pleasure in revenge, the expression of an inferiority complex that she had long suffered, rejected, fought, the memory of two years' humiliation hidden not only from Emilio but also from herself?

Love or pride – whatever the reason – Véve seemed to ignore the bitterness of these humiliations as if they never existed. But day by day, for two years, the poison had mounted in her heart until, with Emilio's departure, it had finally overflowed.

In this way, during those last days in Rome, between the arrival of Véve's letter and his earlier return, Emilio by mulling things over had managed to explain and in a way justify Véve's infatuation for a man she should have hated. And there was something else. Bianchi-Mina was tall, thin, dark. Apart from his mode of dress, he could easily be taken for Emilio. But Bianchi-Mina came from a rich family and at thirty-seven was the managing director of the insurance company Anonima Assicurazioni and other members of the group. He had arrived. He led the sort of life that Emilio coveted in a hopeless kind of way. (Here he was, obliged to travel third class.) Wasn't Véve's choice an object lesson? A perfect object lesson with more than a touch of irony. As if Véve had meant to say: 'Look, Milio, though I've never told you, you know that I would have been ready to marry you even if you'd been a mere assistant to the worst lawyer in Turin, or even if you hadn't got a job or a degree. But you've always said that first you wanted to get a secure position and a lot of money – that life without money is no life at all etcetera. Well, you convinced me. I'm marrying Bianchi-Mina, who is what you may be in fifteen years. I can't wait that long. In any case if I did wait for you I'd finish up by preventing you making money.'

But how did this change things? What difference did it make that she was right and perhaps deep, deep down she did not love Bianchi-Mina? She thought she loved him, she wanted to love him – that was enough. And perhaps she really did love him. Resentment and revenge might well be the right ground to nurture the blossom of love. And now the bloom was tall and bright and all the rest counted for nothing.

In this way Emilio, teetering on an excruciating seesaw of hope and despair, found himself destroying all the arguments which he had thought up from time to time against the sincerity of Vévé's letter, against the possibility that she might really be in love with Bianchi-Mina. But they were not arguments, they were illusions, necessary perhaps as a palliative to allay suffering, a narcotic to deaden his sense of reality. A secret, implacable voice kept telling him not to expect anything from the meeting towards which the train was speeding him, as it furiously wove a path between the Ligurian mountains in quest of the night, fleeing from the pearly blue-pink flush that invaded sky and sea.

And perhaps that murmuring voice was Elena's in the bedroom, when she had breathed – 'intelligent, intelligent, intelligent'. No, that had nothing to do with it. There was no connection between the two. And when Elena's fingers had slipped inside his shirt-cuffs and begun to caress him, Vévé's express letter had been lying buried under a pile of other letters on the great table at San Silvestro in the red glow of the electric bulbs, in the musty, ink-laden atmosphere. Yet he felt the same pang of superstition as when he had stood waiting for Vévé at the corner of the Gran Madre and Corso Casale – if he had gone to meet her, the girl dressed in yellow would have been changed into someone else by some evil, occult, prophetic force. The same force that, as if knowing which way he would turn, foreseeing that he would yield to Elena's caresses, had arranged back in April – perhaps on the very day Elena returned to Rome – for Vévé and Bianchi-Mina to meet in conditions particularly favourable to the burgeoning of their love for each other.

Indeed, it seemed to Emilio that sinister fate had managed to synchronize his affair with Elena and Vévé's betrayal. He continued to think of it as a betrayal, even though he knew that he was being unfair. And Elena's determination to give herself to him (which he had refused to acknowledge), Elena's beauty (which he had refused to admire), the rose, the little table, the new elements of difficulty and violence in his pleasure with her were now merely tokens of some evil spell. No, there was no hope for him.

In spite of a deep-rooted feeling of repulsion, he had found it impossible to avoid Elena during his last week in Rome.

The first day, he spent the evening out and dined in a *trattoria* with Bernardi. He got back after midnight so as not to be seen by Elena, Signora Calandra or Gina. He had not been crying, no – he could not cry – but he knew that he looked upset and he wanted to avoid silly questions. He went straight up to his room, undressed and got into bed. He put out the light without wooing the sleep that in any case he did not expect to come. He only wanted to suffer, ponder over the letter which he almost knew by heart. He had put it under his pillow and as he fingered it he thought of it as the cause of all his misfortunes but also in a way as a talisman which he would not abandon for all the money in the world. Shortly after, in the darkness and the dead silence, he heard the door open slowly. Unfortunately he had forgotten to lock himself in. A tall pale form glided into the room. It could only be Elena and even if he had not heard or seen her, he would have recognized her from her perfume.

She turned the key in the lock. An instant and she was standing over him. She groped in the gloom and stroked and ruffled his hair. This went on for a long time. Emilio neither moved nor said a word. All he wanted was for it to be over as soon as possible. Any remark or gesture could be dangerous and might even produce the opposite effect. So he kept quiet and thought of Vévé while the tall white form by the bed and the fingers running through his hair got on his nerves because they distracted him from the agony in which he was greedily wallowing. But Elena withdrew her hand and slowly stripped off her crêpe-de-Chine chemise. She slid into bed, lay on top of him, began to kiss him, suck him, bite him.

'You're hurting me,' Emilio complained peevishly.

'What's the matter? Don't you want to?'

'No, I'm tired, I don't want to. Leave me be for tonight.' He wanted to say 'Go away, leave me for good and all.' But he had said 'for tonight' with the idea of avoiding arguments. All he did was postpone them.

The following day at lunch, he tried to justify his departure to Signora Calandra, Elena and Rousset, by saying that the examination date had been brought forward to the end of the month.

But as he had feared, the way he looked and spoke must have been a little odd – even Rousset enquired after his health. Night came and he locked himself in his room. Soon he heard someone turning the handle outside. He pretended to be asleep. He would have left sooner but unfortunately he had to finish checking his references. Anyway, it would be a bore to move into a hotel just for three or four days after leading Signora Calandra to believe that he was leaving for Turin, when all he had to do was lock himself in and make sure of never being alone with Elena night or day, which would be easy enough as her mother was always there.

But the third night he realized with a shock that the key had been taken from the lock. Shortly after midnight, Elena came in. She began kissing and fondling him, at the same time scolding and questioning him. He had not bothered to invent any excuses for his behaviour. He kept his answers vague – he was tired, he had to study, he felt conscience-stricken about Rousset. Elena hotly contested each excuse of his, arguing, entwining herself around him in bed and writhing into a thousand different positions. Emilio felt the boredom of it all becoming steadily more intolerable. Finally he realized that the only way to get rid of her was to make love, and although he had not the slightest urge, he tried. Unsuccessfully. The tiniest movement that he or Elena made reminded him of moments of happiness with Vévé, and the pain was such that it enveloped him completely as if his senses were swathed in bandages, insulating him, allowing him only a chink through which to breathe and every breath he took sought Vévé, called her, wanted her.

Elena, grief-stricken, began to cry. 'But why? Tell me! How am

I different from the other night when you liked me a lot? And now you don't want me at all!'

'I don't know, Elena. I'm tired. Maybe I'm a bit off colour. It's the worry of these examinations, which have suddenly been brought forward. I'll see you at the end of July. You'll be passing through Turin. Rousset tells me that the Golzios have invited you to Gressoney.'

'I don't believe a word you say. I know what's the matter with you. Your girl in Turin has jilted you. That's what it is.'

'Rubbish.'

'Emilio, it's a pity we're in the dark. I'd like to see your face when you deny it.'

'Rubbish, I tell you.'

'Mama told me everything.'

'Your mother can't have told you anything because I've said nothing to her and anyway nothing's happened.'

'No, I worked out what's happened to you by myself. I'm not a medium but I'm almost as good as one. Your girl-friend has dropped you. I could see it in your face. And I can feel it now. You're suffering, aren't you? It'll pass. You're still a baby. It'll pass. Mama told me what you confided in her. She made me swear not to say anything. But you've forced me to.'

Once through the tunnels, the train slowed down. Ready to stop at Sestri Levante. A sudden calm. A cool stillness, delicious – or rather Emilio knew it was delicious without being able to enjoy it – rather like having to breathe through an instrument of torture. A voice cried out in a drawling, Ligurian maritime accent: *'Caffeee càldooo!'*

From the steep mountains behind a blue, transparent shadow lay on the deserted station and the red houses of the little port. On the bell-tower the luminous clock-face paled in the dawn light. Just then the quarter hour struck.

'Caffeee càldooo!': the cry rang out again and again as a small boy ran the length of the train with a steaming jug and a cup-laden tray. Each time a little fainter, each time a little more distant, the cry gradually faded into the deep silence of the early morning.

Life was there – a magic spell, a snare ending in anguish. Sea, sunshine, beaches, the beauty of the world – nothing but remorse.

Because he had lost it all, and would never again be able to enjoy it with Vévé. Of course it might be the same for other people. His travelling companions, for instance – that young woman in black, sleeping peacefully with a curly, fair-haired baby in her arms; that sailor smoking and gazing into space with a blissful smile on his face. Poor people who are, after all, the greater part of humanity have the pressing problem of work and shelter, of starting a family and raising children. But they too know the suffering that love can bring. Perhaps in everyone's life there came a moment like the one he was experiencing. Like a universal, hereditary disease that sooner or later made its appearance and for which there was no remedy; and this thought was certainly no consolation.

He did find consolation, however (the first, and a slight one at that, since he had opened Vévé's letter) when he passed the Giovi, came out of the Scrivia valley and felt that he was in Piedmont.

The neat, square fields, the tall, waving corn, the long, straight rows of trees, the low farmhouses of the Alessandria region, the boiling torrents of the Bormida and the Tanaro, then the first foot-hills around Asti clad in the tender green of the shaggy vineyards – all this in the hot sun and golden haze of May which veiled the Langhe and the distant Alps. A landscape growing more and more like that of his childhood. It was like contact with the land, the land where he was born. A confused promise of consent, of remote resignation. But when the train left Asti, the last stop before Turin, he seemed to awake with a start; the pain began again, he felt his heart clenched in an iron grip. He realized that the long journey, lulling him as a mother's hand rocks her child's cradle for hours, had gradually eased his suffering.

Turin: the train was speeding inexorably towards Turin. 'Torino', the name, the sound which he had thought of thousands of times when he was far away and lonely, whose unique, rich sweetness he had savoured with that accent on the 'i' which seemed to irradiate love and total, indisputable surrender, as if it contained all the mysterious goodness of life, a name dearer than his own, Emilio Viotti, which by comparison was petty and fortuitous. Almost a year! He had never been away from Turin for so long. And now (he realized it as soon as the train moved out of Asti station on the last leg of the journey) now the name Turin had a ring about it that it had never had before, fateful and funereal. It contained not only the good but the bad, too, all that was bad – Vévé in Bianchi-Mina's arms.

Nearly there. Villanova, Trofarello, Moncalieri. Emilio read the names of the last few stations as if hoping to see them changed. It would be a sign that reality had changed for him too. And reality had changed – for the worse, oh, much worse than he imagined or remembered it. It was dusty, sad, puny, yes petty and fortuitous, just as if the whole of Turin had become a kind of Emilio Viotti.

The grey, checkered parallele piped Fiat-Lingotto building, the railway lines, the workshops, the warehouses, San Salvario, Via Nizza, Via Sacchi, the dirty, uniform, weatherbeaten façades, a kind of regimental or pedantic imitation of Paris, a relic of provincial France. What struck Emilio with painful surprise was above all the smallness of everything. Not that the old Termini station in Rome was larger than Porta Nuova. But now as he followed the porter beneath the lofty iron-vaulted roof he realized that, carried away by enthusiasms of memory and nostalgia, he had imagined it even higher, immensely higher and larger.

He had arrived. Turin was cruelly encircling him. Vévé was there, quite near – in a few hours he would be seeing her, a torture he longed for. Outside the station the flower-beds were in full bloom and neatly kept, but the fountain jet rose only to a moderate height, not way up (so he seemed to remember) as far as the eye could reach. The monument to Massimo D'Azeglio stood very small and grubby in the sunshine. To right and left, the quadruple rows of trees, plane trees over towards the Po, limes facing the Alps, flanked the Corso Vittorio making it seem not so long as it really was.

'Is this Turin?' – Emilio asked himself. 'Oh, hope! Oh, love! Is this all? Is this all? . . .' As he gave the porter a tip he looked at his face. It was sad and honest, as square and worn as the façades of the buildings.

His own district had the same effect: Piazza Maria Teresa, the house, the steps, the old housekeeper who opened the door and embraced him, her eyes filled with tears, and Mama who was still in bed and Papa who was coming out of the bathroom and finishing dressing before he went off to court.

His emotion, his people's, even the servant's seemed superficial, a fraud. And family, home, town and the rest, they were all a fraud, since in spite of appearances they had only brought him bad luck. He did not want to talk. He said he was exhausted and needed sleep. He went to his room, closed the shutters and threw himself on the bed. Looking at the old, familiar objects in the light filtering through the shutters – the writing-table, the lamp with its green silk shade, the little bronze bust of Napoleon – he suddenly realized that reality made no sense and love was merely a desperate sham in which men believed because they did not have the courage to see reality as it was: senseless. Reality, life, history, humanity, civilization, it would all end as it had begun – in nothingness. Turin too would return to nothing. Arriving that morning at Porta Nuova, Emilio had noticed on the fronts of the buildings, and even in the spring greenery of the trees, the first symptoms of decay and the inevitable destruction to come. There was only one way to fight it – by forgetting; and he could not forget except by believing, or believing he believed, in love. 'Oh, Vévé, why did you leave me? Why did you put your trust in another man?'

He had not been able to sleep for about a week. Being back in his own bed produced a natural physical reaction and before he knew it he fell sound asleep. He had told them not to wake him, not even for lunch. He slept all morning and all afternoon. And when Mama came in with a bowl of soup and two egg yolks, it was half-past-six. Just time to shave, change and rush to keep his appointment. He must get there before her. He dared not risk her getting impatient at not finding him there and going away. He felt a sudden new pang as he remembered Vévé and how proud and adorable she was. Could it really be over?

He had no guarantee that she would turn up. He was so terrified that she would not come that he had not even asked her to reply and confirm the date. It might well have annoyed her!

He ran out of the house. Children were playing in the square bounded by its rows of horse-chestnut trees; their happy cries mingled with the shrill calls of the swallows darting upwards into the tender-hued sky. The sun had just set. Five to seven. 'Vévé, will you be there?' Children were playing on the mound too, stirring up the dust in the small, round earth clearing.

The three seats were occupied and on the one where they had exchanged their first kiss a tramp with a long, unkempt beard and a shabby old hat covering half his face, was stretched out. But he was not asleep, with his right hand delicately poised in the air he was beating the precise time – two vertical and two horizontal strokes – of an imaginary march. Emilio approached him, unconsciously curious. The tramp was quietly humming the tune of an Alpine regimental march. Emilio remembered the opening words:

> *Tranta sold*
> *sun pà trè lire,*
> *e trè lire*
> *sun pà*
> *tranta sold.*

> 'Thirty sous
> don't make three lire
> and three lire
> don't make thirty sous.'

Every now and then an ineffable smile crossed his purplish lips between the bushy growth of beard and moustache. A strong smell of wine emanated from his person. The neck of a bottle stuck out of a haversack hanging from the iron back of the seat. He seemed happy and Emilio envied him. A quarter of an hour to wait. Emilio went off down the narrow avenue leading to Via San Massimo along which Vévé would presumably come from the office. What would he say to her first? 'I love you, I love you, I love you,' that's what he would say. Now he felt a desperate longing to repossess her. Of course he would tell that he was ready to marry her – against his parents' wishes – and prepared to face the consequences, any modest job, poverty. But would it be enough? She was the one now who attached importance to money, so he would be asking her to give up not just the hope but the certainty of an easy life.

The red trams passed along Via San Massimo, bicycles, people going home from work. Emilio felt that everyone ought to know about his torment and the fact that this was the crucial hour in his whole life. But nobody took any notice of him. The huge burden he was carrying was invisible. It isolated him from the rest of humanity, but humanity knew nothing about it. And if anybody had noticed it, it wouldn't have changed a thing. What can one man do for another? Even a friend? It never as much as occurred to him to go to Piero, Serra or Ferrau. He felt that it was all his fault. He and only he had made the mistake and betrayed both Vévé and himself. To complain and cry on a friend's shoulder went against the grain.

He went back up to the mound. The children had gone. Two of the seats were vacant. The tramp was still there, motionless as if he were asleep. What could he do for the man? Even though drink helped him forget, his life was certainly not a happy one. What could he do for him? Only give him money. That's the only thing one man can do for another. And he realized that if he were rich, richer than Bianchi-Mina, he might stand a chance of getting Vévé back.

It was past the appointed time. A slight half-shadow began to gather beneath the great trees. A pair of lovers strolled slowly along the central avenue through the gardens in the direction of the Po. They clasped each other tightly around the waist, whispering sweet nothings and laughing. Just like he and Vévé had been once upon a time. He sensed that she was there. But not because he heard her footsteps. She was still too far away, coming up the path to the mound. Or perhaps he happened to turn around.

He ran to meet her, his heart in his mouth. She was very pale, perhaps because of the failing light or as an effect of the delicate lilac colour of her new suit. Her 'champagne' crocodile purse was new too, and her matching gloves and shoes. The purse was very expensive – a present from *him*, of course. But her whole outfit was different, as if she had gone up in the social scale and was already Signora Bianchi-Mina. She had a new wrist-watch, too, small but of solid gold and very stylish. Like the solitaire which glittered on the ring finger of her left hand, her engagement ring, of course.

And the first words that he said were not those he intended. Pressing her hand, her big motherly hand, warm, soft, dry (that hadn't changed at least) and clutching it desperately in his for a few seconds, he said bitterly: 'You didn't have to put these things on! Surely you realized that I wouldn't like it! Was it too much to ask?'

In reply she gave a short, frank laugh and shook her blonde curls in the usual old way. Then, perhaps to destroy the impression of hardness that her laugh had conveyed, she leant on his arm as they strolled off together.

At once the gentle pressure of her arm made him forget everything – the laugh an instant before and all the torments he had suffered for more than a week. It was like heaven suddenly opening wide to receive him. The gentle pressure of that arm, and her firm breasts with their fresh, natural perfume brushing against him were enough to make him completely happy.

It was like the first time on the Collina which seemed ages ago. Yes, it was just like the old days. Vévé, something sacred, at his side – a treasure he did not deserve in the slightest. Merely to touch her was a favour beyond imagining, to be received on bended knees.

Oh, but did he need to talk? Couldn't he take no notice, keep quiet and walk along with her leaning on his arm? Still, he made the effort and murmured: 'Where shall we go?'

'What?' said Vévé.

He had spoken so quietly that he had to repeat the question.

'I don't know,' replied Vévé. 'Wherever you like. Do you want to stay here?' she said, looking around.

'It was there,' said Emilio, timidly pointing to the seat occupied by the tramp.

'What was?'

Doesn't she remember, thought Emilio, or is she just pretending?

'There, the first time.'

'Yes? Are you quite sure?' She laughed in a wounding, off-hand sort of way. 'I think it was at the Valentino. It couldn't have been here. It was too near your home. Just think if your Mama had passed by . . . the end of the world!'

'Vévé,' begged Emilio, 'you were nasty enough in your letter. Not now, please.'

'Nasty? I don't think I was. I only wrote the truth. And the truth hurts. The truth is nasty, not me.'

'I know. I know that it's all my fault, but you mustn't . . .'

'Anyway, listen Milio. Excuse me interrupting you. I was very doubtful whether to keep this date or not. But I thought that we must meet once more before, and so . . .'

'Before what?'

'Before my marriage. There's not long to go now. The fourth of July. So I thought the sooner the better. I'm glad to see you but what we have to say to each other isn't pleasant for me either, believe me.'

'Then you still love me?' said Emilio.

'Ssssh. Keep your voice down. Look, let's sit here and talk things over. Even though it's not the same seat.'

Emilio had not raised his voice. He realized that Vévé had hushed him to avoid answering. They sat down and he looked into her eyes, her big blue eyes which just then looked a little bewildered. He plucked up courage and repeated quietly and slowly: 'Tell me. Do you still love me?'

Vévé looked straight back at him but her only answer was a shake of the head. Emilio insisted: 'I want to hear you say it. Why don't you say it? Maybe because you feel it's not true, because you really feel that you still love me.'

'No, Milio, you're wrong. There's another reason. It's this. When you fall out of love, it's a bad thing. It's sad that something like we had has gone. That's all. I thought I put it quite clearly in my letter. But if you must be told – Milio, it's all over. I don't love you any more.'

His eyes suddenly filled with tears. He tried his best to stifle them. Since he had received the letter he had not been able to cry. How he had longed for the relief of tears in the loneliness of his room! But in vain. His suffering had seemed hard and solid, a stone which would not melt, a weight continually bearing down. Perhaps this was why only now the tears were forcing their way out – just when he could have done without them, at that.

The tears began to well up, silently, copiously, to his utter amazement. Weeping and thinking how ridiculous he must look but unable to control his emotion, he gently replied: 'But Vévé, I love you, I love you, I do.'

He savoured the sweet pleasure of simply being with her, sitting on the same park bench in the mantle of darkness, gazing at her through a mist of tears and telling her that he loved her. Finally he dried his tears and came out with all the rest. He admitted that it had been his fault, but he did not even dare to ask her forgiveness. He wanted to tell her what he had decided in the last few days. Now it was up to her. For the moment he certainly could not offer her anything comparable to what 'that other person' might give her. But his affection, life, name were hers. He was ready to marry her. He would take his degree in a month's time. He would get a job immediately. His father had never abandoned hope of him becoming a barrister and had kept a post open as deputy. With his degree, a deputy's salary was not to be spurned. Of course for the first year or so she would have to carry on working at the office. But very soon things would improve. He could make his reputation as a counsel and earn a lot of money. He was not stupid. He had taken his studies most seriously. He knew his subject thoroughly. His thesis was an exceptional piece of work and would be a success. He was prepared to marry her once he had his degree, if she liked. He knew it was ridiculous to have waited till now to talk like this, but he could not help it. And he was quite sincere. Now it was up to her to decide.

While he was talking, Emilio saw that Vévé was looking at him in amazement and, so it seemed, overcome by emotion. In the silence and gloom of the mound, dimly lit through the thick branches by the distant lamps in the gardens, she stared at him in that strange way – a mixture of surprise, pity and sadness. She appeared unable to decide whether to speak or not. She opened her lovely mouth as if to say something, then changed her mind. She stretched out her hand, laid it gently on Emilio's, and kept it there for a long time. Then, still gazing sadly at him she said: 'I could say that you're making a mistake. That you're wrong about yourself. That you think you love me but you don't really. That it's a passing infatuation, jealousy, wounded pride. But I won't say any of these things. I know that you love me. I can see it. And I never thought that you loved me so much, Emilio. Honestly, I didn't. You mustn't blame me for that. You didn't even know it yourself.'

'No, but I do now. Well?'

'Well, I can't marry you now.'

'Why not?'

'I told you. I don't love you any more. You love me, it's true. And if I were with you again, perhaps I could learn to love you as I did once before. But it's impossible now, Milio. Something else has happened. Something else . . .' And Vévé, sadly looking away and staring into the shadows, concluded in a weary voice: '. . . you see, I love someone else.'

Perhaps the pain that Vévé's words caused him prevented him from disbelieving them. It never occurred to him that she might be lying, at least partly. And that sadness, that weariness, her compassionate tone sounded sincere and drained him of all hope. At her last words, he was again overcome by tears. Hunched over, his face in his hands, he sobbed like a little child.

Once more she stretched out her hand and placed it consolingly on his knee. But he was not consoled.

'Milio,' she said, 'don't cry like that. Listen. I told them at home that I would be back late tonight. So that they wouldn't wait up, I said I was going to the cinema!'

'To the cinema with him,' murmured Emilio between the sobs.

'Yes, but so I could see you without any fuss. I had to say that!'

'So your engagement is official, then?'

'I told you it was, didn't I? But don't think about it now. Listen to me, listen.'

Emilio looked up at her: 'What?'

'Perhaps we'll never meet again. Shall we . . . shall we spend one more evening together? I've got until midnight, even one o'clock. Do you want to?'

Emilio felt his head reel. His eyes were misty. Could it be possible? Possible that Vévé had actually said what she had said? In a few minutes, would he clasp her again in his arms, press his mouth to hers, that wide, generous, fresh mouth and once more enjoy the intoxicating power of her kisses, and would he have . . . ? Everything that a moment before had seemed irremediably lost and more absurd than the absurdest dream was really happening? But why? Why had Vévé said that?

'Do you want to?' repeated Vévé as Emilio, torn by sudden desire, remained speechless. 'If you like we'll go. Any old hotel will do.'

But why is she doing it? wondered Emilio, looking into her eyes. And Vévé's big blue eyes looked back at him, but alas with the same expression as before – melancholy, they seemed disheartened, drained of desire and passion. Oh, Emilio knew that later the kisses would change them. But did that count? Didn't what Vévé felt at that moment count more?

Suddenly dry-eyed, all tears spent and with a strange heroic toughness in his heart, as involuntary as it was surprising, he said, still staring at her: 'But do you love me?'

Vévé did not hesitate. And her sad expression remained unchanged.

'No, I don't love you. I simply said that if you like we can be together for the last time.'

Implacable to himself, Emilio insisted: 'And Bianchi-Mina? Do you love Bianchi-Mina?'

'Yes,' Vévé replied in a flash, as if she felt rejected. 'Yes, I love him. I love Ettore with all my heart, and I'm going to be his wife.'

Ettore, Ettore – if only she hadn't mentioned his name. Till then Emilio had not been sure whether he was losing or winning. On hearing the man's name he realized that she would never change her mind.

'So you're coming with me because you pity me?'

Vévé looked away. That must be the answer. Emilio also looked away and, though trembling, said quite firmly: 'I'll only come with you if it's for keeps.'

They came down from the mound, slowly walking side by side towards the river, but this time she was not leaning on his arm or brushing against him.

They had nothing more to say to each other but were afraid to separate.

They went along Via Cavour, crossed Corso Cairoli, slowing down to a crawl as they skirted the river parapet, knowing that the last farewell was near and trying to delay it in the vain hope that something, a miracle, would prevent the impending horror and throw them into each other's arms.

The lights dotted about the great, deep Collina were all there: they twinkled, winked, invited them to love. And they were reflected on the swift, black, murmuring waters of the Po.

When they reached the stone bridge, the Ponte-in-Pietra, they stopped automatically at the corner of the embankment.

'Ciao, Milio,' said Vévé, offering her hand.

'Ciao,' said Emilio Viotti. He still felt strong, a hero. Vévé gazed at him a moment longer. Her eyes were the eyes of a mother. She calmly turned and began to cross the bridge. She walked quickly and her step was as springy as ever.

Emilio again admired the curves that he loved so much, her firm waist, her straight, shapely legs.

She swung her light-coloured handbag, the new handbag, Bianchi-Mina's present, in rhythm with her rapid step. And Emilio had the impression that she was swinging it spitefully for him to see it at a distance – the symbol of her triumphant decision.

She vanished from sight and after a little while he turned his back on the bridge. The immense rectangle of Piazza Vittorio with its rows of equally spaced street-lamps came down to meet him.

VII

✤✤✤✤

Was it the wind that had woken him up? Something, probably a loose shutter, was banging fitfully over on the other side of the *baita*.[1] Or was it the icy cold air piercing the roof through the gaps in the great stones and the beams? Or again, a wisp of hay slipping from under the jacket he was using as a pillow and pricking him irritatingly between his neck and his shirt?

Or a nagging pain which showed no sign of diminishing – on the contrary . . . it was the thought of Vévé that had roused him. Vévé was married. Vévé may not have returned from her honeymoon yet. That night, Vévé might be anywhere.

Piero was lying motionless next to him, wrapped in his blanket. Emilio could not even hear him breathe. Piero was used to sleeping in tents and bivouacs. When they arrived he had kicked open the door and then stood aside to let the last glimmer of twilight enter, and after seeing what he could see, he had exclaimed with a laugh: 'Here's the Grand Hotel!'

Emilio stretched out a hand and groped along the wall in the spaces between the stones until he found the little pocket torch that he had left there.

He sat up, switched it on, and looked at Piero. He was sleeping with the peak of his cycling cap over his eyes, and there was a blissful smile on his thin lips which sent a stab of pain through an already painful wound. It was only after a few moments that he understood why. Piero's smile was the same as the tramp's on the park bench.

He put on his jacket to go out round the *baita* and fix the flapping shutter.

He quietly slid down from the hay and made for the door which he could see in the gloom of the hut without the aid of his torch by the dim light filtering through a vertical crack in the wall.

But there was no moon. The mountain towered up before him,

[1] An Alpine hut.

black and sheer. It was the Col of the White Peaks which they would soon have to climb.

In the dark blue sky the stars flashed closely-packed as he had never seen them before.

He walked round the hut and the Matterhorn loomed up – so huge and isolated that the starlight was enough to reveal it.

The summer, Alpine night, the stars, the Matterhorn, coincided with his anguish but neither alleviated nor even modified it. Rather, they seemed to interpret it as if the horror, the absurdity, the torment were part of them, too. From the moment he had seen Vévé disappear across the bridge swinging her handbag, Emilio had lived with a grey, impalpable veil between himself and reality. He had studied, eaten, slept, walked about the town, passed his examinations and taken his degree – all these seemed automatic, unnecessary actions which concerned him only up to a point. Now, in the mountains, in the icy transparency of the night, the veil had fallen away and he felt as if he knew reality as it really was, objectively – marvellous, of course, but terrible in its senselessness.

For days he had been convinced that he had lost Vévé a second time on account of a senseless refusal. The senseless refusal in his reply: 'I'll only come with you if it's for keeps.' Ah, words, words! He thought – 'Words can even decide one's destiny'. When Vévé had said 'Shall we spend one more evening together?' it was not because she was sorry for him. Vévé loved him!

Consolation is retrospect? More like poignant remorse for having been so egoistic and immersed in his own suffering as not to understand. He had thought about it for days and the longer he pondered, the clearer it became. Instinctively or unconsciously, Vévé had made a last attempt as if to say – 'Now I'll put you to the test. If you want to understand, if you can understand, there's still time.'

But he had understood too late. Only now, when it was useless and Vévé was already married. That evening on the mound in the Cavour gardens, he had not fully realized the extent of his guilt – how much and how long he had wounded the working-class girl's pride, inflamed her inferiority complex, her need for revenge, even though it had taken the form of having to marry a man she did not love, or at least was not sure that she loved.

He fixed the shutter with a stone. He went back into the hut and lay down in the hay by his friend. But sleep would not come. So many things had happened in the last few months! A strange destiny had suddenly crowded the very days when he scarcely seemed to be alive with private and family matters, and public ones, too.

He had taken the rest of his examinations reluctantly and passed them with much lower marks than usual. So his average suffered and he got an indifferent degree.

Uncle Sanfront had been at death's door. He had recovered. But it left him paralysed. On his instructions the will had been read to the family. Elisa was the usufructuary. Cousin Alberto, the Papal count, sole heir. And so Papa and Mama had lost the last hope of an inheritance, even a partial one. As soon as Uncle Sanfront recovered, Aunt Vittoria, the sole heir's mother, set about distributing in advance the so-called *souvenirs* – token gifts that after every large legacy the sole heir sends to the frustrated relations. A kind of symbolical consolation prize. But in this case it was more like a practical joke and also a warning to stop hoping and scheming. Emilio's mother had even received a filigree silver brooch as a 'souvenir' of Aunt Elisa who, though old and ill herself, had never been at death's door. As for the Treasury counsel, of all the personal possessions of Uncle Sanfront, now confined to a bath-chair, he inherited the famous malacca cane. Furious, he had it wrapped in tissue-paper and put away in a cupboard. For the Viottis, it was the end of their dreams. And for Emilio there was no escape. He had to get a job immediately in some lawyer's office. His degree, less brilliant than he had hoped for, would unfortunately tend to determine his first salary.

On June 10, Matteotti disappeared after attacking Mussolini and Fascism in the Chamber, and before he could deliver another speech in which he promised scandalous revelations about the budget. People supposed, people knew that he had been kidnapped, tortured, murdered. But the body was nowhere to be found. Right from the first news of the crime Emilio felt an instinctive urge to read and compare different newspapers, follow the details as they came to light – the evidence, the suspicions, the rumours, the revelations of the judicial enquiry. He had never before been so absorbed in political or public affairs. But it was not the indignant reaction of a civic conscience, but rather an attempt to escape from the desperate self-centred thoughts that tormented him. Nevertheless, for the first time he began to understand what Fascism really meant, as if Mussolini had dropped his clumsy but effective mask to reveal all the faults that people were still loath to see in him – his vileness, his brutality, his vulgar ambition. It was a blow for Emilio, but one which failed to provoke a reaction in him; the revelation of a reality which should have stirred and infuriated him but which instead saddened him, confirming his slave status. His visions of Vévé walking away across the bridge, her melancholy expression, the smile she used to give him, the same radiant smile that she must now be giving someone else, added to the desolation and impotence in the visions conjured up by reading the daily papers from June 11. Rome, late afternoon, the purple sun setting behind Monte Mario, between the swollen cupolas and the huge baroque clouds . . . From the window of a small villa in Lungotevere Arnaldo Brescia, Giovanni Cavanna saw a man run up to the parapet of the Tiber embankment followed by a group of other men. He saw him turn round, harried by his pursuers, and slip down the steps leading to the river port. The man disappeared, the others after him, then they reappeared holding him prisoner and pushed him into a black landaulet waiting nearby. Other eyewitnesses had seen a black landaulet speeding along the river road and inside a man held down by three others, struggling and shouting 'Help, help' . . .

Mussolini spoke in the Chamber about the fate of the member who had disappeared in circumstances mysterious enough to presuppose a crime, and hoped that the culprits would soon be traced. And the honourable member Gonzales: 'So it's true. In Rome, seat of Parliament and during a session of the House, an opposition member has actually been attacked, kidnapped and on the third day after the incident while the chamber is still in session, we do not know whether he will be returned to us . . .'

The black landaulet had been hired from the Tommasini garage in Via dei Crociferi, the garage which supplied cars to the various Ministries . . . The garage attendant said that it had been hired for the Minister of the Interior in the name of Signor Filippelli, manager of the *Corriere Romano*. He also mentioned a tall, clean-shaven man dressed in grey, wearing a disabled serviceman's badge who spoke Tuscan dialect and came to collect the car . . . The landaulet with the five men had been seen at the Selva Grossa at Vico. 'The Selva is so dense and impenetrable that it would take months and months to search it thoroughly.' Emilio read the papers and pictured that wild countryside, the sombre green of those forests. A few months before he had accompanied Rousset on a trip to Lake Vico.

Rousset was enthusiastic about it and spoke of 'masses' and 'tone'. But Emilio, faced with that desolation, and especially the dismal, filthy, desperate look of the sparse villages, the sullen, emaciated faces of the inhabitants, the stillness and silence of the dense woods around the lake, had felt thoroughly depressed . . . The black landaulet had been found in Rome, in Via Flaminia, outside the Tattini garage, covered in dust, the windscreen shattered, the inside littered with twigs and leaves, and bloodstained . . . Dùmini the Tuscan, Putato, Albino Volpi, Pippo Naldi had been arrested. The militia had been mobilized. A popular demonstration on the Lungotevere Arnaldo da Brescia had been dispersed by cavalry troops. Dottor Occhiuto, the judge, had examined two of Dùmini's suitcases and found blood-splattered scraps of cloth, a blood-stained knife, a blood-stained car carpet, a revolver . . . The scraps of cloth had been recognized – they came from Matteotti's trousers . . . the existence of the Tcheka was discovered, the secret Fascist organization which had been set up officially at the beginning of that year. Amerigo Dùmini was Inspector-General, Giuseppe Volpi, chief agent in Milan and link with General Del Bono, Chief of Police . . . At the Pedavena Brewery in Milan Albino Volpi had publicly boasted that he had executed Matteotti . . . Despite all this, on June 26 the Senate, with only twenty-one against, voted confidence in the government.

Even Piero, who now maintained that he would follow Mussolini but reject Fascism, was worried. He said that there was no real proof and it was too early to judge. According to him Matteotti had been wrong, but those responsible for his disappearance even more so. Was Mussolini one of them? Piero swore that he wasn't. And he shook his head obstinately even when Emilio reminded him of the statements made by Finzi and Rossi, and of Dùmini's revelations in prison and the bloodstained scissors that Nello Quilici said he found in Filippelli's car and Filippelli's position at the Viminale and the existence of the Tcheka . . . He shook his head, repeating Mussolini's first words to Parliament: 'If there is anyone in this chamber who has the right to be grieved, it is I,' and his reply to Signora Matteotti. Shortly after the deputy's disappearance

Signora Matteotti went to Mussolini and said to him – 'Excellency, give me my husband's body.' To which Mussolini replied, 'I only wish I could give you back your husband alive. Try not to despair, look after your children and remember that the Government will do its duty.' The hypocrisy of these words was obvious to Emilio. But not to Piero. Emilio repeated what Signora Matteotti had said to deputy Sardi outside Palazzo Chigi when she declined his offer to accompany her: 'Thank you, Baron, I'm sure they won't assassinate Matteotti's widow.' Piero admitted that the crime was a horrible one, but Mussolini had explained this, too, in a speech to the Senate. 'You must realize that the present régime is the result of a revolution won by a party barely three years old whose improvised, unruly formation had not yet been brought under the necessary delicate control.'

Piero was due to leave in mid-September with a mountaineering expedition to the Karakoram range. Imports of American films had grown alarmingly. There was the risk of a grave crisis in the Italian film industry. The documentary on the expedition was a big chance for Piero. True, he had just got married at Christmas and he hated leaving his wife so soon. On the other hand, Nuccia was not expecting a baby, she had her own family and could stay with them temporarily. A big mountaineering documentary in an exotic, unexplored region had always been Piero's dream. He looked forward to it with enthusiasm. He had immediately begun his preparations. Good equipment, he said, had to be assembled gradually, patiently, after a series of test climbs. He persuaded Emilio to go with him on one of them. Emilio told him about Vévé. Piero made a suggestion: 'Come with me on August Bank Holiday. You'll stop thinking about it. Mountaineering is the best cure for this kind of thing. Nothing difficult about the climb. I try to tackle the same kind of difficulties that I'll have to face in India. The climbers and the sherpas will go to the top of the Karakoram. I'll only get as far as the base-camps. Long marches at a high altitude. Like our route. We'll cross from Breuil to Fiery in Val d'Ayas and over into the Gressoney Valley. Two cols in one day, White Peaks and Bettaforca.'

Golzio's villa was at Gressoney-Trinité. Emilio had no desire to see Elena or Rousset again, but Piero's suggestion seemed to agree in some strange way with Signora Calandra's, that after taking his degree he should get Golzio to give him a job. Bank Holiday . . . Golzio would quite likely be staying at the villa. The haversack, the boots, the climbing gear would dispel any suspicion that his visit had been planned. Passing through Gressoney on his way back it would seem quite natural for him to call on the friend of his friend the painter. Amid the ruins of his love-life, worries about money, the future, his career continued to harass him. Indeed he seemed to have energy for only one thing – to give up law and try something else. Oh, to start earning as soon as possible, as much as possible! And Piero approved of this.

He was just dozing off when the little alarm-clock, Piero's latest acquisition, rang.

Piero made the tea. His precise, rational movements which Emilio remembered so well, seemed even more refined now The way he placed the tablet of solid fuel on a stone sheltered from the wind, poured water, immersed the tea-infuser – all with the harmonious, magical grace of a technician.

In the dark the path was barely distinguishable. Dawn was beginning to break behind the col they were making for. The top of White Peaks stood out clearly against the growing brightness in the sky, while the surrounding peaks merged greyly with the pale background. Even the Matterhorn was no longer discernible. In the distance, on the edge of a bluish-shadowed hollow, a long, low, light-coloured building perched in isolation. Piero had told Emilio that it was the Giomein Hotel, and Emilio had concealed his wistfulness. It was all right for Piero – he wanted to get used to sleeping rough, but if only he, Emilio, had a little more money! Money, money . . . but surely it was blasphemous and ridiculous to want money in these circumstances, when life should seem rich and wonderful even to a pauper? What better than to climb a mountain track in silence, following a friend in the cold, dark air that nevertheless seemed to be alive with scents and warmth, an insect suddenly buzzing across their path, a white blossom trembling in the breeze between grass and rock, limpid water lapping on stones, the certainty of sunshine and a fine summer's day?

Emilio felt that if only he could stop thinking of Vévé he would be perfectly happy, so why should he worry about money and a job and the future? But that was it, he concluded: he had lost Vévé through sheer lack of money. He could not live for ever high up in the mountains, or with a perfect friend like Piero. He had to have money.

The path was now a narrow, zigzag ribbon of earth rising steeply between meadows of tough, thick, short grass. The joy should have been in the strain and effort, his mind free of all other thoughts; in the rhythm and sound of their slow, synchronized footsteps, and the way he kept his eyes fixed on Piero's boots in front of him, losing sight of them just before each bend and once he had rounded it seeing them ahead again at the same distance. But why was his heart so heavy? Why instead of Piero's boots, the ground, the flowers, could he see Vévé's laughing eyes just as he used to, sometimes, when he was making love and her face – radiant with a happiness which masked the promise of betrayal? And why, instead of enjoying the warmth and calm strength of his own breathing during the climb and the sharp, intoxicating air at three thousand metres, did he remember Vévé's young breath on his face, the softness of her lips, the taste of her saliva, the warmth of her skin? And why did he have to torture himself with an involuntary and horrible day-dream – Vévé in bed that very morning in a dark hotel room, at the seaside, in the mountains . . . somewhere . . . naked in her husband's naked embrace?

Spare, stunted, scattered between the grass and the rocks, the last larches had disappeared. Now the track was crossing a ridge of earth and rubble. The light had rapidly brightened. Turning as he climbed, Emilio could see the Matterhorn peak sun-kissed and aflame with a brilliant strawberry-red cloak, while the shadow of the mountains opposite, slanting down the rugged rock-face, seemed to fall visibly as he watched.

The last stretch of the track merged into a slippery slope of sharp gravel, a mass of debris dotted with great boulders. Along their bases, in slits and cavities sheltered from sun and wind, there were strips of hardened snow.

Emilio wanted to stop and moisten his lips but Piero insisted that they should press on. He was methodical and inflexible – for every hour's march, five minutes rest. Drinking only during the descent.

They got to the col in a stiff, cold wind and with the sun burning down. On the left, stones and rocks melted into the dirty grey clots of the moraine. The glaciers ended just below, stretching down from

203

the crest of the Teodulo, the Ventina, the humped Rollin – gigantic rigid mantles, shining white in the sun, light blue in the folds or shadows, damasked with motionless patterns, marbled streaks, irregular patches – sharper highlights against the background, sparkling like so many tiny crystals.

On the right, a razor edge rose almost abruptly, vertically up to a partly rocky, partly snow-and-ice-clad peak. The col ran between this peak and the glaciers. Lost in wonder, Emilio found himself gazing at the rough and delicate tapestry of yellow, green, lilac and pink lichens on the rocks nearby. Here was a way to forget himself and his suffering! To forget everything and enjoy the air, the wind, the sun, the effort of scrambling over the rubble making the blood throb in his head and throat so violently that he could almost hear it! To forget everything and enjoy the view across to the distant peaks in the glare of the sun, the blue sky, the white glaciers, or over to the two clefts of the valleys opposite with a lingering look at the shadows, the slopes, the green-brown woods behind, the magic stillness of the emerald meadows and fields far away, the matt cobalt of a small round lake, the grey roof of a remote Alpine hut, the tiny, neat, geranium-hued roofs of a village, the last sign of civilization.

Up there politics seemed to lose all significance; as if the fact that Matteotti's body had not been found, and Mussolini's supporters were still covering up belonged, with all its horror and doubt, to another century. But Emilio's remorse at losing Vévé was as cruelly keen as ever. Vévé could have been there with him now. They had so often planned trips which they had never taken – young, sure of their love, they had lightly put off so many other schemes until some time in the boundless future. Instead, for Emilio at least, the future had suddenly shrunk to nothing and he was locked in a blind alley. The altitude, the air, the wind off the glaciers seemed to attenuate the memory of the brutal details, the bloodstained scraps of Matteotti's trousers and the echo of his cries for help. But not of Vévé's handbag. It was more important than the Matterhorn, it swung in the memory beyond joys and pleasures, hopelessly. And there on the White Heights col, while drinking a tot of rum from Piero's flask and with a last glance before the descent at the Matterhorn and the two deep valleys in the distance, Emilio told himself that it should be the other way round. He should have begun to forget Vévé and continue to grieve for the crime that exposed the shame of Italy.

Leaping, running, they charged down from the col to the Ventina valley. At first nothing but rocks and stones, then they came to rhododendrons. Piero jumped through them, deserting the track. They had to hurry if they wanted to get to Gressoney before nightfall. Once down in Fiery, they had another climb up to Bettaforca, a longer one and another descent. The rhododendrons grew over vast areas in thick, dwarf bushes that crunched beneath their feet. The clusters of scarlet blossoms, the tufted, shiny, leathery little leaves filled the air with a subtle, aromatic fragrance. Piero bounded on ahead and Emilio ran after him, intoxicated. Sometimes his feet plunged into the bushes. Flowers and leaves came up to his chest, brushed his face. He did not seem to be running, he seemed to be flying. The perfume of the rhododendrons, the vigour of youth, an animal sense of well-being – for the first time in more than three months, Emilio was thinking only of what he saw with his eyes and felt with his senses. Mountain medicine, as Piero had predicted, was effecting a cure, if only a fleeting cure that worked by surprise.

Oh, the first meadows with their thick, lush grass, the plots of potatoes and oats, light rust-coloured, tall and waving in the wind; the gentians, the sunflowers, the rustic fences, relics of an agricultural system that had pushed up into the mountains in ancient times, the first, touching sign of civilization to meet fugitives from the inhuman cruelty of the hills, the nomads, the shepherds, the newcomers from other valleys and regions beyond the Alps.

The hollowed-out trunk of a huge fir tree flanked the rectangular fence around one of the orchards. From a nearby spring, water carried in conduits of young pine bark flowed into this trough, a crystal-clear stream that sprayed out at the other end like a fountain before hurrying on its way. And the compact red earth mysteriously acted as a kind of sounding-box to the winding brook, projecting its hoarse, yet sweet gurgle into the shady wood through which it flowed.

'It looks like Robinson Crusoe's island,' said Piero, looking around and laughing after he had drunk the icy water which gushed into the trough from the tree-bark pipe.

He sat down by the gate in the fence on a big stone which seemed to have been put there for the purpose. With his haversack between his legs he began breakfast in his usual precise, ceremonial way – bread, cheese, salami, hard-boiled eggs – offering Emilio half of each.

'You *are* Robinson Crusoe,' cried Emilio, laughing too, delighted with the comparison which suddenly seemed to illuminate his friend's true character. 'That's why you're so keen to climb the Karakoram!'

'Look, I'll tell you something.' Piero was looking at the orchard, the row of sunflowers and the oats gently rustling and rippling in the breeze. 'If I wasn't married and I had the chance of living here alone for the rest of my life, I'd take it. See over there? I'd cut down a few trees and build my house on that rise – with a fine verandah in front.'

'And what about the winter?'

'I'd have a big fireplace, even two.'

'And light?'

'Paraffin lamps. The most up-to-date ones are wonderful, they don't smell or smoke. I've bought two to take with me.'

'And what about food? You could get snowed up here until Easter!'

'I'd lay in supplies beforehand.'

'And what would you do all day?'

'For a start, cut wood, light the fire, wash, cook. Then read all the books I've never had time to read before . . . then I'd take photos, shoot documentaries of mountain life, discover all its secrets. Just think – the marmots! And in April the avalanches! And when I was tired of reading and exploring, I'd just gaze at nature. Nothing better. There'd only be one thing missing – something important, very important. But you have to make some sacrifices to be happy, don't you? And anyway you can't expect a girl to live in the wilderness, if you love her. And if you don't, then you couldn't bear to live in the wilderness with her . . .'

Piero broke off, seeing the smile vanish from Emilio's face and guessing the reason.

'What's the matter now? Got the blues again?'

As Emilio gave no reply, Piero did not press him and went on eating in silence.

When Piero mentioned a girl, Emilio suddenly realized that he had not thought of Vévé for some time and that meanwhile he had experienced a happiness which he had believed lost for ever. Mental pain is different from physical pain, largely because the victim does not want it to stop. Those who have suffered from jilted love or the death of someone near and dear, shrink from a cure as the most miserable of solutions, another rejection of the most precious possession, almost a final betrayal. So Emilio felt no satisfaction at being able to forget for an hour or so. He violently rejected the suspicion that for better or worse, it was the first indication of a future, fatal and complete indifference.

But the indifference returned. There were further hours of happiness and oblivion like crossing the rhododendrons or stopping at 'Robinson Crusoe's' small-holding. Arriving at Fiery, for example; the confluence of the Cortoz and the Verra, the emerald meadows, the ice-cold, invigorating stream where they waded. The climb to Bettaforca. And the little rustic march tune they bawled at the tops of their voices as they descended in unison upon Gressoney:

> '*Tranta sold*
> *sun pà trè lire*
> *e trè lire*
> *sun pà*
> *tranta sold!*'

When they reached Gressoney, the sun had long set behind the towering rock-face of Testa Grigia. The first star twinkled in the velvet sky. The valley was enveloped by a great, cool, bluish shadow. Holidaymakers in knickerbockers strolled on the square. The spell was broken when Piero went up to the bar to order two beers and ask what time the last bus left for Pont Saint Martin. Emilio was looking for the Villa Golzio number in the telephone book.

'Is Signor Rousset there?'

A female voice answered with a gasp of joy: 'Well? Don't you recognize me?'

It was Elena. She told him to come up at once. The last bus? Unthinkable. He must stay the night. Engineer Golzio? The *ingegnere* would be delighted to put him up. So he was in climbing kit, haversack and boots? It did not matter a bit. What about his friend, a cameraman? Bring him along too – there were plenty of bedrooms.

But despite Emilio's attempts to persuade him, Piero declined the offer. Perhaps he was shy, or perhaps he had promised Nuccia to be back in Turin that night. 'You see, I'm leaving in September and I'll be away a long time.'

The bus was due to leave in ten minutes. Emilio went to see his friend off. In the square a group of visitors were arguing about the Matteotti crime. After so many days of doubt and obscurity, at last there was news. Somebody had that morning's paper, the fifteenth of August. Banner headlines announced that Matteotti's jacket had been found. A roadman had come across it in a culvert along Via Flaminia, near Civitacastellana, between Scrofano and Riano. Signora Matteotti had recognized it. There were large blood-stained patches on it. One sleeve was missing – it had been cut off. A *brigadiere* of *carabinieri* found it a little further up the culvert. A new enquiry had been ordered and the *carabinieri* search of the area shifted from Lake Vico to both sides of the Via Flaminia.

Up to the last minute, Piero's melancholy smile from the bus window seemed to reflect the conflict between their political ideas.

'Well, ciao! Shall I see you again before I leave? Another climb, perhaps? It does you good. Just one day, and you already look much better with all the sunshine you've had,' Piero had said shaking Emilio's hand before he got into the bus.

Headlights glaring, klaxon blaring to cleave a way through the small crowd of holidaymakers, the bus moved out of the square, making for the Issime highway. Emilio stood watching it until it disappeared from view. Not in the least surprised, he felt a tug at his heart-strings. It was the same old wound aching again. In the melting dusk the bus had vanished into the distance. Just like Vévé over the bridge. Meanwhile a veil of melancholy and indifference had blotted out the clear, starry sky, the shadowy mountains, the little square, everything.

The day of the climb up White Heights already belonged to the past. The mountain and Piero's company seemed, unexpectedly, to have cured him for a short time, but now everything was coming back to normal.

In the gloom of the night the villa, seen through the lower branches of the fir-trees at the end of the lawn, looked like a white wraith in a phosphorescent glow of superimposed lozenges and triangles; perhaps because of the absence of light there was something sinister and unreal about it. It looked uninhabited. Emilio wondered if he had mistaken the bar-tender's directions and this place was not Golzio's. It was a big Swiss-type chalet – three stories with pointed corrugated-iron roof, wooden *transennas*, crossed beams in the form of a cornice. There was a single light – faint and yellowish, it filtered through thick curtains at the corner-room windows. And quiet, staccato piano chords. He knew enough about music to recognize one of Debussy's preludes. Suddenly he felt his face flush hot.

It was his exposure to the sun all day – 'all the sunshine,' as Piero had said. But he felt it now as a wave of embarrassment and diffidence, and could not rightly see the reason for it. Was it due to his shyness at entering the family circle of a man who could decide his future, or to impatience with himself for having accepted Elena's invitation – Elena whom he didn't like, but who liked him.

During the last days in Rome, the arrival of Vévé's letter had helped him to be sincere with Elena. Now he had accepted her invitation so as not to lose an opportunity of seeing Golzio. Elena might go back to her illusions as she had done the first night, after the table-turning experiment. It was Rousset he had asked for on the phone, of course, not her . . . Yes, Rousset's being there would be his best defence. And anyway, since his only chance of happiness had fled irrevocably, what worse could happen to him? What did he care about Elena, or about deceiving her, now that he had lost Vévé? Steeling himself with his own gloom and the thought of Rousset's presence, he rang the bell.

A servant in white gloves and jacket with gilt buttons opened the door. Old, thin, bent, almost decrepit. A dim light and a strong scent of beeswax. The parquet floor creaked. Here and there little Sardinian mats skidded beneath the feet.

Emilio slipped off his haversack, put it down in a corner and followed the servant. The entrance hall was a large one panelled in cherry-wood, with a grand staircase of the same material.

At the far end there was a door with stained-glass panels. The servant slid it open to reveal a drawing-room in darkness. Almost simultaneously, a door opened and Elena stood there against the light. She ran to meet him, blonder than ever, wearing a pleated tartan skirt and a blouse, a cigarette between her lips. She removed the cigarette, grasped his arms, shook her curls and kissed him impulsively on both cheeks like a cousin. Then she took him by the hand and led him from the half-light into the lounge where Emilio saw at a glance that there were only three people – Golzio, Signora Golzio, and a stout middle-aged lady with bobbed hair sitting at the piano. Rousset was not there.

After paying his respects and having been introduced to the pianist, an Englishwoman, Emilio briefly mentioned his climb to Golzio and then innocently asked about Rousset.

'He's not been able to get here yet. Apparently he's very busy on an exhibition in Switzerland,' replied Golzio with his usual ease. But Emilio caught the glint of a fleeting smile in Elena's eyes which meant . . . what? Emilio did not dare guess.

He knew an instant later when Signora Golzio asked Elena to accompany Emilio. He would like a bath, wouldn't he?

Elena again took his hand and led him along dark corridors. 'I felt that something would happen to me today! How well you look! And so handsome and sunburned in that climbing kit! Why don't you say something? Aren't you glad to see me? It's marvellous, isn't it?' After turning on the tap and fixing the plug she planted herself arms akimbo in the centre of the bathroom and wreathed in steam from the noisily gushing water, exclaimed with a laugh: 'Golzio doesn't know yet, but I've broken it off with Rousset for good. Finished. Aren't you happy? Now you don't need to worry about anything.' She stretched out her slim, delicate hand and stroked him under the chin. 'What's the matter? Haven't you forgotten her yet? Serra told me. She's been Signora Bianchi-Mina for more than a month, right? Come on, think no more about it now. Let me help you undress.' She took off his jacket almost violently, opened his shirt and slipping a hand up under his vest, hungrily fondled the hair on his chest. Then she made him sit on a stool, knelt at his feet and insisted on unlacing his boots.

Emilio experienced a feeling of languor, abandon, of strange, sudden weakness. It was not that he liked Elena or wanted to take her in his arms. It was not that Elena's soft touch made him forget Vévé in the same way that he had forgotten her while he was crossing the rhododendron patch. But he had an irresistible need to feel and show compassion, to make a simple gesture, just place his hand on that radiant, blonde hair at his knee and caress it, caress it as if by caressing her he were caressing himself, as if he were trying to take pity on himself, console himself. At last a balm for his wounded pride – after three months of solitude and bitterness: though un-loving, to let himself be loved.

He hesitated, afraid of another lie, anxious for Elena not to inter-pret a caress as a hint of compliance. All the more so now, since he no longer had the excuse (nor she the obstacle) of Rousset's presence. Then naturally he caressed her, at the same time hastening to salve his conscience. After all what harm was there in it? An escapade, a passing fancy – I'm certainly not swearing eternal love.

After unlacing his boots Elena took them off, one at a time. Even Piero – thought Emilio – yes, I'm sure that even Piero would approve. The sensation of guilt was lessened but not abolished. He did not like Elena, therefore there was absolutely no question of a passing fancy or an escapade and by even thinking so he was lying to himself. Elena was something else to him. She was unfortunately a sham taking advantage of that sudden, vague wave of tenderness towards himself and her – she was an imitation of love, a lie. And the real evil was not in the lie but in the knowledge of the usefulness of the lie. Because he needed Golzio. Golzio could solve the most important problem in his life – a job, money and escape from having to settle for being a second-rate lawyer. Perhaps Elena would be generous enough to recommend him to Golzio even if he rejected her? But if he did not, then he was sure of a much warmer recom-mendation. A trade, then. And he did not know whether it was worth the trouble.

Elena's cool hands peeled off one of his socks and fondled his bare foot. It was a pleasant sensation, like the water in the stream at Fiery.

It was well worth the trouble, provided the 'trade' stopped at a few tender words, a little petting, no more than a show of love. But what if Elena were not satisfied? He would have to go on pretending for as long as he needed Golzio. And when would he have no further need of a man like Golzio? In all probability, never. But was it kind, moral or wise to deceive Elena in this way?

The answer he found to these questions was a comfortable one. He must not exaggerate the gravity of the situation. No question of deceiving Elena. All he had to do was not feign an enthusiasm that he did not feel. And in particular he must not say that he loved her. Trembling, Elena rose to her knees and clung to him. He gripped her with his legs and arms, bent forward and kissed her on the mouth. But she broke free almost immediately, whispering breathlessly: 'No, not now. I must go down. What will they say? I've been up here too long already. Later, love.' She ran to the mirror, combed her hair, applied some lipstick and hurried out of the room.

Later? Emilio had not wanted or even thought of anything more than a kiss. But now he could see that Elena from the start had been planning, longing to make love with him again.

He felt painfully weak. There he was, a guest at Golzio's. At that precise moment he was getting into a steaming bath in the guest bathroom at the Golzio villa. In a brass holder were a large, new sponge and a tablet of pink toilet soap. Thick, soft towels of the same colour lay folded on a chair. He would be spending the night with Golzio, perhaps the next morning as well. He would find ways of entertaining and interesting his host, show off his cultural knowledge and his wit. Every day Golzio launched new enterprises – chiefly industrial projects, then horse-racing, archaeological 'digs' in Asia Minor, an art collection and the *Teatro d'Arte* which he was supposed to be opening in Turin the following year with an international programme of plays, concerts and ballet. How could Emilio possibly turn down an opportunity like this to make his fortune?

If Vévé had not got married, if she had been still waiting for him – all right. But as things were he would be refusing a unique chance to make money simply through being too lazy to feign a degree of passion for Elena. Laziness, laziness – nothing else. He wished Piero were there. Piero would have advised him . . . Piero would have certainly urged him not to lose his chance with Golzio – he had mentioned it during the climb. But what about Elena? . . . Emilio, who always told his friend everything he did, had kept quiet about his affair with Elena in Rome, perhaps because he was ashamed of wronging Rousset. So in any case he could not have asked Piero's advice about Elena.

He thought of his mother and father. He remembered their nightly conversations when as a little boy of ten or eleven he listened to them through the half-open door in the old villa at Rivoli. The enveloping warmth of the bath, relaxing and loosening his weary limbs in a feeling of well-being, became the warmth of the bed he slept in as a child. His thoughts wandered in a hazy drowsiness. And the wall on the right of his bed, on the other side of which his parents talked and talked about the Sanfront legacy as the most important thing in their lives, somehow replaced the wall to the right of the bath with beyond it Golzio and his colossal financial power. Instinctively Emilio stretched out a hand and felt the wall – green tiles, damp with steam. But also wall-paper perhaps a hundred years old, stripes and a turquoise floral design on a yellow ground, so smooth and pleasant to the touch. Beyond that wall, then as now, there was wealth. As he lay drowsily in the bath he seemed to be a child again.

The dinner was extraordinarily frugal and badly cooked. Golzio apologized to Emilio for not offering him wine. He kept none in the house as a matter of principle. The absent way in which Golzio, his wife and the English pianist picked at their food showed quite clearly how uninterested they were in eating. By chance or design, Elena was sitting opposite him and never stopped darting those glances and smiles which back in Rome he had taken for some sort of game, mere flirtation, a social affectation, but the sly significance of which he now understood only too well.

Throughout the entire meal they talked about the assassination of Matteotti. Then they went back to the drawing-room where a blazing fire had been lit. Grouped in a semi-circle around the fire-place they resumed their conversation on the same topic. Golzio and Emilio sat in the centre on a small two-seater divan. The ladies made themselves comfortable in armchairs – Elena on Golzio's right, Signora Golzio and the Englishwoman on Emilio's left.

Golzio had very definite ideas. He spoke rapidly and without gestures; his hands, gnarled and crooked like talons, resting motionless on his knees, his head rigidly turned towards Emilio as if he were talking only to him. His Canavese peasant accent, if you listened for a moment without paying attention to the sense of the words, immediately conjured up a cattle market and dealers bargaining among the calves' glossy rumps. Golzio maintained that Matteotti had been assassinated for one particular reason – because three days before the crime, on June 7, at the last session of Parliament that he attended, he had put a question to the Chamber which was prophetic in a way of what lay in store for him and an indictment of his murderers. Matteotti had asked to petition Parliament

213

for information concerning 'the number of personnel attached to the offices of each Ministry, whatever the form of employment and remuneration'.

Said Golzio: 'Matteotti obviously wanted to unmask the Tcheka just as shortly before he had denounced the illegality of elections held under the shadow of violence. A first-rate man. The only really dangerous enemy that Mussolini had. I'm horrified at what has happened. But I can't say I'm surprised. Matteotti was a Socialist. But perhaps you don't know that he belonged to a wealthy family who originally came from Trento? Owners of large estates in the province of Rovigo. He was a serious, well-educated man. He'd travelled and studied a lot in Germany and England – countries which in their industry and labour are now what we shall be in thirty or forty years hence. Matteotti was a new type of politician for us. He wasn't the usual crooked lawyer or tub-thumping revolutionary like Cavallotti or Enrico Ferri. He was a scholar, an organizer, an administrator. Before being elected deputy he had been mayor of Fratta Polesine and as such was in charge of public finance and education. He had even instituted reforms designed to lighten the burden of direct taxation on the poor. In the Chamber he was a member of the budgetary committee and later the financial committee. His budget report of two years ago was a model of its kind. He was not only intelligent. We've plenty of intelligent men in Italy yet things are no better for it. Matteotti was also, and above all, a defender of justice – unbending, meticulous, tenacious. In his private life, a most modest man. Unfortunately I never met him. I could have, you know. More than once. But you know how it is. When I go to Rome all I want to do is finish my business as quickly as possible and get back to Turin. By the way, do you know what somebody in Rome told me the other day? That every morning before leaving home Matteotti used to ask his wife for ten *lire*. Like any wretched pen-pusher. A Member of Parliament! This modesty was a sign of his strength. They simply had to get rid of him. I, of course . . .' and here for the first time Golzio stopped talking directly to Emilio and turned to Elena, laughing good-naturedly and throwing back his small, round head with its flattened white hair, 'I, of course, had to consider myself his opponent.'

Elena, her head reclining against the back of the chair, listened with interest. Her big green eyes wide open, she gazed at Golzio, a fixed smile on her face, arm poised high behind her head, one hand nestling in her blonde hair, the other holding a cigarette between slim fingers, elbow resting on the chair-arm. In the planned half-light of the room and against the sombre leather of the armchair, she seemed to be posing for a photograph. The turquoise moiré silk which sheathed her slender body appeared to respond to the dancing reflections from the fire-place. Every now and then Elena shifted slightly to get more comfortable in the chair; then the pleats and the watering of the gown changed direction and lustre almost as if her body possessed an independent, mysterious life of its own.

Emilio, too, listened to Golzio with interest but for the moment he could not take his eyes off Elena. Golzio went on.

'I'm not speaking of now, I'm talking about two years ago. If I'd thought that the Socialists had any chance of winning, I wouldn't have hesitated to join them. But unfortunately it wasn't like that and it still isn't. In Italy we're too backward and a Socialist government would be the ruin of the country.'

'What about Russia?' objected Elena.

'Don't talk to me about Russia. I've been there several times, before and after the revolution. It's a country I know extremely well. Now I'm telling you that to bring off a revolution like the Russians did, you need limitless wealth, I mean natural wealth of our own, raw materials. Russia had them and still has, so she was able to mount a great revolution and she did and things are progressing. But it's different for us.'

'Then what must we do?' said Elena. And she crossed her legs with a light rustle of her dress. Emilio suddenly noticed her silk-sheathed stomach, wide and very slightly rounded – just enough to make a contrast with her thin legs and slender arms. It was a new and strange impression, a mixture of sadness and desire, of memories and fancies. Vévé's stomach was different – fuller, her hips more athletic, generous and strong. He wondered whether Elena's stomach could change and be like Vévé's. But why need it be different? As it was, so small, convex, delicate, did it not possess an almost painful attraction of its own? Was it not really the promise of a new pleasure, something in the nature of an offer, an invitation to cruelty? Emilio was surprised that he had not thought of it back in Rome. And he remembered a distant cousin of the Viottis;

cousin Emma who was even thinner than Elena but who had eight children.

'What must we do? Nothing,' replied Golzio. 'Just hope that Mussolini is not too stupid, or else that Fascism fades out soon. Unfortunately, hoping for something doesn't mean believing that it will happen. And then . . . and then . . . as Manzoni says, right and wrong are so often mixed together that it's impossible to separate them completely. As far as I'm concerned, I won't make any forecasts and simply hope for the best.'

Golzio, fearing that he had gone too far in his praise of Matteotti, was now trying to tone it down. Emilio understood and partly out of curiosity, partly to give Golzio an opportunity of exercising greater caution and of appearing less anti-Fascist than he might have suggested, said a little hesitantly: 'Excuse me, *ingegnere* . . . do you believe that Mussolini was at least a party to the crime or not?'

'Certainly not,' Golzio retorted without realizing that his prompt denial contradicted what he had said shortly before – that the Fascists and Mussolini in particular needed to get rid of Matteotti. 'Certainly not. Mussolini may be no Richelieu or Bismark, but he's not as stupid as all that. It would have been an unpardonable error for a statesman to make.'

So Golzio based his exoneration of Mussolini from any part in the assassination not on a sentimental or moral evaluation but on objective, almost cynical considerations. Yet he had contradicted himself for the second time in a few minutes, since previously he had not credited Mussolini with overmuch intelligence.

And Emilio, while ostensibly approving Golzio's every word, realized that such contradictions originated from a deep, hidden vanity, a desire common to all elderly, wealthy men to win the favour of young intellectuals and the future élite by appearing broad-minded, non-conformist, almost revolutionary. In other words Golzio pretended to have ideas far removed from his own deep-seated, genuine ones and which he was anxious to correct and qualify. Wasn't good sense right in the middle? Back to Manzoni and all that?

Shortly after ten o'clock, Golzio rose to his feet. 'I expect you're tired after your climb. I confess that these few days' holiday I've been able to take, I like to get to bed early and enjoy the morning air and the colours of the dawn sky which are always marvellous up here in the mountains. I'll see you tomorrow. I'm returning to Turin about midday. You can stay. I'll be very happy if you stay.'

And, wishing each other goodnight, they all retired to their rooms. Signora Golzio and the Englishwoman kissed and embraced Elena – this was obviously a customary rite. Signora Golzio also complimented her on her dress.

'I've not seen it before. You're enchanting. Where did you get it?'

'In Paris, at Schiapparelli's – you were there too!'

'Oh, of course! How silly of me not to remember.' Signora Golzio smiled wearily. Her bobbed raven hair, her eyes heavily rimmed with black liner, her unpainted lips and a dead white layer of powder made her look like a character in an Expressionist film. She was dressed in a black silk tunic, slightly *décolleté* and set off by a double string of pearls – not very different, apart from the colour, from the one Emilio remembered her wearing at the Sakharoff party. Her manner was tired and listless – perhaps because of poor health, thought Emilio, or it might be a pose, or simply because she was too rich and bored, with no interests in life. She had no children.

The Englishwoman had her hair cut like a man's. She was of medium height, thick-set, strongly built and without a trace of make-up. Her face and powerful fore-arms were olive-skinned. At table and since, she had not said a word. She had simply listened and laughed enthusiastically on the rare occasions when Golzio came out with a remark that could be interpreted as a *bon mot*. She then showed a double row of large sparkling white teeth that were probably false. She laughed again in the shadowy hall as she wished Emilio goodnight. And she shook his hand with a vigour that would have seemed far too manly if she had not been a pianist.

Elena followed her and Signora Golzio up the creaking staircase. From the first step, and leaning on the banister, she turned to say goodnight and gave Emilio a longer and more meaningful look than any before. He responded with an uncertain and rather sad smile.

The guest apartment was on the ground floor beneath the staircase. Emilio went to his room and began to undress. He was tired, and thought he would drop off at once. But he could not stop pondering something strange and depressing – even sinister – in

217

the way Signora Golzio and the English pianist looked and behaved. With the result that Golzio's long-winded arguments seemed to lose their brilliance and cogency – and so did Elena's perverse beauty.

He put out the light. Suddenly Vévé invaded his mind again in all her cruel, rosy splendour, effacing all other images. Vévé, his last thought at night and his first on awaking. Vévé . . . But as drowsiness overcame him, the fragrant expanse of rhododendrons, the brook at Fiery, the Matterhorn glaciers and rock-face strawberry-hued in the first dawn light began to superimpose themselves over his mental image of Vévé. Two lost paradises, the first a few months, the second a few hours away, began to merge into each other. And he seemed to hear again, muted and caressing, the noises which had accompanied him for so many hours of the day – the slow rhythm of their footsteps, the crunch of their boots on the stony path. Again he seemed to see the crumbling ground in a halo of sunlight and wind which he felt scorching his torpid limbs, he seemed to see the stony, crumbling ground or the last clumps of grass just before he trod them down, and, looking up to gauge the distance to the col, took in the steep, rubbly slope and there, against the clear blue sky, Piero's red neck as he climbed steadily, doggedly. How marvellous it was to be up in the mountains! But the same sound of slow footsteps seemed suddenly to grow in intensity, terrifyingly – it was no longer a crunch, it was a dull thudding that became a thunderous roar. Emilio instinctively switched on the light and looked around. He was no longer on the Alpine track with his friend but alone and sitting up in bed in the guest room of the Golzio villa. What he could hear was the sound of other footsteps, just as slow but gigantically amplified, coming down the wooden staircase. His bed was in a kind of recess tucked under the first flight of stairs.

He realized a moment too late that the noise was not caused by the steps of a colossus – too late to jump out of bed and lock the door before it opened quietly and Elena, wearing her dressing-gown, slipped in.

His first impulse was to turn her out firmly and honestly. Saying he was tired and sleepy would have been telling no lie.

'I was asleep . . .' he started to say with a smile. But Elena did not seem to hear him. She quickly locked the door behind her, threw herself upon him and kissed him passionately. Emilio let her do it to gain time. While he limply returned her kisses, he wondered how he could get rid of her without offending her and tried to find something to say.

Despite his cold reaction to her burning kisses, he felt a flush of indignation at the injustice of fate. Why wasn't it Vévé in his arms? And this thought was so strong that he suddenly felt an involuntary surge of rebellion, almost mechanically took her by her thin shoulders and eased her away so as to look in her eyes as if their sparkling green could mirror her mind and the reasons why he did not love her, and suggest at least the first words (always the most difficult) of what he had to say. Oh, there were no reasons. It was simply a fact, a reality, nothing more. All he could tell her was that he did not love her. He felt that it was his duty to do so.

'Elena,' he said gazing earnestly at her, but he spoke a little hesitantly, with no solemnity, imagining that a hesitant and humble approach might temper the harshness of his words – the words 'Elena, I don't love you'. So he said: 'Elena . . . I . . .'

But she, quite oblivious and from his tone not expecting him to say anything important, gaily interrupted him.

'Emilio! Good news for you! Guess what Golzio asked me a moment ago before saying goodnight. Guess. He asked me if you had done your military service or not!'

Unwittingly Elena had touched on the only subject capable of stirring Emilio and had grasped the only thread that remained uncut in his heart. Emilio was dumbfounded. He dared not think about it: 'Military service? And what did you tell him?'

'That your father had you invalided out. It was true, wasn't it? At least that's what you told Mama in Rome.'

'That's right. And why do you think he asked you?'

'Before that he'd asked me if you'd taken your degree. He must have something in mind for you. I heard him talk about the Arts Theatre. Ferrau is to be the director. You might be secretary-general. Aren't you glad?'

And Elena's green eyes sparkled as she looked at him with a mischievous smile on her face. In surprise Emilio slipped his hands from her shoulders. Sleepiness and fatigue had suddenly left him. So Golzio was going to give him a job! Emilio was anxious to get up and discuss it with Elena immediately. He wanted to know what she thought Golzio really had in mind. What exactly he had to offer. Ferrau had always liked him, he was a true friend. But Elena stretched out her slim, delicate hands and began to stroke under his woollen vest, his chest, his hips, his belly, then slowly glided to the foot of the bed, pulled up his vest, bent down and gently brushed his skin with her hair.

'Look at me,' said Emilio, clasping her head and forcing her to look at him. Was it mainly to ward off temptation? Or to discover from the way she looked at him whether or not she suspected what he really felt and thought about her? Did Elena realize that he didn't like her? And would she be satisfied to win merely as party to a deal? To get what she wanted only because he could not refuse Golzio's offer which at the time seemed to be the chance of his life?

'Look at me!'

Elena looked at him for the first time sadly, her eyes dull as if she had heard his tacit, insidious query. And she murmured without mincing words: 'I know you don't like me. But I love you, Emilio. You still don't understand. I've loved you from the first moment I saw you as I never loved anyone before. And whatever happens I'll love you as long as I live. I love you.'

Emilio had believed, had found it convenient to believe, that she felt only the whim of a spoilt, depraved girl. But now suddenly, inexplicably, he was sure that Elena was not lying nor was she under any illusion. She loved him all right. Perhaps she loved him even more than Vévé had ever loved him. She loved him and had probably decided to marry him. Perhaps what convinced Emilio was the simplicity of her words, and in particular her confession: 'I know you don't like me.'

Till that moment he had thought that in Rome Elena had betrayed Rousset for the sheer pleasure of being unfaithful. But instead there had been no real betrayal. When she had fallen in love with Emilio, Elena must have felt perfectly sure of what she was doing. She realized that she had never loved Rousset and did not hesitate to act. And now she seemed guided by an assurance, a determination, an extraordinary faith in her own passion. So she could afford to ignore everything – even the knowledge that he did not like her, the humiliation of seeing him surrender so as to get a job from Golzio, the problem of asking Golzio to give him a job, or rather . . . yes, why not? Struck by a sudden doubt as he looked into Elena's serious eyes, Emilio asked himself whether what she had to ignore was *the easiness* of asking Golzio to give him a job. Yes, Elena might well be Golzio's mistress, or she could have been before. Turin (at least the middle-class part of it) was a terribly gossipy and slanderous city. The talk there always ran the whole gamut of conjecture. That Emilio had never heard any whisper of a liaison between Rousset's fiancée and Golzio was in itself almost enough to rule out the possibility. But the favour that Golzio had bestowed upon Rousset was not easily explained simply by the quality of his painting. Besides which, the ambiguous manner of Signora Golzio and her pianist friend and the obvious show of affection that they lavished on Elena justified even odder suspicions, tinging the original one with morbid complications.

Emilio saw these confused, overlaid thoughts reflected in Elena's eyes together with the revelation of her love and sadness. Once again, as he had done in Rome, he realized that he was free to turn the key one way or the other. This freedom, which then had been unpleasant and annoying, was now monstrous, suffocating – a mountain which would crush him either way. If he rejected Elena he would have the satisfaction of being honest both to her and to himself . . . but he would lose a unique opportunity, he would have to go back to Turin and resign himself to his father's dismal plans for him. If, instead, he stopped analysing his own feelings and put aside his scruples, if he yielded without further discussion to Elena's advances, he would achieve what had always been his dream – to make money free from long, dreary routine – but he would have to accept the situation with all its doubts, including the possibility of a secret relationship between Elena and the Golzios; a sombre future in the company of a woman he could neither love nor even want as a passing fancy, whom he could only admire for her intelligence and beauty and pity for her unhappy passion.

By its very nature, the choice was dreadful. To decide meant to be sorry. In either case the first thing to do was to close his eyes and leap into the depths of a dungeon. The first thing to do? Either push Elena violently away, get out of bed and ask her to leave – then goodbye fair, rich world, goodbye beautiful women of all kinds, theatres, shows, travel, summer holidays, hobnobbing with artists and business men, a world which embraced and at the same time surpassed the world of Uncle and Aunt Sanfront, his cousins and Giorgio Badia, the world that Papa and Mama envisaged for him in the way they had brought him up – goodbye to all that! Or, let his hands slip down from her anxious intelligent face to her thin shoulders, crush her against him and, without a hint of emotion or gratitude, receive her adoring, quivering body upon his. Then goodbye memories of Vévé, goodbye dreams of a humble, full life with a woman he loved, admired and desired, a woman like Vévé would have been, or someone else he might yet find! Goodbye, modest, happy, carefree world to which Piero Giraudo with his friendship had unconsciously initiated him. Goodbye bowls matches, goodbye bicycle rides and mountain climbs, goodbye peace and freedom of mind!

But what if after all it wasn't really the case? What if the choice wasn't so hopeless as it seemed at the moment?

Who had said anything about Elena wanting to marry him? Even she had never said so. Why not take things more easily and see what happened as the time went by? Selling himself? Harsh words, but probably just words. It could well be ridiculous to suspect a relationship between Elena and Golzio, just as ridiculous as refusing a job and even an entire career, a life which seemed ideal, on the basis of a suspicion which after all was merely a trick of the imagination. And this affair with Elena might turn out to be nothing more than a night spent together on holiday, just like his flirtation with Gina in Rome.

'I love you,' Elena repeated slowly in the silence of the night, gazing at him as if she had read his thoughts. 'You love me,' thought Emilio. 'Maybe one day I'll love you, too, who knows? This vague, superficial, sympathetic tenderness that I feel for you and which I feel precisely because I don't love you, might it not be the beginning of real love?' He remembered her belly, softly outlined in its sheath of turquoise silk, the moiré fabric glittering in the reflection from the flickering fire; the slight swell that reminded him of cousin Emma, so painfully thin, who had had eight children.

Yes, Elena's belly now seemed all-important – proof that he could love her and was already a little in love with her. Certainly, if he could eventually love her and was almost in love with her now, there seemed no point in further hesitation. And then (as someone had said) there always came a moment when you had to gamble with life. No advantages or happiness were possible without risk. For a few moments he had felt the urge to penetrate that belly once more as he had done in Rome on that night which now seemed so distant and unreal. A few hours later, Vévé's express letter had arrived and for months and months after, he had thought only of her. He thought of her again now, and a spirit of revenge fanned his desire. 'You will pay for her,' he said to Elena with a kiss that resembled a lingering bite. His tenderness had changed into desperate cruelty.

'I don't love you,' he whispered to Elena and added – honestly as he believed at last – 'but I like you – there!'

But when the loud panting first stopped and the silence was broken by a deep, solemn murmuring from outside, like a mysterious reply, Emilio thought 'Those are the firs, the wind has risen.' And he realized that the previous night at the same time he had been infinitely happier on the hay in the rough Alpine hut.

The station bell at Pont Saint-Martin rang out like all bells in small railway stations, but Emilio instinctively paid it particular attention and felt a thrill as he did so. He vaguely interpreted it as the announcement, both sorrowful and exciting, of an end and a beginning. In the Alpine summer, the early afternoon sun blazed down. The mountains rose on both sides of the wide valley, blotched with crude shadows and blinding light. Over towards the sea and the plain, the sky was white. Emilio thought of the heat that awaited him at Turin. What had ended? What was about to begin?

A few hours before, on the lawn in the shade of the firs, a table with a white and red checkered cloth, and breakfast: Golzio, alone, sitting in a basket chair, wearing a chalk-white panama, was sipping his tea and buttering slices of toast. He jumped to his feet and greeted Emilio with extraordinary vivacity as if he had been waiting for him. He invited the young man to sit opposite him and lost no time in firing questions about his studies and what were his plans for the future. And all the time Golzio looked at him fixedly as though not listening to his answers but basing his opinion purely on the evidence of his eyes. In fact, Emilio noticed that Golzio's eyes were quite expressionless; they were two dots or holes and it seemed impossible to establish their colour. The eyes of a statue.

'What languages do you speak?' asked Golzio as soon as Emilio had finished.

'English and French, fluently. German, fairly well.'

'If that's so, you've more than you need,' said Golzio.

'D'you want me to take a test?'

'You'll soon have your chance, rest assured. I'll expect you tomorrow morning at eleven at 14 Corso Valentino. I may have something to offer you,' and he held out a yellow, gnarled claw.

His farewell to Elena had been a romantic one, almost a vow of fidelity. But from Emilio's point of view, pure farce. Waking up that morning in the bed which had been the scene of his nocturnal exploits, he felt neither love, desire nor even tenderness for her, despite all his ingenious and obstinate efforts to register such emotions.

Elena would have liked him to stay another night and leave for Turin early the following morning. But Emilio had convinced her that he must be in Turin the day before in order to prepare for his key interview with Golzio and especially to avoid the risk of arriving late for his appointment.

Elena walked with him to catch the half-past-twelve bus. At the last moment, she did not hesitate to kiss and hug him in full view of the holidaymakers crowding the little square. And it was just like being officially engaged. True, they had never mentioned marriage but it seemed to Emilio that Elena had deliberately avoided any reference to it, happy in the idea that their passion was too intense to bother about conformist consequences. He had clutched at this romantic nonchalance, which might offer yet another hope of freedom.

Now he was here on the platform of the station at Pont Saint-Martin. Two o'clock in the afternoon on August 17, 1924. He was waiting for the train from Aosta to Turin. The sun scorched down. He put his bag on the ground and sat on a bench. Elena had promised to ring him at home in Turin the following evening to know how his interview with Golzio had gone. The call was her idea. And it served to allay Emilio's suspicions. For if she had an intimate relationship with Golzio she would not need to ask him about the result of the interview.

The station bell rang. When would the train arrive? He would climb on, get to Turin and go home . . . Indeed, something had ended and something was just beginning, if as seemed probable Golzio took him on as secretary of the Arts Theatre! For the first time he came back to the old house in Turin with the definite hope of leaving it for good. He would soon have another house. *His house*. After all Elena was quite rich. At least, her mother was rich. Emilio tried with all his might to recapture that sincere tenderness (yes, he actually thought it sincere) which he had felt the previous night, and the desire stemming from his tenderness. Because he was getting away from her and would not be seeing her for a few days, he gradually began to feel a little affection for her. Although he had left her with a sense of liberation, now she was far away he no longer thought her tedious.

Suddenly the bell stopped ringing. But it was not the train from Aosta arriving. It was one from Turin. Emilio could see the plume of smoke peeping round the bend in the valley and rising against the white sky.

'Train from Aosta twenty minutes late,' said a porter coming out of the booking-office – an elderly man in a black dust-coat and a cyclist's cap.

When the train arrived, the man went to the mail van and collected a package of newspapers. Someone came up and bought *La Stampa*. From a distance Emilio saw the headline in thick black type.

It was what people had been thinking for months. Since the previous day and the news that the jacket had been found, all doubt had been swept away. But seeing it splashed across the front page of the newspaper had quite a different effect, just as the long-expected, inevitable death of a father or a relation always has a different effect when it appears in his face during the last moments.

MATTEOTTI'S BODY FOUND

'25 kilometres from Rome on the via Flaminia, not far from Riano station, behind a fence there stretches a dense tangled wood called La Quartarella which belongs to the Prince of Piombino . . .

'Carabinieri Sergeant Amodio Caratelli was not one of the investigating team. He had been on leave for a few days in Riano and was hunting with a gun-dog in the vicinity.

'Here is Sergeant Caratelli's report:

"Last night while I was on the way home, I passed near the

Quartarella wood and noticed that my dog had disappeared. I whistled several times and heard her barking excitedly in the distance. I went back and found Trapani scratching at the earth. She was panting. I let her carry on for a while, then led her away, puzzled and a little worried. I said nothing to anyone but decided to come back to the place early next morning. At daybreak I set out again. As soon as I drew near La Quartarella my dog ran off into the wood. I followed her. She began to scratch at the same patch of ground as the night before. As soon as I removed the first clods of earth I could smell the stench of a corpse. I dug away with my hands and soon came across a damp, cold body. It was a horrible experience. After scraping aside a little more earth, I saw a dead man's head. There was still some hair attached to the scalp, some portions of the face were already decomposed and fat worms swarmed all over it. My dog began to bark furiously. Terrified, I ran to find the *carabinieri*. I met some patrols led by Captain Pallavicini working under the orders of Commissario Cadolino. They hurried to the spot and cordoned it off. It was exactly eight o'clock."

'The news brought a number of Socialists and a horde of journalists from Rome, as well as members of the prosecution, the examining judge, doctors and experts. Deputies Tonello and Mastracchi have informed Commissario Cadolino that Matteotti had a gold tooth on the left hand side of the upper jaw. And in fact the skull has a gold tooth at the point indicated ... The corpse had been squeezed into a hole too small for it and which had obviously been hastily dug. It was bent double with the feet almost level with the head. One of the experts observed that since rigor mortis sets in very quickly after death, Matteotti's body must have been thrust into the hole while he was still alive.

'As the body was buried so near the surface, decomposition is almost complete. It is stark naked. A large file has been planted in the chest ...'

While reading, Emilio had the impression that the reality of what he was reading about – Sergeant Caratelli's report, the bitch Trapani, the decomposed body, the file planted in the chest – must be the only important reality, the only true reality.

Pont Saint-Martin station (he glanced around every now and then as he read) had become Riano station. The vineyards over at Donnaz were La Quartarella.

And yet when he had finished reading, the first thing that came to mind was the lawn in the shade of the firs, the table with its white and red checkered cloth and Golzio in his chalk-coloured panama sitting in the wicker chair, taking tea, raising his cup, buttering slices of toast with his peculiar yellow claw-hands. Once again Emilio could hear the calm voice, the Canavese peasant accent: 'I'll expect you tomorrow morning at eleven at 14 Corso Valentino. I may have something to offer you.' Freedom was more important than life itself: that was what Matteotti's poor remains said. But what would happen? Would the country rise up? Things were happening in Italy which he would never have believed possible. The sun shone and scorched, the birds sang, the wind soughed through the larches in the little garden next to the station. Emilio waited for the Turin train. He thought of Matteotti's last half-hour – his desperate struggles inside the black motor-car, his torn flesh, his gallant fight for life, the certainty that he would die, a certainty that must suddenly have come to him when he glimpsed beyond the hunched backs and the bestial faces of his torturers, no longer the houses of Rome, mute, inert witnesses of the crime, flying past the car windows but the parched pastures of Tor di Quinto and the deserted landslips of Grottarossa. Matteotti realized then that they would never let him live to testify against them!

If Emilio were to search his heart . . . if he searched his heart and were really honest with himself, how could he expect the country to behave any differently from the way he himself behaved? Of course the crime aroused horror and indignation in him. But at the moment all he could think of was that at eleven o'clock the next morning Golzio would be waiting at 14 Corso Valentino to take him into his employ.

PART THREE

I

He got out of the car at the house and turned to glance at Monticone, uncertain whether to tell him to wait or to come Monday morning at eight as usual to take him to the studio. In the hazy light of a summer dusk, the old chauffeur's hoary profile framed in the window of the dark blue Augusta was the unwitting symbol of destiny – that mysterious force which Emilio Viotti had been trying to escape in vain for some time. But was he really trying? Wasn't he still deceiving himself?

Monticone, one of Golzio's two old chauffeurs, had stayed in Rome for the summer driving the Augusta for Victoria Films. Monticone could easily wait for him to have a bath and change and then take him on to San Giovanni to see Piero. There was no need to hide the fact that he was dining with Piero that Saturday evening. Even if the chauffeur told Golzio there would be no harm in that. Golzio knew that he and cameraman Giraudo were old friends.

But Emilio intended to tell Piero everything that evening. Of course that meant betraying Golzio. And so he instinctively preferred to take a taxi to Piero's and not a studio car ...

'Just a minute, Monticone.' He went back to the car. He had left on the seat a film scenario which on the following day, Sunday, he would have to read and annotate – the film starring the singer that was going into production in a few weeks.

Yes, he would tell Piero everything. Perhaps Piero would advise him to leave Victoria and find some excuse to drop Golzio for good. There were other big companies in Rome which had begun large-scale production – ICI and Scalera, for instance.

And as production manager he had made his reputation since the success of the latest films. Yes, Piero would advise him to break with Golzio. That was probably why he had accepted Piero's invitation, knowing that he was alone in Rome without his wife. Monticone, his cheeks hollow, pale, covered with a thick, even growth of snowy-white beard, the shiny black peak of his cap pulled down over his eyes, gazed wearily into the void before him. He was a man who knew his duty, an old man, like Golzio from the Canavese region, taciturn, loyal, melancholy, a man who never questioned orders, who, if necessary, worked twenty-four hours a day without complaining and obeyed Golzio as if he were God. His transfer to Rome with a sick, elderly wife which meant separation from his son, a mechanic at Fiat, and his grandchildren, his new work and the unfamiliar film background, had aroused no enthusiasm in him. Yet he had been there for four years, from 1931, when Victoria Films began, and never a word of complaint, at least not in the presence of his superiors. He was patiently waiting to retire on pension and go back to Turin. Meanwhile he went on working as he had always worked. His only weakness – when Golzio was not in Rome: he only shaved once a week. This irritated Emilio but he dared not pass any comment. He dismissed him.

'That's all, Monticone. I'll see you on Monday. Have a good weekend.'

'Goodnight, sir.'

The Augusta moved away. And Emilio, with the bulky script under his arm, slowly walked to the front door.

It was an ultra-modern building set among the gardens of less recent villas – a grey, sad cube with lifeless angles, awkward lines, big square windows, clumsy little cement balconies and at the top a terraced roof with narrow cement pillars showing through the foliage of a creeper which looked artificial.

His apartment was on the top floor. He opened the door with his key. The maid, whom he had warned by phone of his arrival, came to meet him, saying that his bath was ready. After all, he was not sure that he would talk to Piero. Or rather he was not sure of exactly what he would say to him, how much he would confide in him and ask his help. It would be a whole series of revelations to Piero. He had never told him that he loved Elena of course. But he had also never told him that he didn't love her.

In order to enjoy the coolness of the bathroom to the full, he had not switched on the light. The room was in restful semi-darkness after the glare and dust of the studio courtyards, the stuffiness of the office, the hours that he had had to spend under the metal roof of Stage Three, as red-hot as an oven.

The window was open on to the garden of the villa next door – tall pines and magnolias. A blue and dark-green light entered with the first damp night air.

He had dismissed Monticone and would take a taxi to Piero's. He smiled at his own weakness. So many stupid scruples, still! He really couldn't think of the words 'betray Golzio' without feeling ridiculous. He was the one who had been betrayed, for all ten years since he had married Elena. Betrayed all the more, perhaps, since he had unwillingly profited from the situation. Unwillingly? Why had he not seen for ten years? He had not seen because it had suited him not to see. A mixture of cunning and ingenuousness, of bad and good faith. That's what he should courageously confess to Piero! For ten years he had obstinately refused to see. And it had taken little Luigi's typhoid fever to open his eyes. Golzio spent hours and hours at the nursing-home, neglecting his work as he had never done before to the great surprise of his family and his employees. And then there was the nurse's mistake when she popped her head out of Luigino's room and spoke, not to Emilio but to Golzio, dozing in the armchair opposite: 'The little boy's calling for his daddy.' At the time, torn with anguish and doubt about the child's condition, he had not given the misunderstanding a thought. It was only later that he began to turn the matter over in his mind. Could . . . could it be some kind of proof?

He began to connect Golzio's regular visits to the hospital and his obvious concern for the child's recovery with a host of tiny incidents during ten years of married life.

He went back over the days in Via Guattani when Elena was served at table before her mother, and both her mother and the maid surrounded her with an aura of mysterious respect. Well now, even if enigmas like that could only be explained by assuming that Elena was Golzio's mistress, still it was no proof.

Was Luigino more like Golzio than Emilio? Yes, he was. But was this proof? The only real proof would be a word from Elena. A confession, of course. A denial would be quite useless. That is why Emilio had abandoned the idea of questioning Elena. He was sure that if it were true, Elena would deny it. Because Elena loved him – no doubt about it. Elena's relationship with Golzio was different, a combination of friendship and habit dating from long before her marriage to Emilio, tenderness perhaps but not love. That the only child of the marriage might be Golzio's when he had none from his own wife, complicated matters. And even more the fact that Golzio was Golzio, one of the richest men in Europe.

For a moment Emilio thought to go and see Rousset who had married an art history teacher and was living in Florence. Emilio had not seen him since. But to mention the subject to him would be painful, ridiculous and useless. Rousset owed Golzio too much not to deny it all.

There remained his mother-in-law. Signora Calandra had left her beloved Rome some years before and retired to Quarà. In a wing of the old castle she had had central heating installed. She lived alone all the year round:

> *come quella Contessa Castiglione*
> *bellissima, di cui si favoleggia*

> like that Countess Castiglione
> so beautiful, of whom are told fabulous things.

Emilio had discovered that at the time of Via Guattani, the indomitable Signora was not sixty but seventy, or almost. Now she must be nearly eighty. And she would certainly stand by her daughter and deny any suggestion of her infidelity.

No, a voice within told Emilio that he would never find material proof and that he must be strong enough to be convinced – that is to say, to believe – that Elena had always been Golzio's mistress without seeking proof. He found it difficult to summon up the strength because he was very lucky to be working for Golzio, because Elena loved *him* and because (and this was the most important reason) he did not love her, had never loved her. Someone who discovers that he is being betrayed by a woman he does not love suffers in only the most superficial way. And when other people know nothing about it, then it only wounds your amour-propre – you lose face to yourself but there is no real suffering involved.

More than ten years later, Emilio still hated Bianchi-Mina. Whereas he could not bring himself to hate Golzio. He still suffered at the loss of Vévé. He could not suffer in the same way for Elena. Elena had deceived him? Oh, but she had done it because she loved him and wanted to marry him. So that he could get a job, so that he could make money just as he had always dreamed.

He did not love her. If he had not seen, it was not only because it had suited him not to see; in any case he could not have cared less. Why refuse a relationship that after all did him no harm? Might as well take advantage of it. Might as well. And he could not complain about Elena. He had no right to accuse her. She had given him much more than he had given her.

Ten years of daily lies. Ten years of habitual bitterness and hypocrisy, a continual farce, petty, sad. Sham attentions. Sham consideration. Sham tenderness. Hand in hand in the darkness of the cinema. His exclamations at the sight of the melting brilliance of the sunsets beyond the Monviso peak from the terrace of their house in Via Gioanetti, Monte dei Cappuccini, Turin; and then the baroque clouds, swollen, highly-coloured, spectacular, of the sunsets beyond the cupola of St Peter's seen from their first flat in Rome along the Lungotevere Tebaldi. When they first went to live in the capital, Emilio spent every Sunday with her and the baby.

'Look, dear! Look, my love! What marvellous colours!'

And when Elena accompanied him on his trips abroad, up to 1930 for the Arts Theatre, later for Victoria Films, their first acquaintance with the cliffs of Folkestone, the vast green expanse of Richmond Park, Paris from the steps of the Sacré-Coeur ... Emilio felt sincere enough in his wish to communicate his feelings to Elena and give her proof of his love, but he was unhappy. And he knew that if instead he had been with a girl he cared for, or even alone, he would have been perfectly happy.

He was deceiving her, of course. He had begun to deceive her from the start. There had been no lack of opportunity. In Turin, with the Arts Theatre – dancers, singers. In Rome, even more – film actresses. But he had been careful to keep it all secret. And never to get involved in anything but passing affairs that brought no tiresome consequences.

Moreover, the care and enthusiasm and above all the time he devoted to his work protected him. In Turin as secretary to maestro Ferrau, director of the Theatre, he had eagerly assumed the heavy burden of administration. Ferrau had been delighted. He was Emilio's friend, he had confidence in him. He had shown instinctive liking for the boy since the early days, right from the Bohemian evenings with anti-fascists and Golzio supporters in Serra's studio. Ferrau was a musicologist, a philologist, a serious, genuine person with more talent for study and criticism than for the task of an impresario which required the shrewd conduct of negotiations, practical energy and the ability to work long, tiring hours. So in 1931 when Golzio retired from industry and enterprise, gave up the Arts Theatre and moved to Rome in order to devote himself almost exclusively to film production, Emilio took over the management of Victoria Films. What had happened? Partly because Golzio's financial and management ideas conflicted with the régime's, partly because his patronage of the arts had become an enormous drain on his resources, there came a moment when Golzio's fortune suffered if not a slump at least a severe setback. At exactly the same time the invention of sound films transformed the cinema, and the Fascist government began to encourage the construction of new studios in Rome. Golzio was clever enough to seize the opportunity. Getting on in years and anxious to limit his business activities, he had come out of the battle with honours of war. Victoria Films was a prestige concern of primary importance in the cinema, but in comparison with the industries he had left behind in the North, it represented only a modest investment. In other words, it was a hobby for the great financier and industrialist in his declining years, a fusion of the useful and the pleasurable, an activity which, being a mixture of culture and commerce, had something in common with his former support for the arts.

Emilio deceived his wife in Rome as he had done in Turin and successfully took all the necessary precautions to avoid arousing suspicion. Yet Elena guessed and suffered in silence. Why? Only in the last few months, after the child's illness, when he had come to accept a secret liaison between his wife and Golzio as almost certain, did Emilio realize that Elena was silent because of her own guilt. Besides the habitual hypocrisy in their married life, the hidden deceit of their relationship constantly came to the surface in little things: the choice of food, clothes, an item of furniture for the house, an evening show. Or the friction would start for even more trifling reasons: an open or shut window, words spoken too loudly or too softly. There were fierce quarrels over the child's upbringing, Elena holding liberal views while Emilio was all for strict discipline. They both instinctively approved the methods which their respective parents had applied to them.

Elena agreed with Signora Calandra's relatively modern, broad-minded ideas, Emilio with the old-fashioned, reactionary views of his father and the aunts. And despite his affection for Luigino, he was conditioned by half-hearted love, intellectual laziness and above by all the urge to oppose Elena. For instance – it was certainly not strong religious faith that had made him insist on Luigino taking his first communion, but because Elena was against it and he liked the idea of seeing the child repeating the long-past experiences of his own childhood; it was pleasant and gave him a sense of calm and justice.

They both loved the baby. But Emilio's paternal love was something far apart from his extreme coldness for Elena, while she, on the contrary, seemed to embrace him and the baby in the same affection. So it seemed. Now, the idea that Luigino might be Golzio's son had retrospectively destroyed this link with his wife in Emilio's heart.

The difference in their religious views was clear, right from the marriage ceremony. For Elena, it had been a rite to which she had submitted with romantic, almost mystical enthusiasm. She did not believe in the sacrament, she only believed in love. Therefore it was love that made the ceremony worth while, not vice-versa. But Emilio, simply because in his heart of hearts he knew he was lying, had tried, at least in the months before his marriage and immediately afterwards, to create an illusion of the contrary, to persuade himself that he loved her, to believe that he was not selling himself for the job with Golzio, to blind himself to the truth in every possible way. And the chief one was a temporary return to church-going. He had been to confession and communion several times. Sincerely, or so it seemed to him, kneeling before the altar he had promised to be eternally faithful to Elena. The gold embroidery on the celebrant's chasuble gleamed, the flames from the tall candles flickered in the bare chapel at the castle of Casalgrasso with its low vaulted roof, small arches and slim pillars of grey stone – Golzio's refined but arbitrary ideas of restoration which were being seen for the first time on this occasion. As he knelt, Emilio tried to relive the excitements of his childhood and early adolescence. At his side, Elena smiled at his devotion with an affectionate and emotional air of superiority – of course she mistook Emilio's deliberate desire to love her for spontaneous passion. In the witnesses' pew sat Golzio, sheathed in impeccable morning-dress, his little, round, silvery head rigidly erect, his face pale and lean, his eyes as always expressionless, looking in no particular direction, just like holes. And this enigmatic image was the one that haunted Emilio's anguished thoughts years later, not the active, bouncing Golzio he saw every day at the Victoria office.

But there was something else, perhaps the most important of all. In spite of everything, for ten years their union had gradually grown stronger and not weaker. It was not a question simply of habit, nor hypocrisy and greed of gain on Emilio's part, nor genuine passionate love on Elena's. It was something else. They had struck up a secret relationship that was morbid and enduring, a constant, inextricable, nightly charade which mollified the squabbles of the day, which overcame the daily difficulties of life together, abolished mutual suspicions, settled the quarrels about the child's upbringing. It was the same charade as the first time when they had interrupted the table-turning experiment and sunk to the carpet clasped in each other's arms.

For Emilio, a brief, sterile, violent pleasure, very different from what he experienced with other women. He participated neither with heart nor mind, nor, so it seemed to him, with his senses. A mechanical function (almost as false as fiction) that he performed as if he were alone.

And as for Elena . . . perhaps Elena enjoyed Emilio's coldness more than anything else! So each time the charade began. And Emilio realized it. Sometimes – by, for example, imagining he was with another woman – he managed to feel and show an exception-ally warm tenderness for her, but Elena did not appreciate it. She was only happy when he possessed her with a kind of detachment and a passive brutality. Naturally, he had not told Piero any of this. Perhaps he ought to, that evening? And then mention his doubts, or rather his inward but unproved certainty, of a long-standing liaison between Elena and Golzio. And afterwards, ask his friend's advice on whether he should leave Elena and Victoria Films. But first he should tell him that he had never really loved Elena as he had loved Vévé. True, he had married her believing he loved her but deep down he had only been guided by self-seeking interest.

It was a difficult and humiliating confession. How would Piero take it? He would be alarmed, upset. For this reason, too, Emilio could not make up his mind whether it would be wise to confide in him. Why worry an old friend?

Sprawled on the evil-smelling leather seat in the taxi, he gazed out of the open windows at Rome on a summer night scurrying past – by now a familiar sight but one which still suggested a continual, excessive preoccupation with the futility and brevity of life, a ceaseless meditation on the baseness of mankind. Unlike Turin, Milan, Naples, Paris and London, each in its own way alive and confident, here it was as if everything – avenues, streets, houses, forlorn lights and deep shadows, groups of men and women trudging wearily along, loitering outside bars, entering or leaving cinemas and restaurants – expressed even in any apparent gaiety, merely a constant, mysterious air of resignation. And when Emilio tried to understand exactly what the aspects or the effects of this resignation were, he thought first of the houses, the *palazzi*, the age-old monuments, embracing past and present – the whole of Rome as it was now, and its architecture, symbol of a decadence more nearly akin to decay.

In the old quarters of the city, between the Oppio and the Esquiline, between Piazza Navona and the Circus Maximus or in the Trastevere district, putrescent sixteenth- and seventeenth-century houses, plebeian or gradually sunk to that level, still survived beside the majesty of the pagan ruins and the durability and rationality of the great Renaissance and Baroque buildings.

Even now, from the jolting taxi as it slipped by the white mass of the Viminal before tackling the slope up to Santa Maria Maggiore, he could see on his right the long, dark cutting lined with decrepit, reddish houses – Via Urbana, the Suburra of ancient Rome. He had passed that way once alone out of sheer curiosity, and another time with a film director and cameraman in search of exteriors and interiors for location shots – the outside of a shoemaker's shop, a short flight of stone steps, a porch, which in the film were supposed to suggest an Umbrian village, the idea being to save the expense of transporting the cast out of Rome. Their visit had been a brief one. From the places that they had earmarked there came such a stench that as production manager he had been the first to abandon the idea of cutting down location costs. And the disgust and pity that he had felt at the sight of the tenants, poor people or – worse still – people numbed by long acquaintance with poverty even though it all belonged to the past, seemed all the more poignant in comparison with the lasting glory of the nearby basilica.

He found a similar contrast, more severe perhaps because it was not only moral but aesthetic as well, between the splendid churches and *palazzi* of the ancient Popes and the houses built after 1870, including the more magnificent and luxurious ones. The various styles – 'Umberto', 'Liberty', even twentieth-century Fascist, had something deliberate, cold, immediately tired and tarnished about them, smacked of importation and imposition, were reminiscent of a kind of building that sprang up in remote colonies irrespective of their surroundings and after a while seemed older than the local native antiquities beside them.

Whether from weariness of life or the difficulty of finding a new one, the architecture of Rome as a whole revealed the approach of death. The twinkling lights, the bustling crowd that Saturday night, even the confused sound of voices with their soft aggressive accent which Emilio could hear as the taxi slowed down at an intersection or stopped alongside a tram waiting for it to move off again, made him think of the useless, chaotic bubbling of a spent volcano rather than of vitality and vigour. And the dictatorship, which at that time was beginning to nurse the idea of a new, counterfeit Roman Empire and seemed to be going on for ever, reflected this sensation of prolonged death-agony and set the seal upon a doom-laden destiny. You breathed dictatorship in the air – the warm, damp air of a July night which came at him through the taxi windows and permeated him with the sickly-sweet clamminess of death.

Emilio was still young – only thirty-three. He would not admit it but deep down he had lost all hope of any kind of change. For Italy change would mean the end of Fascism; for him a small private change would be to pack up and go. His fairly frequent trips abroad, especially to Paris, to fix up arrangements for the more important films requiring the collaboration of foreign producers and actors, compensated in a way for the depression of a humdrum life with Elena, but they also made it worse since every time they raised false hopes that one day he might be able to leave Rome. He would have liked to represent Victoria Films in Paris. He had mentioned it to Golzio. But Golzio was against the idea. If he left Golzio now, he would have to be content with some small-budget production in Rome for another company and there would be no chance of an assignment abroad. He had yet to acquire an international reputation while he did not have enough private money to be independent. Certainly, since his marriage he had lived in comfort and with his future assured. But Elena's dowry had not turned out to be what he had expected. She would inherit the bulk only on Signora Calandra's death. So far, it consisted almost exclusively of the little villa in Via Guattani which the old lady had given to Elena when she left Rome and which Elena and Emilio immediately sold to buy an attic flat in a new block on Via Ruggero Fauro, where they lived, and a small villa in the pine-wood at Fregene, Elena's favourite place. Emilio worked at Victoria for a fixed salary, a very good one but not exceptionally so. Soon, perhaps in a few months if business went well, Golzio had promised to give him a percentage on profits. That would be a great step forward, the first real step towards real money. But for the moment he could not afford to live in style or be too extravagant.

For instance, since he could use the firm's car every day, he did not bother to have one of his own. He lunched at the studios. In the evening he went home and dined at about nine or even later, like all the Rome film people. Then he usually took a walk alone for an hour or two. He varied the route, but his destination was always the same – the Termini station. The idea was to buy *La Stampa* which arrived from Turin on the eight o'clock train and would be on sale only the following morning at the other newspaper kiosks. What a comfort to catch up on the news from Turin every day before going to sleep! Some evenings he went to the cinema with Elena. He would take a taxi home and call at the station, trying to get there before forty minutes past midnight, the exact time when the gates closed unless trains were unexpectedly delayed. More often than not he would walk there alone. At the big old carved-wood kiosk in the station booking-hall, he avidly opened the news-paper and ran his eye down the death notices on the last page but one. It seemed ridiculous to think that someone he knew in Turin might have died without his being informed.

Gradually the habit became a necessity, a mania which could only be explained by the discontent he felt with himself and his way of life. He hated (or thought he hated) Rome and Fascism; at the same time he hated (or thought he hated) the ambiguity of his marriage, the bitterness of the continual hypocrisy he was forced into with Elena, the secret, sad solitude of the nights, his daily subjection to Golzio, the devotion that now possessed him to the idea of financial success, the mirage of great future wealth.

He was dissatisfied with himself. And the Termini station seemed the only cheerful, tolerable place in Rome. The place you could leave from, where trains arrived from a long way off, especially the ones from Turin. Under the high, smoky roof, noisy with the puffing and the sharp whistles of the engines, he wandered about for a long time, mingling with the crowds of passengers leaving and arriving, anxiously scanning their faces, straining his ears to catch the accents of his native dialect, repeatedly coming back to gaze at the signs with the magic inscription: TORINO P.M. – the almost incredible and tear-jerking proof that up there in another Italy, in another world, in paradise, lost Turin really existed.

So he found consolation in *La Stampa*, its black-bordered columns with the dear names of the deceased, all dear to him, even those he did not know, because they were part of home and so obviously Piedmontese!

ORESTE CAVAGNERO
has been taken from those who loved him
The friends of the Perotti café share
Pinin's sorrow for the loss of his mother

TERESA BERTONASCO
After an industrious life

GIACOMO GENRE
(Giacu 'l bergé)
horse dealer
has been taken in the Christian faith
from his dear ones.
The sad news has been given by his wife
Barbara Giacotto, his sons Giovanni and his
wife Francesca Deaglio and Rocco and his
wife Giuseppina Chiambretto.

He had told Piero how much he hated Rome. Piero usually opposed him and defended Rome with greater warmth than the many Romans or long-standing residents whom Emilio met every day at the studios.

It was February 1926 when Piero came back after working on the Karakoram documentary. The expedition had unexpectedly taken more than a year. In Turin Piero had found the film industry in the grip of a serious crisis – few films and low-budget ones at that. He had started work again, carrying on for a few years without much hope of improvement. He had begun to think about going back to his old profession and opening a photography studio when the films directed by young men like Righelli, Genina and Camerini, shot in Paris and Berlin, began to point to signs of recovery. Finally in 1930, 'talkies' arrived and with them new studios in Rome or old ones converted.

Then the capital was invaded *en masse* by all the best film technicians from Turin – cameramen, electricians, engineers, secretaries, make-up artists, film processors, scenario-writers, production managers. They were full of enthusiasm for the sudden rebirth of the cinema. The invention of sound was going to save them from ruin and promised bigger and bigger pay-packets. They quickly adapted to their new home, as always happens when people need work but cannot find it in their old surroundings. In a few months they found it quite easy to replace Barbera with Frascati, the neat parallele piped-shaped workers' houses, the scented meadows of Madonna di Campagna, the clear, cool streams, the snow-clad horizon of the Lanzo Valleys and the solemn Alps nearby with the shapeless outlines of the new district outside Porta San Giovanni between the Cines and the Caesar studios set against the dusty background of the Alban Hills.

'Oh,' thought Emilio, 'they must be able to see the difference too. They must feel how much better Turin is, and be stifling their regrets!' Piero more than all the others, because he missed the bowls matches, the bicycle rides over the changing hills he loved, up and down and along the sloping ridges of the Langhe and the Monferrato with a magnificent view of the vast circle of mountains from the Maritime to the Graian Alps!

But (Emilio continued to reflect, trying to find an explanation for their 'betrayal') the idea of ancient Rome's grandeur and world importance had been implanted in them at school with the words of the *Mameli Hymn*, by propaganda as old as the fatal myth that ended and destroyed the Risorgimento, making Rome the capital of Italy. Now Mussolini, the new, inflated champion of the myth, because he feared the power talkies might have on the people, was encouraging the building of new studios in Rome where it would be easier for the Government to control the type of production, and was thus forcing the industrialists who wanted to make films to come to Rome.

So Rome, Mussolini's plans and Fascism went naturally with the job for the majority of the technicians who had come down from Turin. And with their material comfort and that of their families, too. Till then – Emilio thought – they had probably been staunch Communists or Socialists. They were intelligent people, but simple and honest – progressive old Torinese in the Bersezio style. Perhaps they did not think it right, now they were settled in Rome, 'to spit in the plate where they ate', so pretended not to see the faults and the squalor of the city, not even in the districts where they lived and worked. They tried to forget as soon as they could the Turin that they had deserted. And that was why, when Emilio attempted to mention the subject, they sighed and spoke the name of Turin quietly as if ashamed of a nostalgia which betrayed too much affection: 'Turin, my dear sir . . . ah, poor Turin . . .'

Turin was not in the least poor. But it seemed so to them because they instinctively associated the whole city with the poverty they had suffered those last years before moving to Rome. Of course they knew very well that the total number of film technicians altogether did not amount to a hundredth part of the Fiat employees. But as they belonged to that select band and their merit lay chiefly in the serious way they treated their job, Emilio could not blame them for trying, since they had been in Rome, to forget Turin and love Rome – to think of Rome as beautiful, and Turin as ugly, Fascism as right and Socialism as wrong.

The only thing they would not give up was their dialect, which they still spoke amongst themselves. Emilio recognized Piedmontese or the broad Turin accent and sometimes the slang used by the working-class of Vanchiglia and Madonna di Campagna, and he understood: it was a weapon that the Turin technicians unexpectedly found to hand, and which they did not hesitate to exploit for their mutual aid in a sort of natural, open freemasonry, so as to achieve solidarity *vis-à-vis* the Roman technicians who were less well trained, less good at their jobs but who were on the spot and had to be reckoned with.

Of all the Turin technicians who had come to Rome, Piero was the best, or at least the one all the others considered to have most authority. But that did not prevent his reactions being basically the same as the others'. On occasion he too would sigh: 'Turin, ah poor Turin!' Like the others he drank the wine from the Castelli. He differed from them only in the slightly forced air of gaiety he assumed while drinking, and the exaggerated accent he used in conversation with the local technicians and electricians: '*Mannaggia ... Te possino ... Embè, che tte pija? ... Ma va' a mmagnà er sapone!*' (Roman dialect expletives – 'Well what's the matter with you ... go and eat soap!')

Odd, but his Roman dialect reminded Emilio of Signora Calandra's: jarring, forced, an unsuccessful imitation of vulgarity and violence. And Emilio had a vague impression that Piero put on the *romanesco*, praised and even drank Frascati only when he was present. Just to annoy him. To counter openly and good-naturedly his anti-Roman ideas. And at the same time unconsciously betraying a deep bitterness, a kind of sarcasm or a satisfied acceptance of decadence.

'Come on, drink up! It's Marino, drier than Frascati. Why don't you drink it? It goes down a treat. It's just a question of habit. Frankly if someone told me to drink a glass of Barolo I would do it out of respect but I couldn't regularly every night with my meals. Maybe it's something to do with the climate. Anyway, drink up, drink up!'

And he would laugh. Or he would say: 'It's no good you criticizing our Duce! He can foresee everything and never makes a mistake. He understands Italy and knows how to treat the Italians. But no, according to you Benedetto Croce is more intelligent!'

And he would laugh again. He was satisfied with his new life. He was happy to live in Rome and work. But there was a hint of sadness in his laughter. He liked the wine from the Castelli just as he liked being a Fascist and had supported Mussolini right from 1922 – in good faith but only because he could find nothing better.

Through Golzio's decision, Piero Giraudo had been the first

cameraman taken on by Victoria Films. Emilio, without having to put a word in for his old friend, was delighted at his luck in finding Piero working for the same firm. Piero secured an exclusive contract, a high monthly salary and a bonus for every film. He had come to Rome in the autumn of 1930 with his old mother, his wife Nuccia and little Irma. They rented a third-floor flat in a new block in Via Ardea near the studios. Piero would invite Emilio to dinner two or three times a year, doing so naturally when Elena and the child were at the seaside in summer, or up in the mountains for winter sports.

The two friends, jackets off, sat down to eat in the kitchen. Piero's mother prepared the meal. Emilio did not want to 'upset their routine', otherwise he would not have accepted.

The yellow wine in glasses on the marble table. The stuffed aubergines, peppers, cold boiled meat ... The old mother shaking her white head and saying in her naturally soft, tender voice, rather like a whine: 'Piero always likes boiled meat and I try to give it to him. But the meat isn't like it was in Turin. I hope you won't mind, Monsieur Viotti.'

Nuccia was still a very pretty girl. Plumpish and well-proportioned, a round head, light chestnut hair, blue eyes, small delicate features and a little retroussé nose. She hardly spoke at all, as usual. Her expression had not changed either: still the same fixed smile and mischievous doll-like look. From the first time Emilio saw her, he had suspected that Nuccia was not entirely normal – a suspicion shared by all who knew her. But only latterly in Rome, where the two friends met more often at work than before in Turin, had Piero finally talked about it.

The opportunity came one evening when Nuccia, half-way through dinner and without saying a word, got up from the table where they were sitting with the old woman and little Irma and left the kitchen. She did not come back. The three of them, Piero, his wife and Emilio, had planned to go along that evening to the projection room at the studios to see a new German film which Victoria had bought with a view to dubbing the dialogue or remaking it with an Italian cast. Golzio, who had seen it in Berlin, was doubtful. He wanted not only the experts' opinion but also that of ordinary people like Nuccia, for instance. Now, Nuccia who had agreed to go, suddenly refused without giving any reason. Emilio was not particularly surprised. He thought it must be some trivial worry about her outfit, though Nuccia had very simple tastes and dressed like all comfortably-off, unambitious provincial women. Often a slightly unsuitable dress (or one that is considered so) is enough to stop a woman from going out for the evening! But as they walked to the studios in the warm summer night through the gloom of the ugly, dusty streets, Piero told him: 'Please excuse her. You know, you can't be cross with my wife. She's marvellous, she's a darling but ... but ... it's not that she's mentally ill, of course not, she works hard all day, looks after the baby, does all that's necessary. A perfect mother and housewife! But as soon as she has to do something a little out of the ordinary she becomes inert, apathetic – yes that's it. Then nothing will budge her. We all have a little wheel or two missing or not working properly. Well, she has a rather bigger one. It's the wheel of energy. I never told you. At first I got so angry. Then I became used to it. And now I don't complain any more. If that was all I had to put up with! But I'm sorry tonight about the film show and for you.'

Little Irma had been born in 1928, four years after their marriage. She was seven now. Slender, very pretty, with gorgeous Titian red hair, rosy-pink skin and deep dark eyes which sparkled enchantingly and had an expression combining her father's human, intelligent smile and her mother's, which was sibylline sometimes to the point of stupidity. Like her mother, the child seemed a little strange, but in a different way. Instead of sluggishness and apathy, she revealed an almost frantic mobility and activity. In spite of her parents' and her grandmother's warnings – for they lived in constant fear that she would break the crockery and upset the glasses or, while they were drinking vermouth in the lounge before dinner, that she might smash knick-knacks and flower vases – she never kept still. She never stopped jumping, dancing, singing, laughing, but so prettily as to give no offence. With the passing of the years Irma's vitality had not diminished – on the contrary. Now for example, it had become a problem to get her to eat at table. She would tighten her lips, shake her loose tawny curls, laugh, cry – there was no way of making her swallow more than a couple of spoonfuls of soup. Her grandmother and her mother were at their wits' end. According to them the child was wasting away. She had refused to eat for a month. But Piero remained quite calm. He was convinced that the child was perfectly fit. It was just a fad, nothing more. His advice was to leave her alone. She would eat when she was really hungry. Then Emilio said to the child: 'Do you know that I have a child a bit older than you who's called Luigino?'

Irma, all attention, nodded.

'Well, a few years ago when Luigino was about your age, he decided to stop eating. He became ever so thin and ever so ugly. If you'd seen what he looked like! Everybody said: "Who's that child, he's so ugly and so thin?" And those who knew said: "He's a little boy who won't eat. That's why he's so ugly." Do you want to grow up ugly too? Tell me, do you want to grow up ugly?'

No, replied Irma by shaking her head. She would not open her mouth even to speak. She was probably afraid that her mother might seize the opportunity to pop a piece of meat in. Emilio looked at the little girl tenderly and with a pang of sorrow. He was thinking of Luigino, such a darling, too, so pretty . . . Luigino whom he loved of course. But his image awakened in Emilio the old humiliating doubt and he remembered why he had come – to confide in Piero. Would he have the courage to speak? Saddened, he kept silent and gently stroked Irma's soft, tawny hair.

Emilio always found it pleasant to spend an evening at the Giraudos'. Between the bare walls of their flat he seemed to tread solid ground. The injustice, the hypocrisy, the subtle daily harshness of his own life – all forgotten as if by magic. Even Rome was forgotten. Or rather, during the long hours after dinner around the marble table, cleared slowly by the smiling and silent Nuccia, as Emilio, Piero and the old woman chatted in Piedmontese while through the open balcony window floated the night breeze and a quiet hum from the workers' quarter and the shouts of children out late playing in the street below, Rome became the ideal city in which Piero believed, friendly, safe, full of work and peace. The modest flat in Via Ardea, Piero's home, seemed a blessed place and a hint of that blessing seemed to descend upon Emilio, urging him to relax and forget, to imagine that his heart and his destiny were like his friend's. It always happened when he was with Piero – right from the old times when they used to go on cycle-rides or play bowls – indeed whenever they met and chatted, even if only for a few minutes. And now as the moment approached when they would be left alone at the clean marble table with a flask of Marino and two glasses, Emilio realized all the more strongly how difficult it would be to tell his friend about the sadness and uncertainty in his own life, so different from this normal, peaceful setting.

The child finally ate something, picking at her food. Then there was another little scene before she would go to bed. Gradually the hum coming through the dark blue window-space died away. The lamp shone steadily on the marble table and was reflected in the yellow wine. As usually happened after dinner when Piero was contented, he had begun to describe incidents which seemed almost legendary even though they had taken place a mere ten or at most twelve years before. Since with the advent of 'talkies' the silent film appeared to belong to another age. He spoke of the stern authority of engineer Pastrone, inventor of cinecamera tracking equipment and director of *Cabiria* – of the stinginess of Bartolomeo Pagano, a Genoese stevedore who became famous in adventure films under the name of Maciste, and of the trick a group of Neapolitan sailors played on him during an entire day's shooting . . . Maciste was also producer of the film. He had to shoot a scene aboard a pirate ship and for this purpose hired a large fishing-boat at Porto d'Ischia and got his secretary Minotti to fix a cheap daily rate and promise the captain who owned the vessel that there would be several days' work.

'But the weather was splendid, the sea as smooth as oil. The unit had embarked at dawn and as the light was good we started to shoot at once. One shot after another – you know, making silent films could be quick work. By nine o'clock we were already half-way through the schedule. Maciste was delighted. At that speed the pirate scenes would be finished in one day! It was great for him, but a swindle for the sailors. Now it was still early and a cat had to take part in the action – a black cat which was to share the honours of the scene with Maciste. Because Maciste was a prisoner lashed hand and foot to the main mast, and the pirates were so scared of him that they wouldn't untie him even for his meals. So he had to lap his food up like an animal. What does he do, then? He manages to attract the attention of the ship's cat and finally, with accurate aim and strong jaws, performs the spectacular feat of spitting a piece of bacon fat the whole length of the ship as far as the fo'c'sle where the pirate chief is having his lunch. The fat falls on his plate and the cat bounds like a flash on to the table to grab it. The tureen of boiling soup overturns. The pirate chief bawls his head off. General confusion. On board there's a frail young girl, also a prisoner, but unbound. She's all for Maciste, of course. Taking advantage of the pandemonium she runs to Maciste with a knife and cuts him loose. Maciste singlehanded kills or captures all the pirates and takes over the ship.

'Mario Camerini, the director, had told his secretaries to get hold of three or four black cats. Apparently, for reasons of economy, Maciste had said that one would be enough. Frankly I had seen no sign of one. But Minotti maintained that the cat was aboard when we sailed. Still, everything was ready for the first take and the cat was nowhere to be found. The sailors began to rummage in the hold, calling "Miaow, Miaow!" Nothing. Time was passing. The light was good. A worry for Mario Camerini and an even greater one for Maciste who was thinking of the expense. He started muttering in Genoese that the sailors must be lying. The cat had never been brought aboard and Minotti had been cheated. Then suddenly the sailors said they could see it – peering through the hatches into the gloomy hold they pointed it out to each other or to some of us. "There it is! Down there! Look, sir! Can't you see it! Look at the eyes, those yellow eyes, see?" And they got some ham and meat, went down into the hold and pretended to offer it as bait. "Puss, puss! Come here, puss!" Two or three hours passed in this way. Maciste was beside himself with rage. Of course they never found the cat, it wasn't aboard. And the sailors got what they wanted, another day's work.'

'Piedmontese would never have done that,' said Emilio. 'They'd have haggled obstinately about terms, but once the rate had been fixed they'd have played the game. All a question of different economic conditions, different upbringing! Their lower classes have been humiliated by centuries of hunger. Not us, not even the people. Not so much, anyway.'

Piero always defended the southerners: 'But they've got so many qualities that we haven't. They're more intelligent than us. They love life more. In some distant countries that are ignorant of our civilization – Kashmir for instance – you see very few Italians and they've got a very vague idea of Italy . . . Well, for some strange reason Naples is considered there to be the most representative Italian town. To the Indians "Italian" and "Neapolitan" mean practically the same thing. Once when I fell ill . . . they never knew what it was . . . I had a fever, couldn't eat, walk, work . . . twelve weeks of it. Then, just as mysteriously, I got better. I'd had to leave the expedition. And I stayed those twelve weeks I was ill at Shrinagar, in a little house built on piles. See that photo? Well, he was my landlord.'

On the kitchen wall, between a calendar and a figure of La Consolata, there was a framed enlargement: a turbaned Indian with a jet-black hair-line moustache, sharply etched lips tightly pursed as if to prevent himself from spitting or to stifle an insult, very dark eyes shining with a strange light and a severe, disturbing look – perhaps because they were staring at the camera and so followed the eyes of the beholder. Emilio had often noticed the photograph of the Indian (you could hardly miss it) and knew that it was Piero's landlord at Shrinagar. But it was the first time he had heard the story in full.

'He looks like a bandit, doesn't he? But to me he was an angel of kindness. I owe my life to him. If he and his wife had not been there to look after me . . . Shrinagar is a kind of Venice on a lake and nestling among mountains, with all wooden houses. The boats are very like gondolas and they're rowed in the same way – standing high in the bows, and the same twist of the wrist. I was the only European in the whole town. Some of the natives could speak English. But not in the district where I was. We began with sign language. Then I learnt a few words of their language. They were very nice, very kind. And they liked me so much that they cried their eyes out when I left. They didn't want me to go at all. As soon as they saw that my fever had gone and I was a little better, one after another all the members of the family and the neighbours began to talk incomprehensibly to me, making exaggerated gestures that seemed partly deferential, partly pleading. It must have been the same thing because I noticed that they kept on repeating the same words over and over again: "*Kripya apka gyan ho jaye assalimmia!*" Until one evening . . . I had just begun to get up but was not allowed out . . . two or three of them arrived with someone I didn't know. He knew a few words of English. He bowed respectfully as if I were a man in authority while the others stood around attentively. He spoke with great difficulty: "You, Napoli?" – "No," I said. "Not Napoli, but Torino, Turin." But he insisted: "You Napoli!

Napoli! Italian, Napoli. You sing. You sing." And he opened his mouth soundlessly, miming a singer's arm movements. I calmly explained – "I, no, I don't sing. No voice. I no sing." But he, evidently convinced that I was joking, laughed and said "You no sing? You Napoli no sing?" and shook his head in an amused incredulous way. They all laughed with him. And they begged me again, almost with tears in their eyes: "*Kripya apka gyan ho jaye assalimmia.*" And the interpreter: "Yes, sing, you good, you sing *assalimmia*, Napoli!" You know I can't sing in tune. And to have to sing in public!

'But the landlord and his wife who had been so kind when I was ill, bringing me tea, rice and a basin for me to shave . . . now they took both my hands and would have kissed them if I had let them, and they joined in: "Sing! Sing! *Assalimmia*, Napoli, *assalimmia*!" – All right, I thought. All right, I'll sing. But what shall I sing? I racked my brains but the only song I could remember at the time was an old Piedmontese tune: *Mè ideal*. Because it's a song I've always liked very much and I know it by heart. But it seemed too slow, too monotonous a melody to sing to those people. After all they were expecting a Neapolitan song. Well . . . I managed to remember some of the words and a rough idea of the tune of *O sole mio*. I plucked up courage. But I've never been so shy in my life. I plucked up courage and began:

> *Che bella cosa*
> *'na jurnat' e ssole . . .*

. . . and when I got to the refrain, I could see from all their beaming faces that that was the song they expected, the song they wanted – *assalimmia*, o sole mio!

'And now . . . now I'll tell you something that I've never told anybody. Not even my wife or my mother. I've never said anything because I've been too scared. After *O sole mio* I got into the swing of it. There came crowding back a whole lot of songs that I thought I had forgotten. *Fenesta che lucive, A marechiaro, Funiculì funiculà, Torna a Surriento, Mamma mia che vvò sapé, Core 'ingrato.* Once I had started I could go on. There must have been twenty of them listening in seventh heaven and clapping like mad at the end of each song. That evening I must have sung for over two hours, as long as my strength held out. Then I stopped, I was afraid the fever would come back. The next evening at the same time the audience had doubled. And that's how I started giving regular concerts. During the day I studied, practised the songs. I invented words in place of those I had forgotten. Sometimes they didn't make sense. Of course I always included *Mè ideal* in my programme. I had not been mistaken. It was not one of their favourites. I used to sing it for myself alone. Ever heard it? Forgive me if I sound a bit out of tune.

> *Mè ideal? na casota tranquila*
> *ün bel ni, cun pugieul e giardin:*
> *vive sul, tut l'ann sul, mach cun chila,*
> *ël pi bel, ël pi brau dij ratin.*
> *Beive l'aria che chila a respira*
> *pupunéla parej 'd na masnà:*
> *suspiré quand che chila a suspira,*
> *piuré 'nsema s'a l'é sagrinà.*
> *Va, canssun bela, disejlu tì,*
> *ch'i pensu a chila la neuit e'l dì:*
> *disje ch'i seugnu l'ura e'l mument*
> *'d pudeila cheurvi 'd basin ardent.*

'My ideal? A quiet little house,
A pretty nest, with a well and a garden:
to live alone, all the year round, alone with her,
the fairest, the sweetest of darlings.
To drink in the air that she breathes,
fondle her like a child:
sigh when she sighs,
weep with her if she's unhappy.
Go, lovely song, you tell her
that I think of her night and day:
say that I'm dreaming of the hour and the moment
when I can cover her with burning kisses.'

As he sang, Piero sat quite still, holding his glass, his hand resting on the marble table. His wife and his mother listened happily, at the same time looking anxiously towards the door leading to the passage. Beginning softly, Piero had gradually got louder.
'Hush, you'll wake the baby,' said Nuccia.

253

Piero launched on the second verse very quietly indeed:

> *Mè ideal? Ün ratui, na murfela,*
> *cun j'eui neir e lë sguard assassin:*
> *ün-a cosa da gnente, ma bela,*
> *da pié 'n fauda e mangesse 'd basin.*
> *Furse n'aut, indiscret, a seugn'rìa,*
> *le richësse, la gloria, j'unur:*
> *mi m'cuntentu d'ün poch d'puesia,*
> *d'ün basin, na carëssa, na fiur . . .*

'My ideal? A little charmer, a minx
with black eyes and a roguish glance:
nothing special, but pretty,
so I could take her on my knee and eat her with
kisses.
Maybe someone else would rashly dream of
riches, glory, honours;
I am content with a verse of poetry,
a kiss, a caress, a flower . . .'

It was certainly his favourite song. The words, the way the melody
flowed over a calm barcarole rhythm, perfectly expressed his
deepest feelings, the thought uppermost in his mind, his changeless
interpretation of life. According to Piero life made no sense without
rules, moderation, self-respect; the power to discover one's real
nature from early youth, the clue to personal happiness and finally
the discretion not to seek anything else. That was why Emilio listened so attentively right from the start. That was why he stared,
fascinated, perhaps more so than the audience at Shrinagar, at his
old friend's honest face, its expression as genuine as ever, even
during the unexpected song recital, and that intelligent, confident,
gay smile.
But, at the words:

> *Furse n'aut, indiscret, a seugn'rìa*
> *le richësse, la gloria, j'unur . . .*

Emilio felt a sudden pang, almost a physical pain, and a few moments
later he wondered if the words of the song could possibly apply to
him – if that 'rash someone else' unlike Piero, 'dreaming of riches,

glory, honours', were not he himself. Oh, how could he ever talk about himself to Piero? Wasn't his own life the exact opposite of Piero's? He had jettisoned his own tastes, denied his own nature, deserted a woman who might have made him happy, married a woman he did not love or want, accepted being secretly humiliated by her and continued to accept it. And he went on living in a way he disliked in a city that he hated . . .

And yet, who knows? Piero would probably tell him that it wasn't true. That the tastes he cultivated had always been the same. That deep in his heart he felt a need of money more than anything else, so he had nothing to reproach himself for, he did not have to change. Rome? A fixation. That's what Piero said each time they talked about it. A fixation. Emilio fitted in perfectly there and it wasn't true that he hated it. Elena? Piero, after listening attentively to him, would probably say: 'Another fixation. You think you don't love her but you do. And as for Golzio and all the rest, what proof have you got? Before you act you must have proof. Remember, you're a father. Think of your son, you can't afford to do this sort of thing. You can't leave your wife just because of an impression, a vague feeling, moral conviction. You must have proof.' That was the only answer, the only advice he would get from Piero. He was getting them now, though Piero did not realize it. To understand that answer, to take that advice, all Emilio had to do was to look at his rugged, clear-skinned peasant's face while he sang, and listen to his voice, especially now towards the end of the song, which became irresistibly louder in spite of Nuccia's warning – his strong, throaty voice, the voice of a man used to spending whole days in the open air and talking or shouting across the echoless expanses of field and vineyard.

> *. . . Va canssun bela, disejlu tì,*
> *ch'i pensu a chila la neuit e'l dì:*
> *disje ch'i seugnu l'ura e 'l mument*
> *'d pudeila cheurvi 'd basin ardent!*

On the final top note the door opened and Irma, bare-foot and in sky-blue pyjamas, burst into the room, threw her arms around Piero's neck and began to cover him with warm kisses. Her mother and grandma got up from the table in dismay.

'You see? I told you so! Sing quietly, sing quietly! But oh no!'

'Now we've got to get her to bed again. Well, you can do it!'

Piero laughed: 'But she's doing nothing wrong! Even if she stays up another half-hour!'

Irma was astride Piero's knees and, holding her around the waist, he bounced her up and down, petted her, fondled her, kissed her. At the same time he turned to Emilio:

'There you are. Just like in the song – *Pupunéla parej d' na masnà . . .*'

'*Pupunéla, pupunéla, pupunéla . . .*' Irma repeated it with that oddly cold, conventional laugh which children sometimes affect when they are ashamed of not understanding a particular word and try to cover up by doing what they imagine to be the 'grown-up' thing – to laugh at it. She pronounced the *é* in *pupunéla* open and not closed as her father did, and as it should be pronounced. Although the three members of the family spoke in dialect among themselves, and to strangers in Italian with a strong Piedmontese accent, Irma's speech had a definite Roman accent. After the first two years in Rome, the same thing had happened to Luigino. But Luigino was going to school, while Irma had been attending kindergarten for only a few weeks. The spirit of contradiction is strong in all children. Emilio felt that in Irma it was at its strongest.

How pretty she was, though, with her wealth of auburn curls tumbling about her rosy face and how coquettish her kisses, her laughter, her caresses, her plump little hands as she stroked Papa's lean, rough cheeks. Piero closed his eyes in sheer bliss.

Sometimes Luigino gave Emilio moments like that. But it was a happiness that seemed far less than Piero's! Maybe because a little boy cannot be so tender to a father as a little girl? Or because . . . No. In any case, even if he had been able to love him wholeheartedly, calmly confident that he was his son, Luigino offered no solution – if anything he complicated and aggravated the dissatisfaction and disgust that Emilio felt for himself.

But for Piero it was all very simple. At least so it seemed to Emilio. After being married for about ten years to a pretty but strange, listless woman like Nuccia, Piero, too, had his desires and fleeting fancies and sometimes went off on the loose. More often than not it was some little starlet or an 'extra'. On other occasions he had a quick rattle at the brothel. But it was always strictly functional and he gave it only a limited importance both as regards time and sentimental attachment. Piero would never have let a woman upset his life. It would have been like disowning his 'ideal'.

That's how it seemed to Emilio, at least. Because they were good friends, had been happy in each other's company as children and young men. But in the same way that Emilio had never told Piero his secrets, might not Piero have kept quiet about the most important things in *his* life? It was unlikely, thought Emilio. He never managed to catch Piero off-guard as Piero did with him quite often in moments of absent-mindedness, anxiety, sadness that he could not hide. Even in the presence of others, at a technicians' meeting, or on the set, or in the projection room during an interval between two reels, Piero, if he happened to be near, would stare at him with deep-set gleaming eyes and whisper: 'What's the matter? Anything wrong?'

Emilio had never told the truth. He had never admitted to his friend exactly what was wrong. But perhaps Piero guessed all the same. And this is the most genuine sign of true friendship. No need to talk to know each other. No need even to know to understand, at least vaguely. To feel anything you only have to be fond of each other.

At last the child was quiet, she had gradually fallen asleep in Piero's arms. Now Nuccia took her and quietly wishing Emilio goodnight, she went off to bed and so did the old woman. The two men were left alone. A few moments' silence. Emilio thought he would say nothing. Piero got up slowly, almost solemnly and said: 'Are you sleepy?'

'No,' replied Emilio.

'Then I've got something good for you.' And he slowly crossed the kitchen as if it were as large as a film studio. He went out on to the balcony, disappeared. After a few instants he reappeared with a black bottle in his hand.

'I uncorked it and left it outside in a corner of the terrace shaded from the sun. Genuine Barolo, 1923. Twelve years old. But I've tasted it. It's still perfect. Here. To cheer you up.' He opened the sideboard, took out two glasses and poured.

'To cheer me up for what?' asked Emilio.

The wine flowed gently into the glass and sparkled red, clear, transparent.

'To cheer you up for the Frascati,' explained Piero with a sly smile. 'Try it first. Then tell me your troubles.'

'How did you guess that I wanted to tell you something?'

'It was pretty obvious that you were impatient for us to be left on our own. Had a phone tiff with your wife in Santa Margherita?'

'No.'

Emilio raised his glass and sniffed. The delicately sharp bouquet of old Barolo almost took his breath away and made him forget his doubts. But perhaps that particular, unique perfume reminded him of all he felt he had cravenly abandoned and which now seemed irremediably lost. He sighed and finally found a way to vent his bitterness without having to make a complete confession – a compromise between telling and not telling which might give him a little relief.

'I've been wanting to talk to you for a long time,' he said, lowering his voice and looking round to see if the door to the passage was closed. 'A long time, months and months. But you must promise to be honest with me and tell me all you know even at the risk of hurting me. At the studios I get the impression . . . only an impression . . . the way Olga, my secretary, looks at me in the morning when I arrive alone or in the evening when I leave on my own . . . the way the commissionaires and the head porter bow, too . . . I get the impression that it's different somehow when I arrive or leave with Golzio . . .'

'Well, that's quite natural. They know he's the boss and you're only an employee like them after all.'

'No, you see the difference is the opposite of what you say. Because when I'm alone, I seem to detect in Olga, the commissionaires, the porter, the cashier, the clerks, the girls from editing, everyone an air of absolute respect and devotion. But when I'm with Golzio – mind, it's only a vague impression, I may be wrong . . . I seem to catch the merest suspicion of a snigger.'

'You're crazy. And what is this snigger supposed to mean?'

'A lot of people envy my position, especially some of the old hands. You told me so yourself. When I joined, Campolonghi was furious and went around telling everybody that Golzio had been unfair and stupid to put me in charge of Victoria. That he should have chosen him or somebody like him, Negroni, Curioni, Meille – one of the older film-men. That I would make Victoria bankrupt inside a year. Well, everything went fine. But Campolonghi and the others hate me even more. That's why somebody's started a whispering campaign . . . that Golzio is my wife's lover. You promised to be honest with me. I want to know if you've heard these rumours.'

Piero hesitated. 'Who . . . who told you about it?'

'I can't tell you,' replied Emilio.

It wasn't true, of course. No one had mentioned anything of the sort. It was a last-minute ruse, an excuse to bring the subject up. But he knew that he would never have the courage to go on, to admit that he had the strongest reasons to fear the worst. And the mocking sniggers of Olga and the others, the commissionaires' low bows were also pure invention unsupported by any signs or suspicions that the Victoria staff knew about a relationship between Elena and Golzio, but prompted by his fury a few days after the revelation at the nursing-home which ever since had made him look for confirmation, visual evidence, final humiliation in the world around him.

'Well, I'm sorry you can't tell me who told you. Is he a friend of yours?'

'No,' Emilio replied instinctively.

'Is he at least someone you feel you can trust?'

'No idea.'

'Do you know him well?'

'So-so.'

Then Piero raised his voice, his peasant's voice and said with a violence that he could hardly control: 'He must be a liar and a rat.'

'Why?' Emilio's suspicions were aroused by Piero's indignation against the unknown reporter. Piero had hesitated and taken some time to answer. The violence was an attempt to cover up. It looked as if the story he had invented had happened to score a bull's eye. Perhaps there really was talk about Elena and Golzio at the studios. And in spite of his promise Piero would not tell him.

'Why a liar and a rat?'

'Because if there had been any rumours flying around I would certainly have heard them. They know we're good friends but not that we've been friends since childhood. In any case my assistants would have told me. It's envy, slander, filth – you'll find it everywhere. Don't tell me that's why you've been looking so glum these days! Just fancy that! Listen, Emilio, let them talk, it's obvious they haven't got anything else to do.' He stopped for an instant to fill his glass and took the opportunity of gazing more closely at it, looking up at it with his deep-set intelligent eyes. A flash of pain in that glance where Emilio saw as much fear as affection. Piero concluded: 'Is that all you're worried about? Don't make me laugh!'

But Emilio, closing his eyes and pretending to concentrate on the Barolo, wondered what the reason was for the fear he had seen in Piero's eyes. He thought: he's afraid for himself and his job as chief cameraman at Victoria. He knew how keen Piero was on security in his work. He remembered how he had suffered when he came back from Karakoram and had been out of work for some time. He was able to live on his savings for a few months, however. Lately he would often refer nervously to his contract with Victoria which was due to expire in a year's time and which Golzio was in no way obliged to renew. Giraudo was one of the best Italian cameramen, if not the best. As long as films were made in Italy he would always be sure of a job. Yet he was never entirely free from anxiety. Although Emilio had not been the one to get him a post with Victoria but Golzio himself, for purely personal reasons he could not like the idea of Emilio leaving the company.

Emilio had never thought of this before on the many occasions he had wondered whether to confess to his friend. It had just occurred to him on seeing that look of fear. He did not dream of blaming him for that, even inwardly. He knew and loved him too much not to forgive him. Anyway, Emilio was so uncertain himself! How could he expect impartial advice if it meant advice against Piero's interests? It was not even a question of right or wrong. Emilio did not want to know where his duty lay. He was merely trying to decide which of the two solutions would bring him greater or less happiness – whether he should carry on as before, adapting himself more and more to that painful, humiliating state of mind, ambiguous even in his affection for the child, accepting a gradual, sad hardening of his conscience; or whether he should rebel, breaking with a complex of ingrained habits which had their own sweet delights, facing a new life, lonely, uncomfortable, maybe unlucky.

'You think it's a laughing matter,' continued Emilio after a long pause. A mosquito buzzed mournfully in the silence of the kitchen. Through the window came a fresh breeze and the distant sounds, diffused and stifled, of wireless sets.

'I say it's a laughing matter because this is only malicious, slanderous gossip.'

'But suppose there were some truth in it?'

'What do you mean?'

'What I say.' But Emilio did not have the courage to look at his friend. Instead he stared at the Barolo in his glass.

'You can't answer questions like that. What nonsense! Fancy thinking such things and all because some rotten character was nasty enough to come and tell you a load of rubbish.'

'Then you're sure you haven't heard anything of the sort at the studios?'

'I've said so, haven't I?'

'Then . . .' still without looking at Piero, Emilio managed to control a slight quiver in his voice, . . . 'then – swear it.'

'What do you mean, swear it?'

'Yes, swear it. Swear it on . . . on Irma.'

Piero said nothing, then shrugged his shoulders: 'I'll swear to you that you're an idiot!'

'Then you won't swear! You can't swear!'

'You're an idiot! Have you ever heard me swear on oath? I've never sworn on oath in my life except to the King when I joined up and to the priest when I got married. I'll not swear a damn thing to you!' And he got up and went out on to the terrace.

'Then I believe that you won't swear because it's true and because they've told you something . . .' said Emilio without moving.

'Believe what you like. I've got nothing to say. Let's understand one another. I told you quite clearly that I've heard nothing. But I did not swear it because I don't like swearing on oath. It's not the sort of thing that civilized people do, and friends even less. Isn't my word enough?'

'It's enough, it's enough,' muttered Emilio, lighting a cigarette. It occurred to him that they had never quarrelled and they had never been so near to quarrelling as at that precise moment. It also occurred to him that Piero did not smoke. It was the only thing about him that he did not like. Who knows, thought Emilio, if Piero smoked he might be franker with me, he'd tell me what he knows and thinks.

Against the black of night and the vague grey of the apartment-houses opposite he could see his friend's back, shirt-sleeves and his scraggy red neck as he stood on the balcony. The hair was beginning to thin on top of his head. It was still slightly curly, the same light chestnut colour as when he was a boy.

Now Piero slowly turned. He was smiling and scratching himself with one hand inside his shirt. He strolled back to the table.

'You angry? I'm sorry.'

'No, I'm not angry,' replied Emilio, suddenly sad.

He had looked at the time. He would have to leave shortly otherwise he ran the risk of finding the station closed. Once he had bought *La Stampa* he knew how the evening would end. Ten minutes' pleasure. And then?

Piero said: 'It's been very hot today. Since it's been hot, I've got something itching here on my chest, a little red spot like a mosquito-bite . . . Sometimes, specially at night, it drives me mad . . . I don't know what it is . . . maybe my liver.' He sipped a little wine and resumed his train of thought which had apparently been disturbed by the itching, and continued in his characteristically honest, down-to-earth way: 'I know what *you* need.'

'What? What do I need in your opinion?' asked Emilio, surprised and curious.

'Well, it's not easy for you or for anyone to find it. And you can't always find it by looking for it.'

'What is it, Piero?'

'You need to fall in love! What you need is a true, sentimental love . . . You're too much of an egoist.'

At this Emilio looked up and met Piero's eyes, smiling and sparkling with that old, faithful, affectionate friendship. So Piero was even fonder of him and more intelligent than he seemed! Because, without a confession from Emilio, he had realized that his friend's real trouble was not so much Elena's betrayal as the fact that he did not love her or anyone else for that matter.

And that was it. He had not loved since he had gradually stopped loving Vévé. Piero had put his finger on it. His advice was the only one to follow. And Emilio appreciated this, not by reasoning but from the just severity that he had detected (and continued to do so) in the word *egoist*.

Yet for the moment he kicked against it. He felt his eyes brimming with tears and his voice choking. In an attempt to make an impression on Piero he slipped into dialect: 'Me an egoist? Why do you say that? What harm have I done to others?'

'None! You've probably done more harm to yourself than to others.'

'Then why egoist?'

'Because . . . because you think too much of yourself and because . . . listen, forget it and let's finish the Barolo.'

He leapt out of the taxi. The station gates were still open. *La Stampa*, at last! The death announcements, the local news . . . From the familiar print, the particular texture and colour of the paper, its very smell, rose a vision of distant Turin as it must be on that July night. Probably close and hot; the stars barely visible in the mist; but the gardens, the parks, the meadows, the vineyards on the Collina, beyond the river, and especially the woods towards Mongreno and Superga were bound to be wet and cool and luxuriant. On the way up to the Hermitage along the old road from the Fontana dei Francesi to the inn where he and Vévé had bought the cherries, at a certain point you always meet a breeze from the Alps blowing through the Susa Valley Gap.

Yes, Emilio would have liked to go back, start life all over again. But he did not believe it was possible. And that night, before oblivion in sleep, there was something that compensated for everything. The next morning there would be oblivion in work, the whole day till evening! He looked at the time. If he wanted, he could ring Anna Serventi, an extra who would put him up in her little flat in Via della Croce, even without more notice, as long as she was alone at the time. But wait a minute, Saturday night past midnight, not much chance of her being there. The brothel was a better bet. He already knew the girls at Grottino, Avignonesi, Capo le Case. He had yet to make the acquaintance of the one at Cantanella Borghese. He jumped into a taxi. Ten minutes later he was in the suffocating heat of the small pink lounge where a clutch of semi-nude beauties minced around swinging their hips or sat about inert and exhausted. He knew some of them, others not. He saw at once that he would have to look no further. There was Baby, Liliana Bresciana and a new girl, or at least one he'd never seen before, small, good figure, rounded, neat raven hair, big, dark eyes, beautifully shaped lips.

An egoist? All right. But as Piero had admitted he did no harm to anyone but himself and was easily satisfied. The small girl's name was Corinna. She was Tuscan, judging from her accent. She wore a sky-blue slip which threw into relief her perfectly round bottom. Breasts without brassiere, high, large. And she was draped in a transparent white chiffon cape.

'May I? I want to feel,' said Emilio slipping his fingers under the chiffon.

'Perhaps you'd better feel up in my room.'

'Just a second.' He wanted to feel the skin on her hip. Corinna let him do it. 'Let's go,' Emilio said finally.

All he had to do was to take his mind off things; work, sleep, make love and think of Golzio, Elena and Luigino as little as possible. Now Piero's advice began to seem absurd. Now he could not understand what need there was to fall in love.

The chiffon cape was poised delicately on the coathanger. Corinna's skin was not only as fine as satin. It was brown. *Naturally* brown as Emilio discovered, removing her slip and not finding a single part of her body lighter in colour. He pushed her against the bedside table. In a distant mirror he could see by the red glow of a lamp on the floor their two silhouettes, naked, upright, and writhing in a sort of dance-on-the-spot, the man leaning further and further forward, the woman further and further backward as she gripped the table.

There were no problems just then. Finally everything was going as it should.

II

Every morning, even in summer, the narrow avenue which sloped gently down to the administrative building lay in the shade.

The commissionaires had just watered the asphalt. Arriving at the office Emilio always hoped that his working day would be different – a fresher, tidier day. For those first ten minutes he pretended to himself that a film producer's job was different from what it really was – less confused, less chaotic, less hazardous, more like any other trade or profession.

As usual he flew up the stairs three at a time. The two secretaries, Olga and Lauretta, and the production supervisor, the omniscient and omnipresent Martini, were waiting for him on the landing. An obsequious trio, they smiled down at him from the shadows, each preparing some flattering remark.

Martini, his big oblong face tanned by twenty years on location, flashing his gold teeth and spectacles, tried to make his morning greeting as hearty, cheerful and reassuring as was necessary to inspire Emilio with boundless confidence. Technical difficulties, actors, actresses and directors throwing temperaments, vagaries of the weather, a delivery of Kodak film delayed by customs red-tape or damaged on arrival, the unfinished script, the bit-players complaining that during yesterday's fight scene they had ruined their dresses and they wanted compensation, the extras claiming 'meal allowance' or two hours' overtime pay, the insurance company refusing to recognize a three-day work holdup caused by the star's illness . . . Emilio could leave it all to him, rely on his experience, his loyalty, his affection, yes, his affection; because he loved him like a son or a younger brother, he had been the boy's first guide and mentor in the jungle of production. And he who had worked with Pabst and Murnau, Pommer and Nebenzahl, at UFA and Paramount would never let him down! Anyway, he had only one ambition, to collaborate with a big Italian producer now that a big Italian producer really existed, and to make good films.

Martini was honest. He could not fail to be since his private interest was so closely allied with Victoria's. Still, every day he had innumerable small, secret opportunities to 'rob the till', to make money out of Victoria and no danger of being discovered. Confidential verbal deals. Martini and the *other chap*, a small contractor, rapidly agreed what to charge Victoria and Martini got his cut. Emilio had realized this from the beginning. He knew that if he wanted to, he could easily catch his faithful colleague with the golden smile red-handed. But what good would it do? Anyone capable of replacing him would be no more trustworthy. Might as well keep him and pretend to trust him, almost trust him, and finally behave as if he did – be moved by what he said, return his affection, think of him as a true friend. Piero, his real friend, was not very enthusiastic about this. He had known the old supervisor for many years and continually warned Emilio: 'Watch out, Emilio. Martini's an old fox, he'll take advantage of you. Watch him!'

But it was so nice to find him there each morning and wallow in his sham devotion. Sham but genuine at the same time – an inextricable mixture of lies and sincerity. Yes, Emilio felt that just because Martini was shifty and naturally treacherous, he deserved every consideration, a kind of affection. As if Martini's treachery justified his own, or at least lightened the burden. He was the most convenient accomplice even if the complicity existed only in the imagination. For Emilio would never have robbed Golzio or anyone else save himself; but it was his self-betrayal, the theft of the finest, most precious feelings from his own heritage, his deep humiliation that made him almost instinctively recognize Martini as a brother. Sometimes he seemed to be fonder of him than of Piero, who presumably had never betrayed anyone or bribed his own conscience.

Martini was a Lombard from Lodi. He was always boasting about it and made it obvious as often as possible in his speech. According to him, in Roman film circles his Lombard origins were an extremely rare (if not unique) guarantee of combined intelligence and honesty. You couldn't help laughing when he talked of 'honesty' and you saw his sheepish expression. Emilio laughed, too, but he persuaded himself that it was only because he liked Martini.

Emilio's relations with Lauretta and Olga were not, on the whole, very different. Lauretta was from Turin, Olga from Rome. Both were twenty, blonde, blue-eyed and pretty. Lauretta, pale, slender, sunken-cheeked, hollow-chested, a voluptuous image of weak abandon. Olga, plump, domineering, intelligent, her eyes sparkling with perpetually repressed laughter which seemed to hold a promise of happiness.

Without one knowing about the other, he had gone to bed with both of them and continued to do so from time to time, trying to alternate them and thus correct the chance element in these liaisons. It had happened and could always happen again, rapidly, with no words spoken. The first occasion in each case had been late one evening, in the same way and in the same place, when he had stayed behind in the deserted building to dictate a memorandum. As soon as the work was finished, a caress on the ruffled curls, the hot, damp cheeks, an almost paternal (and to begin with almost unintentional) caress, but then immediately a kiss, a long kiss – Olga, clasped round her firm, plump waist and dragged to the leather settee reserved for discussions with the more important guests, foreign producers, top-ranking actors and directors; Lauretta, on the other hand, thrown down with a show of brutality on to the fitted carpet, half-way between the polished mahogany desk and the metal legs of the typist's table, her skirt pulled up to reveal her simple, plain under-clothes. And their blue eyes, Olga's gleaming blue-enamel eyes, Lauretta's languid, watery blue ones, had looked at Emilio for a few moments with a pretence of love that could be deceptive since it made much of the sincere anxiety behind a whole confused range of questions: 'What's the boss going to do now? Will he expect me to break it off with my boy-friend? Does he want me to be his steady girl? If I insist, will he make me an actress? Or will it just mean a small rise in pay?'

As it turned out Viotti's intentions were honourable in their way – a purple patch of passion with Olga, a hint of romance with Lauretta, just a little fun, nothing more. There had been no rise, but presents from time to time – a gold wrist-watch, a crocodile hand-bag, a compact, silk stockings, and, to avoid rousing a family's, or a fiancé's suspicions, a few five-hundred lire notes . . . Olga worked in production, Lauretta in distribution and foreign relations. They were two good secretaries, nice girls who, like so many of their class, worked not because they needed to, but because they wanted their independence or, perhaps even more, the chance of being in a world that would otherwise be closed to them – a world which promised a lucky strike to any girl who was neither stupid nor ugly: a marvellous marriage to a millionaire or a star, or a more modest marriage (but secure) to a technician or to someone in production.

So Emilio felt in sweet, feckless harmony with Olga and Lauretta. He made a pact with both, a pact as valid as it was implied – he would help them to find the best husband possible and they in return would give in to him now and then without making a fuss.

The trio, after receiving him with the usual obsequious smiles in the dim light of the landing, followed him into his office where Giggi, the commissionaire, had finished tidying up and was lowering the Venetian blind on the sun-drenched forecourt and the dust grey palms over towards Stage 1. The other window near the entrance was wide open and a cool green light flooded the large, low-ceilinged room with its bold flowered wallpaper.

'Good morning, Signor Emilio,' said Giggi, 'excuse me, I'll be back at once!' And he hurried off with broom and duster, and a meaning look at the clock which showed that it was not yet half-past eight. Giggi went well with the trio both in his obsequiousness and his shifty devotion. He was generally slack and lazy but not with Emilio, even less so if possible with Golzio. A lightning provider of *espresso* coffee, he overcame all obstacles in his rush to the studio restaurant and back to the office; if there was a queue at the bar he would use his authority and march to the front. 'Management!' he would order, an unaccustomed frown on his face. And while he waited, he stared at the barman without so much as a glance or a word for the crowd of bit-players, technicians, assistants, cutting-room girls standing around.

At Victoria the chauffeur Monticone, representing Turin, was as serious and discreet as any *carabiniere* – and never expressed an opinion on the private life of the management, while Giggi, a Roman of the old school, represented Rome and naturally tended to interpret maliciously what he knew nothing about or only partly understood. For instance, he had very probably known all about the boss and Lauretta and Olga before anything started between them. He would bring in the coffee, the cigarettes or whatever. One of the two secretaries would be at her typewriter or ensconced in the armchair by the desk with her shorthand pad at the ready. Giggi would indicate to Emilio that he was in the know by means of a glance or a hesitation in his step, or, more simply and perhaps more effectively, by half-closing his eyes as he walked from the door to the desk and back. Emilio caught the drift – it was impossible not to. And maybe Giggi's sly innuendoes had given the *coup-de-grace* to the last Turin scruples about correct conduct in an office ('one doesn't do such things') which for some time had restrained him from stretching out his hand and stroking the blonde hair of his two secretaries. If other people, if Giggi himself, thought that he was 'poking' them, then he might as well do it.

Of the two Giggi preferred Olga, and he would have liked her and not Lauretta to be the boss's favourite. Quite understandable, as Olga was Roman too. But Emilio was not sure whether the man was trying to help the girl or to make something out of it himself. It was infinitely easier for dear old Giggi to get along with Olga, whose mentality, perhaps even her family and relations, he knew, than with Lauretta who had only just moved from Turin. To obtain any advantage from Lauretta he would be forced to speak, to blackmail her openly, and nothing was further from Giggi's intentions and habits. To make it clear that he was aware of the situation, well disposed and always ready to do a favour, that was all right, provided, of course, that the friendship was accepted and one good turn deserved another. Olga's attitude to Giggi was the same almost from the beginning. They understood one another. Emilio's only fear was that some time or other Giggi would tell Olga about Lauretta. But once, when the two secretaries were both standing by his desk, Giggi, with a few meaning looks, managed to reassure and convince him that he had nothing to fear. And Emilio showed his gratitude by pulling strings in local government through the head of the Film Division (who happened to be a *Moschettiere del Duce*) and getting Giggi's wife a licence for a meat stall at the market in Piazza Melozzo da Forli.

Giggi left the office and Emilio sat at his desk. Martini handed him the daily expense sheet, Lauretta and Olga their folders of correspondence awaiting signature since Saturday evening. Emilio looked at the silver-framed calendar between the ink-well and Elena's portrait - it was July 15. After that first time, he had seen Corinna again three or four times in one week. And during the day he had often thought of her but without worrying about where she might be. He knew where to find her at night. But now he was beginning to worry. The 15th.

As he opened Lauretta's folder and started to sign, it occurred to him that the date marked the end of a 'fortnight' in the brothels and he remembered Corinna's answer once, when in the enthusiasm of the moment he had asked her where she was going next. 'I'm taking a month's rest at a hotel in Viareggio. But if you want to come and see me . . . it'd be nice, wouldn't it?' He hadn't asked her the name of the hotel. He had let it pass, mumbling that he was very busy. Now he thought about it again. He toyed with the idea of a trip to Viareggio. He only had to ring the brothel. He would later, about noon. He made a note in red pencil on his pad – an enormous C full stop which stood for both Corinna and *casino* (Italian for brothel). He knew what his day would be like – in the mass of discussions, telephone-calls, appointments, he might forget. And if he couldn't manage a short visit to Viareggio because of pressure of work, well, he'd try to keep Corinna in Rome for another week, or perhaps at a *pensione* in Ostia or Fregene, and go to see her every evening. So long as she didn't ask for too much money! Viareggio, if he could get away, would certainly be much cheaper. But simply because it *was* cheaper, he liked it less. Through going with prostitutes, or for some other older, deeper reason which escaped him, he had gradually come to associate money closely with pleasure. Enjoyment meant spending. The more he spent, the greater the enjoyment. But as he disliked the idea of spending, so for him the joys of love were mixed with pain.

A beautiful woman who did not sponge on him seemed almost insipid. He looked forward to marvellous nights of giddy delight alone with Corinna (a week or so his prisoner!) chiefly because he knew that the cost would be exorbitant. He pictured her small, tawny body, lively and so perfectly proportioned that in his mind's eye it seemed bigger. The same sort of thing happened – he thought – in the case of some Venuses, masterpieces of classical sculpture, when you look at photo reproductions.

Corinna, he mused, closing Olga's correspondence folder, and reaching for the costing schedule which Martini had put on the desk – Corinna, 'the little giantess'. And, anticipating the pleasure which would certainly be his if he took the trouble to organize himself (ring her at the brothel, rapidly get her to agree, book a pair of rooms at a hotel, ring her again for confirmation) he suddenly felt quite light-headed.

Meanwhile Martini brought news – he had seen Annunziata. Annunziata had been sitting at the bar since seven o'clock, at work on a draft of the script, drinking coffee and chain-smoking. He told Martini in strict confidence that he had been up all night rewriting the entire script. Annunziata was a middle-aged director who had had a certain amount of success in Berlin. Victoria had given him the film about the singer. It was a commercial production dealing with the career, at first beset by various obstacles, culminating in final triumph, of an opera-singer who came of humble parents, only daughter of a waiter at a second-rate café in Venice. The waiter, now old and tired, had spent all his savings on singing lessons for his daughter. His anxieties, hopes, fears as he followed her difficult road to success in a great opera-house formed the substance of the film. The script had been written by a young intellectual recently engaged by Golzio. Emilio had spent Sunday reading it and found it excellent in its way. But he knew that Annunziata did not share his opinion and wanted to make radical changes.

Annunziata, who had been called by Martini, looked in at the far door.

'Signor Viotti,' he said, 'here I am.'

He walked in confidently and sat down in the armchair near the desk. He was in shirt-sleeves, grey trousers, glossy black silk tie and white cotton gloves.

'Why the gloves?' asked Emilio. Annunziata explained that he had been in the cutting-room trying to match Toti Dal Monte's sound track to the screen-tests of the three actresses in the running for the role of the singer. But Emilio knew that Annunziata had been in the bar till then, so the gloves were part of a childish piece of décor to impress the young man, the lawyer, the dilettante, the greenhorn in the cinema.

Annunziata started by attacking the script. There was no life in it, no verve, no . . . no heart, that was it! As he said 'heart' he contracted his thick, black, sleek eyebrows as if he were about to burst into tears and laid the middle fingers of each white cotton-gloved hand upon the showy monogram embroidered on the breast of his shantung shirt.

Emilio was not so naïve or stupid as to be taken in by Annunziata's partly artful, partly sincere behaviour. The script-writer, exceptionally, had not been chosen by the director, but wished on him by production, indeed by Golzio himself. One of the conditions that Annunziata had had to accept in return for directing the film was the choice of this particular script-writer. It looked as though Annunziata, though he had worked for two months with the young intellectual, could not get along with him. Too much difference in temperament, age and above all culture. The scenario writer was a pupil of Borghese, a graduate of Milan University, an author of short stories and essays in literary criticism. Annunziata, with probably no academic qualifications, had been brought up on Guido da Verona's novels, Dario Niccodemi's plays, revues by Ripp, Manca and Bel Ami and more recently the Ufa musicals produced in Berlin. There could well have been a barrier of incompatibility between the two and hence Annunziata did not like the script. But since a film is a risk in any case and success is never guaranteed, Annunziata had a way of covering himself – if production approved the script, he would agree to shoot it, but first he would send the department a registered letter stressing his doubts on the matter and disclaiming all responsibility.

To prove him wrong Emilio began to flick through the script, to defend and praise it, scene by scene, page by page. Annunziata responded with a cold expression of distaste and denial on his face or curt remarks such as 'Boring. Useless. It's not cinema. It's not funny. It's not human.'

As he made his points, Emilio heaved a sigh of tedium and annoyance. The script was certainly boring, though not in the way that Annunziata meant. It might even be an extremely entertaining show for most cinema-goers. But it had become a crashing bore to Emilio. He had read and re-read it, it was no work of art nor anything approaching it . . .

The last breath of morning freshness had gone. The water, which just before had darkened the asphalt below the building, had evaporated. Through the window, beyond Annunziata's hypocritically pained face and his jet-black Mascagni-style mane which he continually smoothed with his right hand to express utter doubt, Emilio could see the avenue leading up to the entrance; down among the trees he could see groups of extras in evening dress, Tyrolese costume, ancient Roman togas strolling nonchalantly outside the bar; he spotted the chief film editor in his long black, flapping dust-coat and white gloves running across the open space outside, knowing that he could be seen from management and especially from Emilio's window, then immediately slow to a walk as soon as he thought – mistakenly – that the thick foliage of the oleanders would mask him from view; he saw the flushed glare in the sky over the city and as time passed felt the heat and tedium of the day grow more oppressive. When Annunziata finally left, Giggi peeped in to ask if he could admit 'the Commendatore' who had been waiting in the anteroom for more than an hour.

This room, which was very small, opened on to a narrow passage between the management block and the huge cement wall of 'Stage No. 3'. The Commendatore came into the office wiping the sweat from his face with a handkerchief that he had taken from the breast pocket of his jacket. He approached the desk hesitantly, still mopping his brow. He was a distinguished old Venetian actor, now in decline. He needed work. He had agreed to accept minor roles. Now it so happened that Victoria was able to offer him the part of the old waiter in the opera-singer film – in other words, the chief role. But Golzio, crafty as usual, had suggested that the importance of the part should be kept a close secret, so that the old actor could be engaged for a ridiculously small fee, or at any rate a far lower one than he would have expected if he had known about it. This unpleasant task fell to Emilio and there was no time to lose. In a few days there would be a hundred copies of the script and anyone would be able to read it and warn the old man.

Emilio went across the office to meet him. The old man hurriedly replaced the handkerchief in his pocket, grasped Emilio's hand and pressed it for a few moments between his.

'I'm very pleased, very pleased to make your acquaintance at last! I beg your pardon for not coming sooner but your telegram was forwarded from my home in Venice to . . . to Feltre where I was doing a few summer shows with a small company . . . and so I got it terribly late. Well, here I am. At your disposal. What is it all about, exactly?'

His long, snowy-white hair, the anxious, frightened dark-blue eyes, the vague smile and the pale lips, but chiefly the sweat running down his temples and hollow, waxen cheeks from his wide, sunken brow and his desperate, useless attempt to mop it up with that yellow and red flowered handkerchief, inspired sympathy and pity.

Emilio, who till then had not foreseen the slightest hesitation, felt a sudden urge, almost a need to be honest and tell the old man the truth. But Golzio's instructions were clear and precise. Not only must he pull the wool over the old actor's eyes, but he must do it properly, skilfully. So that later he would not question the company's good faith. Emilio had to tell him that the script was not finished and they didn't know how long or important the part of the old waiter would be. As usually happens in such cases the actor in all probability would ask for a contract at a fixed daily fee, independent of how many days were involved. This had to be avoided. Even though the daily rate was low, the number of days when the old man had to be called was very high, so he must be persuaded to sign a contract for a flat fee. He would have to be told that it was in his own interest, and Emilio must refer vaguely to 'a few days' work' but without putting this into writing or, more important still, specifying the number of days. Once the contract was signed, he would be told that the part had become more important in the course of scripting – because *he* was playing it. And if he protested he would be granted, as a token of Golzio's personal sympathy and kindness, a supplementary bonus which would be infinitely less expensive to the firm than a fair contract.

Emilio carried out the instructions to the letter. He was beginning to get used to this sort of thing. The Teatro d'Arte in Turin had been quite different. Golzio had planned it basically as a patron's contribution to the arts and was therefore prepared to lose money. With Victoria Films in Rome he changed his tactics. Perhaps he did not have much confidence in the artistic possibilities of the cinema. Perhaps as people said he had really suffered a serious setback and lost a lot of capital. Or, having retired from business, he automatically brought his instinct and long experience as a maker of millions to film production.

Four years in Rome and Emilio had got thoroughly used to the job. And he used these shabby tricks as much as possible, sometimes even thought up some of his own, but while they were more or less subtle, more or less obvious, more or less unfair, they were also all more or less profitable to Victoria.

Golzio took a passionate interest in film production. He was now talking about launching a sister firm, Victoria Film Distributors, which in addition to distribution would look after the dubbing and marketing of foreign films. He had been encouraged to do this by a new Fascist law which favoured and protected the national film industry with the free concession to the producer of each Italian film of two 'dubbing vouchers', or the right to dub and distribute two foreign films.

Golzio came to the office daily, but only from eleven to one and five to eight. He did not step so much as spring out of the car each time, with a snap of his thin and still very agile limbs, just like a jack-in-the-box. And though they all expected his arrival there was always something unusual about it. On each occasion everyone anticipated some new surprise. He would cross the drive, mount the stairs, walk briskly and erectly along the corridors turning his little round head with its cap of flat, smooth, snowy-white hair to right and left, studying everything closely as if to detect even in the inanimate objects a trace of what had happened during his absence, and more noticeable still were his sharp bird-like movements as he stared at those employees who by accident or design lined the route and gushingly paid their respects in the way he liked – a hint of a bow or a smile in answer to his smile. The whole staff, from the lowliest commissionaire to the secretaries, the cutting-room girls, the technicians, sure of themselves and their ability, felt that there was a kind of magnetism in Golzio's presence. They all knew or guessed that he was sensible, fair or at least not capricious, not gratuitously unfair – a man of whom they had to beware only if their interests conflicted too violently with his. Yet the respect that Golzio inspired in his subordinates bordered irrationally on terror and adoration. As if their whole existence depended on him and on his good and bad moods, as if (and this was where the magnetism came in) those good and bad moods influenced Golzio's decisions, when in fact he never made a move without thinking it over thoroughly and was always prepared to discuss matters.

Even Emilio could not resist the spell of Golzio's authority. He tried to, if not in his actions at least in his conscience, but he was not always successful.

Emilio had known it for a long time, however – the secret of Golzio's power probably had nothing at all to do with magic. On the contrary, it consisted of a very simple, rustic quality – that same basic quality which shone through his peasant accent; in other words absolute, rocklike, burning conviction. A hard, compact block unimpaired by any suspicion of doubt. Golzio believed that his own interests and justice in both large and small issues were one and the same.

Given this premise, it was clear that any outrage, as long as it benefited Victoria, became not only legitimate but obligatory. During his three or four years in Rome, Emilio had gradually learnt to think like Golzio. More often than not unconsciously, he considered right what was useful to Victoria and wrong anything that might be harmful.

Most of the time. Actually there were times when he was aware of swindling someone. He admitted having lost his freedom of action but imagined he had kept his conscience clear. For instance he would say to himself: 'I won't rebel, I'll do what he wants. But it's a dirty business.'

The trouble was that the really obvious cases happened very rarely. Reality is never quite so blatantly simple. And although Golzio was solidly earthy in his self-confidence he possessed a refined, subtle, microscopic talent for detecting and destroying other people's doubts. So Golzio generally managed to convince Emilio, or Emilio convinced himself, that they were doing their best for the artist who had been persuaded to accept a lower fee.

In any case, was it right or not to protect one's own interests, discuss a fee, haggle, try to pay as little as possible? At what point exactly did this lawful practice become abuse? Where did you draw the line between an honest deal and 'dirty business'? In the majority of cases it was impossible to say. Because Golzio was always sensible, always cautious and, on reflection, often generous.

And had not the moment now arrived to show a little generosity? Golzio had fixed everything previously without seeing the old actor personally. Emilio looked at him and hesitated before replying. The old man's shirt was spotlessly clean but creased. He had obviously taken it straight out of his case and changed into it as soon as he arrived at his hotel. And the collar was worn, frayed, almost in tatters.

To gain time, Emilio asked him if he had had a comfortable journey.

'Not very, but it doesn't matter,' replied the old man.

'At which hotel are you staying?'

The old man did not answer. He was embarrassed. Emilio thought that he might be ashamed to give the name of a cheap hotel but that he was afraid to lie in case the producer had to get in touch with him at his Rome address. Finally the old actor smiled and explained: 'You see, I was afraid to be late for the appointment, so when I arrived I went to the Traveller's Rest opposite the station, had a bath and changed . . . If you need me at once, I'll stay. Otherwise I'd like to leave tonight . . .'

At that moment, through the window behind the old actor's soft, white halo-like mane, Emilio spotted Giggi rushing to the bar. There could be no mistake. Golzio had arrived and as usual had sent Giggi to fetch a lemonade. Emilio hesitated. Should he warn Golzio? Get someone to tell him that the old actor was there? Or go to him and frankly confess that he had qualms at the idea of 'twisting' the old man over the part? Of course he wouldn't use the expression 'twisting' to Golzio, nothing would annoy him more. He would simply ask if it might not be better to tell the actor how important the role was. That's what he would say to Golzio. But he still hesitated. Meanwhile he listened to the old man explaining how he had to be in Belluno the following evening for the summer season he had mentioned before; but that it was not an exclusive engagement and if he was needed immediately the company could put on a couple of plays without him . . . Emilio listened but his mind was on what Golzio would almost certainly say a trifle impatiently: 'You do what we decided yesterday, Viotti. Don't worry. In any case I'll see he gets a bonus. But don't let's waste time. Off you go, Viotti, fix it up. When he has signed, I'll be glad to see him.'

Looking at the old actor, Emilio decided that he resembled someone – someone he knew well and perhaps liked very much, someone he had not seen for years, not since he was a child. Whose were those dark-blue eyes, so anxious and frightened, which seemed to be searching for something in space? Then he thought: 'Of course, he'll have a bonus. He'll have nothing to complain about. Of course. Of course.'

Reassured by this thought, he reached for the packet of Tre Stelle cigarettes, offered one to the actor who declined with thanks, lit one himself, inhaled and began: 'Well, my dear chap . . . Victoria hasn't much to offer you for the moment. You've never worked in films, I think . . .'

'I have in silent films, yes. I did something before the war. Not in talkies yet. But I'm a stage actor and . . .'

'We know your excellent work. Signor Golzio remembers you at the Carignano . . . naturally, those were other times. If, as I hope, we reach agreement, you can certainly go back to Belluno this evening. Just be here when we begin shooting -- in about a month, we'll let you know. It's a small part, but a nice one, you'll see. An old waiter who only lives for his daughter. What matters is that this way we break the ice . . . then we'll see. If, as I trust, we're happy with you and you . . . with us, this will be only the *beginning* of our collaboration. Last year Victoria produced six films. We have nine in production during the current year. As you see, there will be plenty of opportunities. And so, my dear chap . . .'

In the contract, prepared by Emilio and approved by Golzio, there was naturally a clause to cover an option for an exclusive on future films in case the old man scored a striking success. But even so, his age and specialization in dialect roles did not fit him for the intense collaboration to which Emilio had referred merely in order to induce him to temper his demands. And if this too was cheating, thought Emilio in an attempt to salve his conscience, then the whole art of business must be considered cheating.

'And so, my dear chap . . . if you'd like to give me your views . . .'

'My views?' murmured the old fellow, wide-eyed, uncomprehending, or pretending very convincingly not to understand.

Emilio remembered that he was dealing with an experienced actor, a man armed at least with one defensive weapon, the ability to pretend. This thought helped him to conclude with the necessary brutality: 'Yes, your views on what your fee should be.'

'But that depends . . . depends on how long you want me,' stammered the old man.

'Oh, I'm sorry but I can't tell you exactly for the moment. We haven't fixed the schedule yet. We're still working on the script. I should say a month, six weeks, at most two months.' Actually the schedule *was* ready and the part of the waiter involved exactly two months' continuous work.

'Here in Rome?' The old man summoned up enough strength to mutter, staring at Emilio for the first time with his eyes like dark-blue marbles. It was a look that spoke volumes – he suspected a trap, he wanted the part, he pleaded for money, he showed signs of the privations of a miserable old age, the drudgery and humiliation of the summer or carnival seasons in the provinces, the lack of funds, even poverty, hence neglected illnesses, late affection unrequited, late vices unsatisfied. From their sunken sockets where the waxy skin became a lilac transparency, the dark blue beady eyes gazed anxiously at him; and for a moment Emilio seemed to glimpse the outline of a skull beneath the taut skin of the actor's face just as if he were looking at an X-ray photograph. The old man repeated breathily '. . . Two months in Rome?'

'In this case, it goes without saying that we should pay you the usual daily expense allowance,' Emilio hastened to add, then a little louder 'Well, tell me how much you want?' And he closed his eyes, unable to meet that beady blue stare any longer. He closed his eyes and inhaled the smoke deeply as he waited for a reply.

'Viotti,' said Golzio from his desk as Emilio came in. The young man held the contract that the old actor had just signed in his hand. 'Viotti, drop everything and go to Head Office. You must be there at one o'clock. I've just been told on the phone that the steel-works project,' (he hesitated a moment and shot a sly glance at Emilio) 'has been approved by the head of the government. He was apparently quite enthusiastic about it. He said – "That's the sort of film to make!" Just as well, eh?'

For years Emilio had known the particular tone, crafty, ironical and intentionally disparaging that Golzio adopted whenever he referred to Mussolini. Since he had come to Rome and worked in films he no longer called him Mussolini, still less *Il Duce* but always 'the head of the government' as if to isolate him, saddle him with all responsibility and disassociate himself, Golzio, entirely. It was clear (and even more so when he talked politics in private) that Golzio had anti-Fascist sympathies, and perfectly genuine they were too. He read and admired Benedetto Croce. In Paris he never lost an opportunity discreetly to meet the more important intellectual exiles. And in Italy he protected and materially aided writers and artists opposed to the régime. Yet he did not hesitate to take advantage of film subsidies and co-operate up to a point with government policy.

He could not afford to do otherwise if he wanted Victoria Films to survive. But could he live with his conscience? Emilio wondered sometimes – about Golzio and about himself. But it did not worry Golzio. He seemed convinced of his immunity, as if his nature and long experience as a financial tycoon set him automatically above not only Fascism but all political creeds, and authorized him within certain limits openly to exploit the régime and reap the benefits without any obligation privately to approve its principles. With his sly peasant's smile, at times quite frankly, Golzio would say: 'What will be, will be. In the long run it will probably come to a bad end. Maybe – you can never tell – it'll turn out all right. Anyway, you've got to deal with them – they're in power. And that's what I'm doing – in the hope I can make something out of it.'

In fact, his circle of friends, the ones he met socially and not his business contacts, had never changed. It was still the intellectual, anti-Fascist milieu in Turin. Government officials, and first and foremost the leader, were well aware of what went on at Golzio's. But Golzio was careful not to indulge in the usual jokes, or as the case might be, actual indictments save in the company of his nearest and truest friends. He, too, was well aware of something – that theoretical anti-Fascism linked in practice to activity in any way favourable to Fascism (the case of Victoria Films) was not at all frowned upon. The head of the government knew perfectly well that there was no better way to neutralize some of the more intransigent anti-Fascist intellectuals than to let them think and talk freely, provided they did not translate thought and talk into action. Golzio accepted this and it did not worry him. But it worried Emilio who barely suspected the whole truth.

Emilio still had no idea who Golzio's contacts with the Ministries and the top people in the government, the banks and industry really were. Once Golzio let slip (or pretended to) that he had a luncheon appointment with the Governor of the Bank of Italy. On another occasion he had been called to the phone by the head of the government's private secretary. But that morning, for instance, who told him that the proposed 'Steelworks' film had been approved? And with whom had he conducted the negotiations? One thing was certain. Golzio never received Fascist leaders or Ministry officials at the studios except during state ceremonies. It was as if the régime did not wish to rob Golzio of his anti-Fascist halo and had everything to gain by letting him keep it. For the same reason Golzio never set foot in a Ministry. He sent Emilio when all the arrangements had been made.

Emilio went back to his office to pick up his jacket and the file on the steelworks project. He was both bored and annoyed, plagued by a vague feeling that he had forgotten something and another, only too definite, which he knew very well by experience, that he must do something he disliked doing – enter by that main-door, take that list, see the sulky faces of those commissionaires, wait in that outer office, snigger softly with the other producers waiting, and finally face the broad smile, flashing with condescension and superiority, of the director-general and find something to say in reply. Lucky Golzio who did not have to haggle or at least could do it on equal terms. Emilio called Giggi – a double bitters! He called Lauretta and he called Olga – the steelworks file. He told Olga that as soon as he left she was to knock at Signor Golzio's door and give him the Venetian actor's contract – he had forgotten to hand it to him. Then she should warn Annunziata to organize another screen test for the singer, a test for Querio at three, no, four that afternoon. When Lia Querio arrived, with or without her mother, Olga was to show her straight to his office, apologize, say that he had had to rush to the Ministry, offer them an aperitif and ask them to wait. Then get a message to Giraudo that he would come along to the theatre during the afternoon. Tell Martini to leave a note of the price of the Kodak, there, on his desk . . . he stopped as he spotted the big red C on his pad. He had nearly forgotten. Twenty-five past twelve. He must phone!

'Off you go, Lauretta, find Monticone and tell him to bring the car to the front door. And you, Olga take the contract to the boss now.' As soon as he was alone, he looked for the number of the brothel in his diary. It was camouflaged, written backwards under the name Fonti which stood for Fontanella.

'Morning, Signora Teresa . . . yes, it's me . . . you recognized my voice? Could I speak to Signorina Corinna?'

Saying formally 'Signorina Corinna' instead of simply 'Corinna' was a part of the pleasure and a prelude to the escapade. He could hear the distant voice of 'Madame' Teresa in the receiver: 'Corinnaa! Tell her to come down! Telephoone!' And another voice even further away: 'Corinnaa! Corinnaa!' His heart pounded as he waited to hear the faint click-click of her mules (she was bound to be in dressing-gown and mules) coming down the wooden stairs from the second floor. A week wouldn't be enough, he would ask her to spend a fortnight with him. He'd book two communicating rooms for a fortnight at the Hotel Quirinale, or the Grand Hotel, or the Excelsior. But would she agree? And at what price? It meant that she would have to forgo a fortnight at Viareggio and in a sense exchange one prison for another – instead of a room in a brothel, a room in a de luxe hotel. Of course during the day she would be free to go and bathe at Ostia. From this point of view maybe his original idea was better – stay at a *pensione* or a small hotel in Ostia or Fregene . . . no, not Fregene! He was too well known in Fregene and he had the villa in the pines there which Elena liked so much and where she made him take her, especially in autumn and winter. At the sudden thought of Elena he instinctively thanked his lucky stars that she was so friendly with Golzio and his wife that she preferred the hospitality at their villa in Santa Margherita and cruising in their yacht to a holiday in Fregene. In that way she left him perfectly free during the summer. He began to hear in the receiver the clickety-click he longed for but much slower than he expected, as if Corinna were tired or reluctant to come down. At the same time there was a knock on the office door. Giggi entered on tip-toe. The way he came in and his suppressed, knowing smile seemed to indicate that he knew who the boss was talking to on the phone. He placed the double bitters on the desk and withdrew in the same fashion. And it suddenly struck Emilio that Corinna could not get away till one o'clock, so it would be too late to go to Ostia and just for one night he could certainly take her to his place in Via Ruggero Fauro. The maid slept at the other end of the apartment and there was no risk that she would notice anything during the night. Of course he would have to be careful the following morning – shut the 'little giant' in the bathroom when the maid came in with the coffee and then smuggle Corinna out of the building . . . the portress would see her but there were other tenants in the block of flats. She would have suspicions but no proof. The real trouble was that Corinna would have to be awakened three or four hours earlier than usual and this too was an important point. But it was such a temptation! Making love in his bed, Elena's bed with another woman and a tart at that! It was a pleasure he had thought about time and time

282

again but had never enjoyed. Such a pleasure seemed to hide a sort of need for justice and revenge – a desire which at all costs must be satisfied.

He turned all this over in his mind as avidly as he gulped down the ice-cold, deliciously bitter drink. Meanwhile the clickety-click on the stairs drew nearer and nearer and finally stopped. A confused sound of rustling silk and heavy sighs indicated that Corinna was there at the phone and in her soft drawl with its genuine Tuscan accent she said: 'Oh, it's you. Forgive me for keeping you waiting. I've just woken up . . . Yes, you did, but it doesn't matter, after all it was the nicest way to wake up.'

Emilio blurted out his proposition and while he was speaking began to regret it – he should have been a little vaguer. Corinna exclaimed: 'A fortnight. You must be mad! Of course, it'd be marvellous. But I'm going to Viareggio for the bathing, I told you the other evening, didn't I? Anyway, we'll talk about it. When are you coming?' Then Emilio told her his plan for that night. He would wait for her outside the smaller door in Via Fontanella at a quarter-past-one. With the car, naturally.

'Come at one, if you like. I'll be finished. I'll get ready before. If you find the door closed, ring the bell. I'll tell them to let you in.'

Was the little giantess's amenability cool calculation or real, unexpected enthusiasm? Perhaps a little of each. A mixture. And the effect on Emilio was mixed too, but through a psychological process contrary to the normal one. The fact that she was calculating excited him. The suspicion that she might also derive pleasure from it depressed him.

✻✻✻

III

In the mock-Empire antechamber which served as the director-
general's waiting-room a group of producers and directors sat in a
circle on settees and light green damask armchairs around the
marble table with the gilt legs, as they always did at that time of day.

They were all Romans or at least 'naturalized' Romans – sons of
Northerners or Southerners who had moved to Rome a long time
ago. And it was the Roman accent, or rather Roman dialect, that
coloured their conversation, the living, irreplacable expression of
the *impasto* that formed their common nature: servility, scepticism,
sentimentality, vulgarity, greed, cunning.

As usual they greeted Emilio with particular, exaggerated
cordiality, due on the one hand to their profound respect for
Golzio and his financial resources, which put their small companies
completely in the shade, and on the other to a double inferiority
complex, a double sense of distrust and suspicion of the Roman
for the stranger from Turin, of the ignorant or relatively ignorant
man for the intellectual. In some way or other they made it
abundantly clear that they were well aware that he was not Golzio
but merely one of his employees.

'How is Signor Golzio?'

'Give him my regards when you see him.'

'Has he taken his holidays? No? Is he still at work in this heat?'

'He must be really crazy about making films!'

'Be honest, now, crazier than you are . . .'

And so on. Until Roberti, the only one he liked, whose company
he liked, took him gently by the arm and led him to a window-bay.
This habit of taking someone by the arm and leading him into a
quiet corner, casually as it were, for a confidential chat was typical
of Roberti and Roman film businessmen in general – at least so it
seemed to Emilio, who each time found it quite fascinating. In
Turin that sort of thing would have appeared normal only between
close friends, but in Rome it was perfectly normal even among

people who hardly knew each other – lawyers, tradesmen, schemers, contractors at the Stock Exchange and in the waiting-rooms at all the Ministries, and at Montecitorio[1] ten years before when Montecitorio still had its importance. It must have been an age-old custom originating in the Vatican or from the East.

Whenever the film-makers noticed one of their number particularly known for his cunning take another by the arm and lead him aside, they would at once remark: 'Another lamb to the slaughter!'

Maybe it was the physical contact that was so seductive, or rather the importance the Romans, who were more instinctive than the Torinese, gave to physical contact. But in that way they had of taking you by the arm and guiding you gently into a corner there was something (and Emilio realized it rather uncomfortably), there was something that smacked of violence and extortion. Anyone unwilling to enter into conversation was forced rudely to disengage his arm; worse still, the other person might take advantage of a compliance due simply to shyness or good manners and read into it an unspoken 'yes', or even try to start up a friendship which was not particularly appreciated.

Roberti was small, thick-set but extremely agile, smooth-faced, fresh-complexioned, balding, with a big nose, sparkling eyes, a broad smile – altogether an extremely pleasant chap. He worked as a free-lance for this or that film company; he had the Ministry's support because he was one of the original Fascists and a friend of the director-general. Yet he had none of the characteristics of the real Fascist, none of the arrogance, the brutality, the simple, provincial ways, or the studied contempt for culture and intelligence. He did not belong to that lower middle class in the valley of the Po from which had sprung the Fascist action squads. Well brought up and behaved, refined, equipped with a civic sense and something of a cosmopolitan flair, he came from the Roman middle class, composed of modest business or professional men, which had prospered until 1870 under the cardinals of the Papal Court and been trained in a matchless school of exclusive servility and subtle diplomacy. Perhaps this was the secret of Roberti's charm which banished the suspicion that militant Fascists aroused in Emilio. Quite apart from the fact that Roberti, unlike the rest of them, was

[1] Montecitorio: the Italian Houses of Parliament.

careful not to flaunt his political beliefs continually; when he could avoid it, he never gave the Fascist salute and went as far as telling and listening to jokes against the régime or criticizing 'the Duce's behaviour'. This at least was the impression that Emilio had of Roberti. And Emilio suspected that it was all calculated to get into his good graces just as it had been calculation that had made Roberti join the Fascist party way back in 1919. Basically the man was a sceptic, full of humanity and humanism. He appeared to be quite cultured. He tried not to speak Roman dialect.

'Actually, Viotti, I pass the Victoria Studios almost every morning . . . yes, on the way to the Caesar lot where we're shooting a short film . . . I pass Victoria and I think of you . . .'

'Why don't you pop in some time?' asked Emilio, flattered, while Roberti released his arm. They had reached the window. The Venetian blinds were closed but through the fanlight and the leafy domes of the neighbouring trees they could see people idly strolling up and down Via Veneto.

Roberti had not lost the thread of the conversation: 'Pop in? If only I could!'

'Why not?' asked Emilio innocently, uncomprehending.

Roberti laughed, and by way of explanation recited: ' "*O belle agli occhi miei tende latine*"[1] – though I'm the Latin in this case . . . so when I pass Victoria I ought to say: "*O belle agli occhi miei tende torinesi* . . . a pity, it ruins the line!" '

'Yes, a pity' . . . Emilio laughed too, completely won over. Quick as a cat Roberti seized his opportunity, putting a hand on Emilio's shoulder like a paw and turning his back on the others so as suddenly to give an intimate, serious tone to the conversation. He lowered his voice and gazed at Emilio.

'Why don't we do something together, Viotti, eh?'

'Well . . . I'd like to . . .' murmured Emilio who still did not understand, 'but as a rule Signor Golzio prefers . . .'

'Yes, I know, he prefers to be a lone wolf. Do you play *chemin-de-fer*? If you like, when we've got a game going one evening at my place or with some friends, I'll let you know . . . just come along . . .'

---

[1] '*O Latin tents so fair to my eyes*' – a celebrated line from Tasso's *Gerusalemme Liberata* (VI, 104). The pagan warrior maid Clorinda sees in the distance the tents of the Christian camp where her lover Tancredi is.

'Thank you,' said Emilio who liked a little flutter at cards but had good reason to believe that he would not enjoy the company.

Roberti went on: 'It would be up to you to persuade Signor Golzio, soften up his resistance which anyway I do not dispute. You know, I'm a friend, a great friend of P.'

'What has P. got to do with it?' Emilio asked in surprise.

'Come on, Viotti . . . Why do you play the innocent with me?' And there was a smile in his bright steely eyes. Then Emilio, completely mystified by the mention of P., realized that the look in Roberti's eyes was equally significant in both cases – whether he really knew that Emilio and Golzio were unaware of facts in his possession or whether he believed that they were pretending. Emilio also realized that Roberti was more interested in stressing the privileged, well-informed position that he enjoyed and in getting him to urge Golzio to recognize the advantages of a future association or collaboration. The mystery was explained a few minutes later. The commissionaire announced that 'Signor Viotti could go in.' Roberti accompanied him, absently so it seemed, as far as the door and when it opened managed to show himself and from behind Emilio to exchange a smile with the man in the room, a mere suspicion of a smile that Emilio was meant to notice and in fact did.

The director-general, '*Moschettiere del Duce*',[1] was a young Milanese. He jumped up, walked round the enormous, massive writing-desk, bending to press a button on the way, and came to meet his visitor. He was tall, dark and handsome, sturdily built and flashing the whitest of teeth in a broad smile. But he did not offer his hand. He patted Emilio on the shoulder and said: 'There you are, Viotti. Good! How are things?'

The gesture, the tone were those of a superior momentarily benevolent towards an inferior. If Victoria wanted to benefit from dubbing vouchers, Fascist law demanded a certain amount of ministerial control but not a strictly bureaucratic relationship. So there was something offensive and menacing about the director-general's reception. That pat on the shoulder seemed to say: 'I

[1] The Moschettieri del Duce (The Duce's Musketeers) were a Fascist Party élite selected for their fanatical support of the régime and their outstanding physique. A guard of honour at public ceremonies, they wore black uniforms, jackboots, belts and silver daggers.

know who you are and I know what you think. I could crush you. But I'm generous and I'll be tolerant.' A commissionaire stiffened into the Fascist salute, lightly clicking his heels to draw attention.

'What will you have to drink?' the director-general asked Emilio with a slightly different, slightly more human smile, which was meant to make up for his previous arrogance, and break the ice. Tantamount to saying 'You see, after all I'm offering you an apéritif, I'm treating you as an equal.'

As Ingegnere Golzio had been informed, the Duce had approved the plan for a film on the steelworks. It was the go-ahead. Now they had to find a story, and a *metteur-en-scène*, a director. At this point the director-general suddenly stopped, burst out laughing and stared at Emilio: 'A *metteur-en-scène*? No, let's speak Italian, let's say a *regista*. Don't you think that's better, Viotti? *Regista, autista,*[1] *fascista*. Or are you one of these people who still say *chauffeur*?'

'It's just a question of habit,' murmured Emilio, smiling at the innuendo.

'Anyway,' continued the director-general, suddenly serious again, 'I expect we'll talk about the director later. Golzio will have his own ideas and the decision will be his. I can only respect and approve his choice because I'm sure it will be a good one. But then there's the story ... the script ... Your plan is to shoot the film in State or State-controlled steelworks. This is absolutely essential as you won't find a setting and all the processes on the grand scale anywhere else. I can tell you that the Duce is explicit on this point, explicit and favourable. But now the script ... the script ...'

'Signor Golzio and I, we thought to launch a competition and offer prizes ...'

'No. You see, we want a big name. That's the only way to be sure of a success. It's the Duce's view, too. P. is to write the script. Believe me, it's a marvellous idea. You'll thank me for it.'

'Of course, of course. I'll tell Signor Golzio at once. But do you think that P. will accept?'

'That's the point!' said the director-general heaving a mournful sigh. 'He must accept! You put it to him. Then if there are any snags ... Well, we must find someone who understands to explain it to him, a friend, a go-between ...'

[1] *Autista* – word coined about 1925 by an unknown Fascist writer to replace chauffeur.

'What about Roberti?' Emilio suggested almost automatically. The director-general looked blank. He frowned and feigned innocence, lapsing into his native Milanese with all the open *e*s: 'Roberti? What a peculiar idea! Why him?'

Perspiring, hungry, slightly muzzy from the drinks (first a double, then one with the director-general and finally another double at the bar in Piazza Barberini with Roberti who had waited for him outside the Ministry), Emilio got back to the studios just after two o'clock. In the shadowy drive, darker now and more suffocating than it had been in the morning, Giggi rushed towards the car as he arrived. His smooth, round, red face, which always seemed to reflect his boss's state of mind just as a mirror reflects light, was wreathed while he was still a long way off in the particular kind of smile that he kept for good news. He panted as he spoke and it was hard to tell whether this was because he had been running or simply because of what he had to say.

'Sir, Signorina Querio's waiting up in your office. She's been there for more than an hour. She's with . . .' Giggi paused intentionally, 'she's with her mother.'

'Well? What about it?' said Emilio, irritated at being caught out again by Giggi.

'Nothing, sir, nothing . . . I meant she's a fine-looking lady, a very fine-looking lady,' Giggi hurried to explain earnestly, contritely as if all he had to do to be forgiven was to praise Mother Querio's beauty.

Oh, Giggi had a sixth sense all right and knew intuitively not only about Emilio's past love affairs but his future ones, too, and sometimes even about his vaguest, most uncertain plans, plans that Emilio was hardly aware of himself. Emilio had already been to bed with the daughter, a pretty girl but a mediocre actress. He had glimpsed the mother, who lived in Leghorn and came to Rome to see her daughter very rarely, one evening among the guests at a film-show. A tall, shapely, bejewelled woman with silvery hair piled high. People said that she came from a rich old Jewish family. Married to a naval officer, she had been left a widow while still young. At first she had opposed her only daughter's stage and film career, then she had grudgingly given up the struggle. And the story was that she lived in hopes of the girl making a good match which would save her from a life that the mother, 'a real lady', despised not so much on moral grounds as out of sheer snobbery. Since that evening at the projection theatre Emilio had been left with a feeling of morbid curiosity. But how Giggi knew about it remained a mystery. As he bounded up the stairs three at a time, a habit of his, but now spurred on by impatience, he wondered not so much if Mother Querio was really beautiful as if she had any suspicion of the relation, something more than friendly though occasional and not at all serious, which existed between her daughter and him. Mothers usually like their daughters to confide in them and when they don't know they guess.

'Don't apologize for being late, Signor Viotti. Believe me, it's quite unnecessary,' simpered the fair lady, offering her hand, glove hanging from wrist, to be kissed. 'When I come to Rome to see my daughter and visit a film studio with her, I know very well I'll be in the colonies . . .'

'Yes, but even in the colonies there's a code of good manners and you . . .'

'All right then . . . in the jungle!'

Emilio kissed the daughter on both cheeks as colleagues affectionately do when they meet after a long time, or are putting on an act of not having seen each other for ages. Then, putting his arm round her firm, fleshy waist, he said with a laugh: 'Lia, be careful! You shouldn't take your mother round with you too often!'

'And why not?' asked the mother, arching her eyebrows and pouting with mock innocence while she waited for the inevitable compliment.

'Because, *Signora mia*, your daughter runs the risk of losing her contracts to you!'

Signora Querio laughed aloud, head thrown back boldly to reveal her lovely unwrinkled neck. Emilio beckoned invitingly, she rose from the divan and, still laughing, came towards him. She seemed to cleave the air with her fresh gardenia perfume. Emilio gazed at her silver hair, thick and curly, the slender neck, the small nape, her bronzed, uncovered shoulders, the waist similar to her daughter's which he still held tight – similar, maybe even slimmer, while her hips were stronger and her bottom rounder.

Emilio felt that he had lived that moment once before. At a quarter-past-two on a July afternoon on the red carpet of his shadowy office; and he remembered going to lunch pressing close to a beautiful girl he had just possessed. A still lovelier woman walked ahead and with her perfume and swaying hips invited him to desire her – the girl's mother. He felt that he had already lived that moment and yet it was not he who had lived it. Someone else, an unknown, had taken his place, someone who had neither his memories nor his past, someone who had always lived in Rome and who was a friend of people like Roberti and spoke more or less like Roberti and even said '*Signora mia*' . . .

As though it were a sudden decision, a whim, he had invited Lia to lunch but without telling her that he wanted her to do a screen test for the film about the singer that same afternoon. He broke the news as a little *coup-de-scène* at the restaurant, in the soft blue lighting of the dining-room reserved for the management, in the cross-current of the ventilators, while Giulio, the manager, in his snowy-white jacket, began to serve hors-d'oeuvres with a eucharistic smile.

The mother sat on his right. On his left, Lia to whom he raised his glass of iced champagne.

'To your test, my dear. Don't eat too much because straight afterwards you must go to make-up.'

The girl flushed up with emotion and joy and gave him a grateful smile full of promises.

Emilio looked in turn at her and her mother. He drank and ate heartily. Contented and gay, though unable to shake off that strange recent feeling of not being himself. But maybe it's a mistaken impression, he told himself. Perhaps this is how I really am. Perhaps Piero is right – I like Rome and I like this life and for instance Corinna . . . Corinna that night in his bed, Elena's bed. Just as magnetized iron attracts iron, the same idea, more urgent and clear-cut, attracted him with regard to Signora Querio. She did not eat so much as pick at her food. She put on too many airs and graces to be the great lady she was supposed to be. She spoke too freely of London, Paris, Monte Carlo and Biarritz for someone who lived in Leghorn. And yet this false worldly-wise attitude of hers, her cosmopolitan poses somehow stimulated Emilio; they made him suspect that deep down she was quite the opposite – provincial, passionate, vulgar.

The conversation turned to art. She said: 'Of course you must understand that I know a lot about the subject. I'm a Modigliani by birth.'

Emilio remembered reading a document in the file regarding Lia's contract with Victoria – 'daughter of Esther Modiglia' and not Modigliani. But he enquired: 'Are you related to the famous painter?'

'He was my cousin,' she replied without batting an eyelid. Even this lie charmed him. After lunch, when the daughter went off to the make-up cubicle, Emilio invited her mother to coffee up in his office.

Giggi brought the coffee. When he had left Emilio sat next to her on the divan. Without a word or opening gambit, without even waiting for her to finish her coffee, he slipped his arm around her waist. As she showed no signs of protesting or moving away, he grew bolder and murmured: 'You know, you look younger than your daughter.'

'I know, everyone says so.' She smiled, motionless, holding the saucer in one hand, sipping her coffee and staring into space. 'But you shouldn't say so, you wretch!'

It was a clear hint and an immediate invitation.

Till four o'clock office work was slack and Golzio would not be back before five. His studio, the divan, the carpet were quite adequate for the occasion. Except that previously, with Lauretta and Olga, the opportunity had occurred late at night when the building was deserted. The night-watchmen, seeing the light on in the manager's office, knew that he and his secretary were working late. At the moment they were shooting two films so Emilio might be needed at any time. A secretary, an assistant would knock, tell him about some stupid snag and ask him to give instructions or come down and sort it out.

There was a solution which he had sometimes thought about but had never yet been able to put into practice – the big bathroom *reserved for the President* which had communicating doors from Golzio's office and his own.

A short, sleepy-eyed engineer, on guard at the door of Stage 2, leapt to his feet with a smile that meant: 'I recognize you, you're Signor Viotti, the studio manager, almost the boss.' And that smile, and the speed with which he handled the heavy bar and opened the little cork-lined door to let Emilio in, gave him as it always did a sense of intense, almost physical satisfaction. A feeling that lingered as he tip-toed into the stifling hot air and semi-darkness, picking his way between coiled cables, switchboards, arc-lamps towards the corner blazing with light where they were shooting a scene, and receiving step by step a tribute of silent respect from electricians, workmen, technicians, make-up artists, extras, actors. They were all employed by him, worked for him, and day by day built up for him the wealth and security he had always aimed at and which only now was beginning to come his way. The smiles of the staff heralded the day, that longed-for day when, as Golzio had promised, he would start to draw a percentage of the profits from the films. Seven, maybe eight per cent. It would be an enormous leap ahead. And yet embedded in the juicy flesh of this hope like a bitter stone there was a strange, indefinable core of anxiety. Emilio pretended not to notice it, to be accustomed to it. He could explain it by the fact that the big money still had to come. But on second thoughts it was not anxiety. It was shame. He had no idea what he was ashamed of. It did not seem possible that his secret suspicions about Golzio and Elena could have this effect. He was studio and production manager at Victoria, he worked hard, did his job honestly. Why should he be ashamed? They were entirely separate things! And yet he had vague twinges of remorse – certainly about Golzio and Elena, but Vévé and Turin and Rome and Fascism came into it too. It was as if a still small voice kept on saying that despite all appearances the cinema was not his métier, not the right place for him; as if his employees' smiles were not merely calculating but ambiguous and unconsciously meant for someone else; as if in fact he had deceived all these people. Oh, why couldn't he follow Piero's example and live a simple life?

Maybe Piero was right – he ought to fall in love. Since that evening, the more he thought about it the more convinced he was that such strange advice, coming from Piero, a man so fond of his home and family and with a traditional code of morality, must be sound advice. He had decided not to follow it – he felt no urge to fall in love. He was all right as he was. Or perhaps he was looking for something else – a woman he liked in bed infinitely more than any other so that he would want to keep on making love to her after the first few nights and not only at more or less regular intervals of satiated lust as had been the case for ten years . . . a woman who would continue to satisfy him in bed? But this was the very kind of love that Piero had suggested. The only woman he had really loved was Vévé. He had never met girls like Vévé since. Intellectuals, concert artists, ballet-dancers, singers, actresses or girls who wanted to be actresses, demi-mondaines, prostitutes. He had never thought he could fall in love with that sort of woman. Perhaps this was his mistake – continuing to imagine true love as a feeling similar to what he had experienced for Vévé which, so he thought, created the need to find another girl like Vévé. Just as he was no longer a university student of twenty-one who had always lived in Turin, so the woman he could and should have fallen in love with was possibly no longer a passionate, intelligent, free girl supporting herself as a typist, but another sort altogether, even one who might seem an absurd choice – Corinna, for instance?

His thoughts returned to Corinna while he watched the scene being rehearsed in a special chair that the prop man had placed next to the director, behind the camera. Piero Giraudo, enveloped in a black cloth, had not noticed him yet. Corinna, 'the little giantess' who would be his in a few hours might well be the woman to love. After all, he had never sought anything else. Apart from Elena, of course, and those very first occasions on Carnival nights when he went to the brothel with his friends, however fleeting the liaison, he had never made love without a secret, implicit hope of discovering in the woman of the moment by means of a shining revelation, a kind of miraculous vision, the only woman in his life. It had been the same with Lauretta and Olga. With Gina, Signora Calandra's maid, too. Vévé was in Turin then. Elena had not appeared yet. Gina, the girl from Trento, a great girl, pretty, tall, slender, healthy – why not her? With Gina as with all the others, the illusion, though momentary, recurred once again.

Elementary logic warned him that what had not happened the first time would be unlikely to happen the second, third or thirtieth time. No matter. Unlikely but not impossible. The time or times before maybe the full force of revelation for some mysterious reason had been denied him. He had failed to interpret the signs. That is why he never asked a woman for a date without looking anxiously into her eyes, not to see if she accepted or offered the promise of pleasure, but in search of a flash, a sparkle the woman herself was unaware of – an indication of an inner quality that perhaps without knowing it she alone possessed. And he had never strolled down certain streets, pushed an inviting door, climbed the stairs to the most sordid brothel without hoping to meet the ultimate woman. So why not Corinna?

True, he had been with Corinna a few times. True, too, she had certainly given him fierce pleasure but not enough to prevent him wanting to leave immediately after and go home. But the disappointment, thought Emilio, absently watching the scene that the director was busily rehearsing (a group of elderly gentlemen in 1880 period costume playing billiards in a provincial club), the disappointment might be caused by the surroundings; perhaps everything would be different at home – at home, that night . . .

The endless repetition of lines, the repetition of movements by the actors around the billiard table in the blinding glare and suffocating heat of the lights, acted upon him like a mild narcotic and helped him concentrate. That night, he told himself, he wanted from Corinna not a few hours of pleasure but the miraculous explosion of a passion which would last for years and years and so give him a purpose in life, solve all his problems.

Then he wondered if he had hoped to find his great love in Signora Querio shortly before. He tried to think so. But he was seized by an irresistible urge to laugh at himself. And this showed as his lips curled into a smile. The director, the actors who at the end of each run-through or after a comic line anxiously studied Emilio's face, thought that the manager was enjoying himself.

Instead, merely smiling at himself and not very pleasantly at that, Emilio came to the end of his reflections and suddenly reversed the meaning that they seemed to have had hitherto.

His hope of a great love was hypocrisy, to allow him to satisfy his every whim without remorse. It was an excuse not to be content with what he could get from life – a pretence in which he felt capable of noble feelings. It was simply wishful thinking, a lack of humility and sincerity, stupid obstinacy that made him think he was much better than he really was.

How could there be any genuine feeling in the desire he had for Corinna when a few hours before his first night of love with her it had never even occurred to him to refuse the famous *coup du canapé* with Signora Querio?

Bells rang out in the studio – the rehearsal was over. Piero appeared from under the black cloth and stepping off the dolly greeted Emilio with a smile which a less honest person would have found very difficult to summon up but which came so naturally to him – the smile of an old friend and at the same time of a subordinate: 'Ciao. How are things?'

It was still the same face – thin, sunken-cheeked, intelligent, human. Still the same look – humorous and warm.

Emilio was fond of Piero uncalculatingly, thank God, without ulterior motives. He was as fond of him as when, one summer Sunday morning long ago, he had found him in the garden of the villa at Rivoli with Bersezio's *La Plebe* on his knees and had said to him: 'I know you, you're Prince's nephew.' He had no doubts about this feeling, at least, nor would he ever have any.

Now Piero was fussing round the actors who were still grouped at the billiard-table. He stopped at each one, showed him the position he would occupy for the scene and checked the direction of the lights. Through his slide of coloured glass he looked up at the battery of arc-lamps and gave instructions to the electricians: 'Tighter, tighter, that's not enough ... Give it another turn ... that's it, good boy!' And if the man was from his own home-town he would shout in dialect – 'A bit to the left. Up a shade. Not that one – the parabolic!' At the studios he had the name of being a martinet. Actually, he was precise, extremely serious about his work, a tireless perfectionist.

When he checked the lights one by one and went back to the camera each time to judge with a glance the general layout of the scene, the particular effect that he had just finished modifying, his face contracted into what looked like a grimace of pain; it was the effort of concentrating his attention exclusively on the intensity rather than the colour of the lights in order to distinguish the slightest variation and graduate them according to the importance of the subject to be lit.

As he watched him at work Emilio admired him – more than that, he envied him. He was marvellous, a real artist – the newspaper critics said so. But he was above all a man in love: yes, in love with his profession, a man with one aim in life.

IV

Twenty minutes to go to one o'clock. A shadow appeared in the slit of light that lined the doorway and momentarily obscured it. Then the man came out and made off rapidly along the dark street and almost immediately the door was closed from the inside with a dull thud.

His heart beating fast, Emilio had been watching for some time, standing a hundred yards away. He told himself over and over again that it was childish to stand there staring at that strip of light. Surely much better to sit in a nearby café, Aragno's or Greco's for instance, and keep an eye on the time?

This ridiculous agitation had begun towards the end of the afternoon. The usual relief at getting out of the studios and offices, the daily surprise and refreshed feeling on meeting the sunset and the bare, squalid courtyards bathed in a soft, bluish light had been superseded by a sudden, anxious desire to see 'the little giantess' again, and he found it difficult to think of anything else.

However, he had thought of a few excuses to stay on at the studios – a run-through of the film which could have waited until the following morning, a check-up with Martini on the last Kodak delivery box by box, number by number – another job which was neither so urgent nor in need of his personal supervision. In the gloom of the projection-theatre, he could vaguely hear the operators in the projection-room above cursing him for making them work late. Even Martini, with all his diplomacy, could not repress a grimace of annoyance when he heard about the extra job.

'All right, sir, if you say so.' And he vented his spleen by shouting to his assistant 'Run to the warehouse, tell them to stay put! After seeing the film, Signor Viotti is coming with me to personally check the new stock!'

Finally, round about midnight, he got Monticone to take him into the city centre and drop him outside a restaurant; but instead of going in he had come to wait for one o'clock here in

Via Fontanella Borghese, not taking his eyes off the slit of light that marked the doorway. He smoked as he paced up and down. He was afraid of being recognized by one of the rare passers-by or by someone coming out of the brothel who instead of making for the Corso might turn in his direction and pass him – a technician from the studios, an actor, maybe . . .

The light from the door seemed in some way to contain all his anxiety. There lay the answer to his doubts. Not because he would see Corinna there shortly but because only now did he seem to be at one with himself and able to find an inner peace in the extreme, growing impatience of the moment. Obviously his aim in life was to manage to live with no interruptions or as few as possible in such a simple, pure state of mind. Maybe like Piero's while he was at work.

At one o'clock precisely he crossed the street and rang the bell. The door was opened a fraction and then only on the chain. The familiar, hard, sad face of a servant appeared in the half-light. Though she recognized Emilio and very probably had been tipped off by Corinna, the old woman said with her usual curtness: 'What's the matter? What do you want? Can't you see that we're closed?'

Emilio was ready for this, too. He proffered a ten-lira note and murmured: 'Will you see if Signorina Corinna is ready?'

The old woman, who had evidently feigned ignorance in order to obtain that generous tip, immediately became all sweetness and smiles and let him in: 'Yes, the Signorina is nearly ready. Come in.'

Emilio slipped past her, crossed the little hall, mounted four steps, stopped on the mezzanine landing. Flanked by a ground-glass partition and a banister of carved wood, a small wooden staircase led to the upper floors. Another flight, between two walls, went down into the basement where the dining-room and kitchen were situated and from which a smell of roast peppers emanated. The old woman showed him into the ground-floor drawing-room and shut the door. He knew it well – low ceiling, no window, armchairs and settees of imitation leather and the glass partition through which you could see the outline of the staircase.

He sat down. Because of the heat he took off his jacket. From the floor above he could hear light footsteps, doors banging, water gushing into baths, the girls humming snatches of songs, the voices and noises together suggesting a sense of relief and gaiety that the daily round of tiring work had at last come to an end.

The sound of a violently beaten gong was followed by a voice drawling in a strong Piedmontese accent: 'It's ready, girls ... *Capelli d'angelo*[1] today, mind. So if you don't eat them straight away they'll be like glue!'

'Coming', 'We're coming', 'Here we are' – answering, laughing voices approached. And all at once the stairs began to resound beneath a stampede of footsteps hurrying down.

The girls looked like a single confused mass through the frosted glass, they passed and disappeared. The voices and laughter continued, mingled with the clatter and clink of cutlery and glasses, and the smell of the peppers drifted up into the drawing-room.

Nothing, thought Emilio, is more delightful than to wait for a pleasure when you're sure that your waiting will not be in vain. Sure? You can never be absolutely sure, but the narrow margin of uncertainty which remains only serves to increase the pleasure.

Emilio had even imagined, and continued to imagine, Corinna arriving at the last minute with a sad look on her face (genuine or false) – a telegram from home, her mother was seriously ill and she could not come away with him. The thought of possible disappointment increased that of a sensual pleasure which would most probably be inevitable and imminent. In fact, he reflected, quite reassured, if some snag had cropped up, the old woman, instructed by Corinna, would have mentioned it to prepare him. Whereas, after taking the tip, she had shown him in, baring her few blackened teeth in an obscene smile. Save that, he thought, seized by a sudden doubt, save that, to give him at least five minutes of illusion in exchange for the tip, the old woman might have had no scruples about not relaying Corinna's message and that smile which Emilio could not help remembering might well have been unpleasantly mocking. To intensify his desire, though he was almost bound to be wrong, he surrendered to this theory.

He looked around at the greasy, worn armchairs of imitation leather where so many men before him and like him had waited and suffered; at the low ceiling, the panels of dirty stucco, the pretentious earthenware or German silver ashtrays full of rank cigarette butts, the orange, gold-fringed, rayon lamp-shade whose

[1] Pasta drawn out into very thin strands.

soft, warm glow seemed deliberately designed for the broad backs and the big bare bellies, the thighs and the huge, flabby buttocks which appeared and slowly gyrated around it while the faces remained in a discreet half-light. And what if after all the little giantess could not or would not spend the fortnight with him? Suppose her financial demands were so exorbitant that he had to give up the idea? The gloom and misery that would then possess his soul seemed, Lord knows why, to be symbolized by these armchairs. Suddenly, through the merry chatter and clinking that rose from the basement, he thought he heard the squeak of a handle turning and a door opening on the first floor; a firm step reached the top of the stairs and began to come down.

Emilio leapt to his feet. The silhouette of a woman – Corinna, surely! – appeared behind the frosted glass. The door opened. She it was, smiling happily.

She held in her arms, white on the sky-blue ground of her suit jacket, a poodle puppy.

'Darling, thanks for the present,' were her first words in response to Emilio whose gaze took in the poodle as part of the joyous picture. 'Careful not to squash him! He's only six weeks old!' she added hastily, a moment before kissing Emilio on the mouth, lightly because of her lipstick. 'You gave me him, you know. Thanks. I thought . . .', she looked behind her, waited an instant for the old woman to get to the street-door with the suitcases, lowered her voice and whispered slyly – 'I thought that as you asked me to spend a fortnight with you, I could have a little in advance! I've wanted him for so long! He's got a pedigree, you know!'

'How much did he cost?' he felt like asking her, but a gay, ruthless greed like the little giantess's was exactly what he preferred. Feeling a little faint between fear of expense and the inversely proportionate pleasure he anticipated, he nevertheless looked steadily at Corinna. Her bright, smiling brown eyes seemed to emphasize the pleasure that her perfect body offered and the pleasure that she wanted for herself. And so, thinking only of the pleasure, Emilio simply said: 'You did the right thing. Let's go now.'

But Corinna had not eaten, she was famished and first wanted to be taken to a restaurant. Emilio had not dined either. He quickly debated where to go. In a small *trattoria*, apart from the fact that it would be difficult to find one open at that hour, he faced two disadvantages – displeasing Corinna and, if he were seen, causing gossip which might reach Elena's ears and against which he would have no defence. On the other hand, in a luxury restaurant Corinna would be happy and if he had to, he could justify himself by saying that he was entertaining a would-be actress and so had gone there quite openly. To invite a pretty girl to dinner was part of his work as a film producer. The taxi was at the door.

'Hotel Quirinale,' said Emilio. And Corinna gratefully threw her arms around him.

'So we'll be able to dance after, won't we?'

'Of course.'

The Taverna del Quirinale was at that time, in 1935, the leading and most elegant night spot in Rome.

The suitcases posed a small problem. To unload them and leave them in the hotel cloakroom and then reload them on to another taxi to go home was a clumsy, embarrassing solution. But to do what Corinna suggested, to leave them in the taxi and pay the driver to wait outside all the time, besides the expense, was not a good idea because the cab would be too conspicuous even if it did not involve anything obviously illegal. That was what Emilio thought. Especially around the Hotel Quirinale where at night-time there was a policeman on every corner. The Taverna was a favourite haunt of the Fascist leaders. And what about the poodle? Almost certainly they would not allow the dog into the Taverna. The only solution was for Corinna to take a room in the hotel. She went upstairs, left her luggage and the dog and came down a few minutes later. She only had her purse but it was all she needed to spend the night with him. And then . . . they would decide what she should do.

Crossing the hall, Corinna spoke with brittle indifference as if the matter did not concern her. On entering the Taverna she fell silent. They followed the maître d'hôtel between the tables and sat down. They would decide, concluded Corinna – whether to go to Ostia, Fregene, another hotel or stay there at the Quirinale. Or she could go alone to Viareggio the next day as she had originally planned.

'Certainly not! You're staying with me for the fortnight! It's all arranged!' said Emilio, looking at her hard and trying to understand what her intentions really were.

The Taverna: three walls of a courtyard pierced by orderly rows of hotel windows, the fourth windowless and masked by a very high trellis of creepers – box plants, black jackets, white jackets, in the centre, a circle of linoleum for dancing, lights which were bluish at that moment. Emilio felt bitterly disappointed, cheated at the thought that Corinna would not be coming to the apartment in Via Ruggero Fauro as he had imagined – with all her luggage. Yet when he stopped to think, he realized that any other solution would have been unwise. As it was, it would be difficult enough to smuggle Corinna out of the house the following morning without the maid and the porteress seeing. With four suitcases, it would be practically impossible. So the fact that he wanted Corinna to come home with her luggage was irrational. But why did giving up the idea seem to mean sacrificing the *complete* pleasure that he hoped for? Maybe because, unconsciously, he wanted Corinna to stay with him *for good* and take Elena's place? That was absurd. Not so much because Corinna was a prostitute as because he hardly knew her. He had been with her three or four times. And now he had been with her for half-an-hour. No matter, knowing someone had nothing to do with the case. This must be it – you could not hope for true pleasure except in a permanent, conjugal relationship. A trick, perhaps, a pretence. But in the same way then that the complicated ceremonial of a religious service may be a pretence and a trick.

The waiters hovering to serve, the menu cards, the champagne, the lights, the shadows, the jazz all surrounded Corinna with a new splendour and she seemed still younger and more beautiful. In fact she seemed completely different from the Corinna of Via Fontanella Borghese.

The neat coiffure, the sober, elegant gown made another woman of her. As she had said, there was no risk that someone would recognize her. Emilio looked at her and, overcome by the pleasure he imagined and anticipated, could hardly eat a mouthful of food. What lovely hands Corinna had! They were the loveliest he had ever seen – small, soft, slender but not thin. Two fingers raised the champagne glass to her lips and the others closed easily around it with natural grace and without curling. Few of the women here tonight – thought Emilio, looking about him – have such good manners.

'My father is a professor of Latin at the *liceo*[1] in Siena,' said

[1] Secondary grammar school.

Corinna, laughing and replying instinctively to the question that Emilio had not dared ask her. 'You look surprised that I know how to behave at table. Admit it. That was what you were thinking, wasn't it? . . . And my mother was Polish. Yes, a Polish aristocrat. I won't tell you her name, not for fear of tarnishing it but because I don't want to appear to be boasting about it. But if you were an expert in heraldry, you might get a clue from this . . .' and she stretched out her left hand across the table to him, gently, almost hesitatingly. On her third finger was a little gold ring bearing a family crest.

To get a better look, Emilio bent over and took Corinna's hand. But he was so taken aback by its lightness and softness that he gazed at the crest without understanding what it represented, without seeing it. Corinna's hand, her dry, warmish, smooth, slightly puffy hand lay in his, fitting as snugly as soon her whole body would fit to his.

He was brought back to reality by a sudden ripple of excitement among the waiters who ran in from all directions while people rose to their feet in the far corner of the courtyard beyond the dance floor. A maître whom Emilio stopped as he was passing and questioned, bowing, explained in a confidential whisper:

'His Excellency, Count Ciano . . . and Countess Edda . . .'

That was enough to make Emilio feel uncomfortable and want to leave. He lived in Rome, worked in 'the cadre of Government-protected activities', tried not to think about it, to forget about it, and seized every opportunity to go abroad. But when, like that morning at the Ministry or now, reality hit him irremediably between the eyes, when he was reminded that Fascism existed by the physical presence of some of its personalities and even more by the immediate, servile confusion of all around – then he felt angry, disgusted, he wanted to rebel or at least make his escape. And he realized that he spent the greater part of his time every day in a kind of voluntary, imaginary, extremely comfortable Paradise from which politics was excluded. So that now he seemed to have abruptly collided with something obscene, brutal and cruel.

'The bill,' he said to the waiter.

'Oh, no, dear, please,' begged Corinna, gently placing a hand on his forearm. 'Don't let's go yet, let's dance, I want to see . . .' Although he had attached no importance to it, Emilio had not missed Corinna's thrill of joy a moment before when she heard the whispered mention of those names that he disliked so much. Happy and excited she had begun to look over towards the far corner where the waiters were buzzing around the new guests like flies on fresh garbage.

'But, look, that's just why I want to go,' retorted Emilio angrily, unable to contain himself.

Corinna looked at him, surprised and puzzled: 'Really? Why? Don't tell me that you're an anti-Fascist!'

He had heard that the prostitutes were all hand-in-glove with the police. He had no proof, but it seemed more than likely and the thought reminded him to be careful if only not to give Corinna an excuse to ask for more money. He knew very little about her and did not want to misjudge her. He had by now long experience of women who plied this trade. He knew that they were just normal women, of course, quite capable of self-sacrifice and love, but in specific cases and obviously not with ordinary clients like himself. Oh yes, no use denying it – he was only an ordinary client. So in all probability Corinna would treat him according to the same rules that other tarts followed – she would try to convert into money anything he might be naïve enough to tell her in confidence. And he suddenly remembered that he had not fixed the 'fee for the fortnight' yet. So he said: 'Anti-Fascist indeed! It was only because when important people come to places like this, it causes an uproar and you can't get any service. And then all this crowd, the music . . . they get on my nerves.' And he concluded, without having to lie – 'because I want to be alone with you so much.'

She laughed.

'But it'll be nicer afterwards. Nicer if we stay and you suffer a teeny-weeny bit. We've all the time in the world! Think of me always cooped up there. Think of the life I lead. My holiday started tonight. It's great here. Some friends told me about it. But I'd never been here. I'm so grateful to you for bringing me. Now, come on, let's dance.'

They went on to the floor and began to dance. Although Emilio strove to keep his eyes off the famous table in the corner while Corinna stared greedily in that direction, he spotted between the waiters' backs the big shining face of the director-general with his broad smile and flashing white teeth. Emilio's last faint hope evaporated – that the maître had simply been bragging about his distinguished guests. That really was the Fascist big-wigs' table and the persons he had mentioned must be there.

Meanwhile the director-general had caught sight of Emilio, was smiling and waving to him more cordially than he had ever done before, arching his eyebrows, pursing his lips in a kiss and nodding approvingly as if to say: 'Congratulations on the piece of fluff you've got with you.'

Emilio, disgusted by this sudden familiarity, almost choked and if he had not had Corinna in his arms, he would have walked out. But she was there, pressing close to him. And following her lead he began to glide voluptuously, at each step crossing her leg with his, gazing into her laughing eyes, dancing cheek to cheek, half-closing his eyes, burying his face in the thick mass of her black hair and breathing in its perfume. To dance, Corinna had taken off the bolero of her suit; she was wearing a pleated white linen blouse which moulded her bosom and left her shoulders bare. The 'little giant' was not so little. And her body was both supple and firm. It seemed to Emilio as if her brown skin gave off some intoxicating elixir. Gradually, holding her tight and dancing, Emilio forgot everything else – troubles near and far, his anxiety about Elena, his self-doubt. All he wanted was Corinna, he believed that he was really in love with her. He wanted to know everything about her, details of her life, her parents and her childhood. Where had she been brought up? In Florence, obviously, judging by her accent. What schooling had she had? She was educated up to a point, evidently. Her age? She must be twenty-seven or twenty-eight. How long had she been on the game? What had made her decide to do it? And what were the circumstances that led to her decision?

He would ask her at home that night and during the next fortnight. He would get her to tell him everything. Now while she was dancing he looked at the smooth, bronzed skin of her shoulders. He could see a sprinkling of freckles which he had never noticed before. He wanted to thank her for the freckles, too.

'I never realized how pretty they are,' he murmured.

'Do you like them? People say they're flaws. You know, normally I don't have them. They disappear as soon as I sunbathe. I lie out on the balcony an hour every morning, summer and winter, when the sun shines of course. That's why in winter I always work the houses in Naples and Rome.'

'I could have sworn that your skin was naturally dark.'

'Because I'm the Arab type? My father who's pure Tuscan, born in Florence, looks more Arab than me. I get the freckles from my mother who had red hair. But I don't remember her. She died when I was two.'

Now he wanted to forget his own life and enter completely into Corinna's, feel surrounded by her memories, sensations, desires, see the world through her eyes.

Was it love? Emilio did not ask himself the question. Holding Corinna close to the gentle rhythm of the blues, he pretended not to see reality – that it was not love but a passing fancy. And that he could not possibly leave Elena to go with someone like Corinna. After all he had to think of his position at Victoria. Golzio would not hesitate to break with him. As the certainty of Golzio's reaction struck him he also suspected, though he dared not admit it, that he had long been aware of another, or rather *the other*, certainty. Yet just then he would have sworn that Corinna was for him an inexhaustible source of pleasure, that the next fortnight would fly and that he would be left with a honey-sweet habit which he could never give up – his passing fancy would be inevitably transformed into true, passionate love. Even if, because of Golzio, he could not live openly with Corinna, he could still rent a little flat and perhaps in the near future, as soon as he began to cash in on his percentages, buy it for her.

She made a lot of money in the brothels. So she would certainly ask him to compensate generously for her losses. And perhaps she wouldn't even be faithful to him. No matter. Without knowing why, he did not feel at all jealous. As long as Corinna behaved publicly with a certain amount of decorum which she was surely capable of doing. And then . . . he would take her travelling abroad. He saw himself with her in a sleeping-car or the cabin of a steamer. He pictured the joy of showing her Paris and London. He imagined the wonder and enthusiasm in her bright, brown eyes. He could almost hear her fresh voice, clear and sincere amid the bustle of the boulevards and Piccadilly.

'Look, there's Edda!' Corinna prattled happily away. 'They've got up from the table. They're dancing. Now we've a good view of them. And how nice he looks! What a handsome man!'

Emilio looked up, emerging from the wavy, soft mass of her

black hair. He saw the two people that Corinna had indicated and absently looked at them in the same way as Corinna – without disgust. If his intention or rather his instinct was to see the world through her eyes, for the moment he had succeeded and never even noticed it.

They arrived home. As soon as he and Corinna were shut in the lift, a box of polished, funereal mahogany where every morning and evening he spent a few moments of deadly boredom, he felt the need to hug and kiss her. Corinna laughed: 'At least wait until I take off my lipstick!'

So in the future the lift would be a blessed, live thing. Every morning and every evening on his way to and from work, in the blank moments he would remember Corinna.

He eased the key very gently into the lock. They slipped inside on tip-toe.

'Darling, forgive me if I don't put on the light, the maid might see us from her room. Give me your hand.'

It was dark and warm. Emilio continued to whisper apologies: 'These rooms are very warm because they face west. But it's better on the other side, you'll see. Come on.'

Still on account of the maid, who slept in a room off the main passage and might wake, Emilio made Corinna take off her shoes and pass through the study, the lounge, the dining-room and Luigino's room. As was the practice of the old bourgeoisie in summer, the lounge and dining-room were stripped of carpets, cushions, curtains, coffee-tables and étagères of their knick-knacks. Divans, chairs covered with white dust-sheets. They were still for the most part the furniture and loose covers that had belonged to Signora Calandra. The two rooms, so bare, seemed huge. Because the windows were kept closed to keep out the dust, the air was even hotter and more stifling than in the hall.

'It reminds me of my grandmother's house in Siena when I was small – ' Corinna said, laughing. 'I thought you were up-to-date. I never imagined you lived in a house like this . . . Oh this is where the little boy sleeps! How nice and gay it is! This room at least is modern.'

She looked around languidly, respectfully. She fixed her bright, brown eyes on the coloured, figured wall-paper. On entering the child's room, the tone of her voice softened.

'Yes, but he's not my son,' said Emilio with a coldness towards Luigino that he had never before dared to express even in his thoughts. During the summer while Elena and Luigino were away on holiday, each time, morning and night, that he passed through the child's room, the sight of the wall-paper with the little figures, the familiar toys lying on the floor, the tiny writing-desk and chair and an ink-stained exercise book left there never failed to move him.

'Oh, was your wife a widow?' asked Corinna.

'A divorcée,' replied Emilio in the same brusque way, lying effortlessly. 'And she'll divorce me, too. We don't get along. She'll keep the boy. He's hers.'

After putting out the light in Luigino's room, he showed Corinna into the double bedroom and locked the door. She stepped forward, slipping off her bolero and dropping it with her purse on to the big bed. He reached her before she could turn round, put his arm about her waist, began to touch her bare shoulders, her freckles lightly with his lips. She twisted around to kiss him.

The first grey rim of light followed the folds of the heavy curtain down to the pale carpet. It was dawn. A pain in his forearm had roused Emilio from a doze. He had slowly slid his arm from under sleeping Corinna's body – that body which only a few minutes before had been endowed with a supreme and exquisite sweetness wherein he had seemed to sink endlessly and almost merge as one single body but which now lay apart, rapt in its own sleep and quickened by its own breath. Actually, maybe because she had smoked too many cigarettes, Corinna was snoring, but only gently and not at all disagreeably.

Having removed his arm, Emilio turned over on his side, leaning on his elbow. He found himself staring with bitter and disenchanted indifference and even a twinge of annoyance at the shoulders of Corinna, naked and asleep – the plumpness of her back, that slight swell of brown skin covered with freckles, which a few minutes before he had smothered in kisses, frenziedly, tirelessly. What had happened to rob Corinna's freckles, her skin, her back, of their charm and even make him see imperfections, something un-attractive and inert about her?

The fine, black down which he glimpsed at the nape of her neck and the dishevelled locks of her thick, dark hair where, gazing deeply, breathing in the perfume, caressing its softness with his lips, he had lost all consciousness of himself and of time, why did it no longer mean anything to him?

That hair, that skin, the crumpled sheets still gave off the same perfume – then why did it give him no pleasure now? Cautiously (he was afraid of waking her and losing the opportunity to reflect quietly while she slept) he stretched out his hand and stroked the brown skin on her hip where it had seemed like silk. Maybe it was silk, he decided as he touched it again. But, stroking it, why did he not feel the same dizziness, the same vertigo as before?

Slowly in the imperceptibly growing grey light the room emerged with its usual, familiar shapes the carved headboard of the bed, the outline of the Récamier divan and the chairs, a small armchair overturned on the carpet with dark garments scattered all around, Elena's dressing-table over in the corner with its three mirrors gleaming in the darkness and a pair of scanties slung across them . . . He remembered, they were Corinna's knickers, he had taken them off her and watched in the three mirrors the triple image of his first penetration between those perfectly round buttocks. And he had tipped the armchair over himself, impatiently stripping off his clothes and leaving his jacket and trousers on the floor. But all these things, the flowered wall-paper, the curtains, the pictures, the frames, the furniture, the objects which till then had been animated, electrified in the soothing, golden glow of the nightlights by Corinna's outrageous intrusion, now at the first grey glimmer of dawn, while he listened to Corinna snoring, seemed inert again amid the general confusion, steeped again in the sadness of their good taste and conjugal destiny.

Suddenly he saw the absurdity of the situation. How could he smuggle Corinna out without someone noticing? Well, he had a plan. When Corinna was ready he would send the maid to get a newspaper at the corner of Viale Parioli. A convincing excuse, as in the excitement of the night before he had completely forgotten to buy *La Stampa*. But the porter would at least suspect that Corinna had been visiting him and mention it to the maid. And she in turn would be sure to tell the porter about the state in which she had found the bedclothes and the chaos in the room. No, it was a useless risk. And would raise a pointless scandal.

He had to wake Corinna and get her out of the flat at once. He got up, hunted for his watch which he had slipped off his wrist and left lying on the floor with his shirt. A quarter past four. He turned back to the bed. Corinna was sleeping face downwards, young dark-haired head buried in the pillow that she clutched to her. He could see the beautifully chiselled mouth, the round chin, the bulge of the eye beneath the closed lid and a breast flattened by the weight of her body. Roundness was the dominant motif of her form and it triumphed in her buttocks which grew luxuriantly from a slender waist, large, firm, smooth.

He still admired that body, but only felt a kind of pity that he no longer loved it, and an impatience to see it vanish. Pity? To compensate for losing her holiday in order to live with him for a fortnight in a Rome or Ostia hotel, Corinna had demanded an enormous sum: ten thousand lire. He had accepted.

Now, to send her away (but of course he would send her away, away from Rome – let her go to Viareggio, he didn't want her any more) he would probably have to give her a third of the money. But he would have to find an excuse, just for appearances' sake.

In the top drawer of the chest-of-drawers there were still a few greetings telegrams which Elena had sent him on his birthday. He took one out and, holding it in his hand, roused Corinna.

'Last night when we came home I didn't notice there was this telegram. I must leave for Paris this morning. So you'll have to go, sweetheart. I'm terribly sorry. I'll call a taxi.'

Half asleep, Corinna murmured: 'As you like.'

'Why? Don't you believe me?'

'Yes . . . yes, of course. How much will you give me? Darling, if it wasn't for you, I'd be on a train for Viareggio now. Maybe already there.'

Emilio had a thousand-lire note ready. He offered it to her.

'You're crazy! The dog will cost me four hundred lire!'

Seeing another thousand-lire note appear, she said: 'And what about the hotel? Who took me to the Quirinale? That wasn't part of the programme. You'll have to pay for that, darling!'

Emilio added a five-hundred-lire note and the business was settled. He accompanied her as far as the landing. As they went back through Luigino's room he saw the figured wall-paper again, the toys on the floor, the little writing-desk, the ink-stained exercise book and it affected him as it had always done. He remembered what he had said to Corinna less than two hours before and was surprised at himself. Maybe Luigino was not his son. Maybe not. But he loved him just the same in spite of the doubt. And why did he confide in Corinna of all people?

'Bon voyage, darling, and give my regards to Paris.'

'And you give my regards to Viareggio!'

They kissed each other on the cheek and Corinna gave him her permanent address: 2 Via Conchetta, Milan.

The marble staircase seemed whiter in the summer morning light; and in the silence of the sleeping building, broken only by the birds chirping in the trees of the surrounding gardens, Corinna's heels clattered on the marble with forlorn indifference, fading down into the distance. Oh, how different the click of her heels had been as she came down the stairs in Via Fontanella Borghese!

He returned to the bedroom and went out on to the balcony. Before getting into the taxi, Corinna looked up, smiled and waved gaily. The taxi left and the sun peeped above the Sabina mountains, tingeing the balconies and the façades of the houses with pink.

He carefully drew the curtains and began to tidy up the room. But he soon got tired and, feeling sleepy, went back to bed. The sheets were rumpled and smelt of Corinna.

It would be better for the maid not to see the room before he finished putting it in order. He ought to get up and lock the door. But he felt too lazy and snuggled down in the bed, in that sweet smell he now disliked, making a mental note not to say 'Come in' when the maid knocked to bring in the coffee and making a mental note . . .

He was awakened by a kiss, a cool face, another perfume. No, it wasn't Corinna. It was Elena.

It was Elena, as large as life, kissing him on the forehead, on the cheek, on the mouth.

She stroked his hair, his shoulders, his hips. And, continuing to kiss and stroke him, she bent low over him, hugged him and fully dressed as she was lay bodily on top of him.

'I've just driven back from Fiumicino . . . yes from Renée's yacht . . .' were the first words that she whispered, detaching her lips from his in the brief pause necessary to slip off her skirt and take immediate advantage of the situation in which she had found him. She lay on him again and began to make love. '. . . Yes, we were on the way to Capri . . . but something went wrong with the car and so Renée preferred to stop at Fiumicino.'

Emilio knew that there is nothing like a night of love to make one wake up in the morning in a state not of calm, as would seem logical, but abnormally excited. And, beginning to squeeze Elena's tiny, soft waist, he thought how lucky he was. In all probability, she had noticed nothing. Even though their sexual relations had become increasingly rare and mechanical, a distance and a separation as in this case of a few weeks were enough to reactivate them. And the violence of Elena's desire when she found him in the semi-darkness and close heat of the room, naked and asleep in that state (thought Emilio) must have prevented her from noticing the disarranged sheets or suspecting that another woman had just been there. What luck!

Out of the corner of his eye, by twisting slightly while still clasping Elena tightly on top of him, he managed to read the clock that he had replaced on the bedside table. Just seven o'clock. There was time to go to the studios. And even if, for once, he arrived late . . . the important thing now was to stir himself, change position, make love in different ways so that in the cold light of day Elena would find everything normal. 'I must cover up all traces of Corinna' – he thought, not without some amusement. And he set to with a degree of relish as if he enjoyed getting his own back for the disappointment that Corinna had proved to be; as if the coldness and boredom which had rounded off his little escapade could be compensated for by the woman Corinna had been unable to replace except for a few hours; in fact as if Corinna were the betrayed wife and Elena his chance lover, his tart for one short night.

And there was something else. The pleasure that he experienced with Elena was completely different from what he had got with Corinna and so often with other women like Corinna. The identical place, the short interval of time and the mental lucidity that he always possessed when making love to Elena led him naturally to make a scrupulous comparison. For they were two pleasures not only different but direct opposites as well. With Elena, cold, clear, deliberate, controllable. With Corinna, warm, confused, instinctive, irresistible. With Elena he relished lying but with Corinna he enjoyed the luxury of absolute sincerity. With Corinna it was like swimming under water but warm, breathable water which transformed and regenerated his nature so that he melted and dissolved in her body. With Elena, on the other hand, he seemed to scale a towering, solitary peak where there was room for only one person and he was that one, master and ruler of the whole world which Elena in some way symbolized.

And the end of both pleasures was disappointing, of course, but the two disappointments were quite different. In a gentle death-agony his passion for Corinna faded away with indifference and boredom. His possession of Elena was abruptly broken by a mixed feeling of pity and hate. The old, humiliating doubt returned about her and Golzio, perhaps even about her and Golzio's wife Renée. There was nothing odd about the yacht cruise. Golzio spent the summer in Rome, he disliked the sea. But Renée adored it and it was only natural that she should invite her girl-friends. Except that Emilio was puzzled by her choice of friends.

And so the old, humiliating doubt returned, complicated by other suspicions, other questions. Emilio felt that he was no longer a mystery to Elena after ten years of marriage. Though still loving him, Elena must have realized that he did not love her in return save in a very superficial cold way. Was she satisfied with that? Or rather, how far was she satisfied? Probably, Elena was busy looking for compensations which she had always promised herself in Renée's elegant, intellectual, cosmopolitan circle. But were they only snobbish, social compensations, or were they sentimental and sensual as well?

When all was said and done, Emilio knew nothing of Elena's private life. But that morning, at that precise moment, he realized that he could no longer hide from himself what he had only suspected up till then. He realized that his ignorance was voluntary. He realized that he had always wanted and at the same time feared to know; that he had found it convenient not to pry or even to think about it. For knowing might be useful from the point of view of his freedom, but it would also hurt his pride. That morning, at that precise moment, heaving himself up in bed and leaning on an elbow where Elena had replaced a woman who was scarcely more of a stranger, Emilio told himself for the first time that to know about Elena could actually be pleasant.

He leapt out of bed and went to the bathroom: 'I must dash to the studios, dear. It's getting late.'

He no longer wanted to delay. His secretly violent relationship with Elena spurred him to go to work, as always, to think of making money and to forget everything else. As long as he was with her he could not avoid distasteful thoughts.

From the bathroom, under the hissing shower, he shouted: 'What about Luigino? Why didn't you take him with you on the yacht? He'd have loved it.'

'Oh, no. There are lots of children of his age this year at Santa. He's much happier there.'

'But are you happy about him?'

'Perfectly happy. I've told you. This year the mademoiselle is a treasure.'

The mademoiselle was the French, or Swiss French governess whom she engaged every summer to look after Luigino.

'Still,' said Emilio at the last minute, as he came back to give her a kiss before leaving (Elena was almost asleep – naked on the dis-arranged bed in the dark room) – 'still, you can't deny that you were glad not to have the bother of the child on board.'

'Silly! Apart from the sailors we were all women . . .'

Elena yawned and turned over voluptuously in the bed, and as Emilio could not fail to notice, unwittingly found the same position as that in which Corinna had gone to sleep.

It was at Scarpone's old inn outside Porta San Pancrazio. The wide pergola with its worn, rustic tables, wicker chairs and the four yellow light-bulbs in the thick foliage seemed isolated in the black, warm night and the empty countryside like the last, ramshackle outpost of a shrinking, dying city. To those who dined beneath it on *fettuccine* and lingered over the amber wine, the world seemed improbable, forgotten.

During the day Elena, unusually, had rung him three or four times at the studios. He too had felt an unaccustomed urge to see her, an unaccustomed vague desire which he had tried to ignore until, while asking about the break-down of the engine in the yacht, he realized that he was afraid she would be leaving that same evening.

'I've slept till now, my dear.' – 'How long will the repairs take?' – 'We don't know yet. Shall I come to the studios for lunch? Send me a car, I'll be ready in ten minutes.'

Emilio hesitated. A tête-à-tête which promised to be new, strange, exciting, would be spoilt if they had lunch surrounded by actors and staff, a lunch bound to be interrupted by phone calls and urgent requests. On the other hand, if the yacht weighed anchor that evening, he ran the risk of not seeing Elena before she left. Sensing his hesitation Elena made the decision.

'We won't be off until tomorrow, you'll see. I'll meet you this evening. It's better anyway because Renée's expecting me now and I'd have to ring and put her off.'

It struck Emilio that the two women must be even more friendly than he had imagined if after almost living together for two months at the villa in Santa Margherita or on the yacht they still needed to lunch together on the one day when it would have been most natural for them to be apart.

The thought occurred to him again that evening at Scarpone's as he raised his glass to Elena's and met her eyes which were sparkling more brightly than the sapphire and the diamond on her slender fingers. Elena was now about thirty-five. Emilio had taken the easy way out of not seeing how much she had changed. Thus he avoided brooding over the years he had spent without getting to know her better.

At first sight, Elena could look very young indeed. 'You've grown,' Emilio would say jokingly sometimes. She had not put on weight, on the contrary she was thinner. She had loosened up, become suppler, lankier. A closer look revealed that only her face betrayed her age – a covert hardness of expression, the grain of the skin which was just a little dry and taut.

The sapphire belonged originally to Signora Calandra and Elena had kept it when her mother retired to Quarà. The diamond was a present from Renée, a recent present to Elena for her tenth wedding anniversary. Emilio was proud of Elena's jewels, he loved looking at them fondly, lingeringly, almost in a state of trance that might have convinced him of the truth of the legend about the magic, hypnotic power in precious stones if he had not suspected a simpler, more concrete reason. To him, Elena's jewels were the clearest, surest sign of the affluence he had sought so greedily and finally achieved. But just then, the sapphire and the diamond seemed to symbolize the whole of Elena and also that part of Elena which, through her mother's way of bringing her up and her friendship with the two Golzios, had always been a mystery to him.

'How is it that you can't stay away from Renée even today?'

'Darling, I rang to ask you if you wanted me to come to the studios . . .' murmured Elena, giving him a strange, intense look and then closing her eyes as though suddenly ashamed. 'If you wanted me to come you only had to say.' In the tone of her voice there was something uncertain or gentle. Emilio, noticing it, felt a slight shiver run down his spine. Fear? But of what? Maybe he was ashamed too. He looked down at his plate.

The food, pungent and tasty, made them drink mechanically glass after glass of the cool, aromatic wine. A feeling of gaiety, of mild intoxication gradually took possession of them. Elena's sunken, restless face seemed to fill out and become calmer – more vulgar in a way. A trick of expression made her chin seem strong and round. Her laugh was different – deep and throaty.

These signs and a trace of fat, something slack and natural between cheeks and neck, something which could well be a momentary indication of relaxation, if not of fatigue, reminded Emilio of Signora Calandra. It had happened before, but very rarely, in their ten years of marriage. Yes, Elena suddenly looked just like her mother. And this time Emilio thought she looked like a woman who wanted to prostitute herself. Once again he met Elena's fixed, knowing smile and for the first time since that morning wondered whether he really had managed to 'cover Corinna's tracks'. Hell! Perhaps Elena had her suspicions and perhaps she was not reacting in the way he had often imagined she would react – with scenes of jealousy and threats of separation. Perhaps she was prepared to take it in a way that till then he had never even remotely expected. And now Emilio realized that almost everything about Elena, including her friendship for Renée, could be quite easily explained.

Signora Calandra was a satisfied woman – a happy woman, within the limits of human happiness. If Elena resembled her that evening, it could be a sign – thought Emilio – that she too had reached or nearly reached in her own way the same state of mind. In her own way. Signora Calandra's tastes were not in fact very complicated. Even in these things they were much more traditional. She had a steady lover, old doctor Bonansea, and did not deny herself other adventures and passing affairs – quite frankly, she liked men.

To ask him to pour her some more wine, Elena held out her glass across the table. As if trying to find confirmation of the revelation he thought he had of her, Emilio had been gazing silently into her eyes for some moments. Then as soon as she dropped her eyes in fear or for pleasure at being found out, he began avidly to study her high forehead, narrow and convex, the small, almost invisible puckers at the corners of her mouth, her thin lips which were so like Signora Calandra's. What did such thin lips mean? Emilio imagined that they had become thinner throughout the centuries, they had shrunk finally as sharp as blades by dint of tasting to the full certain flavours, all flavours. He did not notice the glass or the hand that was proffered. He suddenly felt on the back of his own the sharp hardness of precious stones and Elena's knee brushing his knees as she slipped her leg between his.

It was a pleasant sensation but not of the same intensity and above all not of the same kind as when he had squeezed Corinna's hand at the Taverna del Quirinale and put his arm round her waist as they swung on to the dance-floor.

It was as if they had changed places – Elena now felt for him what he had felt for Corinna, or so it seemed. And maybe what Corinna had felt for him, he in turn felt for Elena – not real desire but the pleasure of being desired, vanity satisfied, a form of narcissism or coquetry. Anyway, he thought, it had always been the same with Elena. A feeling that he knew perfectly well. But that evening there seemed to be something new about it.

Was there something new or not? His intuition told him there was, told him so strongly, and he was about to transform it into certainty from what she said by exploiting his momentary superiority as a man who for once sensed that she wanted him. But as he squeezed the leg which Elena thrust backwards and forwards between his knees, he suddenly doubted whether his ploy would succeed. She might be the stronger and he the first to give in as he had always done, learning nothing – content to imagine and not to know. Or perhaps his imagination had played him false and the roguish gleam he thought he had seen in Elena's eyes had never been there. He had no proof, after all.

Meanwhile he could not resist the temptation of allowing his vanity to be tickled. He suddenly opened his legs, laughed and murmured teasingly: 'Be honest, Nini . . .' it was a nickname that he had invented for her and which he used in moments of tenderness – 'be honest, aren't you sorry you didn't bring her along too

317

this evening?' He saw her go pale, look down, take the packet of Turmacs from the table, give a weak smile: 'Her, Who, darling?' 'Her, your inseparable friend, it seems.'

'Don't be silly. She's your boss's wife, isn't she? When the time comes to argue about five or six or seven per cent . . .'

'Eight, eight! I've already told him,' Emilio retorted.

'Yes, but he hasn't agreed yet.'

'Unfortunately not.'

'There, you see! That's why I must be as friendly to Renée as possible – at least until you get this blessed commission.'

'*Be as friendly?* Do you expect me to believe that you're not on intimate terms with her?'

'I don't expect you to believe anything . . . let me go!'

Emilio had seized by the wrist the hand holding the lighted cigarette. Now, continuing to play cat and mouse, he tried to convince her that he had only done it to get a light. He bent down, dead cigarette between his lips, and once again gloated over the sapphire and diamond on her hand.

'Like to go to the pictures?' he asked, simply to tease her, because he was determined not to go anyway. Elena was fishing her compact from her handbag. She replied at once without taking the cigarette from her lips or looking at him: 'What about you?'

To play it right Emilio should have said yes of course he wanted to go to the cinema. But her question had taken him unawares and he remained silent. Elena had waited long enough. Abruptly dropping her guard, she looked at him searchingly: 'No, let's go straight home. I'm tired.' Her eyes betrayed impatience, if anything. They danced with laughter at the thought of the pleasure to come. She rose from the table. So did Emilio, calling for the bill and a taxi. A single lamp was still alight, the one on their table. The darkness of the countryside seemed to have thickened around the great pergola. Over in a little room with its walls covered in peeling pink distemper, he could see the white-jacketed waiter ringing for the taxi and Scarpone totting up the bill on his marble cashier's desk.

Despite his revived suspicions and the ambiguity of Elena's glances and smiles, Emilio suddenly felt a deep wave of boredom. He knew exactly how it would all end. A few actions and words that were different, especially at the beginning, but then the same mechanical pleasure which had never changed in ten years, from that first night in Via Guattani. Could he really say that he had seen what was happening across the dark, deserted pergola before - the white-jacketed waiter leaving the black telephone set on the peeling pink wall, going up to Scarpone who handed him the bill, putting the bill on a plate and slowly, wearily coming towards him? Of course he hadn't. But it was as if he had seen it hundreds of times; there was nothing new in the whole routine.

So the hope of discovering something seemed to vanish; and it was to avoid boredom, to amuse himself that he now resumed his trial of strength with Elena to test his power over her. He made as if to clasp her round the waist but instead gently brushed her hip with his palm. She immediately moulded her body against his. She had melted and showed it.

Emilio felt embarrassed, not on account of the waiter who put down plate and bill nearby and disappeared at once, but because of his victory which, as always happened with Elena, seemed gratuitous and undeserved. It was an embarrassment mingled with gratified vanity and complacent *amour-propre*.

So, he thought, if Elena felt the same tenderness for him as he did with Corinna, it was probably that Corinna when she was with him also felt that mixture of embarrassment and vanity. And – he mused - a really happy couple consisted of two people capable of feeling mutual and equal tenderness as soon as one touched the other.

Waiting for the taxi, they had strolled out of the pergola into the darkness, their arms round each other. A dusty earth track led up through clumps of couch-grass and reeds to a piece of waste land a few metres above the inn. In the still, almost stifling air there was a stench of dung and the cow-shed. Near the top the path became too narrow for two. Emilio went first. As he climbed he automatically looked up through the stunted dusty boughs at the sky, at the stars hazy with heat. A little further up, he felt Elena clasp his hips and as he stopped in the stubble field she held him close and kissed him. He thought he had glimpsed the fire of a small bivouac under the trees nearby fringing the field. But Elena's mouth tasted of wine and she was kissing him as she had never done before – her tongue darting and fluttering in his mouth with a strange vitality of its own. It was just as if – at least this was Emilio's impression – she had realized that he was different from what she had always believed –

different, so he could and must be loved in a different way. But this new way appeared to come more naturally to her. Then *she* was different from what she had always seemed!

Elena had given him those same kisses that morning. Anxious that she should not notice that Corinna had been there, he had paid no attention. What was this new technique? Had she learnt it from Renée? As she had been Renée's intimate friend for some years, why had she waited till now to use it on him? On the other hand, what if the transformation were simply due to a frolic with one of those semi-intellectual, semi-sporting young men who haunted Villa Golzio at Santa Margherita? Aboard the yacht there were only women and the sailors. But sailors themselves, especially the younger ones, accustomed to going with homosexuals, are often depraved.

In any case, returning Elena's violent, hungry kisses, Emilio too began to enjoy it. He closed his eyes and let himself go, substituting a confused feeling of sweetness for thoughts, or rather fusing them all into that single disturbing, languorous sensation which had first come to him when he got out of bed that morning and which now repossessed him. Elena was like Corinna, like Signora Calandra and knowing the truth about Elena could after all be a pleasant experience. Unless this discovery came to nothing as always happened with anything Elena inspired.

A cough nearby and they started apart. Someone was tramping across the stubble. The glow of a cigarette drew closer. Barely visible in the gloom, it was sufficient to reveal to a glance that took in the camp fire at the edge of the field – a gipsy.

'Evenin',' he muttered sourly, compelled as he was to come past them to reach the path. And there was a sinister yet strangely familiar glint in his dark eyes set between black eyebrows, side-whiskers and moustache. Hate-filled by an age-old grudge, the man seemed not to have noticed the little contretemps; it was as if he had not even seen them kissing. The next moment Emilio realized that the gipsy's face reminded him of the Indian at Shrinagar in the picture hanging in Piero's kitchen.

A lithe shadow among the trees, silhouetted against the soft radiance from the pergola, the gipsy bounded swiftly down the path. In his hand he swung an empty wine-flask.

Silent, motionless, with bated breath, Emilio gazed at the patch of light between the foliage in the direction where the gipsy had disappeared.

'Let's go,' whispered Elena, taking his arm and gently kissing his neck, 'our taxi will be waiting.'

'Let's go,' repeated Emilio. Now that he could no longer see the gipsy's face he felt that he envied him without knowing why.

During the ride in the taxi they said nothing. Elena nestled in his arms, resting her head on his shoulder and holding his erect penis tightly in one slender hand.

In the lift he remembered Corinna and perhaps more because he felt the need to remember her than to compensate Elena for a betrayal that she knew nothing about or merely suspected, he tried to put his arms around her and kiss her. But this time, unexpectedly, Elena did not respond. She avoided his embrace, turned her head away and stood facing the sliding door.

'Why?' asked Emilio after an awkward pause.

'What do you think?' said Elena faintly. 'Do you think I don't understand? On the contrary.'

But that faint voice was not, as Emilio might have feared, angry. Instead it was tender, breathless, as if Elena lacked the courage to speak, as if she could not say any more – just 'on the contrary' which puzzled Emilio.

The lighting on the landing was poor. Elena kept her head bowed. Yet Emilio, once he had opened the door and turned to let her enter, thought he noticed that her expression was still gentler and more hesitant than her last words and that her thin lips were not tightly closed as they would have been had she intended to scold him, but half-open, trembling, smiling.

They went into the bedroom. Emilio slipped into the bathroom and was about to close the door when the faint voice stopped him: 'Leave the door ajar so that I can see you. I'll put the light out here, I'm scared of the mosquitoes.'

There aren't any mosquitoes, Emilio wanted to say, but he kept quiet, suspecting that it was an excuse. And a few instants later Elena, nearer (maybe she was there in the dark outside the door) calmly murmured: 'But it wasn't a married woman, was it? One can tell.'

'I don't understand,' Emilio replied, and meant it.

Elena's voice, still as placid as ever, resumed with a kind of sigh, both melancholy and amused: 'She wasn't a married woman, the one who was with you last night in our bed, in my bed.'

'What are you talking about? You're mad!' shouted Emilio.

Elena answered more quietly still: 'Why do you deny it? Can't you see that . . .' the rest of her words were so faint that Emilio only caught an indistinct whisper. Looking at himself in the mirror he thought how ridiculous it was that they should be talking like that through a half-open door and not face to face. Yet he too lowered his voice to a whisper. And the tone – he was surprised at himself – seemed involuntarily supplicatory.

'Can't I see what, Elena?'

To know at last what Elena wanted to say but did not have the courage to tell him – maybe that was why he sounded so pleading. But Elena would not reply. Emilio repeated: 'Elena, what is it you say I can't see?'

'You can't see that . . .' In the perfect silence of the night, her answer, vibrating on the blue majolica and its highlights, came slowly, pensively, tentatively: 'that I'm not angry.'

She might be pretending not to be angry to make him confess about Corinna. Instinct warned him to hold out.

'Whether you're angry or not, I can't tell you that a woman was here last night because it's not true.'

'It *is* true, darling. And I know that it was not an ordinary married woman.'

'What makes you think so?'

'She usually wears perfume and it lingers.'

'Wouldn't it be simpler to assume that you can't smell perfume because no woman has been here?'

'Actresses, starlets, extras, even the girls in the cutting-room wear perfume too,' Elena went on calmly, giving no hint of any reproach to come. 'You know the only women who never wear perfume because otherwise they would never do business? Oh yes, married men wouldn't go with them for fear of being found out . . . But you know better than me – tarts. Last night you were here with a tart.'

'That's not true,' said Emilio, and put out the light. Slowly in the dark he went into the bedroom. He was convinced that Elena was half-way between suspicion and proof. He was determined to lie to the end. Making love would put everything right.

He clasped her to him in the dark and threw her on the bed. She was in her slip, and yes, perfumed. She must have just put it on while she was talking to him outside the door.

'It's not true, it's not true,' Emilio repeated, his arms tightly about her.

'Yes, it's true. I found lipstick on your shirt.'

'I was working late in the cutting-room last night. I've told you time and again that the chinagraph pencil I use to mark the film is like lipstick - exactly.' He tried to enter her. Elena twisted away, broke free, but as if to explain her refusal she moaned: 'Tell me what she was like! Brunette? Blonde? Fat? Thin? Tell me her name!'

'I should have to invent it.'

'No, it's true, I feel it. At least tell me, was she dark or fair, my love? Tell me! No, I won't make love unless you tell me!' Her body which he knew so well as he clasped it in his arms and covered it with his own, the thin shoulders, the only faintly swelling breasts, the waist still so slender despite her age and the child that he could span it with two hands, the long, powerful legs, the face that now he had become accustomed to the darkness he could see in the faint light from the open window, the blonde hair, high forehead, sparkling eyes and again the body which he took in head to foot. Especially the sudden ample, almost grotesque swell of the hips beneath the tiny waist and the gentle sweep of the thighs down to the knees; that body sometimes admired perhaps, certainly never loved, that body had its own secrets and Emilio had never been able to imagine them. That Elena had been Golzio's mistress and Renée's lover and that she still went to bed with Renée even now – if these were realities, then they were unimaginable realities. Golzio had been old ten years before – wizened, skin like parchment, hands like yellow talons. To think that he had touched Elena's nude body seemed not only repugnant, but absurd! Even taking into account all Golzio's financial power, absurd! And what about Renée's skeletal little body? That powdered face? Those hollow eyes? What could possibly happen between her and Elena? Absurd, absurd! And Emilio had always stopped at the absurdity of it. But now with Elena resisting him and begging him to confess a truth that concerned him – what had happened twenty-four hours previously in that same bed – Emilio instinctively tried to find on Elena's body the truth of her *rapports* with Golzio and Renée. As if there could be visible traces which he had never noticed in ten years of marriage! But he knew he would have to give up due to the unbridgeable gulf between knowing oneself and knowing someone else – each is a stranger to the other, always and in every way.

'I love you but I won't make love with you unless you tell me it's true – ' Elena was sobbing now – 'unless you tell me there was a woman in this bed last night.'

'I love you too,' Emilio had his lips against hers and spoke without detaching them – 'I love you too, but there's something *you* as well must tell me.'

'Yes, so do I, but . . .' Elena paused then restarted, still with her lips against his . . . 'you see, it's true! You've just said – "you *as well*". Now *you* tell *me*.'

'You first.'

'No, you first.'

And as if to prove to him that she was right and deserved to know first, that it could not be otherwise, she slipped from under him and when he twisted on to his back to grab her, she threw herself violently on top of him, kissing him savagely, almost exultantly: 'You first, you first, you first . . .'

'All right – her name was Corinna,' said Emilio. And he tried to enter her again. Though she heard the name she made no attempt to resist him. He was the one who held back. He resisted in spite of the fact that she was grasping his hips tightly and trying to force his penis right up inside. He was the one who resisted, exchanging force for force and holding her poised above him. 'But Corinna is her *nom de guerre* – I don't even know her real name. She's a brunette and she's fat. Yes, you're right, she's a tart. She's a tart I picked up in a brothel. And you're a tart from a brothel, aren't you?'

'Only now you've noticed it? Yes, I am. But why?'

'You must tell me why. Otherwise I'll leave you, get up and clear out. I'll go to Corinna who's expecting me.'

'No, no, my love,' moaned Elena. 'Stay here, you're mine . . . Just as she was yours here. You're like Corinna, you're a tart, too . . . my tart.'

'Yes,' said Emilio, trying with a supreme effort to maintain his resistance. 'Yes, I'm your tart like Renée is, too . . .'

'Yes, she's mine, she's mine as well if you want to know . . . is that what you want to know?'

'Yes. And Golzio, have you been with Golzio?'

'Yes, with him, too. I go to bed with him. He's my tart, too.'

'And Luigino . . . ?' Emilio was still clutching her hips firmly and looked up at her, a black shadow against the grey window. Her face was a shadow within a shadow, lost in her cascading hair; her eyes (Emilio still thought he could glimpse their sparkle) must surely be staring, unobserved, into his. But Emilio shut his eyes tightly, he wanted to see nothing, not even that shadow. He shut them tight, imagining he was falling over a precipice or being swallowed up.

'. . . and Luigino, is he my child or Golzio's?'

'I don't even know that,' sighed Elena, as if it were not true. But by now it was too late for any more answers.

V

It thundered. It poured with rain. The wind, sweeping in gusts across the garden, hurled the rain against the windows, shook and rattled blinds and panes.

He put on the light and looked at the time – seven o'clock. Since he was awake he might as well get up, gain time, go to the studios earlier than usual. It was Saturday – the Saturday fixed for lunch at La Capannina. In all probability Curti would agree to the film about East Africa and enter into association with him and Roberti as Golzio wanted. But before deciding, he would keep them at the Capannina till evening as usual, so that they would be unable to get back to the studios in time to do anything. So he had better finish off as much work as possible during the morning. He rang for coffee.

He could not get used to thunder in January – it always irritated him intensely. He missed a real winter, the tranquil gaiety of the snow, the silent solemnity of the sky over Turin. Thunder in Northern Italy announced the beginning or end of summer, it was a joyful release. But not here! How dreary to go out in the damp, freezing air, in the clammy, fine, monotonous drizzle.

The valet-de-chambre knocked. He placed the coffee and a sodden *Messaggero* on the bedside table. He pulled up the two blinds and opened one of the windows wide. The leafy evergreens swayed to and fro in the wind, lashed by the rain.

'What shall I do, sir? Close it? The rain's coming in.'

Emilio said that it didn't matter, he would close it himself. It was the sixth consecutive winter that he had spent in Rome. Every morning when he awoke he felt as if he were suffocating. Now he sighed with relief for two reasons – the air had freshened the room and the valet had left. For the valet irritated him too. They had just hired him, it was Elena's idea.

At the beginning of October Golzio had renewed his contract as manager of Victoria Films for another three years. He had doubled his salary and given him seven and a half per cent of the profits –

a percentage which met all his expectations. In moments of depression and honesty with himself, Emilio remembered that this had been the end of the doubts which had tormented him throughout the summer. Give it all up, indeed! He had a sneaking fear that he had managed to bring off a successful deal with regard to salary and bonuses only because he knew now how things were between Elena and Golzio. Maybe without wanting to, he was afraid to follow this simple reasoning: 'Before I adapted more or less consciously to the situation, I tolerated it; now I've begun to enjoy it – so I might as well make the most of it moneywise.'

Elena had wanted the servant, she had insisted. His name was Antonio. A Sardinian, an ex-sailor, ex-batman to an admiral at the Ministry. On leaving the service he had sought employment in Rome as a footman with nobility. He was a serious, quiet, hard-working chap. Emilio found him tiresome without exactly knowing why. He should have considered him as a symbol of the growing prosperity that he was at last enjoying and which he had cherished and courted since his earliest childhood when Papa and Mama taught him to envy the Sanfront family principally for the half-dozen liveried flunkies they boasted. There was nothing particularly strange in Elena's request. Yet Emilio had only reluctantly agreed to it. He preferred to be served by women. Antonio's jackets, chosen by Elena, red-and-black striped for the housework, white with white cotton gloves to serve at table, also got on his nerves, they seemed a lot of nonsense – as if the only *real* men-servants were those at the Sanfront house and others like it.

He dressed in the bathroom, a habit he had rapidly acquired since Elena's return from her holidays – so as not to disturb her since she slept till ten every morning. For the same reason, as Elena liked to read in bed for a couple of hours every night and the light disturbed him when he was tired and wanted to go to sleep, they had quietly discussed a plan to convert his study, which was next to the drawing-room, into Luigino's bedroom and Luigino's room, next to their bedroom, into a study, installing a wardrobe and a comfortable bed so that they could sleep apart whenever they wanted to.

But even regarding these marital innovations, Emilio lolled in a comfortable, almost systematic hypocrisy so as not to worry about the reasons why they had thought of them only now, after ten years of marriage; so as to deny that the dinner at Scarpone's and the night in July had marked a turning-point in his relations with Elena; so as to avoid seeing the truth – or perhaps the irreparable lie – which had passed between them.

Truth or lies, some irreparable unhappinesses are like that – suppressed in doubt, shrouded in the uncertainties of the unconscious, just because there is a desire, a determination for them to remain irreparable. It suited Emilio to think that nothing had changed with Elena, and that their new ways of living were the sort of thing that happened normally some time or other in every *ménage*. Indeed, nothing strengthened the new state of alienation which Emilio and Elena were trying to get used to more than the illusion that this alienation either had never happened, or possibly had been accepted and written off by both of them right from the start. Of course, this was not true. And Emilio and Elena, deep down, realized perfectly well that sometimes truth is not only expressed by facts, and that a lie can on occasion be a still more significant truth: the truth of hope, remorse, faith in a higher order of affection even though it be unachieved or unattainable – everything they had given up for good that July night during their loving in the darkness of the room, when they had given up lying for once and allowed each other the brief but intense pleasure of a few words of truth.

He tip-toed in the gloom, leaned over the bed where Elena was sleeping, gently kissed her forehead. A rite, of course, which helped to ease his conscience but which was tinged (and maybe justified) with a vein of genuine pity and tenderness for himself, for his mistake long ago in choosing Elena though he knew he could not love her, and for Elena who no longer loved him as she used to. A sad rite which he repeated once again in Luigino's room. The maid was finishing dressing him – Antonio would take him to school shortly. Another kiss, a ritual like the first. The affection that he felt for the child despite his doubtful parentage (or because of it) was itself a feeling of pity. Luigino was very tall for his age and as often happens to children who grow too quickly, very thin. With his big, dark eyes and round head he looked like Golzio or even Rousset. This resemblance to Rousset, Emilio had noticed only recently. He had begun to doubt everything Elena had always told him about herself, including her statement that she had not seen Rousset again nor had there ever been anything between them. But Emilio was forced to admit that Luigino's expression and character were like his own, especially when he was a child. On the piano in the lounge there was a small photo of him at about ten, roughly Luigino's age now. It was a snapshot taken with the famous Brownie, Uncle Sanfront's present.

Pierino had taken it and printed it on self-developing paper. The faded, sepia picture seemed to reflect the effort needed to conjure up that distant memory – it showed a garden path, the villa at Rivoli in the background bathed in sunlight, and nearer the camera Emilio in vest and short trousers, straddling a bicycle. Pierino had ingeniously stuck a big stone under the pedal so that the bike would stay upright and Emilio could look like 'a race-cyclist in action' and not put his feet on the ground or take his hand off the handlebars to lean against a tree. But perhaps the stone was an insecure support, perhaps Emilio felt shakily balanced, perhaps the snap had been taken in the early days when he was a keen beginner and his face betrayed discouragement and doubt that he would ever learn to ride properly – or perhaps it was simply his normal expression at that time: worried, melancholy, vaguely unsure and pessimistic about the future. Anyway, people who saw the photo all said that Luigino looked remarkably like him and his expression was exactly the same. The same sad look, it struck Emilio again that morning when he went into Luigino's room – the boy's eyes, his face peering expectantly over the maid's back as she knelt to put on his trousers, watching for his father to appear round the door. Luigino knew nothing of the situation: yet he was morbidly attached to both his father and mother. It was as if he felt everything. And he behaved as if he continually feared to be cheated of something that was his due. While Emilio, bestowing his tender, sad, morning kiss on the thin child, also felt cheated in some way. Sometimes he could not help thinking that if he had married Vévé and had a son from her, it would have been different both for him and the boy.

The Augusta was at the front door.

'Good morning, sir.'

'Good morning, Monticone. Hardly nice weather, is it?'

'Hardly,' replied Monticone, relishing his sarcasm. The car moved off in the rain between the grey buildings, the sombre pines towards the forlorn curve of Viale Parioli.

'And they've got the nerve to say that Rome has a Riviera

climate,' sneered Emilio, pulling up his overcoat collar, ramming his hat down over his eyes and settling into the corner of the seat.

'Some nerve!' echoed Monticone.

They reached the studio gates in pouring rain at the precise moment when Piero arrived on his bicycle from the opposite direction. The road for Piero was downhill, for the Augusta uphill. Piero, seeing the car some way off, did not realize that Emilio was inside for he usually came to the office a little later. He stood up over the saddle: four lunges at the pedals, a swerve, a racing skid in his best style and, raising two fans of mud one of which caught the Augusta, he braked to a sudden stop at the gates. He turned and recognized Emilio in the car. His bony face broadened into silent laughter and he whipped his right hand smartly up to the peak of his cap, treating his friend to a mocking parody of a military salute.

The cycle was a sports model, a Legnano racer with Palmer tyres, gear-change, and even a bottle-holder on the handle-bars. The cap, the brown waterproof rubber jacket, wide-belted and gleaming in the rain completed this apparition, unusual for Rome but typical of Piero, familiar to Emilio and one which conjured up names now beginning to age – Sivocci, Gremo, Pélissier, Franz, cyclists famous for their triumphs in storm and tempest, champions who had earned Piero's and Emilio's undying admiration.

The saucy greeting was untypical, different from the habitual respect with which Piero treated Emilio at the studios, yet not really disrespectful and possibly justified by the exceptional time of Piero's arrival that morning and the absence of witnesses apart from intelligent old Monticone.

At all events, with another kind of smartness Piero forestalled the commissionaire who came running up, threw the gate wide open and let the Augusta pass inside. Then he jumped into the saddle and rejoined Emilio as he was getting out of the car at the administrative offices.

'Can I offer you an *espresso*, sir?' Piero was evidently in high spirits that morning and broke into Roman dialect to provoke Emilio.

But once again Piero's presence was enough to put him at his ease: 'I should love one, *cavaliere*,' replied Emilio. For on his return from the Karakoram expedition Piero had been made *Cavaliere* of the Crown of Italy. Emilio was perhaps the only one to know. He accompanied his friend back along the avenue towards the restaurant. It was still raining. Giggi shot out from the office entrance with an open umbrella and handed it to Emilio.

'You free tomorrow?' asked Piero.

'Tomorrow's Sunday. Yes, I'm free, at least I think so. Why?'

'*Voilà pourquoi.*'

They had reached the Doric portico of the restaurant, a building all peeling plaster which had been used a few years previously for some historical film or other: Niblo's *Ben Hur* or *Quo Vadis*. Golzio had taken over the establishment as it was from an old Roman silent film company. Piero leaned the Legnano against one of the columns, on the inside, sheltered from the rain. He unbuckled his belt, opened the jacket, wiped his hands in a handkerchief, extracted as solemnly as ever from his hip-pocket a bulging wallet and from the wallet two yellow and red striped tickets.

'I'm not fussy. If it was the Toro, now! But I thought you might like it. Will you come? Just promise you won't shout too much. At the Testaccio they don't stand on ceremony, not even in the grandstand.'

'Up Rome, sir,' said the dark, hairy, thick-set chief electrician who hailed from the Abruzzi. He was just coming out of the bar and seeing the tickets in Giraudo's hand, he had realized that they were talking about the football match on the following day.

'What's that you say?' Giulio, the restaurant manager intervened smoothly. 'Up, Juventus, dammit! Up Juve, sir, up Juve!'

Since they knew at the studios that Emilio was a Juventus supporter, technicians, office staff and even workmen took advantage of it at every opportunity. Some, to flatter him and get into his good graces, were lavish in their praises of the Turin team that had won consecutive championships. Others adopted a more subtle approach and jokingly ran the team down, despite its victories, so establishing a common basis for good-natured argument with the boss.

In either case, Emilio could well have done without all the remarks, hints, quips and sallies. But there was no question of this as they were not entirely prompted by low cunning. They were an inseparable mixture of calculation and spontaneity, astute servility and humanity. Any employee in a factory or business tries, as soon as he can and in whatever way he can, to vary the rhythm of work and ease his relations with his superiors. So when Emilio was around the studio lots and they tried to involve him in arguments about football he always joined in, albeit reluctantly, hiding distaste even from Piero. Since he was perfectly aware that it was caused not by disapproval of his subordinates' attitude but by his own irrational, unhealthy, even ridiculous, and entirely superficial interest in sport which had begun to take such a strong hold over him after he moved from Turin to Rome.

It was true. If he thought back before his years at the university and the friendly discussions with Piero who supported the red-shirted popular Toro team, Emilio could not remember the time when he was not a Juventus fan. As a child he went to matches with his father who was a club member and had a complimentary pass. Cousin Alberto and his son Vittorio also belonged to the club and at one time had been on the board of management. And Giorgio Badia, when he was too young for cocottes and cocaine, had been goalkeeper in the first team.

The Juventus Football Club was founded in Turin, in the heyday of full-blooded monarchist pride and during the first vigorous stirrings of industrialism, by a hybrid group of industrialists and aristocrats. Feeling obliged to ape the British, they adopted the elegant stripes of the St James Club in Piccadilly, ignorant of the fact that in England football was the sport of the working class. So the black and white shirts had always been for Emilio a symbol of his origin, his upbringing, the family circle in which he had grown up – a passionate, melancholy symbol because his father's notoriously modest financial status had from the beginning relegated him, a Viotti and his father's son, to a subordinate position. Unlike the Ceroni cousins, Papal counts and heirs of the Sanfront legacy, he would never rate a seat on the board of management!

Maybe because of this, while he was in Turin between taking his degree and his departure for Rome in the not particularly brilliant or well remunerated post of secretary of the Arts Theatre, he had paid his annual contribution and gone to matches every other Sunday, following the team's fortunes in the championship with a modicum of interest.

But when his name began to appear in the film credits and both managers and footballers got to know it, and when a rising salary began to give him more self-confidence, then, considering himself 'a Torinese in Rome' and not the least important of them at that, he felt justified in boasting that he was an old supporter of Juventus and this partisan passion became one of the principal emotions in his life, as if humiliating circumstances had repressed and stifled it in the past.

Juventus came down to Rome twice a year to play one of the two local teams. This was an occasion which Emilio looked forward to for weeks with pleasurable anxiety. And when finally he saw his beloved black and white stripes pouring out on to the muddy field, it was as if his whole life had miraculously taken a different turn, as if his childhood had not been betrayed, as if there had been no need to woo and serve Golzio, marry Elena, work at the Arts Theatre, come to Rome, join the film business; as if Uncle Sanfront had left him the entire legacy including the villa at Rivoli and he were now a well-to-do, idle member of the old, incorruptible upper class in Turin, what his father had always dreamt of being and had taught him to to dream of. Oh, those remarks by the chief electrician and sound engineer Cavazzuti, Giulio, the canteen manager, the commissionaires, the film cutters, the actors, the secretaries – what did it matter if they were favourable or not to Juventus? In any case Emilio tried not to listen to them or at least to forget them immediately, because they seemed so insolent.

Juventus was an important thing – perhaps the only important thing in his life since politics did not bear thinking about and there seemed no hope of an end to Fascism; but there was someone to whom deep down Emilio had given tacit permission to talk about Juventus: Piero, naturally. He had the right to. And his remarks about Juventus, invariably cold and unflattering, the remarks of a supporter of the Turin Toro team, were much less offensive than the enthusiastic words of praise spoken in an Abruzzi or Roman accent. Quite apart from the fact that at the match, gradually, almost reluctantly, Piero ended up cheering for Juventus. Faced with the alternative of a team belonging to a city in which, though he claimed to like it, he still felt a stranger, and his old fraternal enemy, he finally chose the latter.

In every match there was always a moment (a dirty foul by a Roma or Lazio player leaving a Juventus man writhing in pain on the ground, a swift, concerted attack by all the black-and-white forwards, full-back Caligaris desperately chasing and catching an opposing winger, robbing him of the ball and passing neatly to the

333

forwards) – there was always a moment when Emilio would hear Piero, who had kept mum up till then, suddenly shout out in his peasant's voice: 'Up Juve!' And then Emilio felt a thrill. No doubt about it, justice and enthusiasm were on the same side!

Juventus had won all the matches Emilio saw in Rome during those years. Besides the two full-backs, Caligaris from Casale, and Rosetta from Vercelli, both of whom seemed to symbolize the peasant strength of Piedmont defending their capital city's colours, there were in the team three star players from South America: forwards Orsi and Cesarini and centre-half Monti. Then of course there was the centre-forward Felice Borel from Turin – very young, pale, thin, on the delicate side, who drove the fans wild with the nimble grace of his attack. Sometimes Borel, streaking through the Roman defence, the ball at his feet, seemed not to be touching the ground. As if on wings he would dodge his opponents one by one as they tackled him, then suddenly, easily, playfully he would plant a goal with a medium-height kick. To Emilio this was the triumph of intelligence and superior education over brute force, sheer animal violence. The superiority of Juventus over the Roman teams seemed to have a political significance, too.

Of course the management of the Turin team belonged to the core of the industrial or industrialized aristocracy which continued to collaborate with the régime – all of them more or less hypocritically Fascist by inclination or necessity, out of conviction or (as in Golzio's case) for convenience. Nevertheless, the style, the elegance of Juventus's football seemed to contradict the Fascist ethos. For though the team came from Turin and was financed by an authority closely allied to the dictatorship, its roots sprang from industrial progress and working-class toil. Shouting 'Long live Juventus' with a certain smile and a certain gleam in the eyes which others, all the true Fascists, could not fail to catch, you could, if you wanted to, imagine you were shouting 'Long live liberty'. It was merely an illusion, a poor consolation, but 'Long live Juventus' was the only cheer allowed at that time to Italians who did not want to shout 'Long live the Duce!'

Piero, aware of these subtle distinctions, did not approve but laughed them off. 'You're crazy,' he would say to Emilio, or talking through Emilio to all the anti-Fascists posing as Juventus supporters. 'You're all mad.' Sometimes Emilio thought that

Piero must be the only sincere Fascist in the whole of Italy. He was certainly one of the few honest men who believed in Mussolini's basic morality and was convinced that Fascism was a good thing for the country.

'See you tomorrow at one o'clock. Will you come to lunch? Then we'll cycle to Testaccio,' said Piero. He had buckled the belt of his jacket and gone over to the column where his Legnano was leaning. He wheeled it back and noticed that Emilio was deep in thought. 'What's the matter? Why so serious? Don't you want to see Juve this time? Oh, I see. I thought that's what it was. They're deciding about the film today, aren't they? And you don't feel like going to East Africa to make your first patriotic film.'

'Fascist film.'

Piero laughed: 'Go on, it's all the same. Let's say Fascist then. So what? Africa's a beautiful country. I've been there. You'll see how marvellous it is. But it beats me why an intelligent, go-ahead chap like you doesn't feel the enthusiasm that all Italians, or most of us anyway, feel nowadays. We need "a place in the sun" too, you know. And you and your Benedetto Croce and that other fellow in Paris, you can say what you like, our Duce is going to give us our "place in the sun". Why only France and England and all the rest and nothing for us? Then again, from what you've told me, you'd make a lot of money. I just don't understand you. What more do you want?'

Fascinated but not at all convinced, Emilio gazed at his old friend's frank, open face. The affectionate humour in his eyes beneath his bony, protruding forehead and the shadow of his peaked cap as he stood there in his tight brown jacket shining with rain seemed at that moment to reflect the entire love potential of humanity. Whereas the plaster Doric columns of the portico and the sickly trees and hedges of the seedy garden expressed the artificiality of everything else – films, women, Rome, politics, everything. The only genuine thing was the affection of a friend like Piero.

Emilio felt just then that by following Piero's advice, even rejecting his own opinion and conscience, he could not go far wrong. How could he trust his conscience implicitly? But the way a friend looks at you – no chance of deception there.

At noon Roberti came as arranged to take him to see Curti. It

335

had stopped raining and the sun had suddenly appeared as if by magic, blinding, piercingly hot over the pool-dotted city, over the evergreens and their metallic highlights. The sky was torn and convulsed – clouds of all shapes and shades of grey opened and closed, revealing wide gaps of bright blue in changing patterns. Maybe there was every reason to be glad. But to Emilio these 'quick changes' were a sign of uncertainty and restlessness, even though for the moment they were changes for the better. The restlessness lay within him and he was trying to attribute it to the weather.

Roberti came in without knocking. He pushed the door open wide enough to see if Emilio was alone, entered, closed the door behind him and marched briskly across the office to the desk. He seemed very gay. Freshly shaved, smooth-faced, almost shining. He stopped at the desk and looked Emilio straight in the eye. Instead of offering his hand he thrust it into the pocket of his light overcoat and pulled out some folded sheets of paper. He gravely presented them to Emilio.

'We've got the treatment. Here it is. Just four small pages. Read it now. If you like it and if . . .' He lowered his voice and turned slightly towards Golzio's office – 'and if he agrees, we'll be all set, see.'

'Did I tell you how much he's willing to risk?' asked Emilio with a slight nod in the same direction.

'It's enough. With that money as a guaranteed minimum on distribution, you'll see that Curti will fork out the cash to shoot the film. And if we play our cards right there'll be big pickings for us two.'

Emilio took the sheets of paper, unfolded them and glanced at the contents.

'All right. I only count up to a certain point. You know very well what I think about it. As far as I'm concerned . . .'

'As far as you're concerned, if we lost the war in Ethiopia and they drove us into the sea, that would be fine? Is that what you mean? I've heard it all before.' During and through the steelworks film Roberti and Emilio had become quite friendly.

Emilio had got Golzio to increase Roberti's commission. Instinctively sure of his gratitude and attracted by his affability, he had not hesitated to tell Roberti his political opinions, arguing and almost quarrelling with him at times. For Roberti too played the anti-

Fascist up to a point, but whenever the system was criticized he re-affirmed his faith, which predated the 'March on Rome'. Roberti's attitude was the same as Piero's and that of a lot of honest people at that time - critical of the Fascist leaders and the various institutions of the régime, enthusiastic about Mussolini, confident that his 'genius' coincided in some way with Italy's 'lucky star" that despite the inadequacy of his collaborators and his own obvious defects and grave mistakes, Mussolini was 'the man of Providence',

Moreover, Roberti realized that Emilio's anti-Fascist views were fanciful – theory not practice. As if to reassure himself, he gave Emilio a sidelong glance and went on to say: 'I don't care a damn what you think or what you want. If we lost the war everyone would suffer, including you. All that matters now is that you want to do this film. Of course it's a Fascist film, you know that very well. That's the reason we're shooting it. We start the day after we win the war. In May or June, they say – the Negus can't hold out much longer. The day after victory, Curti will begin to fork out one after the other all the millions we need and more besides, I don't need to tell you. The money required before then, that is to say, a) fee for the treatment, b) the script, c) advances on the contracts, director, cameraman, principal actors – that comes out of Golzio's guaranteed minimum. Moral: Golzio must believe in the treatment. So don't you run it down to him. If you want to do the film. Of course, if you don't . . .' and Roberti made as if to take back his four pages.

'No,' said Emilio. 'Wait, I'll read it now. The important thing is that the propaganda shouldn't be too blatant. Otherwise the film won't be a success anyway, will it?'

'Important for whom? For you or for . . .' again Roberti motioned towards the door of the adjoining office. Emilio knew that it was not up to him to decide; and he knew that if the decision had been his, he would never have refused for political reasons the considerable amount of money that the film on the Ethiopean war promised. But he also knew that he would never dare to oppose Golzio if he decided against it, nor advise him to do the film.

The four small pages contained a précis written by a journalist or writer whose name Roberti declined to give. The story, vaguely reminiscent of Conrad, concerned an Italian merchant 'gone native' in Ethiopia and engaged in the arms trade for the Negus against his own people: in other words, a renegade who moreover had deserted his wife and son in Italy and lived in Djibouti with a mistress mature in years and loose of morals. The renegade's twenty-year-old boy volunteered for service in East Africa where he was stationed as a radio operator on one of the many road-building sites. An Ethiopian detachment escorting an arms consignment attacked the site and the son was killed, dying in his father's arms. In the end the latter saw the error of his ways and atoned for his sins by fighting for the Italians, who won the war by machine-gunning the almost defenceless Ethiopians from the air.

'I like the treatment...' laughed Emilio, '...I like the first two pages where this chap is on the side of the Negus!'

'All right, all right. As long as you don't tell him,' laughed Roberti. And Emilio went in and handed the papers to Golzio without a word. Golzio, who was already aware of the negotiations, read it at once. Motionless, erect, his white round head erect too, he read without spectacles, his eyelids almost completely lowered, his talon-like hands resting on the edge of the table as they held the pages. Curtains of grey velvet and white muslin framed the sober, elegant office. A steady ray of winter sunshine shone through the only window and projected a lozenge of gold dust on to the beige carpet. On the wall opposite the writing-desk was a landscape by Rousset, all greys and greens – hills around Florence.

Golzio went on reading. Emilio, sunk in an armchair, silently waited and pondered anxiously over what answer to give him if, as often happened in similar circumstances, Golzio asked his opinion before expressing his own. But on reflection he decided that if Golzio thought it a good bet, he would take no notice of a negative opinion: on the other hand if he didn't, an affirmative one would never budge him. So the best thing to do was to be against the idea in order to relieve, at least partly, his conscience of the double remorse of promoting a film completely contrary to his own beliefs and making a lot of money out of it, saving on the capital put up by Curti.

Therefore when the moment came he gave his honest opinion. Laughing, he repeated what he had told Roberti: 'I like it as long as the principal character is on the Negus's side. But to me the second part is the worst kind of *feuilleton*.'

Golzio did not react at once. His face instead of responding to

Emilio's laugh clouded over. Emilio's heart sank. This was the first big rake-off in his life! Too bad, he thought. But it means that I can have a little more self-respect. Golzio began to speak. Slowly, almost sadly he said: 'Viotti, my view is the same as yours, so I entirely agree with you. On the other hand, the risk at the moment is minimal. Italy would have to lose the war and then there would be no film – a possibility which seems out of the question. Have you read today's bulletin? So let's take it easy at first with these advances to the script-writers etc., so as to reduce the risk even more in the improbable case that the war drags on. Tell Roberti that it's on. And get Curti moving too. Between you and me, my dear Viotti, there's nothing in this film that enthuses me. So let's concentrate on the technical side. Yes, on the technical side.'

Emilio had not expected such a quick favourable decision. He was speechless with surprise and the swift violence of two considerations that seemed to tug and tear his conscience two ways. On the one hand he thought happily of the percentage that he and Roberti would get of the money put up by Curti; on the other he felt suddenly crushed at having to do exactly the opposite of what he had always considered his duty. Now he too had to support and make propaganda for a war he had always condemned. Now he too had to hope for a speedy and victorious end to the Abyssinian war, and consequently the consolidation of the odious régime.

But Golzio, misled maybe by Emilio's reservations when he gave him the treatment to read, interpreted or pretended to interpret his silence as frank disapproval. He said: 'Anyway, Viotti, understand that you're free to do as you like. Privately – not as a business man or president of Victoria – I share your views completely. Of course I understand. If you'd rather not enter into the arrangement with Roberti and Curti, that's up to you . . .' Seeing Emilio's scared expression, he went on hurriedly: '. . . No, don't think for a moment that I have anything absurd in mind. You'll continue to manage production at Victoria by the terms of our agreement but we'll relieve you of this film on East Africa. I expect Campolonghi will be very happy to replace you, especially as his ideas . . .'

'Are the opposite of mine,' interrupted Emilio.

'Exactly. Well?'

'What do you advise me to do?'

'The same as me. Your political views are one thing, your job's another. Tell you what, you needn't decide straight away. You started negotiations with Roberti and Curti and you must finish them today. Then when it's time to sign, let me know your decision. I imagine Roberti will sign the day after tomorrow, Monday. You've got two days to think it over. And remember that I'm your friend. Whatever your decision, I'll respect it. Now off you go, give Curti my regards and . . .' he smiled as he handed back the treatment '. . . and mind you don't eat and drink too much. Goodbye.'

Banker Curti's villa was beyond Porta San Sebastiano on one of the pine-clad slopes which looked down on deserted stretches of the old Appian Way and over to the Alban Hills in the background. The area was one of the least disfigured by new buildings. Here and there in the solitude of the untended fields, under the massive, red, abandoned walls, in the silent gardens and orchards of the monasteries, an atmosphere recalling early Christianity lingered on – evangelic, pastoral.

The villa was a low construction of the dreary type then fashionable in Italy. With its smooth surfaces, small arches and slim columns, it gave the impression of being built of papier mâché instead of brick or fine marble. Actually in this house marble was only to be found in the interior and indeed, for the residence of a banker who had made a fortune and was still adding to it, the overall effect was surprisingly modest and simple. Curti, a genial, boisterous, aggressive, expansive Lombard, as impulsive and generous to all outward appearances as he was cunning and grasping in reality, was equipped with a university degree, was cultured (and conceitedly ostentatious about it) and was unusually intelligent and respectful of spiritual values and the arts compared to most of those who filled important positions in the Fascist hierarchy. A *bon vivant*, a devotee of good food and women, he loved all kinds of sport from snob polo, golf and tennis to popular bowls. He kept open house at lunch time for Fascist leaders from all over Italy, Northern industrialists who came to Rome for business meetings at the ministries, writers, scholars, artists, journalists, the occasional foreign visitor, prelates from the Vatican, the odd female intellectual, preferably elegant and broad-minded but generally one of the more attractive and notorious demi-mondaines of the moment. Curti was basically a mean man. His lunch guests at La Cappanina were more or less expected to appear with contributions of food or drink which were consumed at once. That day Roberti had brought a keg of Velletri wine and half a round of Sicilian *pecorino* cheese. But what Curti chiefly wanted people to recognize was his knowledge of classical literature and the independence it gave him of the régime and even of Mussolini's authority. Such was his non-conformist attitude. For instance, he felt authorized to display a freedom of morals which others, leaders and officials, were careful to hide; or he openly criticized some of the Duce's decisions and even joked about him, calling him *il crapa*.[1] He readily quoted Horace, Tacitus, Sallust, Cicero. Still, he too, like all those who counted in the life of the country, was essentially as the official cliché had it, 'conditioned to the directives'.

The lunches were not held in the villa proper but at the far end of the great park, between the kitchen-gardens and the bowling-rink, in a detached cottage semi-hidden in the trees and called La Capannina – the little hut.

In fine weather the table was under a rustic lean-to which over-hung the entrance. A fountain gurgled nearby. The water fell into an ancient Roman sarcophagus which served as a basin and was set amongst small rocks, broken capitals and other archaeological fragments, all covered in ivy and moss. In winter, they ate inside in the only, not particularly large, room next to the kitchen. There would be a great blazing fire with a pot of Lombard *polenta* hanging from a chain over it. In fact one of the 'speciality numbers', the attractions of lunch at La Capannina, was a burlesque anti-Rome act which Curti liked to put on with a wealth of invective in Lombard dialect, even though his fortune and importance in the banking world dated from the day he left Milan for Rome to work with the régime. And his acclimatization to Rome, or rather his satisfaction with Rome, was obvious from the place where he had chosen to build his villa, the style of construction and innumerable little details such as the sarcophagus. Time and time again, forgetting and contradicting his Lombard origins, he would lavish sudden and exaggerated praise on the beauties, the climate and the

[1] 'Big-head' in Milanese dialect. An allusion to the shape of Mussolini's head and his conceit.

other advantages of living in Rome. His persistent, nostalgic elogium of the Po valley and his equally emphatic denigration of Rome and central and southern Italy in general were, in spite of appearances, simply his idea of a joke – a joke which could automatically sweeten that hint of sincere bitterness he felt living far from his home town and quell his haunting remorse at the speed with which he had brushed aside the scruples which might have prevented him from making a fortune. Curti, like so many others, had been a Socialist in the early post-war years.

Emilio's mixed feelings towards Rome seemed not unlike Curti's. That was why the two had got on well from the first time Roberti took him to La Capannina – the Piedmontese and the Lombard striking up an immediate, comic alliance against the Roman Roberti who had introduced them to each other and had known Curti since he came to Rome at the beginning of the Fascist régime.

'Here come our film producers,' Curti shouted in his usual way when he saw them enter, and the words 'film producers' were filled with extreme scorn. The guests were being served roast kid; elegant young women and men of all ages, probably Fascist officials but only one in a black shirt. Curti, at the head of the table, with his curly grey hair, his face a healthy copper red, a napkin round his neck, a brimming glass in hand, called to them: 'You're late, you idiots! You've missed the hors-d'oeuvre, pig's livers!' Then he shouted to the kitchen staff: 'Hey there! If there are any livers left, bring them in.' And to Emilio, making room for him on his left and to the right of an amber-pale, horse-faced blonde with long, white, bare arms: 'Sit here, you bloody Torinese! I've got something for you to get your teeth into, you paranoiac, sex-maniac ponce. Look at this lovely bit of crumpet, she's a Slav from Split, doesn't speak much Italian: *Haec vera est Danae: tempta modo tangere corpus, iam tua flammifero membra calore fluent!* It's Petronius, you ignoramus! And *flammifero* doesn't mean match[1] but blazing – blazing heat in the blood. This is a bit who'll set your blood on fire and she should be in films and if you don't help her you're a fool. Tell Golzio from me!'

They all burst out laughing. The girl, though she did not look a novice and joined in the laughter, was probably forcing herself and blushed with embarrassment. Emilio, embarrassed too, bowed

[1] Match in Italian is *flammifero*.

slightly to her before sitting down. Then the girl, anxious to apologize in some way for the vulgarity of the introduction, murmured with a brief, cold smile: 'Excuse me. I'm Dea Lubini.'

Emilio rose to his feet and bowed again, shaking her hand.

'Oh excuse *me*. I'm Viotti.'

Her hand was warm and dry. It was a large, white hand, strong and yet delicate, like milk, with nails that were neither long nor painted but simply covered by a film of transparent lacquer . . . Why did he like her so much? He liked the girl's face but he liked her hand even more.

Emilio could not get used to Curti's coarse, aggressive language. Each time he suffered as if it were the first. He tried to smile but old-fashioned, well-brought up boy that he was, he looked uneasy, out of his depth. Curti noticed this and seized the opportunity to pile on the agony. It was clear to Emilio that the aggression and the vulgarity were quite deliberate. It was Curti's way of reacting to his own secret feeling of shyness and at the same time he did it to confuse his friends and make them listen to him from a position of inferiority. He considered 'a friend' anyone of a certain importance who was introduced to him; his instinct told him that some day or other he could make use of all of them. His most frequent guests, his closest collaborators had learnt to defend themselves by shouting back at him and, like him, using swear words and foul, obscene language. Curti had a sense of humour and enjoyed being insulted as much as insulting others.

The mock quarrels, the shouting, the arguments on any subject that cropped up, the food, the drink, the girls, cards or bowls – they were all part of his enjoyment, this was the life he liked. It was also his favourite way of conducting business. His guests and friends naturally liked being invited to the Capannina, but very often they came to continue a transaction which had begun that morning at the bank, only to be skilfully broken off by Curti before a conclusion could be reached. Then, with a long leisurely meal, plenty of wine and liqueurs, a hectic atmosphere of fun and games, he would gradually 'soften up' those who had a business proposition to offer and exasperate them by continually postponing final discussion as if involuntarily. And when this eventually took place, his friends' demands were invariably more reasonable than they had been in the morning.

It was the same that Saturday for Roberti and Emilio. Roberti, who was on more intimate terms with Curti, tried to talk to him about the film right from the start. Curti pretended not to hear. Roberti kept on. Finally, after the sweet and before coffee, he managed to give him a rough idea of the theme.

'What a load of rubbish,' was the answer. 'And you expect me to find the money for this crap?'

Roberti patiently fished out a copy of the famous four pages and handed them to the girl from Split.

'Let's have an impartial opinion. You read it, Signorina. It's very short. Then tell me what you think.'

'Is there a part for me?' asked the girl, flushing up again, and hesitantly stretching out her shapely, long white hand.

'But she can't even read!' shouted Curti. 'Of course there's a part for you – so long as you go to bed with all the Victoria managers in turn!'

'How many of them are there?' She laughed, beginning to get the idea that she might as well play along. But then she turned on Curti. 'So I can't read? You don't know what you're talking about. For your information, I got my teacher's certificate at Split. I know this about you, though. You damn well decide that all the girls you meet are stupid, otherwise you feel uneasy with them. Am I right or not?'

This time the laugh was on Curti who got in quickly: 'Bravo, Dea! You're a real goddess! Danae! One up to you!'

'Then let me read this stuff. I can't see a thing in this place of yours!'

For the sky had suddenly darkened as often happens during the winter months in Rome. There was a rumble of distant thunder and the threat of another shower. The Capannina stood in the middle of a wood of holm-oaks and pines. Not enough light to read by filtered under the low, protruding roof and through the small windows. The girl instinctively looked up over the table at an unlit brass chandelier, its odd, elongated shape hugging the ceiling. A chain ending in a large ring hung from it.

'Pull it, Signorina – the chandelier will come down and light up!'

'Pull it and you'll see!'

'Pull, Dea! Pull, light it!'

344

The girl looked around, laughing uneasily. It was obvious – there must be something peculiar about that strange chandelier, something familiar to everyone except her because this was her first visit.

'I won't get hurt, will I?' she asked Curti, still laughing.

They all chorused: 'Hurt? Not at all. Quite the opposite!'

The girl slowly stretched out her long, bare, white arm across the table.

Emilio realized it in a flash – the girl's arm, her hands, even her amber-coloured face reminded him of Vévé, that was why he liked her. She pulled the ring – the chandelier lit up and with a jerk began to descend smoothly. Two large brass wings masking the central part opened out at each side and finally, to the accompaniment of laughter and applause, the centre came into view in the shape of an enormous phallus, winged as in certain ancient Pompeian amulets. Two electric bulbs set in small round cages represented the testicles.

Emilio had already seen it every time he had been at the Capannina and there was a new girl there, too, and it always irritated him. Not for moral reasons, of course. On the contrary. At these mass demonstrations of eroticism he felt a need to defend not morality, but immorality which risked losing all its charm. Immorality requires silence, shadow and above all privacy. It was worse this time. He wanted this girl and he would have liked to slip away with her into the park in the rain and hug and kiss her – or rather, he thought quite honestly, enjoy her. Perhaps in some way she would bring back a particular sensation, remind him of the enjoyment he had had with Vévé! A lost enjoyment? Lost for ever, he mused as he looked lustfully at Dea Lubini's bare arms, amber face, high cheekbones and her blue, slightly Mongolian eyes, knowing that he would go to bed with her that night, enjoyment lost for ever because it was nothing more than enjoyment.

While the girl was attentively reading the treatment, Curti suddenly became serious and said to Roberti and Emilio: 'Crap or not, if you want money to make the film, I'll give it to you. We'll discuss later how and how much. But on one condition – assuming we win this bloody war, apart from that . . .'

'What's the condition,' Roberti quickly asked.

'If you can't work that one out, then you're a fool' – the banker

345

began to shout again. He got up and came towards Emilio: 'Come on, Torinese. Let's play a game of bowls!'

'But . . . it's going to rain.' Emilio hesitated. He looked at Dea Lubini who responded, unnoticed by those around, with a fleeting melancholy expression on her face: eyes lowered, lips slightly parted in the suspicion of a sigh. It clearly meant that she knew he liked her and felt the same about him. Her discretion, though both surprising and touching, seemed hardly necessary given the blatant vulgarity of the company and after Curti's particularly indiscreet introductions.

Curti bawled: 'It's going to rain. So what? Fine, we'll play in the rain! Any bloody fool can play in fine weather! D'you know what Guicciardini said? "The real touchstone of a man's courage is when he is faced by sudden danger." Come on! How much will you bet?'

It did not rain. Something in the Roman air and especially in Curti's garden with the view of the red Aurelian walls through the dark foliage of the evergreens made a bowls match there, however hotly contested it might be, seem to Emilio an imitation or a pale memory of a real match like those he had played with Piero in Turin. No doubt about it, Curti was very good. Emilio could beat him sometimes and always had a chance of winning so he enjoyed playing against him. The rules were the same. On the rink Curti joked and bawled in dialect, he moved and bowled with eye-opening perfection of style. He would not have been able to play like that if he had not spent at least the early part of his youth in the North. Yet Emilio felt that Curti's excitement and interest in the match were forced, studied, almost sacrilegious – like an obstinate urge to dance without music, or repeating amorous acts and movements when love is dead.

Before leaving, Dea Lubini came to the rink-side to say goodbye. Emilio ran over to her and bending to kiss her long, white dry hand, murmured: 'Can I phone you?'

'Hotel Senato, at the Pantheon,' whispered the girl.

Curti shouted from a distance: 'Viotti, fixed up a little bit of cunt, eh?'

And Dea laughed and shouted back: 'Why? Do you want your commission?'

'Of course. In kind!'

Emilio went back to the rink. Laughing at Curti, he quietly

346

corrected him: 'A big bit.' The words had hardly left his lips when he felt sorry and ashamed. Why had he copied the Capannina line of talk? To please Curti? A moment's reflection told him that his vulgar joke was both unnatural and irresistible. He had felt at one and the same time pleasure and pain, a strange sensation of light-headedness (I'm just like these people, like everyone else, I should be a conceited hypocrite if I didn't admit it) and an ache of sadness. The sadness was a memory of Vévé revived by the sight of Dea's muscular legs and slim ankles and her round bottom in the short, tight skirt of her gaberdine costume as her tall figure tripped away down the myrtle-lined drive.

They stopped playing just before dark when the light began to fail. Curti always said that he wanted to install electric light at both ends of the rink, but he never did because of the expense. He expected his guests to bet before playing with him and a part at least of the winnings at the end of the day to be given to the two caretaker gardeners. As he almost invariably won, he gained a double advantage – he paid his staff less and his guests were always received eagerly and with smiling faces.

They washed their hands at the sarcophagus fountain almost in the dark. There was only one small piece of soap – it slipped and fell off the convex edge of the sarcophagus and Emilio groped for it on the ground amongst the grass, the moss and the stones of an ancient Roman road which had been arranged decoratively around the Capannina.

Roberti had patiently watched the match, showing interest, or pretending to, in how the game went.

'Now what about this condition? Tell me what it is,' he asked Curti point-blank in the darkness of the lean-to while the banker was drying his hands on a kitchen apron. Roberti had spoken in broad Roman dialect, perhaps to let Curti know that he wanted a clear, definite answer.

'Where are those crappy papers,' said Curti still drying his hands. 'Did you give them to the girl?'

Surprised, Roberti pulled out of his pocket the four-page treat-ment. Curti tossed his apron aside and went slowly to a table in the middle of the floor where one of the caretakers had placed a lighted candle beside a thick book and a *toscano* cigar. Curti took the cigar and brought the flame nearer.

347

'You two,' he said, turning to Emilio who had just come up, 'bring me this treatment at the proper time,' and he nodded contemptuously towards it as he bent down over the candle and began to light his cigar. 'Bring it back with the mark on it and the deal is on. As simple as that.'

'What mark?' asked Roberti who knew what he meant but wanted a formal promise.

'Come on! Don't be stupid. A mark in the form of an M.'

'With an M, I can find the cash at the Bank of Italy,' exclaimed Roberti.

'Then go to the Bank of Italy, just try the Bank of Italy, you poverty-stricken film characters!'

There was a moment's silence – as if to emphasize that the last two remarks did not count. Curti, drawing great mouthfuls of smoke, sat down at the table. He opened the big book, riffled through the pages and began to read by candlelight. Roberti said calmly: 'All right. We'll get the M. When shall we fix it all up?'

'Eleven o'clock at the bank,' replied Curti without removing his cigar or looking up from the book.

'Thank you.'

Emilio echoed sheepishly: 'Thank you,' and out of the corner of his eye saw that the book was in Greek verse, probably an eighteenth-century edition. Another silence and Emilio managed to glimpse the title – *The Odyssey*. He suspected that Curti was holding the book well up in the candlelight not so much out of a pressing need to read Homer as because he conceitedly wanted to be seen reading it – an extraordinary cultural achievement for a modern banker. Emilio left at the same time as Roberti without being able to verify another suspicion – that Curti was merely pretending to read.

The M, the Duce's famous seal of approval, seemed to hover like a huge, misty patch of phosphorescence in the purple sky over the Colosseum. Emilio, sitting by Roberti who was driving his Augusta, felt just as puzzled as he had been that morning while he was waiting for Golzio to finish reading the treatment. If for any reason the Duce did not like the project and consequently the film was not made during the current year 1936, Emilio reflected that he would be consoled for the loss of money by the satisfaction of salving his conscience. Even though he could take no credit for it.

Either way, it will be all right, he chuckled – if we make the film it will be good for the 'flesh' and if not, it'll be good for the 'spirit'.

The M! The M! Emilio, silent by Roberti's side, imagined the great capital letter up in the Rome night sky and remembered his two casual meetings with Mussolini – once the previous October, the second time in December only three weeks before. He often thought of them, and almost always involuntarily – it was like an obsessive dream, sleeping or waking. But they were two real moments in his recent life and there was nothing extraordinary about them. Lord knows how many people in Rome had met him and would go on meeting him every day somewhere or other, in different circumstances, with one result or another according to the individual's state of mind . . .

The golden roads and the orchards in the warm, clear October air and the afternoon sun; he and Piero cycling off to the Alban Hills. It was a Saturday afternoon and work was slack at Victoria. Piero had phoned him at the studio restaurant: 'Come on. Let's go to Castelgandolfo. We'll have an outing.' They still went on outings, but much more rarely. Piero had two cycles – the Legnano racer for himself and a sports model which he lent to Emilio. Emilio hesitated each time – he had to fight his ingrained laziness. But then . . . but then . . . the golden roads and the orchards and each time the sudden joy of recalling his youth and discovering it again in his muscles. The road rose and fell like a switchback. From the ridge along the Aurelian wall, the same one where Curti's villa stood, the road dropped down to San Calisto, rising again to the mound of Cecilia Metella. Coming up to the top of each slope, Emilio, who was not so fit as Piero, lagged behind – just like twenty years before. And just as he had done then, Piero, as he sailed down the other side, slowed up to wait for him. There, a hundred or two hundred metres ahead, he could hear in the silence of the deserted old road the sound of Piero freewheeling. And against the misty sunshine of a Roman October, Emilio saw his thin frame straighten up and holding the handlebars in one hand turn around to gauge the distance between them.

Then at the bottom of a hill, while Piero was still well in front, Emilio saw two men on bicycles coming from the opposite direction. The cycles were black tourist models and the men wore dark suits and wide-brimmed hats. They were pedalling slowly and as they passed him he took a good look at them. They too stared at him and their scrutiny seemed to have something grim and threatening about it.

Without the slightest knowledge or suspicion of who they might be Emilio felt worried and annoyed by the rude way they stared at him. Who were they? If it had not been for their dark, town clothes he would have said that they were two gamekeepers. Two bailiffs, perhaps, two overseers of a princely estate belonging to the Colonna, Torlonia, Borghese, Odesdalchi families or whoever owned the land the road crossed. Not far from there, the previous year, Piero had shot some exteriors on the Torlonia estate. Emilio, as production manager, had obtained permission from the bailiff, Professor Terilli, and had stayed on location to see that the unit caused no damage to the vines. But why that sinister glance? Perhaps it wasn't sinister but just surprised. From a distance, the Torlonia bailiffs, if that is what they were, seeing two riders on racing-bikes must have thought they were two lads. Then, seeing them close to, maybe recognizing them, they had been surprised. In any case, Piero and Emilio were wearing outfits that must have seemed odd and comic on two men of their age and staid appearance – knickerbockers, long stockings, jersey vests . . .

Shortly afterwards the road climbed again and dropped as quickly. Piero disappeared and reappeared. There was a fork. Piero steered towards the left hand road, while from the right in a cloud of golden dust a confused group of horsemen emerged, silhouetted against the light. They came at a trot. Emilio again had an impression of Roman princes. They might be returning from a fox-hunt.

Now Piero was almost level with the horsemen and seemed to be eyeing them curiously. Then suddenly he slowed to a stop. He leant over to the right to release his toe-clip, put his foot on the ground, straightened up and raised his arm smartly in the Fascist salute. Who the devil was Piero saluting so enthusiastically? An idea crossed Emilio's mind. It must be Professor Terilli, a sturdy man of fifty, bald, smooth-faced who often went riding, hunting, horse-racing and seemed to spend his life in riding-kit. That was why, when the group passed him, Emilio thought he recognized in the dust and sunshine among the horsemen and slightly in front of the others the thickset figure of Terilli. Emilio did not slow down because out of the corner of his eye he could see Piero off and away again. He raised his arm, not in the Fascist salute but to give a friendly wave (Victoria had paid him a handsome fee) and he shouted: 'Good day, Professor! Lovely day, isn't it?'

He just had time to see that his shout and wave had thrown the group into disarray – a horse had been startled. He just had time to see that the 'gentlemen' and Professor Terilli, too, or the man he had taken for Professor Terilli were tugging at their reins and looking back in astonishment at him – astonished or, so it seemed, scared. But scared at what? After all, it was Professor Terilli, wasn't it?

He caught up with Piero who, still pedalling fast, said gaily: 'Did you see how lucky we were?'

'No, why?'

'What? Didn't you recognize the Duce?'

Emilio recalled the alarm on the faces of the horsemen and especially the man he thought was Professor Terilli – the way he turned his head sharply as if fearing an ambush, or at least some unpleasant hoax by the ridiculous cyclist in knickerbockers who had had the impudence to call him 'Professor' – probably a fanatic, a madman! Mussolini would never have dreamed he had been mistaken for someone else. The stocky figure on horseback, the smooth, undefined, almost eyeless face which had turned towards him in that spasm of surprise and fear remained impressed in Emilio's mind like a fold in a sheet of fine paper, a fold that could never be ironed out. The ride, the road up to Castelgandolfo, the snack with the yellow peaches under the portico of the old inn overlooking the lake – everything that day and for some time later bore the crease of the fold.

To think that an important step in his life, the question whether the East African film was to be made or not, depended on that man's momentary reflection, maybe an absent-minded decision, and then – a scribbled M . . .

They crossed Piazza Venezia and from the car Roberti and Emilio, like so many other people who happened to pass that way, looked up automatically (a sort of conditioned reflex) at the balcony, the windows of the Palazzo. They were lit up.

Roberti as if thinking aloud muttered: 'Do you know what? We've got to have that M. You can't blame Curti. For a film of this kind, we've got to have it. So this is where we bring in . . .' he named

the director-general – 'and you'll see that we'll get the M all right.'
Roberti explained to Emilio that the director-general would have
to be secretly in on the affair and take a cut of the profits. So that it
would not appear in the balance sheet Roberti and Emilio between
them had to give him his 'fee' out of their own earnings.

'For a film of this kind . . .' Roberti had said. But of course!
This was no ordinary deal for Emilio. It was a deal based on a
Fascist propaganda film, a film that glorified a Fascist war. If there
was once in his life when Emilio could not claim to be anti-Fascist
or complain about the dictatorship, this was it! Golzio had told him
quite clearly, 'Viotti, understand that you're free to do what you
like . . . you've got two days to think it over . . . whatever your
decision, I will respect it . . .' But should he sacrifice an exceptionally substantial sum that would guarantee him a comfortable, freer
life – travel, luxury, escapades, mistresses – and let him forget at
least for much of the day the existence of Fascism?

The second time he had seen Mussolini at close quarters and for a
few long moments was one evening only three weeks ago at the
entrance to the Teatro dell' Opera. Emilio stood waiting for Elena,
who had dined at the Golzios' and was due to be driven with them
to the theatre. It was a supplementary performance and Emilio
had forgotten to ask for the number of the box. It was raining. As
usual cars crawled slowly, one by one, under the portico, stopped,
deposited ladies in evening gowns and gentlemen in tails, then
moved off. Emilio waited for Golzio's car. He heard the last bell
ringing inside – only a few minutes before curtain-up. Golzio was
generally most punctual but Elena and Renée had a habit of keeping
him waiting. So Emilio was not at all surprised. A big 519, black
like the Victoria car, stopped outside the portico waiting for the
cars ahead to unload their occupants in shelter from the rain. In the
confusion Emilio rushed forward, convinced that it was Golzio,
and spotted Mussolini peering through the rain-lashed car window,
white face, white tie, a motionless phantom in a black car, black
suit. He was staring at Emilio, his enormous eyes dilated with
suspicion and terror. He evidently expected the individual, the
citizen, the Italian standing there on the pavement a few feet away
to recognize him, acknowledge him or at least bow slightly, smile,
give some sign. But Emilio merely stared back, not so much with
any feeling of hate or defiance as with fear and disgust which

paralysed him from head to foot and prevented him from acknow-
ledging his recognition of Mussolini, or indeed from making the
slightest movement. Disgust for disgust, fear for fear, anonymous
citizen against dictator, dictator against anonymous citizen. The
moment was equally monstrous for them both, Emilio felt sure. On
reflection he decided that the dictator's day must be full of such
moments – a whole life of monstrosities, even in the most voluptuous recesses of self-admiration. The dictator's image seemed to
haunt him. And after naturally blaming the dictator for all the
horror that his image inspired, Emilio was struck by a sudden
doubt that part of the horror might be due to pangs of conscience.
Was he trying to hide from himself the sin of complicity towards
which, with the film, he was irrevocably slipping?

But it was such a vague, inarticulate doubt that he could always
dismiss it. Work, better still, love helped. Piazza Colonna – and he
asked Roberti to stop, he had to make a phone-call.

'What is it,' laughed Roberti who had guessed, 'have you got to
ring Lubini? Did she tell you what time? Afraid you'll lose her?'

It was half-past-six and Dea had not given him a time to ring her.
But Emilio knew by experience that this was the right time of day
to find her type of girl in hotels and *pensioni*. They came out of
restaurants about three o'clock, strolled into the centre to do some
shopping, went home, had a nap, a bath, then changed for the
evening. He entered Ronzi and Singer. While he was looking for
the number in the directory, it suddenly struck him that the
Albergo Senato, a small hotel, probably had no room telephones.
It was close by. He might as well call there. He almost ran to it only
to be told by the porter: 'Signorina Lubini?' The porter craned
over the desk and looked out through the glass door – 'She just
went out.' Emilio rushed out and looked around the square. The
first taxi in the rank was moving off. Maybe it was Dea. For a
moment he thought of following her, shouting after her. Then he
flushed with embarrassment when he saw that the porter had come
to the window and was watching him.

He went back in and left a note – a couple of lines to say that he
would call her the following day at the same time.

The first to run on to the field was team captain Caligaris. Emilio
recognized him immediately. Heedless of betraying his sympathies

from the start to the spectators around him, and at the risk of provoking them, he began to shout frantically. Piero caught hold of his arm to try to stop him. Emilio had been shouting almost in isolation, a sign that his neighbours were more or less all fans of the Roman team. For five years Juventus had won the championship and humiliated the opposition. At every match the Roma supporters hoped for a recovery that would break the supremacy of the Turin team. Actually, that year their hopes seemed to stand a good chance of fulfilment. Juventus was beginning to show signs of fatigue. This should have been sufficient reason for Emilio not to count too much on a victory for his favourite team. But below the black wall of the crowd, motionless, silent (save here and there for some grey-green groups of Piedmontese soldiers garrisoned in Rome, waving their little black and white flags and uttering their isolated cries which seemed hoarse in the distance) and under a damp, heavy sky packed with enormous, dark clouds flying madly before the sirocco, when the black and white stripes appeared at one end of the pool-dotted pitch, he felt a breathless tightening in his throat. Throwing prudent pessimism to the winds, he wanted Juventus to win like all the other times – the victory that was sacrosanct and would fill him with joy even though there were other reasons for him not to feel pleased with himself.

Caligaris ran ahead of the rest of the team. He was immediately recognizable because of the large white handkerchief casually knotted round his head, provincial footballers' style. He came from Casale, Monferrat. His red face and big nose, his laughing, half-closed eyes, the curve of his lips and prominent chin revealed peasant wit and toughness. Seeing him run out on to the field that day, Emilio realized for the first time why he reminded him so much of Piero whose parents belonged to neighbouring Asti. One more reason to like Juventus, thought Emilio – no wonder its captain was such a likeable chap. It was as if, through Caligaris, Emilio could transfer to Juventus the friendship, affection and confidence that Piero inspired in him and the attachment he felt for the people of Piedmont. In this way, not only his middle-class traditions and aristocratic aspirations, but also feelings contrary to those traditions and aspirations, his friendship for Piero, the love he had cherished so long ago for Vévé and his admiration for the old tramdriver – they all seemed to flow into Juventus. And today, the dead-line to accept or refuse the East African film, before the choice of deliberately betraying or not his own ideals, today a Juventus victory seemed more essential than ever.

Roberti had phoned him that morning to tell him that the director-general had had to submit the film treatment to Mussolini for his M during the night. But on Sundays the director-general slept until two o'clock in the afternoon, so Roberti knew nothing yet. Emilio would have a definite reply if he rang him after the match. According to the director-general the answer would very probably be a favourable one. Emilio, therefore, felt an urgent need like an ache in his belly for Juventus to win. He shouted 'Up, Juve!' and followed the team's play as if his life depended on the game, as if the Juventus victory he longed for would compensate for everything else. He did not even see the others, the yellow and red shirts. They were just a brute force anonymous, indistinct, from which a player's grim face occasionally emerged – a face that seemed bestial and evil, simply hateful. A hate in which Emilio took a morbid delight, refusing to analyse its true object, telling himself repeatedly that it was a justified hate and realizing however vaguely, through a nagging pain bordering on desperation, that it was hate for himself.

Caligaris had lost the toss. The sirocco with its violent, irregular gusts was to Roma's advantage, blowing the ball directly towards the Juventus goal. Emilio and Piero, in the first row of wooden grand-stand seats and level with the goal, had a close view of the agitated, bewildered efforts of the black and white defenders right from the first minutes of the game to stem the attack of the yellow and red shirts aided by the luck of the wind. The spectators, aware of the situation, roared in joyful anticipation of revenge after a long series of defeats.

In the row behind there was a clean-shaven, pink-faced, hand-some man with raven-black eyebrows and a cruel mouth, a grey worsted overcoat, pigskin gloves, a soft silk-bordered hat, who like all the others around him had been annoyed by Emilio's enthusiasm when Juventus had run on to the pitch. Each time Emilio shouted 'Up Juve!' he touched him lightly on the shoulder and said in a Roman accent whose vulgarity was stressed even more by an affectation designed to mask or correct it: 'Look, sir, take it easy, take it easy. Can't you see that Juve's not in form today?'

And then, when Roma scored the first goal, as soon as the howl of triumph began to die away: 'Poor Juve, what a massacre. It's all over, poor Juve.'

Who scored the goal and how, Emilio could not have said. For an instant he had seen the ball come out of a tangle of legs and shirts, cross a short open space and shoot into the Juventus goal-mouth. And that was it. Whenever he went to a Juventus match he was so keen to see his team win, so keyed up, that he was never able to follow the game properly. Only in brief flashes the passes between players of his beloved team etched themselves in his mind as if dictated by logic, since logic was the chief quality that everyone attributed to the team. Simultaneously he felt so afraid and so hopeful and this fear and this hope vied so strongly within him that he always saw a match even when the issues were clear-cut as an irrational, indescribable sequence of happenings. The skill and class of the black and white team did not come into it. It was not to see them play that Emilio came to the game, but to see them win. To him the clashes between the teams were like lightning mêlées which dissolved too soon for him to observe and judge them. The important thing was for a black and white player, not his opponent, to break loose from the mêlée or for the ball to be passed to another Turin player running up into position. In this way, the swift attacks and lone runs of some of the favourite stars like Borel and Orsi, and even the eye-catching, soaring curved flight of the odd ball sent back up the entire length of the field by backs Rosetta and Caligaris, seemed to have for Emilio a magic, inevitable life above judgment and reason. As chance was certainly part of the game and Juventus had to win at all costs, every Juventus match became for Emilio a struggle between Juventus and chance; every match, and this one in particular, both because of Emilio's peculiar state of mind and the actual conditions of the field, the wind, the team's staleness after long triumph.

It was a tragedy which involved Emilio as witness and participant. A tragedy in which eleven protagonists were fighting a desperate, losing battle against twelve nameless faceless enemies, twelve, because in Emilio's imagination the referee was part and parcel of the opposing team. Two choruses acted and sang their roles around him, one huge, as big as the stadium itself shouted paeans of joy, the other small and puny with Emilio as its bemused leader intoning lamentations and words of loyal encouragement.

Roma scored two more goals in the first half. As the probability of their winning increased, in Emilio's eyes the players melted into a solid, headless, yellow-and-red mass representing Evil; the black-and-whites on the other hand, the champions of Good, became more clearly distinguishable as individuals, much more than when they were winning, for then Emilio, although he recognized them by their features and build, tended in the end to lump them all together in an imaginary single embrace. But now with the luck against them, Emilio thought he could accurately distinguish the individual suffering of each man in each contorted, dogged face and even from a distance in the useless, brave dashes and violent leaps for the ball. Distinct impressions – Rosetta, grey, nervy, resigned already, with his melancholy face and obstinately, uselessly correct technique; Varglien Primo, on the other hand, fierce and indomitable, with his perfectly proportioned limbs and horribly ugly, almost disfigured face; Monti, broad, serious, powerful, scornful today at the probable defeat as he had been many times before at the prospect of victory; Orsi, small, pale, thin, bony, dark, as soon as he had the ball streaking towards the Roma goal in a dash which for a moment gave an illusion if not the hope of victory; Borel, exhausted and breathless, whose running was now a dance lacking in grace. Caligaris was perhaps the only one who refused to believe in the possibility of a defeat.

At the end of the first half, Juventus was losing three nil. The ball had crossed the line and Caligaris, retrieving it and passing to the goalkeeper, looked up boldly as if accusing the wind and shouted so loud that he could be heard half-way down the field: 'Come on, come on, that's enough. Now in a minute we'll start to play.' He meant that with the change of ends in the second half Juventus would have the wind in their favour, so they could score three goals too, maybe win. It seemed like boasting but Caligaris sounded so serious that nobody laughed – not even the affected nouveau-riche shopkeeper.

Something happened which no one could have foreseen – in the quarter-of-an-hour interval the sirocco suddenly dropped, as often happens in Rome. Juventus, baffled, tried in vain to counter-attack, even brought up their backs. And Roma scored again. It was the fourth goal, all hope had gone. Better think of something else – of the time two hours earlier, when hope was almost a certainty, when the world seemed rosy. Emilio had arrived at Piero's flat in Via Ardea, rung the bell and little Irma opened the door. Still on tip-toe, her hand on the bolt, laughing and shaking her Titian curls, she shouted: 'Up Tor!' as her father had just told her to do as a tease. Emilio, taking her in his arms and kissing her, replied: 'No, Irma, no. You must say: Up, Juve!'

'Up Juve and up Tor!' decided Irma.

Piero was in the bathroom in braces and woollen vest. He had nearly finished shaving with a cut-throat razor. Laughing, he said to the child: 'Well now, Signor Viotti's right today. You must say: Up Juve . . .' But Irma had already scampered away. Emilio talked about Juventus, the victory that would be hard-fought but inevit-able and all the time he gazed, fascinated, at his friend's slow, precise movements. Piero cleaned his razor, closed it and put it down, washed his face, dried himself.

'Juve's not playing well. If I were you, to be on the safe side . . .' Piero stopped, made a face and rubbed his chest under his vest (Emilio was surprised to see that he had the same trouble as the previous summer). 'If I were you, to be on the safe side I'd settle for a draw.'

Emilio had bridled at such an absurd suggestion. If only I had, he thought now in the middle of the crowd roaring and striking up the usual mocking refrain: 'We've got them groggy – oh – oh – oh!' If only he had! A draw, playing away, is still half a victory. But what good was it thinking of what might have been. A peal of laughter made him turn round. It was the nouveau-riche shopkeeper. Purple in the face with delight, he shouted at Emilio: 'Where are the Juventus boys now, eh? Where are they?' Emilio muttered to Piero: 'Do you mind if we go now?'

They went. And as they pushed their way through the crowd towards the exit, the shopkeeper hurled vulgar insults after them. Piero smiled ruefully and calmly: 'Don't take it to heart, Emilio. After all, what is it? Just a football match and Juve holds the record for five championships in a row.'

Of course, of course. It was stupid to take it to heart like that. But when, in the bar on the other side of the avenue where he could still hear the wildly enthusiastic shouts of the crowd, he tele-phoned Roberti, and when Roberti told him it was all fixed, he had the treatment signed with the M, the go-ahead for the film in East Africa, it seemed to Emilio that the defeat of Juventus was really a deeply sad event. Luckily he was sure to make a lot of money out of the film. In his whirling imagination he saw all the women he had ever wanted but could not have, and all those he had had but not enough. He decided that when he went to Africa with the unit, he would take along as secretary – a bogus secretary, of course – Mimma or Livia or Gloria or even Dea Lubini. Why not? In any case he would know something soon. He looked impatiently at the time. It never occurred to him to pass up the chance of meeting her.

He followed Piero on his bike. And he thought of the girls, and of how when the film was finished and he came back from Africa he would go alone – or with Elena (why not?) – to Monte Carlo and Paris, and would stay there at least a month ostensibly on film business but really to have a good time. The sirocco had left behind damp, warm air and a subtle perfume which came from the countryside, like the first promise of spring, the walled orchards skirting the road beyond Porta San Paolo, Porta San Sebastiano, Porta San Giovanni. Over in the west the sky was overcast, but narrow luminous streaks of yellow and violet marked the course of the setting sun. In the opposite direction, where Piero and Emilio were pedalling, wide rents of cold, matt blue opened up and a few stars were beginning to peep. Emilio got to Via Ardea, left his cycle with Piero and took a taxi. He had told Piero that Roberti wanted to see him urgently about the African film. It was not true, naturally. In ten minutes by taxi he was at Hotel Senato in Piazza del Pantheon. It was the time he had promised to ring Dea.

'Signor Viotti? There's a message for you.'

Dea's pencilled note said that she was so sorry but something had unexpectedly cropped up and she had to leave at once for Milan. She did not know when she would be back. If he still wanted to see her when she did get back she would get in touch with him through Curti. The note ended: 'Love and kisses, your Dea.'

Emilio thought immediately how right it was, it had to be so. Dea was like Vévé, and like Vévé he might never see her again. In any case for the present it was no good thinking about her. He asked the porter, slipping him a tip: 'Excuse me, can you give me Signorina Lubini's address?' And back came the reply: 'The Signorina checked out without leaving a forwarding address.'

PART FOUR

I

Happiness exists, thought Emilio, motionless on the bed. A faint light reflected by the age-old blue ceramic floor and the white paint on the wardrobes glimmered in the summer siesta air of the room. This was happiness – no Elena, no Luigino, no servants, no girls, the realization that he was alone for a few hours in his fine new home, the little Baroque palazzo in Via Gregoriana which he had just moved into. Alone at four o'clock on a late September Sunday afternoon, gazing at the sun mirrored in the windows of the inner courtyard and filtering through the shutters and silk curtains – still warm, still a Roman summer.

He had stayed in the office until one o'clock. Then he had preferred to lunch alone and put off his date with Grazia until later. He would pick her up about six and take her to Fregene where there might be time for a quick dip. After dinner back to Rome and they would spend the night in Via del Mare. Grazia was a twenty-two-year-old girl from Marseilles – tall, slender, dark, passionate and sweetly tender. He had met her a few days before at the Trocadero, a Naples night-club. And he was not tired of her yet, no, on the contrary! So happiness in a general way was the knowledge of having passed the stage of financial security to the comfort and luxury he had always wanted – in particular the expectation of an evening and night with Grazia. That love and acts of love were only a pretence and a function, a kind of ritual repeated each time with exquisite little variations, no longer irked him in the least. Indeed, it all seemed quite right and wonderful. He believed he had finally found a way to avoid the torments and troubles brought on by real passions and derived more enjoyment by acting out those passions for an evening or a night than by actually living them. Romantic lovers, he thought, would call me a hedonist, an egoist. But fundamentally what difference is there between my type of passion and theirs? None at all, except that there comes the moment, after being ruled by my passion in much the same way as they are by theirs, when I can control it, abandon it as soon as I see the pleasure flagging and become enslaved once more whenever that pleasure revives.

Self-dissatisfaction, remorse stemming from his early youth, Vévé's desertion and his pretence of love for Elena, the vague longing for a great new love and the thought which Piero had suggested that this love was necessary to his peace of mind; Emilio believed at last that he had conquered all these doubts and anxieties.

And it was true that between the year of the African war and the film with Roberti, and the first two years of World War II, he had felt them gradually diminish – perhaps because his economic prosperity, with Golzio's help, had been increasing. 1943 and 1944 saw the end of financial problems. With his usual cold, realistic calculation, Golzio had managed to exploit the war so that events disastrous for the great majority of Italians turned out to be extremely profitable for him. And his calculation had been simple. If Europe is destroyed, capital savings will be useless. If, on the other hand (and it was obvious to anyone with common sense, at least when America and Russia came into the war) Europe survives, the best thing to do would be to invest all the capital available in land and real estate in Rome, Milan, Turin, Genoa, everywhere. These were the worst months of heavy bombing raids on Italian cities. The prices of land and real estate plummeted and would continue to fall until they reached rock bottom. Emilio had wisely arranged to transfer to Switzerland a large proportion of the money he had accumulated from film production. Golzio knew about these deposits and offered to treat them as security for equivalent sums he was prepared to advance Emilio for new purchases. In this way, small new real estate societies sprang up in the chief Italian towns during those most terrible days. Most of the shares belonged to Golzio, or to Golzio in partnership with Emilio. Golzio knew that Emilio was a shareholder who would never try to squeeze him out. Everything worked smoothly. From '41 to the spring of '43, Emilio performed the functions not so much of a film producer as of a travelling salesman. He travelled in style, but the work was tiring and sometimes not without its dangers. Following Golzio's directives (he did not move from Rome) Emilio toured Italy visiting sites and buildings, negotiating purchase prices, setting up companies. When the Americans landed in Sicily, Golzio, without even waiting for July 25, retired to a remote spot deep in the Maremma near

Roccalbegna and between Grosseto and l'Amiata where he had bought a castle and renovated it with every modern convenience.

The estate was large and well cultivated, sufficient to provide a regular supply of food. The castle itself was spacious – Elena and Emilio rented an entire wing where they lived separately. Luigino, who was now seventeen, had been previously sent to an expensive college in Switzerland where he continued his studies safely until the end of the war. At Roccalbegna Golzio had no difficulty in dealing with both the German soldiers and the few partisans in the area, avoiding trouble from the former and currying favour with the latter whom he supplied regularly with provisions. Helped by Emilio, he hid English prisoners and sheltered people sent down from the north by the Committee of Liberation on the way to Rome or to cross the lines for political reasons. Golzio's former unbroken contacts with anti-Fascist circles were now paying off, all the more because he had always been privately opposed to the régime. Allied troops liberated Roccalbegna on June 17, 1944. Emilio left immediately for Rome, a few days earlier than Elena and the Golzios.

Victoria's new studios and the new offices in Via Pergolesi, headquarters of production and most of the real estate companies, were occupied by the Allied Military Government. But Golzio had not lost touch with some very influential friends in London and New York and here too he managed to avoid losses and confiscation. Under the pretext of producing propaganda documentaries for the Allied authorities, he obtained a work permit, a stock of film, ultramodern American equipment and English projectors.

Victoria began to operate again with a considerable start over the other film companies. Emilio himself struck up a profitable friendship with a man called Adams, a British official in PWB.

The house in Via Ruggero Fauro was invaded by Allied officers, writers, artists, actors and actresses, politicians, beautiful women, the élite which remained south of the Arno in 1944. They finally came out of their various hiding-places. Happy with the return to life and security, anxious to tell one another about their adventures and stake their claims for the future, they all met again in liberated Rome. The celebrations lasted several months. There was a constant round of parties, at least twice a week at the Viottis'. Elena worked hard at it. She was happy, too. She and Emilio were beginning to taste the fruits of the comfortable living which they had always longed for, had achieved in the last years of peace and the first of war, but had only now become able to enjoy openly.

During all this time Emilio's parents had been in Northern Italy – his father ill, both too old to accept his invitation to come to him in Roccalbegna. From the time of the earliest bombings they had sought refuge in the old Viotti house at Trino Vercellese, a township on the left bank of the Po a little more than thirty kilometres from Turin.

Emilio had had central heating installed there. The Crown Counsel and his wife, realizing how readily their son had undertaken the not inconsiderable expense, heaved the first great sigh of relief in their lives, saw the first tangible proof that films or not, Emilio was at last 'home and dry' – at least that was how his father put it. Up to the moment when with the Allies' advance, Northern Italy was isolated beyond the Gothic line, Emilio still received good news from his parents.

But in December of that year his father died and he only learned of it a few months later after the liberation. Signora Viotti returned to Turin. The apartment in Piazza Maria Teresa was now too large for her on her own. Emilio bought her a little flat in the aristocratic Via della Rocca nearby. The old lady, able to bask in reflected glory and count upon an easy life, began to devote body and soul to a single purpose – making up for lost time and cultivating once again the oldest and best Turin society where for too long the Ceroni-Sanfronts had admitted her only at Christmas, Easter and the few other regular holidays. Emilio's mother had always believed it to be the only society that mattered. Moreover she had always entered it, head held high, with exaggerated dignity, even during the worst years when her son was first away in Rome 'making films'. But a head held high and dignity had not been enough. Signora Viotti, though accepted everywhere, had been officially considered only as the mother of one of 'Golzio's employees'. And Golzio, in spite of all he had done for art and culture in Turin, had always been considered a 'profiteering shark'. His removal to Rome had been looked upon as running away, an admission of defeat. Now the time had come for old Signora Viotti to get her revenge.

Alberto Ceroni, her husband's first cousin, had managed to be appointed a Papal Count and had become sole heir of Uncle Sanfront who was his uncle as he was Emilio's father's. Continuing along the same line, a few years later and still under Fascism, the son Vittorio Ceroni, Emilio's second cousin and contemporary, had changed his name by a royal decree which gave him the right to add 'Sanfront'. When old Signora Viotti embraced her son again after a year of enforced separation and in mourning for the recent death of her husband, the subject she broached most urgently was the transfer of his remains from the cemetery in Trino Vercellese to the Sanfront family mausoleum in Turin where all the Ceronis were buried, even before they took the name Sanfront, and consequently where the Viottis had to be laid to rest. Emilio promised to see to it and try to mention the matter to his cousin Vittorio at the first opportunity.

His mother was right. Emilio knew that thanks to his sound financial position he had overcome the last traces of the Viotti inferiority complex vis-à-vis the Sanfronts, the Ceronis, the Badias. If Vittorio Ceroni-Sanfront and Giorgio Badia, both forty-five years old like Emilio, had preserved a spark of their youthful 'gay dog' spirit, *they* must be envying their cousin now! Or they would be, thought Emilio, as soon as they knew about the stability and future possibilities of his financial stake in the building trade, the glamour and enjoyment he derived from film production and his two establishments in Rome – the bachelor flat in Via del Mare and the small mansion in Via Gregoriana.

One of the last transactions that Golzio had concluded before leaving Rome for Tuscany was the purchase as it stood of the Palazzetto Stroganoff in Via Gregoriana. A building dating from the end of last century but in eighteenth-century style, it belonged to an old lady of the Turin aristocracy who also intended to retire to the country, but in Piedmont. Fearing the immediate future, she realized more than enough to live comfortably in the provinces. So as not to leave the premises empty Golzio rented it to three of his employees' families who had been recently evacuated to Rome from the north. The rent was ridiculously low given the house's location and the value of the furniture and fittings; but the tenants undertook to maintain the property and move to new accommodation which Golzio would find for them after the war. In June 1945 Emilio acquired the entire mansion, paying Golzio the equivalent in real estate company shares, and moved in at the beginning of September.

Now the happiness he had won and the happiness of that Sunday afternoon, too, depended partly on his new home. At last he was beginning to glimpse a reconciliation with Rome that had never been possible in the flat on Via Ruggero Fauro. Here, in the Rome of Piazza di Spagna, Trinità dei Monti, Via Sistina, Via Gregoriana, it seemed real – that famous clear, warm light which Rousset and others had lauded with such stupid persistence that he could see it only as an aesthetic, almost oleographic, reflection. He opened the bedroom window wide and saw beyond the old russet roofs of the house opposite a huge untidy expanse, pink and dirty-white, of flat roofs, small hanging gardens, domes, steeples, baroque copings, rough porous stones, grey, honey-coloured, corners and sections of houses with pale yellow or apricot plaster, an infinite number of details or fragments superimposed and criss-crossing half-way across the horizon from the sombre green of the Janiculum to that of Monte Mario – and between the two hills the great dome of San Pietro, silvery in the morning, golden at noon, blue against the light at sunset. The front of the house opposite was apricot, too, beneath the russet roof. That strange, vivid colour in various lights and under different skies always made him feel incredibly gay – it somehow represented *joie de vivre*.

During the first weeks Emilio had chosen for his afternoon siesta the spacious dressing-room, paved with Dutch tiles, blue and white, which was between the bedroom and the bathroom and where he had installed a divan. Cool. Quiet. One wall was entirely lined with large white-painted wardrobes topped by narrow gilt cornices. Opposite, three windows shielded by grey shutters and white silk curtains opened on to the inner courtyard which was enclosed on all four sides by walls that were part of his property.

He wanted nothing more. He had worked steadily in the morning, then eaten and rested well. Elena and Luigino were on Ischia. He had given the two servants, the maid and the cook, the day off and anyway they occupied a flat on the top floor. He would have to wait until six o'clock before picking up Grazia at the *pensione* in Piazza del Popolo. How long to go? He checked the time on the gold Rolex he had bought in Lausanne a month before when he went to fetch Luigino. Half past three. It was still early. As he sauntered into the bathroom he wondered what he could do until six o'clock. He thought about it calmly, lazily, entirely undisturbed at the prospect. He could read. He went back into the summer rest-room, his name for the dressing-room. He crossed the bedroom which was in semi-darkness apart from thin shafts of gold filtering through the shutters that overlooked Via Gregoriana. He entered the studio.

The furniture was partly some of his own from Via Ruggero Fauro, partly some of the former owner's more valuable pieces which he had chosen to keep. In one corner there was a big eighteenth-century inlaid writing-table and on it lay an English novel which he was reading. But beside the book was the telephone. And the sight of the telephone disturbed him – it was the first unpleasant sensation for hours. So unpleasant that he only remembered why after a few seconds' reflection. That morning Piero had rung the office to tell him he wanted to talk to him. For a reason he would explain later, he begged Emilio to call at his house in the afternoon or evening. It was Sunday – surely he could spare half-an-hour? There were people in the Victoria office while Emilio was on the phone to Piero and so, almost absent-mindedly, he had said that with the best will in the world he was not sure he could make it but in any case he would ring him about four. Piero had insisted: 'Do me this favour, I really must talk to you.'

Emilio glanced at the time again – a quarter to four. He was free until six, he might as well go now. And since he would certainly find the sight of his sick old friend more painful than on the previous occasion, he consoled himself with the thought that every passing minute brought him nearer to Grazia. At six o'clock, Grazia's face, her strange lips and her strange brown eyes which changed expression so rapidly from severity and sadness to innocent joy, in a flash would make him forget everything.

He did not bother to ring Piero. He hurriedly finished dressing and went down to the car parked outside the small door in Via Gregoriana. He set off across Rome, dominical, golden, exhausted in the long summer heat and post-war transport of joy. As he drove, he thought of Piero's illness which had become steadily worse during the last few years. It was a skin disease – a form of psoriasis or eczema – which had gradually spread from a small red spot like a mosquito bite until it covered his chest and sides round to his back. Inflammation, swellings, pimples, sores, scabs which continually changed their location. Sometimes over periods of weeks or months they peeled off and seemed to abate, but then they erupted more fiercely than before. The worst part was an incessant irritation, sometimes merely annoying, but specially at night or in the summer, most distressing. Piero had been to a number of doctors and specialists who gave the most varied and contradictory diagnoses – a nervous allergy, an infection of the skin due to liver trouble, degeneration of the epithelial cellular tissue . . . and no one could say how it would develop or how long it would probably last. The treatment, according to each diagnosis, varied enormously but the remedies were all equally ineffective against the disease and its painfully slow, inexorable progress. The only relief for the itching consisted in bathing the rashes with olive oil. Lately the trouble, serious in any case, had been aggravated by Piero's financial situation.

In 1943 film production was almost at a standstill throughout the whole of Italy. Piero had lived in Rome with his family – his mother, wife, and daughter Irma – and like so many others had spent all his savings. The war over, he could no longer keep the old lady with him, so she had gone back to Baldichieri d'Asti in the country, to her daughter who was slightly younger than Piero and was married to a vine-dresser. Meanwhile film production had gradually picked up in Rome after the liberation the previous year. But although the doctors all agreed that there was a general improvement in Piero's condition and foresaw a rapid cure, he was still not fit to work. He had tried – one day he came to the studios to do some tests. The nervous strain had immediately aggravated the irritation and made his eczema worse.

Emilio had got Golzio to see that Victoria paid Piero a year's wages, half as a bonus for past service, half as an advance on what he would earn when he returned to work. But the sum was barely sufficient to cover his debts – doctors' bills, medicine, above all the X-rays in which they had such confidence. So Piero had tried to raise a loan. Before the war, with many years' savings, he had bought in Rome beside the flat in Via Ardea where he lived, two other apartments in the same district outside Porta San Giovanni. The three flats were all he possessed and they had to provide a small dowry for Irma as well. 'If only she gets married soon,' Piero would say. But for the moment at least, the girl seemed to have no intention of doing so. Naturally, he could get the loan only by mortgaging the flats – something which went very much against the grain. Seeing his hesitation and gloom, Emilio had given him a cheque for the same amount free of interest and conditions of repayment. But Piero returned it saying that it wasn't right; he himself was responsible for having contracted this grievous debt.

So that Sunday visit to Piero was not particularly cheerful. But the Roman Sunday was gay enough – there was still a little of the bustle and festivity of the Liberation – Americans still around in shirt-sleeves, jumping on a truck at four in the afternoon and arriving in Ostia in time to see the sunset. And Piazza Venezia was as gay as it had been sad during the long years of Fascism. Then, Emilio always tried to avoid it. Now, he took every opportunity to pass that way. To cross Piazza Venezia freely, to pass by the great brown building lightheartedly, not to see the surly faces of the sentries – it was like a whiff of oxygen, a spurt of vitality, the last surge of happiness. But Piero who had obviously wanted the war to end like everyone else had not felt the same joyful release as Emilio and so many others on the day of Liberation. Piero had been disillusioned by Mussolini, but even at the end did not go so far as to hate him. He said that those around him, the Germans, everybody had betrayed him, ruined him, but that he was a good man and had done a lot for Italy. This too, not only his illness, made him sad.

And now what did Piero have to tell him? Was there some new trouble on which he wanted advice?

Piero must be cured, thought Emilio. The only thing wrong in his life, the only shadow on his happiness was now Piero's illness. The week before, without telling Piero, he had written a long letter to his friend Adams accurately describing the symptoms of the disease. Adams was in London for a brief holiday. Emilio asked him to find out who the leading skin specialist was. He planned to get the specialist to come to Rome and to pay all his expenses, or to take Piero to London although he knew that the patient was not really up to travelling or movement of that kind.

Adams had not yet replied. But Emilio was sure that his old friend could be cured.

He parked outside the front door in Via Ardea. He looked up at the windows on the fourth floor; the blinds were down. He imagined Piero inside, in bed in the dark, alone with his cruel irritation, nauseated by the smell of the olive oil on his skin. Emilio felt glad he had come. The squalid yellow facade of the building faced west and at that moment the sun beat down upon it pitilessly. It had been built in 1928 or 1929, was almost new when Piero came to Rome and went to live there. Now it seemed decayed and ramshackle like the pavilions built on the sites of exhibitions and trade fairs, originally destined for rapid demolition but which linger on because even demolition costs money. There were large patches of damp in the peeling yellow plaster. The false neo-classical architraves and the large ornamental cement balls alternating with them looked like papier-mâché. Ten years before Emilio had noticed the ugliness, but then there was something infinitely more important which served to neutralize the impression and almost make it seem beautiful. Piero, still young, strong, healthy, full of enthusiasm for his work and confident of the future, lived there with his family. Piero, one of the few sincere Fascists in existence, certainly the only one Emilio had ever known. In 1935 the building was in Emilio's eyes the very image of Piero's Fascism – in bad taste but good faith. Now, in 1945, it was still the image of Piero's Fascism – utter ruin.

Piero in vest and pants opened the door. He was alone in the house. The sickening smell of oil and ulcerated skin seemed stronger than before. True, it had been an exceptionally hot day. But it was also true that Emilio had not come to see Piero since the beginning of the summer. Three months, a long time, he thought ruefully as he entered and saw at first glance in the half-light of the hall, from the bandages around Piero's neck and arms down to the wrists, and under his vest round his shoulders and chest, how much worse his friend had become. As Piero told him regularly on the phone, the only parts of his body unaffected so far by the disease were his face and hands. His freshly shaven face was the same as ever, though paler and thinner. His hair over the great bony brow was still curly and light chestnut, but thinning. His deep-set eyes burned more brightly, but humour and laughter were gone. The expression on his face was different chiefly because of a grimace of pain which Emilio had noticed on previous occasions – a sad contraction between the upper lip and the cheekbones which recurred at long intervals. Now (Emilio noticed it as soon as Piero opened the door) now his face contracted almost continually, a sign that there was no respite from the torment of the terrible irritation.

'Forgive me for receiving you like this,' said Piero slowly, after closing the door but not moving from the spot. 'Thanks for coming, anyway. I don't know where you can sit down. Forgive me. The

372

house is in an awful mess. Nuccia and Irma have been for a fortnight with my mother at Baldichieri for the grape-harvest. I don't go out or see anybody. A male nurse comes in the morning to give me an injection. Then the porter's wife brings the shopping. I do my own cooking. Apart from the injections, I treat myself too. I might as . . .'

'But what about X-rays?'

'They cost the earth. Look, I've had them, a lot of them but they've given me no relief. Sometimes I feel that for diseases like mine they may even be harmful. So I've stopped them . . . I don't know where you can sit down.' And he led Emilio slowly into the flat looking for somewhere to make him comfortable.

The drawn blinds at all the windows let in very little light and air. The stench of oil, lotions and sores was even more unpleasant in the other rooms. Scattered all over the chairs, the tables and the beds were traces of the treatment – bandages, lint, bottles of oil and ointment, greasy vests, towels, handkerchiefs.

'You must forgive me,' repeated Piero. 'It's a filthy, rotten disease and it goes in phases . . . At the moment the skin is peeling off and the irritation is terrible. The only relief I can get is by oiling myself, scratching the skin and scabs off, then oiling and scratching again. Now I'm alone I spend my days wandering about the house . . .' He suddenly fell silent and turned away. Emilio did not dare say anything. He saw that Piero, erect, facing the wall, motionless except for an almost imperceptible tremor in the thin shoulders, was soundlessly crying. Emilio tried to think of a few words of consolation. But he could not find them. Finally he just said: 'Don't be like that, Piero.'

'It's nothing, nothing. It'll pass,' Piero replied brokenly; then, suddenly brightening up: 'Wait, I've got an idea. Let's go into Irma's room. I never go there normally, it's clean. No, don't sit down there. Come on.'

They went back to the hall. Piero pushed a door open.

'You go in and sit down. I'll sit outside, I'll only make a mess if I come in. We can talk through the open door.'

Emilio brought a chair near the door and sat down. Piero did the same outside. Irma's room was small and prettily furnished – flowered wallpaper, furniture of light-coloured wood. On the bed, sheets and pillows of pink, green-embroidered linen.

'You see?' A first, fleeting smile struggled for a moment with the continual wry grimace and seemed to transform it. 'Wherever I go I can't help leaving traces. My skin keeps on peeling. That's why everywhere in the house is filthy and stinks. It's partly the stink of the oil and other preparations I'm trying in the hope of finding a cure. It must be these boils, too. When they burst they give off a foul smell. I don't notice it so much now, I'm used to it, like the men who work in the tanneries. But Irma won't have me in her room and she's right, poor girl.'

'What do the doctors say?'

'What do you expect? I've learnt to understand doctors inside out, don't worry. The best ones, or at least those who seem the best, are the ones who say least, keep quiet and don't make rash statements or forecasts. They don't make mistakes that way, at least. The only conclusion I've come to is that in some cases, and mine is unfortunately one of them, medicine . . .' and he seemed to smile wickedly again like in the old days . . . 'medicine is a science that only helps you to understand one thing – that you'll never understand anything. Unless . . .' he stopped and the smile was gone. 'Unless the doctors have their suspicions . . . just suspicions without being sure, and they won't tell me for fear of scaring me.' He was silent again. Then slowly and quietly he went on: 'Look, I've done something that perhaps I shouldn't have. If you know what a rigmarole I had to go through. Taking advantage of the fact that Nuccia and Irma are away, I phoned all over the place. I finally found an actor whose son is studying medicine. I won't tell you who he is – after all what does it matter? I've done it. Well, the actor didn't know that I was ill. I made the excuse that I wanted to imitate for make-up purposes some of the symptoms of skin diseases for a film I told him I was shooting and asked him if his son could lend me a manual on the subject.'

At these words Piero's eyes momentarily lit up with a smile. 'You see, he's as proud as Punch that his son will be a doctor next year. I told him that he could leave the book with the porter as I'm always at work and never at home. So he had no need to come up and didn't see me. Here's the book.'

He got up slowly. Sitting in Irma's room Emilio saw Piero cross the hall and go into his bedroom, open a chest-of-drawers and take out a thick dark-red volume which looked like a dictionary. He came back just as slowly to his chair. But instead of sitting down he stood and gazed at Emilio in silence, clutching the book as if it were a sacred relic. And now Piero's eyes seemed to be burning feverishly.

'I've read it from cover to cover. I had time and to spare. Of course I can't say I understand it all. But from the description of the symptoms I discovered what my disease might be. And if it is what the book says . . . then it's terrible . . . terrible . . .' He could not go on. He looked down and began to cry again, motionless, silently. He murmured through his tears: 'It's not death I'm afraid of, it's all the suffering before you die.'

Emilio wanted to ask him the name of the disease. But he dared not. He realized that the name which he neither knew nor could imagine was ever-present in Piero's mind like a death-sentence which might have no reprieve. He realized that Piero, then and always, would only think of that name and if he refused to reveal it the reason was because he was too afraid of it.

Piero slowly took the book back to the chest-of-drawers. Then Emilio got up and said brightly: 'I haven't told you before because I'm still not sure whether it's possible. Through Adams, that friend of mine in London, I hope to get the best English specialist to come and see you' . . . he began to explain his plan. As he spoke he saw that Piero was staring at him and the grimace of pain became more frequent.

'Thank you,' Piero suddenly interrupted him, 'but hang on a minute. I must go in there and scratch myself. I can't stand it any longer.'

He went back into the bedroom and closed the door. After a few minutes he came out, visibly relieved. They sat down again and resumed their conversation across the threshold of Irma's room.

'Thank you. From what the doctors tell me I seem to have some sort of tropical disease. I may have caught it at Karakoram years ago. Perhaps at Shrinagar where I spent all those months in that house built on piles. I know the English are the finest specialists on tropical diseases in the world. But, look. That one . . .' and he motioned towards the other room where through the open door Emilio was still instinctively staring at the chest-of-drawers . . . 'that one's a tropical disease and if I've got it there's no hope.'

'You can't be sure. How old is that book? Maybe ten years! Medicine has made enormous progress in recent years. Think of penicillin!' Emilio tried to cheer him up, give him some hope, but in his mind's eye there suddenly appeared a hostile figure – the face of the Indian at Shrinagar, the big photograph hanging in Piero's kitchen.

Piero was saying: 'Thank you, thank you . . . but time's passing. You'll have to go in a moment, I know and I . . .'

Actually, Emilio had forgotten about everything, even about Grazia. Piero's words reminded him. He looked at the time. With a heartfelt sigh he agreed that he would have to go soon. Piero went on: '. . . and I haven't told you yet why I asked you to come. And I can't put it off till the next time because Nuccia and Irma are coming back tomorrow and I must be alone with you to discuss this matter. Believe me, Emilio, with all my suffering, the sleepless nights, the disgust I feel for my body . . . an even deeper suffering comes from something else. I can't talk to you about it in front of Nuccia because she doesn't understand these things. She's always been the same – apathetic, anyway you know her very well, she's never changed. Apathetic, nothing worries her – she says I'm exaggerating. My sharpest anxiety and concern is for Irma. You haven't really seen Irma since she's grown up. You left Rome with Golzio for that castle in Tuscany in 1943. Irma was still a child then. The few times you've been here since the Liberation Irma didn't happen to be at home.' (Emilio could not detect the slightest note of reproach in Piero's voice, only and always his desire not to embellish reality but to see it exactly as it was – with the same precision that he brought to his work and which everyone called Piedmontese fussiness, with the same appetite for scientific knowledge which had made him read an entire volume on specialized medicine in order to learn something about his disease.)

'Physically Irma is a woman now. But mentally she's a child, a spoilt child. Don't misunderstand me, Emilio. She's a fine girl, basically. But like her mother she's a bit scatter-brained. I can't get it into her head that since my illness has prevented me from working and bringing money home we're living on our savings. And so unfortunately her life can't be what she had always dreamed until three years ago. I sent her to a typists' school and paid for a term's tuition in advance. At first she went very much against her will. Then she began leaving the house in time for her lesson but instead of going to school, she would go for a stroll or to the pictures. When the time came to pay for the second term she told me frankly:

"Papa, don't throw your money away. I'll never be a typist. I don't like it." – "But you must do something, Irma," I said. It's useless. I can't get her to understand that she must look for a job . . . all right, she's pretty and intelligent and if she finds a husband so much the better . . . but she's not going to waste day after day and never raise a finger. The trouble is that her mother does everything at home - shopping, cooking, the beds, the cleaning, the whole lot. It's always been the same. And so the child has got used to being waited upon. "Try Irma in the kitchen!" Oh, yes, you can imagine it. It was like talking to the wall. She doesn't even get her to make her bed. She could at least do that, couldn't she, keep her room tidy instead of lolling about all day doing nothing? But no. She's a "lady" and that's all there is to it. So it's not Irma's fault. It's her mother's fault. And mine, too, a bit. Before, I used to work and everything was fine. I realized that the child was getting spoilt and I was against it. But I could not foresee this trouble and so I let it ride. And that's why the girl, like so many others, only has one thing in her head – to enjoy herself, go to the cinema, go dancing, off to Ostia, Fregene, full stop. Moral: for the last two weeks I've been alone I've thought and thought. And since I'm sure that Irma isn't a bad girl, I've decided that there's only one solution. I mustn't wait – I told myself – for her to make a move and go round looking for a job. If I wait for that then I'll get nowhere. But if I find her a job and all she has to do is say "yes", go to the office and draw her wage packet once a month then she won't refuse, I'm sure.'

'Shall I take her on in the cutting-room at Victoria?' asked Emilio who had caught Piero's drift.

'That's it. Great. I see that you're still my best friend . . .' replied Piero. But the sound of his words seemed to affect him. He looked away into space to summon up courage. 'Yes, in editing as a checker – just to start. It's not so boring as working in an office. Especially if you put her at once on a film in production and not in distribution or copying. You know how it is, there are the rushes in the evening – she'll see the director, the actors and actresses. It's interesting, she might get to like it a lot, at least I hope so. After all, she's my daughter. She knows film work already, I should say. She's born to it.'

'Don't worry. As soon as Irma comes back, get her to phone me one morning at Via Pergolesi. I go to the studios as seldom as

377

possible. And anyway all the editing has been in Via Pergolesi since July.'

'I don't know how to thank you,' muttered Piero.

'You don't need to. But let's hope we get some good news from London. If I do, I'll let you know straight away . . . And tell Irma to ring me.'

'Tomorrow. As soon as she gets back.'

'Tell her I can give her a job immediately. There's a film starting next week. The editress is Gisa, Gisa Levi. If Irma wants to learn the job, she couldn't be in better hands!'

The time came to say goodbye. Emilio, conquering a moment's hesitation and hoping to conceal it, embraced his friend. He felt Piero's chest against his. He felt his thin shoulders through his woollen vest and lint bandages. He brushed Piero's cheeks with his own and plunged long enough to take breath into that sickening smell.

'Ciao,' he said and went out on to the landing. Piero stayed inside, holding the door ajar.

'Ciao,' he repeated, turning round half-way down the first flight of stairs.

'Ciao, and . . . thanks, eh?' replied Piero still not closing the door.

Emilio went down the stairs slowly, maybe more slowly than was natural. He was now thinking irresistibly of Grazia and he feared that Piero might notice his urge to rush away.

II

꩜

More than a week had passed and still no sign of Irma. So Emilio
rang – the film had started and Gisa urgently needed an assistant.
Piero explained that Nuccia was back but not Irma. The harvest
had not finished. Irma was staying with her grandmother for a
couple of days longer, no more.

Another week, and one morning about noon the commissionaire
(Giggi had gone, now it was an ex-customs official Golzio had known
at Roccalbegna and taken under his wing) knocked and
announced: 'Signorina Giraudo is here.'

Surprised, Emilio called his secretary. Since the management of
Victoria had been in Via Pergolesi, Emilio's rule was that only
announced visitors who had made appointments were brought
straight in. Those who arrived unexpectedly were received by his
secretary, Signora Bruscantini. A pretty, pert woman of forty, a very
rapid shorthand typist in four languages, she appeared at the communicating door, surprised in turn that Emilio had not used the
office inter-com as usual.

'Did you fix an appointment this morning for Giraudo's
daughter?'

No, Signora Bruscantini knew nothing about it. Emilio rebuked
the commissionaire who said in his own defence: 'The Signorina
told me that she had an appointment with you at noon sharp.
Otherwise I wouldn't have announced her.'

'It doesn't matter. Show her in and don't say anything to her.'

Irma walked in quickly. She came straight to Emilio at the desk.
There was such decision in her step that Emilio involuntarily rose
to his feet. She seemed older than eighteen. Tall but not thin, fresh-
complexioned with little make-up, regular features, dark eyes, she
was wearing a light camel-hair overcoat tied at the waist by a belt of
the material. Slender legs, slim ankles. She coolly slipped off a pale
leather glove and offered her hand. The gesture, her clothes, the
way she moved were those of a girl both unaffected and elegant –

379

natural yet perfectly stylish. The only thing to remind Emilio of Irma the child was the artistically dishevelled shock of Titian red hair and something about the warm, intelligent, humorous expression in her glance and her smile that she perhaps inherited from her father.

'So it's you, Irma! I'd never have recognized you!'

'Well, I'd have recognized you!' said Irma, laughing. 'I remember you very well.'

As if to get a better look at him, she stepped back so naturally, so gracefully that it added to Emilio's surprise. 'Yes, you've changed a bit, but you're really just the same.'

'I'm older and . . . greyer,' laughed Emilio, 'but I'm no fatter.'

'Who said you were fatter?' the girl retorted. She spoke with a slight Roman accent as she had done as a child, but with a middle-class almost intellectual touch of refinement.

'Well, did you have fun? How did the grape-harvest go?'

'What grape-harvest?' Irma seemed puzzled.

'At Baldichieri.'

'Oh yes! Sorry – it was fine. I was miles away. Everything is so different here!' And she looked around as if struck by the elegance of the office.

'A grape-harvest at Asti!' exclaimed Emilio. 'I wish I'd been there, too.'

'It's easy to see you've no idea what the country's really like.'

'What?' replied Emilio, surprised again at the girl's quickness. 'When the Germans were there, I spent more than a year in Tuscany . . .'

'Yes, I know, Papa told me. In a castle with bathrooms and hot and cold running water. I mean in the heart of the country, in a farm, an old farm . . . certainly I'd rather have been in this lovely office!'

The negotiations, if you could call them that, were rapidly concluded. Emilio told her what her weekly wage for the first film would be. Later, if all went well as he hoped – indeed expected – and if Gisa Levi was happy with her and she with the job, then Irma would be taken on by Victoria at a higher salary as established monthly-paid staff. The girl did not seem embarrassed but had become serious and said nothing in reply. She was very beautiful. Emilio admired her while he continued to tell her about the hours of work, overtime and other details concerning the job. Filtering through the white muslin curtains, the autumn sunshine invaded the Liberty bow-window which looked out on a small garden adjacent to the pine-grove in Villa Borghese. The grey velvet hangings, the pearl-grey carpet, a few bright paintings by Morandi and De Pisis, some huge hide armchairs, the enormous desk covered with the same leather, with its rectangle of pale green blotting-paper (a complementary colour to the hazel of the leather), glass inkwell from Bohemia, two vases of the same glass (one for a bunch of fresh anemones, the other for penholders and pencils), little six-calibre Beretta which he had bought before escaping to Roccalbegna, had never been called upon to use as weapon and now utilized as a paperweight (letting visitors think that he had been a partisan in 1943–1944), two ivory paper-knives (the big one for correspondence, the small one for books), leather and glass lamp - even the Bristol writing pads of three different sizes in their trays, also of Bohemian glass: everything from the heavy curtains to the smallest knick-knack or item of stationery which he never tired of looking at belonged to the extraordinary happiness of his present life and had been the result of a long pro-cess of preparation and selection in which Elena had helped him.

Emilio sometimes told himself that even if his harmony with Elena was limited – almost exclusively – to furnishings, it was at least a perfect one.

Against this background of colour, *objets d'art* and happiness, Irma with her young, personal, vigorous beauty, her Titian hair, her camel-hair coat, her dark laughing eyes and their deep, intense expression, seemed entirely at ease. She was certainly no less in her natural setting than the majority of visitors to the office – English or American officials from the PWB Film Section, actors, actresses, famous directors, Italian film producers.

When he thought of Piero's nineteenth-century provincial slow seriousness, he was amazed that Irma could be his daughter. But the glamour of the film world in which she had grown up was probably the answer. No doubt, as she blossomed into a woman, Irma had instinctively, eagerly emulated the latest, most refined examples of a world from which her father with endless vetoes and warnings, had striven to keep her apart. But Piero himself, for good or evil, lived in this world – he would bring photographs home and would inevitably end by talking about them every evening. So the warnings and the vetoes had backfired into incentives.

Emilio took the girl down to the ground floor where he was going to introduce her to Gisa Levi, chief editor at Victoria and assigned to L's film. 'Start tomorrow morning at nine o'clock,' he told her, 'and be on time.'

At the lift the attendant, who had leapt to his feet as soon as he saw them coming along the corridor, was waiting to press the button.

'I'm very glad you came. I was expecting you as you know,' said Emilio to Irma in the lift. 'But why did you tell the commissionaire you had an appointment? You were lucky. But I might not have been in or I might have been busy . . .'

Irma laughed.

'I'd have waited. As soon as I got back the night before last, Papa told me to ring you to fix an appointment. I should have done it yesterday morning but I forgot. I went home for lunch: "Did you phone?" he asked me at once, anxiously like all invalids. I didn't dare to tell him I'd forgotten so I said you were expecting me this morning at noon. Can you imagine it? He woke me at eight for fear I'd be late! When I came out, I saw the sun shining brightly. Oh well, I thought, I'll go along and chance my luck! Even if he's become so important, he's still my father's best friend and just as I remember him so he'll remember me all the better when I was a child. Was I wrong?'

'No, you weren't,' replied Emilio, laughing too.

'You won't tell Papa, will you?'

'What?'

'That I came without phoning first. As everything's all right it would only vex him unnecessarily.'

'Don't worry, Irma. I won't say a thing. What do you take me for? I'm not crazy. I'm worried stiff about his health. I don't know if he told you but I hope to get a specialist from London to come and see him.'

'Mama and I are both worried too. Believe me, it's terrible having him always about the house in that state. He's worked steadily all his life. Now he doesn't know what to do. He complains, complains, it's one long moan from morning till night. Even then he wanders about the house groaning and moaning.'

'He's suffering,' Emilio thought it only right to point out.

'Yes, I know he's suffering. But so are we, I can tell you.'

382

The cutting-rooms, each with a french window, opened on to the small garden. Seeing the boss come in, Gisa Levi in white overall, white cotton gloves, silver-haired with big blue eyes, pretty, calm, smiling, respectful, got up from the moviola.

'Good morning, sir. To what do I owe the honour of your welcome visit?'

Emilio introduced Irma, explained the situation and concluded: 'My dear Gisa, I ask you also on behalf of Signor Golzio to take Signorina Giraudo under your wing and give her the benefit of your valuable experience. You know her father and so . . .'

'And so there could be no better recommendation,' Gisa hastened to say. 'Then be here tomorrow morning at nine, dear.'

'What about the overall . . . and the gloves?' murmured Irma. Emilio noted with relief that in the presence of Signora Levi the girl was at last beginning to show a little respect.

'Don't worry. We've got everything here, dear. And if the overall's a bit big for you, you can take it home and alter it. Good day, sir.'

'Good day, Gisa.'

He accompanied Irma to the street door. He lingered for a moment watching her as she walked away in the dazzling sunshine towards Villa Borghese – her strong straight legs stepping out briskly, her camel-hair coat fitting snugly, her Titian hair glowing in the distance like a rare flower.

Emilio's feelings at that instant were equally rare and pleasant – he seemed to be breathing a new, strangely light air. It was the first time, he told himself, that he had ever admired a woman without wanting her.

Irma started work. Emilio saw her only occasionally, when he came down to editing which happened very rarely, or in the evenings at about half-past eight in the projection room, when L, the director, and a few leading actors and actresses were also there. But they did not run film every day and Gisa had two assistants, so Irma was not always on duty. He asked Gisa a couple of times: 'How's the Giraudo girl coming along?'

And Gisa with her inscrutable Turin smile replied: 'Fine, sir.'

One night, after midnight, during the showing of an American film which he had to see with L to choose a possible lead actor for *La Bufera*, the big feature scheduled for the following year, he felt himself drifting off to sleep. It happened to him quite often at showings, especially night sessions. Sitting in the front row between Gisa and L, he had asked the latter to wake him as soon as the actor in question, who was playing a supporting role, appeared on the screen. The boredom of the film, the softness of the seat, the bluish light irradiated by the screen, the aroma of L's Havana cigar all acted as soporifics. And even more so, maybe, the calm 'after-glow' of Paola, his new mistress. He thought of her in connection with this English expression, meaning a joy which lingers on after a pleasant experience. He had made love with her until shortly before in his bachelor-flat on Via Del Mare, compelling L, who was unaware of the reason for the delay, to postpone the screening which would have taken place normally about ten. Long forgotten were the times when the erotic act left Emilio troubled, full of remorse and yearning for a vaguely different pleasure. That only happened now with Elena. But he made love with Elena too seldom for it not to seem a novel experience each time and for this illusion not to correct in some way the old, perennial dissatisfaction. With all the others he always achieved his aim now. He felt he had learnt to know not so much women as his own tastes, his own vices – and when they were satisfied he asked for nothing more. From the roots of his hair to the tips of his fingers and toes, he felt a still tenderness, an empty, bottomless calm invade his whole being. He would lie in the dark and think to himself that complete satisfaction could be interpreted at one and the same time as supreme happiness or supreme sorrow – a temporary, conscious, painless death.

He had just experienced it again – with Paola. Then, leaving her asleep, he had got up, dressed and come to the screening. When it was over he would go to Via Gregoriana and sleep there. Alone and contented. Elena and Luigino were not yet back from their holidays.

Sitting between Gisa and L in the front row of the comfortable soft seats of the little hall in Via Pergolesi (built to his own specifications and choice of grey carpeting, plush upholstery and velvet curtains) he lapsed into sweet sleep, thinking of how the happy string of events which had begun last summer was continuing: it all seemed fixed and unchanging, and even the flattest hours of work seemed to fit comfortably into it.

He was awakened by a telephone ringing somewhere. He opened

his eyes and saw that there was a woodland scene on the screen. The telephone was ringing at regular intervals. Gisa had left her seat. Emilio turned round lazily. In the semi-darkness he saw her unhook the receiver on the little table at the back of the hall behind the last row of seats. He heard her talking quietly – in Piedmontese dialect, it seemed. It so happened that the sound track of the film which was already low became even quieter – an outlaw on the run (it was a film about Robin Hood) was escaping from a wood, wriggling on all fours across the heather, careful not to make a sound or stir a twig. Gisa did not want to disturb the showing of the film or perhaps she didn't want to be overheard by Emilio and L. Either way, all her efforts to speak quietly were in vain.

'Yes, she's here, she's here . . . don't worry, Signor Giraudo . . . as soon as we've finished running the film, she'll come straight home . . . no, I'm sorry, I can't call her now, she's in the projection-room . . . No, Signor Viotti's not willing . . . don't worry about the tram . . . there's a company car for her and me. Good night . . . don't fret and look after yourself. We all want to see you back on the dolly . . . And soon! Don't say that, Signor Giraudo! Good night.'

As soon as the film finished, Emilio took Gisa aside and asked her innocently enough but with a shadow of suspicion if Irma was really up in the projection-room, and why. Gisa flushed scarlet and the colour seemed all the brighter in contrast with her magnificent silvery hair and her big blue eyes. But she tried to control herself and smile.

'Forgive me, sir. I didn't mean to tell you about it, at least not for some time. But now you've caught me in the act, so to speak . . . if you like I'll tell you everything. Yes, as you've gathered, Irma's father was on the phone. When there's a late evening showing, the girl takes the opportunity of going out with her fiancé. Her father knows nothing about it. What can you expect? The way things are today, it's no mystery. She calls him her fiancé but he's just a . . . mind, I've never seen him, I don't know him or what sort of chap he is. He may be a nice boy . . . I'm not saying . . . but it's certain that neither of them is thinking of marriage, not for the moment anyway and that's why the girl can't tell her father. She's got permission to go to the cinema once a week, every Saturday evening. So she asked me to help her out the other evenings. If her father phones I'm to tell him that she's here and she'll take the car home with me. I know it's not right but I'll do anything not to hurt the poor man. And then . . .' Gisa stopped and blushed again.

Emilio prompted her encouragingly: 'And then . . . what?'

'I was hoping to tell you about that too at the end of the work on the film. Because you can't expect a pretty girl, young, elegant, full of life and who's never worked before to suddenly start winding film for twelve hours a day . . .'

'Why not? D'you think the work's too much for the Giraudo girl and we should take on another assistant?'

'Good gracious, no, sir. Thank you but that's not what I mean.' She hesitated for a moment, then: 'It's something else, a simple matter really. I think she's a good, intelligent girl, a bit odd sometimes but with an original sense of humour. It's just that . . . that she doesn't want to work. Or rather she has no *intention* of working, that's all. She comes here for one reason only – so as not to grieve her father.'

'Does she get here on time, at least?'

'She can't fail in the mornings, because they wake her and see she leaves the house in plenty of time. But in the afternoons . . .'

'Why, doesn't she go home to lunch?'

'No. She confided in me on the second day. She told me about her boy-friend. How he took her to lunch and they stayed a while together. At home they think she gets a sandwich in a milk-bar near here like so many of the other girls do.'

'And what time does she come back in the afternoon?'

'She should be back at three. But she appears at five o'clock, six . . . sometimes she doesn't even bother to turn up again.'

'What does her "fiancé" do for a living? Doesn't he work in the afternoons?'

'Seems not. He's an actor.'

'An actor? What's his name?'

Gisa didn't know. Emilio felt saddened and as if stabbed in the back. After an instant's reflection, he told himself that it would have made more sense to be surprised if the opposite had been true – in other words if a pretty, self-possessed girl like Irma had been prepared to work with the same enthusiasm as all the other women.

Gisa apologized again for having kept quiet about it. She repeated that she believed she had acted for the best. Every day she took the girl to task and she had intended to tell Emilio at the end of work on the film. Certainly things couldn't go on like this. Irma would not be engaged for another film. And anyway she was a bad example to the rest of the girls.

Emilio wondered what was the best thing to do. He decided not to give Gisa away and told her so, thanking her and explaining that he did not want to distress Giraudo. For if Irma knew that Gisa had reported her absences to the management she would complain about her to Papa and Mama, without admitting anything, and vent her spite on her. No, better find another way. Emilio would ask the commissionaires on the ground floor who certainly saw her come in or go out even if she slipped through the garden. That way he would gain proof of her negligence without involving Gisa. The first day Irma arrived very late, Gisa was to phone him – then, when she finally appeared, tell her he had been looking for her and send her up to his office.

Once again Irma's entrance was a surprise. In her white overall and cotton gloves she crept slowly forward, weeping and wiping away her tears with a tiny handkerchief. She kept her head down like children do when they know they're in the wrong, but her pose seemed involuntarily seductive since the beauty of her mass of Titian hair was even more evident.

Irma went on crying bitterly. Had the commissionaires warned her? Or Gisa herself? It was possible, thought Emilio. But even so it meant that the girl was expecting a terrible scolding and was trying to inspire pity right from the start, and this was strange. Emilio knew very well that unlike Golzio he did not have a reputation as a tyrant with the staff. Nobody could have scared Irma into such a torrent of tears. Unless . . . unless, Emilio pondered, a little worried, the girl's shortcomings were more serious than Gisa had reported.

This time, protected by his huge leather-covered desk, Emilio did not get up; he waited until Irma, head bowed, sobbing, slowly stepped nearer. Then he said gently: 'Now sit down, Irma . . . sit there.'

Irma, without taking the hand holding the handkerchief from her eyes, peered round and gingerly perched on the edge of one of the huge armchairs. She sat there still crying, stiff as a ramrod, chin sunk on her chest.

'You just cry,' Emilio went on, well aware that the only sure way to stop a child crying is to encourage her to cry for as long as she wants. 'You just cry, you'll feel better then, don't be afraid – I've got some free time today and nobody will hear us. I'll show you what I'll do.' He pressed the key on the inter-com. The distorted voice at the other end said: 'Yes, sir?'

'Signora Bruscantini,' Emilio kept the key down while Irma almost automatically controlled her sobbing, 'do not disturb me for any reason whatsoever, I'm not in to anybody, not even to my wife. Only to Signor Golzio.'

'Signor Golzio has gone out.'

'Very well.' He realeased the key and Irma began to cry worse than ever as if the bottled-up sobs and tears had to find a natural outlet. But why – thought Emilio – why see malice in the girl when maybe there was none? What did he know about Irma? She was pretty, smart, self-possessed, witty, modern, not fond of work and in love with – perhaps the mistress of – a young film actor. Well? Did that necessarily mean that she was a bad girl? In any case the tears were natural enough. Only now were they beginning to abate, the sobbing to slacken off.

'There's no hurry,' repeated Emilio. 'You'll tell me later, won't you, why you're crying like this?'

'Yes, yes,' said Irma, still looking down.

But Emilio seemed to detect on the girl's full, finely-chiselled lips the suspicion of a smile.

When she finally spoke, she began very slowly, averting her face: 'I had made up my mind for some days to come and talk to you ... because ... I know, you've always been so good to my father and to me, too ... and that's why I didn't have the courage to ask you for something else ... but today ... today I was so desperate ... and as you're the only person in the world I know who can help me ... I made the effort and told myself – I must go today!'

'But it was I who called you!' murmured Emilio, astounded.

'Yes, I know ... talk about a coincidence! The very day I decided to come and speak to you ... you've called me for the first time since I've worked here.'

As he listened to her, Emilio felt more and more amazed. Irma's defence was really extremely clever. But, he concluded, he had to face the harsh reality of an Irma who, while she might not be bad, was at least precociously experienced in the ways of the world.

'And what did you want to ask me?' he said, humouring her, trying to understand her. He imagined vaguely that the girl wanted to ask him for shorter hours – permission to come only in the mornings, without her father knowing, of course.

Instead: 'I want you to know . . . I'm telling you this but Papa knows nothing about it and he mustn't know a thing . . . Promise you won't tell him?'

She had finally looked up, her face tear-streaked, her eyes red but shining with a deep, soft light. Her lips were sinuous, clearly etched, slightly protruding and parted as she waited for a reply.

'I shall never tell your father,' Emilio said with a gravity that even he thought a little exaggerated. 'And does your mother know?'

'No, she doesn't either. Oh, mother can't keep the tiniest secret. She runs to tell father at once. No, I haven't told Mama or Papa about it. You're the first person I've confided in. I'm engaged.'

Irma fell silent and closed her eyes as if to summon up the strength to continue. Emilio asked: 'Since when?'

'Since about . . .' she stopped and frowned. It was obvious that she had not expected the question and the length of time was something she never thought of . . . 'yes, look, since a few days after the Americans occupied Rome. And so about eighteen months.'

'You've been engaged for eighteen months?'

Another question that seemed to take her by surprise. But now she answered instinctively without thinking and gave herself away.

'I first met him eighteen months ago . . .' She stopped, realizing her mistake. 'Fiancé' was clearly a term of convenience for use in company but it was equally clear that between her and the young man, whoever he might be, there had never been the slightest suggestion of an engagement. Emilio feigned ignorance.

'And who is he?'

'A nice boy, believe me . . . kind, sensitive, intelligent. We're very much in love . . .'

'How old is he?'

'Twenty-two.'

'He works, I suppose?'

'Yes . . .' replied Irma and she stared at him, dry-eyed now.

Emilio seemed to notice for the first time how extraordinary her eyes were – two sparkling points in the centre of the pupils, surrounded by large, dark irises sharply separated from the white, filled with a poignant expression, maybe of anxious waiting, maybe of a numb void, something between the hope of surrender and the agony of not finding anyone to surrender to. The way Piero looked at people certainly had a particular intensity and keenness, and Nuccia's doll-like expression was unusual. But Irma's appeared to combine the keenness of the former with the fixed gaze of the latter in depth that was different – very sweet and disturbing.

'Yes . . . he works . . . when someone gives him a job.'

'Why? What does he do?'

'He's a film actor. Perhaps you know him. He's had a few parts . . . His name is Giorgio Gentili.'

Emilio seemed to have heard the name. On the inter-com he asked Signora Bruscantini to see if there was a photo-file on him. Irma, sunk in silence, still stared at Emilio as before, as if she wanted to speak but dared not. Emilio, who thought he understood, now kept quiet deliberately. Signora Bruscantini came in, handed him a large envelope and went out again. It contained photos of a boy in bathing-trunks on the beach – muscular, slim, and with long, thick, curly hair, almost certainly artificially blond. The face was typical of extras or small-part actors in Roman films – smooth, sharp-featured, giving a false impression of a thin frame, nervous energy, virility. From the photos, a type who could have success with homosexuals or smart women of a certain age. Maybe Elena would like him, he sneered inwardly. But odd that Irma was in love with him and even odder that the boy was in love with Irma.

Irma, hesitant, leaned over to see. Emilio asked her: 'Is this the chap?'

The girl nodded.

'But here it says that he's twenty-six,' Emilio remarked on turning over one of the photos.

But Irma did not turn a hair: 'He's still such a boy. He must have said he was older to get people to take him seriously. He needs to work. His parents don't want him to be an actor and his father who works in a mail-order firm would have found him some sort of job as a clerk in Milan. But Giorgio refused because he doesn't want to leave me and has decided to carry on in films. But he hasn't been able to get into a film for two months . . . and unless someone gives him at least a bit part, he'll have to pack up and go back to Milan.'

'Is this why you were crying?'

'Yes.'

'And what you wanted to ask me about the last few days?'

'Yes.' She said 'yes' firmly and each time the beautiful, curved, pouting lips closed determinedly. Her eyes: now Emilio saw that Irma's deep, dark eyes were gazing into his trustingly, almost gaily. Suddenly, he felt like smiling, too. It so happened that in L's film there was the confounded part of a second lover which, through a series of stupid circumstances, had not been cast and might suit the young man. Strange how difficult it is sometimes to find actors for roles which only require the most ordinary faces! Film production, thought Emilio, is like a chain assembled haphazardly link by link. By doing Irma a favour, he might solve a casting problem. Anyway, first he had to see the boy and so would L before arranging a screen test.

'Do you think if we ring . . .' and to avoid saying 'your fiancé' he glanced at the photo and read the name which he had forgotten . . . 'Giorgio Gentili, we'll find him at home?'

'Yes, until seven. He's waiting for me to call him,' said Irma, jumping up and lifting the receiver from the telephone Emilio had pushed towards her.

'Waiting? Do you mean that he knew you were going to talk to me today?'

'Yes,' Irma repeated with that attractive air of assurance which Emilio interpreted as a guarantee of innocence. And now to dial the number she sat abstractedly, naturally, on the edge of the leather-covered desk. Emilio could not recall any of the secretaries or actresses who had been his mistresses daring to do that, not so much out of respect for him as for the impressive piece of office furniture.

'Tell him to come at once,' suggested Emilio while she was on the phone.

'It was his mother. She's gone to fetch him. He's downstairs in the bar.'

'How can this damned girl be the daughter of Piero and Nuccia, even if she's like them both?' wondered Emilio, lost in admiration.

Sitting on the edge of the desk in her white overall, her mass of hair dark copper in the last light of a November afternoon still filtering through the bow-window, Irma made a strange, unexpectedly, vital picture. Emilio thought of putting on the light but hesitated, afraid to break the spell. Just then the girl, to fill in time at the phone, caught hold of the Beretta paperweight and began to play with it. She laughed, opened her eyes comically wide and breathed 'Is it loaded?'

'Yes, hey, watch out!' replied Emilio, laughing too and in a dramatically hushed voice. Irma, continuing the joke, stretched out her arm, closed one eye to take aim and pointed the Beretta at him. Then she put it down, her 'fiancé' was at the phone.

'Darling, Signor Viotti wants you to come straight away to Via Pergolesi. There may be something for you.' She looked at Emilio anxiously, questioningly. He hadn't said anything. Was she right to tell her boy-friend that? Emilio reassured her with a smile as she hung up. But, quite apart from her 'fiancé' and the proba-bility of a part for him in L's film, Irma still did not understand, or she pretended not to understand, that she could not go on neglecting the work she was paid to do. Whether it was ingenuous-ness (as Emilio secretly hoped) or cunning, she had not apologized for arriving late or not turning up for work, nor had she even remotely mentioned it. Emilio decided that it was high time to reprimand her seriously. He began cautiously, so as to confirm and explain the smile with which he had reassured her concerning her boy-friend.

'Yes, perhaps there'll be something for him in the film you're working on now. It's more than a bit part, it's an important one, the second or third after the star role.'

'That's wonderful! Thank you, thank you!'

'I'm happy about it, too. Because when your boy-friend's working perhaps you'll be able to come to work on time, as you should, Irma. I see you're blushing. Why do you think I wanted to see you? No, don't say anything. There's no point. I know every-thing that goes on here. Gisa tried to defend you. Unfortunately, hours are hours and anybody can check exactly when you arrive and when you leave. Just think. If you were employed by one of the many firms where you've got to clock in, how would you manage? But the worst thing about your slackness is this. You're too intelligent, Irma, not to know that I love your father like a brother, more than a brother. That's why, sick and suffering as he is these days and worried about your future, I will on no account distress him by telling him that you're always late for work and don't care a damn. Because of this, knowing this, knowing that I can't punish you, you ought to be perfect. Instead, you're the opposite, you take advantage of your privileged position. Take care, though. I can only shield you up to a point. I'm not referring to Gisa who's an angel and above this sort of thing. But if one of the other girls reports you then I'll have to sack you!'

Irma jumped up. She tore off her gloves, unbuttoned her overall and threw them on the chair.

'Very well, you're right. Then throw me out now. I'll deal with my father. I'll tell him I don't want the job. Will that suit you?'

Emilio was speechless. Both fascinated and scared, he looked at Irma and she stared back at him. In her eyes was an expression of bitter hate that he would never have thought possible. Just as he would never have thought her, Piero's daughter, capable of such a savage outburst of violence. Then he suddenly remembered what Piero had told him once – even apathetic Nuccia was subject to unexpected fits of rage that were fortunately extremely rare. And Piero himself, the calmest, coolest man in the world . . . Emilio had never seen him really angry. But at work they all said that when one of his assistants or a technician tried to pull the wool over his eyes, then he went berserk.

'Irma, calm down. You're crazy' . . . was all Emilio could say.

'Crazy? Thank you for all you've done for Papa. Thank you again. But I didn't ask for this job. I came back from Capri and found it all settled. Take it or leave it. What could I do? I love my father, too . . .' She could not go on and began to cry again. But not, this time, as a confession of weakness and an appeal for help. These were tears of indignation. Capri, Emilio reflected. So that's where she went after the grape-harvest and Lord knows what lies she told at home. Now, in her anger, she had unwittingly let the cat out of the bag.

'If you really loved your father as you say, you'd make the effort to work and be here punctually every afternoon instead of seeing your fiancé.'

'Yes,' replied Irma, tossing her head proudly and stifling her tears, 'yes, of course. But it's got to be a job I like.'

'And what sort of job *would* you like? Come on, tell me.'

Irma did not answer immediately. She looked down and finally, like a sulky child, said: 'I don't know. All I know is that this job is not for me, so there.'

Emilio, eyeing her closely, suggested: 'Maybe . . . maybe you'd like to be a film star, eh?'

'If only I could!' She looked up, laughing, amused at the idea, but not at all convinced.

'You're certainly photogenic.'

'Yes, I know, but I can't act.'

'We'd have to arrange a test. And only tell your father if it's OK.'

'Papa is dead against it. But it's not that. If I thought I had the makings of an actress, I'd manage to persuade him. But I'm no actress. I know because I've tried a couple of times. Just the thought of being in front of a camera . . . scares me to death.'

By now the room was in semi-darkness. And Irma suddenly stopped talking.

'Well, when you find a job that suits you, let me know. For the moment I advise you to stay here and be more punctual. For your own self-respect, chiefly.'

'I see. You feel that as Papa mustn't know I'm . . . what's the word? . . . I'm blackmailing you.'

'Exactly.'

'Look, I feel that instead *you* are blackmailing *me*. Yes, if Papa weren't ill, I'd never have come here.'

'Not to work. But maybe to ask me to give Giorgio Gentili a job?'

'Oh, you're terrible! You never miss a trick, as they say in Rome.'

She laughed self-confidently and turned to sit down. 'May I smoke a cigarette while we're waiting?' She fished a packet from the pocket of her overall which lay in a heap on the chair. Emilio offered her one of his. He was more astonished than ever at Irma who at times seemed experienced and perfectly sure of herself, at times, childlike, impulsive, wild – scatterbrained as Piero had called her. He looked at her across the desk as she inhaled the smoke deeply, voluptuously – an exaggerated pose as if she were striving to pass for a girl who had 'lived' a lot, almost a vamp. The gloom prevented Emilio from catching the expression on her face, but nothing could be more innocent, childish, almost ridiculous than the sweeping gesture with which she took the cigarette from her lips and held it in mid-air. He decided to put the light on. Break the spell? What spell? Of course he couldn't think of courting Piero's eighteen-year-old daughter and he knew that he had never entertained the idea for one moment! Come on now! He switched the desk lamp on.

'When you go home this evening, can you remember to give your father a message? Tell him I received a letter from London yesterday. My friend has talked to the greatest specialist in the world, Higgins. Higgins hopes to come to Rome during the Christmas holiday and then he'll examine your father . . .'

'Why don't you ring Papa if you don't trust me to give him the message?'

'Because I know, child, that since he's been so ill the phone's a nuisance, gets on his nerves and he only uses it when he has to. Like that time after midnight when he rang Gisa and asked for you.'

'You *don't* miss a trick, do you?'

'Irma, don't you realize that you're being cheeky?'

'Oh no, pardon me. I'm in the right this time. If I'm cheeky, then you're a snake.'

He was not offended. He couldn't be. He admired her too much at that moment. He admired her for her impulsive retort and the presence of mind with which she had found the right word to hurt him.

'A snake? Really? Why?'

'Because you tell me things gradually one by one. You do it so sneakily. I've already told you. If you want, though it'll hurt Papa, I'm ready to leave Victoria now and never come back and I'll take all the blame. I've decided I don't want to work any more. Understand? The only thing I ask you is not to break your promise about the job for my fiancé! That's all I ask.'

'All right. But before I give him the part can I make one small condition?'

'More blackmail. Tell me.'

'Nothing. I just want you to promise me something. If he gets

395

the role try to come to work more regularly,' he said slowly, paternally, severe-faced. But he repeated to himself 'Snake'! Beneath the kindly moralizing of Papa's old friend, so concerned about the future of a rebellious little girl and determined to put her on the right road, he felt a creeping, glowing desire – he did not want to lose the chance of having the girl below him on the ground floor of Via Pergolesi, and of being able to see her easily at any time.

'I promise,' replied Irma calmly, but looking away. She was staring at something on the desk. 'Yes, I promise. But pardon my curiosity. Why do you keep that revolver there? Is it always there?'

'Always. It's a war souvenir. There was a raid . . .' he had told the story more than once to more than one actress. It was too effective a lie, especially on a young girl like Irma, for him not to yield to vanity and the innocent temptation of using it. 'There was a raid. I had to escape to the mountains and hide out with the partisans near the top of the Amiata. Oh, if you only knew . . . This revolver saved my life!' And Irma gazed at him in admiration.

Giorgio Gentili was like his photographs – a good-looking, well-built boy, typical of the effete, violent fringe of the film business which flourished in the Roman working-class areas and suburbs. He gained, however, by being fully dressed. He seemed taller, leaner. His hesitant step and smile as he entered and the correct, almost military bow with which he introduced himself suggested to Emilio a more sensitive, or at least a more discerning mind than the beach photos had led him to expect, for there the young man was probably too concerned about showing off his muscles. Now, seeing and hearing him, Emilio realized that Irma's choice wasn't so odd after all.

The boy had a technical college diploma – at least he had enough culture to understand that he must claim to have a certain amount of culture. He had worked before – small parts in small films and he listed the titles and the directors. He could drive a car and ride a horse. Age, twenty-eight. The photos had been taken two years previously . . . When Emilio's normal preliminary interrogation reached the question of the boy's age, Irma, caught in a lie, tried to laugh it off. She was sitting in the same chair as the young man and Emilio was not at his usual place behind the desk but in the chair facing them. She pressed close to her fiancé.

'I told Signor Viotti just now that you were twenty-two,' and she gently kissed the blond, downy nape of his neck. But at the same time, as if to ask Emilio forgiveness for her lie, she winked flirtatiously at him.

'Little minx! Silly girl!' murmured Gentili with an indulgent smile, half-closing his eyes in the cigarette smoke.

'Why?' retorted Irma, lapsing into Roman dialect, 'I'm honest, that's all. I'd just like you to be even more of a boy than you are, Giorgio.'

Emilio felt that the little scene in the armchair opposite was a piece of spontaneous acting by Irma prompted by a sense of more or less unconscious devilment and put on specially for his benefit. It was now clear that if Irma liked Gentili, this was because of his experienced, adult ways. And by saying that she wanted her fiancé to be 'even more of a boy' Irma clearly intended to tease Emilio who, she knew perfectly well, was forty-four – an age borne out by his greying temples. Emilio began to explain rapidly to Gentili the part he would have to play in the film in the event that L agreed to sign him up.

But all of a sudden he felt distracted by what he saw – the two lovers listening and looking at him, motionless, were pressing more tightly to each other. Gentili had his arm round Irma's supple waist and she was leaning languorously against him. There was definitely something equivocal about Gentili. As he talked Emilio studied him. The bracelet, the watch, the gold signet ring. The snugly-fitting shirt cuffs. The too-smooth face. And in particular the boy's smile, all flashing white teeth and sparkling apple-green eyes, which conceitedly, confidently proclaimed his erotic bravura. 'It's obvious that they go to bed together,' thought Emilio as he went on explaining the plot of the film. 'I was certainly naïve to think otherwise! And there's no doubt about it,' he concluded: 'Irma was in Capri with him. Unless she had someone else.' He felt tempted to discover the truth. He knew that he should not try but could not help himself. He finished the plot.

'A nice part, don't you think?' Then he said 'Tell me the truth, you two. Did you have fun on Capri?'

'Oh yes, a lot,' Gentili rejoined, hiding his surprise and embarrassment, while Irma looked sharply at Emilio with a far from friendly expression on her face. 'The weather was marvellous. They told us that the Americans and the English had made a shambles of the place, but it simply wasn't true. On the other hand, as a permit is needed, they're the ones who defend the island. Anyway, Irma and I thought we had got away . . .' he smiled broadly and gave her a significant squeeze . . . 'got away secretly. But I see that you're very well informed, sir!'

Irma seemed exasperated. She wrenched free of Gentili's arm and stood up.

'I told him so, a few minutes ago. I was angry about something else and I let it slip. So what?'

'Keep calm, Irma. In any case you needn't worry about me. Irma knows that. I shan't tell a soul. And certainly not Irma's people, of course . . .'

'Thank you, sir,' said Gentili, convinced that he was giving a noble answer to noble words.

Emilio went back to the desk and rang L at the studio where he was shooting.

'See this revolver?' Irma said to Gentili and laughed as she caught hold of it again and began to toy with it. 'What d'you think, Signor Viotti says he was a partisan and fought against the Germans but he's boasting really. Because I know it's not true.' And she laughed again, eyeing him defiantly. Emilio laughed too even louder as if to indicate to Gentili that it was all a joke. He turned to the young man and, shaking his head, remarked: 'It's true I had this Beretta in Tuscany during the German occupation. But I wouldn't dream of making up yarns like that!'

Sly or innocent, Irma burst out laughing yet again and said to Emilio: 'What? You dare to deny it?'

Luckily the phone rang. It was L. Emilio told him that the actor Giorgio Gentili was coming to see him at once. Could he give him a screen test for the part still remaining to be cast?

Paola's perfume was heavy, fragrant, somehow oily and dusty, though Emilio could not understand if the latter sensation originated from an invisible and impalpable but actual cloud of dust or whether it was just the memory of incense and old satin folded and lying at the bottom of a chest of drawers. It was certainly an expensive, modern Paris perfume, otherwise Paola would never have used it, but it also contained – at least for Emilio – something antiquated and mystical: perhaps bergamot-orange which his

mother loved, perhaps the camphor and the opoponax given off by
the chinchilla stole when his mother, getting ready to go to the
Teatro Regio, used to take it out of the big wardrobe and strip off
the gauze protective covering, or perhaps even incense, the
imperishable recollection of benedictions every October evening in
the little church at Rivoli.

In any case he noticed and enjoyed Paola's perfume only in the
first few minutes of each meeting. Later he felt enveloped,
saturated in it. It was the aroma of her golden skin and he breathed
it automatically, even though his nerves probably registered it as
an aphrodisiac.

These were the first minutes now as, behind her, he climbed the
four flights of stone stairs set in the walls of the old palazzo on Via
del Mare. The bachelor flat had one drawback – there was no lift.
Paola mounted the stairs, tall, slim, strong, sheathed in her gold
silk jersey gown, her champagne mink stole thrown over one
shoulder. Even her blonde hair seemed golden; and her perfume
like incense, radiating from all that gold, revealed to Emilio for the
first time what was probably the secret of Paola's fascination – a
kind of profane memory of chasubles and copes.

The bachelor flat consisted of one very long room, almost a
gallery, with five windows overlooking Via del Mare and in the wall
opposite five small doors leading to the kitchen, the larder, the
entrance, the dressing-room, the bathroom. At one end of the
gallery was an oval table; at the other, fitted into a sort of alcove
and near the bathroom, a double bed. Black carpet. Huge divans
and armchairs. Low tables. Large sombre pictures. Beige shantung
upholstery like the curtain which could, if so desired, seal off the
alcove.

Besides a glow reflected on to the low, white ceiling from a
battery of bulbs concealed behind the cornice, illumination was
provided by eighteenth-century night-lights, porcelain lamps of
different shapes and colours. Emilio had started to collect them,
saying that it was his hobby. He kept at least a hundred of them on
show in four glass cases which filled the wall spaces between the
five windows. The less valuable ones had been converted into
lamps with light-bulbs strong enough to penetrate the texture of
coloured porcelain. A complicated system of relays and buttons
allowed Emilio to light the lamps as he wished, in groups or singly.

While the electricians, the carpenters and the decorators were busy, he had felt that so many refinements might be rather ridiculous, but once the work was done he felt a satisfaction each time he entered the flat that he never experienced in Via Gregoriana and Via Pergolesi, where Elena had had ideas and made suggestions. Here at the flat, he had done it all himself, altering and improving the furnishings of the previous owner, a Swedish diplomat from whom he had bought the apartment. Elena knew about the flat and tolerated it. She pretended that Emilio needed it to give parties for 'elements' from the film world, actors, actresses, starlets, dancers, whom it would be awkward to entertain at home. She wasn't being honest, of course. In Roman society, any hostess could receive any 'elements' – apart from the small fry whom it was quite useless to invite anyway. No matter, between her and Emilio there was an arrangement that the apartment in Via del Mare should be used for this purpose, and they called it in private 'the studio'. By tacit agreement, Elena undertook never to set foot there. She had been there only once when Emilio invited her along to express an opinion after the workmen had gone. On the oval table, near a vase of flowers, he had the idea, malicious rather than tactful, of putting one of her photographs in a silver frame for her to see – not one of her recent ones but a very attractive one all the same. Elena had laughed, then slightly moved the photo so that it seemed to be looking directly at the alcove along the length of the 'gallery'.

'This way,' she had said, managing to suppress any hint of sarcasm in her voice, 'this way, if you ever happen to spend the night here, before you go to sleep, I shall always be able to see you, a tiny figure away in the distance.' Emilio replied: 'No, on the other hand I shall be able to see you.' And she persisted: 'Well, let's say that we'll be able to see each other at a distance.' Emilio had concluded: 'But of course!' and they had both laughed heartily. At the time he was sure he would remove the photo as soon as possible. Later he realized that he might as well leave it there. It was always nice to have a ready, polite answer for his girl friends, his 'birds of passage.'

'Tell me, that very pretty woman, who is she?'

'My wife.'

Emilio would go to Via del Mare of a late afternoon in summer or in the evening after dinner. He rarely stayed later than one or two o'clock in the morning, and preferred not to stay the night there except on very rare occasions. This was one. Irritated by Irma's visit, disgusted by his introduction to the curly-headed gigolo with whom Irma seemed absurdly in love, he had felt in no mood to face Elena just back from holiday, full of society chat, faded, vicious, bored. Besides, Luigino had left that morning for Trani to attend a cadet's course. And Elena, as she always did in similar circumstances, would certainly try to rekindle a fire since she persisted in seeing glowing embers where there were only ashes.

With Elena the conventional sign which they had immediately agreed upon from the beginning and with no need of mutual explanations, was the following telephone call: 'Ciao, Elena. Look, I'm off to Milan tonight. I'll be back tomorrow.' When the trip to Milan was genuine Emilio instructed Signora Bruscantini to inform his wife: 'Signora, your husband asks if you will please pack his bag – he's leaving for Milan tonight.'

This time everything had gone smoothly and was continuing to do so. Paola knew the flat. She walked quickly down the long gallery to the bathroom. Grazia had left a few weeks before. She had gone to Marseilles to see her parents from whom she had been separated for the last two years of the war. He did not know when she would be back, so Paola had taken her place.

Paola was different from all the others, thought Emilio, sitting in an armchair and taking off his shoes – a determined girl from Trieste, whose determination consisted of a perfect imitation of love. Smiling, Emilio summed her up like that. Grazia was 'more genuine'. Paola had closed the bathroom door. Emilio undressed slowly and looked at the lighted *veilleuses* – the little blue and gold lion at the head of the bed; the crimson and orange dragon on the bracket at the opposite end; the pink and black shepherdess near the larder door.

He corrected himself – every woman when you know her a little seems completely different from all the others. That's why making love is always such fun! A heavy object slipped out of his trousers which he was taking off and fell with a dull thud on the carpet. For a moment he was surprised. He had forgotten that he had put his Beretta in his pocket. After taking Irma and Gentili to the lift he had gone back to his office and seeing it on the desk he thought that Irma was a pert, rude brat but that her sarcasm was basically justified. Yes, to keep the weapon on his office desk was ridiculous. To avoid the temptation of boasting, as Irma had accused, he had decided to take it home and leave it there. Better still, he could leave it here, at the flat. He pushed it to the back of the drawer in the oval table which was very deep so that unless it was pulled right out, the revolver would remain hidden. He switched off two of the lamps, leaving on only the little lion. He finished undressing and went to bed to wait for Paola. He lit a cigarette. Suddenly it occurred to him that for some time he had been aware of a vague, new sensation, slightly unpleasant . . . a kind of discomfort. But not physical discomfort. It was a sort of uneasiness, anger, regret. Was the happiness, that beautiful, unclouded happiness which now filled his life, perhaps impaired? And when did it happen? Some time ago, a short time ago. Just a few hours. He concentrated, trying hard to understand. This was it. The moral discomfort that he was feeling resembled an insect's sting – or better still, a burn, which at first seems to have healed but instead continues to hurt. Wounded pride, he thought. Naturally. But what a little fool. What does she see in that gigolo? Is she really a little unbalanced? Going about with a vulgar, corrupt fellow such as Gentili is bound to be – let's face reality and say, *going to bed with* Gentili – she'll end up by being corrupt and rotten herself, gradually becoming vulgar and coarse and even worse. But what can I do? When I think that she's Piero's daughter (and I have to make an effort) I seem to be dreaming. I can do nothing except say nothing to Piero, whatever happens.

The door of the bathroom opened. Paola appeared in a night-dress of very transparent pink crêpe-de-chine. She was almost as tall as the doorway. She switched off the bathroom light and disappeared. An instant later Emilio smelt the dusty, religious perfume approaching. Finally he saw her emerge from the gloom. In the light of the little lion, her long bare arms were all golden. Emilio, stretching out his arms to hers, told himself that the burning sensation had stopped hurting for the moment. This was the first step towards recovery.

III

The blue of the cassocks – the cassocks worn by the porter who had opened the door and let them in, of the hospital orderly or lay brother who had taken them along a glass-lined corridor to a ground-floor room enclosed on three sides by windows, of the monks whom Emilio, sitting waiting with Piero, could see passing to and fro in groups or couples between the rows of thin shrubs already sprinkled with spring green – the particular, unexpected blue of the cassocks seemed in some way to confirm the reputation of an Order dedicated entirely to the study and treatment of skin diseases. It was as if – thought Emilio – that cold, sombre hue were itself a sort of remedy; as if it possessed some healing power over mysterious, incurable sores.

Higgins did not come to Rome for Christmas as he had said he would. He had gone to the United States. Back in London about the middle of March he had written to Emilio explaining that his visit to Rome, besides being problematical, would be useless, because at the monastery-clinic of La Madonna del Ripose in Rome there was always available for consultation the greatest authority in the world on tropical dermatology, the Czech Father Stablum. Known to scientists of all countries for his publications, Stablum had fled to Rome from Prague during the last year of the war – a fact which Higgins had unfortunately been unaware of before, and only learnt by chance on his recent trip to America.

Piero's sufferings had become infinitely worse since the previous summer. Emilio had gone to pick him up in the car and taken him to his appointment with Father Stablum. During the ride Piero told him that the disease, as it developed, had revealed the worst symptoms mentioned in the book. Nodules, or disgusting ulcerous growths, were forming all over his body with the exception of his extremities and head. They were growing in size and number, merged together in twos or threes, sometimes healing but mainly on the increase. Like fungi, they caused such terrible, continuous irritation that now he had only light, fitful sleep. It was not even real sleep, but a series of dozes, day and night, when the itching abated from time to time under various treatments or perhaps through a kind of exhaustion. Piero's face also showed signs of deterioration. Staring at him without meaning to in the clear, cold light of the glass-paned room, Emilio saw that he had never been so emaciated. His eyes burned.

'Do you get fever sometimes?' he asked him.

'Not so far,' explained Piero. 'No, I must confess that apart from lack of sleep and the itching I feel reasonably well inside. I get hungry and eat and drink regularly. My organs, heart, liver, bowels, lungs are all healthy. And I feel that they are healthy. It's the envelope around them that's sick. Because I feel all right inside, I'm afraid that it'll be a long business, a very long business . . . whether I get better or not. Now, thanks to you, Irma likes her work at last. It looks as if she realizes for the first time that life's not only having a good time, but in one way or another, sacrifice, discipline . . . after all, you know it was my biggest worry. I was worried stiff. Now thank God and thanks to you, I don't worry any more, not about Irma anyway. I feel a bit easier in my mind at last, and I want to make a decision – a painful one but in my opinion a necessary one. I'll talk to the professor then I'll tell you everything. Here we are, this must be him.'

A monk had appeared on the other side of the glass, tall, massive, pallid, in a voluminous dark blue cassock. He entered smiling with bloodless lips and a steely glance slightly softened by the gold rims of his spectacles. He said: 'I am Father Fidelius, Doctor Stablum.'

He had such a high, prominent forehead that it obscured the view of his hair – thick, fairish hair which was cut very short and made him look bald. He asked Piero to follow him to the consulting-room.

Emilio, left alone, tried to imagine what Piero's decision could be and how it was connected with Irma's change of heart. A genuine change, thought Emilio, which perhaps had a logical explanation, but since Gisa had pointed it out it continued to surprise him and hardly seemed possible. Since the beginning of March Irma had been coming punctually to the studios and even working with a will. Piero was not mistaken about Irma, but he was wrong to thank him, Emilio, who had nothing to do with it. Ever since the first moment, since the evening of the phone call from

San Remo, he had been careful not to try to influence Irma. And it was since then that Irma seemed to have changed.

L had called from San Remo where he was finishing shooting the film. 'Helen Christis is accusing Giorgio Gentili of theft.' Emilio's first thought had been for Irma. Should he tell her about it or not?

Christis, the American star of the film, said that Gentili began an evening with her at the casino, where he had played and lost heavily, and ended it in her room, where he made love to her and neatly stole some jewellery which had gone to pay for his losses. She had not reported it to the police yet out of personal regard for Signor Golzio. She had locked herself in her hotel room and refused to continue work until the jewels or their value were returned to her. Golzio instructed Emilio to leave at once for San Remo and settle the matter. Emilio went down to the cutting-room. He had an excuse – to tell Gisa that if the reels of new film came out from printing in time she should have them delivered to the train, to such-and-such a carriage and sleeper. He would take them to San Remo himself. He could just as well have rung Gisa. He had gone down to the cutting-room because of an instinctive need to see Irma. No, the more he thought about it, the surer he was. He had nothing to blame himself for except a longing to see her. He had never thought it necessary to warn her, put her on her guard against Gentili. He had come down just to see her.

As he entered, Gisa got up and began the usual ritual: 'Oh, sir, to what do I owe the honour?' Irma, in her white overall, her mass of tawny hair bending over the moviola, didn't move or look round. One of her usual perversities? That was what Emilio thought at the time, but later he became increasingly convinced that she already knew, or at least guessed, that something was wrong and had decided to break it off with Giorgio Gentili. In San Remo, once the jewellery had been redeemed and restored to Christis, shooting resumed without any further scandal. The film was near completion. Emilio, on Golzio's advice, stayed until the end. And that was how he happened to learn the truth.

L had asked him to play a small part in the film – a single scene among palm trees at sunset with the sea in the background, the heroine, Christis, giving a lingering kiss to a distinguished-looking forty-year-old man in order to make the character played by Gentili jealous. Emilio had taken a few small parts in Victoria Films before as a joke. This time he consented to give the director, who was in difficulties, a helping hand. For Christis had turned awkward and refused to be kissed by an 'extra' or an unknown actor. And even an average actor would refuse a 'silent' part and such a short one, unless he was paid a ridiculously high fee.

Helen Christis, a slim, smart woman of a certain age, contrived to look youthful by careful make-up and was after all extremely attractive on the screen – even in real life, at a distance and for a few moments. It was enough to lunch with her for her to lose all her charm, and even worse when one had to talk business, as Emilio did when he drew up her contract, and now had to do again about the theft of her jewellery. It became apparent then that she was a precise woman, extremely self-controlled; every action, gesture, glance was calculated and her measured, sophisticated polish concealed something revolting: a vicious, avid, almost masculine coldness.

The kiss sequence had the couple standing near a balustrade. Emilio was to put his right arm round Christis's waist while he stroked her hair with his left and tried to look into her eyes. Christis had to bend back pretending to resist his kiss and avoiding his glance, while Gentili approaching out of the corner of her eye. Watching. When she was sure of being seen, she had to pretend to yield and kiss Emilio first. Gentili would come still nearer and finally see her. Then Christis had to break free and look for a moment at Gentili (who was out of shot) over Emilio's shoulder. The look was to simulate surprise and express love and the savage satisfaction of revenge.

After the business of the jewels Christis and Gentili obviously did not kiss and make up. They worked together, of course, and in scenes much more sentimental than that one. But apart from work, they did not speak to each other or even pass the time of day. Yet, as they repeated the scene time and again, Emilio seemed to detect a glow of sincerity in the way Christis looked at Gentili. Laughing, he told her that she really did look as if she were in love. Christis snapped back, 'That's silly, coming from you. I'm a real artist.' The harshness of her reaction confirmed Emilio's suspicion that the theft was a cunning trick thought up by the two of them to get the company to pay for their losses at chemin-de-fer. Gentili was the one who had sat at the gaming-table, but rumour had it that he was 'in partnership' with her.

Once the film was finished, Emilio could still report the theft to the *carabinieri*, or at least withhold the last instalment of Gentili's fee which was only slightly less than the sum Victoria had paid to redeem the jewellery. In spite of everything Gentili continued to brazen it out. He had never admitted theft. He said that the jewellery had been 'given' him by his friend – at least, half of it had, the other half having been used to cover her losses. Emilio believed that this, too, was part of the couple's 'arrangement'.

In the blinding sunshine of a March midday, at a window overlooking the sea, Gentili laughed with all the tiny wrinkles of a face that looked young but was not youthful, carefully kept but tired-looking. 'Why won't you believe me? I haven't pinched anything. What do you think I am? Anyway that American female's a bitch.'

He had had the cheek to come and draw his last pay. Emilio stared at him and thought of Irma. For a moment before signing the cheque he thought of making a condition that Gentili would have no difficulty accepting: extracting a promise that he would leave Irma alone. But he refrained and did not mention Irma, not even vaguely. A promise from Gentili would be worthless. Besides which, it would be a mistake to show too much interest in the girl with a man of this sort, like giving him a weapon; not, of course, that Emilio's interest was hypocritical or due to anything but his old, fraternal friendship for Piero.

Emilio forgave Gentili and paid him off generously without saying a word. Gentili took the cheque and saw it was for the full amount. He was surprised – he had not expected to get more than half. He thanked Emilio, shaking his hand vigorously and gazing earnestly at him. That look, more potent than words of thanks, scrutinized him, tried to discover the real reason for his generosity and detect a basis of connivance and complicity. It was a look which said 'We understand each other.' Or at least, 'We will understand each other.' And in the depths of his sparkling, apple-green eyes there was something hard and cold – the same lack of scruples and refinement that marked the way Christis looked and behaved.

Emilio asked himself why he had decided to be so generous. Had he done it for Irma and Piero? Or so that Gentili would feel in no way tempted to sue the company and provoke newspaper publicity? This, of course, was the reason he gave to Golzio when he returned to Rome. If Golzio disapproved, he was ready to pay out of his own pocket. But Golzio, who had always been against any form of scandal, approved.

He said nothing to Irma. He did not even try to see her after his return from San Remo. Those days work was lighter – Gisa came alone to the viewings. And it was Gisa who gave him the good news one evening. Irma had changed, she always came punctually to work and stayed late without complaining as if she had finally taken a real liking to it. 'She's left her fiancé,' concluded Gisa, 'or her fiancé's left her. Anyway they don't see each other any more. She must have suffered at first, perhaps she still does. But he was a no-good, apparently he was kept by women . . . and men. And even after what happened, it seems he went back to Helen Christis. At least, they were seen together the other evening at the Taverna dell'Orso. If you want my opinion, sir, those two were never apart . . .' A few days later the newspapers announced the return to Hollywood of Helen Christis with Giorgio Gentili, her future husband.

By chance, that evening Emilio found Irma in the projection theatre instead of Gisa, who had stayed at home with influenza. Pulling aside the grey velvet curtain, he had looked into the room and seen the girl in Gisa's place. She had jumped to her feet, smiling pleasantly just like Gisa. And she had even greeted him with a trace of Piedmontese accent: 'Good evening, sir.' At first glance she seemed transformed. To begin with she had changed her hair-style – it was combed back from the brow and temples and tied into a chignon at the nape of the neck with a wide black ribbon. She looked completely different – serious, self-confident. At the same time she appeared to be younger and fresher – she looked no more than sixteen.

During the showing and for a few minutes immediately after, just as he always did with Gisa, he dictated notes and remarks to Irma. The girl wrote carefully, her notebook held in one hand, without raising her eyes, without saying a word that was not connected with her work. The projectionists had gone. The building was deserted apart from the caretaker who lived with his wife in a little house at the bottom of the garden. The theatre was in the basement. The plush, the carpeting, the curtains plunged it – in the heart of the night quiet of the aristocratic residential quarter – into a deep, almost unreal silence. As Emilio went on dictating he watched Irma, bent over her notebook, and it seemed impossible that this could be the same impertinent girl of three or four months before.

When the dictation was finished, Irma ran to pick up the overcoat that Emilio had left on an armchair and helped him to put it on as Gisa always did. They went out together and met the caretaker coming down the stairs to pull the curtains, open the ventilators and put out the lights – as he always did. He was a son of old Monticone. More than fifty years of age and pensioned off by Fiat, he had agreed to replace his father as chauffeur when the old man died. But then Golzio had promoted him caretaker at Via Pergolesi, a more responsible job. He was thin like his father, but taller and just as taciturn. Although he had lived in Turin until a few years before, he affected not to speak the dialect. 'Good night, sir. Good night, signorina.'

Emilio, crossing the vestibule, wondered what he should do now. It was half past twelve. There was no film on the floor at the moment and so no production car available. What should he do, take Irma home or let her go by tram? Still undecided, he went through the gateway, made for his car parked outside, stopped and turned round.

'Ciao, Irma' . . . The girl was close to him, motionless, in her tightly-belted camel-hair coat, and she was looking at him with her brown eyes which seemed full of expectation, tenderness, anxiety. Via Pergolesi between the villas, the gardens and down at the end the great dark mass of pines in Villa Borghese, was absolutely deserted. The moon rode high in the sky playing hide-and-seek behind the scudding clouds. In the air there was a bracing, tingling wind which smelt of the sea and the spring.

There was something painful in the way Irma looked at him – it scared him a little. But he had said to her 'Ciao, Irma, shall I drive you home? It's no trouble.'

'No, thank you, sir. I'll get the tram in Piazza Fiume,' and she hurried away before he could insist.

While Gisa's illness lasted he found Irma in the projection theatre on several other evenings. He was not always alone with her.

But in any case he did not offer to take her home again. Her behaviour was invariably impeccable. So when Gisa recovered and they both asked permission to take it in turns at the evening showings, Emilio made no objections.

Irma had changed, then. Piero was pleased and so was he. But he tried in vain to convince himself that his own pleasure was the same as Piero's: fatherly, disinterested, based on the knowledge that the girl had finally realized the need for sacrifice, discipline, work. Emilio knew very well that the evenings when Gisa was on duty did not have the same attraction for him as those when it was Irma's turn. Sometimes, when Irma was on and he went to the bathroom after dinner to wash his hands before leaving for the projection theatre, he found on looking into the mirror that his shirt was grubby, and he changed it. Sometimes he noticed that his beard had grown, so he had a quick shave. Those evenings he avoided dates with Paola or other girls – for no particular reason, just because he felt like that. In the end, gradually almost imperceptibly, his visits to Via del Mare became less frequent.

Irma had changed and there was no denying it, he liked her more than before. But if before, seeing her rebellious, insolent, mischievous and knowing her to be the girl-friend of a fellow like Gentili, Emilio had supposed her to be experienced, even depraved, and had been tempted to toy with the idea of having a love-affair with her some day, now that she had become serious, grave, chastened, he felt a sense of respect. 'Stop that,' Irma seemed to be saying with that intense expression on her face and her correct behaviour. 'Watch what you're doing, and above all what you're thinking! Better still, don't think about me, you mustn't think about me . . .' Those warning brown eyes seemed to contain a new depth of grief and passion which she had probably learnt through the bitter disillusionment caused by Gentili.

Irma had changed. In a few weeks she had become a real woman. Naturally, he preferred her like this but for the same reason he felt that he must banish her from his thoughts for ever.

A faint tinkling roused him from his reverie. Father Stablum had opened the glass door.

'Your friend will be out in a moment. The orderlies are just finishing his dressings.'

'Tell me, Father. How do you find him?'

Father Stablum threw his arms wide. He spoke Italian haltingly but correctly and almost without a trace of foreign accent: 'The same as all the other doctors have found him.' And he added with a wry smile, 'I'm not a magician, they don't exist. Though I must say that in the case of skin diseases, diagnosis and prognosis are sometimes not only difficult but impossible. And that's why it looks as if magicians have plenty of opportunities.'

'But, tell me . . . I think my friend has been honest with you. Last summer he told me that he had read a medical book and recognized from some of the symptoms in his own affliction an incurable tropical disease . . .'

'Fungoid mycosis?' said Stablum calmly.

'I don't know, he didn't say . . .' replied Emilio, feeling that at the same moment the new name, 'fungoid mycosis', was being engraved in his memory.

'The symptoms appear to be the same as those of fungoid mycosis. But symptoms where skin diseases are concerned count only up to a point.'

'Then it's not an incurable disease?'

'Like leprosy? That's the common belief. But I've seen several cases of leprosy cured. And fungoid mycosis, too. It depends.'

'On what?'

'On the treatment, on the organism attacked and on the particular form of fungoid mycosis. There are a lot of different varieties. I've prescribed treatment that should at least bring him a quick relief – if he has the patience to follow it strictly. By the way, I think your friend's right in wanting to go into hospital. In this sort of case treatment at home is unfortunately inadequate and on the whole more expensive. Without counting the serious inconvenience that the disease causes for the family – and if I'm not mistaken that is the real reason why your friend wants to move out.'

So this was the painful, urgent decision that Piero wanted to talk about. Emilio realized that he had refused to envisage it and immediately tried – but in vain – to quell his misery by linking this resistance with a prejudice which took him back to his childhood: to be treated in hospital or a nursing-home was then considered something shameful, indecent. He could see Aunt Vittoria's thick lips curling in her usual scornful sneer: 'Just as I expected, your friend's gone to hospital like all paupers. After all, what was his father? A labourer. And his uncle? A blacksmith. And his great-uncle? A peasant. Everyone gets what he deserves in the end.' Emilio told himself that nowadays no one felt humiliated at going into hospital. He and Elena did not hesitate to take Luigino there when he had typhoid fever. Yet in spite of this, at the thought of Piero going to hospital, he felt his heart miss a beat. He understood now why Piero's decision had been influenced by the change in Irma. Her irresponsible frivolity while 'engaged' to Gentili behind her family's backs had made it impossible for Piero to think of entering hospital, if only because he wanted to be sure she came home every night.

'Unfortunately,' concluded Stablum, 'I can't take him here, because we're full. But I've given him a note for the director at the Policlinico where they'll certainly be able to accommodate him.'

There were sounds of footsteps and voices in the corridor. Emilio suddenly had an idea and asked quietly: 'Forgive me, Father, but tell me . . . this disease . . . is it contagious?'

'Fungoid mycosis?' whispered Stablum, turning towards the glass partition through which he could see Piero and a hospital orderly coming. 'No, it's not contagious. Not in the slightest.'

He took Piero home. Piero seemed to be looking at the street – the squalid, filthy streets of La Madonna del Riposo. But really he must have been looking into space. He asked: 'What did he say?'

'He told me there are hopes you'll get well.'

Piero smiled. 'Yes, he told me too. They always say so. He's like all the others. And they're right. What's the good of telling someone he's going to die? If you happen to pull through, then the doctor looks a fool. On the other hand, if the patient dies then he's no longer around to blame the doctor for making a mistake or not telling him the truth.'

'But look, he would have told me surely?'

'Yes, yes, I know . . . I may get better gradually . . . but when? And how long must I go on suffering like this? I tell you, Milio, if only I didn't have to put up with this continual, continual torture . . . look, now I'm talking to you . . . but I've got a mad urge to strip off and scratch, scratch, scratch myself . . . Nowadays I can't sweat. Not even in a Turkish bath. It's because I don't sweat that I get this terrible itching. Of course, I soak myself with oil –

it's a life's work. Either I scratch or I oil myself. That's how I spend my time. But the oil doesn't do much good, sometimes nothing at all. If only I could be let off this suffering for three, even two years so that I could start work again on a few films. Irma would get married and I'd die leaving something to my wife, poor thing. She says she doesn't want me to go into hospital but I know it'd be a great relief for her – for Irma too when she comes home from work in the evening – not to find that mess, smell that stink, and hear me walking up and down all night.'

'When are you thinking of going?'

'Before the summer, in any case. Before the hot weather comes.'

Emilio said he would take him but he would have a chat before-hand with the authorities at the Policlinico to arrange for a comfortable private room. Piero protested that it wasn't necessary, he had decided to go into a ward. Then Emilio said he would look after all expenses and Piero was not to worry.

When they arrived in Via Ardea, unlike on other occasions, Emilio insisted on going up to the apartment with him. He wanted to say hello to Nuccia, he said. He hadn't seen her for so long.

He discovered that she was grey-haired. Smooth hair combed to the back of the head which was as he always remembered it, small, round, nicely shaped. Smooth hair and a chignon, like Irma. But Irma had absolutely nothing in common with her. Even the mother's fixed, startled look was not at all Irma's strange, intense look. And on reflection he realized why he had felt the urge to come up and see her. It was not mere politeness. Piero's eyes, even though clouded with melancholy as he gazed lingeringly and as if starved of affection at Emilio as he left, still had a sharp glint of intelligence and common sense.

When he got back to Via Pergolesi, night was falling. He still had to sign his letters. As he stepped out of the car he could see through the gate and into the garden, to the brightly lit french windows of the cutting-room. 'Irma's there,' he thought – 'she's there working.' In the dark blue air, those long yellow windows which threw their light on to the gravel paths in the garden, had, he told himself, a significance that was quite precise and new, or maybe so long forgotten that it seemed new. It was no longer the sting of wounded vanity. It was a thought like the solemn, inevitable one of Piero's perhaps imminent death, though at the same time a profoundly different thought, painful but also vital, elating. In comparison, all his usual and pleasant thoughts – interest in his work, pride of command, enjoyment of beautiful furniture and the pleasures of food and wine, curiosity about new women, delight in the softness of their skin, even the intoxication of possessing them – all these seemed to have lost their charm. Worse still – he could not understand how they could have given him so much pleasure in the past. As he gazed at the warm, yellow light of the long french windows in the blue shadows of the garden, he seemed to discover the poverty of his happiness. 'I thought I was happy,' he concluded, 'but actually I was merely satisfied with what I had.'

And what now? In any case, he felt sure of himself . . . he would not raise a finger . . . instead he would invent some excuse to get rid of Irma from Victoria, finding her a job with higher wages and equal security in another film company. That was what he would certainly do to protect her. And he himself would work harder, travel more, make love more often. If, with Golzio's approval, he could find a good production manager to replace him temporarily, he would spend June and July on a visit to the United States with Elena. He would be back in August to follow the location shots for *La Bufera* which were scheduled to begin then in the countryside around Turin. He would be with L for the entire duration of the film. Three or four months in Turin and Piedmont for the first time for years! That was his programme. There was a cure for everything except death – he repeated the proverb, thought of Piero, felt sure of himself.

But still the feeling coming from the cutting-room windows was hard to shake off – and he didn't want to shake it off, even if he ought to. It was painful, but it was also – almost miraculously – like being twenty again.

Following his intention, next day Emilio began to ring other film companies, but without success. Either they had no films scheduled for the moment or they were fully staffed. Perhaps later, in June, there might be something . . . in fact, even for someone like Emilio with a great deal of influence in the film world, it was difficult to place an assistant-editor from one day to another. Lieutenant Pilade of Paramount was the only one to offer any hope.

Meantime, he avoided Irma except when he had to see her or when it might seem odd to her and the others. If he had to talk to

Gisa, instead of going down to the cutting-room, he rang. And if it involved long explanations he told Gisa to come up.

The only sacrifice that he was still not prepared to make was the evening viewings. Gisa and Irma took it in turns to be there. All he had to do was instruct Gisa to come every evening as she used to. He did not have to explain why. Or, those evenings when Irma was on duty, he could invite other people so that he would not be alone with the girl. But just think of it – two nights a week in the quiet and secrecy of the theatre, spending a few hours alone with Irma, he in the centre seat, front row, she back in the corner at the editing-table; knowing, feeling even without turning round that Irma was just a few yards away, silent, motionless, on call to write any notes he might care to dictate; arriving, pushing aside the grey velvet curtain and finding her there; and before leaving, stopping for a moment to ask about her father, shake her hand and see her running along the deserted, night street to catch the tram to Piazza Fiume; gazing even for a moment at the smile on her Etruscan lips and the dark depths of her brown eyes – the sweetness of all this was too much for him to give up. Nevertheless he continued to ask around and to recommend her for other jobs. He knew that he would soon find something; then he would never see her again. And the imminence of total sacrifice seemed to justify the trifling, harmless consolations of those evenings in the projection-theatre. Finally, he thought he could define Irma's lips – he had discovered their exact shape in Etruscan sculpture, fleshy, sinuous, prominent, laughing. He had rummaged about in the antique shops in Via del Babuino. He had bought a woman's head of eroded stone with an ineffable smile almost the same as Irma's. He put it in a glass case and kept it on his office desk. In this way Irma's secret image would always be with him even after she had gone for good.

It so happened that Gisa came on two successive evenings. Emilio was so disappointed on raising the curtain and not seeing Irma that he was afraid that it showed in his face. He went straight to his seat, murmuring good evening and not daring to ask for an explanation, but Gisa hurried over to give him one in her sing-song voice. The next time, on Saturday, when it would be her turn, Gisa was afraid she could not come. She knew it was important, it was the showing of the first editing of L's film. But Gisa was expecting some of her husband's relations on a visit from Lecce and did not know if they were coming Saturday evening or Sunday morning, so she had asked Irma to stand in for her and had come on duty this evening instead.

Emilio spent the whole of Saturday anxiously wondering if he would see Irma or not. Normally it would have been no problem at all. To press the key and ask 'Signora Bruscantini, who is on duty in the theatre this evening, Levi or Giraudo?' was simply the most trivial form of office routine. He realized it. But his courage failed him. He suddenly saw the measure of his sense of guilt. He felt again that it was high time to finish. He gave Lieutenant Pilade another call at Paramount, telling him that he had to find a job for the girl at all costs – she was first class but had to leave Victoria because of a clash of temperament with her chief. Emilio regretted having to repeat this lie but it was the best excuse he could think of and a necessary one. He told Pilade he would return the favour in kind – by signing over the distribution of a film that the company wanted to Paramount. Pilade promised a reply for the following week and indicated that in all probability it would be a favourable one. But now Emilio had to think up another lie – for Gisa, Irma, Piero. He would have to say that Paramount urgently needed a good assistant in the cutting-room, someone hardworking and reliable. No other girls were free and he could not refuse to do this favour. Wages would be higher than at Victoria. That was it – and this evening would be the last opportunity for him to be with Irma in the projection-theatre. But he was not even sure of this, Gisa might be there instead if her relations from Lecce were coming the following morning . . .

How long that Saturday seemed. The same daily reality – the bowing of the commissionaires, Signora Bruscantini's constantly triumphant smile; the daily chat with Golzio, the withered, white idol behind his onyx desk, polished like a mirror, Golzio who was capable of keeping him a whole hour talking about figures, comparing box-office takings of various films, percentages, taxes, government subsidies, production costs; the actor Nazzari coming into the office, monumental, cordial, his big hand outstretched; producer M, smooth-faced, obsequious and shrewd like a major-domo from the *belle époque*; L himself, dark, excitable, passionate, saying that he had made up his mind about the three stars for his next film, *La Bufera*, but not talking about the previous one which had just been completed and skimming over the subject of the 'first cut' though he knew it was planned to run it that evening (this intelligent man – thought Emilio – is staring at me with his dark eyes but does not suspect what tonight's 'show' means to me!); the gentle gradation of light and shade on the pearl-grey office walls; and outside, over Villa Borghese, the April sky with its great baroque clouds of all shapes and shades of white and grey – the same daily reality seemed airy and insubstantial. It was a vision, nothing more. Because the true reality, the only one that mattered was different – every passing hour, minute, brought him nearer to the moment when he would see Irma again and be with her in the projection-theatre for the last time.

He went home and changed. Elena was already at table with guests – two new English friends, one a journalist the other a mannequin. He made a brief appearance, said 'hello' and apologized for having unfortunately to dine out. The three women, all very elegant in their cocktail dresses, were in the old dining-room, still as Prince Stroganoff had originally furnished it, the most valuable part of the palazzetto, entirely lined with great panels of tooled, painted and gilt Cordovan leather. Thin gilt threads winding between fleeting, blackish figures which it was impossible to make out from a distance – mythological, hunting scenes, woods or crags and floating here and there in all that dark brown, long white forms, hounds, maybe. The three blonde, pink-and-white women with their sparkling jewels and bare shoulders, their bodies sheathed in shiny black silk, seemed also in some way to be part of the Cordovan leather panels. To Emilio they were less presences than a feature of the ancient, patinated decoration of the room. Watching them as he heard them without listening (the two English women were probably admiring the splendour of the house, the richness of the furnishings, and Elena was giving them technical and historical information), Emilio wondered what he would do on another evening. Yes, on another evening like this one, in the too-near future, when he would again find Elena and the Englishwomen, or Elena and two American women, or Elena and some other guests, all belonging to the same cosmopolitan snob set, dim-witted and hard-hearted . . . what would he do when he could no longer look forward to seeing Irma? Suddenly, as he asked himself this question, Elena for an instant became real. It was Elena's fault, or at least because of her, that he had lived so long without caring about what really mattered. He looked at Elena in her reality – she was hateful and he hated her. But it was stupid to blame her. He thought – suppose Elena disappeared, ran off to America with one of her girl- or boy-friends, asked for divorce? What difference would there be? He would still be forty-five and Irma barely eighteen and she would still be Piero's daughter.

He left the house. He was still early for the film. He drove to Villa Glori. He went to see the new bridge over the Tiber, work on which had been resumed after the war and which was due to be opened shortly. In the violet sky the columns and eagles rose squat and graceless as if made of *papier mâché*. Emilio could see their ugliness but without a hint of surprise. It seemed to him that the bridge was a natural reminder to the Italians of Fascism. And wasn't he himself up to a point responsible for that ugliness? Emilio thought bitterly of the East African film and so many other mistakes for which he should take the blame. But here too, what did blame matter now? What did the past matter?

The curtain, at last – the grey velvet curtain was before him. He touched it, stroked it with his fingertips before grasping it. Oh, God – he thought – if Irma were not there after all it would be all the better, there wouldn't be a last time, the last time would have gone by without his noticing it . . .

Irma was at her post. She got up as usual, neither too slowly nor too quickly. She greeted him. Emilio thought that she blushed slightly. As if – it struck him as he went to sit down – she too knew something. Ah, yes, he must talk to her about Paramount later. But he would tell her in Gisa's presence to simplify matters, and only when the transfer was settled.

He had seen the film in bits and pieces before it was assembled. It now flowed rapidly, stripped to its essentials in L's usual style. Helen Christis was thoroughly convincing in the role of a refined aristocrat whom the romantic myth of Mediterranean passion plunged humorously into violent, unconventional adventures. A first-rate actress! 'A real artist', Emilio remembered when he saw the shot on the terrace. In the dim half-light of the park skilfully exploited by the cameraman, he hardly recognized himself – fortunately – in the middle-aged gentleman embracing Christis. For the moment he knew who it was mainly from the director's voice off-mike, a voice which would be eliminated in the final sound-track as it gave continual instructions during the scene – 'Helen, look, wait, wait, yes, it's him, yes, now . . . Viotti, careful now . . . look at her, fondle her, look around, Viotti, look at her . . .' Apart from the relative brevity of the scene, Emilio was not worried about himself. But he was worried every time Giorgio Gentili appeared in shot. For then he seemed to sense behind him Irma looking at the screen. He tried to imagine her reactions. Then he remembered that the girl had seen the same scenes over and over again for months on the moviola so they probably no longer made any effect on her. When the scenes were silent, Gentili in the part of a provincial gigolo set on the conquest of a rich American seemed natural and plausible enough. But in those with dialogue, his acting was too self-conscious and off-key, his accent too vulgar and Roman.

But to judge properly they would have to wait for the dubbing. Of course he realized that he was not worried by Gentili's capabilities as an actor. What disturbed and haunted him was that Irma had fallen in love with a chap like that and had almost certainly gone to bed with him for months. Each time Gentili's face appeared on the screen, especially in close-up, Emilio scrutinized it, studied its lines. There was an obscene softness round the mouth, an almost childlike devilment in his often half-closed eyes, a fleeting gleam in his pupils. And he cruelly tried to imagine that face poised over hers, those eyes looking into hers, the long, strong embrace and how Irma's rose-pink arms (he had never seen them bare, it was not warm weather yet; he had imagined them from the skin of her wrists, forearms, neck, face) – how Irma's rose-pink arms would clasp the smooth, muscular body of her lover. Could all this have happened, he asked himself in an agony of doubt. Of course it could. He might as well abandon any stupid hopes in retrospect on that score. It had definitely happened. But there was one great consolation and it was sufficient to raise his hopes for Irma's future . . . Afraid of his own hypocrisy, he interrupted his train of thought and wondered if he really cared about Irma's future. He came to the conclusion that he did, although he could only summon up trite old formulae such as 'she'll find the right boy', 'she'll be a good wife', 'she'll make an excellent mother'.

This was the consolation, then: when Gentili left her for Christis, the immediate, incredible, entire change in Irma showed how much she was suffering and how completely she had misjudged her lover.

Irma, for all her posing as a little vamp, could not have had the faintest idea of what her boy-friend was really like, the vileness and vulgarity in Gentili's nature. This was the secret of her conversion and at the same time the best proof of her essential innocence, even if she *had* been Gentili's mistress. Although he had thought about it a lot, Emilio realized the truth only now while studying Gentili's face on the silver screen. And as he studied the face he had to admit that it was 'Etruscan' too, though the features were softer, weaker, more exhausted than the lines in the stone sculptures of the proto-types. That – he concluded – was probably what had attracted Irma to Gentili: a mysterious similarity or affinity.

The film came to an end. As usual, Irma got up with notebook and pencil and came over to Emilio who was already on his way to her. He told her that he wanted to make a lot of notes, so would give them personally to L on the following day, which was what always happened after showing the first cut of a complete film. So as not to forget he would only dictate a brief summary of the various points now.

'Just a dash and a couple of words for each remark. Write. One . . .' Irma wrote standing quite close to him, notebook against her chest. While he dictated, Emilio was thinking that he only had to stretch out his hand to caress her forehead fringed with tawny curls, caress her gently just as he had caressed hard, artificial Christis in the film. Irma had changed her hair-style again. Not that she had returned to the dishevelled mop of a few months before, but neither was it brushed smoothly back. It was a compromise – a pony-tail bound with a black ribbon and round her forehead and temples part of her hair was prettily free and loose. It was the loveliest hair-style that he had ever seen. And the colour of her hair (he had a close view now while he was dictating) was the most extraordinary, the most marvellous colour that a woman's hair could have. A deep burnished copper red with the same impact as a brunette's hair but strangely glowing and somehow liberated from the sombre weight of sexuality. While he dictated he watched Irma's hands as if for the first time, and perhaps it really was the first time that he had watched them so intently. He told himself that he must study them closely to remember them later – he would never have another opportunity. They were a little girl's, a schoolgirl's, hands – pink, long, not thin, soft, with plain, pale oval nails that were unvarnished and had something gauche and childlike about them which was accentuated by the way she gripped the notebook with one hand and the pencil with the other. He could not look into Irma's eyes because she was bending low over the notebook – intentionally, so it seemed to Emilio. He therefore continued to watch her hands which, after the eyes, are the most expressive personal features. But Irma's hands, clutching notebook and pencil, were merely expressive of her honest application to her work, her anxiety to keep up with the dictation even though Emilio was doing his best to go slowly. Irma's hands expressed nothing else; but Emilio realized while dictating that he was thinking of something quite different – the caresses which she had certainly lavished on Gentili's body. Was it possible? More than that, it was a fact. He was suddenly interrupted by the rattle of curtain-rings over at the entrance. He turned and saw the caretaker.

'Good evening, Monticone . . . We'll be finished in a moment.'

'Take your time, take your time, sir. I'll do the rounds on the floors above first. Good night.'

The sound of Monticone's footsteps receded slowly up the stairs until he was out of earshot. Now Irma was staring at him. Now at last he could look into her eyes. His list of notes for L was almost finished. One more thing . . . Irma gazed at him, waiting for his last few words to add them to the rest. But Emilio, as he looked back at her, realized that he had forgotten what he wanted to dictate. The deep silence of the night seemed to press heavily all round and the fact that he and Irma were standing there so close to each other seemed to mean something, demand something. Irma was not smiling. Her brown eyes looked unwaveringly at him like two candles in a closed crypt. And her lips were motionless, closed – the corners which always shaped her smile by some indefinable change now expressed something else, something very different – a dark, anguished determination, thought Emilio without stopping to ponder over it because he was seized by a sudden desire: the desire to know what Irma's determination meant, and to respond adequately to it, to penetrate her mysterious soul with his own. His eyes fixed on hers, he could only murmur: 'Irma . . .'

She fell against him, opening her mouth on his, clasping him tightly in her arms, crushing her firm full breasts against his chest, gasping out a kind of long lament or sob.

Bewilderment, the frenzy of sudden pleasure, her fresh, natural perfume, the thick mass of her Titian hair. He pressed her to him with all his strength and returned her kisses with an energy as savage as her own. Simultaneously thoughts were jostling in his mind: Irma liked him! But since when? Since Gentili had left her? Or right from the start? Was that why she had been so cheeky when she first came to see him? Perhaps she already liked him then without knowing it. And the change in her, her 'conversion', was at least partly due to this feeling? All these questions crowded through his mind, overlapping each other in tangled confusion, mingled with the pleasure of a kiss from which he could not break free though he was afraid of Monticone coming back and glanced every now and then towards the wide open entrance with the curtain drawn to one side. He felt Irma give in his arms as if she were going to faint.

'Irma,' he whispered, and realized with delight that he was saying her name in a new, loving and intimate tone, 'Irma, we can't . . . we must go . . . come on, we must go.'

'Where?' asked Irma, not looking at him but pressing even closer as if to resist in case he tried to leave her. 'I don't want to go home, it's too early.'

The word 'home' conjured up for Emilio the Via Ardea, Nuccia, Piero, Piero ill, bandaged, with his bottles of oil, his itching, his dreadful disease and he could see no connection between that reality and the present one – he and Irma clasped tightly in each other's arms.

'No, you're not going home. Will you come to my place?'

Irma nodded, laughing, then kissed him again.

Driving across Rome on a late April night with Irma beside him; downhill swiftly, smoothly, Via Veneto, Piazza Barberini, up again, Quattro Fontane, the Quirinal, down again, Via Ventiquattro Maggio, Piazza Venezia and finally gliding into Via del Mare; stopping at the glossy, green front-door; Irma's wondering, intoxicated gaze; opening the door; running up the four steep flights of stairs; entering the small hall; closing the door behind them and bolting it; along the dim gallery; kissing, standing as they were; kissing endlessly . . . Emilio was amazed that life could still give him such pure joy.

Irma showed no sign of embarrassment. There was no silly

nonsense, no stupid resistance – so tiresome, thought Emilio, when they are false, so depressing when they are sincere! He had to admit, though, that she *had* been Gentili's mistress, and perhaps in spite of her youth there had been other men as well. She was experienced in love. It was equally certain that the experience had not spoilt her. Her natural grace or the genuine affection that she felt for Emilio produced the most correct and delicate reactions. When Emilio, while he was kissing her, tried to draw her towards the alcove, she stopped, slightly withdrew her lips and whispered slowly, gravely: 'What if you don't love me any more afterwards?'

Emilio was deeply moved. He could not find a ready answer. At the moment his only thought was that it was the first time in years that he had heard the verb 'love' used seriously. Evidently, he realized with a stab of pain, Irma expected a serious answer. But isn't this what I've wanted so desperately for so long? Yes, I wanted it because I never believed it possible. And now?

These reflections took only seconds, but time was passing and he had to reply and he had to be serious. She was right. Afterwards he might not . . . want her any more. The word 'love' – no he dared not think of it as far as he was concerned. But he had to answer.

'Afterwards?' he said, trying to turn it into a joke, but without lying. 'Afterwards? But how can I know unless I try? Perhaps you won't be satisfied either.'

'What has satisfaction got to do with it? I love you, Emilio and I shall always love you. This I know.'

These words sounded absurdly like a life sentence. Was it the word 'always' that rang like a funeral-knell? For an instant Emilio had the terrible and fascinating impression of being face to face with destiny. Destiny was Irma's pure face, those deep, dark eyes, wide open in the shadows, fixed upon him, searching for a definite, straight answer; destiny was those soft arms clutching him, it was that sweet breath mingling with his, that full, throbbing breast, those hips he was gripping, that belly pressed against his penis. That was destiny. And he felt a momentary need to reject or rebel against destiny which could not be anything but a mixture of pleasure and pain. Without understanding which of the two – rejection or rebellion – might count and cost more. For a moment he was afraid. He told himself that there was still time to avoid the worst, to escape. Instead of going nearer the bed, he began to kiss her again, at the same time trying desperately to think. He thought of Piero. And the fact that Irma was his daughter seemed again not so much improbable as downright unreal. But, while attempting to find the strength to say 'no' to what seemed to be his destiny in thoughts of Piero, he found instead a reason not to believe in fate. It's impossible – he thought – for complications to set in, for a long and serious relationship to develop. It's impossible simply because she's Piero's daughter. It's a passing fancy, nothing more. Or rather, two passing fancies. The perfectly normal one of a slightly dirty old man who has an affair with his best friend's daughter. And the also perfectly normal one of a rather passionate little girl who has an affair with her father's old and experienced friend. Two fancies meeting in agreement. Not to let them have their fling means the risk of something worse, of the whole affair ending in drama, passion, real love. Natural that the girl believes she 'loves' me. A pity if she didn't. 'For ever' she says now. But she'll be the first to get tired. And I'll be the one left in the lurch and I'll suffer the most.

That was how, comforting himself with the certainty that he would soon suffer, Emilio overcame his last doubts. They reached the bed and fell on to it. Still embracing her, he began convulsively to take his own clothes off, and hers. But Irma broke free and murmured: 'Don't look, darling . . . please don't look for a moment.' He obeyed, felt her slide off the bed, heard her go into the bathroom. He finished undressing and slipped between the sheets.

They were superfine, slightly starched, blue linen sheets – a colour which suited Paola. Though he had not seen her for a fortnight she was still the 'favourite' of the moment – at least up to that moment. Emilio had seen coloured linen sheets for the first time at Signora Calandra's house and they had impressed him as a revelation of what a 'life of luxury' meant. He had never forgotten it. He had once even confessed jokingly to Elena: 'Perhaps I wouldn't have married you if I hadn't made love to you the first time in salmon-pink sheets.' Before that nothing could surpass in elegance the coronet of nobility and the big S for Sanfront embroidered on the sheets of Aunt Elisa's bed. Embroidered sheets, liveried flunkeys, a coach, an automobile, a box at the Regio, the best tailor and the best shoemaker in Turin – his idea of luxury in those days had been solid but provincial, a little stuffy and austere, like that of his mother. It was natural enough that in opposition to the antiquated world of his aunts and his mother, and as a kind of nightly celebration of the new ideals which had first inspired him at the end of his adolescence in the person of Signora Calandra and in the unexpected salmon-pink linen, he and Elena, in perfect agreement, should have devoted special attention to coloured sheets. But Elena was unaware of his flights of imagination at Via del Mare. Here he had four sets of sheets – four colours, sky-blue for blondes, salmon-pink for brunettes, pale yellow for grey-haired women, grass-green for red-heads. The 'guests' reacted according to their class and personality – some of them thought the thing to do was to hide their surprise, others came out with coy remarks, but they were all without exception 'impressed'. Irma, too, would certainly like them. And the next time she would find 'her very own' sheets – grass-green ones . . . He stopped his musing, realizing that he was already considering 'the next time'. But why not, he asked himself?

The bathroom door opened quietly – Irma was in her slip. Like all the other women before, she was silhouetted against the light which snapped off almost immediately. But it was long enough for Emilio to see her shoulders and full breasts, her slender waist, her hips, surprisingly powerful and rounded, a mature woman's hips. And it was the weight of a woman and not a young girl that Emilio now felt getting into bed.

He had left the usual little lion alight. And Irma did not ask for complete darkness as he had feared she might. Slowly, very slowly, she slid up to him under the sheets, fixing on him her big brown eyes with their anguished, poignant expression which seemed to contrast violently with the sensual fullness of her 'Etruscan', often ironical lips; those eyes which he never expected one day to study closely, and even to understand. But as soon as Irma began to enjoy his love-making, their expression changed, or so it seemed to Emilio – an effect, he thought, of the pleasure that he was getting. It became (contrary to his recent, cogent conjectures) a more distant, a colder, a more reserved expression like the appearance of a smooth, mysterious wall with something frightening about it. At first, Emilio wondered if Irma was disappointed, discontented. He loosened his hold and breathed – 'something wrong?'

Irma shook her head, smiled and held him close so that he could penetrate her again. Emilio thought he recognized the melancholy, almost painful smile of true, profound pleasure. And he could tell now that Irma was not disappointed from the gentleness and the violence, the insistence and the variety of her embraces, her kisses, her caresses. He had alarming confirmation of this when he happened to glance at his luminous Rolex: a quarter past three! He could have sworn that they had been in bed for only twenty minutes; instead they had been there for three hours.

Piero must be frantic with worry. Irma could not stay a moment longer. When he told her, she sat bolt upright in bed.

'Yes, I'm going. You'll see me home, won't you? It'll only take five minutes. But we can do something first.'

'What?' Actually, Emilio knew what she meant and was getting ready to refuse.

'Phone. If he hears your voice, too, and you say that we've just finished running the film, he'll know everything's all right. After all, it's already happened once before. I was with Gisa until half-past two, three. And tomorrow is Sunday.'

'Impossible. I can't speak to your father . . . No!' He tried to stop her. She wrenched free with a violence that astonished him even though she had already shown how angry she could get.

'You must. Don't you understand that you must? It's for his own good and peace of mind. Come on, what sort of man are you?' And there she was dialling the number and handing him the receiver.

'You talk to him first, at least!' Emilio begged.

Irma saw his embarrassment and spoke first, naturally, calmly, gently, in a tone that was no less amazing than her rage a moment before.

'Yes, Papa, I'm still at the theatre, the film's only just finished. There are fourteen reels with separate sound track and the film kept on breaking . . . yes, it's the working copy. They print on old film and the acetate's poor quality . . . Here's Signor Viotti, he wants to speak to you . . .'

Emilio took the receiver, quaking. He was scared of giving himself away if only by a note of uncertainty in his voice. His heart was thumping. He thought rapidly. After all, Irma had explained why she was late. Further excuses could be dangerous. Better leave things as they were.

'Hello. Piero. It's me . . .' He hesitated, wondering how to go on. Piero spoke.

'I'm not very well tonight, Emilio . . . I must really pluck up

426

courage and go to the Policlinico. I'd made up my mind. Then I thought, let's wait a few days more and see if this new treatment Stablum prescribed will do any good. But nothing, see. Nothing to report on the Western Front. I've got to call back Monday for confirmation. Are you in Rome all the week?'

'Yes,' replied Emilio.

'And can you still come with me or get someone else to without much trouble?'

'I'll come, any time, any day . . . just let me know a bit before. I'll come. Because I want to see where they put you and have a chat with the director . . .' and he went on in this way, promising to help, trying to cheer him up, asking about his illness. Meanwhile, his eyes were following Irma who had quickly finished dressing, put on a light and was now walking about barefoot, looking curiously around at the other end of the gallery.

Irma turned in a flash as soon as she heard him replace the receiver. In her hand she held Elena's photograph in its silver frame.

'Listen,' she said firmly and her voice was again strained with anger: 'listen, you must do me two favours. One: I don't want to see this photograph again . . .'

'But it's my wife,' murmured Emilio who could not believe his ears and, in spite of himself, admired Irma's self-assurance – her erect figure, her ruffled hair, the arrogant way she held the photograph.

'Your wife? Worse still. I hate your wife.'

'Irma!' It was all that he could say.

'Oh, not for herself, poor thing . . . I only hate her because she's your wife, because of all women she's the one who has the most right to be with you . . .'

'But wait, Irma. I haven't told you anything yet . . .'

'I don't want to know.'

'. . . my wife and I, we're . . . we're just two good friends, as if we were divorced and we live together for . . . partly for our son's sake, partly because, practically speaking, there's nothing between us any more, we're free . . . and so we don't feel any need to separate.'

'I don't understand. Anyway, I suppose your wife doesn't come here. Or does she?'

'No, she never comes here, don't worry.'

'Then if she doesn't – hide this thing, throw it away, take it home!' She laid the photograph on the table, face downwards. Emilio, laughing, put it in the drawer.

'Now, will that do? What's the other favour?'

But he could see that Irma was in no joking mood. Her lips were trembling, her eyes glittering. And she was even more beautiful in a rage.

'The other favour . . . maybe I'm being stupid. It's something that makes me feel uncomfortable . . .' She came to him, put her arms around him and kissed him on the mouth. She was smiling now.

'Tell me.'

'I don't know if I'll come here again . . .' she smiled artfully as if to contradict what she was saying . . . 'but if I do, be a darling and let me have some ordinary white sheets!'

Emilio was ashamed to tell her that he didn't have any. But of course he would buy some. Yes, Irma continued to amaze him. She was a really exceptional creature.

Exceptional, fascinating, disturbing, too, he thought as he came back after taking her home. And what was deep down in Irma's heart? Was it really love? A sudden love, so overwhelming and jealous that to find anything like it he had to look back more than twenty years to Vévé? Usually, if he left Via del Mare late at night to take a girl home, he preferred to go to Via Gregoriana to sleep. He had discovered that the change or simply the comfort of a made bed helped him get better rest. But this time he went back to Via del Mare. He felt the need to go to bed where he had possessed Irma, which seemed incredible; he needed to see again in his mind's eye as clearly as possible her strange, dark, almost absent look while she was making love, those deep, brown eyes which seemed to lose all their variety of expression, the anguish, the tenderness, the poignant melancholy, the anger as they dimmed and grew lack-lustre so that Emilio continued to think of a mysterious, smooth wall looming between them.

Lying motionless in the dark, and too curious to woo sleep, he began to reflect that women's eyes while they are making love can be divided into several categories. He wanted to understand what Irma's look meant and hoped it would be useful to compare it with that of other women he had known.

There were eyes, usually light-coloured eyes, which at that

moment seemed extraordinarily luminous and transparent – wide-open windows through which you could see the soul. He tried to remember them as accurately as he could. Eyes, he thought, which hid or withheld nothing and which said: 'Here is my heart.' And he saw no shadows, no mysteries. His trust was complete. As he looked into those eyes he found another self. Such were Vévé's eyes.

Then there were eyes, usually light-coloured too, but sparkling, reflecting light rather than transparent; they expressed at the time egoistic joy, the deepest satisfaction of personal vanity. They said: 'Look and see how happy you're making me with your happiness.' Eyes like mirrors. Elena was like that. And there were eyes, generally dark ones which, instead, received and cherished you with natural warmth. Eyes which said at that moment: 'I'll shelter you within me, lose yourself in me, disappear, I will completely envelop you, you're mine.' Women of this kind had been the tenderest, the surest, those from whom he had never had anything to fear, even when he offended them, even when he humiliated them. 'Grazia is one of them. Grazia is like a mother, she could never betray me.' Finally, there were eyes which at the moment of love-making became frighteningly opaque. They seemed to be seeing nothingness and this secret vision seemed to rob them of every spark of life. They could be light or dark eyes – blue, green, yellow, hazel, grey, brown – all colours. 'Eyes which at the moment in question I have happened to see more often than any other kind. Women incapable of experiencing pleasure, or more accurately, of experiencing it *with me*. Lots of them. The majority.' Conclusion: should he deduce that Irma, contrary to all the other evidence, got no pleasure with him?

Of course not, it was absurd. But then, what about the way she looked at him?

Perhaps, as he had noticed in other very young girls, Irma was childishly afraid of not being experienced enough. Or perhaps she felt a sense of guilt in giving herself to a middle-aged man and a friend of her father's. Or, without knowing it, she was still in love with Gentili. Anyway, it was premature to judge Irma's character and feelings from a look in her eyes which he had only seen once and in such extraordinary circumstances.

Emilio began to get lost in these fruitless reflections until he gradually drifted off to sleep.

Ah, at last, no more darkness.

Streaks of grey light were filtering beneath every window. What time was it? He found it difficult to breathe. No more dark, no more dreams. Reality – happily different. He was . . . of course he was in Via del Mare. Irma . . . what time? He wanted to look at the Rolex on the bedside table; he would have liked to turn over, to move, but he was afraid of forgetting the nightmare from which he had just awakened – the darkness . . . his parents' bedroom in Piazza Maria Teresa, Turin . . . the bedroom or rather the bed itself, his parents' big, high bed.

What time was it? Early May, it got light sooner and from the silence he would judge that it was . . . oh, the dream was fading like a wisp of straw or some other light object in a basin which darts away in the water if you try to grasp it and is there to see only when the water is still.

Well, he was in his parents' big, high bed, like when he was a little boy. But it was happening now – his father was dead and his mother . . . his mother was not there, perhaps she was in one of the other rooms. He was alone in his parents' bed and in the dark. He was afraid. Of what? He did not know. He had raised his arm to press the light switch. He could not find it. He was small. The switch was high up and he could not reach it with his tiny hand. His fear grew as if the mysterious cause were creeping nearer in the pitch dark and about to seize him. Finally he managed to grab the switch and press the button. He heard the click. But the light did not go on. A short-circuit perhaps. It was then that he realized what he was afraid of. His dead father who was probably near him in the dark. He pressed the switch again, he tried and tried. Why wouldn't the light go on? Only rarely was there a failure. Why did it have to happen now when he had woken up, most unusual for him, in the dead of night and needed the light so much?

But his dead Papa did not have the long, thin, sad face that he remembered, with small grey moustache and bushy eyebrows. He had no face at all. And perhaps there was a reason; a few minutes later, remembering the dream, Emilio thought for a moment that he had found it. He had learnt of his father's death only after the Liberation. He had not been there at the end: he had not seen him die. Or, there was another reason. The invisible presence in the dark was that of another Papa, a Papa whose face he dared not look at.

Skeleton hands which he could feel, imagine behind him in the dark, stretching out to touch him now. Desperately he again pressed the switch – darkness, pitch blackness. Until in a spasm of agony he woke up.

Beneath each window the bands of grey light had rapidly brightened. The meaning of the dream did not matter, nor did knowing what time it was. He looked at the bands of light which seemed to brighten and strengthen before his eyes, gradually revealing the depth of the gallery lined with beige shantung, the black carpets, the doors painted pale green, the Venetian glass cases and the collection of night-lights, the far table, the armchairs, the divans, all the exquisite fittings chosen by him for his personal pleasure, and he told himself that this was the hour of truth. Suddenly he realized bitterly that he was laughing at himself: his attempt to classify 'women's eyes while they were making love' had been so stupid! Why compare poor Irma's strange look to that of women who experienced no sexual pleasure? It could also be described as profound and rapt rather than gloomy and absent. And his curiosity to discover its meaning had been – he could see it now – an artificial curiosity about an artificial, perhaps non-existent peculiarity; an imaginary problem which he had invented in good faith to hide from himself the fatal disenchantment which he was beginning to sense and which he knew so well, having already experienced it an infinite number of times until he had got used to it, even derived satisfaction from it, but which this time he had believed and hoped he would not have to experience again.

He had thought he was in love with Irma. For a few months he had believed he loved her. And the strength with which he had decided to give her up – he had believed he had found it in love, true love, not in his friendship for Piero, not in a sense of morality or prudence. He had been convinced that he would give Irma up not to prevent a scandal but simply to avoid hurting her. Unfortunately, he thought now, seeing the light of day implacably flooding the room, the taboo with which he had surrounded the girl had automatically misled him; his renunciation had created in his mind the mirage of a second youth, the certainty of being in love, which was not true.

He had liked Irma. He would like her again. He would probably continue to commit the indiscretion of going to bed with her. But

431

he did not love her. And he must have the courage to admit that after giving her a last kiss and seeing her run off to the corner of Via Magna Grecia, turn and disappear into Via Ardea (he had not taken her to the door for fear that Piero might be at the window), he had heaved a huge sigh of relief. Then he had immediately started thinking about her again and considering the question of her strange look. The truth was that he felt free and delighted to be able to sleep on his own.

But now, in the sadness of the stronger light and the reborn day, he did not want to be alone. He did not miss Irma. He missed Grazia, who for some time had been the only woman with whom he liked sleeping as a perfectly natural occurrence. Odd that he could have forgotten her, even though he had thought he was in love with Irma. Grazia had sent him a few postcards from Marseilles . . . My God, it suddenly struck him: perhaps he had thrown them away! If so he would not know where to reach her. True, Grazia would write to him again. But when? And unless her address had changed she would probably not mention it again. Any moment now he might need her – to help him to do without Irma if she went on this way. What about Grazia's address then? He jumped out of bed in a panic He started to rummage in the bedside tables, on the shelves in the dressing-room, in the drawer of the oval table which now contained the Beretta and Elena's photograph – any place where he might have put at least one of the cards delivered to Via del Mare and which he had certainly not taken home or to the office. Then he remembered that due to his absurd conviction of being in love with Irma he had torn them up one by one as he received them.

He went back to bed. Perhaps because he felt annoyed at losing Grazia's address, for a moment – oh a mere fraction – he thought of Irma as a confounded nuisance. There was a secret, brutal language which he permitted himself on certain occasions with the exonerating certainty that in similar circumstances any other man would do the same. He recalled Irma's violent behaviour, her dark, furious eyes when she said 'Your wife, I hate her'. Christ, thought Emilio in his secret, brutal language, who knows what mess this girl will get me into? But what a situation to be in! I realize that I have no feeling for her, I don't love her. It's sad but no drama. The trouble is, how will she take it when she knows the truth? Oh, well, let's hope I haven't got myself in a trap.

He turned over and covered his head with the sheet. The light was too bright and stopped him from going back to sleep. He had thought he could do without curtains at the windows here in Via del Mare – the ceiling was low and he felt they would make the décor too heavy. The Venetian blinds and the shutters should have been enough. The shutters were supposed to fit the window-frames closely and turn day into night. But this too was a disappointment. The wood, by drying or swelling, perhaps on account of the paint, had warped and let the light in. He certainly needed very heavy curtains!

'No, I didn't fall in love with you at once,' replied Irma quietly, calmly: 'Do you want to know when?'

'That's what I asked you,' said Emilio and he slowly stretched out his hand on the sheets until it met hers. He squeezed it gently.

'Can't you guess?'

'No.'

'Try to guess! Think.'

Emilio tried. He began to think back. But his mind was a blank. He seemed to have forgotten everything about the beginning of their love affair. He never thought about it. He was only worried about the present and what had happened that month. He had been going to bed with Irma for more than a month now. But this time was different from the others – it was the first time that they had spent the whole night together.

Piero had kept to his decision and gone into the Policlinico. Emilio went with him and insisted he be given a pleasant single room on the first floor with a southern exposure and a balcony overlooking the garden. True, summer was near, but sun-bathing seemed to be beneficial for his sores and if it did not make him sweat caused a reaction, a circulation of the blood that eased the irritation. Piero entered hospital on May 9. A few days later Irma made no mystery of her impatience to spend the night at Via del Mare. Emilio had tried to dissuade her, saying that her mother would put two and two together and get suspicious or even, with her usual naïve indiscretion, tell Piero. He had managed to put off this folly of hers, as he called it, for a few weeks. But he was only able to put it off. Anyway (he kept on saying to himself as he lay beside her) anyway the whole thing was pure folly.

After his discovery, that first morning on awakening from the

433

mysterious dream, that his heart was as cold and unmoved as ever, Emilio continued each time, before each rendezvous with Irma, to quell the increasingly urgent objections of common sense, nervousness and remorse with two contradictory arguments. One: Irma was a very lovely girl and he liked making love with her a lot; he almost loved her, he had taken the plunge now, the damage was done; it would be stupid not to take advantage of it, not to yield to a passion – a more or less genuine passion – which they both felt; stupid not to enjoy it until it was spent and harmless. Two: Irma was a young girl and as everyone knows young girls easily become inflamed with passion which dies just as easily; they get a tremendous kick from pretending to be in love and that's all. It was this which had led him to ask: 'When did you realize that you loved me? Straight away? The first time you came to the office?' He wanted to see if he could cause the first crack in the romantic castle of eternal, indestructible love which seemed to be Irma's belief.

In order to simplify the delicate problem of meeting – he naturally had to arrange things so that they weren't seen and talked about – he had given Irma a set of keys for Via del Mare. And almost every evening through May, from half-past nine on, Irma had been there waiting for him. Sometimes he arrived punctually but more often he was late. They stayed until about midnight, then he drove her home. On a few occasions he had rung her to say that he was detained at a business dinner or something of the sort. He could not come and she was to make her own way home. He was not lying. But neither was she. Her devotion was obviously genuine and indeed disturbing, because words were not enough and she had given him no peace until she had proof each time that it really was work that had kept him.

Grazia had not sent any more cards for some time. But Emilio, wanting one but afraid that it (or a letter from some other woman) might arrive at any moment and Irma might see it through the glass in the letter-box, had given instructions to the porter to hand him his mail personally.

Finally, more than once, the phone had rung while Irma was there, and she, pretending to be Signor Viotti's secretary, had intercepted messages from girls, dancers, starlets. Each time there had been a violent scene afterwards – sarcasm, insults, even blows. Emilio put up what defence he could, protesting truthfully that they were all 'ex' girl-friends. But Irma would not listen to reason and Emilio

434

would certainly have found it very difficult and tedious to placate her if right from the very first quarrel he had not realized that he possessed an invincible weapon – he only had to gaze into Irma's eyes and stroke her face gently and the girl turned pale, calmed down immediately and fell trembling into his arms. At those times his reassuring idea of Irma as a superficial, childlike little girl, aflame with a lively passion that would soon fade and die, seemed rather improbable. And the power which he found he had over her acted on him, too. It satisfied his vanity, tickled his senses as a result, and despite his final conscience-searching that morning, left him again with the dangerous illusion of believing himself to be in love.

From the beginning the quarrels had been frequent. For instance, when the editing of L's film was completed, Emilio thought he was doing Irma a favour by transferring her from Via Pergolesi to the developing and printing works where she would have in addition to a higher salary, a simple job of checking and shorter hours. He had mentioned the matter gently and, so he believed, in good faith. The post was coveted by all the girls. Emilio remembered Irma's laziness and negligence during her first months at work and was convinced that he would be doing her a good turn; so convinced that he had forgotten the underlying reason for the offer – his wish to get Irma away from Via Pergolesi, reduce the opportunities of seeing her and gradually eliminate the embarrassing sensation of having her beneath him in the same building all day. But it was as if Irma sensed only this – as if she had guessed behind Emilio's words his original intention which he himself had so completely forgotten that he was frankly surprised when she turned on him savagely.

'You beast! So you want to get rid of me? You don't want to see me during the day? What's that? You never see me? But you know I'm there. You know I can come up on some excuse or other at any time. You're afraid I'll catch you with one of your tarts. Is that what you are afraid of? Tell the truth. Well, I'm not going to the developing section. I don't care a damn about working longer hours for less pay. I've learnt to work well, haven't I? My father has always worked and I'm a chip of the old block. So you think I'll go just to please you! You poor fool! Shut up, you're only making things worse! You're an idiot and a hypocrite! I'm staying here whether you like it or not, my fine feathered friend. I'm staying here with Gisa. Here, on the floor below. Checking developing and printing indeed! I'm going to keep a check on *you*.' And so saying, she stared at him even harder for a few seconds. That was the end of it. Emilio had smiled, thought of an answer and could not resist the temptation.

'Yes, keep a check on me.' He had caught hold of her and kissed her, repeating: 'Yes, keep a check on me.'

After these quarrels their love-making was – if possible – more impetuous and crazy than at other times. The pleasure seemed greater and more real. They would fall on to the bed closely entwined.

She was always the one who started the rows. But it was not only jealousy that caused or provided an excuse for them. One evening during the first week of their liaison Emilio came in and found her half-naked, kneeling on the carpet at the end of the gallery, busy winding string round a wet towel which she had tried to fold into the shape of a ball.

At the other end of the gallery near the bed, Irma had lined up on the carpet all the night-lights from the cases and most of those converted into lamps which she had taken from their sockets.

'What are you doing, you crazy girl?'

'Going to play skittles,' replied Irma mock-seriously.

'But don't you know they're worth millions?'

'I know. You've told me a hundred times. It was one of the few things you told me when I came here the second time. Not the first time, that was the only time you gave me your whole attention and said only nice things to me. But from the second time you thought it necessary to warn me to be careful . . . not to knock over one of these . . . these . . . because it might be worth a lot of money. And those in the glass cases, those were even more valuable. Millions, you said. Well, I hate them, these . . .'

'*Veilleuses*,' Emilio, rather anxious, hastened automatically to prompt her.

'What? . . . well, these gadgets . . . I hate them. Is this supposed to be an apartment? It's more like a museum. If you don't promise to take all this stuff away, take it home to your wife, she'll go mad about it, if you don't promise, do you see what I'm going to do? I'm going to play skittles with them. I'll begin with that duck there . . .'

'What duck?'

'That black, white and green one.'

'That's a penguin.'

'Well, it's the one I hate most of all. I'll begin with that one!'

'Stop. It's worth seven hundred thousand . . .'

'If you tell me once more what they're worth, I'll smash the lot. Let me go! Let me go or I'll smash them! Let my arm go . . . darling, my darling, I love you.' Emilio, scared that she might really break them, had seized her wrist, then, without letting go, had knelt down facing her so that his body touched hers. As usual she quietened down immediately. In these situations, Emilio, as he held her, felt a sudden change in her body – a weakening, a tenderness, a wave of sweetness that mounted swiftly to her face, wiping the rage away as if by magic and replacing it by a relaxed smile of bliss.

Confused, even annoyed, he did not however lose his temper. If only because it would have seemed overdone. The next day, thinking calmly about it, he came to the conclusion that Irma with her working-class instincts was not entirely wrong. The collection of *veilleuses*, whichever way you looked at it, was rather ridiculous, a chi-chi hobby or rather a maiden aunt's delight. Worthy of the Swedish diplomat who had been the previous tenant. The same day he had the nightlights from the glass cases taken to Via Gregoriana and arranged in Venetian shelves which had held books. The books were brought to Via del Mare and put in the cases. As for the lamps, he cut them down by half.

Perhaps the true secret of Irma's charm lay in the fact that she was unpredictable. He found her different every day. And he had no need to lie to himself or believe that he was in love. Love had nothing to do with it. But the genuine pleasure of being with Irma and chatting to her, of witnessing her often spiteful scenes, always new, never boring, was enough to make him continually postpone the decision which he had considered wise and desirable right from the beginning – the decision to reduce the number of dates with her in Via del Mare. For that pleasure and nothing else he had committed the indiscretion of taking Irma to dinner on two or three occasions at the Castelli[1] or along the Via Aurelia in one of the more modest and less crowded *trattorie*. He thought it a big sacrifice not to be able to go out with her freely, not to be seen in public with her at the cinema, the theatre, the café.

[1] Castelli Romani: hills south-east of Rome, noted since classical times for their wines. The most famous is Frascati.

Irma's surprises were endless. She had dreamt up the latest that evening. At six o'clock she had left the cutting-room with the excuse that she was going to have tea. From the bar on the corner she had rung him in the office. Taking him by surprise she admitted that she had been to Via del Mare during the two-hour lunch break, had done some shopping and made preparations for them to dine there. 'The only thing I still need is wine. What wine shall I buy?'

Emilio did not have the presence of mind to say that he was busy that evening; now it was too late to oppose the idea which anyway, he had to confess, amused him.

'Which wine, then?'

'Don't worry about it, we'll drink champagne, there are always a couple of bottles in the fridge.'

But that wasn't all. After dinner, planned and excellently cooked by Irma, he had got up to look for a box of Havanas, a present from Irma, and discovered in a corner half-hidden by an armchair, a small suitcase!

Irma had finally decided to spend the night at Via del Mare and worked it out on her own, telling her mother a lie which she could pass on to Piero without his getting suspicious. A Victoria unit was shooting exteriors for *Eugénie Grandet* on location at Pescasseroli in the Abruzzi, a few hours' drive from Rome. Gisa was actually leaving that evening to take the director some cans of film for him to 'view', and to agree the first editing with him. Irma had told her mother that Gisa wanted her to go with her to Pescasseroli. To be on the safe side, as Gisa lived outside Porta San Giovanni and sometimes met her mother in the street, Irma made an arrangement with her, but without telling her how or with whom she was spending the night away from home.

As soon as Irma confessed all this to him, laughing, Emilio felt that the time had come to take a stand. He could invent a business engagement – midnight at the Grand Hotel with Adams, for instance. But on reflection he realized that it would only make her angry uselessly. Irma would tell him to go, she would wait for him in bed. He could come back when he liked, two o'clock, three. So he had better do what she wanted. She was the stronger. The fact of Irma's superior strength, which from time to time shone through, emphasized her charm and provided in Emilio's eyes a morbid but by no means unconscious substitute for real love.

They lay naked, motionless, close together in the big bed after making love. The room was dark, the windows open. Through them came the glow of street lighting and the reflection of a hundred spotlights from the marble monument to Vittorio Emanuele. Fortunately, opposite was the Capitol escarpment, dark-clad with pines; the nightingales were still singing through the last nights of dying spring. Emilio no longer had any doubts: it was sad, but Irma loved him. And it was without much hope of sowing doubts in her mind that he had asked her: when did you realize that you were in love with me? After slight resistance and some strangely fascinating hesitations, Irma told him.

'It was when I saw your scene with Christis the first time in the projection-theatre. We were alone, Gisa and I. I recognized you at once. I recognized your hand caressing her. I remembered your hands. I know them. And then when you held her tight and kissed her. That's when I began to love you. Who knows? Perhaps I fell in love with you simply because I saw that scene. That's what I tell myself sometimes. It made such an impression on me. In the evenings when Gisa left I used to stay behind with the excuse of waiting for a phone call. Gisa believed me. As Giorgio was up at San Remo, she thought I'd already found another boy. She was right, of course. I had found one – you. As soon as Gisa had gone I would put the reel in the moviola and time after time I'd watch that scene with that trollop Christis – but you were there and I never got tired of looking at you. I imagined that I was there instead of that trollop.'

'And so,' said Emilio, 'when we saw the film together in the theatre, you had already decided that something would happen that evening.'

'You take too much for granted. On the contrary, I had decided not to flirt with you ever and I thought that if you tried to kiss me I would say no.'

'Then why did you change your mind?'

'I don't know. I was in love with you. Every time I saw you, it was like seeing . . . something that made my head spin. Honestly. It was just like that. And when you spoke to me, I felt weak at the knees. Just think then how awful I felt that evening you dictated the corrections and they went on and on. Awful? Awful and marvellous at the same time. So when you looked at me and called my by name, I couldn't think straight any more. But by that time I loved you, working it out logically, too. I thought that you were a nice man. Maybe I've made a mistake. Now that I know you, I'm sure I've made a mistake. But then there was something that made me believe you were nice.'

'Can I know what it was?'

'Of course. Because I've no more doubts or illusions even though I'm still in love with you, and I love you more than before . . .' Gradually sliding down and moulding a place in his body with hers, she finished up by nestling against him and resting her head on his shoulder. '. . . Yes, I love you more, much more, and I know very well that you're a rotter. But since I know it, I don't care if I tell you everything. I thought you were nice when I saw you didn't mention to me that Gentili was carrying on with Christis, and you didn't tell Gisa either. Honestly, the way you had treated me till then, I thought you would have. Every day I expected you to call me at any time. A sermon, that's what I expected: "Be careful who you go with, my girl. This is what your Gentili has done. This is what he is. I could have sent him to jail if I'd wanted to, but I didn't. I could have refused to give him all his money, but I didn't. I could have refused to forgive him, but I didn't." And honestly I expected you to say that you were being so generous because of your regard for me or my father.'

'But how did you know all this?'

'Giorgio told me himself. When he came back from San Remo I already knew all about Christis. We had practically broken it off on the phone. But when we met again I told him there was no point in going on. Guess what he said. He blamed me. According to him, it was *I* who had left *him*. And for whom? Guess. Well, he said that I was your mistress, yes, and I had been for a long time. He had kept quiet because he had to think of his career, but right from the beginning he had known perfectly well that he owed his booking for L's film to this. And so if he had to thank anyone for your kindness re the business of the stolen jewellery etcetera etcetera it was not you but me. Telling me all this rubbish, he stared at me and laughed. It was obvious that he believed it.'

'The funny part,' said Emilio, 'is that it's true.'

'Oh, yes? Why? Am I your mistress? I didn't know. Tell me I'm your mistress. Tell me now, I like that.'

'You're my mistress.'

'That's not enough. Now you must tell me something else.'

'What?'

'Silly! Why can't you guess?'

'Because I'm silly. What must I say?'

But Irma did not answer. He imagined her usual indifferent, inert, mysterious expression which he had noticed from the start and learnt to know so well. He had accepted the mystery, but the inertness and the indifference – he now knew how deceptive they were. Irma loved him, unfortunately. Gently slipping his shoulder from beneath her, Emilio raised himself on his elbow.

'What are you doing?' said Irma.

'Nothing. To guess what I must say I must be able to see you.' And he looked at her in the half-light; her big, dark eyes flashed naughtily; her full, fleshy lips were closed, curled in their Etruscan smile; her whole face, fresh, young, firm, expressed the ripening, the bliss of a deep passion when it is completely satisfied.

Irma loved him, unfortunately. And the fact could still gratify his masculine pride. He could also enjoy himself with her and he never wearied of her fantastic company. But he felt the need for freedom growing within him. Grazia had written at last and sent her address. She was in Paris, working at a night-club, and was ready to come at the first call. Emilio had replied that it was impossible for the moment – he was too busy with new films, but there was a chance he might come to Paris or get some free time when he would call her. He wanted her to write and tell him at what time and phone number he could be sure of finding her – possibly at night at the club.

Possibly, possibly . . . the opposite of what he had hoped in the beginning when he had yielded to temptation was happening. Irma was sticking closer to him every day. Every day it seemed more difficult to break it off. 'You'll be in trouble' she had told him a couple of times, suddenly freeing herself and giving him a threatening look, 'you'll be in trouble if I find out that you're deceiving me. I'll kill you!' And both times she had burst out laughing. But Emilio liked the laugh even less than the threat, which Irma gave the impression of having uttered in all seriousness, although she then tried to pass it off lightly.

Following his own train of thought, Emilio lay down again and sighed deeply.

'What is it, love? Why do you sigh? Is it because you can't guess?'

'Can't guess what?'

'So you weren't thinking about it, then? And I believed all this time that you were thinking of nothing else!'

'Oh, I see . . . what you'd like me to say to you,' murmured Emilio, remembering at last. 'No, I can't guess. That's why I sighed, yes. Excuse me.'

'No excuse. You should have guessed it. Obviously you didn't guess it because it's not true for you, it's not something that you feel. Now I, you see, think of nothing else. From the time I wake up in the morning until I go to sleep, I'm sure that I think about it every minute of the day. Even when I'm at the moviola. A . . . what is it? . . . a fraction of a second of each minute, but I think of it. I think of it and I tell you to myself.'

'What are you telling me?'

This time, Irma raised herself on her elbow. Slowly she bent over Emilio as he lay there on his back. Staring at him in the semi-darkness as if from an insuperable distance she replied: 'I'm telling you – I love you, I love you, I love you.' And she embraced him impulsively, pressed close and almost suffocated him with kisses. Then, like children when they are about to reveal a secret, she said mysteriously, gravely: 'Emilio, listen!'

'Tell me.'

'Emilio, listen. Let's do something – let's die together.'

'Yes,' said Emilio lightly, paying little attention to this new fantasy.

'Let's die together, let's kill ourselves!' continued Irma, hugging and kissing him wildly.

'All right, you little silly. But when we are dead how shall we be able to make love?'

Soon the big dark eyes, misting over as if by an inner frost, seemed to lose vitality and light. Again, just at the moment when he should have felt Irma in his arms as a part of himself, he realized that instead she was a stranger. Trust her? Let himself go? He was beginning rather to be scared of her. And he could not really blame her. Irma loved him. And perhaps the sudden chill in her gaze, like her baroque notion of wanting to die, sprang only from the sad certainty that her love was not requited.

IV

The flavour of potato soup and parsley; foaming, violet Barbera;
the *tumin eletrich*;[1] the cool shade of the pergola; the castle in the
background, radiant in the late summer sun, with its silver cupola
and a stag as its crowning glory; the shining, black bottles on the
coarse, clean tablecloth; the round, ruddy, smiling faces of the
elderly landlady and her little granddaughter; the traditional
courtesy of their welcome expressed in polite, rustic variations of
dialect as a prelude to the enjoyment of the exquisite, simple meal . . .
so many other sensations, so many of the sights belonging to this
golden September afternoon seemed to tell Emilio over and over
again that he had come home, that he was back at last deep in the
heart of the Piedmont of his childhood and adolescence, the
countryside near Turin. Meanwhile L, sitting on his right, gay and
talkative in the euphoria of the first day of shooting; on his left,
the delicate, Gothic profile, the high, prominent forehead of Alida
who had come to table in her film costume – Liana's pink dress
when she meets Massimo on the avenue leading into the Villa
Robelletta; opposite, Andrea Checchi, lean, dark, with big black
eyes and that honest, melancholy, forlorn air so well suited to the
character he was playing, the Jacobin Doctor Ughes; and pale-
faced Gérard Philippe, the young and already famous French
actor, in the leading role of Massimo Claris, his blond hair
combed casually in the Directory style, his flashing blue eyes –
they all seemed to reassure him and confirm that the film had
begun, that he was really in Turin and would be there for the
shooting of all the exteriors, two whole months, far from Rome,
far from Irma, calm, free!

He recalled the satisfaction with which he had looked at himself
that morning while shaving at the hotel. Just a few days had been
enough – his well-loved, thin-featured face looked ten years younger;
his skin was rested, his eyes, with their greenish-brown irises, were
clear and gay. It was the first time since he had gone to Rome with

[1] Small fresh cheeses soaked in a piquant sauce (garlic, pepper, pimento):
rebaptized in recent years 'atomic'.

Golzio that he had been able to enjoy the quiet happiness of a real stay in Turin – his other visits had been rare and fleeting, two or three days at most – but if he felt rejuvenated, it was in relation not so much to his sixteen years in Rome and away from Turin, as to the last four months of his liaison with Irma.

From early May he had seen Irma every evening at Via del Mare. And now that he was in Turin he received a letter each morning and a phone call each evening. Irma had the key of his bachelor flat and she went there after work at about nine o'clock, to write to him, call him, think of him. Thank goodness, he thought, thank goodness that he had managed to get away! Thank goodness that he had put a night in the train between himself and her, created a material rift, achieved the first, indispensable stage of that final separation for which he was striving with every nerve.

Meanwhile, he was free. At least temporarily. So, as soon as he arrived in Turin, he thought of getting Grazia to join him. She was still in Paris; she had written to him saying that he could ring her when he liked between one and three in the afternoon, at her sister's where she was staying. He had put it off day after day – partly as a sensual ploy to obtain even greater gratification than he was already confident of deriving from their next meeting; partly because in the few days before the cameras begin to turn a producer is usually extremely busy; and lastly because he had to carry out what he had promised his mother – to arrange with his cousin Vittorio for the purchase of some resting-places in the Sanfront mausoleum in the Turin cemetery and organize the transfer of his father's remains from the cemetery at Trino Vercellese. Now everything was settled. The places were acquired, though at an exorbitant price. The transfer day was fixed. And the film, *The Storm*, had been launched. That morning the first scenes had been shot outside a wing of the Castle of Stupinigi representing the Villa Robelletta.

During the break technicians and extras had scattered into the wood with their snacks. L and the actors had gone out in search of an inn, insisting that Emilio come with them. They crossed the vast, dusty square in the scorching sun. Over at one end of the avenue leading to Turin was an inviting pergola. Facing west, it was shaded by one of the two long, low buildings opposite each other just outside the castle, formerly stables and storehouses of the

House of Savoy. Now they had been converted into a dairy-farm, and flanking the road there was a row of shabby shops – a baker, a barber, a butcher, a tobacconist, an inn – all the essentials for a small township and the farm-labourers of the surrounding district who worked the fertile land of the present owners, The Knights Hospitallers Saint Maurice-et-Lazare. Just as in his memories of boyhood bicycle rides alone or with Piero, the place still had an air of solitude and abandonment, but the effect was strange and different. No cars passed. The cicadas chirped. The plaster flaking off the façades of the four wings; the windows here and there shattered by bomb explosions; the great main gate, twisted, torn up or missing altogether in places; the disappearance of the gravel which should have neatly covered the whole square outside and its replacement by a thick layer of dust; the untidiness and dirt of the long buildings reduced to farm outhouses and poky shops . . . all these signs of the recent war seemed magically to liberate the castle and its immediate surroundings from that frigid, inert perfection characteristic of museums and official monuments and restore them to the past, to the actual period of *The Storm*, about a century and a half before, when the armies of the new French Republic invaded Piedmont, trees of liberty were planted in village squares, the king fled to Sardinia and patriots rebelled against the age-old privileges of the aristocracy. That too had been a time of pillaged castles, villas and palazzi, torn-up railings, shattered windows. Then the Austrian and Russian allies, until the Battle of Marengo, re-established the *status quo*. This historical analogy, in reverse of course, with events in Italy from 1943 to 1945 had inspired Golzio and Emilio to produce the film. In any case they had always had it in mind. Edoardo Calandra was a distant relative of Elena. *La Bufera* (The Storm), *Juliette* and other novels and stories of his had always had pride of place in a special bookcase in Via Guattani, Via Ruggero Fauro, Via Gregoriana, rather like trophies of family glory.

Here as everywhere in Turin and Piedmont, the monuments and the relics of the past evoked the omnipotence of the House of Savoy much more than the privileges of the aristocracy. It was a vague, melancholy, omnipresent atmosphere of solemnity and uniformity, to which every Turin man and Piedmontese (and consequently Emilio) remains attached all his life, unaware or forgetful of cause or meaning, accepting it indiscriminately as the essential, profound, irreplaceable atmosphere of Piedmont and Turin. There were also precise characteristics of rationalism and order to which the mind of a child conforms once for all: topographic symmetry, with Stupinigi as the masterpiece or supreme image, and the long straight roads planned in military fashion to the specification of the only central authority, without interference by petty local administrators.

Vitality of a harsh coercive past, melancholy and indestructible legacies of a small, provincial monarchy, they had resisted at the time of the 'storm' and were still resisting today at the time of the film beyond the démise a few months earlier of that same monarchy. And Emilio, talking about it to L as they crossed the enormous dusty open space between the castle to the inn, combined the deep pleasure of understanding the past of a country in its historic reality with the no less intense joy of feeling, almost at every step and breath, far from Rome, safe from what was for him (and Lord knows how long it would go on) the saddest of despotisms – Irma's love.

As he entered the pergola of the old inn, he saw a public call box. He handed the proprietress who came hurrying up a piece of paper with Grazia's Paris number written on it. What was the good of freedom if he did not take advantage of it? L and the cameraman would not doubt for a moment that it was a business call.

During lunch Spartaco, the youngest of the production secretaries, arrived from Turin on a motor-bike. He had called at the hotel to collect the mail. Naturally it included Irma's daily letter. Emilio opened it as soon as the others went back to work, leaving him alone with the last *tumin*. A letter of four tightly-packed pages. It began: 'Dear Emilio,' then went on for four pages of just three words repeated over and over again: 'I love you, I love you, I love you, I love you, I love you . . .' and finished: 'For ever yours, Irma.'

He sighed. Ordered a small *grappa*. And chased up the Paris call. Contrary to an elementary rule observed by every good Havana cigar smoker, he relit the Corona Corona which L had offered him and which he had absent-mindedly allowed to go out because of the anxious, even anguished reverie into which he had fallen on seeing Irma's letter.

The flies came swarming, perhaps because of the stables nearby, buzzed over the table littered with food remains, landed now and then on his forehead or hands, stinging him painfully. But he noticed that the smoke tended to keep them away. Gradually as he went on smoking he passed into a kind of half-sleep. His mind followed a succession of involuntary reflections. Pity that the Havana lost so much of its aroma when relit. This was a fault that the modest *toscano* did not have – its flavour was even better if you let it go out and then relit it . . . Irma was the Havana, he concluded before dozing off, but the *toscano* was Grazia . . .

In his sleep he heard, distant and muffled, a bell ringing, ringing, then the piercing voice of the proprietress: 'Paris, sir.'

What made Grazia exceptional was the knack she had of always being desirable. Her moods varied like those of any other woman or human being – in turn gay, melancholy, calm, irritable, lazy, active. But on all occasions her nature remained simple and sincere.

For instance, she had never told Emilio that she loved him, only that she would always rather be with him than with any of the others and given the same money she preferred his to anyone else's. No complexes, no complications, no ambitions, no stupid, tiresome conceit. She expected nothing but the money, which was agreed in advance. She never complained. Emilio booked her a large room in the hotel where he was staying. The two rooms were on the top floor but not inter-communicating. He slept with her every night. He dined with her almost every evening, late, at a restaurant in the city or the surrounding country. In the morning, at lunch time and for the rest of the day, Grazia was free. She stayed in bed until noon and went out for a stroll along the arcades in the afternoon. She looked in the shop windows, bought a few little things, went to the cinema.

Except for the short walk from the lift to the car, across the hotel lobby and the forecourt outside, Emilio avoided being seen with her. And if, in spite of the late hour, they happened to meet some of the unit at the restaurant, he made a formal introduction but did not offer to join the company. Grazia had never asked him to. On two or three occasions when he felt obliged to accept an invitation from L or Gérard, he asked her to stay at the hotel and dine alone. And she had not complained even then. Nothing seemed to offend her. Emilio who had known her quite a while but was living with her for the first time wondered if that imperturbable mildness were due to humility or pride. In any case, he accepted and enjoyed her the way she was. To come back to Grazia at the end of the day was at first like stretching out full length in a soft, green, shady, restful meadow. A moment later it was unfailingly something better. So that after three weeks with her in Turin, he thought he had practical, final confirmation of what he had only supposed or guessed in Rome the previous winter – Grazia was for him by far the most agreeable of all possible female companions. Gentle, serene, even-tempered, reasonable in the social and intimate relations of every-day life, but in bed the opposite – a tireless catherine-wheel of desires, inventions, tenderness, violence, peculiarities. Her pleasure seemed to consist of a nightly liberation (yet sudden and unexpected) from the usual calm and common sense of the daytime. Perhaps that was why Emilio always wanted her – because she always wanted him.

'Better at forty-five than never,' he whispered to her gratefully before going to sleep as usual in her arms.

'*C'est mieux, quoi?*' said Grazia without turning and pretending not to understand – but her bantering tone proved that she did. Her deep, husky voice, how many times had it made him fall in love with her all over again! Instead of answering, Emilio kissed her lingeringly on the soft down at the nape of her neck. He was thinking that at last he had been lucky enough to find the perfect woman and she knew it, too. So there was no answer needed. But would his luck hold?

Unfortunately he had been indiscreet. Determined to confide in her and tell her about his affair with Irma, he had so far only mentioned it vaguely, putting off a complete confession day after day. Not that he was afraid of Grazia's reaction – no, not in the least. Grazia was quite certain (and it was no illusion) that at least for the moment she was the woman he preferred – therefore she had no reason to be jealous. But Irma's morbid obsession and violent nature worried Emilio deeply.

He tried to be in his room between nine and half-past nine at night, the time when Irma phoned regularly from Rome. Then, when he received the express letter in the morning, he would open it, read it once and put it into his pocket. Back at the hotel he put it with all the others in the inner compartment of a box. His instinct had told him to destroy Irma's letters immediately. But he kept them so as to be able to give them back to her when they separated, even though he had never written to her and so had no letters of his own to be returned. Apart from these three moments – the phone call, reading the letter, opening the box – he spent the rest of the time like an ostrich: he buried his head in the sand to avoid seeing the danger, tried to forget Irma's existence and almost imagined that the shooting of exteriors for *La Bufera* would go on for ever. That was why he hadn't yet told Grazia about Irma – he wanted to forget, not even to think about it.

One evening he had to leave the hotel for some night filming – it was the scene of the fake ghost in the country house at Murello. He looked in on Grazia who had already eaten and was in bed, surrounded by newspapers and magazines. In the warm glow from a yellow skylight, the pink, filmy chemise, the brown skin on the shoulders and arms, the jet-black, glossy hair, the smile, the motherly look in the brown eyes . . . Emilio stood looking at her, breathless. Perhaps because he knew that L was waiting for him at the hotel bar, he told himself that he wanted nothing different, nothing more in the whole world. Forgetting everything, he sat on the bed, took her in his arms and began to kiss her as if for the first time. She gently broke free: '*Non, chéri. On t'attend, en bas.*'

'But when I get back, you'll be asleep.'

'*Tu rentres à quelle heure?*'

'Three or four in the morning, later perhaps.'

'*C'est parfait. Je dormirai. Je ne fermerai pas à la clef. Tu rentreras. Et tu me réveilleras . . .*' A fleeting look in her eyes told him exactly how she wanted to be awakened.

Emilio, imagining what Grazia meant by that look, raised the receiver mechanically, called the bar and made his excuses for the delay.

A few minutes later, after he had driven off with L, Irma's usual evening phone call came through. The operator innocently put it through to Grazia's room where she thought she would still find Signor Viotti. Irma, hearing Grazia's voice, immediately asked who it was. And Grazia, with great presence of mind, said: 'The chambermaid.'

At least that was what Grazia told Emilio a few hours later that same night. When he got back he found her asleep. After a few instants a thread of light from the bathroom door was enough for him to make out her opulent, dark figure on the bed. Grazia was sleeping peacefully and her generous curves rose and fell with her regular breathing like the calmest of seas if the shore is exposed and rugged. Even asleep Grazia inspired calm, security and self-confidence. He undressed slowly, then did not have the heart to wake her. He sat quietly in a chair at the foot of the bed, smoking and watching her sleep. Before the cigarette had finished, Grazia woke up naturally and gently. Without moving she saw him and said slowly: 'I was dreaming you were back. Come to me,' and she opened her arms to receive him.

When she knew all about Irma, she seemed very worried. She sat on the bed, her arms embracing her knees, and smoking. Emilio was near her, lying on his side. He had just finished telling her, and lost in admiration he assured himself that she would give him the strength to leave Irma – and not only strength but the most useful advice, too.

'*D'après ce que tu me dis, mon chou . . . cette fille, eh bien, j'ai peur qu'elle ne soit pas . . . tout à fait normale. J'ai peur, d'ailleurs, qu'elle ne le fasse exprès, qu'elle ne joue la folie que pour t'épouvanter. Un chantage comme un autre. Surtout, elle sait très bien que tu feras tout ce qui est en ton pouvoir pour ne pas faire de peine à son père, c'est à dire pour éviter un esclandre. Voilà sa force, et elle le sait très bien, la petite . . .*'

Grazia could see only one solution. It was difficult but the only safe one – very slowly, almost imperceptibly to ease off; on his return to Rome to see Irma less frequently; and hope that something would turn up to help him. The girl was very young, she was pretty – she might change her mind suddenly and accept the attentions of another man. It was important for her to meet a lot of people and to be seen about. Why not get her a part in a film? Maybe that would take care of everything. Emilio explained sadly that Irma knew perfectly well what a camera was and hated the very mention of it. But – Grazia remarked – what if Irma was saying she didn't want to be a film actress because she wanted it too much and was afraid she would never make it? This might be the explanation. In any case – Grazia concluded – it was worth trying again. But Emilio must not act directly, he must pretend to know nothing about it to avoid arousing the girl's suspicions. It was up to one of the Victoria directors to notice her and offer her a job.

'*Tu verras, mon chou, tu en sortiras. Pourvu . . .*' she turned towards the bedside table, extinguished her cigarette, then stretched out languorously. She finished the sentence, smiling sweetly: '. . . *pourvu que je suis toujours auprès de toi. Et ça, mon vieux, ça malheureusement ne dépend plus de moi. Je ne suis comme ta petite, moi. Ca dépend de toi-même.*'

Just so, Emilio thought, putting out the light and stroking Grazia's bare thighs. I'll get out of it as long as Grazia stays with me. And that unfortunately does not depend on her. She's not like Irma . . . It depends on me, only on me.

Grazia went back to sleep almost immediately. But Emilio realized that perhaps because he was overtired sleep would not come till much later. He could not get Irma's phone call out of his mind. And suppose Grazia, admittedly in perfectly good faith or so as not to alarm him, had not told him exactly what happened? What if she had hesitated before saying she was the chambermaid? Wasn't Grazia's foreign accent suspicious? Of course there were Swiss hotel maids with a French accent. But Irma probably did not know that. Who knows? Maybe Irma had suspected something.

No, he could not sleep. He slipped quietly out of bed, collected his cigarettes and *Stampa Sera* and locked himself in the bathroom. He pulled the blind up gently in order not to awaken Grazia. As soon as the slats moved he could see the light of day. And what a day! He opened the window wide and leaned out to look. Only October could perform these miracles. The hotel was a small sky-scraper and from the window, as though from the top of a tower, you could see the whole city, northwards, eastwards, spread out in the plain between the hills of Superga on one side, black against the sky translucent in the first rays of the rising sun, and on the other the range of Alps already thickly coated with snow which in the exceptionally limpid, windswept atmosphere seemed higher and nearer than Emilio pictured them, even in his most affectionate, exaggerated memories. The Alps, because of their altitude, had their peaks bathed in sunlight; the criss-cross of roads on the lower slopes was veiled in a bluish mist, while above, the ridges, peaks, passes and gorges were clearly defined: the white of the glaciers and snow-fields rose-tinged, the wide violet-red wooded belt of the Alpine foothills which sloped gently down to link mountain with plain almost as far as the edge of the city. In the distance, obscured by the smoke of innumerable factories, dotted here and there with the white patches of workers' flats under construction, it seemed as if Turin had expanded to occupy the entire, vast plain. It was still his city. From the shape of the roofs, the copings, the steeples, despite the damage caused by the bombing which was just beginning to be repaired, Emilio recognized one by one the ancient palazzi and the churches; from the clumps of yellowing foliage which sprouted among the houses he recognized the avenues, the public parks, the royal gardens and those of the nobility; the straight furrows, a deeper grey-blue in hue, each had a name – Via Arsenale, Via XX Settembre, Via Lagrange, Via Carlo Alberto . . . and beyond, still wreathed in fog, the bizarre black pinnacle with its lofty spire, not a lordly tower, not a church belfry, not a cathedral steeple like in any other Italian city, but a kind of abstract temple to the nineteenth-century idea of progress, the Mole Antonelliana. Places, people, events of his childhood, adolescence and the early years of his marriage crowded back into his mind, summoned up by the living topography below him. And gradually the image of Rome became alien, unreal. How could he possibly have left Turin? How could he possibly not live here now? He knew very well that Rome had presented the only opportunity for him to realize his dearest ambitions – that prosperity which had always been his goal and which, once achieved, he could never imagine being without. So if he had hated Rome in the past, he had ended by loving it. But he thought sometimes that nothing in the world would make him want to die in Rome. He had even told Elena. If a sudden, supernatural, categorical warning of his imminent death ever reached him in Rome – he said – the first thing he would do would be to leave immediately for Turin.

While the sun began to shine forth over the rim of the hill and the mist lingering over the roofs and in the streets of Turin turned gaily gold, the most recent memories jostled with his old ones. He looked towards the Po.

Wasn't that the cupola of the Holy Sacrament church? It was one of the churches of the old aristocratic quarter of Borgo Nuovo, very near Piazza Maria Teresa where Emilio was born and lived until his marriage, also near Via della Rocca where his mother was living now, and Via Bonafous where stood the palazzo which his cousin Vittorio Ceroni-Sanfront had bought in Fascist times and which had remained miraculously intact under an aerial bombardment which had flattened almost all the houses in the block. It was at the Holy Sacrament that his mother had arranged the solemn service of a few days before for the transfer of his father's body from Trino to Turin. An interminable sung Mass that went on for more than an hour! At first, Emilio thought of his father. But then he cautiously began to look round. There was his mother, his cousin Marie Rose Ceroni-Sanfront, the other relatives and his mother's oldest friends and acquaintances – all shrouded from head to foot in long black veils and rustling black crêpe-de-chine, just like the old aunts in their time. There was cousin Vittorio's red neck, at its reddest when, during the elevation of the Host, he knelt low and hid his face in his hands, pretending to pray. Suddenly, Emilio feared that he was going to doze off and fall forward. Vittorio was the same age, forty-six – tall, thick-set, fairish, red-faced; he had come to look exactly like Uncle Sanfront even though he did not have a drop of Sanfront blood in his veins, no more did Emilio. For the resemblance to be complete – Emilio sneered to his mother – all cousin Vittorio needed to do was to saunter around with the malacca cane. Now he thought of it, he could send him the cane as a gift with the cheque for three millions for the three niches. He was furious at having to pay out the money. To make matters worse he had discovered that his cousin, in spite of the addition of the name Sanfront to his own, had no more legal right to the niches than all the other descendants including the collateral and female branches, and therefore the Viotti line!

Emilio took no legal action because he did not want to grieve his mother. He found sufficient outlet in inflicting these little tortures on her. The old lady lacked nothing, but the slightest reference to the Sanfront inheritance was still liable to infuriate her. According to her, there did not exist a more flagrant example of injustice in the whole wide world. She had insisted on such a solemn service at the Holy Sacrament with one purpose in mind, and Emilio knew it. She wanted to show triumphant Marie Rose, her old adversary, Marie Rose's daughter-in-law and Vittorio that the widow Viotti could spend with the best of them.

To get the niches, Emilio had had to exercise a great deal of patience. Vittorio had begun by saying that he could do nothing, that it was an exclusive right of the Sanfront family which had

453

passed with the name to his poor father. In any case the expense of maintaining the graves, and the taxes, had been his responsibility for several years. Then, little by little, he had confessed that if he did accept the idea of giving up some of the niches, he still could not do it, for – although he found it distasteful to mention it – he was obliged to consider the financial aspect of the matter. Finally, after Emilio had pleaded with him for a few days, he had consented to quote a figure. Three millions was absurd. But Emilio, out of stupid vanity – no different from his mother's except that he knew it – paid immediately. A moment later he regretted it. Cousin Vittorio had cheated him. A swindle, perhaps bordering on fraud. And behaviour (*that* at least) which bore no resemblance to Uncle Sanfront's. But cousin Vittorio, just like his father Alberto and his grandfather, old Uncle Ceroni, was Janus-faced – one face all conformity, respectability, nineteenth-century Piedmontese, aristo-cratic attitudes, *vieux jeu* and *grande allure*; the other, skill, greed, modernity, practical acumen, lack of scruples. Back in Fascist times and two years before he died, Alberto had sold almost all the Sanfront land on the outskirts of Turin, including the Gerbido stables and the villas at Rivoli and Santa Margherita, and had invested the proceeds in the purchase of most of the shares of a large vermouth firm. Now, at the end of the second year of peace, the business seemed to be flourishing; the first machinery was being delivered from abroad designed to increase production tenfold in relation to cost, and new factories were under construc-tion.

After the Mass, black-veiled relatives, friends and acquaintances, and with them their husbands and sons and a few old colleagues of Emilio's father, drove behind the hearse to the cemetery. From the cemetery gate they followed on foot. It was a sunny afternoon towards the end of September; the air was mild and still; a white haze thinly veiled the sky. Beyond the variously sculpted tomb-stones, beyond the small slate roof over the wall of the *primitivo*, the oldest enclosure in the cemetery where the nobles and the wealthy were buried, beyond the tall box hedges and the rows of cypresses, one would have said that the hills with their great orange patches of woods and small reddish oblongs or triangles of vineyards were in some way part of the cemetery, or that they sheltered it in their majestic span as if it formed a natural part of the whole.

Cousin Vittorio also followed the coffin, dignified, silent, bare-headed, his cheeks and neck almost purple, a grey vicuna suit from London fitting tightly to his large frame. A little neo-classical temple, the Sanfront mausoleum, was near the entrance. A short way to go.

When the undertakers took the coffin from the hearse, carried it into the tomb and lowered it into the vault, Vittorio, as if in duty bound to do the honours, came forward slightly and stood at Emilio's side. The ladies had stayed at the door, praying. Emilio thought again of his father. Certainly, if Papa had known that he would be buried there, he would have been very pleased. But disappointment and frustration had always been in his destiny and in his nature. And what about him, Emilio? What, he asked himself, was in his nature and destiny? Before he could answer his own question, automatically and without understanding why, he thought of Irma again – certainly not because he wanted Irma to play an important part in his destiny, perhaps because he was afraid she might. 'Careful, gently, gently,' exclaimed Vittorio to the workmen who as they pushed the coffin into the niche had knocked a bronze handle against the corner and loosened a brick; a few tiny fragments had fallen on to the marble floor.

'It's nothing, Signor Conte,' said one of the men. 'We've got to wall it up, anyway.'

'Yes, but don't forget to clean up the floor,' snapped Vittorio and turning to Emilio with an immediate change of tone: 'You have no idea what the upkeep of this place costs.'

Emilio stifled a smile as he reflected on his cousin's meanness and remembered the very different tone he used long ago when the Viottis were poor. Turin, from the top of the skyscraper in the transparency of the day, seemed infinitely lovelier than Rome – it really was, as Corbusier had said, the city with the finest natural position in the world. But if to become or stay rich in Turin, you had to be mean like Vittorio . . . well, he was not sorry to be in Rome. Again he saw Irma – her searching, dark, passionate look. He had to solve this problem as soon as possible.

He had no objections to the cautious, gradual tactics advised by Grazia. But there was one difficulty. The news of Piero's health, which Emilio received regularly by phoning the director of the dermatological section at the Policlinico, was not good. The end was not imminent – so the doctor had said – but it was approaching inexorably. Emilio wanted Piero to live on a long time yet. He tip-toed into the bedroom. Seeing Grazia's dear sleeping form again, it seemed easy to conquer hypocrisy. He told himself that he only wished Piero long life because he was thinking of himself. Piero's sufferings – he knew – were becoming more and more atrocious. To alleviate them the doctors had prescribed morphine. But Piero, while he was alive, was a brake on Irma, perhaps the only brake that would work on her. What would happen when he was gone?

He slowly eased himself into bed near Grazia, near her warmth, near her breathing. After such tiresome, distressing thoughts, this was calm and security. After those thoughts of death this was the tranquil pulsation of life. He was surprised to find himself thanking God or whoever was up there for having given him Grazia, and begging that he could keep her.

The run-through of all the material accumulated during the first month and a half of shooting was fixed for Friday and Saturday nights at a big cinema in the centre of Turin, at about one o'clock, after the show. He had just sat down in the middle of the stalls between L and the cameraman when Irma appeared, light-hearted and smiling in a short scarlet overcoat. He was so surprised that he temporarily lost control. Before greeting her or waiting for her to do the same he said: 'What's this? Wasn't Gisa supposed to come?'

Apart from anything else, the remark was rude. Irma blushed, shot a murderous glance at him as only she could, then recovered immediately and laughed. 'I'm sorry, sir, but Gisa was too tired. You understand, she spent all night in Via Po sorting out this week's material too, the sequence of the arrival of the Russians, and at the last minute she didn't feel like travelling by train all day. Why? Don't you like the idea that I've come? The director does. Don't you, sir?'

'Come, come,' replied L, cheerful and conciliatory, speaking between his teeth and half closing his eyes while he lit his Havana, and in his sly look there was the firm conviction that he had understood what was up. Things were very simple in L's mind: the showing was an important one, Emilio wanted to have the opinion of a canny veteran of the cinema like Gisa, especially as they would very likely have to face the expense of reshooting some of the less successful scenes. And Irma with her childishness, her desire to get on and shortly become chief editor had been hurt by Emilio's aggressive tone. How difficult it is, thought Emilio, even for the shrewdest and most intelligent people, even for an intuitive artist like L, to capture the truth.

Realizing that neither L nor the cameraman had the slightest suspicion of how things stood, he tried his best to remedy the situation. He was charming to Irma throughout the viewing. And thanks to his previous rudeness, he felt he could risk asking questions apparently designed to correct that impression and which otherwise would certainly have aroused L's suspicions. Where was she staying? Irma replied: 'At the Nazionale.' It was a moderately cheap hotel-boarding-house, headquarters of the production unit, and occupied almost entirely by technicians. At this news Emilio heaved a sigh of relief. It was obviously impossible for him to go to Irma's room during those two days and nights; and luckily just as impossible for her to come to him at the hotel where all the actors and L himself were staying. But so what? On reflection he saw exactly how illusory that feeling of relief was. It was hardly likely that Irma, who had not seen him for six weeks, would calmly give up the idea of being with him at least once. She had to be back at work in Rome on Monday morning. It was up to Emilio to arrange to meet her secretly, possibly on Sunday.

The viewing finished at three o'clock in the morning. Irma was ready with pencil and notebook to take down editing notes to pass on to Gisa. But it was too late. L said that he would dictate them the following morning in the car on the way to the location. It was nearly an hour's journey and there was plenty of time.

The next morning at half-past seven, Irma was sitting on the corner of a divan in the deserted lobby of the hotel. There was something menacing about how she sat bolt upright, the stiff way she held her purse, gloves and notebook on her knees, the very positive colour of her coat, bright scarlet in the grey, gilt, somnolent atmosphere of the hall. It struck Emilio as soon as he saw her from a distance through the lift window. The night porter who was reading a newspaper propped up on the counter, rose to greet him. In the main hall, beyond the marble columns, two men were cleaning up. Emilio approached Irma casually and whispered to her that during the day they could certainly talk in the Varáita

457

woods and arrange how to meet without anyone overhearing them. Suddenly he noticed a strange mocking expression on the girl's face. He asked her: 'Aren't you happy?'

'Yes, of course.'

'Why are you laughing like that, then?'

'Because of how you're behaving. All your precautions. You're looking around suspiciously. You seem afraid. If you knew how comical you look.'

'Of course I'm afraid, darling. Do you think it would do you any good if someone in the unit came to suspect (let alone know) that there's something between us?'

'I think it would,' replied Irma without the slightest hesitation and laughing out loud: 'What am I now? An assistant editor. But as the boss's mistress I should have an important position, wouldn't I?'

'Sssh! Please, Irma, I beg you, keep your voice down. And don't talk rubbish. Just think of your mother and father. They'd soon get to know about it and that would be terrible.'

'For daddy maybe,' said Irma, becoming serious. 'But as for my mother, and I swear to you because I know her well, she couldn't care less, she's indifferent to everything and can't wait for father to go and for me to get out of the house, married or not.'

'Irma!'

'Well, what's the matter? Didn't I tell you about mother? No, I never did, but I'm telling you now. All right? No, you're afraid . . .'

'I'm afraid for you.'

'Yes, yes. Pull the other one. You're scared stiff for yourself and it sticks out a mile.'

'For myself? Why should I worry? You know that with my wife all I have to do is to keep up appearances.'

'You're afraid I'll compromise you in front of other people, all your contacts . . .'

'Excuse me, are you speaking Roman dialect just to spite me? Yes, you do it on purpose when you're mad because you know how it annoys me!'

'Don't change the subject. I was saying that you're the one who's afraid that people will know about us. Because to the others, especially the other women in the unit, you always want to give the impression that you're available!'

'Don't be so silly, love. Anyone would be proud to have a mistress like you – a young, beautiful, intelligent woman! Especially a man of my age! But everybody would envy me if they knew!'

'Then do me a favour and don't be so mysterious. After all I don't get anything out of it.'

'You're crazy, Irma. And if you carry on like this I'll have to . . . well . . . I won't be able . . .'

'You won't be able to see me. That's what you mean, isn't it? You've been dying to tell me! That's all you've been waiting for. But do you think I'm an idiot? That I'm blind? . . . No, don't bother to turn round to see what the porter's doing. He's reading the paper and listening. He's listening and taking it all in. He's got the whole story now. He looks a real copper's nark!'

Emilio, who was beginning to be scared not only of Irma's behaviour in general but of a scene, some sort of scandal that morning there in the hotel lobby, tried instinctively what had never failed before. He glanced at the time.

'I see the director's late. We've got time for a coffee, come on.' And he took her by the arm and stroked her hand. On the way to the door he tried to press Irma close to him and calm her with the heat and contact of his body.

It worked this time, too.

'I thought you didn't love me any more,' murmured Irma, mollified, as soon as they were outside in the clear, fresh air. The sun was already gilding the top floors of the highest palazzi.

A few hours later, in the wood at the confluence of the Varàita and the Po, he was pleasantly surprised to find Irma in the same affectionate mood. Had that brief contact and discreet caress really been enough to calm her down? L was rehearsing the walk scene with Alida, Andrea and Gérard. Nearby a path followed the river upstream. There the wood was thicker and wilder. There at the mouth of the Folia was the actual place described by Calandra. Emilio had re-read the episode that very morning, coming out in the car from Turin while L was dictating editing notes to Irma.

L with an eye on the grandiose, had preferred to move the scene a few kilometres downstream where the river widened and the Po appeared in the background. And there was another difference between the walk in the novel and the walk in the film – the former took place in the middle of summer, the latter on a beautifully clear autumn day. According to Calandra: '. . . they entered the great green shadow impregnated with plant odours and through which the sun's rays filtered: the path, snaking along the bank, followed it for a while, went off at a tangent and disappeared into the depths of the wood. Quickening their steps, they reached the mouth of the river in a few minutes and there they paused. The Varàita flowed down a nearby bend into a wide bed of sand and gravel; it calmly received the Folia and the water turned slowly and in depth; it soon resumed its course, now rippling and silvery, now golden with the sun's kisses, then lit up with broad blue reflections, then green or brown in the shade of the trees, finally vanishing towards the horizon in the azure haze of other distant curves.' Now, however, the trees were partly bare, partly decked with the gay, ever-changing hues – yellow and rust – of the leaves; the ferns had dried into delicate tones of beige, brown, grey; the Varàita was deep blue; the sand and gravel white; and the mountains which the summer mists usually shrouded and cloaked in a whitish curtain appeared clearly-defined between the yellow foliage and the slim tree trunks – black, white, violet. You felt you could touch them – rocky ridges, sharp peaks, snowfields glittering like silken trains. But towering above them all, isolated sovereign, Monviso, the lofty black and white triangle so familiar to all the Piedmontese of the provinces of Cuneo and Turin and also to him. For Emilio it had remained the Monviso of the sunsets observed from Monte dei Cappuccini in the days of Vévé.

The path had become narrower – Irma had started to walk in front and he behind. Either because Irma really had calmed down, or because the beauty of the place and the day, the scent of the autumn woods, the lapping of the Varàita against the bank had conditioned them to serenity, till then they had talked with mutual tenderness, very differently from early that morning in the hotel lobby. Emilio had asked her and she had told him about her work and life in Rome without him, and about her father's illness. Three or four times a week, after working at the moviola until six, Irma went to the hospital. Piero was getting worse and he knew it. He said to her: 'You'll see, Irma, I haven't got long to live. I won't last till Christmas, I won't.' But the doctors whom she had consulted a few days before assured her that there was no imminent danger and that in their opinion he could last for months and months, maybe years. Leaving the Policlinico, Irma caught the bus, bought something in a rôtisserie and dined alone in the kitchenette at Via del Mare while waiting for a line to Turin. She was sad to be alone and far from Emilio – but happy too because, simply by being alone and far from him, she had realized without a shadow of doubt that she loved him more than anything else in the world.

She told him that without looking at him, when the narrow path made her walk in front of him. She walked more and more slowly, crunching the dead leaves and brushing the withered ferns. Suddenly she stopped and stood with her back to Emilio as if gazing at the swift, blue current of the sunlit Varàita. In the abrupt silence which had followed the noisy crackling of the leaves beneath their feet, the low, hoarse swish of the water seemed to gain a deeper resonance like a voice with a mysterious but not necessarily unintelligible message of warning, regret or consolation. Without turning and still looking ahead, Irma concluded very slowly: '. . . I realized that I love you in life and death.'

Emilio was glad that Irma could not see him – he would have betrayed his fear and anguish. How could he answer words which Irma had spoken simply but which were made solemn and definitive by the place, the moment and the time he was taking to reply? Yet he must try to neutralize the effect – by saying something, doing something. He could think of nothing better than to take her and stroke her hair, which was shining and the same colour as the reddest leaves in the wood.

Irma reacted to the caress like someone who had been waiting for it for an age. She whirled around and began to kiss him passionately, stopping only to gasp: 'Darling, darling, darling . . . If you knew how much I have thought of you, how much I've wanted you! Every day . . . every hour, every hour and every minute . . .'

And Emilio, his will weakening, had the impression that what he had never wanted to happen was going to happen. Almost in self-mockery he longed for the day when impotence would finally enable him to be sincere.

In the deepest part of the wood he spread out his raincoat on the dry leaves. He lay on his back, motionless and silent. Irma was face down on top of him, her face buried in a hollow between his neck and his right shoulder. 'This is my nest,' she whispered. 'Let me stay here. Don't speak, don't say anything. I'm happy.'

461

Now he felt the girl's weight and breathing on him, and listened to the incessant but everchanging murmur of the river not far away. He looked directly above him at the sky, between gaps in the foliage; it seemed too pale a blue, almost grey, but he thought that it was an effect of the noonday sun against the light, framed by leaves which for the same reason, though yellow or red appeared to be black. Suddenly the topmost leaves rustled as if shaken by the wind. Then they were still again. But a cool breath of air, the suspicion of a breeze seemed to kiss his cheek. And all the time he was listening to the Varàita. Automatically his thoughts returned to the sweethearts' walk, the episode he had read in the car on the way from Turin. He wondered whether Massimo's romantic love for Liana was still possible in 1946. He, for instance – had he ever experienced such a love?

The Monviso had reminded him of Vévé shortly before. If he had known that kind of love, it had only been once. The other women, starting with Elena, had all been something different. Grazia herself – the most desirable of women, at once mother, nurse, perfect confidant, was something different. During the night he had discussed with Grazia how to solve the problem of Irma; and with her he had decided what was the wisest thing to do. The following day, Sunday, he would spend entirely with Irma – he would take her out to Lake Maggiore; in the evening he would accompany her to the airport of Malpensa nearby and put her on a plane for Rome. And so for another short month, time enough to finish shooting the exteriors, he would be rid of her. Of course, he would instruct Gisa to come herself to Turin for the next showing. On his return to Rome he would gradually space out the appointments and on every occasion try to get Irma to understand the absurdity and danger of their liaison. Whatever her reaction, she would then have to realize that things had changed, a new phase was beginning, and that it was inevitably the beginning of the end. And so much the better if in the meantime he managed to persuade some director – as Grazia suggested – to give her an important enough part in a film to keep her occupied every day and to change her way of living. It was not impossible, but very likely too much to expect. Damn! At this point, Emilio could hardly refrain from heaving his usual sigh. Oh God, he felt Irma's weight upon him like something enveloping and possessive. Oh, his calculations were wrong,

Grazia's advice was too optimistic! Unless Irma changed her mind spontaneously, it wouldn't be so easy to get rid of her. He looked at the time, murmured gently that they must go, otherwise they would miss the break and the whole unit would be suspicious; as it was, they had been rash to stay so long in the wood.

'What the hell do you care?' said Irma so sweetly that there was none of the vulgarity and aggression that the expression usually suggests.

'Now, no more talk like this morning,' smiled Emilio as he got to his feet. 'Don't let's spoil it. I'll scold you another time. Let's go now. Tomorrow . . .' As they went back he told her what he thought of doing the next day and fixed a place and time for them to meet.

When she heard about the plane, Irma threw her arms around his neck and kissed him.

'I've never been in a plane! You're a darling, thank you!'

'I thought of the plane,' explained Emilio, 'because otherwise, either you'd have to leave at midday and spend the day in the train, and then we wouldn't have any time together, or you'd have to go by the night train and arrive there tired.' He wanted to show her how much he thought of her, put her in a good mood for the following day when he planned to reassure her of his sincere affection but also tactfully to instil the first doubt in her mind that perhaps their love could not last for ever, as she kept on saying, if only because he was almost forty-six and she eighteen.

Suddenly an unnatural voice resounded in the wood. It was L. With a loud-hailer he was giving orders to a boatload of fishermen for a scene where they were going down-river. Emilio still had his arm around Irma's waist. He broke free sharply. He had not looked towards the river, had not thought of the fishermen. Irma burst out laughing.

'What harm is there? We could be husband and wife, couldn't we? All right, just to please you, I'll run on ahead and you can come the long way. Then they won't see us come back together and from the same direction.' Irma ran off along the path. As if to receive her, away down among the trees the silvery rays of the arc-lights shone out rapidly one after another. They were only used for night and twilight scenes, or in bad weather. Was it possible that the sun, so brilliant when they arrived that morning, had clouded over? He made his way down the bank through the brushwood to the river's edge in order to see a wider expanse of sky.

Yes, wispy, shapeless, grey layers of cloud were encroaching on the sun. The tip of the Monviso was covered. And behind the peaks, over towards France, darker, distant clouds had appeared and seemed to be approaching.

Emilio looked down at the stream below. Very fast and transparent but with flashing grey or blue reflections, it showed up the tiny pebbles and sand at the bottom. Like the sound of its murmur and like the flames in a fireplace, the waters of the Varàita were never the same. Infinitely varied, always fascinating were the frolics of the cool liquid, scattered, jerky, darting, gliding, skipping, foaming. And like their voice they seemed to indicate the existence of a mystery, maybe the mystery of life. They melted from the snows, filtered through black, splintered, sandy stones, united in rivulets, then torrents, then a river; they joined another river and this river flowed to the sea. That water – thought Emilio, gazing at it – must contain a truth: why, if he had the patience to stay there for hours just watching it without thinking of anything, he might draw nearer to the truth. But what truth? He had never cared to seek any kind of truth, only to live as happily as possible. Was the same thing happening to him as to philosophers and poets when, to achieve happiness, they must needs seek a kind of truth?

He preferred to think that these thoughts sprang from his grave and growing concern about Irma. And his burning desire, almost a prayer, was that the day would soon return when the waters of the Varàita would again be for his eyes and ears only a pleasant caress, without meaning, without questions.

He knew that he would see her again that night at the projection theatre. He did not count on meeting her before. So he judged Grazia's caution excessive when in the evening they were about to leave together as usual and she asked to go down in the lift alone.

'I'll wait for you in the car. It's better that way.' A wise precaution! He followed in the lift and through the glass window he could see Irma's scarlet coat. She was leaning on the counter with a few other people and talking to the porter. What about? Was she daring to ask for information, to spy on him? In any case she could not do anything with L fortunately there beside her. Emilio had not recognized him for the moment.

'Oh, there you are – why don't you come to dinner with us – ' said L on seeing him. L had invited Irma before going with her to the showing. And this was obviously the result of the conversation Emilio had had with him that day during the break, while they were picnicking on the river bank: 'Take a good look at the little Giraudo girl. Don't you think she's very, but very photogenic? It happens like that sometimes. We look around for new faces and don't notice those under our very eyes. In my opinion she has an exceptional face. Especially the expression in the eyes. She's always refused up to now because she's only been offered tiny parts. You see, she's a cameraman's daughter and knows only too well what the film business is and that it's not worth a damn unless you get into the big time. If you talk to her about it, she says no. I've tried more than once. But I'm sure that if you offer her an important part and show you've got faith in her, she won't refuse.'

From this point of view, then, it would have been smart to let Irma dine alone with L. But L knew nothing of their liaison. Emilio regretted not having followed up a sudden inspiration while he was talking to him that morning about Irma. He should have taken him into his confidence or at least given him some idea of the situation. Now disaster threatened. Irma, her suspicions aroused by the phone call when she had been wrongly connected to Grazia or because of gossip in the unit, could easily raise the subject if she were alone with L; and L might innocently let the cat out of the bag and tell her that a French girl-friend of Signor Viotti had been staying at the hotel for some time or – just as damaging – that a pretty French-woman dined with Viotti almost every evening.

He hesitated for a second, then decided to accept the invitation. At that moment he gave L a significant, intense, even pleading look. L caught his meaning and responded with a glint in his dark eyes, indicating Irma who had her back to them and was asking the porter for her identity card which she had presented to get her plane ticket. It was obvious what had happened. L had told Irma to ask the porter to call him. Naturally, Irma had given her own name. And the porter had remembered that it tallied with the ticket which Emilio had asked him to book.

They left the hotel. It was raining. The weather had certainly changed. L's car was parked outside the hotel but luckily on the opposite side from Emilio's. Grazia was there at the wheel, waiting.

L who must have more or less sized up the situation, took Irma's arm and hurried off with her as if to avoid the rain. Emilio followed them and turning slightly saw Grazia smiling approvingly.

They dined at the Borgo Medioevale restaurant on the banks of the Po. Irma was in the best of spirits all evening. She laughed and joked with a continuous spate of witty, original, amusing repartee. L saw that she was not only a beautiful girl but an intelligent one, and could well become an actress. The next morning Emilio got up cheerfully and full of confidence, even though from the bathroom window the roofs, the houses, the streets of Turin seemed to stretch to infinity in the rain and fog; and in all that blackish grey the last yellow patches in the parks and avenues had already almost disappeared. Grazia was sleeping peacefully. To wish her good morning he kissed her tenderly on one shoulder peeping bare and rounded from her filmy pink nightdress with the brown skin smooth and shining. Without opening her eyes, half asleep, Grazia returned his kiss and asked him what the weather was like. When she knew it was raining she laughed: '*Ça vaut mieux. Tu vois? Le bon Dieu est de mon côté. Fais donc attention, ne roule pas trop vite avec l'auto, et ne me trompe pas trop . . .*'

He thanked his lucky stars again for Grazia. She was the only girl it gave him no pleasure to betray. And so the only one he should live with. At that time, some important people in the film world, profiting in one way or another from the inevitable bureaucratic and juridical confusion that followed five years of war, had obtained divorces or annulments. Emilio had never dreamt of divorcing Elena; why should he? Anyway after the first few months of 1946 it was no longer so easy to get a divorce. But, he concluded not without a vague feeling of surprise, if Elena wanted a divorce, he just might accept to marry Grazia.

His appointment with Irma was at a bar in the arcade outside the Porta Nuova station, away from the unit technicians' haunts although they were probably still in bed at that time of the morning on their day off. In any case the place was central and always crowded so that it could be taken for a chance meeting.

But Irma was late. Emilio stood in the bar waiting and looking through the window. He watched the usual Sunday morning passers-by strolling to and fro. He thought he recognized one person out of every three or four despite all the years that had passed. Or maybe he was wrong and they were complete strangers. But they were also typical Turin faces with a family likeness or resemblance to others he had always known. He liked them all and felt that he was one of them. And for some reason that he could not understand, he liked the unpleasant, nasty, mean ones even more. Not those which reminded him of his years and friends at the university and the Teatro d'Arte – Serra, Ferrau or again Rousset – but the ones belonging to the family circle and his childhood, his father's colleagues, officials, bourgeois types, clerics, aristocrats whom he sometimes saw at home or at his aunts' and who were thought highly of by his father and mother.

An elderly tramdriver came into the bar and as he passed Emilio touched the peak of his cap with two fingers by way of salute. It was of course a mark of politeness – a habit still alive among elderly people in Turin when they go into public places. But for a moment Emilio thought that the tramdriver might know him ... No, it couldn't be. Vévé's father would be more than eighty now, and retired. It was not he, thought Emilio, looking at the old man's erect figure and serious face while he was sipping a small *grappa* – it was not he but someone who looked like him. It had been so long since he had thought of Vévé's father! If he was still alive he must have worked with the Resistance, or at least done what he could to help. And at the end of the war with what enthusiasm he must have hoped for a world, an Italy that was new and different! Since the war many things had changed. But not enough. Not what the old tramdriver had hoped for even then.

In June Emilio had naturally voted for the Republic. He had also voted for the Socialist party. He believed he could do it with impunity just as he believed that he could pass as a progressive and proclaim his anti-Fascist past. He would certainly have liked to have been anti-Fascist. Indeed, he had been one – but only up to a point, and this he always remembered. He had not, for instance, refused the first big money in his life; he had allowed his name as general organizer to appear in the titles of a film which glorified the most stupid and cruel form of Fascist violence, Italian aircraft machine-gunning unarmed Abyssinians. So now he was a Socialist. This was not inner conviction but vanity, snobbery, an intellectual pose, almost bantering opposition to the Christian Democrat Golzio – who, however, did not disapprove of his chief-of-staff supporting a left-wing party. He watched the old tramdriver pay the cashier and walk out, erect, sad, dignified. He went along the arcade and into the square and disappeared in the rain and the crowds, obviously making for the terminus in Via Sacchi. The sadness, thought Emilio, was not so much in the tramdriver as in the look with which he followed him, like a stimulating remorse departing and vanishing into the distance. Emilio knew very well that he was lying, and he also knew that he had a reason to lie, secret to all but not to himself. He knew in fact that he was a hypocrite, but not such a hypocrite that he didn't realize that he was supporting Socialism only because he believed with absolute and mathematical certainty that the Italian and foreign opponents of Socialism and Communism were too strong in Italy, and that therefore Socialism and Communism would never win.

Irma appeared in her scarlet coat and carrying a suitcase. It seemed like fate that she always had to surprise him. Contrary to how he had left her the previous night after dinner with L and the showing, she seemed depressed, irritated, almost upset. It even looked as if she had not bothered to comb her hair properly – her red hair was partly too bouffant, partly too flattened in untidy, careless disorder. With one hand she pushed back a thick lock from her brow: 'Order me a coffee. I haven't had anything yet.' She spoke in Roman dialect – this was nearly always a bad sign.

'You're late,' said Emilio, looking absently at his watch and without thinking that it would have been better to keep quiet.

'Oh, I see, you're scolding me now. After me getting up so damned early. With such a marvellous day we're going to have a marvellous trip, I bet! And to think that I could have slept on in peace until two o'clock!'

'If you want to go back . . . Irma . . .'

'You invited me to see Lake Maggiore and as I've never seen it, you're going to take me. Let's go.'

In the car she looked straight ahead without a word. Every so often, with an almost mechanical gesture, she raised her hand and pushed her hair back from her forehead. Emilio tried to get her to talk to find out why she was sulking – if there was a reason. But Irma replied in monosyllables. Suddenly, as Emilio kept on, she turned like a Fury, telling him to leave her alone. There was nothing wrong with her, she simply didn't want to talk, that was all.

'Maybe you're sleepy,' Emilio tried again, pointing to his shoulder. 'Lean on me and go to sleep. In this rain I'll have to go slow.'

'No, thanks, I'm all right like this.'

Equally fruitless was his attempt a little later to coax her with a caress. Irma pushed his hand away. She had never done that before, at least not so sharply. Emilio did not know what to think. He settled for silence and the radio which was broadcasting hit songs. He tuned in to Montecarlo: *J'ai ta main dans ma main*, sang Charles Trénet.

'Turn it off, please, I can't listen. It's getting on my nerves.'

Emilio imagined that while she was paying her bill at the *pensione* that morning, the hairdresser or the costumier of the unit might have told her there was 'a French girl' staying with him at the Grand Hotel; this would explain her late arrival, her bad temper, and her irritation at hearing a French song. But how could he put things right? If Irma spoke first he could defend himself. If, however, Irma refused to talk, then it would be stupid to take the initiative.

Even though the sky brightened slightly towards midday, the rain did not slacken. The flooded rice-fields, the rows of poplars stripped of almost all their leaves were a magnificent spectacle in their grey uniformity and geometric regularity. He did not even try to communicate this impression to Irma of whom he could only see the obstinate profile, her lips clamped shut, her eyes staring grimly at the centre of the *autostrada* and her hand stubbornly pushing back the red hair from her brow. Even without taking his eyes off the road and looking at her, Emilio felt that this gesture was so frequent, so monotonous, so identical each time that it could not fail to suggest an involuntary reflex, a nervous tic. And consequently the movement was all the more irritating. He wanted to shout: 'Stop it, stop it! Haven't you got a comb?' But he said nothing. Not that he feared Irma's probable reaction – a string of insults – but because he found any reference to that gesture, albeit with the intention of stopping it, mysteriously repugnant.

At Novara he left the *autostrada* and took the fork for Arona. The scenery was gradually changing. Oleggio, Marano, the first hills. But Irma's sullen expression, the stubborn, fixed gaze and the movement of the hand continued exactly as before. Not even the lake interested her. As soon as it came into sight, Emilio pointed it out eagerly: 'See, there it is. Look at that castle up there – it's the fortress of Angera!'

'You don't have to explain everything, I've got eyes, too, you know.'

But Emilio saw that she was not looking to the right, towards the lake. She was still staring into the void in front of her. Nor did she show any interest a little later in two islands which through the silvery, vertical rain (a huge curtain that never stopped falling) and on the surface of the lake, livid, bristling with tiny needle-sharp waves, looked like two big ships at anchor, strangely and harmoniously armed: houses, grey, rose-pink, blue, yellow, stone balustrades and statues, gardens with assorted evergreens and other trees which the wind and the rain were stripping of their last yellow leaves. Meanwhile, a real boat, blue and white, was heading out into the lake to a point where, between the distant opposite banks and the mountains, almost hidden in the mist, it seemed to stretch to infinity like a sea. The boat moved so slowly against wind and wave that each time he looked Emilio had the impression that it was still in the same place. He would have liked to say to Irma: 'See those islands? They look like two ships.' Or: 'Look at the boat, it seems to be standing still.' But he kept on seeing her hard, withdrawn profile and preferred not to risk or get another dusty answer.

The boat was making for the top of the lake. Up there on the left, just before the Swiss frontier, was Cànnero. He remembered a small restaurant, a small hotel; one day before the war he had gone there from Milan. With a girl, of course, but he could not remember who it was for the moment. Perhaps a dancer from Galdieri's revue, or some tart or other, or a starlet. Lord knows. He thought that, without mentioning the girl of course, he might suggest to Irma that they stopped in Cànnero.

'Are you hungry?' he asked, finally breaking the silence.

'Whether I eat or not, it's all the same to me. Act as if I didn't exist. It's much better. And more honest, you see.'

'What? What are you saying? What have you got against me? What have I done to you? It's ridiculous to go on like this. Explain, for God's sake. Or shut up altogether!'

She did not reply. Emilio realized that Irma was working to a plan. First she had provoked him, accusing him implicitly of hiding something from her ('Act as if I didn't exist . . . It's more honest'); now, by keeping silent again as she had done all the way from

Turin, she was trying to exasperate him so that he would talk, ask questions and gradually give himself away. And he had almost fallen into the trap. He stopped himself in time. The only canny answer to Irma's sullen, accusing silence was an absent, indifferent, innocent silence. On no account would he be the first to mention Grazia. And he would only defend himself against a concrete charge. He had his story ready. He would say: 'Yes, she's a French lady I've known for some time. I chanced to meet her again in Turin where she has relatives, friends, business. I had dinner with her a couple of times, that's all.' But Irma said nothing. And neither did he.

When they got to Cànnero, it had stopped raining. He looked in at the restaurant to order lunch, then joined her in the avenue of plane trees by the lakeside.

With her hands deep in the pockets of her scarlet coat, Irma was walking along, grazing the iron railing, trampling the rust-coloured, rotting leaves. Every now and then she pushed back her hair from her brow, but, thank goodness, less often than before. The lake beneath the bank was lead-grey and getting calmer; in the distance, all around, lighter-coloured, almost green and still choppy. Flossy clouds, grey, white, hung half-way up the mountains on the opposite bank and even lower. In the mingled haze of factory and fog, touched here and there on roof and house-front by a fleeting, pale ray of sun, you could make out a town – Luino . . . Irma had stopped. She was not looking at the scenery. Without taking her hands out of her pockets except for the usual business of her hair now and then, she was leaning over the railing and staring down into the lake.

He went to join her and looked down, too. The water, dark blue, black, greenish, after a few instants when the eye had become accustomed to it, seemed to teem with life – there were big fish, black or the colour of pewter, now stock-still, now darting after invisible prey. He began to follow their unpredictable movements, fascinated and oblivious to everything else. The life of a fish, so mysterious to us – he thought – also has its laws, its reasons, its dramas, its joys. Those evolutions, flashing, winding, recoiling, intertwining, the moments of immobility traversed by quivering or broken by sudden departures, seemed at first senseless and purely decorative though they were surely the result of agonizing desires, mortal terror. Who could say? The more he looked, the more terror seemed to be the strongest instinct of a fish – terror continually

471

vying with hunger or lust, the fear of dying competing every moment with the desire to live.

A yellow leaf from a plane tree slowly floated past him and fell into the water. He came back to earth. From the corner of his eye he could see near his left elbow the sleeve of Irma's scarlet coat – she was still motionless and leaning like him on the iron railing. Looking at the fish, he had forgotten all about Irma. It had happened again, just like the previous day at the river. He had been daydreaming. And like yesterday he evidently, instinctively wanted to avoid the serious problem that Irma presented. Suddenly it seemed to him that Irma was no longer eighteen but the same age as Elena, and that *she* was his wife not Elena. Because he felt so much her prisoner and feared and hated her so deeply. He would have . . . yes, the idea crossed his mind for a second, just the idea . . . he would be glad if Irma died in an accident or committed suicide or (this of course was a better, a much better solution) found someone who would fall in love with her and make her love him and take her far away for ever!

'Signor Viotti, your table is ready.'

He crossed the avenue with Irma in silence and entered the ground-floor dining-room. There were very few customers – the bad weather had discouraged the usual Sunday trippers.

They sat down opposite each other at a little table near a window. They began to eat, still in silence. Meanwhile the sky was darkening again. They reached the fruit course without exchanging a word. Irma kept her eyes fixed on her plate. She looked up two or three times and met the gaze of Emilio who, with growing and ill-concealed anxiety, had never stopped staring at her. A strange vertical seam furrowed her brow. Her fresh pink face with its strong, straight nose framed by her untidy Titian hair seemed unconscious of the external world, obstinately locked in her unhappiness. And there was something absent and deranged about the way she put her food into her mouth – exactly like the gesture with which she had tidied her hair in the car or on the banks of the lake.

At one moment, as he passed her the salt, he could not resist the temptation to touch her hand lightly. It was of course a wrong move. He should never have done it. Irma whipped her hand away violently as if she were scalded. Perhaps she expected him to protest. But he did not say a word. It was an effort to keep quiet. He told himself that now, with a smile, a caress, a sweet word, Irma would probably relent. This hate was hell! And it wasn't two o'clock yet, the plane did not leave till eight and from there to Malpensa airport would take less than an hour. How would they pass all that time if they didn't make love? On the other hand this mortal boredom, this bitterness, this coldness . . . perhaps this hate which he was trying, sincerely and bravely, to keep up all day would be his salvation – he knew it. Irma could not fail to notice his attitude, she could not delude herself any longer, she must begin to suspect that it was all over between them.

It was raining again. The water was beating hard against the window near their table. On the sill outside two small geranium plants in a box with their few red blooms shivered pathetically. Luino, the other bank, the mountains, had disappeared in the streaming greyness. Inside, a cushion placed along the bottom of the window frame to stop the draught was gradually becoming sodden; here and there rivulets were slowly creeping down the rustic plaster on the wall. Without thinking he looked at Irma again and saw her smiling for the first time that day, smiling sweetly and gazing at him. What had happened? If she were really sensible she should be sad, but instead she looked delighted. And while her big, dark eyes, suddenly shining, smiled naughtily at him, he felt her leg pressing against his under the table. Her pink hand came gently across the table as if to apologize for her previous rudeness and rested warm and vibrant on his. He must have been wrong. Irma had discovered nothing, suspected nothing. She was simply annoyed at having to go straight back to Rome and be away from him another month. He knew Irma, didn't he? She was odd, capricious, silly. Perhaps she had sulked so long out of a purely instinctive, childish desire to try him out. Well? Well, had he not decided to avoid quarrelling for the moment? Grazia herself – hadn't she advised him to spend Sunday with Irma as peacefully as possible? He returned her smile and murmured: 'Irma, baby . . .'

She blushed and looked down. Still smiling she seemed to hesitate and tremble, but with relief, like someone coming out of a nightmare. She turned towards the window and said: 'Look at the rain! . . .' but her tone was not at all bored or depressed – on the contrary it was affectionate and optimistic as if she had said, 'How happy we could be . . .' At least that was how Emilio interpreted it.

473

Almost sure he was not making a mistake, he tried: 'Want to rest? Shall we go upstairs?'

'Yes?' asked Irma joyfully. 'Do you think we could? I didn't dare say anything. But remember, I'm under age. I wouldn't want to get you into trouble.'

Emilio caught himself smiling with a kind of self-satisfaction as he stretched out a hand: 'Give me your identity-card. We'll take two rooms and I'll come to yours.'

'You're experienced, eh?' Irma laughed with only the slightest trace of jealousy in her voice.

'I'm older than you, that's all.' But what had happened, he wondered, to change Irma's mood so suddenly? What had cured her? It must have been the rain with its furiously gay drumming on the windows and the asphalt of the lakeside walk, the rain with its rustling veil of light grey silk which enveloped and hid lake, bank, mountains, the whole world.

When he entered Irma's room a few minutes later, he found a grey, all-embracing half-light, an immediate allusion to love. The shutters were closed and through the cracks filtered a silvery glimmer from rain and lake. And the pattering, the dripping of the water seemed to isolate the room, like the cabin of a boat strangely motionless in the middle of a storm. Irma? . . . At first he could not see her and thought that she was in the bathroom. Then he noticed that she was already in bed and had swathed her head in the top of the sheet like an Arab, leaving an opening for her burning, dark eyes.

'Come on, be quick!' she said through the sheet. Emilio undressed rapidly. But before he finished Irma flung back sheets and blankets in a single movement, lying stark naked and beautifully pink on the cold, bluish-white background. She looked at him, frankly wanton. Without stirring she repeated: 'Come on!'

She had discarded the pillow. Her red hair, tumbling like Medusa's around her flushed, laughing face, looked almost violet in the blue-tinted penumbra. Her body was that of a mature woman as if in the last month she had grown and filled out – her breasts erect, firm, yet broad, springing from beneath her armpits, her waist slender but not thin, her pelvis and thighs sturdy, almost matronly. And her sex, luxuriantly covered with hair even more brilliantly red than that on her head, expanded and pouted in a way that was both animal and natural, sweetly tender.

'My love!' said Emilio; but at the last moment she had nimbly pulled herself up and, hands against his chest, was pushing him away, her muscular arms tensed in the effort.

'No,' she said: 'not now. First you must promise me something.'

'Yes, of course, dear. Anything you want . . .'

'Anything I want? You must promise me clearly first. Word by word.'

'Of course. Tell me darling, tell me what it is.'

'Then I'll see if you really love me.'

'Tell me, sweetheart!'

'Well then – promise me that as soon as possible . . . You repeat after me: I promise that as soon as possible . . .'

Emilio, laughing, began to repeat: 'I promise that as soon as possible . . .' He stopped, waiting for Irma to go on. But in that brief pause he saw that if she had laughed at first, now she had become terribly serious.

Looking at him steadily with that inert, sombre expression which he had never been able to explain, she went on very slowly: '. . . as soon as possible I will divorce my wife and marry you.'

He realized that Irma was not joking – she was crazy and she was not joking. But he tried to laugh it off.

'All right, darling . . . as soon as we get divorce in Italy.'

'Oh, you can get it now,' and she quoted some recent cases of people well known in film circles who had obtained a divorce by taking on fictitious foreign nationality. 'All you need is money, with money you can do anything. And don't tell me you haven't got any.'

'But then, how could I marry you, silly? Let me get into bed and let's pull up the blankets. I'm cold . . .'

'No, you must promise first.' She was still serious. He tried to stroke her bare thigh. At the first touch she hit him hard, screaming furiously – 'leave me alone!' The pain made Emilio get up and hold his forearm where she had struck him. Then he became serious, too.

'Look, just think. How could I marry you, silly? Don't you know that I'm twenty-seven years older than you? Don't you understand that in ten years' time I'll be almost an old man and you'll still be a young woman?'

'That's a lot of rubbish! Do you know why you won't get a divorce? For the simple reason you're in love with your wife.'

'Like hell I am! A likely story!' And he told her as he had told

475

her before that he did not love Elena and had never loved her; that he had only married her because she was a close friend of the Golzio family, to further his career; lastly that he wasn't even sure that Luigino was his son.

'Then if it's like that, you *must* divorce her. What are you waiting for?'

'It's not so easy to get a divorce as you think. And then, what's the point? I told you at the start that I no longer have any relations with my wife; it's no more than a friendship, a superficial friendship because we don't confide in each other . . .'

'What's the point? So that we can get married!' And she looked at him with her great dark eyes which seemed to want to bore right through him. She held her gaze in silence for a moment, then went on quietly: 'If it's not because you love your wife, then it's . . . *me*. You don't love *me*.'

'It's because I love you that I don't want to hurt you and . . .'

'I hurt your arm just now, didn't I? I'm sorry, I didn't mean to . . . Please forgive me . . . but the pain, who felt it? Not me. You felt it. It's not the one who gives it who feels the pain. What do you know of the pain you can give me?'

In the logic which seemed momentarily to have cut across Irma's madness, even more perhaps in the calm cadence of her speech, Emilio recognized Piero's intelligence. Only rarely did Irma show that she was his daughter. What she had from her mother was clear from her look, which sometimes had the same fixed glassiness as Nuccia's and never the keen, witty sparkle of Piero's. She took after Piero chiefly in her obstinacy. Emilio decided to take advantage of that moment of calm: 'The pain that I give you, you won't feel it now but in the future. I've told you – if we get married, you'll still be young when I'm old. Well, let's put aside this reason even though it's sufficient. There's another very strong one you haven't thought about.'

'And what's that?'

'Your father. You didn't think of that. You couldn't possibly tell him what has happened between us. That we're lovers and I've decided to divorce my wife to marry you . . . You can see very well that it's ridiculous. It would be like a knife in his back.'

Irma was silent and looked down. Emilio immediately regretted what he had said. It was clear that if Piero were to die, that reason would no longer be valid. Irma must have thought the same thing. Without raising her eyes, she murmured: 'At least you could begin to . . .' Then she snatched her slip from the bedside table and put it on, continuing with a surprising, spiteful snigger: 'At least you can't say that if you begin to take steps for a divorce, you're going to grieve Papa. To start with, you needn't tell him anything.'

'Why are you getting dressed? Wait.'

'Leave me alone. Don't touch me. I don't want it today.'

'What is this? Just now . . .'

'Just now was just now. If you'd done what I wanted, then I'd have done what *you* wanted. That's the end of it. Until you promise you'll marry me, no more love-making.'

'I'm glad you can laugh about it.'

'I can laugh because I'm pretty sure of what I say. Of course I may change my mind. But I don't think so. In any case if I do change my mind, I'll let you know. We can all change our minds. You as well – right?'

'Irma, you're crazy.'

'Who knows? Maybe. Here are your keys. I shan't need them.' She took the keys of Via del Mare from her handbag. She threw them on the bed, ran to the bathroom and locked herself in.

Emilio picked up the keys and slowly began to dress. This was freedom, the freedom he longed for. Look, he held it in his hand like the keys. It had all been much easier and quicker than expected. Now the only problem was to see the afternoon through and get her to Malpensa.

But how sad that the affair should have finished like that! Before slipping on his shoes, he paused to listen to the patter of the rain in the great Sunday silence over the lake, to watch the silvery light filtering through the shutters, to look at the almost undisturbed bed and imagine the pleasure which he had lost. Oh, well, you couldn't have everything in life. He'd come back there with Grazia, why not? But no, no. It was useless to try to deny it. Irma was mad, Irma was dangerous, Irma was hateful. But now that he had lost her, he realized that he loved her more than he would have thought possible. Loved her? That wasn't the word. What did the word matter? He knew perfectly well that supposing he had been absurd enough to marry Irma, he could never have given up other women, if only for a month. He seemed to need her and the others as well. The trouble

was that Irma expected him to be faithful. The trouble was Irma's
jealousy. Why couldn't you be honest? Why couldn't you love now
one woman, then another and be loved in return? The instinct of
exclusive possession also exists in animals. And human civilization,
with all its artifices and superimposed institutions, instead of freeing
us from that instinct, has endowed it with the power and authority
of moral law. Would it always be so? Was there no hope of progress
in this field, too? He interrupted these general considerations and,
in view of their very spontaneity, realized that he was . . . yes . . .
sad, but not too sad.

The afternoon passed. They went to Locarno and did some shopping in Switzerland – chocolate, cigarettes, cigars, cashmere pull-
overs and cardigans. Irma left by plane from Malpensa as planned.
Emilio returned to Turin to finish the film.

He was hoping to spend a month with Grazia – a month without
worries. But Grazia was sceptical: *'Tu crois d'en être quitte à si bon
compte? Tu te fais des illusions, mon chou. Tu verras.'* On the phone
to Gisa regarding work, he asked her casually about Irma. The news
seemed good. Irma was turning up on time, she was quiet, just a bit
sad. The reason, according to Gisa, was that Piero's condition was
deteriorating day by day. Then Emilio called the Policlinico once
again and spoke to the doctor. For the moment there was absolutely
no danger.

The worries started up again the following week. Irma began to
phone. She called every two or three evenings at the usual time from
a public phone box at San Silvestro. Grazia was right. On the phone
Irma's voice sounded calm. But she was not submissive. On the
contrary. She said that she was not sorry and had not changed her
mind. She still hoped that he would change. Meanwhile she intended
to remain a 'good friend'. She said: 'Why shouldn't we stay good
friends? If you didn't lie to me when you told me that you loved me,
why shouldn't we stay good friends?' Emilio told her that he was
sorry she was spending so much money on telephone calls. And she
laughed: 'Don't worry. When you get back I'll present you with the
bill.'

Shortly before the middle of November, the film exteriors were
completed. There remained the snow sequences for which L planned
to return to Turin with a smaller unit in December or January.
Emilio went back to Rome with all the others. And Grazia left for

Paris where she had an engagement lasting on into the New Year. Naturally she could have cancelled it but they decided that a period of separation would be the wiser course. If Grazia went to Rome, Irma would find out sooner or later. Irma must know for certain that it was all over since the Sunday in Cànnero – but not because of another woman. The idea seemed so good to Emilio that once back in Rome he went, almost naturally, to see Elena. He began to spend evenings with her at home, at the cinema or with mutual friends.

For the moment he did not want even to set foot in Via del Mare. He saw Irma at the office – they were alone for a few minutes on the first day. She was all smiles and seemed contented. Perhaps she was expecting him to try to caress and kiss her. It would have been a very stupid thing to do and Emilio felt strong enough not to yield to temptation.

He found Piero very low, much thinner than when he had left him two months before. He had stopped shaving and on his neck and wrists Emilio glimpsed the reddish swellings of new nodules. Perhaps because of strain, perhaps because of a slight, stubborn fever, his eyes seemed to be larger; they glittered constantly in laughter and tears as if absorbing and expressing all the love that Piero still felt for life.

He was in a new room, a bigger one on the ground floor but shabbier than the room Emilio had arranged for him to have. The skirting-boards painted glossy light green were peeling. Here and there large untidy patches had fallen on to the floor. In the corners between the floor and the wall there were small heaps of rubbish which the orderlies had not bothered to clear up. There was only one electric light bulb and that was blinding. It hung without a shade, tied by its own flex to the iron head of the bed. Piero said that they had moved him into the room a few days before. Emilio remarked that it was not right, that he had personally arranged for him to have the other room and he would complain to the director immediately. Piero begged him not to do it. He explained with a smile: 'You see, these rooms on the ground floor are given to patients they can't do anything more for. That way, it's easier to cart them away.' He smiled again: 'I swear to you that I'm not making it up. I long for the day when it'll all be over.' He began to describe his sufferings in detail. The irritation was continuous, as was the pain in his skin and his whole body apart from his face and hands. It eased a little during the night when they gave him an injection and he managed to snatch a few hours sleep, but the effect of the injection was getting shorter and shorter. Now he was waking up about four o'clock or three o'clock and could not go back to sleep.

'It's like being on red-hot coals – little ones that pierce my skin and burn me all over. And it's getting worse and worse!'

He asked Emilio to come and see him again on Monday evening at seven o'clock. Was that all right for him? And on the way he would like Emilio to call at Cànepa's and collect a nice roast chicken and a bottle of barolo and to come and have dinner with him like in the old days. Emilio promised he would. He murmured a few words of comfort and encouragement, trying not to show too much emotion. He had to go now. He got up from the chair and went over to Piero. He made as if to embrace him but was unable to. Leaning over the bed, he could not stomach the stench.

At the door, he turned. In the great, dark, empty room, the electric bulb was hanging almost vertically over Piero's poor head as he wagged it gently in farewell: 'See you Monday, then!' His voice was still strong.

'See you Monday,' echoed Emilio and went out.

It was a Saturday evening.

V

❧❦❧

He was walking slowly, clutching two bottles of barolo and the parcel from Cànepa carefully wrapped in greaseproof paper. He had left his car close by in Piazza San Bernardo. He studied the shop windows. He had promised and meant to keep his promise. And he was glad to do so. Piero had said seven o'clock and he did not want to arrive late. He looked at the time – twenty-five past six. A sad business though. Once he would have gone to dinner with Piero so gaily, so light-heartedly, forgetting everything else. For so many years and in any circumstances dinner with Piero was a form of security, absolute security. Standing outside a window full of hardware, locks, padlocks, monkey-wrenches, brass bolts, he felt that for the first time he was assessing himself absolutely clearly. He had always sought selfish, superficial, vulgar pleasure with the sole exception of his affection for Piero – the only fine, noble sentiment in his whole life, the only sentiment that seemed worth a sacrifice. And now, perhaps soon, how would he replace it? What other sentiment could induce him to renounce satisfaction, vanity, fleeting joy?

He paused outside another window – a florist's. How many times, coming out early in the morning from the Grand Hotel opposite, he had only to cross the street to feel polite and refined, to order the roses, lilac or gardenias for the actress, almost invariably foreign, with whom he had spent the night! A large glass vase, squat and round, was filled with little white flowers, the pointed petals closed, the long leaves bright green. He tried to think of the name which he believed he knew – but he could not remember it. He had never seen so many. He would like to buy them all and send them . . . to whom? To Elena? Yes, he could. But why? This sudden idea of sending Elena flowers had certainly not occurred to him because he wanted to please her. He simply felt the urge to go into the shop, to smell those white blooms which had a very subtle perfume or perhaps no perfume at all; in any case to find out, ask the florist what they were called, have the pleasure of buying them. The only woman he was seeing in Rome these days was Elena. That was the only reason why he had thought of sending them to her. Was his pleasure in buying flowers vulgar? It seemed to be the opposite, but actually, yes, it was vulgar, even brutal – not only because it was a selfish pleasure but because he enjoyed it too greedily, exhausted it too quickly, detaching and isolating it from his other pleasures.

Diomedi, luxury leather goods. What he feared most was not being able to hide his revulsion and distress from Piero. Not being able to pretend. But he must – he must act as if he did not notice the nauseating stench of the sores, the flakes of dry skin and scabs littering the floor round the bed and he must look into Piero's eyes as if he did not see the tears welling up.

He went into the shop. In the window, between some English articles in leather, silver, ivory, was a green crocodile bag in the shape of a travelling-case. He thought of sending it to Grazia in Paris for her birthday, December 2nd. While they were wrapping the bag, he noticed a stand of elegant umbrellas and in the middle a malacca cane identical with, or very like Uncle Sanfront's with its wide, flat golden band just below the handle. He had never wanted Uncle Sanfront's cane. He knew exactly where it was – carefully wrapped in tissue paper at the bottom of the big wardrobe which, when his mother moved to Via della Rocca, had been put in the maid's room. And he knew perfectly well that there he would find it the day he lost his mother. He also knew what he would do with it then. Who carries a cane today? He would not keep it in the hall in Via Gregoriana among the walking sticks and umbrellas in the wood and leather stand he had bought at Diomedi, as it happened, back in the days when they lived in Via Ruggero Fauro. Nor would he use Uncle Sanfront's cane, as he sometimes used one of the other sticks for a country walk on a winter week-end. Or if, as had happened in the past, he should sprain his ankle. No, he would not use it. That object, a mocking reminder of the saddest fact in his life, the loss of the inheritance – when his mother died, he would sell it to a second-hand dealer, give it or throw it away. Not the saddest 'fact' – he corrected himself, looking at the cane that Diomedi had hurriedly taken from the stand to show him – but the saddest 'circumstance', since the Viotti family, though having the same legal rights as the

Ceronis, had never had any serious hopes of inheriting. He handled the wood, so light and smooth, warmly, brightly coloured; he admired the sprinkling of a strange, pale speckle so similar to freckles on a smooth skin, on a woman's back or arms. His faults, which he had recognized shortly before as clearly as the neatly arranged tools in the ironmonger's window, were the story of his life, mismanaged even before giving in to Elena, mismanaged from the moment the thought crossed his mind to drop Vévé. And if the fault was his, the cause was the loss of the inheritance. He bought the cane, uncertain whether to interpret his sudden, naïve whim as a sign of regret or as an incentive to forget all about it. Now he had 'his own' malacca cane. And it was with this idea that after getting into the car and starting the engine, he climbed out again and went back into the shop to ask Diomedi to have his initials engraved on the gold band. He waited to see that the assistant wrote them down correctly: E. V.

Then Emilio remembered – bouvardia, that was the name of those white flowers – bouvardia.

Piero's movements were still the same, calm, rhythmical and measured. Following his instructions, Emilio drew up an iron table to the bed on the opposite side to the commode and Piero laid out tidily the potatoes, the ham, the chicken – half for himself on a plate, half for Emilio on the Cànepa cardboard tray, two rolls, two bunches of radishes, two apples, two stainless steel penknives, one bigger than the other, and an aluminium egg as a salt-cellar. Emilio recognized the penknives and the aluminium egg – Piero took them everywhere with him in his haversack, on location and bike-rides. There were also two glasses. They looked dirty to Emilio; he said nothing, tried not to show any sign of distaste and thought that he had managed it. But Piero must have caught his glance. 'There in the corner you'll find running water. I'm sorry you've got to wash the glass yourself.'

The wash-basin was one of those small, enamelled, funnel-shaped ones. Emilio rinsed his glass carefully. Coming back to the table he examined it against the light. Piero, laughing, said: 'It's not dirty, it wasn't before, I got the sister to wash it. It's just the quality of the glass. It's one of those they give away with pots of jam. They brought it from home. Because here they don't give you a thing. Everything you see comes from home. But, see, I only want them to bring stuff they don't want, that otherwise they would throw away. When I'm dead, I don't want them to have to take anything back home. Apart from the fact that Nuccia and Irma might feel for Lord knows how long that they had taken my disease home, I don't want anything to remind them of me as I am now, sick, with this stinking, filthy body of mine, but instead I want them to think of me as the husband, the Papa when he was sound in wind and limb. See, Emilio, that's why— I don't want them to come here too often or stay too long. Nuccia comes every morning for ten minutes; she brings me something she's cooked . . . look, it's usually something like this . . .'

From the marble top of the bedside table which was crammed with tubes, phials, boxes of ampoules, packets of powders and tablets, all kinds of medicines, he picked up with an effort a big, round box covered in a napkin. It was the usual old aluminium box with a lid that screwed on and off and served as a plate – the workman's lunch box. He laid it gently in his lap and began to un-screw the lid.

'Look, as it's not a quarter past seven yet and I thought that you had dinner much later . . . I'll eat this before the chicken and ham. I'm sorry, I should have told you to come later. But after nine o'clock visitors are not allowed in except in exceptional cases and we have to talk quietly. I wanted to be with you a while so we could take our time eating like in the old days.'

Emilio who felt a lump in his throat tried to laugh: 'Don't worry. Just because I knew that we were having dinner at seven, I ate practically no lunch.'

'Bravo! Thank you,' said Piero. 'I know you're a friend and will be right to the end . . .' He looked down and suddenly began to weep, silently, motionless. Emilio wondered if he deserved Piero's trust or not, whether he had betrayed him. Piero would certainly not have spoken like that if he knew. Yet Emilio did not really feel guilty, he did not believe that he had hurt Irma.

Piero recovered almost immediately. He simply said: 'Excuse me . . . there, you see, the food's this sort of thing.'

He went on unscrewing the lid. He did it delicately, carefully, keeping the lid perfectly horizontal so as not to strip the thread, just as if it were a lens. In fact it was the same movement, and Piero did it as meticulously as when he used to unscrew a Cook from the camera to clean it with a linen handkerchief. He showed the contents

484

of the lunch box, laughing: 'Guess what it is. A mixture of bread pudding, tomatoes, oil, salt, pepper and garlic, lots of garlic – in this there must be four cloves of garlic . . .'

'But isn't it bad for you?'

'What harm can it do me now? Even the specialists have given me permission: "Eat what you like". So I'll enjoy this at least. You know, the itching has lessened since yesterday.'

'A good sign, I'm glad.'

'No, it isn't a good sign. When I told the specialists they said the same as you. "Good sign". But I looked them straight in the eye. Either it's the body not reacting any more or it's those injections they give me – they've increased the dose. They must have said amongst themselves, see, "Well, there's no hope for poor Giraudo so we'd better relieve his suffering a bit even if it means that he'll snuff it a few days earlier . . ." No, I'm not joking. I've been telling myself this all the time since yesterday – as soon as I noticed that the itching was less but the little strength I've got left was giving out too. I couldn't tell Nuccia when she came this morning. Nor Irma. Irma came today too, during the lunch break. I can't tell them. They've heard me complaining for two years. Now they just don't believe that I may go any time. They've got used to it and think I'm immortal. But believe me, my dear Emilio . . . that's enough, I'm talking too much and the fever will rise. I'll eat my garlic hors-d'oeuvre. If you like you can open the barolo. Look, in the penknife there's a corkscrew.'

Emilio had brought a corkscrew. He took it from his pocket and, laughing, showed it to Piero. He opened the bottle, sampled the wine which didn't seem at all bad, filled Piero's glass and then his own. Piero asked him: 'Listen, tell me something . . . Have you ever been to Barolo?'

No, Emilio had never been there.

'What a pity. You've no memory of the place. You can't see with me what I'm seeing now. It's all here now . . .' He looked into space, his eyes shining with joy, and seemed rapt by a wonderful vision of sunshine, countryside, warmth, blue skies and the chirping of the cicadas.

'What I remember in particular is when the road bends and suddenly you see barolo at the top of a slope – the red houses, a crest among the vineyards. Do you know why I remember the climb up to

485

Barolo so well? Because up there at the first houses was the finishing-line. It was the Giro delle Langhe cycle race for amateurs – junior amateurs, boys, we were all lads of about fifteen, sixteen. Still the tour was a hundred and fifty kilometres and more. Start and finish at Alba. The first stage was from Càstino, Cortemilia to Cairo Montenotte and Ceva. From Ceva up to Murazzano, Bossolasco, down to Dogliani, then almost a level run to the bridge at Nàrzole. From there up to Barolo. This was the crucial climb because then, from Barolo to Alba it's only slightly over thirteen kilometres and downhill. The route was, to coin a phrase, tailor-made for me. Even then I was a stayer and a good climber, above all a good climber. Racing for the finish in a bunch, I didn't stand a chance, in a sprint anyone could beat me. I was too thin, and could only forge ahead uphill. And so I had made my plan. I had gone there from Turin the Sunday before. To practise on the route of the Tour. I knew all of it. At Dogliani I began to take the lead. At the Nàrzole fork I was away like a streak. It was the middle of summer. The road after the fork . . . there was dust on it, thick dust, I'm not exaggerating, at least five centimetres thick. Never mind, I was away and when I turned round, I couldn't see the pack. I pushed and I pushed. I felt fine, I wanted to win. I gave it everything I'd got. But I knew nothing about the others. How far behind were they? Cycle races, especially amateur ones, were not at all like they are today when there are more team cars than competitors. In ours at that time I believe there was one car and one motor-cycle and that was a lot. So I couldn't get any information about the advantage I had gained since the fork. Whether they were near or far I had to keep on pushing and that was that. At last the road curved. And suddenly I saw Barolo and the last three or four bends on the way up. Great! Look, maybe it seems ridiculous to you, yet even now after all these years, if there's one moment which made me glad to be alive, that was it. Once past the first bend, I turned round and saw the road empty a long, long way back and the first of those following me down there in the dust, standing over their pedals. Good, in six or seven kilometres I had maybe gained two on them. I turned towards the red houses of Barolo and stood up on the pedals too – something I never did. But I realized I had won and that only a puncture could stop me. And I wanted to get far enough ahead to be able to change a tyre and win even if I did have a puncture. I didn't. I arrived at Alba six minutes before the runner-up. I was sixteen. Without a shadow of doubt that was the most wonderful day in my life.'

He fell silent and closed his eyes as if to savour more fully in his memory the happiness of that moment. But the effort he had put into his reminiscences left him panting. Emilio, fearing a total collapse, wondered whether he should ring the bell for the sister. But Piero opened his eyes and said with a laugh: 'It's nothing, my heart . . . it always plays up like this when I get excited. It's nothing, really. Sorry, but I don't want to disturb the sister. Do me a favour. Bring up that glass trolley, that one there.' The top tray of the trolley was full of drugs, too. And the lower one held an assortment of bed-pans and bowls of various sizes half-covered by a towel.

'Please turn around . . .'

Emilio turned around. And Piero went on: 'Do you know what I say when I urinate? . . . I've got to make water as much as possible, according to the time of day, in one or other of these things . . . I say to myself – this is my dolly. And these are my cameras – the bed-pans. I've given them all names. There's the Bell and Howell, the Mitchell, the Debry, the Ariflex and the Pathé Baby, too. Excuse me, won't you. You can turn around now.'

After making a start on the chicken, he finally tried the wine. 'Isn't it all right?' asked Emilio, studying his expression.

Piero shook his head slowly: 'Well, you know . . . real barolo doesn't exist any more. These bottles on sale with their labels . . . it's all more or less adulterated wine. This comes from one of the few reliable firms, I know. It's not too bad, I suppose. But the bottle itself is corky. You didn't notice it, you're always satisfied.'

'I'm sorry,' said Emilio, and felt himself blushing. 'Let's open the other bottle.'

'No, no, leave it. I want to give it to the sister. I'm not saying that the wine is undrinkable. I'm only saying that it tastes of the cork. I purposely ate a bit of chicken before sampling it. Because after garlic you can't taste anything and any old wine seems good. What I can't understand is why this disease hasn't ruined my palate.'

He relapsed into silence again as if exhausted. After a few more mouthfuls of chicken, he seemed to lose the strength to chew. He closed his eyes once more and asked about Irma, if Emilio was still satisfied with her, and how the filming was going, how *The Storm* had turned out. It was a picture he would have loved to work on.

Emilio felt it was his turn to talk now. If only to give his friend a rest. He began by telling him all the news in detail as he had done each time he had visited him during the last year or more. But suddenly he stopped, noticing that Piero was not listening: 'Am I boring you? Perhaps you want to go to sleep?'

'No, no. I was sidetracked. I was thinking of something else.'

'What?'

Piero opened his eyes. He was smiling.

'I was thinking that Father Stablum came to see me the other day.'

'And what did he say?'

'A lot of nice things.'

Emilio saw that now Piero was looking at him very sadly. He tried to cheer him up.

'So it means that Stablum has reason to think . . .'

'No, not at all. There's no Stablum in the world who can . . . believe me, my dear Emilio, when your time comes you can feel it.'

He spoke of the arrangements that he had made to be buried near his father – years ago he had bought a plot in the Turin cemetery.

He also said that he had been to confession and communion and received extreme unction.

'Is there or isn't there? Is there really something on the other side? Nobody knows. But, I asked myself, what harm is there in believing? I can't see anything wrong in what the priests tell you on these occasions. To me it seems that the whole of morality can be summed up in a few words – try to do the least possible harm to your neighbour. That's all. I don't say it's easy. Sometimes people get the urge . . . not only to do harm but what is more serious, to derive pleasure from it. Sometimes they thoroughly enjoy it. I've made my mistakes of course. But not too many, not too many. At least I hope not with all my heart.'

The silence and the complete stillness that followed these words appeared intolerably long to Emilio. What could he say? What could he do? Anything he might say seemed out of place. But perhaps Piero was content to be like that with Emilio there close to him, motionless, silent.

Finally he heard the sound of the glass door opening behind him. It was the sister.

'Signor Giraudo, we'll be along to see you in five minutes.'

'Must I go?' Emilio asked him.

'They're coming to give me an injection. When will you come again?'

'When you like.'

'Come on Thursday.'

'I don't know if I can. But if I can't make Thursday I'll be back to see you on Friday.'

'O.K. Thursday or Friday,' said Piero. He threw back the bed-clothes, swung his legs out, eased two deformed, purplish feet into slippers and stood up. 'Moving about is very painful all over but I must do it every so often. At least that's what the specialists say. I'll come to the door with you.' He leaned on Emilio's shoulder and limped forward. The dirty, wrinkled sheet on the bed bore the imprint of his body. Before leaving, Emilio had automatically glanced around.

At the door they met an orderly pushing a trolley, then the sister to whom Emilio gave a note of his office and home telephone numbers, asking her to call him at any time or for any reason, even if it were simply a question of Signor Giraudo wanting to see him urgently.

'Thanks, thanks,' smiled Piero, 'but it won't be necessary, don't worry. But thanks all the same. What makes me feel good is the idea – the idea that you're ready to come at any time. Thank you.'

The sister had followed the orderly into the room. Emilio could see that they were remaking the bed.

Now they were alone in the long, deserted, gloomy corridor. In the darkness Piero's eyes glittered at him. He repeated quietly, on the verge of tears, 'Thank you so much.'

Emilio felt that he wanted to embrace him, embrace him properly this time. He hesitated for a moment. Then the need overcame everything else.

While he held him tight and kissed him on both cheeks, unable to avoid the evil smell from the sores and medicines, he told himself that he loved Piero more than he had ever loved his father – yet with that unique, irreplaceable, deep love that one has for a father.

Almost outside the entrance to the Policlinico, across the avenue and under the plane trees, he remembered seeing a little fountain as he was parking the car. He ran to it. The nearest street-lamp was half-hidden in a ruddy mass of foliage. The trees still had a lot of leaves in Rome even in the middle of November. He washed his face and hands thoroughly. In the shadow of the trees and the cool fresh water he seemed to be able to shake off other things too. Death, true love for a father or a friend were irksome thoughts.

The telephone woke him up. It was over on Elena's side of the bed. Since his return to Turin he had begun to sleep with her again.

'It's for you.'

'Who can it be, this time of night?'

'Someone said to wait.'

He took the receiver and looked at the time. It was four o'clock. He thought immediately of Piero. He would be going to see him that afternoon because it was Friday. A woman's voice – the sister.

Piero had died in his sleep a couple of hours earlier.

VI

❧❧❧

Between Alessandria and Asti, in the early dusk of November, he began to make out the Alps cloaked in the frayed clouds nestling on the distant, bluish peaks. The big, black motor-hearse leading the way along the arrow-straight road glistening with rain, seemed to point directly at the mountains. Nuccia sat next to him and Irma was behind. Every now and then he glanced at her in the driving-mirror – in mourning like her mother, pale, her eyes red-rimmed. And each time he caught her looking at him with a peculiar, cold, glassy stare that was terrifying.

From the mortuary chapel at the hospital they had followed the big, black car along the Via Aurelia, then from Genoa they took the Turin road. Emilio kept on thinking of Piero as he had last seen him, when they lifted him from the bed to take him to the mortuary. He could still see the same imprint of his body on the sheet as when he was alive and had got up to go to the door with him.

Now the Alps had appeared in the distance, shrouded in fog and rain. And suddenly he remembered more long-forgotten images – for instance, a thin, red neck, Piero in front of him slowly, silently climbing the path up to Colle delle Cime Bianche. The stones crunching beneath the deliberate tread of his heavy boots. He had thought of it so many times! But never as now while he followed the black limousine taking Piero back to Turin. That night in the hut on the Breuil . . . the breakneck race down among the rhododendrons . . . And the little field and Robinson Crusoe's trough. The water running into the red earth channel with a soft, harmonious sound; the shade under the fir-trees and the sun filtering through the branches in needles and blades of gold; the deep blue sky; the breeze; the snap and crackle of the oats; Piero's movements as he opened the haversack, unpacked the food, cut the cheese and bread with his pocket-knife . . . He had thought of it so many times. And remembering it as another Eden through which he had been miraculously privileged to pass, he had never lost hope of trying again, never abandoned his intention of making the same trip once more. 'Piero, it's settled. In July when the film is finished we'll go!' But they never did. Not a chance. Twenty-two years had passed and he had never gone back to the mountains.

Why not go this time?

While he was driving, even without looking into the mirror, he was physically aware of Irma's grim stare. He suspected some new, absurd fit of jealousy or maybe a desire for revenge, and he was afraid. Who knew what was in Irma's mind? Piero's death had probably shattered her nerves. Now Emilio had the distinct impression that his mere presence was upsetting her. Only the black car in full view ahead acted as a restraining influence, a constant reminder that it would be in the worst taste to make a scene. After, it would be different. After, Irma might not hesitate to say something even with her mother there. Fortunately the burial was to take place the following morning in Turin cemetery and Nuccia and Irma were not returning to Rome with him. They were going to Baldichieri to stay for a week with Piero's sister and brother-in-law. His old, ailing mother was there and they had to tell her the sad news. Thinking of the next day, he felt relieved, if only because he would not have Irma's eyes upon him, something he had been unable to avoid hour after hour. But he also thought of the sadness of an immediate return to Rome . . .

When it was all over, why not go up alone to revisit the Cime Bianche and pay a secret tribute to Piero's memory in a place where they had been happy together? Since last winter a ski-lift had been operating up there. The Breuil was no longer called Breuil. It bore a Fascist name although it had been invented after Fascism. Why not? In two days' time, he would ride up to the Breuil.

When the grave had been filled with earth and the three wreaths laid upon it – one from the family, one from Emilio, one from Piero's fellow-cameramen – the gravediggers left but Nuccia, Irma and Piero's sister stayed there kneeling and praying. Emilio, the brother-in-law and a friend from Baldichieri stood just behind them, bare-headed.

It was nearly midday and the sky was still overcast. The mountains were no longer visible. Even Superga and the other peaks of the Collina, so near, were hidden in a fog creeping almost down to the plain. The undertaker approached Emilio who had insisted on making all the arrangements and asked his permission to withdraw.

'What shall we do about the headstone?' murmured Emilio. 'I'm leaving tomorrow.'

'If you come back today at half-past four the monumental mason will be outside the office at the entrance to the cemetery.'

'Very well,' said Emilio. Meanwhile the three women had risen to their feet. Nuccia and Piero's sister moved away, their heads bowed. But not Irma. Irma passed him with that same fixed stare.

Slowly and silently the group walked through the cemetery. Piero had been buried in the most recent extension. It took almost twenty minutes to reach the gate.

The two cars, Emilio's and the friend's, were parked close together in the deserted square. The three women and the brother-in-law were going straight to Baldichieri. But first they had to collect a suitcase from the *pensione* where Nuccia and Irma had spent the night, the same one Irma had stayed at when she came up for the film.

Emilio went to Nuccia. At last, time to say goodbye. He kissed her on both cheeks. He tried to kiss Irma but she abruptly turned her back on him and slipped into the car. Luckily Emilio was not taken by surprise and passed on to the sister and the brother-in-law as if he understood that Irma's behaviour was understandable because of the strain of the funeral.

When he came back that afternoon to give instructions for the headstone he decided to return to Piero's grave. It was raining. And nearly dark already. A thick fog blanketed the gravestones and the trees so that only the nearest ones were visible. It was difficult to find the way through the maze of new plots. Several times he thought he was lost. He did not meet a soul – not a gardener, not a gravedigger, not a living soul to help him. When he finally realized that he was only a few yards from Piero's grave and turned towards it, he saw a dark shadow in the fog, a shadow following him. His heart began to pound. He thought for a moment that it might be Irma. But then he rejected the idea, saying to himself, 'Don't be absurd! Irma's in Baldichieri by now.'

He reached the grave and knelt down. It was cold. He took off his hat and recited a requiem. He remembered Piero's words: 'Is there or isn't there? Is there really something on the other side? . . .

But what harm is there in believing?' . . . Then again, 'Try to do the least possible harm to your neighbour, that's the whole of morality.' At first the ground had seemed soft but now his knees were beginning to ache. And what about me – he asked himself – have I respected this morality so far?

He suddenly heard footsteps on the gravel, very near. He turned. It was Irma. He leapt to his feet. Irma there, coming nearer, staring at him.

'Why haven't you gone?' he asked, managing to hide his fear – or so he hoped.

'We're leaving this evening, in an hour. Mama was too tired, she's gone to bed. My aunt's with her. I came back because I knew I'd find you. I must talk to you.'

'What is it, tell me, Irma dear . . .'

'Irma dear nothing. I don't want to hear your lies, understand? Your *lies*.'

'Excuse me, Irma, but whatever you want to say to me, I don't think this is the most suitable place . . .'

'On the contrary, it's just the right place because you won't dare to lie here. You try!' She had a purse under her left arm and her right hand thrust into her coat pocket. For a second, Emilio thought she might be armed. He again tried to persuade himself that he was exaggerating and being ridiculous. But the hate or whatever it was in her eyes suggested that anything could happen.

Irma said sharply: 'Swear to me here on Papa's grave . . .'

'What do you want me to swear, Irma? But this is absurd!'

'Swear to me here on Papa's grave that you will divorce your wife and marry me.'

The way she was looking at him was so terrifying that Emilio thought it might be safer to swear. She was mad – there was no longer any doubt about it. So he'd better humour her, then see what he could do. But what was he letting himself in for? A scandal was inevitable.

'Be reasonable, Irma. I told you at Cànnero that it was impossible.'

'That's not true,' Irma retorted violently. 'You're lying again. You told me it was impossible, yes, but only as long as Father was alive. Deny it if you dare!'

'I said that was one of the reasons.'

'It was the only one to convince me that it was better to wait. But you haven't even got that reason now. So?'

'So there are others.'

'Yes, shall I tell you what the other reasons are? There's only one, a very simple one – you don't love me. Well, I can put up with that, you can't make somebody love you. But you're a rotten, lying swine. You make me sick. Do you understand? You make me sick! Because I know everything, everything you're doing, everything you have done – with that French slut you had at the hotel in Turin . . .'

'Slander, gossip. I'll prove to you that it isn't true.'

'Oh yes? You poor thing, and do I have to listen to you?'

'No, not here. When you're calmer. Come on, let's go back. It's getting late and they'll be closing the cemetery. Let's go, we can talk on the way back, or come to my hotel and we can discuss it there. Or at your *pensione*, wherever you like . . . but, come on.' He tried to take her arm. Irma recoiled towards the grave and tripped over the nearest of the three wreaths.

'Keep your filthy hands off me. I don't want to hear anything. We'll finish it here. I saw her with my own eyes, that whore. She passed me, laughing, with all those gold bracelets and the jewellery you'd given that brothel tart, you miserable cuckold!'

'Irma, look . . . you must listen to me . . .'

'Even if you swear you'll marry me now, I don't want any part of you, see? I don't want you because I'm going to kill you,' and she pulled her hand out of her pocket.

Emilio immediately recognized the Beretta pointing at him – the Beretta which he had been stupid enough to leave in the drawer at Via del Mare, and he thought of what Piero had said: 'Believe me, Emilio, when your time comes, you can feel it.'

He only had the strength to murmur: 'Irma . . .'

'Don't worry. Don't worry, I'm not going to kill you. The safety-catch is on.' And she laughed. 'Do you think I'd keep a revolver in my pocket without putting the safety catch on? Oh, you've gone pale. Do you know that? You've gone pale. Just think. If I kill you here like a dog, I can run away in the fog, nobody will see me, and then they'll find you and everyone will think you've committed suicide. Well, it's your revolver, isn't it? They've all seen it on your table in Via Pergolesi.'

'That's enough, Irma!' and he plunged towards her, grabbing for the gun.

He never reached her.

He clutched at his chest and fell on his face.

He was not thinking of Irma. 'Someone will come now,' he told himself confidently, 'they must have heard the shot.'

Was it all going to end more quickly than he had thought possible in his stubborn optimism?

He tried to raise his head and see if someone was coming. Lashed by the rain, monstrous, enormous, green, violet, crimson, there were the wreaths – Piero. He thought again of Piero's words. The next instant, his last, he thought of the taste in his mouth of blood and sodden earth.